THE GAY GALLIARD

The character of Mary Stuart is still a riddle, and her love for Bothwell, the Gay Galliard whom even his enemies called 'this glorious, rash and hazardous young man', forms one of the strangest episodes in history. Yet from their story Miss Irwin has forged a drama of two human beings as moving and exciting as anything she has written.

In the furious turmoil of her Scottish kingdom, Mary's aptitudes for statecraft and affection were constantly at war; it was only in Bothwell's courage and his love that she found serenity and a momentary happiness. But fate and their own nature worked against them, though no destiny could conquer their spirit. 'I am myself, myself!' Mary cried in revolt against the political tyrannies of her time. It became a battle cry flung against the world by two fiercely individual souls.

THE GAY GALLIARD

MARGARET IRWIN

UNABRIDGED

PAN BOOKS LTD : LONDON

First published 1941 by Chatto and Windus Ltd.
This edition published 1966 by Pan Books Ltd.,
33 Tothill St, London, SW1.

ISBN 0 330 20136 0

2nd Printing 1971

*Printed in Great Britain by
Richard Clay (The Chaucer Press), Ltd., Bungay, Suffolk*

CONTENTS

To

MY SISTER, E. J. IRWIN

&

MY HUSBAND AND COLLABORATOR

J. R. MONSELL

FOREWORD

This book was planned before I read Robert Gore-Browne's vivid and forcible biography of Lord Bothwell, but owes a great deal to it, although some of the conclusions I have drawn are directly opposite to his.

That does not lessen my gratitude to him for the first historical work I have seen on Bothwell that does not faithfully follow the view of him set down in his enemies' propaganda, however inconsistent.

The facts and incidents in this book are drawn from contemporary records, and so are much of the conversations. Practically everything John Knox says is in his own words, as he himself recorded them.

The names of the four Maries were Beton, Seton, Fleming and Livingstone, not Hamilton and Carmichael as mentioned in the Ballad of Mary Hamilton – who was, in actual fact, executed in Russia at the Court of Peter the Great, at a much later date.

There was never any Mary Hamilton at the Court of Queen Mary, nor any such execution.

ACKNOWLEDGEMENT

The portrait of Mary, Queen of Scots shown on the cover is reproduced by permission of the National Portrait Gallery, London.

ON THE BORDER

For the Galliard and the Gay Galliard's men –
They ne'er saw a horse but they made it their ain.

THEY WERE in the saddle again, out on a night-ride again, but what a night for it!

All Hallows' E'en, when all honest folk should be either in bed safe from hobgoblins, or else ducking for apples in a bowl with the lassies and playing tricks on them when they sat brushing their hair in front of a burnished steel mirror and watching it to see the face of their future mate, or if they were bold enough, running out into the kailyard at midnight to pull a kail runt to see if it were straight or crooked, for so would be the shape of their man – and if it had plenty of earth on its roots that would be the best luck of all, since earth meant money.

Some of the younger lads on this ride, Long Fargy and Dugall Quin and wee Willie Wallocky, out for the first time, had planned to black their faces and rig up some turnip lanterns and go round with the youngsters to all the neighbours' houses at Haddington, singing their song of 'the merry guisers', which changed in the last verse to 'the thirsty guisers' as a broad hint for drink to be served them.

But it was another sort of raid they were on now, called out on the instant by their lord, as was his way, and bad luck and a sore back to the lad who wasn't in his steel bonnet, and his boots in the stirrups, within five minutes of hearing the order to horse. Their leather-jacks were all the armour on their bodies, nor did their lord wear more, except that his sleeves were of linked chain-mail and he wore a light modern sword where a few of his men carried the heavy two-handed weapon or for the most part a Jedburgh axe slung at the saddle-bow.

They had been told to leave their dags and pistols behind – it was to be a quiet job, then, as was fitting to this eerie hour – and wee Willie was not the only one to stick a bunch of scarlet rowan berries in his cap as defence against the goblins known to be abroad on this last evening of October. Only the Galliard would choose such a night for a foray, a night moreover when the Merry Dancers, those spirits like streamers of red fire, were out riding the Northern Lights.

So they grumbled to each other as they rode, but very low, in obedience to the order for silence, their stirrups and harness bound in rags to keep from jingling; it was as bad to be the Galliard's disobedient servant as his enemy – worse, in fact, for he did not kill unnecessarily on a foray.

But what foray could it be that even the Galliard would lead, now they were at peace with England? Their lord had won that French nickname for a gay reckless rake from a noted freebooter who 'ne'er saw a horse but he made it his ain'. But only a year ago the Queen Regent of Scotland had made him her Lord Lieutenant of the Border, Warden of the Marches, Lord of Liddesdale and Keeper of Hermitage Castle, and he would hardly flout his royal appointment so far as to break truce with England, still less to ride on some private quarrel, least of all to lift his neighbours' cattle. Only two dozen had been called out – on what errand?

When they were clear of all walls and out on the wide moor, that dark figure at the head of their troop drew rein, and waited till they came up round him. It was too dark to see his face; but his height and broad shoulders showed up against the torn, stormy dusk of the sky above the hillside, and there was a faint glinting on the dark mail of his sleeves and on his steel helmet from those red flickering lights in the sky of the far North.

A young man, not more than twenty-four years old, he was as stalwart as any of the older, hardened moss-troopers in his train, and one and all felt his eye upon them, even in the darkness, as he spoke in a low yet rather harsh vibrant voice.

'Well, lads, we're out for a bag of English gold! But don't wag your jaws open, for it's for none of our keeping. This is no march-treason, stealing English gear in time of truce. We are riding against traitors, and the gold is being brought from England to pay the rebel troops. Last week the Lords of the Congregation declared the Good Queen was no longer Regent, and stamped their declaration with a forged seal. They asked England for a thousand men to help them fight against their lawful ruler.'

There was a deep angry growl at this last; it was worse than treason, worse even than march-treason against the Border law between the countries, for it was inviting the ancestral enemy of centuries to come and invade their homes yet again. There was not a man there who had not suffered from the last invasion just

10

over a dozen years ago, when the English had tried to capture the baby Queen Mary of Scots as a bride for their boy King, Edward VI.

The little Queen had been sent safe to France; King Edward had died in his sixteenth year; but the vale of Teviot and the fair fields of Merse and Lothian had been turned into a desert, and hundreds of villages and many market towns and castles and monasteries had been burnt and smashed to ruin.

'Then let it be a killing job tonight, sir,' said an older, gruffer voice. It came from the heavy shape of a man who leaned with bowed shoulders over his horse's neck. 'I'll not hear it said that an Englishman lay under me and ever got up again.'

'That's old Toppet Hob's growl, I'd know it a mile off. No hope of your lying tonight on top of an Englishman, Hob; it's a neighbour we're out after, John Cockburn, a far cousin of mine by marriage, and you'll keep your grimy fists off his throat or you'll have to reckon with his kinsman. Aye, John Cockburn's a traitor, and double-dyed; he is taking English gold again and carrying English gold to his fellow-rebels, curse him! But we'll lift that last burden from his conscience. We'll wait for him in the wood below Hailes Castle as he skirts the bog on his way from Berwick, and spring an ambush on him. So wind your scarves well round your necks, my lambs, lest you get a sore throat from cold steel. When you get to the wood, keep silent as death, and remember that if you're scared of the dark this All Hallows' E'en, John Cockburn's men will be more so when such ugly goblins as yourselves spring out on him.'

He swung his horse round and thudded over the moor, his men after him in the same sweeping movement, for there was no dallying when the Gay Galliard led a raid, and no wish for it. The wind was in their faces, sharp and damp from the east, with a salt tang in it from the sea. They sang low as they rode, in a curious laughing mutter of voices, the raiding song of their clan:

> 'Little wot ye wha's coming?
> Hob and Tam and a's coming,
> Fargy's coming, Willie's coming,
> Little wot ye wha's coming!'

And so on through all the names of their company in turn over and over, until they came down the moor into the shelter of the hollow and saw the hill of Traprain rise above them, a black sleeping monster hunched against the dim sky and racing

11

clouds. There in the scanty wood the Galliard halted his men, and their muttering song died on the wind.

There was wild weather in the upper air, may all the saints hold it there and not let it come down on them in heavy rain and rack his old shoulders with cramp again, prayed Toppet Hob devoutly, wishing the New Religion didn't prevent his vowing a candle to Our Lady if she'd keep the wet off his back. A chill comfortless business this New Religion, warning a man off the saints and any hope of driving a fair bargain with them.

Now the men were all huddled together under the bare soot-black trees. An owl went blundering heavily up out of the low scrub of heather and whin, and Willie Wallocky let a screech out of him that he hoped to God would pass muster as that of the bird. It didn't, but a muttered curse and warning was all that it called down on him for the moment.

The sour smell of hot wet leather from the sweating horses cooled to a chill steam. The darkness settled on them, deepened slowly; the silence widened to an enormous gulf. Farther and farther off, the sounds of night reached out to them, the cry of a startled curlew, the sough of the wind in the sedges, the whisper and rush of dead leaves swirled up from the wet ground and scurrying on the wind.

And always close round them were the sounds they made themselves for all their care, the stifled yawns that broke in a gasp, their whistling breath as they blew on their hands to keep them from stiffening with the cold and damp, the squelching of a horse's hoofs in the mud, stamping and fidgeting, and once or twice, shatteringly, the sudden trumpet of his sneeze. But this was rare, for these small rough-coated beasts that could leap so nimbly over the peat-hags in the dark and find a foothold in the slippery morass knew on what sort of errand they were out.

The wind whistled shriller; more than one man could have sworn he heard the thin cackling cries of witches in the upper air. But the furies that drove down on them were gusts and spurts of rain, swishing down on their heads and shoulders, trickling under the thick folds of the rough woollen scarves wound so closely round their necks for defence against sword thrusts, groping with icy fingers farther and farther down against their shrinking skins as they shivered in this wet chasm of utter darkness.

To their leader all that mattered was that the night was all but past, and had he missed his prey.

The rain stopped. The trees that had waited with him all

12

these hours, so close to him that he could smell their wet mossy bark, now began to take their shape slowly with the dawn. The stars between the racing clouds were growing small and dull; the hump of Traprain was black once more against a rim of pewter; the night was over, then the quarry had escaped his grip. John Cockburn must have got some warning of his movements and smuggled his bag of gold safe across the Border to Edinburgh, into the hands of the 'Bastard of Scotland', Lord James Stewart, leader of the Lords of the Congregation, and of his prime agent, Mr John Knox.

He heard the thudding of hoofs on the wet moor. At the distant sound every man tightened his horse's girths and clambered into the saddle, stiff with cramp but ready before the scout reached them with news that their quarry was coming. The Galliard thrust a numbed foot into his stirrup, the fierce joy and heat of action already warming his blood. Not for nothing had he held his men in leash all this chill night.

It was still quite dark in the little wood, but John Cockburn knew the ground almost as well as the kinsman lying in wait for him, and he and his men would be off their guard, nearing the end of the night and of the journey. That end would come quicker than Cockburn thought for; he would see these familiar trees suddenly come alive and moving, rushing round him like demons in the darkness.

Now the Galliard could hear the creak of saddles, a clink of harness, and horses clumping heavily, slowly, tired with their journey. He stuck spurs into his horse, and Corbie sprang forward with a shrill whinny, as eager for the fray as his rider, who answered with a yell of joy, taken up by his men. They swung in among them, scattering them, a man shrieked that the devil was upon them, there were shouts and oaths and the clashing of steel.

The Galliard's eyes, said his men, could see in the dark, and they saw at first glance the heavy lump of the portmanteau jingling at Cockburn's saddle-bow. With a blow of his sword he cut Cockburn down from his horse, another cut severed the strap that fastened that clanking bag, and the Galliard swung it on to his own saddle, and galloped off with a halloa to his men.

'Hey, my night hawks,' he called to them, laughing, 'has that warmed your cold feet as it has mine?'

Said Long Fargy, 'That was a grand ding you gave him, sir.'

13

Said Toppet Hob, 'I'm thinking Your Lordship kept my hands off your kinsman for the pleasure of cracking his head yourself!'

'Is he dead?' asked wee Willie in an excited squeak, for he had not yet seen a man killed.

'Not he,' said his lord. 'It takes more than that to cleave our family's brain-pans.'

They joked together, the men as much at ease with their lord as with each other, now that their job was over and he was well pleased.

'There'll be great cursing at Cockburn's the night,' they prophesied. 'It's they who'll be crying this time – "Fy, lads, cry a', a', a', my gear's a' ta'en!"'

'And Cockburn's lost gear will cost him more than the lifting of a herd of cows.'

'Aye, and it will cost his masters more,' the Galliard told them. 'We've put a good chapter of Lamentations into Johnny Knox's next sermon.'

'I mind him well as a lad in Haddington,' growled old Toppet Hob, as though the worst thing that could be known of a man was his birthplace.

'Will they raise the Hot Trod on us?'

'They'll not dare,' said their lord, 'they'll have to keep this night's work quiet. The Queen of England won't thank them for bringing it into the open!'

But he did not feel as sure as he sounded. And it was for his castle of Crichton, not the nearer one of Hailes, that he was making.

A streak of angry red had begun to fire the iron edge of the clouds; it showed the black shapes of horsemen riding fast up over the hillside, and far behind them, on the moorland path below the wood, a pair of seagulls swooping and screaming over a group of bent forms huddled round a prostrate figure.

*   *   *

Big Bess was trying to whisk eggs to stir into her pan of Friar's Chicken with the one hand while with the other she turned the spit on which a haunch of venison was frizzling and sputtering.

'I have but the one pair of hands,' she was wont to tell her mistress with untiring insistence on an indisputable fact.

The kitchen door of the Laird of Sandybed's house at Haddington stood open to the stone-walled passage that in its turn

14

was open to an oblong slice of sky and running water. This was not because the kitchen was hot to suffocation and reeking of roast meat, fried fat and cinnamon, nor yet because Bess liked to get a hurried glimpse of the shallow Tyne that flowed outside her master's back door, very convenient for the rubbish and slop-pails; but because the grey oblique light given her by those two doors was all she had to cook by.

And suddenly that was obscured.

'If that's yourself, Simmy o' the Syke, for the Lord's sake have the sense to come in and not stand blocking the light on me,' she yelped on a high yet full-throated note like that of a hound.

'It's not himself,' said a strange voice, deep yet rather harsh, that sent the blood tingling through her veins.

She swung round so quickly that she spun the bowl with the eggs on to the floor.

'Mary have mercy!' she breathed, crossing herself, before she remembered that both words and action were a legal offence.

In the doorway was a tall stalwart young man, splashed with mud to his head and shoulders and with water dripping from him as he stood with his legs apart, his arms clutching a heavy portmanteau to his chest, his swarthy head cocked and his eyes scanning her with so merry yet ruthless a scrutiny that poor Bess felt hotter than the kitchen fire had made her. Only wee Simmy o' the Syke knew that inside that great gawky frame was a timid and modest being that leaned on his tenderness for protection, although he barely reached her shoulder.

'What are you doing here – staring like that at a decent body?' she demanded.

'That's a poor word for your splendid body, my Queen of the Amazons!' And he let the bag slide to the ground with a jing-ling crash and came over to her at one stride.

'I'm not your queen, and my name's not Agnes, it's Bess, and – and – the men don't like me as a rule, I'm so big,' she finished weakly as he put an arm round her waist and stood with his shoulder touching hers, which was almost on a height with his own.

'The very thing I like best about you at this moment. I want your clothes. Will you take off your petticoats for me, Bess?'

Instinctively she swung out a fist like a ham to box his ear, but thought better of it as she saw the flash in his eye. This was not a man to anger lightly, even in fun, and he was a noble, she had seen and heard it from the first really.

'I'll do no such thing!' she exclaimed in shocked tones.

'You will – for the Lord Lieutenant!'

'Oh mercy! I might ha' known it!' she cried on a note of terror. 'But I've never set eyes on Your Lordship, I've been away with my married sister since a bairn — '

He snatched off her apron.

She gasped out, 'You'll not force a poor girl!'

'I'd never force a girl my own size! What d'you think of me?'

'What I've heard,' she stammered ruefully.

'Then hear this: I've no time for raping, I'm on the run, so off with those things – hurry now or I'll tear them from you. They're after me.'

He was dragging off his wet leather-jack and breeches as he spoke. She was quick enough then to strip herself of her bodice and skirt and help him to bundle himself into them, while he laughed and joked like a schoolboy dressing up for a prank. She dealt with their fastenings for him before she flung a plaid round her massive shoulders.

'Now look out of the back door and see if anyone's following,' he commanded. 'If there's no one, then shut and bolt it. Never mind your shift.'

She did as she was told and came back with a grave face. 'Not a body to be seen, my lord, but I heard the bay of hounds far upstream.'

'They'll lose the scent at the water. I turned my horse loose there and came down the river-bed.'

'Eh, sir, is it the Hot Trod?'

'Aye, Bessie, they're after me with bug'es and bloodhounds and all. Now fetch Sandybed to me – and I'll turn this spit for you in case anyone comes.'

The Laird of Sandybed was another Cockburn, a distant and humble relation both of John Cockburn and of the young Lord Lieutenant. He came padding down the kitchen stairs in his slippers, neighing feebly with anxiety, an elderly man with reddish-grey whiskers, his fluffy face at this moment very white about the gills.

He had already heard flying rumours of the portmanteau raid, and fondly believed that the author of it was safe, or not, in his castle at Crichton – but here he was in Sandybed's own kitchen, and in his own servant-maid's clothes, and here – God help him! – was that ominous black portmanteau plump in the middle of the kitchen floor, along with an overturned bowl and a creeping mess of raw eggs into which he stepped before he noticed.

'Eh – eh – my lord! – you here, and in such a guise!'

The Galliard swept him a curtsy, eyeing him with cruel amusement. 'This is a bad day for you, Sandybed, but I'll make it a good one both for you and your heirs if I rid myself of this cold feeling round the roots of my neck.'

'What feeling, my lord?'

'Why, a foretaste of the axe, man!'

'You're not outlawed? They'd never put the Lieutenant to the horn!'

'This is not a horning, it's a hanging job. The Bastard and his spaniel the noble Earl of Arran are at the gates of Crichton with cannon and a couple of thousand men – if they're not inside the Castle by now. I've told Somerville it's no use to defend it.'

'Eh, dreadful, dreadful! Crichton – the fairest of all your castles! All the expense your father put himself to, getting those stonecutters from France – I always said – I always said —'

But he had better not say what he had always said of such extravagance, so he only neighed plaintively, 'Eh, what evil times we live in! No man is safe, no man! After all the care I've taken to keep out of it all! You'll not be staying the night?'

'Three or four, more likely.'

At this, Sandybed, quite unaware of what he was doing, pranced feebly up and down and wiped his eggy foot against the side of the portmanteau.

'I never knew you spurned money,' observed his visitor; 'there are £3,157 in that bag, all counted out by Queen Elizabeth herself on the floor with the help of her minister, Cecil. It's a weight, I can tell you, to carry downstream in one's arms.'

Sandybed hopped back as though the bag had burnt his foot.

'*You* carried it here! But where is Your Lordship's body-guard?'

'What use of a bodyguard against two thousand men? I only had a quarter of an hour's warning before they got to Crichton – time enough to leap on a horse barebacked, but no time for saddle or spurs, or boots either for that matter. But I've got the bag.'

'Ah, God be praised!' Bess bayed from the doorway, wrapped in her plaid. 'Your Lordship will have Tom Armstrong's to-name from now on – "Luck i' the Bag"!'

*　　*　　*

After three days of wearing Bess's clothes and making a show of turning the spit most of the time, the Lord Lieutenant managed to get himself and his bag to Borthwick Castle. There his Captain, John Somerville, arrived with the enemy's terms. The money must be handed over to them instantly, and reparation made to 'that honourable and religious gentleman' John Cockburn, who had shown himself so 'very diligent and zealous for the work of the Reformation', and was now as a result lying grievously wounded. If the Lord Lieutenant refused to obey these commands, then he would have his castle of Crichton sacked and burnt and his property confiscated.

'And they've left Captain Forbes and fifty hagbut men in charge until they carry out their orders,' John Somerville finished on a dour and heavy note.

'Where are the Bastard and Arran?'

'Gone back to Edinburgh, sir, and none too soon for them. D'Oysel took the opportunity you gave him by their absence to lead a sortie from Leith against the rebels and drive them back to Edinburgh. They put up hardly any fight.'

'Why, where were the rest of their leaders?'

'In church, listening to a "comfortable sermon" by Mr John Knox.'

'He'll need to make it a deal more comfortable after that repulse,' his lord remarked, 'the more when he knows they've no money to pay their troops.'

'He knows it – "deadly news", he called it.'

'Well he may. Their men are beginning to desert already; if it goes on they'll never be able to hold Edinburgh.'

'Your Lordship won't give up the subsidy to them, then?'

'Don't be a fool, Somerville!'

The Captain, a gaunt man with a bleak nose and grizzled grey hair, looked at his master in some perplexity. This young man was as tough a customer as many of the robbers that he was privileged to hang, yet he had no second thoughts about flinging his property to the flames, since he could thereby preserve the spoils he had won for the Queen Regent instead of letting them fall into the hands of her enemies. 'Ah well, it's a great thing to be only twenty-four,' the Captain finally summed it up to himself.

Aloud he said, despondently pulling his long nose, 'It's little luck Your Lordship has got out of the bag.'

'Has Bess handed on that nickname, then?'

'Bess? I have not the full list of Your Lordship's wenches.'

Somerville sounded mortally offended, but relented enough to add, 'It's your own men are calling you "Luck i' the Bag".'

His Lordship for all answer flung himself out of his chair and was marching up and down the room, running his fingers through his rough black hair, tugging at it, his hot reddish-coloured eyes bright with anger.

'Curse the Bastard!' he burst out. 'As to that sickly whey-faced moon-calf Arran, if he dares set a finger on any of my goods I'll send him a challenge to mortal combat.'

'He'll not accept it,' said the older man dryly, but his master looked so black at this that he tried to cheer him by telling him that d'Oysel had written of his raid to the French Ambassador at the English Court, and told him to tax Queen Elizabeth with her double dealing in subsidizing the Scots rebels.

'She'll deny it of course, she'll deny anything, and her Envoy is trying to make the Lords of the Congregation deny it too – much they care if her face is blackened, when they never mind the grime on their own!'

The Earl of Arran, son of the Duke of Hamilton and Châtel-herault, and the heir to the Scottish throne most favoured by the rebels and their English party (there was considerable talk of marrying him to the young Queen Elizabeth), was put in charge of the punitive expedition on Crichton, with three hundred horsemen to carry off all that could be carried, and to destroy the rest. Only the walls and the work of the French stonecutters would outlast the flames.

John Somerville, grimmer and gaunter than ever, came back again with news of it; and he and his master went up on the tower of Borthwick Castle where they could see the dun clouds of smoke rising in huge columns, flame-reddened at the lower edges, and spreading on the wind for miles round.

'They've taken all the furniture except the big beds,' said Somerville with the sour relish of one who knows and tells the worst; 'and those they're burning with the rest. The oak coffers and treasure-chests are halfway to Edinburgh by now.'

'And the charter-chest?'

'Aye, sir.'

'I wonder they didn't use the title-deeds and family papers to light the fire!'

'They didn't do that' – Somerville never perceived irony – 'but the rare glass that the Fair Earl brought from Venice has all been smashed by the troopers. It's well he didn't live to see it, for he set great store by those toys.'

The present Earl, who was anything but fair, knitted his black brows together, seeing again those opalescent goblets, light as bubbles, and fantastic ships and dragons, that his father had packed and brought home from Italy with such infinite care, and which he himself as a boy had never been allowed to touch.

'What odds?' he broke out roughly. 'My father lost more in his time than a little glass too brittle to use. And it's like enough I'll lose more than a houseful of gear. I'm not an inland Scot to sit snug at home and never smell the smoke of my own barns.' He suddenly burst into a roar of laughter, and told his astonished Captain, 'It's your face, man, squinting down your long nose at that smoke! What are you looking so glum for? Am I to yelp like any old wife for her cow or the three coverlids off her bed? The Black Douglas was right, "It's better to hear the lark sing than the mouse cheep." '

Those odd reddish eyes were gleaming with an excitement strange to Somerville. Yet the Captain had borne the loss of his own house and goods more than once; it was the common lot of those who lived on the Border.

'Aye,' he said, 'but I had thought to see the end of that in my time. The last King worked hard enough to make the furze bush keep the cow, but it's little use to hang the robbers and reivers, if rebellion is fostered by the highest in the land. It used to be cattle raids, but now it's civil war.'

And he let a groan out of him ('like a sick bullock,' the Galliard remarked in exasperation); he was past fifty, and tired, and his wife was expecting her tenth, and what was the use of bringing more and more children into a world that never seemed to get any nearer to a breathing space of peace – no, not for all its new laws and new religions and new books of the gospels to make every man feel he was as wise as the priest – aye, and discoveries of new countries filled with gold, and new weapons to make war more deadly and therefore more certain. But people were just as poor, property as insecure, life as difficult and unsafe. 'The world changes damned little,' he mumbled in conclusion to his thoughts.

His master was not listening to the monotonous growl of his Captain's voice. He was leaning on the parapet of the tower, looking out over the wide rolling hills, and those clouds and wreaths of smoke that darkened the horizon of this bright autumn sunshine. His blood still tingled with that strange exultation – let them take his goods, burn his house, batter it to the ground if they care to waste so much powder on it –

what odds did that make to him? He'd have the less to worry over!

In this moment of loss and defiance he was at one with the host of his fellow-countrymen on the Border, known only by their nicknames in the songs that were sung and never written down, such names as the Galliard and Luck i' the Bag, more his own than any of the hereditary titles in his charter-chest, since they had been won by himself. He was the Queen's Lord Lieutenant on the Border, the highest office to be held by a Scottish subject, with absolute power to send letters in the name of his Sovereign to command his neighbours on pain of death; yet he was part of that remarkable commonwealth of the Border, hardly to be distinguished from his men in battledress, and now, like them, made to realize that his castle, like their cottages, was a thing to be left quickly and without care.

> *A fat horse and a fair woman,*
> *Twa bonny dogs to kill a deer —*

that was as much property as a man could wish, if he would ride light in the saddle, and only so could he ride light of heart.

Nothing of this came out in words, even to himself, only a sudden whoop of rage against Arran that rang out on a note of fierce joy. 'By the faith of my body, I'll get my pleasure yet of yon straw-coloured tatter-boggart – I'll pull his house about his long asses' ears and himself inside it! Let Arran slug it in bed while I take to the heather – I'll wake him yet to defend his life – aye, and I'll light my candle at the flames of his house to lead me in the darkness better than moon or star.'

'Your Lordship cannot,' came the dry reminder, 'for he has my Lord James Bastard's armies behind him, and you have only your own men.'

'You are right as usual, damn you!'

And he rattled down the winding stone stair of the tower to write instead his challenge to single combat 'armed as you please, on horse or foot, unto the death'.

But there too John Somerville was right. Arran sent back a dignified reproof that it was the 'deed of a thief to beset a gentleman's road and rob him of his goods', and promised to uphold it by force of arms 'the next time I come that way'. But he wrote this from as far away as Stirling, where he was well guarded, and seemed in no hurry to come out of it by any way.

The bag of gold safely reached the Queen Regent, and the

21

effect was what its captor had hoped: the rebel troops besieging Leith, short of both pay and food, deserted in ever larger numbers; the next attack of the Regent's troops broke their ranks; and within one week of that 'dark and dolorous night', as their preacher, Mr John Knox, always referred to that night of All Hallows' E'en, the army of the bastard Lord James Stewart had to retreat from Edinburgh to Stirling.

They made the move at midnight in a disorder that was all but a rout, the rabble of Edinburgh, risen from their beds to run after them, throwing stones, flouting and hooting at them. 'The sword of dolour passed through our hearts,' as Mr Knox lamented, even while he contrived to lay the blame of it on his allies, telling his noble leaders, the Lord James and the Duke of Châtelherault, that they were nothing but 'a bragging multitude'. It was not a comfortable sermon.

Yet he too had his moment of exultation in loss, when he told them in that same sermon that 'whatsoever shall become of us and of our mortal carcasses, I doubt not but that this cause, in despite of Satan, shall prevail'.

But for the moment Satan, the generic term for all who opposed Mr Knox, prevailed; the siege of Leith was raised, and the Queen Regent able to march out of it and back into Edinburgh. She owned to the luck the bag had brought her, and told her Lord Lieutenant to name his reward.

He asked for eighteen hundred men to lead against the rebels at Stirling, with leave to pause a few hours on the way to burn and loot a castle of Arran's.

This happened in 1559, just over a year after Queen Elizabeth had come to the English throne, half a year before the Queen Regent of Scotland died, and while her daughter Mary, Queen of Scots in her own right, was away in France, married to the little French King, François II.

Part I

FIRST MEETING

CHAPTER ONE

HE FIRST saw her walking down a street in Paris, swift and shining in the sunlight as though made of Venetian glass. Her tall childish figure so glittered with jewels that it seemed translucent to the hot rays of the evening sun behind her; a halo of pale gold shimmered from the loose threads of hair round her bare head, fine as spun glass. She wore a tiny mask of black velvet which did not conceal the fair skin and broad forehead, nor yet the direct untroubled eyes.

Beside her walked the scarlet figure of a young-looking man, fair and slender like herself and very tall; so lithe, soldierly and arrogant in bearing that it gave a slight shock to the traveller, watching from the doorway of his inn, to perceive that those gorgeous robes were those of a Prince of the Church, and that it was a Cardinal who was swinging down the street like a young Captain of the Guard.

'Who is she?' he demanded, though he had known even before he saw her, from the cries of the people who came running down the street, out of the narrow doorways, thronging round her, throwing up their caps, shouting 'La Reinette! La Reinette!'

So this was their 'little Queen', and his; Queen of France for the last fifteen months; Queen of Scotland for the whole of her short life; Queen of England to all who admitted the bastardy of Queen Elizabeth. He had known her too from the sight of her, for she had some likeness to her mother, whom he had been proud to account his friend.

That gallant Frenchwoman, Mary of Guise, Regent of Scotland, he had seen for the last time this summer, stricken down with the illness that was to be her death, yet still with the splendid physique, broad shoulders and erect carriage to balance her unusual height, which had led stout Henry of England to offer her marriage, 'since he was so big himself, he needed a big wife'.

'But my neck is small!' she had answered.

Would this girl ever fill out to the same sturdy quality? He

23

doubted it. At this first glimpse, for all she had the height of her mother's family, there was more trace in her of her Scottish father, that delicate racehorse of a king, with fine golden hair and a smile for any lass, but tragic eyes. He too used to walk boldly through the streets among the common people and talk familiarly with them, just as his pretty daughter, whom he had never seen, was now doing, attended only by her uncle of Guise, the Cardinal de Lorraine.

She was wanting to stop and talk to the people who pressed about them; she held out a hand to a ragged woman who had dropped on her knees crying out that she was an angel from heaven. The Cardinal flung a coin to the woman and scattered a few more among the crowd, whereupon a thin cheeky lad, going one better, shouted, 'It's either Jesus Christ or the Cardinal!'

Her uncle hurried her on, perhaps because the sweating, chattering crowd was none too pleasant in this dusty heat. She swung easily into step with his stride; she walked like a boy and as though swift movement were a delight to her.

'A nimble filly,' thought the young man in the doorway of his tavern, 'though still a long-legged foal. If she be anything but a virgin yet, I know nothing of women.'

But the Galliard knew women nearly as well as he knew horses. And he knew Mary Stewart, and a good deal about her, as soon as he set his bold eyes on her. But 'Who are they?' he asked again, for it amused him to play the ignoramus abroad, one got a deal more information that way.

The thin lad, cheerful, disreputably shabby, with a nose as pert as a sparrow's beak, and a sallow, pock-marked but not ill-looking face, swung round at the question with a squawk of laughter which he instantly checked at sight of the stranger.

Incredible! Did the foreign lord not know Charles de Guise, the great Cardinal de Lorraine, 'the Red Phalaris', the 'Tiger of France'?

The soubriquets shrilled higher and higher off his tongue in a crescendo of national pride. The Galliard took his measure at a glance, balancing the wiry strength of the fellow against his high voice – a lively rascal, nervous, but all the quicker for that, should be useful in a tight corner. Master Cock-up-Spotty (so he named the talkative youth) was telling him that the Cardinal and his eldest brother, the great soldier, Duc de Guise, were known as the Pope and King of France; and 'the Pope', that suave, scholarly courtier, had been the fiercer of the two in

24

quelling the Huguenot rising this summer – 'such a rage he flew into, he tore the biretta from his head and trampled it underfoot!'

My lord was unimpressed. 'The more fool he,' he remarked in easy French, but with a strong Scottish accent, 'hadn't he his brother's hat within reach?'

But if a man must wear the long robes of a woman, it was something that his blood should burn like a man's inside them. He liked also that the Tiger minded the hatred and gossip 'no more than the barking of a dog; he collects all the lampoons against him and keeps them with his rare pictures – and some of *them* ought to be rarer, they say!'

It gave the Scot a twinge of patriotic jealousy that 'the Cardinal's Niece' seemed here a prouder title than Queen of Scotland in her own right, and even of France by marriage; 'La Petite Sauvage' they were actually calling her, though with a chuckling admiration. 'Ah, she's bred from barbaric stock on her father's side!'; so Cock-up-Spotty told him with a grin that split his face and was instantly wiped off as the Scots lord stiffened, for this was not the way for a French gutter rat to talk of the Stewart Kings. But his Border blood answered with a throb of amused sympathy when he heard that the Little Savage's wild blood was not to be tamed even by her severe mother-in-law. Catherine de Medici's own children were terrified of her, but nothing could make La Reinette afraid, she only tossed her proud little head, despised the Medici for her lack of breeding, and even said in one of her naughty fits that she was only the merchant's daughter of Florence.

'Damned careless of her,' grunted the Scot. La Reinette's mother had fondly told him of the Medici's glowing praises of her daughter-in-law; 'this bewitching child,' she had written, 'has only to smile to turn all heads.' With any sense, she'd have smiled at her mother-in-law most of all; but he could not help liking the spirit of the lass, for he had no love for people who remembered to smile in the right direction – as he must now do himself!

And at that the Galliard shrugged and grinned mockingly at the Parisian youth's instant compliment on the shrug, that Monsieur had the air of a true Frenchman, a Gascon *par exemple*. It was inconceivable that Monsieur should not know Paris as well as himself, but if by any chance he required the services of a guide through the streets, he, Hubert, would be enchanted to render them.

'Hubert of what?' It might be useful to know of this fellow some time.

'Hubert of Paris,' replied Cock-up-Spotty with a superb air, and was rewarded with a short laugh like the crack of a pistol.

'Of all Paris, are you? Get out of my way, fellow. I don't need a guide to the Tuileries, *nor* your introduction to the Queen Dowager!'

And thus unashamedly answering boast with boast, the splendid stranger pushed past the street loafer into the mean inn where he was lodging; pulled up his soft leather boots and roared to his page to fetch a brush for them, picked up a pair of gloves embroidered in seed pearls by his latest mistress, and swaggered off to the interview he had been promised with Catherine de Medici, Queen Dowager of France.

He had to save on his lodging, but his clothes were fine enough to bear comparison even with her courtiers, or had been, though perhaps they were getting a bit worn-looking. But his bearing carried that off; his hat was cocked triumphantly on the side of the dominant head; his doublet was rather shabby, but that did not prevent his swinging his short scarlet-lined cloak far back in gay insouciance as to what it might reveal; and his gloves, the only new and perfect garment, he flicked against his knee in rhythm to the tune he was whistling, as though he were urging his horse to the gallop instead of strolling through the streets of Paris.

His stride showed the born horseman, the long, lean-flanked, slightly bowed legs and the easy swing of the long arms from the broad shoulders. His reddish-brown eyes were the colour of bog-streams on a sunny day, alert and quick-glancing, as they had had to be from childhood against sudden danger; but now alight only for the women, scanning each that passed in cool, arrogant appraisement of her points, as he had just now scanned those of a young Queen.

And would he need then to be afraid of an old one? Not he! Here he was again in Paris, which he had not seen since he had finished his education as a boy; he had gone far since then; he would go farther, and Queens, young or old, would be the pawns to help him on his way. His father had tried to work that line, and bungled it, but his father had been a bit of a fool and more than a bit of a traitor; he himself knew better. He had shown he could not only win a Queen's trust, but deserve it.

For that reason he could now be tolerably sure of a good reception from Queen Catherine. The Medici's only possible game at present lay in subservience to those great brothers of Guise who ruled all France between them. And it was their sister, Mary of Guise, Queen Dowager and Regent of Scotland, dead these two months past, who had proved this young man to be the most audacious and loyal of her servants. She had given him the highest office in the land, to guard against England, and this two years ago when he was still only twenty-three. And early this summer, when Mary of Guise lay sick to death and besieged in her castle of Edinburgh, she had sent him to Denmark to enlist the services of the Danish Fleet, the most important at that moment in Europe, against her enemies of England and those of her subjects who were in league with them against her.

Her new Lieutenant of the Border had carried out her mission with as much success as a diplomat as he had shown as a soldier; he had drunk deep with King Frederick of Denmark, undeterred by the three-litre capacity of that monarch's wineglass, and discussed with him the breeding of horses and bloodhounds; the King and his brother had been so taken with him that they had gone out of their way to escort the young Scottish Envoy across the sea from Copenhagen to Jutland on his way to Germany.

It was on that journey that he heard of his Queen Regent's death in Scotland; heard too that both Scotland and France were now signing a treaty with England. There was therefore no further use in his mission, and he travelled direct to France to lay his sword at the service now of the daughter, Mary Stewart.

Of all this, Catherine de Medici, Queen Dowager of France, showed due recognition when James Hepburn, Earl of Bothwell, Hereditary Lord High Admiral of Scotland and Lord Lieutenant of the Border, was presented to her that evening. She was walking in the midst of a little group of courtiers and ladies and her favourite dwarfs in her gardens of the Tuileries. The sun had not yet set, but slanted behind the late blossoming rose trees and monstrous forms of giant toads and diminutive dragons of green majolica; they threw their squat shadows on the path where that tall stout lady in black walked up and down between two hunchbacks not three feet high.

As she walked, a fretted gold ball containing a pomander, suspended from her girdle, bounced up and down against her stomach – her sporran, the Scot instantly dubbed it in his ribald mind. Her cold and glassy eyes, brown, blank and opaque as chestnuts, took with shrewd accuracy the measure of this tough weather-beaten young adventurer, the swaggering self-confidence of his splendid chest and shoulders and sturdy horseman's stance, as she turned to him with a dirty jest about his amorous career.

It brought back to him with a flash of amusement the gossip he had so lately heard: 'banker's daughter', 'shopkeeper's daughter'? – what was the epithet given by the girl who should wear three crowns to the lady whose family emblem was three gold balls? Whichever it was, it fitted this stout Florentine dame as snugly as her own tight black brocade as she cushioned her beautiful hands in the yielding flesh of her hips in the determined gesture of commercial *bonhomie*, and asked him if it were Scotland, France or Denmark that had most contributed to his reputation as Don Juan. And she followed this compliment with a loud, purposefully jolly laugh.

He'd no love for shrinking modesty in woman, God knows, but there was something in the coarse-grained fibre of that hearty matron and mother of ten that struck him as more unnatural than even the chastity of a nun. Of this he was not really aware, but thought her repellent because her chin fell away like a rat's beneath the sensual lips. But he found himself no whit at a loss in answering her badinage; they exchanged one or two low stories of an ancient pattern, and the Scot was certain that his was the less hoary.

The heavily robed figure pushed its way on through the humming sweet-scented air of the rose-walks, out on to the open squares of chequered marble, her erect head and wide skirts making a wedge-shaped block of shadow, narrow at the top, wider and wider at the base, cleaving its way so purposefully through the late evening sunlight.

Yet she had no fixed purpose; she changed her mind a dozen times a day even in quite small matters; she valued common sense above all things, and was fond of saying that the end justified the means; but she had no end, no aim, except first to win the love of her husband, and second to get power for herself. The first aim had died with the death of her husband a year ago; the second – well, that remained to be seen.

She was a clever woman, she knew how to be all things to all men, she studied medicine, mathematics and astrology because she liked them, but Greek and Latin because they were the fashion. She had encouraged the Reformed religion because it was the fashion, said rude things about the Pope, who was 'no more than a man', and had liked to sing the Huguenot Marot's psalms with the late King Henri II, her husband, perhaps because his mistress Diane de Poictiers had been a staunch Catholic. But, like everyone else, she had to obey the Guises; and though the tastes and interests of the Cardinal de Lorraine all leaned towards these new experimental ideas (he had even attended their prayer meetings for a bet), his policy was firmly Catholic.

Queen Catherine took trouble to explain this to the young Protestant from Scotland; she even, as though she were one of his warmest admirers, quoted the Cardinal's very words on the subject, warning them that the true danger of these new doctrines was that they struck ultimately at the root of all government. And for proof of that, the Lord Lieutenant could furnish only too many instances, since nearly all the other nobles of his faith had banded themselves together as the Lords of the Congregation, in league with England against their Regent.

'But you, my Lord Bothwell, almost alone, have contrived to reconcile your advanced ideas in religion with a loyalty that is alas now old-fashioned.'

'Madam, my ideas are no more advanced than my boyhood's lessons, where I learned them – such as they are,' he added deprecatingly as he shot back in his mind, trying to remember when he had last attended any service. 'We of the Border ride light, we don't take more religion than we can carry with comfort' – but no, that was not too safe even with this old pagan. He was on surer ground as he went on: 'But loyalty is my true creed, as it is the motto of my house – "Keep Trust". I cannot see why men should not worship as they choose and let others do so.'

It was a bold remark to make to the lady who had signified her approval of the executions at Amboise this summer by watching them from the Castle balcony; and so she hinted, with a glance at him from her blank eyes as they rolled round in her fat, flat face.

But he answered the challenge as coolly as he had provoked it. 'Those executions were for rebellion, not for religion. If the Huguenots plan to murder the rulers of the kingdom and kidnap King François your son, what can they expect but to lose their heads?'

She winced very slightly at his reference to the Guises as the rulers of her son's kingdom, but agreed enthusiastically: 'No one can call me a bigot. I have brought up my own children in the doctrine of the Huguenots, and have always said that anyone of intelligence must think much as they do. But one must be practical. It is results that count. "By your fruits ye shall know them," as Saint Paul said, I believe, and if he did, it is magnanimous in me to quote an apostle who paid scant regard to my sex.'

'Madam, you are right. In Scotland, at any rate, religion is being used by rebels chiefly as a decoy duck.' ('And much Saint Paul would care for being quoted by you, you ugly old bitch!' he added to himself.)

Yes, it was good to walk out from that interview, to take a deep breath, remember that he was going to sup with a couple of men, and look round him in free solitude on the familiar town which now looked fantastically beautiful in the September dusk. A single star hung over the piercing loveliness of the spire of the Sainte Chapelle; Notre Dame lay like a couched lion in the dark mass of little buildings round it; the river flowed broad and pale and gleaming under the quiet sky. After this hot day its smell was as exotic as its beauty. 'Edinburgh is as strong but not so rich,' the Scot decided. In the capital of his native land the predominant smell was of stale salt fish; here, of rotting garlic.

But it was for the cool pungent smell of bog moss, of heather and bracken after rain, of dew on the tough hair-grass in these misty September dawns, that his finely cut nostrils were longing. All this summer, and longer, he had been away; what had happened since then at home? What raids had been ridden in spite of the treaty? What mischief had his rascals been getting into?

*　　*　　*

The inn where he was meeting his two friends was a better one than that at which he had to lodge. He saw them sitting waiting for him on a bench outside the house under some dusty plane trees, with wine on a rough table in front of them. They hailed him cheerily; Monsieur d'Oysel, the Commander of the French forces in Scotland, in co-operation with whom he had fought this last year, waved a fat gracious hand as he rose to embrace him, complaining in comfortably lethargic tones of the heat; while Long Geordie Seton had that lantern-jawed grin like a pike's on him, and whistled the tune of 'The Gay Galliard's men' by way of greeting. They told him it was too hot to sup indoors and asked him, chaffing him, about his interview with the Dowager of France – had he been successful with yet another widowed Queen?

'What are we eating?' Bothwell demanded before he would answer, and put down a mugful of wine at a draught – 'Ah, I needed that! Thirsty work, dowagers.'

Nor was he only joking; there had been something oddly exhausting about that large, deliberately jovial woman; she used up all the air round her.

'She told me of the tosses she'd taken. That one take a toss! She'd fall like a load of pig-iron!' And he sang the ribald rhyme of the Paris streets about her:

> *'She is fat, so fat,*
> *Forty stone in nothing but her hat:*
> *Think of that!'*

It was good to relax at ease with his fellow-campaigners of this last year and stretch his legs before him, grinding the dust up with his heels as he leaned back against a tree trunk and looked up at the broad leaves cut out against the glowing dusk.

Below him the river flowed and gleamed and stank. D'Oysel loosened his collar and released the roll of fat at the back of his neck, its crimson hue slowly paling. He sat, large, contented, and apparently immovable, speaking hardly at all at first and then in dulcet tones, moving his hands with a very slight flapping gesture, or his shoulders in a faint shrug, as he listened with a lazily benignant smile to the talk of the two Scots, Bothwell's quick, curt voice and Seton's slower, grinding, burring tones.

They had ordered trout baked in cream and chickens stuffed with mushrooms; meanwhile here were some sardines pickled in red wine, and plenty of the crisp fresh white bread of Paris. Lord Seton was wolfing it as a schoolboy would cakes.

'You find this better than our dry oatcake,' said my Lord of Bothwell.

'Horses' fodder!' murmured d'Oysel on a soft note of horror; 'strange how you Scots can gnaw oats and barley, even drink them in your barbarous whisky.'

'A deal better than a *ragoût* of baked horse and *vol-au-vent* of roasted rats, anyway, *mon capitaine*,' Seton remarked quickly before Bothwell should bristle, and d'Oysel responded with a wheezy chuckle.

'Aye, this lucky dog missed all that,' and Seton turned to Bothwell, ' – and a queer sight it was when the truce was settled, to see all the soldiery feeding together, friend with foe, on the sands of Leith, the Scots and French with their siege rations of horse or rat, and the English with their bacon and beef and chickens. I will say, though, they shared handsomely with our fellows.'

Bothwell showed little pleasure in that. 'All over by June,' he said; 'and I need never have lost the half of my stout fellows in that foray I led on Easter Monday.'

The Frenchman blinked his little blue eyes but still seemed too comfortably placid for the effort of speech. It was Seton who protested:

'You caused more than double that loss to the enemy.'

'And what of that? When those that were left were all sharing their chicken and rats together in three months' time! But old Toppet Hob o' the Main got an Englishman under him that never got up again – but nor did Toppet Hob. And young Kirsty, who was learning to be a handy fellow with a horse, will never go home again; and Jock o' the Lamb-hill will have to sit like an old woman at his door from now on, since the marrow of his shin-bone ran down on his spur leather.'

D'Oysel's solid calm suddenly exploded. He bounced up on his seat in a bubble of fury. 'Never have I heard such impractical sentiment! Do you hope to make omelettes without breaking eggs, or battles without breaking bones? This Border warfare makes you Scots too soft; you think of war as of a raid in which you all know each other by name, even the enemy, and carry off what loot you can with as little loss of life as possible. It is a ridiculous convention – and most dangerous.'

The younger man cocked an impudent eye across that palpitating bulk at Geordie Seton's ironic grin. It was the first time James Hepburn had been accused of being soft. But his chief amusement was in seeing the fat hot Frenchman blowing up with excitement. He watched him delightedly, murmuring, 'Up he goes again! No restraint!'

'An amateur soldier!' d'Oysel shrilled, then broke off abruptly. 'It seems I make you laugh.'

'As any Scot would,' the Galliard replied airily, 'when he hears a squeak like an exhausted bagpipe.'

It was a bad start for a pleasant evening. Seton wished his frugal mind hadn't suggested a Dutch party for this supper; if he had agreed to d'Oysel's wish to invite Bothwell, who was notoriously short of funds, as their guest, then both would have had to behave better. He quickly turned in a conciliatory way to the Frenchman, talking in his most deliberate fashion, determined not to be interrupted by either of them.

'You think, Monsieur, in terms of the new artillery and massed armies, where we, as you say, think of our men as persons known by name and generally nickname; it is a habit due to generations, no, centuries of fighting between those who can be friends, and even of the same family, when they are not enemies. But you know well how heartily my lord of Bothwell believes in the modern methods of warfare, the value he places on cannon in siege —'

'Aye, well he knows it!' broke in the irrepressible Galliard in spite of him, 'seeing I led off Harry Percy's forces on that Christmas wild-goose chase at Haltwellsweir and thought Monsieur d'Oysel and his highly professional soldiers would take the opportunity to besiege Norham Castle. Maybe he'll tell us now why he didn't – if it isn't beyond the comprehension of an amateur!'

'Lad, you are incorrigible!' growled Seton in deep annoyance as d'Oysel, with fat hands, fierce blue eyes and tufted eyebrows all upraised together, went off into a stream of Gallic oaths, explanation and abuse. If they got through this supper without the Galliard flinging down one of his challenges to mortal combat, he, Geordie Seton, would need all his wits about him – and just when they were all hoping for Court favour!

But thank God the stuffed chickens had appeared and – 'Gentlemen, gentlemen,' he protested, 'if you must quarrel, leave it, I beg you, to the end of this course, and not let these mushrooms, the first of the season, cool on your plates.'

The poignant appeal went home, d'Oysel admitting with reverence that it would be a crime to spoil their flavour by letting them congeal in the grease of the gravy.

Bothwell laughed and said, 'Aye, we should keep our breath to cool our porridge, not to fan such tender morsels as these,' and filled his mouth with them.

Seton knew better than to hope for any sort of apology from him, and got on to politics as soon as d'Oysel showed signs of ceasing the really important discussion of the evening. ('C'est bon, ca, hein? – A suspicion more of the garlic vinegar in the sauce perhaps. – It is possible that the nutmeg has been applied a thought too freely.')

They questioned how long the peace would last between England and the allies, France and Scotland; and Bothwell, what odds that would make, since the new Queen Elizabeth would work against them whether in war or peace. Or at least her minister, Sir William Cecil, would do so.

'And our precious new Secretary of State for Scotland, Master "Michael Wily" Maitland of Lethington, is hand in glove with them, I'll swear.'

'Aye, I've heard him described as a sort of Scottish Cecil,' said Seton, 'and the English Queen calls him the flower of the wits in Scotland.'

'Then the flower bears a rotten dry husk for fruit,' Bothwell remarked sourly.

He had once caught a glimpse of Elizabeth before she was Queen – a fine upstanding whippy young woman with a wary eye. She would be rising twenty-seven by now, and still too soon to see how she'd shape on the throne; besides, as was to be expected at her age and yet unmarried, she was too busily engaged in making a fool of herself over a man.

Wave after wave of scandal about her and handsome Robert Dudley had been going on for the past eighteen months and had just broken in a storm over the news that Dudley's inconvenient wife, Amy Robsart by birth, had been found dead at the foot of a staircase in extremely suspicious circumstances. Ambassadors who had been making delicate investigations on behalf of their masters, anxious to know whether they were indeed wooing a Virgin Queen, were now talking openly not merely of immorality but of condoned murder. Her Ambassador in Paris, Sir Nicholas Throckmorton, was nearly beside himself with shame. 'There are too many people here,' he had burst out, 'asking what religion is this, that a subject shall kill his wife, and his Queen not only bear with it, but marry him?'

Bothwell's roar of disagreeable laughter followed the question with another: whether Elizabeth had lost her virginity at thirteen to her stepfather Admiral Seymour, or had waited for Dudley. But unchastity was a slight matter, marriage a serious. If she married her lover, the general view in England was that she would go to bed with him as Queen Elizabeth of England and rise the next morning as plain Mistress Dudley.

A most blessed conclusion, in all their opinions, since this would leave the English throne in the undoubted possession of their young mistress Mary, Queen of Scotland and France and (since Elizabeth had been doubly declared a bastard) of England. The late King Henri II of France, her father-in-law, had insisted on Mary bearing the Royal Arms of England quartered with those of Scotland and France, and had sworn to lead a crusade to win her rightful kingdom.

'He wished to be young again, a knight errant, a champion of

old, for the sake of that charming child – but what would you?'
D'Oysel's hands outspread in gentle despair; his voice, now
loosened and tender with good wine, rocked on mellifluously:
'He was killed by his valour, his chivalry, his desire to shine
before the eyes of his mistress, his wife, his daughter-in-law.'
(D'Oysel's own eyes were moist at his touching picture of the
royal domestic circle.) 'And so, the sport, a tournament, the
chance thrust of a lance in his eye, ended all hope of his
championship of this unfolding rosebud.'

'And what of her?' asked Bothwell, unbuckling his belt and
leaning back in his chair to drink his wine and stare under
drowsy lids at the steel-dark river under the purple sky; even
here under the dusty plane trees of the little inn garden it was
stuffily close.

The gossip his friends repeated bore out his fleeting impression of that tall, grave, glittering child. She was seventeen and a
half, and ripe therefore to be a wife, but most people about the
French Court doubted that the marriage had ever been consummated, for King François, nearly two years younger than
herself, was wretchedly backward and delicate, and had grown
far worse in the eighteen months since their marriage, shooting
up into a sudden height that overtaxed his already feeble
strength.

And as for other affairs, there was still – it was really very
odd, almost scandalous, d'Oysel seemed to think it – no hint of
them. No doubt she was too closely guarded by her six magnificent uncles, and it would be a rash man who would dare to
brave the fury of the Guises. Sheltered, pampered, treasured as
an infinitely precious jewel from infancy, hers had been an
utterly different upbringing from the smeared, scared girlhood
of Elizabeth of England.

Elizabeth had been branded with bastardy by her own father,
had struggled with the drab dangers of her over-familiar stepfather, Admiral Seymour, of her slyly sensual brother-in-law,
Philip of Spain, of her bitterly jealous half-sister, 'Bloody
Mary'.

But Mary Stewart had been the First Lady of the Land since
her birth, the object of passionate care from every one of her
relatives. The Cardinal de Lorraine watched over her with far
more careful intimacy than over his own bastard daughter
('Devil doubt him! That's easy seen!' muttered Bothwell); the
late King's elderly mistress, Diane de Poictiers, had vied with
his wife Queen Catherine in supervision of her education and

appointment of her governesses, showing that strict perfection of respectability that is only to be attained by a French royal mistress; and the little Queen on the whole spent less time at Court than in the remote country home of her maternal grandmother, the Dowager Duchesse de Guise, an old lady of severe charm and shrewd sympathy, as much a saint as an aristocrat.

Yet even as d'Oysel sketched these extenuating circumstances in a slow trickle of words like the dropping of sweet oil, he evidently found it a grievous oversight that in all this chattering Court, where it was only paying a woman her due compliment to tell tales of her lovers, there were as yet no such tales to tell of its young Queen.

'But she's not a woman yet, nor will be for many a day,' observed Bothwell, with a grunt at the obtuseness of the French gallant, for he himself knew as well as any, and rather better, that women do not all grow up at the same age.

The Frenchman, unheeding, spoke hopefully of 'a certain foolish fellow we all know, who they say is in serious danger – but yes, literally – of losing his wits for love of her.'

This was the young Earl of Arran, who had lately been Commander of the Scots Guard in France. Bothwell's knowledge of the family history of that pale gaunt young man with the eyes of a startled hare led him to remark that the loss of his wits would make small odds to him.

'Well, he'd wit enough to answer your challenge from a safe distance,' Seton said with a grin at his companion's strong long arms and nervous fingers that curved inwards in their instinctive grip – a grip that tightened at mention of Arran and memory of his sack of Crichton.

So Arran was losing his head over the Queen, was he? What chance was there that he might work against himself, Bothwell, with her? But Arran, no, that gawk with the lank untidy hair, he was too futile, Bothwell decided, to have any effect on his fortunes.

Those fortunes were surely at the crux of his career. His chances in his own country, on the face of it, were pretty small, with the Lords of the Congregation in power. The Regent had been his only powerful friend, and his faithful and forcible service of her as faithfully rewarded —

'And well it might be!' he suddenly broke out, as the wine glowed more and more warmly in his stomach, and the comfortable dusk dimmed the faces of his companions, so that d'Oysel's seemed only that of a large pink moon rising through

36

the early autumn mists, and Seton's the sharp profile of some distant rock; 'it's not only Scotland, it's France, Denmark and Germany, aye, *and* England, to her cost, who have recognized me as the handiest servant of the Scottish Crown. But now that the Regent's dead, all that that will do is to make me a marked man for my enemies. And they are now running the government of Scotland!'

'You don't suffer from too small an opinion of yourself,' came in a growl from the distant rock.

'It is known,' came in soft agreement from the moon.

But the young man was hot on his career, that career of such enormous, glorious importance that it was inconceivable that the others could be with equal eagerness considering theirs. Nor could anything be strong enough to down it.

'If Scotland's finished for me, who cares? There is the rest of the world. My ancestors travelled to Egypt and the Holy Land, my father lived in London and Venice. And I've clinked glasses with the Danish King, and his was big enough to float a turbot; I've seen the sun at midnight and chased pirates up the Norwegian fiords. That's a good life, a pirate's.'

'I've no doubt it would suit you fine,' said Seton, with a wink at d'Oysel.

'It would,' said Bothwell simply. 'There's an old Roman writer in my library at home' – he paused for the effect this should have on his companions – 'who says of them: "The sea is their school of war and the storm their friend; they are sea-wolves that live on the pillage of the world."'

'I take it the book is a translation,' came that dry, exasperating voice again.

Bothwell ignored the challenge. He tilted back his wooden seat till it all but overturned, and sang, in a powerful though somewhat husky and not entirely sober voice, the refrain of a song by the poet king, James V, father of the young Queen he had seen today:

> *'So we'll go no more a-roving*
> *So late into the night,*
> *We'll go no more a-roving, boys,*
> *Let the moon shine ne'er so bright.'*

'Well, I've no objection to roving farther. The world is widening. It's a grand thing to live these days and hear every month or so of some fresh discovery on the other side of it. Why should the Spaniard and Portuguee have it all their own way there?'

'They would not have had,' said Seton, 'if that stout ruffian Henry of England had had his way.'

'Oh, he set about building a navy, but his miserable children have let it all go.'

'Little King Edward and Bloody Mary did. We've yet to see what Elizabeth will do.'

'Damn Elizabeth! I'm Lord High Admiral of Scotland and I know what I'm talking about. The English navy's finished. There's no reason the Scots fleet shouldn't start again. And I'm the man to do it.'

D'Oysel still kept silence, but Seton took warning from various soft shiftings and heavings of his bulk on the hard seat. He had no wish to have to act as peacemaker again. He gave him a friendly nudge with his elbow to show his amused irritation with the young braggart, and said in a humorously sensible voice, 'Man, you are clean daft to talk so. It's bad luck for me as well as you that the Regent died just as we'd convinced her of our excellent qualities – but the Galliard is not the lad to think he can't convince her daughter of that fact!'

'If only she weren't so young!' the Galliard remarked pensively.

It was the last thing they expected from him, even in this wine-warmed and unguarded mood, and their roar of laughter stopped any explanation from him, though they demanded, even begged it. He was too soothed and complacent by now to be furious at their laughter, but he felt he had made a fool of himself and fell into sullen silence.

But his remark had been perfectly genuine. That girl he had seen today was young even for her age, which was bad enough. He found no attraction in young girls, had no experience of them, since he had always preferred older women, and in his rough and dissolute boyhood, deprived of his mother when nine years old by a peculiarly cynical divorce suit of his father's, he had had no chance, as well as no inclination, to meet any such delicately nurtured and guarded specimen as now awaited him in the person of his Queen. He would do nothing to precipitate his meeting with her, but await his chance for an introduction. He planned this as policy, but in fact felt a most unwonted and uncomfortable shyness at the prospect, a sensation that would have astounded his companions could they have known it.

They were even at this moment twitting him with the latest scandal about him – what was this tale of a young woman of good family who had followed him from Denmark? Where had he tucked her away? In some country corner of France, or in Flanders on his way here through that country? 'The farther the safer, hey? Wouldn't help you to turn up at the young Queen's court with a foreign mistress in tow!'

But he rapped out a surly answer, and neither was such a fool as to wish to cross his temper again.

He lounged deeper into his chair, stretched his legs out farther, enjoying his hopes, the warm night, the wine that was again benevolent, the stars that seemed brighter and bigger in this velvet sky than the stars at home, the distant harsh foreign voices, even the foreign smells. But behind this mellow present mood, and the eager visions of his future, there stood in his mind an unwilling picture of the girl of whom his companions had reminded him, Anna Throndsen, the Norwegian Admiral's daughter.

He would not think of her. There were other women to think of, God knows!

And, as if to exorcize the spirit of that importunate lady, there rose in his mind the image of three Queens: Elizabeth of England of whom they had just been talking scandal, taut, erect, alert, with ever wary eyes; the gross Dowager Catherine de Medici with whom he had talked this evening; and her daughter-in-law, Mary Stewart, a young shining figure that looked as though it were made of Venetian glass.

CHAPTER TWO

THE COURT went to Fontainebleau, and Bothwell followed. He also followed the royal hunt in the forest there, but he was hunting another quarry than the stag, a slight figure in dull green velvet on a dapple-grey horse, who kept well to the fore of the riders, even of that urgent, desperate boy, King François. If he rode furiously, that companion of his rode superbly, with unconscious daring and swiftness, never noticing the strain her rivalry was laying on the panting boy. Her firm hands and easy seat, the grip of the long lithe thighs, showed her more than a pretty horsewoman; the wind tossed aside her skirts and gave a glimpse of the strong young knee in a turquoise silk stocking. 'By God, but she'd manage a raid as well as any lad in my train!' thought the Borderer, who followed behind.

'Your hair is coming down again,' said King François.

'Bah, let it!' exclaimed Queen Mary.

A long strand of it had slipped from beneath the little jewelled and feathered hat perched like an impudent bird on the side of her head; it tossed out like a torn banner on the wind, a banner of pale shining chestnut, the colour of the blown autumn leaves that scurried past her, more and more of it rippling down in haste to join that truant wisp. If only her hat would blow off and give him the opportunity to return it! It gave a leap, a flutter, it was just about to fly into the free air when her whip hand shot up to catch it and crushed it in a secure hold against her hunting-crop. No chance there for the opportunist behind.

If only his luck would stand in and help him to rescue her from something! She had outstripped that over-impatient boy by now and left him winded while she sped on. She rode too well for an accident to be likely, but perhaps some assassin – a lurking Huguenot now — ?

But his luck wasn't in. It was no Huguenot that came galloping after her, but a tall slender figure in green velvet hunting-dress and soft white leather boots, with a ruby cross blazing on his breast, who laid his hand on her rein to bring her horse to a standstill, and scolded her for outriding the rest.

Bothwell pushed his horse alongside. 'I was taking care to keep abreast with the Queen, Your Eminence.'

'Who is this gentleman?' the Cardinal de Lorraine asked of his niece, not too cordially (The proud rascal, the sneaking red fox, thinks he can keep a girl like that in the family, does he?). Still, he had got his chance to introduce himself to his young Queen in an unconventional and therefore interesting manner, though not near as good as he'd have made for himself if this jealous guardian hadn't come to spoil sport.

'I have not yet introduced myself to Your Majesties' Court,' said he, 'but I am James Hepburn, Earl of Bothwell, whom Your Grace's mother — '

He had hoped for some sign of recognition at the name, but he was not prepared for the delight that leapt up in the girl's face – he positively saw it flushing through the transparent skin of her little throat up into her now rosy cheeks.

'My Lord of Bothwell!' she cried. 'Oh, but indeed I know you well. It is the Lord High Admiral of Scotland, whom my mother appointed Lieutenant of the Border,' she told her uncle eagerly, and hurried on to Bothwell; 'she gave me your name in a list of those nobles in Scotland that I was to trust. Guess how high it was placed! Higher than — '

'The Queen's pleasure is no less than mine,' the Cardinal interposed, too smoothly and cordially for it to seem an intentional interruption. It was no wonder he checked the lass's imprudent tongue – God's blood, will she often let it wag so freely?

The little Queen, well aware of her uncle's unexpressed rebuke but by no means taking it to heart, sped on, though on a less dangerous path, her manner as boyish, free and casual as ever:

'You have been helping her cause in Denmark and Norway – yes, she told me in the very last letter she wrote. So you were not there when she died? I wish you had been – she had so few friends by her.'

'I was with her when she fell ill,' Bothwell answered, 'but it was not much I could do then to help. We stocked Edinburgh Castle well with provisions for her lying sick there and in a state of siege – plenty of the French peas and figs and medlars she loved, and salted fish from Leith. One of my sailors caught a sea monster and begged leave to send it up stuffed to show the good Queen. I let him. It made her laugh.'

Her daughter laughed too, though at the same moment the tears rushed up into her eyes, chasing that warm flush of pleasure at their meeting. She was suddenly white, sad and drooping all in an instant, and had to turn away her horse to hide the fact that she was crying. This was no Court mourning, it was uncontrollably genuine. But she tossed her head to shake off her sudden sadness, and turned back to him with a smile so brilliant it made the tears still in her eyes shine like jewels. 'You must come and see me tomorrow,' she said, 'and tell me of my mother and all you have done for her. Please do not be modest, it is so tiresome when brave men will not tell the exciting things they have done; I have often had to speak to my uncle the Duc de Guise about it.'

It was certainly the first time James Hepburn had ever been asked not to be modest, and the bold laugh he gave showed it.

'Madam, your request has done so much to overcome my modesty that I shall swagger for the rest of my life.'

The smile she now flashed at him from under her long eyelids was full of amusement. 'Do not put your nature to too severe a strain, my lord. It is dangerous to change the course of one's life too abruptly!'

Damn her, had her mother said he was a boaster? He felt himself flushing, not under the girl's merry glance, but under the subtle eyes of the Cardinal. *He*'d never trust this girl to the 'Pope of France'! He knew what priests were like – he had not been brought up by his great-uncle, the Bishop of Spynie, for nothing. He had once heard him coyly confessing after dinner to a round dozen of mistresses, and seven of them other men's wives.

He could make friends with the Queen in spite of that flick of mockery, indeed it acted like a spur, but her uncle was leading her away and here came her 'husband', wan, puffy, woe-begone.

'Marie, where were you? I lost sight of you – but all the rest lost sight of me,' King François added in quick determination to prove himself the leader.

Nor would she disprove it. 'You have tired them all out, sir,' she said. 'And look at your poor Bayard, he is sweating all over,' but as she said the tactful words, her eyes widened in frightened question on that bluish distorted face.

'François! Are you well?' she asked.

'Of course I am well. For the love of heaven, don't pretend that I am ill again,' the boy answered pettishly.

They rode on together, the Cardinal beside them. Just before the trees swallowed them up, the Queen turned to wave her hunting-crop to Bothwell, and with it the little feathered hat crumpled in her hand. He heard King François say, 'Who is that?' in his rather nasal thick voice that sounded like a perpetual cold in the head, and the Queen's answer, clear as the note of a bird, 'A faithful servant of my mother's,' all very right and proper; and then the green and golden beech trees hid from his sight that pair of royal children, the one so sick and sorry, the other – but here Bothwell's admiration took a form very unusual in him when dealing with a woman. 'By the faith of my body, it is a pity that one was not born a boy!'

*　　*　　*

Mary Stewart had a small adventure to tell her four Maries when they dressed her for the Court that evening. They were four girls who had been chosen from noble Scots families to be her companions from early childhood, of near the same age as herself and of the same Christian name, so that to distinguish them they called each other by their surnames, which was apt to give a jaunty mock-masculine air to their conversation.

Mary Beton with her frivolous curls, her bright watchful eyes, her mocking smile, was the most excited to hear of the encounter in the forest. 'Oh, but, Madam, I can tell you all about the young Earl of Bothwell. You must be careful of him! They call him the Galliard in his own country.'

'But that is a French word.'

'Many Scots words are. They use it for a gay rascal – as he has proved himself.'

'And it is the name of the Dance Royal. But I promise you he shan't lead me one,' laughed Mary.

'As he did my aunt, Madam! Yes, he is, or was, the lover of my wicked aunt, the Wizard Lady of Buccleuch —'

'Sorcery – you?'

'It's in the family,' said Mary Beton, unabashed, for sorcery was not yet a pervading terror in Scotland. 'Her father learned it in the University at Padua, where the Devil held a fencing class and nearly caught him, but only got his shadow. That was why my grandfather cast no shadow to the day of his death. And Janet, my aunt, learned magic of him and has taught it to Bothwell, they say, but all the proof she's given of it that I ever heard is her power to win a handsome young lord for her lover —'

'Handsome? No, I'd never call him that,' murmured Mary.

'Monsieur Brantôme says he is hideous!' exclaimed Livingstone.

'That is probably because he has triumphed over Brantôme in some love-affair,' said Beton wisely. 'In any case, it is good proof of magic power in my aunt to win him when she's past forty, and has already had three husbands and a lover whom she called her husband in the sight of God.'

'God must have squinted then,' observed Mary Stewart. 'And is my lord of Bothwell her husband in the sight of God?'

'Oh no, the affair is over, I believe, though they said he was handfasted to her.' Her mistress looked rather thoughtful; was she disapproving? She hastened to tell her that her aunt had a great spirit. 'She took a battleaxe and broke open the church door with her own hands when Kerr took sanctuary at the altar, after he'd murdered her husband, Sir Walter Scott of Buccleuch.'

Ah, that might explain the affair! That dark, bold glance that had scanned her so keenly in the forest would appreciate a daring and revengeful temper. Mary herself felt a thrill of pleasure. If anyone dared hurt her poor François she would much enjoy breaking in a church door to get at them! (Her image of the malefactor was no ferocious Scot, but a stout lady in black with a flat blank face and receding chin – to wit, her mother-in-law.) But all she said in a cool, purring little voice was: 'How encouraging are your glimpses of family life in Scotland! I am glad I have a husband in France and no chance of going back.'

Mary Livingstone disclosed more up-to-date gossip of Bothwell.

'He's left a woman behind in Flanders, though he really *is* handfasted to her, so I've heard.'

'What varied tastes the man has! A great Flemish mare, I suppose, as a change from Beton's aunt.'

'No, she's a Norwegian lady of good family who followed him from Denmark.'

'The more fool she!' observed their Queen. 'I've no patience with women who make such fools of themselves over men. Look at Queen Elizabeth – she has lost her head so completely that she is likely to lose her crown as well.'

'And we all know where that crown should be!' cried Livingstone, and the rest of the dressing time was taken up with discussing Elizabeth. But Mary was still thinking of their gossip of Bothwell. All this tittle-tattle of women here, women there! What did it matter to her how many ladies of quality Bothwell had seduced in France, Flanders, Denmark? What she had to consider was that her mother had proved this young man so staunch and able in her service that she had found she could trust him as she had been able to do no other of her nobles. The damage he had done her enemies had been valued by the French Ambassador to Scotland at as much as £1,400.

That was the way a Queen should think of her servants, not as lovers, as that uncontrolled Tudor woman was doing.

CHAPTER THREE

Mary, Mary, quite contrary,
How does your garden grow?
Silver bells and cockle shells
And pretty maids all in a row.

JAMES HEPBURN was reminded of the English song when he was brought to his private audience with Mary Stewart, whom he found singing Italian madrigals with her Maries, sitting in a circle on bright cushions like the five petals of a flower. They sang of 'passion's burning sighs' in voices cool as drops of water – 'Ardente miei sospiri.' He stepped back as though

44

afraid he might tread on them, and certainly his boots seemed far too heavy in that company.

Mary put up a warning hand to him till the tiny song floated away like a thread of gossamer on the scented air; then they uprose with a winglike flutter and rustle of silks and she seated herself gravely, very much the Queen, on a gilded chair, with the other girls behind her in a fan-shape of wide coloured skirts and young slender bodies rising from them in their tight stiff bodices like the sticks of the fan. Their Queen seemed the youngest of them. He stood looking down on her, scrutinizing her as they talked.

Indoors she was different – he would scarcely have recognized her for that radiant creature he had met in the woods. She sat in that high-backed chair and pulled a gleaming silver thread in and out of some damned church embroidery. Was it, then, a waste of time to talk with him unless her hands were also occupied? With her head bent to her work and her eyes downcast to it she looked like a demure schoolgirl – the thing he detested most in women. He discovered at this close range that she did not attract him physically, she was too young and slight, unformed in every way, unaware of his manhood.

His taste, like most young men's, had been formed on much more mature charms – on those, first and chief, of Janet Scott of Buccleuch, née Beton, the aunt of one of these girls – (and there she was, he'd know that impudent chin and cool stare anywhere, the living spit of Janet!). That extraordinary woman had been old enough to be his mother, but had an inexhaustible vigour and zest, whether in love or blood-feud or forbidden learning. She and the foreign Anna, left behind in Flanders, his two most permanent mistresses, would make a round dozen of this variable, unawakened creature.

'The man's a fool that would think either to get or hold you easily,' he thought, and quickly added to himself, 'or to want you.'

But in one respect she was wholly admirable; she wanted to hear all about his exploits on the Border.

'My mother has told me —' she began, but, too quickly for good manners, he broke in:

'Aye, Madam, and her enemies could tell you even better. The proudest testimony I bear is their proclamation a year ago that "the Earl Bothwell and Lord Seton are the only two of all the nobility who keep company with her".'

His flash of angry pride made her flinch; he seemed to feel no pity for her lonely mother, surrounded by her enemies, only pleasure in his prowess on her behalf.

He glanced round that audience of smooth pretty faces, eyes and mouths all ready to open in admiration like daisies in the sun. How the hell was he to make them understand the wild joy of those silent watches in the winter dusk, and then the sudden onslaught, the crash of armed horsemen meeting like the clap of a thunder-cloud?

He drew a deep breath. 'Well,' he began, 'you'll have heard how the Percies all but grabbed old Huntly, so slow he was to get his bulk across the saddle, though all the corn-bins of Duns and Langton had gone up in flames to warn him?'

It did not seem to have been quite the right beginning. But he was not going to be put off by the faint lowering of the temperature.

'We got the news of that English raid by beacon – not much needed, since the corn-bins looked as though a dozen towns were afire! I got two thousand horse together, dashed across country through the night, and cut off the Percies' retreat at Swinton just as the dawn was breaking. There they were, straggling home with their spoil – herd after herd of kine and sheep – never dreaming but they'd be safe in a few hours across the Border – and all their gunpowder damp in the early rising mist – hagbuts missing fire everywhere – that's where the superior English musketry has to give way to cold Scottish steel.'

'Oh, but my uncle says — ' began Mary, and stopped, suddenly shy.

'Your uncle the Cardinal, Madam?' demanded Bothwell, as suddenly grim.

'No, my eldest uncle, the Duc de Guise. He says the musket has supplanted the arquebus as surely as the cannon will in time supplant the musket.'

'I was not speaking of arquebuses' – (his impatient tone was certainly forgetful of to whom he was speaking) – 'but of getting to grips in a hand-to-hand fight when the enemy is unprepared in a misty dawn. No time then for the taking of aim, still less for slow and uncertain loading.' (He suddenly remembered the Duc de Guise.) 'Not but what your uncle, Madam, is entirely right. That is a giant; he belongs to a time when men were cast in another mould.'

'Oh, you think so in Scotland too?' Mary had flushed with pleasure.

'How could anyone *not* think so after his retaking of Calais, in seven days, when England had held it for more than two hundred years? In one week he reduced her to a third-rate Power.'

'I wish you knew him.'

'I wish so too, Madam,' ('especially if I fail to find further employment in Scotland,' he added to himself). His bold eye roved round the little group; there was one girl there that had already caught his eye, Mary Fleming, larger, riper than the rest, possibly the most beautiful. Aye, she was 'fair o' flesh'. His gaze rested on her as he continued: 'It was after the success of that counter-attack that the burghers sent a petition to your Lady-mother to appoint a nobleman for the protection of Edinburgh, and put my name first on their list. So Her Grace made me Lord of Liddesdale and Keeper of Hermitage.'

'Ah yes, Hermitage Castle!' Mary was anxious to show her knowledge of her country, though mostly acquired at a distance. 'That is a lonely fortress on the Border, isn't it?'

'Aye, Madam, it stands watchdog over the whole of Liddesdale; no light job with all the Elliots and Armstrongs there for ever spoiling for a fight! But there's little I'd ask better than a fight with Elliots or Armstrongs – they can follow gear quicker and wind the chase with bugle and bloodhound better than any family on the Border, bar the Hepburns — '

'The Hepburns?'

'My own, of course, Madam.'

'Oh, of course, sir.'

Not exactly a lowered temperature this time, but a hint of irony which Bothwell did not like – if he did not lead it. There was an unexpected dimple in that small chin. So he flicked his eyelids in something very near a wink: 'We Border robbers are somewhat shady gentlemen, Madam; we work best in the bright dark.'

She was quick to be gracious again. 'Then it is true of you, as they said of my uncle the Duc de Guise – "the night brought out his star".'

But to Bothwell the night was a fact, not a metaphor.

'Aye, Madam, the day is our night, and the night our day, and our over-word, "We shall have moonlight again." We are no milksops brought up by the fireside. We are used to win our meat by the sword; but for all that, it is we who bear the brunt of all the attacks from England, while the inland Scots sit safe in their castles. Yet it's not often that royalty deigns to recognize us, unless our King comes down on us with a punitive expedition as your royal father did on my father's friend, Johnny Armstrong, and strung him up in a withy of a cow's tail. Yes, your father had mine imprisoned when he was but seventeen, for protecting "the robbers". But your royal mother dealt more kindly and, I think, more wisely with him; she set a thief to catch a thief and made him Lieutenant of the Border – and she did the same by me when she took the Lieutenancy from that asthmatic bag of guts, old Huntly — '

(There was a gasp at this description of the most powerful Catholic noble in Mary's kingdom, but he did not stay to heed it.)

' — and gave it to me, with the Keeping of Hermitage – aye, and with Hermitage went a subsidy of twenty-three pounds a month, very handy after all the lawsuits left by my father's death, and the sore necessity I was in to prove my grandmother a bastard.'

The silver thread quivered over the embroidery. Mary had started a ripple of laughter that ran all round the semicircle of girls. But she could not get him to tell her why he had needed so sorely to prove his grandmother a bastard; he had become self-conscious and actually wondered whether it had been a trifle sordid of him to do so. Besides, his grandmother had been mistress to Mary's grandfather, James IV, before she had married the second Earl of Bothwell. Their disreputable grandparents might prove a common ground between them of a not altogether convenient nature, and he hastily sheered off them to tell her that as Lieutenant of the Border he had the power to command his neighbours, and if they disobeyed, ride upon them with fire and sword and besiege and cast down any houses held against him.

There was a faint gasp of a different kind at this; the young man who stood before them, his eyes flashing as he gave instance of his power, seemed alarmingly ready to put it into execution.

'And did you?' asked his Queen a little faintly.

'No, Madam, I got to work on my enemies quicker than on my neighbours. If Edinburgh had seen I was the man for them, London soon paid me her compliments, for she had to reinforce the garrisons all along the English side against my attacks. Did your mother – did Her Grace ever tell you of the Raid of Haltwellsweir?'

Mary blinked and paused for the fraction of a second. Some such terrible name flashed back into her memory, which had been praised for its royal quality. If only she could prove it now!

'Was that,' she began tentatively, 'when you all but captured the Earl of Northumberland and his brother Sir Henry Percy?'

Thank heaven it was, for this fierce Borderer was nearer smiling than he had been yet. 'Aye,' he said, 'and if it had not been for their fine Arab horses, the best that English gold can buy, they'd have been with the rest of the prisoners I took that day, rising two hundred of 'em. But my main object was to draw off the strength of the enemy while our French allies burned the Percies' outpost, Norham Castle.'

His face had blackened. Mary thought it must sometimes be as dangerous to be his ally as his enemy. 'And didn't they?' she only just dared say.

'No.'

The answer fell like a stone, and his Queen did not venture to ask the reason. The amazing young man seemed positively to forget that he was talking to her; he stood brooding on that fight in the icy dark of the winter before last, as though it were more present to his mind than the lovely young Queen who sat before him, her shy down-dropped eyes now opened wide upon his face.

'The deep sluggish Till was our best ally that day,' he suddenly broke out. 'Did you ever hear the verse of the two rivers before you left Scotland, Madam?

> *Till said to Tweed,*
> *"Though I run slow,*
> *Where ye drown one man I drown twa."*

'It was a day or two after Christmas in the dead hour before dawn that we took our Christmas cheer crossing that black swollen water, eight hundred horsemen and as many foot, each of them clutching a stirrup-leather to keep him from getting swept away by the current, though God knows it was a near thing for many of the horses too.' He gave a short bark of laughter. 'It was a bit of a shock to my men, though they took it like lambs, when I turned my horse to tell them where I was leading them.'

'Couldn't you trust them before?'

'Trust a Borderer to keep trust? Aye, Madam, through hell itself. But trust him to keep a secret from leaking out through his wife's brother or his son's wife, that's another matter. For all the laws against intermarriage, the moss-troopers have relations

49

on both sides of the Border, and are apt to take a fight less seriously than a football match. Why, they'll stop and gossip in the very midst of a battle – aye, and not even stop for it, for I've seen a Northumberland man and a Scot hacking at each other good and hearty, and asking between the strokes how sister Annie fared in childbed with her seventh.'

An amazed titter rustled through the group; he cocked a merry eye at Mary Fleming in acknowledgment, but went straight on.

'No, I had to keep my true plans to myself. There was only one of the Percies I really had to reckon with – the younger, Sir Henry, a hard man, so his own fellows report him, but the finest soldier I've ever had the luck to encounter — '

('I think he likes his enemies better than his friends,' Mary reflected.)

'As for his brother Northumberland – that easy lord isn't going to forgive me for getting him out of bed by candlelight at two in the morning, after his Christmas dinner, to gallop with his men to meet his brother. But it was I who met his brother first – on the wooded slope of Haltwellsweir, on the bank of the Till behind a swamp of willows. There we couched in the wet dead bracken, waiting, God knows how long, while some of my best prickers fired the haystacks of Fenton Town to lure Harry Percy by the flames, and so led him in pursuit of them past our ambush. It was "Fire and sleet and candlelight" that night, but Percy's candles were lit too late. I gave the word to fire. The best thing about these modern firearms is the din they make. Percy must have thought there were three times our number hidden in that wood; their horses took fright and bolted, so did the riders. I hallooed my fellows after them along the river bank. God, what hunting! I'd sent on the foot to turn them at Ford; Harry Percy's horse out-galloped them and escaped across the river at the shallows, so did some others, but the rest were caught between us and the Till in spate with winter rains, and preferred surrender to cold steel or colder water. It was a bonny fight.'

He was ruminating happily on it again, then remembered that the real point of the story was not the harrying of the Percies by that steel-dark swollen river, but to impress his new Sovereign with his importance.

'It spurred on the English to an armistice, there's no doubt of that, and Percy and I had another sort of river rendezvous some six months later, when we met on the banks of Tweed to settle peace on the Borders – aye, and I saw to it that the English had to cross to the Scottish side for the conference.' He chuckled wickedly. 'The Bishop of Durham gobbled like a turkey-cock over it, and Harry Percy was fit to be tied.'

Mary had heard that the new young Lieutenant of the Border was too fond of baiting bishops, and that Sir Henry Percy had indignantly demanded someone more 'wise and discreet' to represent Scotland. Should she tell him that? Why should she be afraid of him? 'I would have told him instantly in the forest.' But she did not tell him here.

'We signed the papers for your appointment as Scottish delegate,' she said; 'my mother wrote of "the probity, industry and loyalty of our chosen cousin".' Here she was quoting praises again instead of criticism, and why in heaven's name, when he surely had as good a conceit of himself as any man that ever came out of Scotland?

And he paid no heed at all to her compliment.

'There was underhand dealing, Madam, all through that commission, the English using their chance to get in touch with the disloyal Scots. We signed the peace terms at Ladykirk near the end of last September, a year ago. A bare month later, the Lords of the Congregation dared to "depose" your royal mother from the Regency, and were demanding help from England – English soldiers, English money to pay their troops – when the ink was scarcely dry on the treaty. Nothing open, of course. John Knox the preacher wrote to Cecil suggesting that he should send English troops into Scotland and then declare them rebels!'

'What? But this is incredible! How dare you make such a charge without proof?'

Mary had certainly lost her timidity now; she had sprung from her chair, her eyes blazing. He scanned her with cool appraisement. She was better like this.

'Madam, the only proof would be the letter itself, now in Cecil's files.'

'Then how could you have seen it?'

'John Knox himself showed it me, when he was offering me their bribes to make me swerve from my allegiance to the Crown.'

'Which you refused – '

'No, which I haggled over, and so learned all I could. Knox, as an upstart tenant (his family have been dependants on the Hepburn lands for generations), was out to brag as well as bribe, by showing how he had given his orders to Queen Elizabeth's Chief Minister of State.'

'Then he is dealing direct with my enemy against me!'

'As practically every Protestant lord in your kingdom is doing – Madam.'

'Protestant? What has it to do with religion? Elizabeth is not so Protestant.'

'No, religion has nothing to do with it. Elizabeth dislikes John Knox's views as much as yourself. But, as her Ambassador here said, it is to her best interest to "nourish the garboil in Scotland".'

'These are Machiavelli's doctrines, utterly devilish —'

'And the groundwork of every statesman's principles since he formulated them nearly half a century ago.'

'Then if that's how they've come to understand statecraft in my father's country, I thank God I'm never likely to see it again!'

If she had lost her temper illogically, so did he, as quick now to be up in arms for the Scots he had just been accusing.

'Is it only in your father's country, Madam? Would the statecraft here of your mother's fine relatives, the Guises, aye, and your husband's mother, the Medici, breathe a cleaner air?'

'This is intolerable, my lord. You need not stay longer to insult me.'

Yes, he had gone too far again; he had seen it even as he did so; curse his unlucky temper! 'Madam, you are right to be angry. I spoke like a fool. We are both hating the same thing, so why should we quarrel?'

She wanted to say she had not quarrelled but dismissed him, but he gave her no time.

'Statecraft has come later to Scotland than to Italy and France, and therefore is the cruder in treachery. We have ever been a race of hardy ruffians —'

'And apparently proud of it!' she shot at him.

'Aye, Madam, proud of it, though my father was so damned modern and cultivated that he thought it the clever thing to break his faith, both to Queen and wife – having been paid so ill by your royal father in his youth for keeping it to his neighbours!' he could not resist adding.

He longed to shake the confidence of this childishly unconscious creature; to tell her that her father had annexed his father's 'Lands and Lordships' – that his father had called hers 'the murderer of the nobles'. Before he should be mad enough to express the blood-feud in words, he rushed on: 'He was a fool. Let him go! The rest of our house have followed our motto, "Keep Trust". And that is the over-word too of the Border. So our society rests on secure foundation – aye, even though we keep little gear, except a score or so of horses lest we be called out at any moment to attack or defend. But now that foundation of a man's word is being cut away, and no man will be able to trust his enemy.'

'But why should my people hate me – or my mother? She was called the Good Queen. She was kind to everyone, she forgave her enemies again and again, she allowed more freedom to the Protestants than they have known under any other ruler.'

'It's not freedom they want, it's power. That is why they hounded your Lady-mother to the grave, as they will Your Grace if they get the chance – and sought English aid to do it. And I've not yet told you how I baulked that for them, when I frightened the portmanteau of English gold out of John Cockburn's grip.'

But Mary was still hearing those other words, 'hounded your Lady-mother to the grave – as they will Your Grace.' What terrible things this man told her, and so roughly and casually! Never in her life had anyone spoken with so little regard for her feelings.

And had there not been the hint of a threat in his voice when he had told her, twice over, of the harsh way in which her father had punished his? He might be a loyal servant to the Crown of his own choice; but it was as a Borderer, loyal to his house, his neighbours, even his enemies, that he thought of himself first and foremost – and he had utterly ignored her command just now to him to go. She must show him that she was to be obeyed.

She rose in as stately a manner as she could muster, and held out a hand which to her intense annoyance she found was trembling a little. Her voice, she hoped, was cold and ironic.

'I regret, my lord, that there is not time at present for yet another of your adventures' – and then she must needs repent and spare his feelings, adding impulsively, 'but you will tell it to me some other time, won't you?'

'I will, Madam.'

('I'll swear he will!' muttered Beton.)

He knelt to kiss the Queen's hand. This interview seemed to have gone agley, but that should not matter much; she was a young thing and flighty as a weathercock. Now that her hand lay on his, he saw how slight and white a thing it was on top of his hard brown muscles, and felt it flutter a little. A vague, annoyed perception came to him that he had been talking to a child and frightened her; against all etiquette he took her fingers in his grasp as he raised them to his lips. It was done only to reassure her and pledge his loyalty, and he did not know how he crushed them.

Then he went, and all the girls drew a deep breath. The painted walls seemed to close in round them and the room seemed very small.

'Woof!' they exclaimed; and Livingstone, 'I feel as though I had been buffeted in the wind!'; and Seton, 'Or tossed at sea — '

('Or on a bed,' murmured Fleming, but not loud enough for the rest to hear.)

'Can we breathe now? And speak?' asked Beton. 'It seems we didn't dare just now!'

That gave the cue to their exclamations.

'*How* he talked to you, Madam! and at us!'

'The words he used! "Bag of guts" for my Lord Huntly!'

'He could not even remember to call you "Madam", but had to jerk it in every now and then.'

They went on talking about him a surprising amount. You would have thought they were in a convent and never saw a man, Mary said wonderingly.

'Nor do we often—a man like that,' said Fleming.

She thought Monsieur Brantôme had been wrong about his looks; the swarthy Borderer was not handsome; his thrusting nose, which should have been straight as well as short, had evidently been broken, but he had a fine head, well carried, broad in the brow, the thick rough hair very high at the temples as though the furious exertions of his twenty-five years had already thinned it there a little.

Seton said his mouth looked cruel, the full sardonic lips shut so hard under the short moustache; Fleming had noticed the quick commanding glance of his eye; Livingstone was enraged by it – 'he would not even wait to command, but just seize you with those long gorilla arms — '

'All the better to hold you with, my dear! What heated imagination! Your dislike is more improper than my liking!'

'Extremes meet,' observed Seton in her quiet little voice, anxious to hush the small flare-up before their mistress should notice it. 'At first touch one does not know ice from fire.'

Mary Stewart was surprised they should talk so much about

54

him and never take note of what had excited herself far the most – his tale of the fight and chase along the river Till. She sat staring out of the window at a graceful fountain that her husband's grandfather, François I, had set at the end of a rose-walk, and behind it formal gardens like a bright new tapestry, stopping abruptly at the edge of the dark old forest of Fontainebleau that grew for miles all round this lovely palace.

So it was with her life here, bright, sheltered, social, with people always telling her pleasant things in polite voices, paying her compliments on her beauty, her grace, her learning, and above all, her manners; but all round it, behind it, and perhaps some day in front of it again, there lay, far in the bleak North, the far-off land of Scotland that she had left long ago.

There in the 'bright dark' (those two words of the Borderer would remain with her always) stood a bare hillside and a dark loch and a gaunt castle like a thundercloud, carved out against the scudding clouds and the light like silver behind them. For years she had been homesick for the sight, as she had been for her mother, whom she had left behind in Scotland at six years old. Would she ever see it again?

'We shall have moonlight again,' she heard his voice answer her with a promise. Yes, those words would remain with her too. She did not care how unpleasant he had been, he did not matter enough for that, but she was glad she had met him, for he had brought back Scotland to her, here in this small painted room with the marble salamander of François I prancing delicately over the fireplace, and her Maries gossiping behind her; he had brought back something to which she belonged more passionately than the fair, flat fields of France.

CHAPTER FOUR

BOTHWELL WAS not ill pleased with himself as he walked away from the palace; he had told a good tale and held their attention – that was a fine girl, that Fleming girl, good hips. He had rammed it well home to the Queen that he was a useful fellow, good at need, but one to be reckoned with too, if she did not treat him according to his deserts.

He swung through the gates into the dusty square of the great courtyard outside, to the inn where he was lodging, and there saw a slight, shabby, perky figure lounging back against the doorpost, and recognized him instantly.

'Halloa!' he called. 'Has all Paris come to Fontainebleau?'

The youth sprang to attention and bowed profoundly. 'My lord, this letter reached your lodging in Paris; it would never have reached you here if I had not brought it.'

Bothwell took the letter, flicked it over, looked sourly at the seal and superscription. Now he would have to pay this fellow handsomely, and heaven knew how he was to do it!

The lad must have guessed his thought, for he was hurrying on: 'I ask no payment, only a reward.'

'And why should I reward you for bringing me a letter I don't want from a whore I've left behind?' he muttered inaudibly. Paris looked at him like a puzzled dog that has performed a trick which failed to please its master.

'Well, what are you asking?' demanded Bothwell.

'To enter my lord's service.'

The answer came with a harsh laugh: 'What pickings do you hope from that? I've not money enough for the fellows now with me – none for any more.'

And he twisted the letter this way and that as he thought how he had had to let Anna Throndsen give his men their long arrears of pay in Flanders when he had run clean out of cash, and how proud she had been of doing it, and how she would probably remind him of it again in this letter that he would have to read as soon as he had settled with this fellow. He began to feel in his pouch for a coin, but Paris threw out a hand.

'My lord need not trouble. When my lord has been lucky at play he can give me something, and in the meantime I can scratch along for myself if there are not too many questions asked. I would be of use to you, sir.'

'How? There's not much of you.'

'I am quick with my hands for all that. And with my wits. I can read and write – yes, and in English too. I was one of the ragged scholars at the Sorbonne when I thought to be a priest.'

'But why do you want to enter my service?'

'I have a great desire to see the world,' said the lad, throwing out his chest.

'And a great notion that you'll make your way in it,' said Bothwell, with a laugh that sounded less harsh. It struck him that this boy had much the same notions as himself. Anyway, to take him on would save a crown-piece at the moment – or, wait a bit, there was that slack dog Maltby, untrustworthy too, he'd already told him he'd get rid of him as soon as he'd found another to fill his shoes.

56

'If you can find clothes to do me credit I'll not ask where you got them, and you can serve me,' he told him, and went to his room to read his letter.

God, how long it was! The French not near as easy as he could write it, and the sentences all tied up because she wanted to be learned. What was all this high-falutin' stuff about a bracelet she was making him with a pattern of skull and bones and pearls for tears, which he was always to wear, but which nobody must see? Difficult to manage, that. If she'd stick to gloves, that would be a deal more useful.

And here was another of those 'sonnets' of hers, full of the usual complaints that she had left her home for him and was crawling at his feet – and apparently imagining he should like her the better for it! He'd liked her better when holding her head when she was sick from a debauch together – she'd had good reason to complain then, of his leading her on to drink more than she could hold; but she hadn't done so, for all her shame at it she had helped him laugh it off, and had been grateful for his self-reproachful tenderness. He had been nearer real fondness for her then than at any time since they had left Denmark – but this stuff about living only to make herself good enough for him, these 'pearls for tears', etc., made him more sick than his drink had made her. He would tear it up as soon as he had answered, for answer he must, there was some matter here about her being with child, and he must read it more carefully.

He sat down, frowning, at the table, spread the letter before him, drew pen, ink and paper towards him, and sat chewing the end of his quill till the damp feather tickled his palate, and finding his throat uncomfortably dry he shouted for wine. It was brought him swiftly, silently, and it was only as the bearer whisked out of the room again that Bothwell noticed it was the new lad, 'Paris'.

He was not writing, though he could write, as easily in French as in English, in a fluent, even elegant hand founded on the Italian script, owing to the education he had had at the Paris University. It was an unusual accomplishment among the Scots nobles, who wrote mostly in a vile old-fashioned crabbed script, if at all.

His mistress, Janet Scott of Buccleuch, had been the only person in his own country to share his educated tastes after he had come of age; she had enjoyed with him his French translations of the classics, his 'One Hundred and Twenty Stories of Battle', even his books on arithmetic and geometry, a taste so unusual that it saddled them both with the charge of necromancy. 'Charms' certainly she had taught him, for the young ruffian of the Border whose instinct was to take forcibly any woman he had a fancy to, as he would carry off cattle on a raid, had learned great cunning as a lover from his experienced mistress. That had stood him in good stead (or maybe in evil) when provocation, opportunity, and his own furious blood, impatient of any delay, had led him to take Anna by storm; and his practised ability to give pleasure had won her consent soon enough – and all too permanently.

There was nothing of the coy schoolgirl in Anna – a fine showy young woman, the second of seven daughters, all wanting husbands and the solid cash to buy them, for all their brave show of jewels and parents' promises! Why had he been such a fool as to promise marriage to her? True, it was with her money that he had been able to come to the French Court now. But that was only common sense, since this adventure was his best chance to repair his fortunes – by which Anna herself would profit.

And if it came to fair dealing, then by God she owed him every penny of it, for he had been lured into that very same promise of marriage by her family's promise of a dowry of 40,000 silver dollars. It had come at a moment when his fortune seemed desperate, for he had just heard of the Queen Regent's death, on top of all he had lost in her service. But devil a dowry had he got or would get out of Anna he had found – so why should she get her part of the bargain?

If it came to that, he had been 'hand-fasted' to Janet Scott of Buccleuch before he had ever met Anna, though that had been only for appearances' sake and they had both of them chuckled together over it, especially on that absurd occasion when Janet had been summoned in a law-case before him as sheriff of his county, and the plaintiff complained of a case in which the judge bore so intimate a connection with the defendant!

A promise of marriage didn't count for much when marriage itself went for so little these days that there was the proclaimed bastard Elizabeth reigning as the legitimate Sovereign of England. And the marriage of Bothwell's parents had been dissolved without any prejudice to his own legitimacy – dissolved because, so Patrick the Fair Earl had boasted again and again in his cups, the Queen Regent of Scotland had won his doubtful loyalty by promising him marriage 'even to the fixing of the date'.

It was only four years since his death, four years since he had sat at table complaining in his weak querulous voice of the fair French Queen who had played him false, and of all the wrong that she and hers had done him.

At the other end of the table the saturnine face of his son had watched with a certain sardonic pity that flushed consumptive beauty of the Fair Earl as he sat stooping over his table, fingering the Venetian bubbles of blown glass of which he was so proud, counting up the great expenses of his vain courtship of the Queen Regent, all the fine clothes and jewels he had bought in order to brave it before her at Court in rivalry with the Earl of Lennox, another aspirant to her hand – 'all for her, and all to no end!'

But the expense that he did not mention, and his son silently counted, was that for her he had divorced his faithful wife, the mother of his children. James Hepburn well remembered his mother going, sent disgracefully, needlessly away, and her anguished tenderness over leaving his small sister and himself, a savage, scowling, bewildered boy of nine.

Where parents and sovereigns set such an example, what wonder if sons and subjects followed?

So he argued with himself, thinking of Janet Scott's worn but vivid face laughing in the county court; of his mother crying and the queer shock it had given him to see her face crumple up, all red and ugly; of Anna kissing his hands in passionate subjection – things so different and happening at such different times, and yet all a part of his own life. And he bit his pen and drank his wine, and knew that he must now give ease and comfort to the girl who had been so eager to leave her home and family for him. If he went back to Scotland he would take her with him, and the child should be brought up as one of the family. That decided, he pulled the paper towards him, wrote quickly and shortly, sealed it, stood up and squared his shoulders, finished his wine at a draught and gave a long 'A-ah!', then picked up her letter and poem to tear them across.

But he did not tear them. His vanity reminded him that this was the second learned as well as beautiful lady who had loved him; he thought of her flashing dark eyes, unusual in a Scandinavian, which had led her to fancy herself in a Spanish dress her father had brought home from one of his voyages; she had worn it whenever possible (and sometimes when Bothwell had thought it impossible, but this he did not think of now) – a damned fine woman, who had helped him in Flanders and loved him enough to throw away everything for him.

So he opened a silver casket in which he kept his papers, threw letter and poem into it and locked it again, and went down the rickety little dark stairs, whistling, and out on to the square, and there sat at his ease on the rough wooden bench and looked across at the great wrought-iron gates that François I had set up in front of the drawbridge to the royal palace.

As his eye followed the fantastic convolutions of their pattern, black against the golden evening light, he found himself thinking, for the first time since he had left her this afternoon, of the young Queen who had just given him audience; but not as he had seen her then, scarcely distinguishing her among the other girls, but in his first view of her, walking with her uncle the Cardinal, the two so much alike in height and bearing and that transparent mother-o'-pearl fairness.

An odd pang of jealousy, of a kind quite new to him, shot through him at the mental vision of those two creatures of a beauty bred to the highest point of race, of a culture far beyond his small, prized collection of books and his understanding of modern warfare and his learned mistress's long-winded verses which he kept for trophies though they bored him. Anna Throndsen the Norwegian admiral's daughter seemed at this moment unbearably crude and provincial, a woman of no importance.

And he whistled happily the refrain of that song of 'the good poor man's King' that had shuttled from mouth to mouth of soldier, sailor, tinker, tailor, until even the English sailors had got wind of it and made their own version of it:

> 'So I'll go no more a-roving
> With you, fair maid!'

for that was what they would go on saying through all the ages to the maids they left behind them, left rather as no maids.

CHAPTER FIVE

H E S A W her again, surrounded by her uncle the Cardinal de Lorraine and her other uncle the Cardinal de Guise, a jolly red-faced young man distinguished from his elder brother by the soubriquet of the Bottle Cardinal, and by still younger and jollier uncles, Claude Duc d'Aumale and that famous sailor the Grand Prior, and the soldier Marquis d'Elbœuf – in fact, by the whole galaxy of the six superb uncles, and at head of them that great and gay and generous Commander-in-Chief of the army, the Duc de Guise himself. These 'heirs of Charlemagne and Saint Louis', with eight royal quarterings in their coat of arms, were the tallest, handsomest, most powerful men in France, too arrogant even to count themselves as of France, but as half-foreign potentates; and the chief aim of these 'Princes without a fatherland', whose father had been buried with more royal magnificence than many French Kings, was to found a reigning dynasty. They built their hopes of it on this slight docile child; they domineered over her and her even younger husband, the impotent little King of France, and were watched furtively, patiently, by the blank inexpressive eyes of his mother, Catherine.

The Court had moved again, the Court was always moving, partly as a precautionary measure, since it was unwise to stay too long in any country palace to be a settled target for Huguenot conspirators. So the Court moved to Orléans, and a magnificent reception was given by the city. The splendour of the processions, the triumphal arches, the decorations, gave James Hepburn, after the rough poverty of the little towns along the Border, a dazed sense that he had come to another world, even another age. He was invited to a ball, where the young King led out his Queen with a torch in his other hand which he passed to her, and she to the Duc de Guise behind her, and so on to every couple, its leaping flame flickering up on to the glinting jewels, the suddenly bright face of one dancer after another, until all the dancers swung into a ring for the Branle des Lavandières, clapping their hands in mimicry of the washer-woman beating out the linen on the stones by the Seine.

It was a wild movement, a fantastically courtly copy of the rough peasant dances; and as Mary led it, her delicate head tossing back on the long slender throat like a flower stalk, her eyes were dark and brilliant with excitement, drunk with happiness.

The girl ought to be always moving – riding, dancing or ablaze with sudden anger; no wonder no painter could ever show her.

He made a brief comment of the sort to d'Oysel, who shrugged, mopped his pink forehead, which was steaming gently after the dance, and remarked with dry French finality, 'But of course. It is known. The connoisseurs have pronounced her the best dancer of the day.'

'Damn the connoisseurs!' muttered Bothwell.

D'Oysel was not the only one to want to cool his head. Both

King and Queen were wearing their crowns in compliment to the State reception; she found it very hot stepping up and down with a crown on her head, her face was flushed a brilliant transparent rose; when they gave her red wine to refresh her, Bothwell could have sworn he saw it pass down her throat, for the white skin had flushed there too for an instant.

The musicians were now playing the strange Oriental music that the late King Henri II had loved, and half a dozen gilded ships were propelled into the hall by some mechanism, rocking backwards and forwards as if on real waves. In each ship stood a prince who invited a lady from the company to share his magic voyage. King François stepped from his boat and handed his Queen into it; and they sat looking up at sails of blue Cyprus silk spangled with gold stars, listening to the singing of sirens whose glistening tails and silken hair of inhuman length were coiled about the crystal rocks.

In the boat beside them another King, the handsome young Antoine de Bourbon of Navarre, turned his head and looked at them with a half-smile on his weak, sensitive mouth.

'What are you looking at?' his wife demanded in her emphatic fashion.

'At those children.' But Queen Jeanne saw that his eyes were fixed only on Mary, and her delicate nose wrinkled in exasperation. Poor Antoine – he was always so transparent!

Mary did not notice their companion royal couple. She was examining the boat.

'How does it move?' she asked.

'I don't know,' François confessed. 'My mother arranged it all. I am sick of hearing her say my grandfather had to get Leonardo da Vinci over here to do his shows for him. Now she's got other mechanics from Italy. Do you feel seasick?'

'I never do,' said Mary proudly.

'I don't usually, but somehow — '

'Oh, François! Had you better — ?'

'No, I am all right.'

'Ah, thank heaven, there is supper!'

'You are always hungry,' grumbled François. 'I don't feel I can eat a thing.' He looked at her enviously, but forgot his discontent at sight of those dancing eyes. 'And you are always happy,' he said in wonder.

'I am the happiest woman in the world. I once wrote and told my mother so – did I never tell you that?'

'No. When was it?'

'On our wedding day.'

'Oh, Mary —!' he sighed, and then, 'what did you tell her?'

'Only that, the happiest woman in the world, because my husband loves me so much that I can wish for nothing more than to live and die in that love.'

She had written that because of him! He could not speak. Her genius for love awed him.

She took his hand in her strong warm clasp. His was very cold for all the heat of the room.

'You have a headache again,' she said; 'it is only because you are growing so fast. You always said it was unfair my being nearly two years older and taller, and that you'd never catch me up, but now you're doing it so quickly that I shall have to wear high heels!'

He looked at her with the shy adoration that he had felt ever since his father had led him up to the 'most lovely child I have ever seen, and one day you will be her husband'. The Duc de Guise had given him a toy suit of armour on his fifth birthday, and François had challenged him to single combat in the hope of winning the favour of 'a certain beautiful lady'. The children had played together and quarrelled, and in the middle of some assembly would trot off into a corner by themselves to whisper some secret plan together, the little boy frequently interrupting the conclave to fling his arms around the older, stronger child in a fierce hug. And eighteen months ago they had been married in Notre Dame under a golden canopy, and she had moved to music beside him, high up on a platform above the vast swaying, roaring crowds of Paris, moved in the dazzling radiance of her dress like a lily swathed in gossamer.

But still he had had to wait before he could be her husband, 'only a year or so,' the doctors had said, as though a year or so were so short a time, and so it was to them, slow old fellows with their fifty, sixty, seventy odd years, all too many and too long; but to François, who could never go fast enough for his wishes, who tired out his companions, far bigger and stronger than himself, by the fury with which he rode to hounds as if determined to prove himself a man before his time – since later there might not be time – to François II of France 'a year or so' spelt a lifetime, as indeed, deep down in his inner self, he knew that it would prove.

*   *   *

Marble supper-tables were carried into the hall by innumerable pages in white and scarlet. Bothwell found himself seated near the high table; he watched the Guise brothers as they ate and talked, their rings and earrings flashing as they moved, their teeth smiling in their fair pointed beards ('Aye, there's the grin of the fox,' he thought as his eyes fixed on the Cardinal de Lorraine); he listened to their crisp French accents, sharp and light as the clapping of hands in the Branle, certain as commands. Every now and then they turned towards their niece, drawing her into their conversation, smiling at her, petting her.

'Yes, tell us, Madam. Who should know, if not "the Little Savage", how it is pronounced, that cacophony?'

'Ker – ker – ker – nochs? Is it possible? All their names are alike – you have only to imitate water hissing on hot iron.'

'But of whom are you speaking?' she asked.

'Why, of your countryman, the Scottish preacher who gave your mother so much trouble. It is he, we have just discovered, who was the author of that anonymous pamphlet from Geneva.'

Bothwell's ears, as well trained as the mountain deer's, listened acutely. They must be talking of 'The First Blast of the Trumpet against the Monstrous Regiment of Women', which John Knox had written to prove that it was against nature and the laws of God and man that any woman should have the supreme rule of a nation.

' "Woman," ' the Cardinal's soft ironic voice was quoting, ' "having been accursed of God, is to be for ever in complete bondage to man and daily to humble and subject herself to him." '

'He must be very ugly to hate women so,' said the Queen's grave childish voice.

They all laughed, and the Duc de Guise said, 'Hate rulers rather – ever since he was embroiled in that English plot to murder Cardinal Beton, and served a couple of years in our galleys for it.'

'Then why was he ever let out to plague my mother?' she demanded indignantly.

No one could remember at first; then one of them said it was through some negotiation of England's.

'Ah, then England acknowledged him as her agent!' she cried triumphantly.

'Very right.' The Cardinal de Lorraine smiled with pleasure to hear her talk politics so wisely. He held the floor with light graceful gestures of his beautiful hands. 'This particular agent was even acknowledged so far as to be made King's chaplain to the boy Edward VI. He took the chance in his sermons to abuse all the chief councillors to their faces under the thin disguise of Biblical names!'

'A bold fellow!' There was a note of admiration in the deep voice of the Duc de Guise.

'Bold as brass – while under royal protection. The moment the Catholic Mary Tudor was on the English throne he bolted and left his friends to burn.'

The Cardinal's amused eyes glanced at Queen Catherine to see how she took his account of the Reformers, her former protégés. But she was busy capping the classical quotations of the Lord Rector of Orléans University; she was also busy eating, 'shovelling all the food she can into her mouth', as Mary noticed – and without any discrimination, although she was worried by her growing stoutness; no doubt she would outwalk all her courtiers after this in order to counteract it!

The Bottle Cardinal remarked that all Reformers were treacherous to their friends, and the Duc de Guise said, 'Because they are so to their foes. If a man cannot keep faith with his enemy, then he will do so with no man, nor with God.' ('This is as great a man as I've heard,' thought Bothwell, but he was staggered the next instant by de Guise's example of the Reformers' lies.) 'Their Bible is supposed to be the book of the gospels, written fifteen centuries ago, and yet today I saw a copy, and the date in the beginning was only last year's!'

There was a second's hushed gravity in respect to the head of their house; then, it was irresistible, all his brothers began to laugh, until he, puzzled at first, suddenly saw his blunder and laughed too.

'We simple soldiers, sir, should leave these matters to the clerics,' René de Lorraine, the Marquis d'Elbœuf, said to him, grinning with the impudent delight of a younger brother.

'Got it wrong, have I? Well, anyway, I'd have got it right in the galleys and let the traitor sit on there till he'd worn through his – breeches.'

'If it is any consolation to you, brother,' said the Cardinal de Lorraine, 'I am told that his session was long enough for him to contract a certain distressing complaint.'

'Ha, ha, undermined his constitution, hey?'

'But,' said the Cardinal, turning yet again to that tall pretty child, taking, as Bothwell noticed, any chance to hear her clear voice, 'you have still not told us, Madame la Reinette, how is one to say that name – K-N-O-X?'

'You do not say the K at all, sir; it is pronounced "NOX", like the Latin for "night".'

'Then may night never fall on you!' he answered, smiling, and Bothwell was hastily suspicious of so lewd a gallantry from an uncle. But she took his remark literally and gave him a bewitching, rather tired little smile.

'My crown is so heavy,' she said. 'May I take it off?'

She lifted it from her head and put it beside her, although she saw her mother-in-law give an involuntary gasp. The Medici was so superstitious with her astrologers and slavish belief in dreams and omens, she was always afraid, thought Mary with the irritation of one who is never afraid. She pushed up the damp reddish tendrils of hair that the crown had pressed down on her forehead, and gave her head a little shake to free it from the sensation of that weight.

As she did so she caught the eye of a young noble at a neighbouring table, and recognized the Earl of Bothwell. She was so tired that she gave him exactly the same bewitching shy sleepy smile before she remembered that she had dismissed him in anger at their last meeting. But why should she bother about that? It was tedious to go on being angry; and her mother had told her she would be wise to make friends with this young man.

So, for she did things thoroughly, she beckoned him to her side after the banquet and introduced him to her uncle the Duc de Guise, 'who has heard so much of you.'

De Guise was gracious, his keen eyes sweeping the strong figure before him, the alert head and great shoulders. 'My sister the Regent has told me something of your doings, my lord, and so has our Ambassador to England. You have not only done some very pretty work for Scotland; you have actually brought a blush to Queen Elizabeth's maiden cheek!'

'No man could have the face to do that, sir!'

'At least you gave her an awkward moment when you robbed her baggage.'

'And gave your Ambassador the opportunity to call her one,' was the instant retort.

De Guise chuckled at his impudence. 'Yes, you forced her underhand dealings into the open.'

'Wars nowadays,' said James Hepburn, 'seem to be less a matter of men and weapons than of the lies told by their governments.'

He spoke quickly, forcibly, as if he were dealing strokes in battle, for he knew that the greatest captain in Europe was summing him up, and he might only have a minute or two in which to give a decisive blow for himself.

De Guise's next words were obviously designed to give him an opening: 'What did you think of our cannon? Do you believe in a future for that weapon?'

'Its best effect, sir, is no doubt in siege, but I firmly believe there is a great future for it, though we may not live to see it.'

'I hope not. For I have heard it said that with improved artillery the individual soldier will make precious little odds.'

'Don't you believe it, Your Highness! What counts, as always has and always will, is the kind of man you've got behind the big gun, as behind the musket, behind the bow and arrow or the stone in the sling.'

'Personal leadership – and well you've proved it, young man! The Galliard has made war *gaillardement*.'

So he even knew his nickname. Bothwell saw why the Guise's men worshipped him. And the great man gave him his best chance by asking how he had combined with his French allies.

'I fought side by side, sir, with the Sieur d'Oysel all through that last siege of Leith this spring, and ask nothing better. There was a sortie I led of French men-at-arms and my own light horse which swept the English trenches clean – and I never saw better work done in unison by horse and foot, though more than half could not speak each other's language. But French and Scots are a grand mixture.'

'We have good proof of that,' said the Duc de Guise, with a smile at his niece.

Bothwell did not want any distraction in the way of feminine compliments; he hastened to tell of the night sorties he had led, riding down with his prickers from Edinburgh Castle under cover of darkness to cut off the English supplies as they came up from Berwick – 'We Borderers have a good nose for plunder'; how he and Geordie Seton had led the sally last Easter Monday, the hottest bit of fighting in the whole siege; they had succeeded in spiking the enemy's guns, and Bothwell in his furious charge had himself unhorsed and wounded the two best leaders on the English side – 'we cracked their Easter eggs for them hard enough,' he said gleefully, with no trace now of the regret for his own men that had enraged d'Oysel.

'Easter,' said de Guise thoughtfully, 'when discipline was slack, the men drinking and gaming in their trenches. Then All Hallows' E'en – and wasn't there a Christmas raid of yours which startled London into reinforcing her northern garrison?'

'Yes, he told me,' murmured Mary, but neither paid attention, and the Guise was saying:

'You have the secret of guerrilla warfare, a sense of the season, the right moment at which to strike a surprise blow.'

He turned again to the girl who had been content to stand and listen, though accustomed to be the whole centre of attention: 'Take note of that, my Reinette, to think always what your enemies may be thinking. But why are you not dancing? It is dull for you to hear of sorties and surprise attacks.'

'It is what I like best in the world,' she answered, and her eyes were shining. 'I wish I had been in Edinburgh with my mother this spring'; and it was plain she saw herself fighting for her, riding down from the Castle at the head of Bothwell's light horse.

Her uncle smiled at her indulgently, then told Bothwell, 'You must have a talk with my brother the Cardinal de Lorraine about the situation in Scotland. I gather that my sister's death has left the Protestant lords in charge of affairs there.'

'Of whom I am one, Your Highness, though no longer in charge.'

'Hey, what's that? You a Protestant? I thought you a loyal man.'

'So am I, sir, to my Sovereign *and* to my faith.'

'Warning me not to try and change it, hey?'

'I have too much respect for the value of Your Highness' time.'

De Guise gave a short laugh. 'I'll take the hint. But I don't like your creed.'

The young man stiffened. 'Loyalty is my creed. It is also my line of action. I've no other to fall back on.'

'It has done you no good with the bulk of your co-religionists.'

'No, sir, they are my enemies, because of my allegiance to the throne. For that reason they sacked my house at Crichton; and for that reason I am unlikely to find further employment in Scotland.'

'Humph, yes, and your diplomatic mission to Denmark pulled up in full course. Short of cash?'

'Very.'

'We must see to that. If you are still at a loose end later on, there's always employment in France for men of your calibre. Remember that I should be glad to see to it, and if I'm not handy, I'll leave word with my brother the Cardinal.'

He left them. 'There!' said Mary. 'He is thinking of the Captaincy of the Scots Archers in France – I thought he would,' and she nodded to Bothwell like a benevolent fairy god-mother. He suddenly remembered that he owed this interview to her, and gave her a smile of real friendliness.

'Your Grace has been kinder to me than my deserts.'

'Now, that you know to be nonsense,' said she, snatching at her momentary tactical superiority. 'You do not honestly rate your deserts as lower than the last Captain's!'

The last Captain of the Scots Archers had been the Earl of Arran.

'But he,' said Bothwell, with a sudden glint of amusement at her, 'had the disadvantage to lose his wits for love of his Queen.'

'You are wrong, sir, it was Monsieur Calvin who unsettled his wits. My lord of Arran paid him a visit at Geneva and came back raving that he was damned, or that everyone else was. Monsieur Calvin must be an unsettling person. He has eleven diseases, but none of them succeed in being fatal.'

'Your Grace knows a deal about the Father of the Reformed Religion.'

'I can just remember his patroness, my husband's great-aunt Marguerite, the sister of King François I. That is her pretty daughter over there, Jeanne d'Albret, with her husband of Navarre – can you see her?'

'I can see,' said the uncompromising Scot, 'that the King of Navarre keeps a grey mare in his stable.'

As his Queen stared bewildered, he explained his native idiom by another: 'I mean, it's she who wears the breeches.'

She laughed at such frank criticism. 'Certainly Queen Jeanne is more of a managing Reformer. But it was her mother, La Marguerite des Marguerites, who sheltered Calvin for years at her home in Meaux, to prevent his being martyred for his doctrine. Yet he has remained a martyr, and made everybody else one, to his digestion. He was always scolding her. He even quarrelled with Monsieur Rabelais, the most good-natured of men, who was also in her protection.'

Again Bothwell felt that half-unconscious pang of wonder and envy at this glimpse of a life beyond the scope of his own.

'I would give all France,' he had often said, unthinking, to express the quintessence of wealth. Now for the first time he had some perception of that wealth in the terms of civilization and the beauty prepared by men's minds; all these fair châteaux whose images glimmer in the smooth waters of the Loire; all the songs of these new poets, Ronsard and du Bellay, weaving fantastic arabesques in praise of her woods and sedate gardens, and of this young girl whose shy beauty they watched unfolding like the petals of a flower; the stored wit and wisdom of Rabelais and Montaigne; the humanity of such spirits as La Marguerite des Marguerites, whose power of love was wiser than all learning; a country that had been the spiritual as well as the material heaven of the Scots through the preceding centuries.

'They say,' he said, apparently inconsequently, 'that good Scots go to Paris when they die.'

CHAPTER SIX

IT WAS the first of several conversations between them, sometimes in her mother's language, sometimes her father's. 'Do I talk Scots well?' she asked, preening herself for a compliment, and he told her, grinning, 'With a braw French accent, Madam.'

'It is too bad, I am always the foreigner. When I came here I could not speak a word of French, and they took my Maries away from me so that I should not chatter Scots with them.'

He liked her, especially when her eyes flashed at some tale of adventure, daring or absurd, such as that of Dickie o' the Den who drove off a flock of sheep and disappeared with them, until the bloodhounds stopped dead at an enormous haystack where they scented the whole flock, and Dickie, completely covered with hay.

'Ah, but that's the grand lad! He'd lift anything that wasn't too hot or too heavy. It was only the lack of four legs to it that kept him from driving off the haystack itself.'

The sympathies of her Lieutenant of the Border (and his Queen's) were all with the robbers that he had sometimes to ride down and suppress. He told her of a respectable matron who at dinner would put a dish before her son, empty of all but a pair of spurs, as a hint that the larder needed replenishing and he must ride again on a cattle raid. 'Ride, Rowley, naught's in the pot,' was the maternal injunction given by the Lady Graham of Netherby.

These Border women were of a piece with their men, gay with silver brooches and bracelets to show their men's success in plunder, but their houses very bare of furniture, to be left lightly.

'And I,' Mary exclaimed, catching in her excitement at the fabulous pearls round her throat, given by Solyman the Magnificent to François I, 'I do not care for possessions.'

He laughed at her, scrutinizing her narrowly. 'Aye, it's fine to talk so when one's safe and snug with a hundred baggage-wagons piling up the furniture to move on to the next palace!'

For all that, he remembered that her father, with the same fine-drawn beauty and a constitution not strong enough to last more than thirty-one years, had been bred up in his boyhood in effeminate luxury by the Douglas family, who hoped thus to keep the power to themselves, and how he yet had the force and determination to break away from them when only fifteen, seize the reins of the throne, and govern with a resolute hand.

This lass looked like inheriting his spirit – his constitution also, the more's the pity.

This was largely the reason why she still had no physical attraction for him. She was not of a stock he'd care to breed from; it was too highly bred, from a hundred kings, from Charlemagne and Saint Louis; apart from such practical considerations, she personally was too undeveloped, for all that she was nearing eighteen; she was also too delicate. The courtiers might rave about her beauty, but that was their business. He had no taste for a woman he could crush like glass; nor for one who might faint at any moment and have to spend days or even weeks in bed. Weak health was in itself exasperating to a man of his own full-blooded strength; if one were ill one had better die and make an end of it.

The Scottish Secretary of State, Mr Maitland of Lethington, was frankly banking all his policy on the likelihood of Mary dying of a consumption within the next year or two. But there Bothwell did wonder whether Master 'Michael Wily' (the Scots version of Machiavelli's name) was quite as clever as he thought. Was he not counting on the wrong horse to fall on the course? To his eye there was something far more deadly in the thick puffy pallor of King François than the brilliant, swift-fleeting colour of his Queen.

She was always having to console and encourage him, and the robust vigour of the Borderer came as a relief to her. As she grew less shy of him she told him something of her troubles. She never seemed to have enough money for all she wanted to do ('Then we are like enough in one thing,' he told her); she had recklessly given away too many of her dresses and jewels to the wrong people and so had not enough for the right ones, 'and I am afraid they will say I am not at all like my mother, who was always so generous.'

Her worst trouble had been a very unkind governess, but the

Cardinal de Lorraine had dismissed the old hag before even she had complained to him. That would show my Lord Bothwell what reason she had to adore her kind uncle – yes, and once he had even got up in the middle of the night to come to her.

'And wouldn't any man!' exclaimed Bothwell with irrepressible amusement.

'No, he would not – to a greedy child who had made herself sick, and he a terribly fastidious young man. But after that he ordered my diet himself, and as carefully as he did my lessons. But my mother-in-law, Queen Catherine, has always continued to teach me Latin,' she ended on a note of despair.

He bore with these schoolgirl confidences from policy rather than patience, and led her to speak instead of what she could remember of Scotland. It was not much, for life had moved so fast with her that it scarcely gave her time to notice what it had poured through her childish hands.

She was born; in a few days her father died and she was Queen of Scotland. Then that ogre across the Border, King Henry VIII, uncle to her father, whom Henry's armies had defeated at Solway Moss and thus killed of a broken heart, proposed to marry his son Prince Edward to the baby Queen in the North; insisted that he was to be her guardian, and that if she died in childhood the Scottish crown should pass to himself. Children died easily; in the guardianship of so wicked a great-uncle (he had already beheaded a couple of wives as well as countless numbers of his nobles and servants) Mary might die very easily indeed.

Her mother refused to part with the infant, and King Henry's reply was his army order to invade Scotland and 'put all to fire and sword – burn Edinburgh and raze the city to the ground, sack Holyrood and as many towns and villages as you may conveniently, exterminating men, women and children without mercy.'

James Hepburn had watched that 'rough wooing' as he called it; again and again in his early boyhood he had seen the countryside round his home laid waste, and the flames and smoke swirling up from the nearest towns, the beautiful old Abbey churches of Kelso and Dryburgh and Melrose smashed to ruins, and the peasants flying in terror from the English and the German hagbut men that King Henry had hired to help his invasion, since the English soldiers, themselves peasants, refused to destroy their neighbours' harvest.

'But he did not get Edinburgh,' he said – 'nor you. He was

told that the women and small boys of Scotland would fight for you with distaffs and stones – I was a small boy myself, and had my stones and catapult ready!'

'You can remember it and I can't! I had my first night-ride at seven months old when my mother took me out of my cradle and galloped with me to Stirling. But later I can remember hearing the English guns, and rushing away again from Stirling among huge silent overhanging mountains, and the man who carried me on his saddle said, "It'll need be a bonny hunter who'll run ye to earth in the Highlands." But after that I even had to leave my mother and be taken away in dead secrecy to a monastery on an island in a loch – Inchmahome, the "Island of Peace", they called it, all those kind black-robed men whose cowled faces I never seemed to see, they were so far above me.'

Six months later she had been sent with her Maries to France to escape the clutches of the English 'alliance', and her convoy had had to dodge the enemy's fleet all through the voyage.

A harried infancy, never bringing, as her devoted French grandmother, the Dowager Duchesse de Guise, lamented, a moment's 'rest and repose for the little creature'. The little creature had not known that, but she had known how important she was – Queen of Scotland from the week of her birth, told that she was also to be Queen of England, until the day she was told she would instead be Queen of France. The hurried journeys, the changes of scene, the different people who looked after her so anxiously, petting and playing with her, were all pleasantly exciting; while in the background there was always her mother, that tall calm woman with the low voice and the amused mouth and clear considering eyes, who lived only that she might look after her small daughter and her interests, and with so selfless a devotion that she sent her away to her own country, 'like a small bird', as she herself wrote, 'that makes a nest for its nurslings'.

In France all the countryside came to welcome her with pageants and toys and fireworks and dances, and an army of a hundred and fifty children in white uniform, banging drums and shouting, 'Way for the Queen of Scotland!'

And in France was an adoring new papa, the King of it; a devoted little slave who would be her husband; six kind gorgeous uncles and their mother, her grandmother, like an old fairy, wise and gay, an aristocrat of the old school ('there are no ladies like that now'), with whom she stayed more often than at Court, in her country home of Joinville, learning the arts of embroidery and fancy cookery and garden-planning, hearing legends of royal and pious ancestresses who had talked with the ghosts of Saint Francis and Saint Anthony.

She still had her four Scots Maries, and in a few years her mother came to visit her, and for the first time Mary saw elephants, seven of them, swinging slowly down the streets of Rouen in the procession to welcome her.

Certainly, if time had moved fast in those early years, it moved in the sunlight.

To Bothwell, getting glimpses of it in contrast with his turbulent, dissolute boyhood, it was incredible that anyone, even a girl and a Queen, should have been brought up, in spite of all her adventures, so remote from reality. She seemed to take it for granted that all the men and women she met were her guardian angels; she knew nothing of them, nor, he guessed, of herself.

*   *   *

The Duc de Guise had been as good as his word; Bothwell was given a grant of six hundred crowns and a temporary sinecure as Gentleman of the King's Chamber; there were promises of more solid benefits in the way of Abbey lands in Scotland should he return there. This he had now made up his mind to do, 'despite of all men', and work up a party there in the interests of the absent Sovereign.

He was admitted to private discussions on Scotland with the Duc de Guise and the Cardinal de Lorraine, the greatest honour in France. The Venetian Ambassador in France, a lively old fellow who had been a crony of Bothwell's father during the Fair Earl's enforced sojourn in Venice, told Bothwell that the Cardinal, Controller of Finance, was regarded by the Doge and Senate as in himself an independent European Power; and the Duc de Guise's victory in retaking Calais, the last of the Black Prince's conquests left in English hands, had given his family 'such repute that the administration of France will remain in their hands for ever'. That was good hearing for the young man whom the Duc de Guise obviously liked and trusted.

Altogether life was good, the soft autumn weather mild as milk, the boat-hunting with spears a new sport, and the tame-cat existence as Gentleman of the French King's Chamber, though intolerable if for any length of time, made quite a pleasant interlude after the furious activities of the last few years.

He decided to return to Scotland in about the third week in

November, when the Court was going to move on to Chenon-ceaux on a hunting expedition and remain there till the end of the month.

The curtains and tapestries were taken down, the rugs taken up, the beds taken to pieces, and all the furniture piled on to barges instead of baggage-wagons to glide on down the Loire and be put up again at Chenonceaux before the royal party arrived.

It suddenly turned bitterly cold on the Monday that they were to start, and Mary shivered in a white furred mantle while waiting for François on the water-steps. Their gilded barge was moored ready for them, rocking very slightly on the iron-grey water that had been lashed into little waves by the bitter east wind. The wide sands had turned from pale gold to lead.

François was always late; she wished she had waited for him inside, instead of running out here in her eagerness to be off. She saw one of his gentlemen coming towards her; it was the Earl of Bothwell.

He looked grave as he came towards her, and said, 'Madam, the King's headache is worse, it is giving him ear-ache, and violently. He cannot start just yet.'

She turned very white. 'He fainted in church yesterday. I've done that several times, but it is worse for a man. He had got a cold again – can it be that that gives him ear-ache?'

She went on talking as they hurried back to the house; all the time she was thinking, 'It's unlucky to go back' – unlucky, that horrible word, suggesting that there was no order in the scheme of things, only the working of blind chance, as Queen Catherine believed. She had, so her Maries whispered to their Queen, con-sulted astrologers here as to the length of life her sons could expect. No one could read the answer in that enigmatic face, but Mary thought her mother-in-law had been graver of late.

The dismantled house was chill and desolate. François was lying on a bare mattress laid on the floor, and shivering vio-lently though several cloaks had been laid over him. He still had his boots on. A page was making up the fire again, blowing it with a huge pair of bellows, but the logs were damp and hissed and spluttered without sending out much heat.

'It *would* happen today,' François was muttering, 'just the very day we were to start.'

She knelt down on the floor beside him, threw her arms round him, and said, 'It will make no odds. We will go on in a day or two, you will be better then.'

'But there's nothing here – everything gone on. It's all cold, cold, cold and wretched.'

'Your mother has sent for some bedding. You'll soon be warm and comfortable in bed, and your poor head will ache less then.'

He had covered his head with his arm. She looked out over it to the uncurtained window that showed the grey sky and the dead leaves blown past it, silting up on the smooth lawns in brown untidy heaps. She felt frightened and miserable, but François must be feeling far more so. 'You will soon be in bed,' she said again, 'and then you will feel so much better.'

But François got worse. He had high fever and terrible pain in his head and ear. There was soon no question of their going to Chenonceaux, and Mary asked Bothwell not to leave just yet for Scotland as he had planned. So he stayed, though every day enhanced the danger of the journey, it being an ancient seaman's law in Scotland that no ship should sail between the day of Saint Simon and Jude and Candlemas, the most stormy season for the Northern seas.

The Duc de Guise sent for Ambroise Paré, the famous surgeon who had brought him back from the grave when wounded at Metz, and Mary talked hopefully to Bothwell.

'Paré will cure the King. He is a Huguenot, but surely he could never let that influence him towards the King?'

'Rest easy, Madam, if the man's half the doctor he's reported to be, he'd never let religion foul his work.'

It was an odd way of putting it, but Mary was reassured, until there came a new fear. Paré came, with his long duckbill of a nose and bushy moustache and face like an honest bourgeois until you saw the unswerving, considering eye. He believed he could cure the King by an operation on his brain, but Queen Catherine thought the risk too terrible.

'She is afraid, always,' said Mary.

Bothwell wondered. The Medici knew well enough what she was about; she had extremely advanced ideas in medicine. It had begun by now to be evident that there was no other chance for the King's life. But – how much did she really wish that life to continue?

It was a monstrous thought; Bothwell was rather appalled with himself for thinking it, but facts were facts; as long as François lived, the power of his wife's relatives, the Guises, was paramount, and that of his mother nothing. She had ruled her son by fear, but he worshipped Mary; with every year of advancing manhood his wife's influence would grow, his mother's lessen.

Could any mother not a monster reason so? Bothwell's first impression of Catherine had been of something unnatural, though there had been nothing positive in evil, nothing positive at all, only – nothing! That was it; there was nothing behind those blank eyes but an immense indifference. She was insensitive to all except her own lust for power, which she had never had a chance to excercise.

If François died, she had three other sons to take his place, and the next in age, Charles, only ten years old, was and would be completely under his mother's thumb for a long time. If François died, she would rid herself both of her daughter-in-law and the Guise domination.

Bothwell thought it extremely likely that she would not allow Paré to operate.

November froze into December. On the 8th, Mary would be eighteen. The snow was falling lightly, soft as feathers, covering the scaled tourelles like the inverted tails of mermaids. The statues in the gardens stood all wrapped in snow, their white outlines blurred against the iron-grey sky. The King of France was dying, and the Queen of France and Scotland moved like a ghost about the palace, pale and ill from her constant watching by his bedside. She was now too full of fears to confide them to Bothwell; it was he who blurted out to comfort her:

'Remember, Madam, if the worst comes to the worst, there is always Scotland.'

'And is that the worst that can come to me?' she laughed sadly.

But as he too laughed he took her hand and said again, 'Remember Scotland. If you come to it, Scotland will always remember you. You would be such a Queen as they would make songs and stories of until the end of time.'

She had never heard him say anything so flattering, and yet it did not sound like flattery, it had been jerked out of him as though he were not aware of it.

'Why did you say that?'

'I don't know.' For an instant he seemed almost abashed, certainly puzzled, then pulled himself together. 'Come, Your Grace, am I so great a boor that I should not tell a Queen her country would remember her beauty?'

That came like a cold douche; she shook back her head and said, 'I know why you said it. You are going away.'

'Madam, yes. I must go at once.'

'Must you?' She paused, her tired eyes gazing up at him – a forlorn child, he thought, ready to drop from weariness; never had he seen her look less beautiful; the light had all gone out of her face these days, she was quite plain really, and he did not know why he had suddenly seen her just now as a spirit lighting Scotland like a flame.

He must be getting maudlin in this sick-bed air of hushed anxiety and sympathy – Christ! why couldn't a fellow leave the world quickly from a clean blow instead of dragging his maimed life along for days and days!

He towered over her; his solid yet springy strength seemed almost overpowering to her who had just come from that painfully dying boy; if only he could give some of it to François – and to herself. An almost pleading note came into her voice as she said:

'You were my mother's friend – and I think you are mine.'

'Haven't you friends enough here with all your fine uncles round you?'

His voice was unexpectedly surly even in his own ears. It was no wonder she looked bewildered; only fatigue and anxiety prevented her being angry. He went quickly down on his knee and raised her hand to his lips.

'Madam, I must go,' he said. 'Will you forgive me for what I cannot forgive myself?'

'What is that, my lord?'

'That I must go,' he said.

CHAPTER SEVEN

THE REASON Bothwell had to go, at the very moment when people were giving up hope of King François' life, was that a frantic summons had reached him from Anna Throndsen, who believed herself to be dying in Flanders of the child that he had given her. He had to go, to see that she was provided with the comforts he could now afford for her; he had to go at this most critical moment in his Queen's life, which might well prove as critical in his own.

He left his new servant, Paris, behind, to 'use his eyes and ears if he valued his skin', and follow with full news of King François' death – or life. The Queen had promised to write herself.

Battles were raging over her head; the Queen-Mother was telling the Court physicians to forbid Paré's operating; the Duc de Guise was swearing at them that he would hang the lot of them if they forbade it; his Huguenot enemies, the Bourbon princes, were hurrying to get into touch with Catherine; and Catherine had already summoned to her side the Guise's other great enemy, the Constable of France.

But Mary knew nothing of all this; she was with François night and day, for even in delirium the boy seemed quieter when she put her hand on his.

Bothwell had been only three days in Flanders when Paris tumbled into his lodging, stiff and blind with continuous riding and lack of sleep, and held out a paper to him. It was carefully sealed, as Bothwell had seen Mary seal her letters, with threads of coloured silk twisted in the scented wax to form her monogram.

He did not break it at once, but asked: 'Well? He's dead?'

'Dead as mutton, sir.'

'What happened? Nothing, I suppose.'

'Just nothing. They didn't operate. The Queen-Mother wouldn't have it. They say the Guise roared at her, "Madam, you have killed your son!" She said nothing.'

Paris' imitation of the lion roar of the Guise was exact. Bothwell told him not to shout, as the lady upstairs was ill. Paris repeated the gossip; there had been some ironic comments on the King's last prayer, dictated by the Cardinal de Lorraine; it was believed to be: 'Lord, pardon my sins and impute not to me those which my Ministers have committed in my name.'

He had died just before midnight on December 5th. The Queen was there, and Queen Catherine and the Guises; no one else was allowed in except the doctors – 'but a marvellous lot got out! Keyholes are wide in Orléans.' And Paris told how, as they left the room after the King had died, Mary remembered to draw back and give Catherine the precedence to pass out first, just as Catherine had done eighteen months before when her husband, King Henri, had died, leaving her as only the Queen-Mother, and Mary as the Queen of France. But now Catherine was again the first lady in the land.

'Is the old Queen being unkind to the young one, do you know?'

'No, sir, kind, in her way; she told her to dress comfortably and not to grieve over what couldn't be helped.'

It was the authentic Medici touch – advising the removal of a corset as consolation in bereavement. 'Got into the innermost circles, haven't you, hitting the Queen-Mother below the belt like this! How did you do it?'

'I made it my business, since it was my lord's, and chose the ugliest girl I could in the old Queen's service. The ugly ones are the most grateful. She told all she could.'

He winked at his master, who had an absurd feeling that his page was play-acting in imitation of himself – badly, he hoped. He asked what use Catherine had begun to make of her power.

Quick use, as Bothwell had expected (hadn't she stripped her husband's mistress, Diane de Poictiers, of all the jewels and possessions he had given her, and within a few hours of his death!) And now —

'The Constable has hurried to Orléans with eight hundred gentlemen in attendance,' Paris was saying, 'and has disbanded all the troops there of the Guise. The Guises are down in the mud. All they can do is to shoulder along as best they can in the crowd and forget they were ever above it.' He rubbed a bleared, dusty eye and went on:

'People are wondering they don't escape from the town, but I'll say that for the Guises, no one sees much of their backs. All the courtiers went scampering off to congratulate the new little King as soon as the breath was out of t'other's body. They say he wants to have his brother's wife as well as his crown, but his mother will have a word to say to that. It isn't going to be much of a funeral, they've only got a leaden vase to put his heart into, it can't have cost more than a few crowns. Nobody is thinking anything about it, or him.'

He swayed on his feet and nearly fell. Bothwell gave him a drink, and told him to go off and get some food and sleep.

'You'd make a damned good spy.'

The lad put down his drink at a gulp and grinned up at his master. 'I did, sir. I found out that the handsome Englishman with the horrible name, Throckmorton, was in the devil of a fidget when you went off so suddenly – to Scotland by way of Flanders too! He wrote to London to warn them to look out for trouble, and I saw the letter.'

'Did you seduce his valet as well as Catherine's slut?'

'Only with drink,' said Paris with simple pride. 'We had a merry evening in the Englishman's lodging while he was at the Court, that was all, and I ran an eye over his papers.'

But Paris had found only an estimate of his master's character which showed how keenly the English Government was on the watch for all his movements.

'This glorious rash and hazardous young man,' Throck-morton had written (and Bothwell did not flatter himself that Sir Nicholas intended any more complimentary meaning of 'glorious' than 'vain-glorious'), and advised that 'his adversaries should both have an eye to him and also keep him short.'

'The shorter by a head – if they could do it!' said Bothwell with a laugh, and gave Paris one of the remainder of the six hundred crowns. Paris went off yawning and grinning at the same moment.

Bothwell turned to his letter.

But when he had broken that elaborate seal and shaken out the paper he could find no letter, only some lines of verse with words scratched out here and there, evidently the first rough draft of a poem. Having turned it all over in vain search for anything to show that the Queen had intended it for him, and not sent it in mistake for her letter, he read the verses:

> *Si en quelque séjour*
> *Soit en bois ou en prée,*
> *Soit sur la Vesprée,*
> *Sans cesse mon cœur sent*
> *Le regret d'un absent.*

> *Si je suis en repos*
> *Sommeillant sur ma couche,*
> *J'oy qu'il me tient propos,*
> *Je le sens qui me touche;*
> *En labeur et requoy*
> *Toujours est prez de moy —*

He found himself oddly moved by the utter simplicity of the grief, the bewildered sense of loss, not of a husband but of a childish companion.

He read it through again, and heard the soft cadences ringing in his mind like a peal of muffled bells.

Had she really meant to send them to him? He hoped she had. Anyway, he would keep them.

He opened the casket in which he kept his papers, and gave an exclamation of brutal amusement and disgust at the sight of Anna's last 'sonnet' lying on the top. Those heavy-handed verses made odd company for this childish lament, crystal-clear as drops of dew – 'but it's odd company you'll get, my Queen, if you trust me with your fancies!'

Part II

SECOND MEETING

CHAPTER ONE

HE DID not see her again for nearly eight months, and by then she had changed, as was natural in a girl of late development who had just begun to grow up when suddenly all her life was changed, changed in one frozen black December night, when the boy who had been her playfellow lay dead upon the pillows, and the Cardinal de Lorraine lifted his smooth white eyelids and looked at her across the still form, telling her with those fine pale grey cat-like eyes that she must remember to stand aside and let her mother-in-law pass first out of the room.

The heavy black silks rustled out before her: in the hush of that moment they made a monstrous noise, harsh as the rattle of sabres, telling her that the familiar ground of her whole life and of her home for the last dozen years was being cut from under her feet, cut in every direction.

François died at midnight; early next morning Mary sent back her royal diamonds to the new King. She was no longer Queen of France; her uncles were no longer the rulers of the kingdom; the great rival house of Bourbon with its Huguenot sympathies was now paramount; Antoine de Bourbon, King of Navarre, lately in daily fear of arrest, was made Governor of the new boy King, Charles IX; Antoine's brother, condemned to death for his share in the Huguenot conspiracy at Amboise, was released and restored to full honour and power; a match was even suggested between Antoine's son, the little Henri de Navarre, and Queen Catherine's youngest daughter, a precociously clever child of seven, always known as Margot.

Mary was now only a guest in the country that had so long been her home, and Queen Catherine made it abundantly clear. During the weeks prescribed for mourning Mary followed all the accustomed regulations, wore robes first all black, then all white, stayed all the time in her own rooms, which were kept religiously dim, saw no one but her servants, her Maries, her nearest relatives and Queen Catherine and her eldest son.

King Charles IX was a quick-witted, excitable, odd-tempered boy, unhealthy, with thin legs and a big pale head that narrowed suddenly to a tiny sharp chin – 'the Goblin of France' my lord of Bothwell had called him in one of his daring irreverences, and she disliked but could not help remembering it as the boy talked shrilly to her, waving his nervous hands.

'I don't know how you stand it here, all those candles and black curtains, and you who like being out so much! The Loire's frozen all over the shallows – do come out and skate with us. I wish you'd marry me, you'd be the Queen of France again then and I'd give you back your diamonds, and my mother couldn't go on having it all her own way. Do marry me; I may be a bit younger than poor old François, but I'm much stronger and I mean to be a great soldier just as he wanted to be, I know I could be if I married you. Just think of all the things we'd do together! – France and Scotland leading the world, and down with all the old shams. Yes, I'm for the Reformed Religion. I took away Margot's Mass-book and boxed her ears – she howled like anything. Mother is encouraging the Huguenots for all she's worth, and if you joined us, how exciting it would be! Besides, I shall never want to marry anyone else,' he added suddenly, wistfully.

That was the only time he came to her without his mother and without her knowledge, the only time Mary heard him talk.

She did not much mind the long seclusion; she wanted time before she took up the business of living once again. If it were dark in these rooms it was not much darker than outside, this iron-grey winter. Life had moved so fast, bright and shifting in these past years, hurrying her from one place to another, always to cheers and speeches of welcome, always among crowds of faces, eager, curious, peering to look at her. Now she had to make a pretty speech of thanks; now she had to stand up before all the Court and the foreign Princes and Ambassadors and deliver a Latin oration of her own composition (or most of it), urged thereto by the continual maddening reminder that the Princess Elizabeth of England (but *she* was ten years older) could talk Greek with the learned Oxford dons. Now she had had to amuse her father-in-law, King Henri II, whose heavy Spanish-looking face had seldom lit into laughter except with her; now she had had to cheer poor François and make him believe he would soon be well.

But now – *now*, she had nothing to do but sit in a dim place and wait, wait till life should begin again, knowing that it would be something entirely different from all that had gone before. So, swathed in her white robes and veils, she waited in

83

the dark like a chrysalis for the hour when she should burst her bonds as a butterfly.

There were already offers from that life ahead. The King of Navarre was so anxious to marry her that he was actually planning to divorce his strong-minded wife, Jeanne d'Albret. King Philip II of Spain, the austere and terrible monarch of half the world, who had tried to marry Elizabeth of England, now sought Mary, in his usual secret and ambiguous fashion, on behalf of his young son Don Carlos. And many other wooers of Elizabeth turned their attentions to this young, lovelier Queen who had so suddenly entered the lists of matrimony.

The young Earl of Arran was the most unblushing, for only that autumn he and his fellow-nobles had been pressing Elizabeth to marry him as 'next in place' to the throne of Scotland, with a strong hint that the papist Queen Mary would then be prevented from ever returning to her country. Yet before any reply had been received from Elizabeth, Arran was already urging his suit on Mary as soon as François was dead. The stolidly jovial King Frederick of Denmark, whose drinking bouts Bothwell had shared, also promptly transferred his wooing of Elizabeth to Mary; so did young Eric of Sweden, one of the handsomest men in Europe, half genius, half madman; so did his brother the Duke of Finland; so did the Emperor's two sons. The Earl of Lennox, who had rivalled Bothwell's father for the hand of the late Queen Regent of Scotland, was planning for his son Henry Darnley to follow in his father's footsteps and win the daughter of the lady who had rejected himself. And Darnley was a possible heir to both English and Scottish thrones.

It was noted in the English Court that all this was having a rapidly souring effect on Elizabeth's already rather acid comments on 'My dear sister of Scotland'.

Nor did it soften Catherine's tone to her former daughter-in-law. 'All France will soon not be big enough to hold your suitors,' she remarked in that fat jocular voice that always made Mary feel sick with rage and disgust. 'Had you not better find another country to contain them?'

Yes, but which? Her own did not want her; she was very tired; she only wanted to 'give it all up and become a nun', so she sobbed out to her grandmother the Duchesse Antoinette de Guise, when after her retirement she visited her at Joinville.

The old lady smiled very tenderly, looking down the enormous bony hook of her nose at the fair head buried in her lap.

The head lifted suddenly, caught the smile, and tossed back in indignation.

'And why not, Grand'mère? I would not be the first Queen in our family to become a nun. Look at my great-grandmother Queen Philippa of Guise – she is famous.'

'And so may you be,' replied her grandmother, 'but not, I think, as a nun.'

A thrush perched on a branch of white pear blossom above them and burst into shrill song. Mary looked up at the tiny ecstatic creature.

'No,' she said, 'it does not sing Mass to me as it did to Queen Philippa.'

'Does it sing of nothing else?' asked her grandmother, and saw that quick flush race upwards into the cheeks that had grown so much too white in her long seclusion. They were sitting out on one of the first warm days of spring, the old lady, in her black robes, on her favourite garden seat on the lawn that sloped down to the placid stream, a tributary of the wide Marne. Mary had slipped to the grass at her feet, her long limbs in their white dress lying as though spilt on that bright green, in a languor that would have enchanted her lovers but was disturbing to the shrewd old eyes now looking down on her.

The child had been ill again. Luckily she was here where a close eye could be kept on her; the Duchesse had seen to it that she should be troubled with no diplomatic interviews. But she could not keep her from such for ever; even now she would have to tell her of visitors from that far-off fierce Northern kingdom that had given her mother so much agony of spirit. Years ago the Duchesse Antoinette had written to that mother, her own daughter: 'You have had so little joy in the world, and pain and trouble have been so often your lot, that I think you can hardly know now what pleasure means.'

Would she ever have cause to feel the same about that daughter's daughter?

No, she would not, for even as she wondered, the girl laughed and whistled back at the thrush, imitating his note, then broke into the tune of a song, whistling it first like a boy and then singing:

> 'Worship ye that lovers be this May,
>   For of your bliss the Kalends are begun,
>   And sing with us: "Away, Winter, away!
>   Come, Summer, come, the sweet season and sun!"

'That is what he is singing to me, Grand'mère – the Spring Song of the Birds that my ancestor, the first King James of Scotland, wrote when he was in prison. New life, new hope, new adventure:

> *And amorously lift your heads all,*
> *Thank Love, that list you to your mercies call!'*

And she turned eagerly to that wrinkled face, pillowing her elbows on the stiff black knees as she had done ever since a child, propping her chin between her hands.

Whatever happened to this girl, she would certainly 'know what pleasure means'.

'My dear,' said the old lady, 'I hope you will always be able to "thank Love". I think you will, for you are of a generous spirit.'

'New adventure' – Mary had just seen what that might open for her. Since six years old she had thought of herself only as the predestined wife of François; but now, with the ruin of her former position, there had opened new prospects from a new unrealized source of power – her own attractions in the marriage market.

To be Queen of Spain, of the New World and half the old, would she have love to thank for that? For, as was suitable in a proud Princess, love, in her mind, was only the handmaid to ambition. A sharp flick on her cheek recalled her attention. The Duchesse Antoinette was telling her, 'What I should have told before, but that I did not want you to worry your head over the matter before it arrives.'

'Before what arrives, Grand'mère?'

'Why, these visitors from Scotland.'

She had no reason now to complain of Mary's inattention. The girl's white face flamed, her eyes opened aghast and with more than astonishment; there was startled anger in those usually cool depths.

'He is come back! Without a word to ask if it is my wish? How dare he?'

'Are you not being unreasonable? You must remember that he expected to be made Regent instead of your mother, that to her he owed no personal loyalty. But his action in coming here to urge your return to Scotland seems to show an honest loyalty to yourself.'

'But, Madam, what are you saying? Are we all gone mad? He never can have hoped for the Regency, not even his impudence could go so far.'

86

'I should advise you to bear in mind,' the old lady answered dryly, 'that he is not only your elder, but very nearly your legitimate brother. If your father had been able to contrive the Lady Margaret Erskine's divorce, then the Lord James, and not yourself, would have been the Sovereign of Scotland. That must be very galling for a proud and ambitious man, and you should the more welcome any sign of his goodwill.'

'O-o-oh!' Mary's sigh was so long-drawn that it blew the dandelion clock she had plucked in her nervous agitation into a cloud of airy dancers. 'You are speaking of my half-brother, the Lord James!'

'And of whom in the name of heaven could I have been speaking?'

'Oh, I – I don't know, Madam.' She rallied herself under the old lady's severe scrutiny. 'But yes I do, and I am so glad it is not he. I thought you meant the Lord Bothwell.'

'And how has he offended you?'

But Mary with sudden animation was asking questions about the proposed visit of the Lord James, to which the old lady crisply replied, 'Let us walk. This stone seat is finding its way through the cushion to my old bones.'

*　　*　　*

For the first time in her life Mary was experiencing jealousy, though she naturally did not recognize it as such. She had lately heard the true reason why the Earl of Bothwell had left her in her hour of worst need, within a few hours of François' certain death. It was not to go straight back to Scotland to work for her cause, as she had thought, but to the woman in Flanders whom he had kept there for months. That was why he had ridden off in such a hurry, though she had actually begged him to stay. No wonder that he had asked her forgiveness 'that I must go'. He had left her to go to a woman in Flanders, and taken her back to Scotland and kept her there ever since.

'How many more of these half-wives has he in Scotland?' Mary demanded indignantly of her own Maries. 'He's both right and left hand-fasted – a case, I suppose, of not letting his right hand know what his left hand doeth!'

She could joke about it, for it was not that that was hurting her, waking her sometimes in the night with a sudden little cry like an angrily startled bird. The reason for that pain she told to no one, it was too deeply mixed with shame and self-reproach; she could not bear to remember (and was always doing so) that she had sent him those verses on François' death. She had exposed their tender companionship, now sacred because sealed by death, to the man whose hard reckless eyes had scanned her up and down, stripping her, as she now felt, of all she had ever believed and wished herself to be.

More and more stories of him were being brought to her ears, stories of debauchery, of 'terrible vices', the more terrible to her since these were left vague and unexplained. She listened eagerly to them, from her Maries, who saw that she had developed an unwonted taste for scandal where Lord Bothwell was concerned, and even from Queen Catherine, who told them with the impartial zest she always gave to any dirty story.

But most she listened to the contemptuous silence of Lord James.

*　　　*　　　*

The Lord James was thirteen years older than the Queen, his half-sister; and his father had been only eighteen years old at the time of his birth. All his life James had seemed older than his father, whom he in no way resembled. He had inherited his mother's black hair and the dark pallor of her skin, also her solid gravity, which was utterly different from his father's wild melancholy, shot through with a gaiety as wild. James was never melancholy nor gay; he was unchangeably, imposingly grave. He made a deep impression in France by this unalterable gravity and the dignified composure of his bearing. He was the Bastard of Scotland, and no man could look less like the result of light love.

But it had not been light love that his father had borne for Margaret Erskine, wife of Sir William Douglas of Lochleven. He had done his best to marry her, and had remained faithful to her after his fashion, through scores of other mistresses and a couple of wives.

James as a sallow, solemn youngster had seen his father bring home to Scotland a fragile little Princess, Madeleine, daughter to King François I, whom he adored as he never adored even Margaret Erskine. For Madeleine, just sixteen, already doomed to death by consumption, King James V had loved with the hopeless agonizing tenderness of one who knows that the thing he loves cannot last. She lasted in Scotland only a few weeks, and when she died it was with difficulty that James could be persuaded to take another wife, by the necessity for an heir. Those words struck a sardonic mirth in the precocious mind of the King's eldest bastard, so nearly his heir.

Every available Princess had been suggested for the King of

Scotland: among them Henry VIII's eldest daughter, Mary Tudor; and the Pope's niece Catherine de Medici, then a child of fourteen. But the Pope considered the expense of posts to Scotland a barrier, thrift which won Mary Stewart's shuddering gratitude whenever she considered the possibility that her former mother-in-law might have been her mother.

But the King turned again to France for his bride, to the tall young widow with the calm eyes and smiling mouth, eldest daughter of the house of Guise. Two fine sons she bore him, but they died of smallpox within a few weeks of each other. All the hopes of James the Bastard, now a prematurely wise youth of twelve, destined for the Church, that comfortable sanctuary for the inconvenient sons of royalty, raised themselves anew.

His father was only just past thirty, but his restless spirit was burning his frail body like a flame; he had always had to fight to keep his kingdom from the ruffianly nobles who hated him as they hated any check to their power; from his dread uncle, Harry of England; and from poverty, the most grinding, humiliating struggle of all. Ten thousand sheep in Ettrick forest were all the wealth he possessed with which to build up again the splendour that Scotland had begun to show in his father's day, when James IV had made her a European Power; to turn the rude old fortresses of his kingdom into palaces as fair as those of France; to mine the vein of gold that had been found on Crawford Moor; to explore the uncharted Northern seas that roared beyond his kingdom, and bring those savage isles beneath his sway.

He never drank; his wine was his poetry, his mad adventures in disguise, his snatched fleeting love-affairs. But now through his furious pursuit of life he was showing signs that death had already beckoned him. Old 'wise women' to whom the Bastard listened avidly (though he said, and even thought, that it was only for the purpose of collecting information against the Black Arts) told him that his father was 'fey'; even as his grandfather James IV had been when he rode to Flodden Field.

And James V, that gay lover and 'good poor man's King', whose dearest joy was to make his escape, or 'outgate', as he called it, for a few hours from his royal duties to taste life in disguise as pedlar or beggar – James V who had such sovereign remedies for the disease of sovereignty now abjured them all, and lived like a hermit among his courtiers, shut off from them in a cloud that dimmed his quick light eyes, those 'twà merry winking e'en', a ghost walking among living men.

The defeat of his armies at Solway Moss gave him his *coup de grâce*. The King who wrote 'The Jolly Beggar' died of grief. Yet he died on a little smile of laughter, as though when he saw those sad anxious faces crowding round his bedside he knew suddenly in that last moment what small reason there was for sadness or anxiety in this transient flash of sunlight and shadow that is called life.

Three days before his death, his only surviving legitimate child was born, his daughter Mary.

The Bastard, now thirteen, saw his hopes dashed to the ground yet again. A girl baby had made void those aching ambitions, inextricably woven into the day dreams of childhood – 'if I were King'. But James was not King. He was made instead the Commendator of St Andrews.

In compensation, his manner, speech and behaviour became more judicially royal than ever his father's or grandfather's had been. The English Minister, Cecil, had his own reasons, and those of his royal mistress, for his opinion that James' person and qualities would fit him admirably to be a king. Mary, whom he accompanied on her journey to France when she was a small child and he already a young man, looked on him with awe except when she laughed at him for being seasick.

She had seen him again only as one of the myriad faces that had crowded round her and François at their wedding three years ago; she thought she scarcely remembered him, but when she saw two tall figures walking towards her on the terrace at Joinville she knew instantly that the dark one beside the Cardinal de Lorraine was the Lord James.

He stood before her, a man just over thirty and looking older, with a sparse black beard narrowing his sallow face; he had kissed her hand as his Sovereign, then embraced her, and now stood looking at her with grave, deep-set eyes. She felt she had done him an injustice in being born to be Queen of Scotland.

'We must do what we can for him,' she said later to her uncle, who firmly agreed with her – from quite different motives. The Lord James had behaved abominably towards the Cardinal's sister, the Regent of Scotland, but there was no sense in remembering that now. What was far more to the point was that he had a brain of the statesmanlike calibre of Cecil's, which might be used against the Englishman instead of in alliance with him, especially if he could be induced to revert to the old religion. As a Prince of the Church ruling Scotland for his sister when she became Queen of Spain, his power would be as great as that of any monarch.

The Cardinal exercised all his charm in painting this happy prospect. Mary saw the two talking together, her brother so grave, deliberate and downright, as though determined to be honest whatever it might cost him – or anyone else; her uncle with his light graceful gestures and magic eloquence, the more insidious in that it was so airy and casual. It was impossible that he should not win James over to whatever he wanted.

But even he could not persuade James to accept a Cardinal's hat.

'He speaks of loyalty to the new faith and old friends,' the Cardinal told his niece in some exasperation, 'but I fancy what is more to the point is that he has a mind to marry. One should not blame this too severely, since he has passed the age of thirty without a mistress – incredible, but he is determined to play for virtue. Lacking any positive impulse to it, he can only deny himself those vices for which he feels no temptation.'

He advised his niece to be guided by her brother at present, return with him to Scotland and follow his direction there, especially in religious matters, since all that could be done as yet was for her to 'serve the time'. The Earl of Huntly, 'Cock o' the North', wanted her to throw in her lot with himself as the most powerful Catholic noble in her kingdom, to land on his shores and march with an armed force against Knox and the church-wreckers.

But Mary refused to enter her kingdom with an army to promote civil war. Nor did her uncle advise it (a more important factor than her sentimental objections); he thought Huntly an 'old wind-bag' – he had given the Queen Regent a deal of trouble – and the Catholic party in Scotland was too weak at present. The Lord James had a far longer head than Huntly's, and his alliance with Knox had brought him into line with the burghers, a newly powerful middle class whose importance in Scotland the Cardinal dimly guessed.

He encouraged Mary to make friends with her brother, in the confidence that her charm would win him as it had won all the men with whom she had to deal in France, including the cautious English Ambassador, Throckmorton, obliged though he was to work against her in the interests of his own Queen – including also himself. He could not suspect that the half-brother, so inexperienced in women, would prove less susceptible than the practised and worldly uncle. For it was Mary who was charmed by James' inaccessibility. It was her first experience of the dour Scot, and she saw him as a tragic figure, fitted to play the highest role in the State but doomed to a lesser by the accident of his birth; whose thwarted ambition had led him to act wrongly towards her mother, but who now nobly strove to make amends to herself. Her romantic imagination, while it coloured her opinion of her brother, had no effect on his opinion of her. All that she confided to him he passed on to Throckmorton, who reported it to Elizabeth.

Monsieur d'Oysel was sent to Elizabeth's Court to ask for a passport of safe conduct through England in case Mary was forced by storm or sickness or the shipwreck of any of her fleet to land on English shores. It was the mere formality of courtesy between two countries at peace with each other; the French Court could scarcely believe it when they heard that Elizabeth had flown into a blazing rage at d'Oysel's request and flatly refused it. She gave no reason for this extraordinary scene until later; and then complained that Mary had not yet ratified the Treaty of Edinburgh. The Treaty required alterations which Mary must first discuss with her Scottish Council; it enjoined her to lay aside all claim to the English throne, not merely for herself, but for her heirs. Nobody therefore expected it to be signed as it stood. It was no excuse for this insult, which startled Mary's enemy Catherine as much as her friends.

Mary showed Throckmorton what she thought of his Queen's conduct – and manners – with a frankness, yet delicacy, that made that unfortunate gentleman even more ashamed of his royal mistress.

This was no new thing, Mary told him ironically; the English had been determined on her capture or destruction when she came to France, but she had braved the danger of the seas and hostile ships and was not afraid to do so again. If she fell into her cousin's hands, well, then, 'she may do her pleasure and make sacrifice of me'.

The watchful composure of her cousin's Ambassador could not restrain a movement of pity, but Mary stopped his gesture with a look so clear and calm that it seemed to be looking through his eyes at something very far away. She said, 'You do not know. That casualty might be better for me than to live.'

What did she see to make her say so strange a thing for a girl of eighteen, for whom the world was opening in colours more dazzling than for any princess of her time? He asked her, but she did not seem to know even that she had said it; fancies raced through her mind unsought, almost unaware, in bewildering contrast to the deliberate calculations of his own Queen. He was relieved that she instantly shrugged off her unnatural fatalism and told him with a flash of angry spirit that she would follow her own course in spite of Elizabeth, and had friends who would help her do it.

These friends had already been summoned from Scotland by the Lord Cardinal, to undertake the perilous voyage and 'steal the Queen out of France' in the teeth of the English fleet. Chosen with an eye to their hardihood in seamanship, they included the sailor Bishop of Orkney, the Lord Eglinton, whom the English called a pirate, and chief, as was natural, the Lord High Admiral of Scotland.

CHAPTER TWO

'WHY DID I leave France, then? Do you need ask? I have been busy enough on Your Majesty's business in Scotland.'

'Oh, very! I heard that.'

'What have you heard?'

'A great many things. I heard of – of — Well, I heard of some mighty business of a race-meeting, and that Lord Ruthven had to send to England for geldings to match yours.'

'Aye, the horseflesh in his stables was poor stuff, as needs be since he chose it. You'll not say a race-meeting took up eight months of my time?'

'No. There was some – some — Well, there was some slight matter of the Abbey of Melrose — '

'Which you gave me, and its fee.'

'I did not give you leave to bully the monks into yielding that fee by threatening to take away the keys of their chambers and heating them to brand their cheeks.'

'Pah! If they didn't like hot keys they could pay the fees – and did. Will you tell me a better way to get money out of monks – Madam?'

'You abuse my authority.'

'Who says so? The Lord James?'

'No. He says nothing of you. But your Liddesdale men have been raiding the Border. Sir John Forster, the English Warden, has sent complaints.'

'Twenty-three. He sent the list to Lord Borthwick at Hermitage. Old Borthwick's answer was that he held the place for me, and he gave point to it by stealing the messenger's horse and gear.'

'He'd never have dared do it if you had not been back. Sir John said so.'

'Sir John was right. A man must have compensation for reading through twenty-three complaints. And isn't the crest of my house a horse's head, and its song, "They ne'er saw a horse but they made it their ain"?'

He had hummed the words to the tune of the Galliard, looking down into her angry face with laughing eyes. She struggled for an instant to keep it up, then burst out laughing.

At which he was quick to give serious heed to her complaint.

'I was back in Scotland in time to convoke your Parliament at your request. I saw to it that in the coalition Your Grace's nominees should be at least as strong as those of the Congregation. Unfortunately they saw it too – that they wouldn't get their own way with me in the saddle. That is why they've sent their leader to ask you to come back and rule your kingdom yourself, in your name – and in their interests.'

'*Their* leader – *their* interests! Is that how you interpret my brother and his motives?'

'How else, Madam? My memory can stretch as far as a year ago.'

'The circumstances are clean different.'

'The characters are not.'

'You are a severe judge of character, my lord – in other people.'

'Christ's blood, Madam, how am I to take that?'

'Do you use oaths to your Queen?'

'If my Queen were the one your brother serves, she'd use 'em herself.'

'How dare you say the Lord James serves Elizabeth?'

'I dare say more – that now, while he's applying for the arrears of his pension from the French Crown, he's also drawing pay from the English.'

'This is intolerable!'

'Then do not tolerate it.'

'Is nobody honest but yourself? Am I to trust nobody but my Lord Bothwell?'

'Precious few.'

'It is ridiculous. You have warned me against nearly everybody in Scotland. You don't like Lethington because he can make you look foolish —'

'I'd make *him* look foolish if I got my hands on that canny old tabby-cat!'

'That is your one idea of dealing with people. To you everyone clever is false. But I know my brother is honest; he may be blunt, you call it "dour" — '

'No, Madam, I call it dyspeptic. Would you trust Calvin too on account of his sour stomach?'

'I know more about my brother than you do. Blood is thicker than water.'

'It's stickier. I know more about blood than you do.'

'I will *not* join the Worshipful Guild of Backbiters. I will *not* believe that if anyone shows honour or kindness it is either from self-interest or stupidity. I had rather die from trusting too much, than kill my soul by never trusting at all.'

He stared at her passion that had suddenly burst through long years of restraint in the dry disillusioned air that Queen Catherine breathed all around her, that jocular blight in which Mary had felt her tenderness for François, her devotion to her uncles, withering as though discovered to be ignoble.

As he dimly guessed, for he said, 'But, Madam, you are not thinking of me?'

'No-o-o,' she breathed in a long sigh. 'I believe I was thinking of my mother-in-law. And now,' she turned on him, 'I find you of her company.'

'God forbid! I don't ask you not to trust – only not to trust the wrong man.'

'In fact, to trust only you.'

'I can naturally answer best for myself. Why are you so angry, Madam?'

His voice was gentler. To her horror, she found that tears were mounting to her eyes. In another moment she would be telling him that she was angry because she had trusted him with her verses on François' death while he was disporting himself with a woman in Flanders.

So she cried instead, 'I think the Devil's been let loose in the world. Don't you think it's the Devil's work to sack churches and monasteries? Mr Knox is commanding them all to be destroyed and so "keep the rooks from returning by pulling down their nests". And me too – he preaches openly against the return of the "idolatrous Queen".'

'Well,' he said coolly, 'and are you going to be deterred by that?'

'No. I mean to return, and teach my subjects their duties.'

He nodded with an approving smile. 'But you'll not bring in the Inquisition to teach them their duty to God?'

'I'll not meddle with their religion – nor let them meddle with mine. You'll find my constancy to my faith a deal less dangerous than Queen Catherine's sympathy with yours.'

'Devil doubt it!'

'But if I give my subjects freedom, they must give freedom to me.'

'They'll never do that. The first Mass you hold at Holyrood will be the signal for an organized riot.'

'My brother swears I shall hold it, even if he has to guard the chapel doors himself.'

'The trusty watchdog, hey? Growls, but faithful. And you'll set him to guard the door against his own allies! The thing's plain enough, Madam – you'll always trust the wrong man.'

'Go!'

*   *   *

As soon as they met and talked again they quarrelled again. It annoyed her intensely that she had to discuss her plans with him: her plans for the voyage, or rather his; even her plans, or rather those of others, for her marriage, for these too had to be submitted to his approval. So the Countess of Lennox had evidently thought, that termagant niece of King Henry VIII, for no sooner had Bothwell been given the governorship of Dunbar Castle than she had written to sound him as to his views on a royal match for her handsome long-legged lad, Henry Lord Darnley: 'a baby face on top of a pair of stilts, is that your Grace's fancy?' Bothwell asked his Queen, laughing at her attempts to make him tell her what he had written in answer to the fond mother's hopes.

He would not tell her; he stood with his legs apart, his hands on his belt, his eyes narrowed, mocking her. A mere Border ruffian, as her brother James plainly thought, but would not descend to his level by saying so; while Bothwell had no such gentlemanly scruples; he decried everybody she wished to hear praised, first her lords, now her lovers.

The King of Sweden? An erratic giant three parts mad.

The King of Denmark? A sot who sagged in drink to the pattern of his own heavy jowl and buttocks.

King Antoine de Navarre? A nincompoop; that jolly young rascal his son Henri was already more of a man than he.

My Lord of Arran? That zany!

But his breath failed him at the Prince of Spain.

This was the match she most desired. It was much the greatest. Queen Catherine, having secured the father, King Philip, for her eldest daughter Isobel, was now busily intriguing for her youngest, Margot, to marry the son, Don Carlos. It did not at all suit either her policy, or Queen Elizabeth's, that Mary should make any important continental alliance. Mary saw them, not unfairly, as the wicked stepmother and stepsister, determined to thwart her chances. Their antagonism greatly stimulated her ambition.

There were other, more tender reasons, though these did not include the bridegroom. It would be thrilling to go to Spain, yet it would not be at all strange, for she would be going to her dearest schoolfellow, François' sister Isobel, the gentle dark-eyed girl who had set off to Spain two years ago, at fourteen, to be King Philip's third wife. She and Mary had done their lessons together with over thirty other noble children of France, had written their Latin exercises in the form of letters to each other, had acted their favourite romances of Launcelot and Amadis de Gaul in the little wood above the castle at Amboise, where Mary, the elder and taller, had always been the adventurous knight and Isobel the distressed damsel. If she married Don Carlos, she told Bothwell, a little intimidated by the look on his face at mention of the plan, she would be again with her former sister-in-law.

'Who would now be your stepmother-in-law. I quite see that the relationship is more important than that of a husband!'

Why should Don Carlos not make her a good husband? His father, King Philip, had been kindness itself to Isobel; he had sent her cloth woven from the gold and silver of the Indies for her trousseau, and underwear of the finest Flemish linen, and silk stockings from Grenada, some red, some blue – he had even sent Mary some too, of turquoise silk.

Bothwell remembered the hunt at Fontainebleau and the glimpse he had had of a slender leg in a turquoise silk stocking. The discovery that it had been sent her by King Philip most unreasonably augmented his anger against the Spanish marriage.

'You'll do well to remember, Madam, that we Scots are not the tame cats of England to stand a Spanish Prince over us as *they* did when their Bloody Mary married Philip. And I swear he never gave her any stockings,' he added inconsequently.

'Well, she adored him all the same, and so does Queen Isobel. All his three wives have done so.'

'Because women like a man to be a brute.'

'You are mistaken, sir. They may like the steel hand, but only when concealed by the velvet glove. I think you ride bare-handed, sir.'

He was furious. It would need his whip to teach her manners! He longed to break the icy quiet of her voice. He burst out, 'Carlos – that sickly abnormal boy! He makes the Goblin of France here a fine healthy lad by comparison! But I forgot – there's an alternative plan to marry Your Grace to him too – I beg pardon, instead. Are you never to have a man in your bed to teach you what marriage really is? Are you always to think of it as a matter only of treaties and alliances, and have no care who is to sire your sons, who are to be Kings of Scotland?'

Her hands trembled, she gasped out, 'Never, never speak to me again!'

But he would not take her command. 'You *shall* understand what you are doing,' he said, and gripped her hands in his furious determination. 'Do you know that that boy is stunted, almost deformed? That he roasts hares alive for his sport, and goes into such rages that he foams at the mouth? Have you thought what it would be to give your body to the sickly frenzied lust of such a boy – as if it weren't bad enough to give it to a boy at all?'

'*Stop!*' He was making everything come back – her fear of François' feeble passion, her relief and gratitude that she had never had to endure it, her tenderness that gave her remorse for both emotions. 'Your foul mouth blackens everything. It's true what Lord Arran says of you – you hurt both body and soul.'

He dropped her hands. 'I didn't know I was hurting you – or holding them. I beg Your Grace's pardon. What is Arran's complaint of me? I'd best hear it.'

'I don't remember.' She was nursing her fingers, and her voice sounded sulky and tearful.

He looked at them in disgust; he hated a woman you couldn't touch without bruising. 'Will you find the Spaniard gentler, do you think?'

'You are never to mention any plan of my marriage to me again, do you understand? No one has ever dared speak of it as you have done, not even my grandmother, and oh!' she burst out, suddenly remembering the delicate reticences and austere humour with which the Duchesse had prepared her for matrimony, 'You are utterly unlike my grandmother!'

She laughed wildly as she heard her own words, and his hearty roar echoed her on a distinct note of relief.

'Last time we quarrelled you confused me with your mother-in-law, and now you compare me with your grandmother!'

'We quarrelled!' Was there ever such impertinence! But she could not rebuke him with dignity while she was sobbing with laughter.

A haze of blue forget-me-not was spread at their feet, shimmering in the late sunshine as though it had dropped from the sky; it spread up to the delicate Renaissance staircase of the miniature castle. They were walking in front of the modern house built by the Duchesse Antoinette's husband in their youth, as a peace-offering after some love-affair with a peasant girl. Mary looked up at its slender turrets.

'Do you know what this house is called? It is the House of Love Repented. That, I think, is what you are telling me to avoid.'

'Madam, I am not presuming to tell you anything of the sort. I am not so foolish as to imagine you would ever repent of love with Don Carlos, since it would be impossible for any sane woman to feel it.'

Now he had made her angry again, he simply could not help doing it; besides, she looked so pretty in a rage, her very hair seemed to flame up, along with those curious light eyes, opalescent eyes, whose colour you could not determine even when they flashed open.

He took his leave abruptly without waiting for the lofty dismissal that she was evidently preparing.

Was this an earnest of the way her nobles would treat her in Scotland? If she were married to Carlos, she would at least have the safety of formality, so barricaded with the stiff Spanish etiquette that it surely would not much matter what her husband was like.

She tried to sound her brother on the subject, but could not do so without giving away the fact that she had discussed it with Bothwell, and of this he was so disapproving that she felt she had been grossly indelicate. The Earl was no fit counsellor for her – 'a violent and dangerous man,' he called him, 'whose power depends solely on his leadership of all the thieves of Liddesdale and Teviotdale, reckless and impoverished younger sons of the nobility.'

'At least he used that power to his utmost for my mother,' she answered, fixing innocent eyes upon him and wondering if he would blush – which he did not.

But James' dignified presence, his austerity, even his disapproval, was rather comforting to Mary; it showed his deep concern for her, she thought, as he stood looking down at her and laid his hand on hers in tender reproof. Excited, a little frightened by the prospect of her great new adventure, she felt that his solid respectability promised her something of the restraint and spiritual security she had always found in her grandmother's home.

The Cardinal, who had handed over the guardianship purely from a policy of prudence, would have been astonished if he had realized how the impressionable girl of eighteen interpreted it.

*   *   *

Bothwell's plans for the voyage were completed, though not to Mary's satisfaction. Everything ordered by him she wished to flout, for even if he were her Lord High Admiral, she was his Queen, and how dare he give his commands so plainly? She had set her heart on returning to Scotland as she had come, that summer thirteen years ago, by the far Northern route first adventured by her father two years before her birth. It was only right, she told Bothwell, that she should now visit those remote islands, since her father on that voyage of discovery had annexed their Lands and Lordships.

It was an unfortunate reminder, since Bothwell's forefathers had been Lords of Orkney and the Shetland Isles. But a gleam in his eye was the only sign of his feelings about that.

He said dryly, 'One thing is plain, Madam, that you are a remarkably good sailor.'

'And you are not, I understand, since you oppose my wishes.'

'It doesn't need a bout of sickness, Madam, to determine me that you shall not show your fear of the English Queen so far as to travel all round the Northern seas in order to avoid passing near her coasts.'

He had no trouble after that about the route of the voyage; only the difficulty of getting it to start. France, it seemed, could not bear to let Mary go, nor Mary to leave her. All her friends and relatives were planning fêtes to detain her. Would there never be an end of the mummery and dressing-up, thought the impatient young Scot, eager for the new adventure in his own country when he should make himself chief adviser to the young Queen, overbearing all the sly counsels of these 'Scottish Cecils', Master 'Michael Wily' of Lethington and the good Elder-bastard-brother James with his down-dropped glances and admonishing pats of the hand ('the best that one dares do with a woman!').

But he had to wait while mermaids hailed Mary as their Queen, and Venus abdicated in her favour, and all the poets in France sang their farewells to her. That was the homage she was used to: the hands that he could not grip without hurting were poems in the mouth of Ronsard; she was a puppet of the State, a pretty doll for courtiers to praise respectfully, a subject for painters and poets and the letters of Ambassadors to foreign Princes who had never seen her, but were nosing hot on her track like dogs on a scent! Was there anything of her that belonged to her alone, and to the man who would ever be fool enough to love her?

So he grumbled to himself, furious with impatience at this delicate, crisp yet pensive culture that was holding her from the real business of living in the land where she belonged.

It was mid-August before he at last succeeded in getting her away. The packing alone was a tremendous business; all her favourite books, French and Italian romances, English historical chronicles, collections of poems; most of the Latin classics and some of the Greek, with which she meant to continue her education; a sprinkling of theology, Luther's works and Calvin's Institutes, so that even Mr Knox would have to admit that she had studied their side of the religious question.

There were rich carpets from Turkey, thirty-six of them where her mother had only had two; forty-five great carved and painted beds, five times as many as her mother's; and her jewels, the finest in Europe: the diamond called the Great Harry from Harry of England; a set of black and white enamelled buttons given by Diane de Poictiers, with her crescent moon in diamonds; an agate-hilted dagger, studded with diamonds and emeralds, with a huge sapphire in its head, a present to her father on his first brief marriage, from his father-in-law, François I.

She gave away quantities of parting presents: a necklace of rubies and diamonds to the young Duchesse de Guise, a huge emerald ring to the Cardinal, silver-plate to her friend the enemy, Sir Nicholas Throckmorton, so beautiful that he thought it advisable to say nothing about it to his own Queen.

Bothwell insisted that the final day of departure be kept secret till the last moment. The Lord James had left in advance to prepare for her arrival. The Duc de Guise saw her aboard at Calais, the scene of his greatest conquest. She cried and clung to him, but young René de Lorraine, Marquis d'Elbœuf, cheered them up with his absurd jokes as he stood by them, a rare blue-ruffed pigeon chained like a hawk on his wrist. He had brought it as a present for his niece, but not a parting one, for he and two more of her younger uncles were to accompany her, Claude Duc d'Aumale, and François de Lorraine, Knight of Malta, Grand Prior and General of the French war fleet, leading the noble escort. Three uncles, four Maries, and the Chevalier Bayard's nephew, Châtelard, and all the rest of the gorgeous young company went on board the Queen's galley, which was all white, with white flags bearing the arms of France.

It was true then, she was really leaving France; nothing, after all, had happened at the last moment to keep her at home. Her life there was over. The Duc de Guise stood on the shore that he had wrested from England, the tears running down his scarred cheek. His farewell had been the last.

But the strangest had been when she said goodbye to Queen Catherine. The two Dowagers of France had confronted each other, the one in her white robes like a young willow tree in the snow, the other a wedge-shaped block of blackness, peering up into the tall girl's face with those bulging short-sighted eyes.

'You have been crying,' she said, 'but think how fortunate you are that you may cry. Only the slim and lovely may do that. When I came to France I had to learn to laugh.'

For one shamed instant Mary had realized that though she was suffering exquisite grief it was certainly satisfactory to be so constantly assured that she herself was exquisite – that the 'gift of tears in the voice' had been cited as one of her rarest charms. Whatever she might have to endure, she would never know the agony of being the dumpy, pop-eyed, entirely friendless bride of fourteen that Catherine had been when she came to France to marry a boy already devoted to his beautiful mistress. Catherine had 'learned to laugh' to please his father, that jovial satyr, François I; of her husband she had been always too much afraid.

A horrid memory, from which Mary had always turned her mind away in disgust, came back to her in a sudden new light; she had heard it said that Catherine used to lie on the floor and look through the chinks between the boards at the room below, where her husband was with his Diana, that crystal goddess whose moon never waned, nor hold on him slackened, until the day he died.

'But I,' Catherine said, on a note as flat and dull as if a lump of earth had fallen from her mouth, 'have never been loved at all.'

CHAPTER THREE

THERE WAS no need of the lamp at the mast-head, said young Châtelard, for the eyes of their Queen were bright enough to light them through the darkness.

It was an unfortunate moment for his metaphor, for her eyes were red and dim with crying. She had stayed up on deck to look her last on the shores of France, luxuriating in her sadness with the rich youthful egotism of one who must taste every sensation to the full. The galley-slaves toiling below, chained to their oars, filled her with unbearable pity; there was too much misery in the world; at least she would lessen what she could of it, and she ordered her sailor uncle, the General of the Galleys, in nominal charge of the voyage, to see to it that not one of them should be struck by the slave-master's whip, however lightly.

She would not go below even when it was dark, neither for supper nor bed. She had a salad brought her on deck and a great golden melon, like the August full moon that had swung mistily over the edge of the sea, and she was nearly as greedy of this as she had been of her homesick tears. Another exquisite sensation she would enjoy, and that was to sleep on deck. She had her bed made up there, and lay listening to the lap, lap of the waves and oars, the creak of the ropes, the occasional flap of a sail, until she saw the clouds floating like islands in the golden dawn. Its light did not reach the edge of the sea: that distant water was cold as moonlight, corpse-light, the twilight at the edge of the world.

Were these the islands she had longed to see again? She knew they were not, that they were mere wraiths of mist, disappearing even as she watched; but what did it matter if they were of land or water? They were lovelier than any she remembered, her own as much as if she looked on them to say, 'I am Queen of Orkney and the Isles.'

Her hair was all wet and curling from sea-mist; four Maries could not get the tangles out of it. But she continued to sleep –

or not – on deck for the five nights of the voyage. She composed some charming verses in farewell to the pleasant land of France, in obedience to family tradition, remembering the sad little Princess Margaret, poet daughter of the poet King James I, who had also sung her homesickness – in her case for Scotland, which she had left to be the bride of the cruel Louis XI; had kissed the ugly mouth of the Court poet as he lay asleep in a garden, 'because it had uttered the fairest words in France'; and, so the chronicle briefly related, 'died of scandal'.

Girls must have been more sensitive a hundred years ago, Mary decided. No Princess now would die of scandal. Certainly not Elizabeth. There were shocking scandals about her. Gone was that Good Princess who had always been so tiresomely held up as an example to her own childhood, so much older and cleverer than herself; gone was the poor motherless girl who had succeeded in making all her four stepmothers so fond of her. From the moment she became Queen, Elizabeth did not care to possess a single woman friend; in fact, you might have thought there was no other woman at her Court. She played all her lovers off against each other, refused none of her suitors, and had managed to avoid both war and matrimony with Philip of Spain.

And Elizabeth would now be her nearest and, it seemed, her most dangerous neighbour. Mary accepted the challenge with a tingling of excitement. Elizabeth was almost twenty-eight, an appalling age to eighteen; it was high time now for her to give way before the younger and fairer rival.

And Mary thought with a spice of malice of all the red and orange-coloured sails of the princely suitors that came up the Thames to woo the Queen of England; now she would be taking, had already taken, the wind out of those sails!

*   *   *

As if in prompt revenge for these mischievous imaginings, Elizabeth's fleet managed to capture two of Mary's ships, the two containing all her stud of horses and most of her possessions, and detained them for something over a month. Short of capturing Mary herself, the revenge was perfect, since it prevented her making the triumphal entry into her capital on which she had counted. Riding down the Royal Mile in her white robes on her white thoroughbred, Madame la Réale, followed by the gorgeous chivalry of France, she would have made a dazzling first impression on her subjects, and knew it.

But now there were no horses, no jewelled harness.

Everyone had been taken by surprise by her swift arrival; there were no preparations for it, and she had to sit in a bare shabby house on the quayside at Leith and wait while a messenger went to inform her brother; and there was a thick east wind sea-fog, so that though it was past nine o'clock on a mid-August morning she could scarcely see across the squalid streets of the little port.

Night had fallen on her, as her uncle had prayed it never should – and fallen before noon. It frightened her unwontedly, that unnatural darkness. She was miserably angry – with Elizabeth for spoiling her very first move in the game, with James for not being ready for her, with her younger uncles for showing the obvious disgust that she was trying to hide in front of her impromptu host, with herself for finding the tears running down her cheeks as she sat among her luggage, with Bothwell for striding in on her, obviously in the blackest of tempers himself, and scolding her for crying.

'But I've been sitting here for hours and nobody's arrived to welcome me, and they can only find some wretched hackneys for us to jog to the Palace like a party of tinkers – *is* this the way to welcome a Queen? – and it's so cold and dark it might be night.'

'It's a haar, that's all. You'll get plenty such in Scotland. What if it *is* night? If you can't be a Scot, Madam, you can be a Guise, and remember that it was the night that brought out your uncle's star.'

She blew her nose furiously, preparatory to snubbing him, but had no time. 'Good,' he said, grinning, 'that's a fine trumpet call; now follow it. The Lennoxes' envoy is coming down the street; let him see you are as good a Queen on a packing-case as on a throne.'

She shot him a dagger glance, flinging up her head, and he chuckled, almost restored to good humour himself by seeing how royal she was the moment he put her in a rage.

She told herself she would have no peace unless she quelled him or let him rule all, and that last was impossible and he would have to see it. But all the same, she set herself to charm Lennox's envoy, and her host, Captain Lambie ('But no, it has been so refreshing to rest here before riding into Edinburgh; and your wife's porridge is delicious – I remember the taste of it in childhood and have always wanted to eat it again.') and even Lord James, whom she would not allow to apologize ('But how *could* you know, dear James? We have done the voyage far more quickly than was thought likely – you must give thanks to the Lord High Admiral for that.').

So she continued to charm and be charmed by everybody; she made her State entry into her capital on a dreadful little hackney, and treated it all as the greatest joke, and though nobody called her an angel from heaven, a fishwife did call out, 'God bless that sweet face!'

She listened to the pipes and the melancholy chanting of psalms and begged to hear such sweet music yet again, and when her uncles chaffed her for her hypocrisy she indignantly protested that it was true, as far anyway as the pipes were concerned – 'I have been longing to hear that wild skirling.'

She watched pageants prepared in her honour but far from complimentary, since they contained strong hints as to her future conduct, showing 'worshippers of idols' burnt in effigy, children who presented her with a Bible in the Scots tongue, more children who sang a petition to her to put away 'that wicked idol' the Mass. The three Guise brothers were astounded at the insult; Mary only told the actors, and truthfully, that she had never seen such a show in France.

But she had a chance to show real sincerity when the Edinburgh prentices begged her royal pardon; they had been put to the horn for breaking into the Tolbooth to rescue one of their company condemned to be hanged last May, and had imprisoned the whole Burgh Council in their own prison; in fact, there had been a first-class riot dispelled only by Lord Arran's guards, and all owing to the ruling of the ministers of the Kirk to prevent the prentices' traditional right to act their mumming play of Robin Hood on May Day.

'But why shouldn't they be allowed to act it?' she demanded, and was told that Mr Knox's Book of Discipline had expressly forbidden such heathen mummeries.

'Condemned to death for a mumming play? Are they all mad? Indeed it's time I returned to my country!'

She granted the pardon and told them she wished she'd been there to see their play. 'I am certain I should have liked it better than any in Scotland!'

The ministers grumbled, but her action restored quiet to the city, which had been in a state of insurrection all this spring and summer. The prentices rushed out of their shops to cheer her wherever she went.

'I shall be Queen of the Commons as my father was King,'

she told Bothwell who, more canny than usual, remarked, 'The ministers are more powerful than the people. Keep in with God.'

'Keep up my Latin rather – they might be good for that.'

And she asked one of their chief lights, the learned Mr George Buchanan, to read Livy with her every afternoon.

It was like a game, seeing how quickly she could get these dour Scots to eat out of her hand, as Bothwell called it, laughing at her small triumphs and telling her to beware of getting her fingers nipped. And he would not stay to watch the triumphs, he went straight off to his Border fortress 'to see what the rascals have been up to'. Many of them had been up to no good, but he soon stopped that.

On her first Sunday at Holyrood she attended her own private Mass in her private chapel as James had promised, and, as he had also promised, with himself to safeguard it. At the most sacred moment of the Mass, when the priest was in the act of elevating the Host, rioters burst into the chapel with drawn swords, shouting, 'Death to the Idolater!'

And above those shouts of fanatics and ruffians, led by the ferocious Lord Lindsay, was another wilder cry that held more suffering than the screams of the women, 'Save her – save my darling from the power of the dog!' Mary had a glimpse of the very tall shambling figure of a young man who was flinging his limbs in all directions, of a distraught face and eyes pale and glistening like two protruding bits of glass; it was the young Earl of Arran whom she had not seen for over a year; he seemed to have changed for the worse.

In a moment the Lord James' quiet efficiency had driven out that shocking rabble, and the service proceeded, though with a shaking priest and sobbing women. Mary herself showed no sign of nerves until they left the chapel, her two younger bastard brothers, the Lords Robert and John Stewart, themselves escorting her priest with their servants. She found Lord James with his sword drawn, guarding the door, and laughed, with a catch in her throat that turned the laugh into a sob as she caught his arm and gasped out, ' "The trusty watchdog!" Who said that of you? Oh, I know now. But it's true for all that, it's true!'

He put his arm round her very tenderly. 'Little sister, you are overwrought – it is no wonder.'

There was a genuine quality in his kindness. His sense of decency had been outraged by the vulgar row in the Chapel Royal and the effect it must have on all those noble guests from

107

France, outraged too by the perverted workings of Arran's mad passion for this lovely girl. Lust was unseemly enough in itself, it was doubly so when cloaked by religion. With Mary clinging to his arm, her eyes shining with tears, looking up to him (as they ought to look), James became conscious of a new feeling towards his half-sister. If she continued to be modest and humble (as a woman ought to be), to acknowledge his superiority, be grateful for his protection, and do all that he told her, then he would serve her faithfully, and so he now promised.

'It's true I'm your watchdog – what else should I be?'

She heard the bitterness in that question. What could she do to show she would stand by him as he had just stood by her?

James smiled rather sheepishly and hesitated. She urged him eagerly; amused, incredulous. *Could* James be bashful? It seemed he could.

'You could help me to marry after long love,' he blurted out at last. 'Her father is proud.' He let the bitterness creep into his voice again, this time slightly overdoing it. 'A bastard, even a king's, isn't good enough for his daughter.'

'Oh, James, who is she?'

'Agnes Keith, the Earl Marischal's daughter.'

'The Lady Agnes!' Mary hoped her exclamation had not shown her disappointment. It would have been so delightful if James had wanted to marry a gay and charming girl, one of her Maries for example, who would have warmed and softened him. But Lady Agnes' chill manner and rapacious eye did not encourage such hopes. And how could James have had 'long love' for anyone whose chest was flat as a board? But perhaps that was why, and poor Agnes had grown thin and cold and wary under the stress of her long engagement. Mary was instantly sympathetic again. She would speak to the Earl Marischal herself. Now that she had just made James the Earl of Mar, he would surely think the match good enough.

But her brother shook his head. The Earl Marischal was a great noble on the Border, and only a Border dignitary would impress him sufficiently. He had as good as told James that he wanted his son-in-law to hold the Lieutenancy of the Border.

'He surely doesn't hope to marry Agnes to the Earl of Bothwell!' exclaimed Mary in an uncontrollable burst of laughter. Bothwell – and that cold acquisitive eye upon him – that would indeed be incredible!

James thought so too, from another angle.

'That unprincipled ruffian! Indeed he would not wish or allow it. But Bothwell has been Lieutenant of the Border for three years now, and the office is one that should be changed constantly.'

He gave a great many further reasons why he should now be made Lieutenant instead of Bothwell, but his instinct had been sound in giving that of his marriage project first. It was that that made her agree in the end, though reluctantly, and all the time she thought of Bothwell's twisted smile when she heard that he was to be supplanted by his enemy. Would he understand how she must work in friendship with her brother? How all her advisers had told her it was the one thing she could do at present?

And in return James was now eager to work in friendship with her and so was William Maitland of Lethington, the 'Michael Wily' who had also hitherto backed Arran and Elizabeth. It was very gratifying to hear them discussing instead their plans for her advancement as against the English Queen, talking so wisely and interminably in the Council while she sewed at her embroidery, catching every now and then a glance of amused superior pleasure from these men who were well content to have so pretty and docile an audience. Often they appealed to her merely for the pleasure of hearing that low magical voice – *'vox Dianae!'* the Parliament exclaimed after her speech at its opening, as much moved by its music in French-toned Scots as the French had been when she gave her Latin orations as a schoolgirl.

Of more comfort than all his other support, Mary found James standing shoulder to shoulder with her against the storm of protest aroused by her service of the Mass. James, 'whom all the godly did most reverence', was severely reprimanded by them; but he stuck to his guns and declared that, while he would never consent to a public Mass, 'for the Queen to hold it privately, who had the right to stop her?' Many asserted that right; eminent Protestants from all over the country hurried to Edinburgh to protest against the Queen's infringement of the law laid down in Knox's Book of Discipline that the Mass should be abolished; with death as the penalty for the third offence of hearing or celebrating it.

Yet once they came to Court there was a strange slackening of their indignant resolution. The more they saw of the Queen, the less they protested; old Campbell of Kinyeancleuch, a purblind misogynist, simply could not understand what had happened to

109

all his ardent colleagues. 'I think,' he wrote, 'there be some enchantment whereby all men are bewitched.'

Not all. Mr Randolph, the English Envoy, writing of that same enchantment which was drawing all men round the Queen, added: 'There is not one who absents himself, saving John Knox who thunders out of the pulpit.'

Never had he thundered louder than on the Sunday following the Mass. All that past week he had been waiting hopefully for the Lords of the Congregation to rebuke the Queen and banish her priest; instead of which he saw them dancing attendance on her, jostling their horses against each other to get the nearest to her as she rode up the Royal Mile, swarming about her, as he bitterly remarked, 'like flies about a honey-pot'.

She was bringing back the old gay Edinburgh of her grandfather's day, so the old people said who could remember the city as it had been before Flodden, the booths of silks and gold thread worked on fine linen, the many-coloured processions of knights and ladies riding up from Holyrood to tournaments in the windy tiltyard before the Castle.

Flodden had ruined the country, the Reformation dulled it. But this young girl from France was bringing back the old colour and gaiety, perhaps also the old greatness and splendour, so they said; and Knox, writing in his window, heard them; and watched his own servants (or the servants of God, it was the same thing), led away from him by the wiles of a woman, competing for her favours with each other and the fools she had brought from France, as they passed right under his window and never even troubled to look up and see if he were observing them.

Never did he fail to observe them; his house at the top of the Canongate and foot of the Netherbow might have been built for the purpose, each story butting farther out over the street than the one below, so that the window of his study on the third floor had an excellent position both as an observation post and occasionally as an impromptu pulpit.

He told his congregation at St Giles' that the private Mass last Sunday was a worse disaster to Scotland than the landing of ten thousand armed enemies; he prayed God to 'purge the heart of the Queen's Majesty from the venom of idolatry and deliver her from the bondage and thraldom of Satan, wherein she has been brought up and yet remains'; and to allow 'that this poor realm may escape the plague and vengeance which inevitably follows idolatry'.

'This,' exclaimed Mary, aghast when the words were repeated to her, 'is a direct attempt to stir up rebellion. He ought to be arrested instantly for sedition.'

But the rebellion, the sedition had taken place long before she set foot in Scotland. Knox had been virtual monarch for the last year; she could not uproot him so easily, they all told her, even Lethington, who shrugged and sneered at his 'devout imaginations'; while the English Envoy warned her that the voice of the preacher 'put more life into the Scots than six hundred trumpets continually blowing in their ears'.

She sent for him to Holyrood, and once again James was on guard, while Beton and Seton stood in a window at some distance. She watched him curiously, this 'little man who rules the roost', as Bothwell had warned her; he was considerably shorter than herself, but made up for it by an inordinately long beard which gave him a gnome-like appearance. In the midst of all that dark grizzled hair his lips were surprisingly red and full, 'like a ripe plum in the middle of a withered furze bush', she thought on a spasm of distaste, remembering the dirty jokes she had heard about all the women who clamoured for his spiritual guidance. In odd contrast to the prophetic beard and fierce sunken eyes under heavy brows, he was natty, almost dapper, in his dress, his taffeta bands sewn with gold rings and even some jewels – a jauntiness that made her smile when she reflected how carefully severe had been her own choice of dress for this interview. But the thing that surprised her most was that voice of greater power than six hundred trumpets. It was not the least like a trumpet – unless it were a child's tin trumpet, for it was high and weak, always a little hoarse and inclined to go into a husky croak when excited. It very soon got excited.

He stared up at this tall slim secretly smiling creature. Unwomanly, he instantly dubbed the plainness of her dress – a queen masquerading as a young student; her hair drawn back and hidden under the little black-winged cap; her black dress fitting so closely to her lissome figure; the immensely long cuffs and collar of fine white muslin fluting out like tapering, transparent petals from the slender hands and throat. He would have enjoyed the challenge of a parade of her feminine charms and regality, and did not recognize how subtle was her concealment of them. Did she think to meet him on equal ground? Then she should learn her lesson!

Certainly she invited it with manly frankness, for she charged him at once with stirring up sedition against her; not only on account of her religion but her sex, since he had published a book to prove how 'monstrous' it was that any woman should have 'regiment' over men.

His denial was not so direct, but more invidious. If his country suffered no inconvenience from the rule of a woman, 'I would be as well content to live under Your Grace as Paul was to live under Nero.'

After which, as he himself recorded with satisfaction, she remained silent for nearly a quarter of an hour.

During that time she heard his voice going on and on. If only the Cardinal were there to confute these interminable arguments, or rather attacks!

He called her Church 'that Roman harlot polluted with all kinds of spiritual fornication'.

At which she blinked, and said her conscience did not tell her it was so.

'Conscience,' he replied, 'requires knowledge, and I fear that of right knowledge you have none.'

'But I have read and heard of it,' she modestly suggested.

'So had the Jews who crucified Christ.'

And he proved to his satisfaction that even they were not as degenerate as the Catholics, until his voice cracked and had to clear itself with coughing.

'You are too hard for me to answer you, but I know those who could,' she murmured almost inaudibly. But James heard the sigh, and unexpectedly, even to himself, was by her side.

'Your sermon last Sunday,' he told Knox, 'was a very untimely admonition.'

It was hardly a severe condemnation to a man who in any other country would now be under arrest and probably sentence of death. Mary gave him a grateful glance but felt she could do better than that herself. Knox ignored Lord James and told Mary that Princes were often the most ignorant of God's true religion, and that the highest dignity on earth was to obey His Church.

'*Which* Church?' she demanded innocently.

He shot a furious look up at her from under those shaggy brows, and advised her to read the Scriptures.

'But you interpret the Scriptures in one way, and the Church of Rome in another. Which am I to believe?' she asked, still in that gentle voice.

James began to wish he had not encouraged her by his support. It would have been far better for her to have remained silent. Knox, expounding the Scriptures, embarked on an alarming digression as to whether Melchizedek had brought bread and wine as an oblation to God or a gift to Abraham – a controversy that he had already argued with the Abbot of Crossraguel for three days. Mary began to tap the table, then at last broke in, half laughing.

'Mr Knox! Mr Knox! Mr Knox!!!' And she rapped out three knocks as she repeated his name. 'You tell me to follow the Scriptures, but you reject them whenever you choose. Did you not disagree with Saint Paul himself, saying that you "greatly doubted whether those particular words of Paul's were inspired by the Holy Ghost"? Are you then of God's Privy Council that you alone shall determine which even of the Apostles has received His commandments?'

'A proud mind' – 'a crafty wit' – 'an obdurate heart against God and His truth', – Knox revolved all these phrases in his mind against this pert chit, not yet nineteen, who dared to confute him in argument because she happened to be called a Queen. He warned her that it was the duty of subjects to disobey their Princes when their conscience told them to do so; and smacked his full lips over this threat, shooting it savagely out of his thick beard, for he was greedy of his anger, it affected him voluptuously to taste the bitterness of his own words.

Again she stood silent and very still, and this time even Knox was silent. A hush like death fell on the room that she had already made lovely with painted walls and curtains of Cyprus silk.

'Why then,' she said at last, so softly that the words were scarcely heard, 'I perceive that my subjects shall obey you and not me.... So must I be subject to them and not they to me.'

Then, as if what she had just said had no significance, she held out her hand with a charming smile. The interview was over.

Mary, her imprudent victory won, sobbed her heart out before her brother and her two friends.

'What is the use?' she wailed in answer to James' judicial remarks that it was never wise to get the better of a man in argument, certainly not of a preacher who is accustomed to speak unanswered for three hours on end. 'He hates me, he hated me long before he saw me. He doesn't even *want* me to do what he wants. He wants me to fail, he is praying for it daily, nightly.'

113

'Oh, Madam, Madam!' moaned the gentle Seton, frightened by her hysterical words.

Beton was instantly practical.

'He is jealous of you, Madam, that is why. He looked at you like a woman whose lover you had stolen.'

James softened it, but in agreement. 'He has had absolute power this last year in Scotland. Now you have taken it from him and he is driven into opposition. He is great in making, in doing, but bitter in criticizing. You must deal gently with him.'

'Gently? I would have him broken on the wheel if I only could!'

James frowned, pulling at his thin black beard. She tried to justify herself.

'Where is he great? Not as a Christian! Buchanan himself says he's read every word he ever wrote, and not in any of them can you find any single reference to the sayings of Christ.'

James inaudibly cursed Buchanan, that Learned Pig with little eyes sunk deep in the fat of his cheeks, currying favour with titbits of gossip and criticism.

'You had best get Mr Buchanan to read you the Book of Discipline,' he remarked dryly. 'Even if you deny its Christianity you will have to admit its noble polity. Statecraft has never achieved anything greater than its ideal of Commonwealth, a Trinity which shall co-ordinate a National Church, National Schools, National care of the poor and sick. Your Church complains that the wealth of its religious houses has been seized, but it could be for no greater purpose than to provide every Scot, the wildest upland peasant lad as much as the Earl's son, with the finest education in Europe.'

Lord James spoke with such grave and disinterested enthusiasm that Mary could not bring herself to ask how it was, in that case, that he had enriched himself with the Church lands of Pittenweem and St Andrews. She put it more generally.

'I thought that much of the Church property has passed into lay hands?'

'To some extent,' said Lord James in that vague yet severe statesmanlike manner that she had often observed when men talk politics so as to obscure rather than explain them; 'there are, naturally, various adjustments which will have to be made, slowly.'

She was certain that in James' case the adjustment would be at least as slow as his lifetime.

The mixture of hypocrisy and sincerity in him baffled her

114

clear young mind. If only people were all villainous or all virtuous it would make it so much easier. Perhaps there was something to be said even for Mr Knox – but she was sure she could never say it!

*　　*　　*

Knox's next move was to inspire the Provost and bailies with a proclamation coupling 'priests friars and nuns' with 'whoremongers drunkards and other scandalous livers' and banishing them from Edinburgh.

The Queen, with the approbation of James, Lethington, and the rest of the Council, promptly had the Provost and bailies clapped into the Tolbooth, and ordered a new election of them.

Mary had won the first round against Mr Knox.

CHAPTER FOUR

BOTHWELL WENT back to Crichton to see what more it needed in the way of replenishing from the furniture of his other castles; the main damage caused by Arran's raid two years ago had already been repaired.

It was a cold autumn day and all the firs were turning up their leaves in the wind with a rustle of steel among their dark thunder-green. He saw his sister Janet (Jan, he had always called her) come riding down the slope of the hill towards him on a tall bay horse, her short rough dark hair blown behind her like a fox's brush. She was riding astride, in a pair of his old breeches and a leather-jack faded almost white with age and far too long and loose for her slight shoulders, buckled in with a broad scarlet belt. In his cast-off clothes, it might have been himself as a boy coming towards him; she was slim and long-legged like a boy – or the Queen, he thought, for the first time comparing them and realizing that Jan must be some months older than Mary – nineteen then, and what was she doing with herself all alone at Crichton instead of in their mother's house at Morham?

And for that matter, what had she been doing with herself all these years since their father's death, when she had begged him to let her off her engagement to Robert Lauder of the Bass, 'an old man at least thirty, and looks cross'. She'd not been quite fifteen then, and he had already thought it rather hard of his father to force the match, so sent her out of his way to live with their mother instead, and had since seen very little of her.

115

Now, as they drew rein and swung out of the saddle at the same instant, he found himself looking into a pair of tawny-dark eyes and decided with satisfaction, 'she's like me, but pretty.'

'Here's a fine rapscallion stravaiging the country!' he told her, taking her chin between his finger and thumb in a hard pinch as he tipped up her face for a kiss. 'Where's your manners to the head of the house? Can't very well curtsy in my old breeks, can you? Why are you here?'

'Why shouldn't I be? It's our house.'

'Mine, you mean. You should be at Morham with your "ain minnie dear".'

'You've given her enough to do looking after your brat. She's got no time for her own.'

'What's *his* mother doing?'

'Crying mostly and writing verses, and then stitches up a petticoat with sequins and says what a great lady she is at home. I will say she can cook, though – all sorts of savoury side-dishes – and how she eats – pouf! Tell me, sir,' she took his free arm confidentially as they strolled back towards the stables, leading their horses, 'why did you take up with Anna? A fine figure of a woman, is that it? If I stuffed my chest with a cushion would I get a lord to my lover, do you think?'

And she stuck out her chest, bending backwards like an acrobat, and burst into laughter all the more sudden and transforming because she had omitted any smile of greeting. He shook her arm roughly, pulling her upright again, and quieted her horse, which had plunged as she jerked backwards.

'Whoa there! You're both in need of the bridle – and the whip too, I fancy. So you're wanting a lord to your lover – do you mean to tell me you've not had such a thing about you?'

'Not seriously.'

'Lightly then?'

She laughed again; it had a more conscious sound than that first free shout of merriment.

'You'd best answer,' he said a trifle grimly. He had suddenly remembered a meaning smile on the astute face of 'Michael Wily' of Lethington at some mention of Bothwell's female dependants; he had thought it directed at one or other of his mistresses, now for the first time it occurred to him that it might have been intended for his sister. 'That canny cat!' he burst out, thrusting off her hand on his arm. 'Have you given him the chance to jeer at us?'

'I've had no cat for a lover, I can tell you that.'

'Whom then?'

'It doesn't matter. It's over. I'm thinking of Archie Douglas now.'

'Then you can stop thinking, if you ever did such a thing in your life. Archie Douglas! A useful fellow, would earn his hire, to stick someone in the back. Is that your notion of a match for our family?'

'Well, he's a man. T'other's a boy.'

'Who is t'other?'

She looked round at him mutinously.

'Nothing to do with you, since it's not matrimony – *ow!*' as he caught her arm again.

'And now you'll tell me,' he said quietly.

'Not till you let go my arm.'

He dropped it and she nursed it ruefully, with a sidelong glance at him to see if she mightn't even now evade him, but his face showed her it was useless. Five minutes home and he had got everything out of her! How had he done it?

She gulped and said, 'Well, it's Johnnie Stewart.'

He whistled. 'That imp! Is he as old as yourself?'

'Just.'

'Did he get you with child?'

'No – luckily.' She spoke with swaggering nonchalance and stole a look to see how he had taken it, but could not make out.

He said carelessly, 'And now he's tired of you, and you've got no one better than Archie Douglas to fall back on?'

She flared up. 'He's *not* tired of me; it's t'other way round. Or is he? Have you seen him with anyone else? Is it true about that pink pudding – Alison Craig?'

He flung back his head in a roar of laughter.

'You damned little fool!' was all he would say in answer to her startled and indignant eye. It was plain as a pikestaff that the little bitch was still in love with that young rascal. If he were too, a very pretty match might be made of it; bastard royalty wasn't aiming as high as his father had done, but all the same it would suit his game to marry his sister to the Queen's half-brother, and the one she was fondest of too. Bothwell liked the lad himself; Lord John was as unlike his eldest brother, the Lord James, as he was like the King his father – a fair, quick-glancing, lightly moving youth, with all his father's gaiety and love of songs and dances, and none of his melancholy.

117

He had shown himself eager to be friends with Bothwell, so much so that that cynic had begun to wonder what he wanted of him. If it were his backing for a match with Jan, why had he not mentioned it to her? He asked her, and found that Johnnie had done so, but there had been difficulties. James didn't approve and kept him short of money, and she had wanted to show she didn't care and so flirted with others, and so he did too, and they had quarrelled and he'd told her she'd the manners of a stable-boy ('And so you have,' growled her brother), and she'd told him he was an impertinent puppy aping royalty from a left-handed litter.

'Did you tell him that, after he'd had your body?' he inquired, with an admiring grin.

'Yes, why not?'

'And so now you've split for good?'

'Oh no, we made it up and then quarrelled again.'

'I'd like to knock your two heads together,' was his final genial comment.

*   *   *

It was the Queen who unintentionally gave him his best chance to speak with Lord John.

In spite of her swift boldness in punishing the Provost and bailies, she was determined on a peaceful policy; she had resolved to make friends with her subjects, even John Knox as soon as she could get the chance; and still more to make her subjects make friends with each other. She had made James Lieutenant of the Border instead of Bothwell – very well then, James must do his best to make it up to Bothwell, and so she told him in her frank laughing fashion, as though to make a joke of these ridiculous feuds that were always rending Scottish public life.

They should keep the Border quiet between them, hold their Courts of Justice together, and together lead a friendly deputation to Berwick to improve relations with the English officials.

So together they went, at the head of an enormous party, both Scots and French nobles. Everything went off perfectly. Mary got up specially early to see them off, waving her handkerchief till they were out of sight, and then, as it was raining, went back to bed to read a book, for there were only two attitudes in which it was possible to keep warm in Scotland, either to ride at full gallop or lie in bed. So there she stayed in exquisite solitude, with not even her Maries with her, for she had sent them to start the cavalcade on their way as far as Mary Seton's home, where her father's pike-like grin threatened to split his face at the sight of James Hepburn politely conversing with the Bastard.

They dined well at Seton House; they supped better at Dunbar Castle, where Lord John showed René, Marquis d'Elbœuf, how to dance a Highland fling, and the fat Earl of Huntly insisted on joining in, until he fell and put an arm out of joint. Lord James made speeches to the English at Berwick next day, and d'Elbœuf complimented them on their artillery with cheerful Gallic mendacity (to Bothwell he muttered under his smiling moustache that his brother de Guise would have had such gunners hanged). The English, by their own account, returned more solid compliments in the shape of 'a bellyful of good cheer' and the present to each nobleman of a gelding 'finer than any they brought out of Scotland'.

On the way back they spent a night at Lord John's house at Coldinghame, and Bothwell enjoyed a private chuckle with his young host over all this excellent behaviour.

'Another of those halter-grins of James and he'll crick his neck!' remarked the irreverent younger brother as he kicked his bedroom door to, and carefully deposited a couple of bottles of light claret on the floor.

They were all sharing beds, those who could have any bed at all, and Lord John had invited Bothwell to his. A brace of hounds were already in occupation of it, and the host cuffed them aside to make room for himself and his guest. The room was very bare, lighted only with a glowing peat fire and a single rushlight in an iron pan on the floor; there was neither table nor chair, since all were in use below, and Lord John had to stoop to the ground to fill the two leather and silver cups he had carried tucked under his elbows.

'This is a better way of making merry than below,' he said with a shy, ingratiating smile, the low yellow flame of the rushlight flickering up on to his face.

'You were merry enough leading the fling at Dunbar, and seeing fat old Huntly break his funny-bone.'

'Wish it had been James! Wish it had been his neck.'

'What's your trouble with your brother?'

But Johnnie Stewart shied away like a colt. 'Oh, he's too thick with the ministers, foul swine that they are! I will say he stood up to them over the Queen better than I'd thought – you know, that time he kept the door of the chapel and Rob and I had to frog-march her priest through the rioters. I said frog-march because he's a French frog, ha ha! The ministers blame us for it too. The way they rail against the Queen is sheer treason. I sent word to the chief of 'em – *you know who* –' (he wagged his fair tousled boyish head portentously and laid a not entirely steady finger to his nose) – 'that if he troubled the Queen's Majesty too far, I'd leave him stickit to his pulpit with my dirk. That's the best way to make a stickit minister, hey?'

'What did old Knox say?'

'Said modesty wouldn't permit him to repeat the filth that came out of my stinking throat and mouth.'

'Modest fellow!'

'Aye, he's noted for it. When the Queen Regent lay dying last year he said a dropsy had swelled her belly and loathsome legs!'

Bothwell's face was black with fury.

'By the faith of my body, I'd like to make *his* belly and legs loathsome!'

'*And* I'd help you. Do you think we'll ever get the chance?'

'No. The Queen wants us all on our good behaviour, saying pretty things to each other. Geordie Seton and I have promised to sign a truce in the middle of next month with the Bast— with the Lord James and John Cockburn, promising "to leave each other's lives and property undistroublit".'

'Will you be able to keep it?'

'Might be done. It's only till the first of next February.'

Johnnie Stewart seemed to think two and a half months' 'undistroublit' truce just possible.

'You know,' he said as he filled up their cups again at that uncomfortable angle, spilling a good deal on the floor between their legs, 'there's something to be said for that notion of my sister's – and she *is* my sister, mind you, though only half and left-handed, as your sister is never tired of rubbing in – well, there's a good deal to be said for this notion of all being friends together, don't you think? Here Lob, here Luby, come lap this wine-puddle, there's glory for you! Look at 'em getting as drunk as lords – as us two lords!'

His impish glee as one of the hounds slithered on the bare boards, scrabbling with his claws out to get a footing, made him look about fifteen. Bothwell got impatient of waiting for this flibbertigibbet to come to the point.

'Why is my sister never tired of insulting you?' he asked.

'Oh well, you know what she is. She's a little devil. Mind

120

you, I like her for it. Other women are always preening themselves. Jan would clout me over the head if I paid her a compliment.'

'Paid her some, though, haven't you – of a kind?'

His host shot him a glance like a guilty schoolboy.

'Did she tell you?'

'I made her.'

There was real alarm now in young Stewart's face. 'Why, there's no — ? She isn't — ?'

'With child? No. Small thanks to you, I take it.'

'No, but – damnation! This is devilish awkward.'

'Why? You wanted to talk to me, I suppose, or you wouldn't have asked me to share your bed.'

'Yes, but – it's like this. I want to marry her – I do indeed — '

'Mighty kind of you.' The legitimate noble stiffened forbiddingly at this condescension from a bastard prince, but the prince was too intent to notice it.

'I didn't at first,' he admitted, 'I wasn't thinking of marrying. I wasn't thinking at all. She wasn't either. But she makes other women seem like a lot of lumps. I don't feel I could stand any of 'em for more than a bit, now there's Jan.'

'Is there?'

This time the ironic note was unmistakable.

'You don't mean — God's blood, Bothwell, you'd never let her marry that blackguard, Archie Douglas?'

'She's got to marry someone since she's started playing the fool like this.'

'But I tell you I want to marry her, only she's such a damned perverse little wretch I don't know that I can make her – even now when most women would be grateful for it. It ought to be child's play — '

'It is,' muttered Bothwell, leaning over to pick up his cup. He could not believe in this boy's age when he thought of himself at nineteen. It had been as easy to get what he wanted from him as from Jan. Now it only remained to tackle Lord James – a very different matter. But the Queen would help. She owed him compensation over the Lieutenancy of the Border, and she liked this gay lad – he liked him himself. He'd see to it as soon as he returned from hanging thieves at Jedburgh with James.

'You stand well with the Queen,' he said. 'She should be able to manage your brother. I'll manage my sister.' And he rolled back on the bed, kicking over what remained of the wine as he swung up his legs.

Lord John began in ruminative solemnity, 'You know, it's a funny thing about women — ' and saw that his guest was already sound asleep, the insensitive block, in spite of the importance of their talk.

The hounds lapped up the rest of the wine and were sick. Lord John considered calling a servant to attend to this, but reflected that most of them would be in a like condition. *He* wasn't going to sleep. He was going to make a song about women, like his father's. Would he himself 'go no more a-roving' when he married Jan? He'd swear he would – it would be she who'd have to mind the bridle then. But would she, if he himself roved too far? He must give that up if he were going to keep his Jan – she was worth it. He must give up sweet Alison Craig, so easy-tempered and admiring, who loved him so faithfully, but never reproached him for his neglect.

Poor Alison! He must break the blow gently to her, and he thought with pitying regret of the submissive downward sweep of her eyelashes on her soft pink cheek, and of her modest ways (she'd be shocked by Jan's speech) for all that he'd seduced her – but her boor of a husband (to say nothing of his own attractions) was good excuse for that. Yes, he must say farewell to Alison and give her a parting present, do the thing handsomely as his father had always done, whether with countess or beggar-maid.

He stretched himself back where he was sitting at the foot of the bed, wondering for one drowsy instant why it was so lumpy, until a kick enlightened him, and a deep voice growled, 'Get off my feet.'

*   *   *

Lord James believed in 'Jedburgh Justice'; it meant hanging first and trial after, a method which had the advantage of speed. Bothwell refused to allow it in the case of the Liddesdale men, but even so, the Raid of Jedburgh only took a fortnight. On his return to Edinburgh to attend a meeting of the Privy Council (he had been appointed one of the twelve Councillors), Johnnie Stewart sought him out in high excitement.

'You've missed all the fun of the fair,' he began.

Bothwell thought he meant a masquerade tourney led by the Marquis d'Elbœuf on the sands of Leith, but young Stewart exclaimed, 'Lord, man, it's not d'Elbœuf's foolery I'm talking of, but the scare of Arran kidnapping the Queen.'

James Hepburn's silence was so fiercely peremptory that the youth went on instantly: 'You know he's not been near the

Court since he led the riot in her chapel – all the Hamiltons have kept away, in fact, but now they're showing their face again, an ugly one too, it strikes me. Arran's precious cousin James Hamilton, the Primate, I mean, came riding up the High Street t'other day, and eighty horsemen at his back. Then Châtelherault himself comes and pays his respects to the Queen.'

'And his son?' demanded Bothwell as Lord John paused.

'Arran? Wait a bit. On Sunday night we got an anonymous letter telling us that danger threatened the Queen's person. Assassination was what we feared. The Court was in a panic, everybody accusing someone different, the Frenchmen foaming with rage, swearing they'd take her back to France next day – women in hysterics – not Mary herself though – God, I was proud of her! But it was devilish, feeling responsible for her. I'd never wished before for James to be there, but I did then! Well, Rob and I did what we could, set a special guard round the Queen herself, called up armed men from the town, set pickets round the Palace, sat up all night outside her door, with only water to cheer us, so as to keep our heads cool — What are you grinning at?'

Bothwell was thinking that this lad had shown a remarkably good head, for he, and not his elder brother Lord Robert, was always the leader of the two. 'The Queen's got reason to be grateful to you,' he said.

'Yes, and she is too – it couldn't have happened more luckily for me. Besides, she likes making marriages, she called herself my "Marraine" and said she was James' also! But she laughed over that. I fancy I'm the pet godson of the two! She's going to talk James over and come to the wedding herself and bring him too, worse luck, but it's a good thing, of course – can you stand the expense of a royal wedding?'

'Oh aye,' was the imperturbable answer, and then, 'Where does Arran come in?'

'Next morning. We heard he'd crossed the Forth with horse and foot behind him, that he was going to join with Gavin Hamilton's force inside the city and kidnap the Queen. I kept the burghers' guard on as a permanency and set every courtier in the Palace on sentry-go in turn. I even got the builders to block the entries to her rooms. The Court had just settled down to it all happily – you know how different it is the moment one knows what's to be done – and they were making jokes on it and Mary writing a masque about it – when Châtelherault comes up to say it's all a mistake; Arran had only come home the night before to see his father, with no armed force, nothing but a couple of servants and a page, and he can't think how these ridiculous rumours can have got about! It made us look foolish, I can tell you. We disbanded the emergency guard, and it all fizzled out. But I stuck to it that her bodyguard of a dozen halberdiers must be doubled. I've wanted to do that for some time, though it's raised the cry of armed tyranny – as if one could be a tyrant on the strength of twenty-four halberdiers!'

'You don't think the warning was just a hoax?'

'No, I don't. I still think Arran's dangerous. He's been sulking ever since the chapel riot, and says it's a crime to allow Mary to hear Mass. And yet he's mad for love of her – it's as though he's jealous even of her God. But the worst is, he's been saying how easy it would be to kidnap a Queen from Holyrood. There was once a plot to kidnap her mother there, wasn't there?'

'And he thinks it might succeed with her daughter? He'll learn!'

CHAPTER FIVE

ALISON CRAIG was the stepdaughter-in-law of that grandmother whom Bothwell had been at such pains to prove a bastard. This complicated relationship is best explained by a brief glance at the grandmother in question. She was Agnes Stewart, illegitimate daughter of the Earl of Buchan, and was first the mistress of King James IV (Mary's grandfather) and then the wife of the second Earl of Bothwell. Both King and Earl were killed, with nearly all the Scots nobility, at Flodden; the Earl while leading a counter-charge so furious that it was sung by succeeding poets for three hundred years, the contemporary epitaph being:

> *The Earl of Bothwell then outbrast,*
> *Into the enemy throng he thrust.*

That 'hardy heart' ceased to beat when he was only twenty-one: his widow Agnes was left with his infant son Patrick, and made up for her early bereavements by three more husbands. The last of these was Cuthbert Ramsay, a youth of twenty, who had already proved himself a family man with a baby son, and now married the indefatigable dowager, aged fifty.

Agnes died within a few weeks of the death of her son, Patrick the Fair Earl; and her grandson, James Hepburn, fourth Earl of Bothwell, promptly patched up what he could of his father's debts by proving the illegitimacy of his recently deceased grandmother. By this he secured the escheat of her property from Cuthbert Ramsay, and the disconsolate widower fought the action unavailingly.

'A twittering sparrow of a man,' as Bothwell called him, who had married a woman thirty years older than himself for her money, and lost it, Cuthbert was still determined to make what capital he could out of sex. His son had married a merchant's daughter called Alison Craig; she continued to be called it even after her marriage, for there was little reason to remember her husband. But several nobles showed their gratitude to her father-in-law, for it was at Cuthbert Ramsay's house that they were able to meet her without any open scandal.

Among these was the Earl of Bothwell, to whom Cuthbert now showed his forgiveness for his financial injuries by getting back through his daughter-in-law a small modicum of what he had lost through his wife. So accommodating was he that he twittered almost effectionately over his stepgrandson; he enjoyed the consequence brought him by his even more accommodating daughter-in-law; he was in fact that very rare bird, a natural pandar; his withered pink cheeks, his twinkling pale blue eyes and thin hair streaked with silver, showed the faded remains of the effeminate beauty that, combined with a happy shamelessness, had helped him at the romantic age of twenty to his unromantic marriage. Even so it had not been all for money; he had taken a vicarious pleasure in his wife's career from the bed of a king and of an earl to that of his own. And he chirped with pride over Alison's beauty and soft passivity that made her attractive to such widely different men – a rare girl that, for whom even the Earl of Arran was not too pious, nor the Earl of Bothwell too rakish, nor the Lord John Stewart too young and inexperienced.

But the Earl of Bothwell was not so accommodating when he paid a tactlessly impromptu visit and met his prospective brother-in-law walking down the steep garden path at the back of Ramsay's house in St Mary's Wynd. Lord John twirled his budding moustache and glanced with an absurdly proprietary air at the bee-skeps that bordered the cabbages, as he sauntered through the warm early December dusk. Bothwell, coming up the narrow path, was the first to see the other, and stood still, waiting for him. Lord John pulled up short and gave a sharp whistle.

'What!' he exclaimed. 'Do *you* know Alison?'

'Who doesn't? – if you speak biblically.'

Johnnie Stewart could hardly flush deeper than he had already done, but he laid his hand on his sword. 'How dare you insult her — ' he began, but James Hepburn struck his hand off the hilt before he could get any further.

'Put that away, you fool. Have you nothing better to do than defend the honour of a whore? Forgotten something, haven't you?'

There was an instant's pause while Lord John still made an attempt to keep his hold on the heroic, but the grim amusement in the other's eye was too much for him; he grinned and said airily, 'Ah yes, that little matter of your sister. Let's go back and get married.'

He took his arm, and Bothwell swung round and marched him back to his house in the Canongate, where he set him down on the opposite side of his hearth and scanned him from the corner of an ogreish eye.

'Now,' he said, 'what's this foolery a few weeks before your wedding? If Jan got wind of it, you know her temper and the chances she'd pay you back in your own coin.'

Lord John's explosive reply to this was entirely satisfactory to the other. But he did not so much like his excuses about his old friendship with Alison, his necessity 'in common courtesy to say farewell', and his insistence that Bothwell had maligned her – a gentle creature, with a churlish husband and an immorally mercenary father-in-law. It was plain that he half blamed, half flattered himself with having seduced her, and so paved the way for her falling to a cynical ruffian like James Hepburn, who was, he implied, incapable of understanding the essential innocence of any woman.

These high-toned sentiments made the affair much more dangerous from the point of view of the cynical ruffian, who knew how restful insipidity could prove after a fiery jade such as his young sister. At least he should have no chance to compare Alison's mealy-mouthed modesty in his mind with Jan's frankly boyish crudity of speech.

'Would you still believe in the virtue of that squashy pink plum if you found her with Arran?' he demanded. 'You'd not call *him* a seducer like me, I take it, or think no woman could resist him, like yourself.'

But his reputation for rough irreverence went against him. Proof was needed, and it would be an amusing revenge on Arran to blast his reputation, which stood so high with the godly. The sack of his house of Crichton had never been wiped out; and only last week he had had to send out a force of armed horsemen to collect his tithes at Melrose, since Arran's men were out doing the same thing. To crown all, Arran's father, the Duke of Châtelherault, had snubbed a friendly overture of his, made in compliance with the Queen's wishes, with the reminder that he wanted no such assurances from an inferior in rank. Inferior! He, a Hepburn, inferior to any man in Scotland, let alone a Hamilton cockered up with a brand-new French title.

'Duc de Châtelherault!' he suddenly exclaimed. 'If *he's* a Duc, then I'm a drake!'

A cruel grin spread slowly on his face. 'We'll root up this "young plant" of Johnnie Knox! We'll show his pastor and master just how deep Arran's virtue grows. We'll make a Christmas revel of it and catch him supping at the old pimp's house: the godly won't believe, whatever you do, that he goes there to say his prayers.'

Johnnie Stewart was relieved that Arran had become the centre of attention, so much so that he presently plucked up courage to ask if Bothwell had found it tolerably easy to 'manage' his sister as he had promised.

'Oh aye,' said the other airily, 'she said she'd no mind to stay a Hepburn always, for she hates a name that sounds like a hiccup!'

Johnnie hurled himself upon him, and the brotherly rebuke ended in a rough-and-tumble.

*   *   *

When Bothwell presented himself to the Queen next day he found her and the Court in deep mourning for the anniversary of King François' death. Everyone with whom he spoke urged him to hurry home and change his scarlet velvet for a suit of sober black. But he refused, and was no whit disconcerted when he met the raised eyebrows of his Queen.

'Did no one tell you?' she asked. 'But of course you will change for the memorial service in the chapel this evening.'

'I can remember a year ago, Madam, without any memorial service.'

She gave him a startled look as though she resented his memory of a year ago. 'Do you mean you will not come?'

'I am a Protestant,' he said. 'I don't attend services of the Mass.'

'So are more than half my nobles, yet they are attending this one out of courtesy – and sympathy with me.'

Her voice shook a little with indignation, but he remained unmoved.

'Then, Madam, you have from them what you expect. You've never found me a courtier, and as to sympathy —'

'Yes?' she said as he paused. 'Are you going to tell me you never had sympathy with me – a year ago?'

'That was another matter.'

'It was indeed!' But she must not show her anger so plainly, for though he was being insolent, intolerable, she somehow felt that it was giving herself into his hands.

And so it proved, for standing there so nonchalantly, yet every inch of him alert with his powerful vitality, he was getting the mastery of her so that it was possible for him to say, quite easily and coolly and without rebuke from her, 'You're thinking more of your next husband than of your last, so why should I help you mourn him?'

And it was he who turned away, not she who sent him, it was that that angered her more than anything as she thought it over; for she did think it over, all through that memorial service, she in her white veils and her courtiers in black, and now holding a great white candle draped in black velvet to her husband's memory – and how heavy it was, and how overpowering the fumes of the incense-perfumed wax, and how dazzling that tapering heart-shaped flame flickering just in front of her eyes, now leaping, now guttering in the icy draughts that always blew through every building in Scotland.

> *The wind it blew frae north to south,*
> *It blew into the floor.*

She must not think of those rude country songs, she must think of this solemn Requiem the choir were chanting.

But she was thinking neither of her last husband nor her next, whether he were the Prince of Spain or the new little King of France, or the King of Sweden or of Denmark, or either of the Emperor's two sons, or the Earl of Arran, or Lord Henry Darnley, but of the forcible, arresting face of the man who never cared whether he pleased her or not.

Three days later it was her nineteenth birthday and she gave a ball ('One moment she is pretending to mourn her husband, and the next leaping and dancing,' Knox complained to the citizens of Edinburgh). She wore Highland dress as she had done sometimes at the French Court, when they had declared that 'rude barbaric costume' the most becoming she had; it suited the lissome grace of her strong young body far better than the stiff gorgeous robes in which she never really felt at ease. She had learned the reels and flings years ago, and danced them now in an ecstasy of enjoyment. This cold grim country had provided the liveliest dances in the world, and here she was dancing them, the Queen of that country, and beautiful, and nineteen today. She called Mary Beton to her to pin up a long shining wisp of hair that had tossed out from under the eagle's feather on her head. The reel had stopped, the music stepped into the stately royal dance of the Galliard. She turned to the man behind her who was talking with her youngest half-brother Johnnie.

'Are you not dancing this, my Lord Bothwell? You should, for I think it bears your nickname.'

'No, Madam, it is the Dance Royal, and the Galliard should not dance it except with royalty.'

The music flourished a magnificent panache and he swept her a bow in time to its rhythm. She flushed, scarcely knowing if he were laughing at her or asking her to dance; in either case an impertinence, to ask her so. She no longer felt a Queen – or nineteen; this odd teasing fellow always managed to make a child of her. She would not bother with him, and turned away to dance with Lord George Gordon, the Earl of Huntly's eldest son, a magnificent young Highlander, as tall and silent as his father was fat and talkative. He had never taken his eyes off her since she had entered the room in their native dress.

Bothwell's glance followed them as Gordon handed her across the floor, bowed, advanced to her again, took hands and swung her into the lovely postures of that formal measure. But all he said to Johnnie was, 'My fellow Paris will bring word when he's at Cuthbert's; in another week or two will be best. The Christmas revels will be beginning then, and we'll have an excuse to wear masks.'

'What revel is that, my friends? May I make one at it?'

The Marquis d'Elbœuf was taking his arm, smiling under the waving line of his moustache, affable and almost ridiculously handsome.

'May I tell him?' asked Johnnie eagerly, and Bothwell

nodded, and Mary's young uncle was allowed to share in the plot – one after his heart, for here was a chance to expose the hypocrisy of that insolent canting knave who had dared insult his niece at her Mass. He insisted that he too should be allowed to 'testify' – to use their own jargon – 'to the impurity of the godly'.

'Aye, it will be a Christmas sport for you as good as your mumming tourney that I'd the bad luck to miss,' Bothwell conceded, and the three young men stayed in their corner so long, talking low and laughing loud together, that the Queen had to send her Maries with a royal command to dance. But she was not entirely satisfied with the result, for though her uncle and half-brother both clamoured to dance with her after that, the Galliard danced only with Mary Fleming.

Nor was Mr Maitland of Lethington pleased. Forty years old, thin, dry, delicate, a little wizened, he could not deny to himself that the two made a splendid couple; Mr George Buchanan, now fulsomely intent on showing himself a courtier, wheezed heavily into his ear that Mary Fleming was a venus for beauty, a Minerva for wit, and a Juno for wealth.

'And her partner,' said Lethington in his gently dispassionate fashion, 'is, I suppose, a Ganymede for beauty, a Joseph for chastity, and a Moses for meekness.'

When the dance was over, he complimented Bothwell so elaborately on his dancing that the young man began to have an angry suspicion that he had somehow made a fool of himself, and their political animosity was much increased.

*   *   *

Christmastide set in fine and frosty. The dark goblin figures of little boys were running and squawking, pelting each other with snowballs in St Mary's Wynd that moonlit evening, when three masked revellers knocked at the door of Cuthbert Ramsay's house, and were inside it before their 'host' had discovered who they were.

'And who did you think we were?' demanded Bothwell as Cuthbert twittered and fluttered before him, overcome by such embarrassment of riches as two of his daughter-in-law's lovers at once, and in company with the young foreign nobleman whose armorial bearings (as Cuthbert could have told you on the instant, having always nursed a wistful passion for heraldry) included the lilies of Anjou and Sicily, the crimson bars of Hungary, the double cross of Jerusalem, and hovering over all, the silver eaglets of Lorraine – the arms, in fact, of the royal house of Guise.

He chirped insistently that he had expected no visitors, but was delighted to have these; he called to Alison to bring them wine, and she came at once, all fluttering eyelashes and shy smiles. There was no sign of Arran. Paris must have mistaken.

'The women of your country are indeed wonderful,' murmured d'Elbœuf as they strolled down the hill again to Holyrood later in the evening. 'At what stage, if any, do they cease to simper?'

Paris' information was wrong by twenty-four hours; it was the next evening, he discovered, that Arran would be at Ramsay's house, and thither went the three indefatigable gallants yet again – to find the doors barred and bolted against them, sure proof that this time their scent was not at fault. They had dined at d'Elbœuf's expense before coming out, the cold night air acted powerfully on his warmed Armagnac, and the opposition of the barricaded house gave a final stimulus to their rampant spirits.

'To me, one and all!' roared Bothwell, and the three of them rushed at the door and smashed it in with their shoulders.

They were in time to see Cuthbert's hinder parts crawling under the stairway and Alison's scampering up it, but again no sight of Arran. Bothwell leaped at the back door on to the garden and dragged it open. A tall shadow was visible for one moment running and stumbling downhill. Bothwell yelled to his comrades, hallooing them on to the hunt, and led the charge through the cabbages. Here was sport indeed, with that skulking shadow ahead of him and the frosty air sharp on his face, his blood tingling with the force of that mighty drive against the door, and the crash of rending timber still echoing in his ears – but here he fell headlong over a bee-skep.

Johnnie reached the bottom of the garden to find the door there open, the quarry fled. It was useless to seek him outside in that rabbit-warren of twisted passages, dark courtyards and low shadowy archways. But he returned in some triumph, for at the bottom of the garden he had found Arran's hat; this he waved proudly before the eyes of his fallen commander, who was picking himself up and blinking at the stars that bounced about so inordinately above his head.

The two champions of virtue returned at leisure to the house, where René d'Elbœuf, now disappeared upstairs, was presumably testing the extent of Alison's capacity to simper. That of

131

Cuthbert's was unlimited; he was waiting for them with a coy smirk, and only giggled when Johnnie shook Arran's hat in his face in righteous wrath.

'Te-he-he!' he tittered. 'If your Lordship could but see yourself!'

'I'll wring your scraggy neck,' growled His Lordship, but was distracted from this purpose by a yelp from Bothwell, who was busy shaking some sleepy bees out of the flaps of his boots. In the warm air of the room they were beginning to zoom and fly about, and one had already stung him. The two champions departed in haste.

But it was a hornets' nest they had aroused rather than a skep of drowsy winter bees.

Arran sobbed out his complaints, not only to his clan but to his Church. Knox made a thunderous attack on the Court; James came to his young sister with a face as long as Knox's beard, and dark hints of a matter 'so heinous and horrible' that he could not bear to sully her ears with it.

'Well, if you can't tell me I can't deal with it,' she snapped, 'so why speak of it at all?'

But James was fully determined to speak of it; he would 'think himself guilty if he passed it over in silence'.

'And why not think yourself guilty for once, dear James? You might enjoy the change.'

She spoke in her most coaxingly teasing voice, taking his arm and laughing up into his face; but he went rigid under her touch and his face red with real anger. It was no use, she must never again make the fatal mistake of laughing at James.

His account was still veiled and allusive in regard for her modesty, but as far as she could make out, a citizen's house had been broken into, and a citizen's wife dragged from her husband's bed to please these outrageous rioters. She flatly refused to believe it either of her uncle or her delightful brother Johnnie. The Earl of Bothwell was another matter, he seemed to enjoy showing there was nothing of which he was not capable.

James heartily endorsed this opinion, and added that my Lord Arran and the whole great clan of Hamilton were mortally offended with him.

'Arran! But what has he to do with the matter?'

James was reluctantly forced to explain that the citizen's wife had also pleased Lord Arran; then, when pressed, that she had been the mistress both of Bothwell and Lord John; finally, that the outraged house had not been that of her husband, but of her father-in-law, an acknowledged pimp in the matter.

'But this throws an utterly different light on the business,' she declared, and rounded furiously on him for bothering her with such an ugly silly affair. Her Uncle René was a foreigner and did not understand the sanctity of a Scot's home (even when it was a pandar's); Johnnie was a lad not quite twenty, his two companions only half a dozen years older: Bothwell had the excuse of his quarrel with Arran, who had shown little regard for the sanctity of Bothwell's home when he sacked Crichton.

'That was political,' said Lord James stiffly.

'I have yet to learn,' she replied, 'that a crime is any the less a crime when it can be labelled political.'

He looked at her pityingly and reminded her that she was a woman and had only just had her nineteenth birthday. She just restrained herself from hitting him.

Finally she promised to reprove the roysterers, and did so, but it was not the end of the riot.

Knox accused her publicly of 'maintaining impiety, and whoredom in especial'.

Arran was out for blood. Three hundred of his clan planned to attack the three gallants on Christmas Eve as they returned from supping with the Queen, and Paris, more Cock-up-Spotty than ever at proving himself 'a damned good spy', brought word of it to Bothwell when he was already at the Palace. His master tapped Johnnie on the shoulder.

'The Hamiltons are on the street. Warn d'Elbœuf and tell him to send as many men as he can muster instantly to my house. You do the same. But keep the Guise himself out of it. We don't want his death in a street brawl.'

'Hadn't we better leave a hint here how matters stand?'

'We'll do that when we've mustered our own men – and rather more too than the Hamiltons! Bring Arran's hat. We'll stick it on a pole for our banner.'

Within the hour Bothwell's faithful lieutenant, Black Ormiston of the Moss Tower, had gathered together a mixed bag of Hepburns, Lord John's men and d'Elbœuf's 'Papishes', amounting in all to between four and five hundred. Johnnie had the devil's own work in keeping René d'Elbœuf out of the fray, for he at once grabbed a halberd, and a dozen men were barely able to hold him back, but as luck had it Johnnie had already taken the precaution of locking the inner gates on him.

Gavin Hamilton, the warlike Abbot of Kilwinning, was reported to be in command of his kinsmen at the market-place, and the whole city was buzzing with the news that the Hepburns and Hamiltons were out for a Christmas Eve row; the shopkeepers and their prentices left their mince pies and plum porridge and were busy sharpening their spears and axes in the little lighted booths throughout the town, for every merchant was bound by law to keep a stout weapon handy so as to be ready to rush to any fray in the streets, should the Common Bell summon them to keep the peace. So the tinsmiths and braziers in the West Bow were clanging noisier metal than their wares; the linen merchants in the Lawnmarket and the goldsmiths of Elphinstone Court near the Mint were handling weightier weapons than scissors and trinkets; the butchers just below the Netherbow and just under John Knox's window were preparing for bigger game than calves and sheep.

The preacher was writing his sermon against the superstitious observance of Christmas when the 'dreadful noise of armour pierced his heart'. Brave as he was in words to any man's face, he could not bear the actual sight and sound of an armed clash. It did not help to steady his nerves when the door flung open and Mrs Bowes, the mother of his young wife who had died last year, threw herself on her knees beside him.

'Oh Master,' she sobbed, 'Maigret says they're fighting up by the Tron, hundreds and hundreds of them, and we'll all be murdered and raped and burnt in our beds. Stop them, Master!'

'Maigret's a fool. It's only some fash of the Hepburns and Hamiltons. The citizens will deal with it.'

But the mistress was a worse fool than the maid. She seemed to think he had only to put his head out of the window and preach to them, for them all to disperse quietly. She went on nagging at him:

'Oh Master, save me, save us all! I came here for your sake – do this for mine.'

She was sobbing hysterically, and he pushed her away as she clutched at his knees. 'I asked for you to come and take the burden of housekeeping from me, not add to my burden by weeping and howling' – and as this produced a still louder howl – 'There, there, woman, I'm only telling you to have sense.'

But the women that John Knox preferred to have about him were singularly lacking in sense. Mrs Bowes continued to plead for 'one trumpet note' of that voice which in his own ears sounded weaker and hoarser every time he spoke.

For the uproar was thickening in the street below – 'Hoo! Hoo! Hoo for a Hepburn!' came the cry; 'Fye Tyndale, to it!';

and 'Bide me fair!' Farther up the hill it was answered by 'A Hamilton! A Hamilton!'

Knox found to his intense annoyance that his knee, still clutched by Mrs Bowes, was shaking.

'For my life,' he said severely, 'I count it not a rush. It is my Maker's, to be called back by Him when He so pleases. I say this of my deliberate mind to my God. But for this infirmity of the flesh I cannot answer; it comes, I think, from the time when I suffered the continual fear of the lash in the galleys.'

That was a time he seldom spoke of, and would not have done so now, but to excuse his trembling. But Mrs Bowes mistook his meaning, as she usually did, and thought he referred to his complaint of the stone, the galley's painful inheritance; she was at once busy with hot possets and logs for the fire, forgetting her own fears and drowning those of her son-in-law in his helpless irritation at her fussing. But even as she rushed at him with a fleecy plaid in one hand and a steaming bowl in the other she dropped them both, for into the little warm room so closely shuttered against the wintry night outside, there came the muffled clanging of the Common Bell.

Men below were running, shouting, dogs barking, women shrieking, and rushing to and fro went the bells above them higgledy-piggledy in a hideous clamour. Down went Mrs Bowes on her knees again, instinctively mopping up the mess of the posset with the plaid, while she screamed and prayed in alternate gusts of breath, and her son-in-law silently asked God what devil-sent impulse had ever betrayed him to get her to leave England to look after his household.

He stormed at her to stop mopping up the slops with his best plaid, then checked as other noises came swinging uphill from the Canongate into the Netherbow, sweeping on up towards the market-place, the steady run of disciplined armed forces and shouts of 'In the name of the Queen!' Law and order were on the march against the riot. In a spasm of irritation, relief, and determined courage, John Knox sprang up, away from that tousled sprawling bundle of dishevelled hair and clothes, and flung open his shuttered window.

The Lord James and the Earl of Huntly were in command of the guards from Holyrood, and shouting to their respective religious sects that any man who stayed in the streets would be put to death. Mr Knox shut his window hurriedly. In twenty minutes neither Protestant nor Papist could be found out of doors.

135

The religious question was certainly obscure in this controversy, for when the leaders had to answer for their action before the Queen next day, Bothwell appeared at the head of as many Papists as Protestants, while large numbers of the godly, even of Knox's own congregation, were following the Papist Abbot of Kilwinning, Gavin Hamilton, in their anxiety to avenge the insult to his kinsman, Arran.

Arran himself declared that the proposed attack on Bothwell had been organized by his kinsmen, but that he knew nothing about it, nor did his father.

'Maybe you don't know your own hat either?' demanded Bothwell, flourishing that now disreputable piece of headgear.

Mary, betrayed into an incautious giggle, instantly turned it to a severe frown.

'If it amuses you, my lord, to make a mock of our justice, you will find it harsher than you seem to expect.'

The Lord James made a brief aside to her against the superstitious Christmas revels which had helped lead to this disturbance; the Queen replied rather tartly that she did not see that it would have made it any better if the disturbance had been helped instead by the non-superstitious New Year revels.

But it gave her her cue, for she made a charming little speech to the delinquents, reminding them that it was Christmas Day, and whatever 'some in our kingdom' might think of the superstition of observing that day with reverence, yet surely both Protestant and Catholic might give thanks for the birthday of the Prince of Peace, and even if they gave each other no other gifts on that day, should agree to give peace and brotherly love. And she turned to the Duke of Châtelherault as the most important of the protagonists, and asked him to accept her arbitration.

The head of the Haughty Hamiltons refused, standing very stiffly and looking like a handsome sheep. Only one political idea had ever penetrated behind that classic profile with the pink and white skin under the silver hair – that but for this skittering lass before him, now making her schoolgirl appeals for his good behaviour, he himself should be King of Scotland. He would show her he was not going to be coaxed into making up the quarrel; he declared that he could listen to no overtures of peace until Bothwell had withdrawn his charge against him and his son – 'publicly at the Market Cross.' As an afterthought, during the startled pause that followed this announcement, he added triumphantly, 'With sound of trumpet.'

This imbecility made any reconciliation impossible. If the armed forces of the Hasty Hepburns and the Haughty Hamiltons continued to stay in the town, a pitched battle would be inevitable. The Queen looked in desperate appeal at Bothwell. He was leaving in any case in a day or two, to go and arrange for his sister's wedding at Crichton, and Mary would be attending it and staying the night. He must see how absurd was her pretence of 'banishment' and that she only made it for the sake of peace. So she commanded my lord of Bothwell to leave Edinburgh with all his men for the present, and as he bowed his submission and laid her hand on his to raise it to his lips, she gave his fingers a little secret nip as if to say, 'You do understand I have to play this solemn farce?'

His answer was so hard a pressure with his lips upon her hand that it left a mark. She felt it was done more in anger than in friendliness; it was certainly not the least like a caress.

CHAPTER SIX

THAT WAS a wedding. Generations of Hepburns of every ilk talked of it afterwards; four hundred years later, people about the place could still point out the haugh where the sports were held that sparkling January day when at last the mist cleared and the frosted grass crackled like tiny flames as it melted in the sun. The hills in the distance were transparent-looking; the pearl-coloured morning hung breathless in suspense for its first bright hour; then the scene became crowded with noisy, hurrying figures, dark and bright coloured, running, jumping, blowing on their fingers, calling to each other, shouting commands, riding up on horseback to clear a space for the sports; and now, louder, more piercing than all the loud human voices, came the skirl and drone of the pipes tingling through the thin air.

There rang out a shout that drowned even the pipes, a blood-curdling yell of loyalty as the Queen came out of the Castle with the bride and bridegroom, led by her host, Lord Bothwell, and leaning on the arm of her half-brother, Lord James.

Mary had already attended the service in the Castle, showing no such scruples over her presence at a Protestant ceremony as Bothwell had shown over his at her Catholic service; and so she hinted to him with a mocking flicker of those long white eyelids that made her look as though she were pretending to be solemn even when she was laughing.

137

He did not take up her challenge except to laugh back, 'Well, what's the use of a Protestant if he doesn't protest? Or a Catholic if she doesn't show a Catholic taste?'

Jan had been awed at first by her wedding robes and the presence of the Queen. Johnnie, proud of his advantage, had assured her beforehand, 'Oh, you needn't be afraid of the Queen. Mary's a darling and sure to like you. Besides, she adores me. Just wait till you see her.'

When Jan had seen her, she pulled her brother aside and gasped out:

'She's like a pearl or a flame – and I'm so ashamed of my hands so brown and rough, but she doesn't seem to mind. I've seen her bath – an oval silver basin curved like a shell. Is it true she bathes in wine?'

'I couldn't say. I'm not her Companion of the Bath.'

'She has nightgowns sewn with jewels, and fairy slippers over little coloured feathers. Look at this ring she's given me. If I were a man I'd fight for her to the end of the world. Aren't you mad for love of her?'

'Lord, no,' he replied, much amused. 'She's well enough for a Queen. A pretty piece, but not much to her yet. She's a baby like yourself.'

'Lord, what a dolt, a block you are!' And his young sister thumped him in the chest and darted away.

But for all his teasing, grudging, brotherly answers to Jan, Bothwell was showing Mary a new and unexpected charm as her host. He had always been rather on the defensive with her, but now he was wholeheartedly anxious to please.

Mary too was in the happiest mood. The burgesses of Edinburgh had just sent her 'a right jolly New Year's gift' of three tuns of wine, one of which she had brought with her to contribute to the wedding feast, among many other wedding presents, and this early tribute to her popularity with the city had made her very proud. In spite of all Knox's efforts to undermine it, she was gaining steadily in the affections of her people, and she told Bothwell that her pleasure was 'not so much in their present as in the spirit it represents'.

'Is the wine as strong as all that?' he asked in reply.

They seemed to be joking together all the time. And they had more congenial guests to help them than the Lord James. René, Marquis d'Elbœuf, was there, so handsome and gorgeously dressed, so charming and courtly and complimentary, that Jan, who had been only momentarily awed by the Queen, was paralysed by her uncle. The two liveliest Maries were there, Beton and Bothwell's favourite, Fleming; his friend Lord Gordon, Huntly's eldest son, with a large company of his Highlanders; Geordie Seton, the Lords Home and Borthwick, and Hepburns of every branch. Also a dark forcible looking woman who said little, the Lady of Morham, Bothwell's mother, of the Highland Sinclair family.

So that there were many hundreds crowded together on that white hillside, their breath going up in little blue clouds in the rare and shining air. Below them the Tyne wound its sluggish course through the valley, and following its intricate mazes went a host of alders and drooping willows, the elaborate traceries of their bare branches now all frosted white as if in honour to the bridal occasion.

'Your Grace should see Crichton in early summer,' Jan eagerly told the Queen; 'we have glow-worms sparkling all over this haugh on nights in June; and the Tyne – you are only seeing it now as a sulky oozy old snake, but you should see it in May and June when the spreat and deer-hair are all out in flower.'

'Spreat? Deer-hair? What pretty names! and for what?'

'Water-rushes and a pointed grass with a wee yellow flower not half the size of a buttercup,' Bothwell told her; 'these are the rare glories my sister promises you as if from the Sultan's garden!'

But he too was eager to show off Crichton to her. He was delighted that she noticed the scutcheons carved on its walls and the anchors on the graceful portico in honour to his hereditary title of Lord High Admiral; that she praised the stone cordage with twisted knots interlaced with roses that decorated the stairway, and compared it with Anne de Bretagne's motif of the knotted cord in the châteaux of the Breton Queen.

'Here is yet another lovely reminder of our "auld alliance",' she said as she pointed out this unusual elegance to her French uncle. Both he and her Scottish host wondered if that alliance with France, that had brought Scotland all that she had known of the beauty made by man and a gracious way of living, were indeed ending in favour of this new idea of a religious alliance with England. They instinctively glanced across at the austere figure of the Lord James, who plumed himself on being the man of the future. The future wore rather a bleak air. It was cold work watching sports.

But there were few who only watched. There was wrestling and jumping on horseback and on foot and with a pole. Bare arms like knotted whipcord were busy tossing the caber or putting the weight or pushing at a large stone boulder to see who could drive it farthest. A game of football with a blown swine's bladder seemed to engage about a hundred a side. Mary thought the game looked as murderous as a pitched battle, and was not surprised to hear that attempts were always being made to suppress it by law. But that was because it often formed a pretext for different clans to meet together and ride on a foray – so much so that the Wardens of the Marches had only to hear of a great football match at Kelso for them to clap on their buff coats and steel caps and call their men together. In spite of the law, it was the favourite sport on the Scottish Border.

The nobles were jousting on the haugh and tilting against each other, and soon there was a farce that brought yells of delighted laughter from the crowd. D'Elbœuf in a kail-wife's bunched petticoats, and a flapping kerchief on his head, had ridden into the ring. From the other side Johnnie Stewart rode to meet him, dressed in the long black gown and Genevan bands of the minister who had married them. He wore a beard provided by one of Gordon's Highlanders, to wit a shaggy goatskin sporran tied round his chin. He had painted his lips as full and red as a scarlet button, and his bands were sewn with curtain-rings; when he wagged an admonishing forefinger at the shouting crowd and thumped the saddle in front of him as though it were a pulpit, there was no possible doubt as to whom he represented.

The roars of merriment all round them, and the unfamiliar flapping skirts of their riders, startled the horses so much that it was difficult to keep them from bolting. Johnnie's mare did indeed charge a little way into the crowd, who scattered with cries of 'Go easy with us, Mr Knox!' 'You'll find no Cardinals here!'

The kail-wife proved herself the more experienced jouster, and the minister was unhorsed. He quickly scrambled to his feet while the pages caught his madly careering mare; flinging his arm aloft in the prophetic gesture of the preacher, he called out, 'Be warned by me, ye ungodly swine! No man, but a woman, has downed my knocks!'

The applause was deafening, to Mary's relief, for she had looked anxiously at Bothwell and asked if all his clan were

Protestant, and might take this absurdity as an insult. But he only laughed.

'They're Protestant enough not to mind robbing a church. The Border hasn't as much peace and quiet for religious controversy as the safe inland counties. It's little enough they've ever cared about prayers except their neck-verse to patter on the gallows, should the English swing 'em at Carlisle or the Lord Lieutenant at Jedburgh.'

The applause was, in fact, largely a tribute to Knox. To this company he was not so much the prophet and inspiring national leader as that more popular thing, a great public figure who could also be a common butt. Here he was private as well as public property; he had been Johnnie Knox, a lad from Haddington whom nobody had thought of much account, who had indeed been called a jail-and-gallowsbird since he had been among the men who took pay from Henry VIII to murder Cardinal Beton, and had served in the French galleys for his share in the crime. Yet he had risen to be cock o' the walk, crowing it over the whole country and the Queen herself; he could carry off anything he had a mind to, even his mother-in-law from her husband and family, giving out that it was all for her soul's good; and now that his young wife was dead, he was said to be wooing the daughter of the Duke of Châtelherault, the proudest noble in the land – he, rising sixty, from the back streets of Haddington! There was nothing that one couldn't get over; he'd a voice like a rusty saw, but he banged the pulpit about until you thought it would fly to pieces under the wrath of God – and whatever he threatened against anyone of that wrath, it was sure to come true; it had done so again and again, as he himself was always pointing out. He was a nuisance and a tyrant, but there was no denying that he was a great little man, this Haddington lad who'd become cock o' the walk and ruled the roost.

So that the cheers that greeted Johnnie's performance were complimentary as well as derisive, and the rude comments were in pleased recognition that the great man was human like themselves. The pipers started playing and the crowd singing:

> *'The minister kissed the bonny kail-wife*
> *And couldna' sleep for thinking o't.'*

They rocked uproariously as Johnnie took the hint and embraced d'Elbœuf, addressing him first as 'Mother-in-law' and then as 'Mamselle Châtelherault'.

141

'Why should the men have all the fun?' Mary whispered to Jan. 'Let's see what we can do!'

They went back into the Castle with the two Maries on the excuse of warming themselves.

A little later, four gallant youths galloped on to the haugh, two from either side, and rode a tilt against each other, but fortunately none of them got their lances within striking distance of their opponents. It was seen at once that they were girls and —

'God's blood, the Queen!' shouted Bothwell as he dashed into the ring to part the jousters, in imminent danger of a thrust from their unpractised weapons. D'Elbœuf and Johnnie were hot on his heels, the Lord James followed, all four horses were firmly held, and the girls leaped from their saddles, laughing and excusing themselves, pushing up stray curls underneath their manly caps.

Bothwell swore at Jan for this fool prank that might have brought the Queen into danger, Mary declared it was all her doing, and the two looked at each other and laughed like a couple of mischievous urchins. Both made likely lads with their long slim legs and narrow hips, and knew it, swaggering with jaunty gestures, but Beton and Fleming were too plump for the part and looked self-conscious. Bothwell, moreover, perceived that the beautiful Fleming, his 'pick of the bunch', was not only short-legged but knock-kneed, a discovery which made him thoughtful for a few minutes.

Mary swung her short blue cloak over her shoulder and clapped him on the back with manly camaraderie, reminding him that it was not only his sister's wedding day but the 6th of January and Twelfth Night: 'So kneel and he dubbed my Lord of Misrule,' and she drew a dagger whose agate hilt flashed with jewels in the now faint and slanting sunlight, 'or will your Protestant conscience protest also against heathen mummeries?'

He looked at her as she stood there mocking him, flaunting her cloak and dagger – at her teasing smile, her provokingly pretty figure pretending to be a boy's – and forgot the repartee he meant to make. He dropped on one knee, and her dagger tapped him on the shoulder. He rose, Lord of Misrule, whom all the rest must follow whatever he did, and called the guests round him back into the Castle, Mary darting after him at the head of them like a dragonfly with her green silk legs flashing out under the flying wings of her cloak.

Soon they were all careering out of it again, astride on hobbyhorses of broomsticks and coloured rags, wearing whatever absurd disguise they could find to put on their heads, bunches of cocks' feathers or rabbit skins or hats cut out of painted paper, and all playing some instrument, beating drums or tin cans or humming on jews' harps or combs covered with paper, or blowing on trumpets made of cows' horns or whistles of elder stems. The whole mad procession came clattering and whooping after the Lord Bothwell, who rode his hobby-horse at a gallop, hung all over with bells and flying ribbons, and blew a bugle that made every bloodhound in the place bay furiously in the belief that he was raising the Hot Trod. He led them through the crowd on that now darkening hillside and down through the little bare church and into the churchyard. There the villagers waited to hand him cheesecakes and ale, which he ate and drank, and then knelt again before his Queen in her boy's dress, who solemnly placed a crown of silver paper on his head.

For an instant the figures in that dim scene were still. The frosty mist hung over the whitening ground; only a dull and smoky red light in the west showed where the sun had sunk. But soon those goblin forms with the fantastic heads leaped into wild movement and noise again, for now, at the moment of his crowning, the rule of the Lord of Misrule was over. He had to dash back to the Castle, chased by the company, and when they caught him they tore his crown from his head, and his bells and ribbons, and cried out that he was deposed, that he must die, and once again he had to kneel, this time to Johnnie Stewart, who struck off his head with a sausage.

Then, hot and panting, they all pulled off their mummery and looked at each other, laughing. Bothwell said low to the Queen, 'Is it true you sometimes go about the streets of Edinburgh dressed like that?'

'Yes, why not? I keep my cloak over my face. My father was always going about in disguise.'

'You're a woman.'

'So is Queen Catherine, and most respectable for all her gross stories, and she used to walk about the streets as a burgher's wife, in Paris of all places.'

'And that's different too. Is no one ever going to show you what it is to be a woman?'

He spoke in impatient exasperation and regretted it the same instant. 'I did not mean to offend you,' he began, but she was quick to take his apology before he made it.

'And you have not. Nothing could spoil this day, the day I have enjoyed most since I came to Scotland.'

Yes, she was generous, she gave with both hands, he'd say that for her.

She had brought an exquisite dress for the banquet that evening, of silver tissue, and a wing-shaped coronet of pearls. When they cut the Twelfth Night cake before they went to change, the bean was found in Jan's slice, which meant that she was to be Queen for the evening – 'And so you shall,' said Mary mysteriously, leading her away, and when they came down into the great hall, Jan was wearing Mary's dress and crown. Never had Jan seen anything so lovely, and never had Johnnie seen her half as lovely; his face as he looked at his bride gave Mary her reward.

That *was* a banquet. Bothwell's preparations had been thorough; for days past he had kept his men busy hunting to stock the larder, and nearly two thousand wild does and roes had been slaughtered to provide venison, as well as so many plover and partridges, ptarmigan, herons, cranes and wild geese and wild duck, moorfowl and rabbits that nobody could keep count of them.

'Aye, there's enough to eat,' he assented grudgingly when Mary exclaimed at the vast quantity of dishes.

For the first time he felt a personal regret for those glass toys his father had brought from Venice, which Arran's men had smashed. They would have been the right thing to have put before this dainty little French Queen. And, also for the first time, he saw his familiar home as barbaric and uncouth; it struck him how chill and draughty this vast stone hall must be to her, its mighty walls steaming with damp in the heat of the feast, in comparison with the small snug painted rooms of Fontainebleau, and all the curtains and rugs and cushions to give them warmth.

At least a score of logs six or eight feet long were piled fanwise on his huge hearth, their burning noses all meeting together in the red centre of the fire; their flames roared up the great chimney, sucking all the draughts towards them so that the wind blew in icy gusts from the shuttered windows and along the floor under their chairs. Mary had been glad to forgo her gossamer dress for one of pale grey velvet and white fur. Like a winter fox in the snow she looked, in its pale winter coat but keeping the reddish tinge in her shining hair – he wanted to tell her so, but of course he could not.

144

Did she think it all very restless and noisy? – the servants clattering about so clumsily, the shrill mew of the hooded goshawks and merlins perched high above them on the great oak beams, flapping their wings and shaking their bells and feathered jesses in answer to the barking of the staghounds that wandered about in search of bones, and above it all the pipes playing,

Noble Lord Bothwell he dwells on the Border.

He saw the warm enjoyment and interest in her delicate face, and with a very new shyness he said hesitatingly, 'I can't turn the tables into gardens with green lawns and flowers and singing birds as I've seen you do in France. I wish I could.'

'I don't want this to be like France,' she answered him, 'I am in my own country now. I had rather look at the faces of my friends than at a garden on the table.'

And she raised her silver flagon to drink to him with as airy a grace as if it had been any Venetian goblet. He drank to her, put down his cup, and with his eyes still fixed on her, said, 'There are tales here of magic that will make some broken-down shieling seem a palace, and the cobwebs on its walls fine tapestries. I think you have that gramary, to transform this rough feast to a royal banquet of France. You'll do it with all Scotland and make her a fief of Elfland, like the Eildon Hills near here.'

She was amazed, even disconcerted. The Lord Bothwell had paid her a compliment! She had to cover her surprise like any bashful schoolgirl by asking about the Eildon Hills. Bothwell's answer was an order to the minstrels, and one of them sang how True Thomas had kissed the Queen of Elfland and followed her to her realm through a door in the side of Eildon. It was a charming fairy-tale, but Mary wished she had not interrupted her conversation with her host by asking for it; she never seemed to do the right thing when with him; no one else had so much the power to put her at a loss.

And was her hope of reconciling him to James being furthered by this festivity? She was not at all sure. James was looking rather glum. It might be merely that he was having to eat and drink more than his weak digestion would stand.

But that was not the reason. James had not taken part in the mummery of the Lord of Misrule, but sauntered chillily about the Castle by himself and in a spirit of dispassionate inquiry strolled down a dark passage and opened a door into another world – the world of kitchens and domestic servants all busy over this gargantuan feast. For a second or two he stood spell-bound; he saw women running in all directions, their bare red feet slapping the stone floor, their loose hair streeling behind them, their faces scarlet with furious intensity; he heard the screeching of feminine voices and the sizzling of fat; he smelt the raw meat, and meat roasting and feathers burning.

And then, feeling slightly sick, he side-stepped into another passage through another door, and saw more salt beef hanging up than he could have believed possible. This time a scullion perceived him and asked what he wanted; James admitted to having lost his way, but inquired at the same time about the salt beef.

'Martinmas cows,' replied the fellow; 'every parish pays a cow to the Lieutenant at Martinmas to be salted for the winter.' Grinning familiarly, he added, 'Puts you in mind of Jedburgh Justice, don't it, to see 'em all hanging there!'

His grisly wit got no response from James, who, as the man most responsible for 'Jedburgh Justice', should have appreciated it; he was reflecting that, as he had superseded Bothwell as Lord Lieutenant of the Border, he should have been the re-cipient of the Martinmas cows this year. It was a comparatively small matter; his increase of wealth this autumn made a drove of cows equivalent to the loss of a few shillings; but no matter was small to James that made him feel he was being deprived of his rights.

He was still brooding on salt beef, looking down his long nose, even when the supreme dishes were carried in to the applause of the guests – the boar's head, tusked and holly-crowned, surrounded with miniature banners of the host's baronial colours and achievements, and the roasted peacock, reinvested in all the glory of its plumage with spread tail, and fire coming out of its beak from the sponge it held there, dipped in spirits of wine. In old days knights used to vow to do some chivalrous deed within the coming year 'before the Peacock and the Ladies'.

They now revived this custom with modern frivolity; d'Elbœuf vowed never to refuse a drink; Johnnie to entertain this same party at his house at Coldinghame next New Year's Eve, and Bothwell that he would claim that hospitality even if he were not asked. James with a determined effort flung off the cloud of salt beef, and vowed to discover a wooer to whom the

Virgin of England would say 'No' – a piece of malice that delighted his sister. Only George Gordon reverted to the earlier spirit of the custom, and dropping on one knee before Mary swore that her will should be his, whatsoever it might be. The passionate quiet of his earnestness made an odd shy little hush in the midst of all the noise and laughter.

The minstrels had reached the complimentary stage; they sang Bothwell's most famous raids, and even the events of a fortnight since in Edinburgh, when, as they triumphantly proclaimed —

> 'We gar'd the Hamiltons hold their jaw.'

They praised their lord as more skilful than any moss-trooper on the Border, to lead them through the fords of Esk or Liddel on the Solway sands or Tarras Moss. Quiet days were on them now, but

> 'We shall have moonlight again!'

The feast was finished; the servants cleared away dishes and tables and trestles to leave the hall bare again for dancing.

Mary asked where all the rest of the men were that had gathered in hundreds on the haugh that day. Bothwell ordered the great doors at the end of the hall to be flung open, and she had a brief vision of the darkness outside, torn by the leaping flames of a huge bonfire in the courtyard, of dark forms strutting with the pipes or jumping and dancing, of faces suddenly aflame in the red firelight. Fierce shouts rent the night, men were calling the names of their clans as though they were music —

'Hoo for a Hepburn!' 'Fye Tyndale, to it!' 'Bide me fair!' 'A Gordon! A Gordon! Bydand!' And then the queer growling mutter of a chant that rose louder and louder like the howling of wolves:

> 'Little wot ye wha's coming!
> Hob and Tam and a's coming,
> Dick's coming, Jock's coming —'

With a blood-curdling yell the kilted Highlanders joined in:

> 'Colin's coming, Donald's coming,
> Mony a buttock bare's coming'

She seemed to be looking on the war-dance of savages.

Then that wild scene was shut outside again, and the company gathered round the fire in the hall.

Johnnie was singing now, some ribald verses of his royal father's:

' "Oh, kind sir," she said, "be civil, or ye'll waken my dada." '

The older men there nodded together and said how like he was to the late King; too like, that was the pity, he had the same flushed look of delicacy even as he stood and sang so uproariously, waving his wine-cup in rhythm to the tune and calling to the rest to join in the chorus:

'He cadgily ranted and sang,
"She's off with the gaberlunzie man!" '

Yet he never seemed to tire, not even when at the end of this active day he danced flings and reels one after the other without any pause, leaping higher than anyone, snapping his fingers, yelping against the fierce music of the pipes. Never was there such mad music and dancing; to Mary it was as though the cries of the curlews and the sea-birds had joined with the storm-wind to play the tunes.

But the music changed; fiddles and harps were now playing the stately music of the Galliard, and this time she had no doubt as to whether Bothwell had asked her to dance, and sufficiently respectfully; he bowed low before her and together they swept into the measure of the Dance Royal. It was the first time he had danced with her; he danced well, and she was the best dancer of the day. In her grey and white dress she moved like a shadow in the flickering light of the fire and torchlight, and he like the red flame of a torch beside her.

To many who watched among the retainers and rough 'led-captains' of the house of Hepburn, the formal grace of that measure to the old grave music was the loveliest thing ever seen in that hall. To the young Highland lord, George Gordon, who watched with the blank blind eyes of one who sees other scenes from the past or future behind the present, the beauty of that dance did seem indeed unbearable, for before it was finished he turned his head away.

The music paced on to its last long note, the red dancer and his shadow were still, then smiled at each other without a word, and Bothwell led her back to the fire. She stood with one foot on a log, tapping the white wood-ash that had blown back from the fire over it so that it fluffed up in a little whirlpool. Her knees were being roasted while her heels and the back of her shins were icy; one needed to sit on a turning-spit to get warm all over in Scotland. Her finger traced an inscription carved in the stone of the chimney-piece:

> *They have said – What*
> *Say they?*
> *Let them say.*

'Who had that done?' she asked.

'My father,' her host answered. 'There was a deal said against him, so he put that up. I don't know why he troubled.'

So the father had made the gesture to show he didn't care – and did. The son would never care enough to think of the gesture.

She stole a sideways glance at the rugged powerful face. He was too sure of his power, that was the danger; he thought he could stand alone against everyone.

'Do you then think me a coward?' she asked him, 'that I could not take the course I wished at Christmas and order the Hamiltons to leave the city instead of you? But I *cannot* follow my own road yet. I am in my kingdom on sufferance, and barely that. Until I am strong enough to speak myself, I have to listen to what others say.'

He glanced at Lord James huddling his cold hands in his sleeves as he talked with forced geniality to Lord Gordon.

'For "others" read "brother",' he remarked.

'As you will.' She gave him a subtle smile. He began to realize that his warnings against Lord James had not been entirely in vain. It was not so much now that she refused to believe anything against him as that, whatever she believed, there was no way as yet in which she could take action.

'Well,' he said, 'don't ask me to do the same as yourself.'

'I do ask it.' She was vehement now, even commanding. 'Does it amuse you to have enemies? I have read history, and I see that these private enmities between great families have been a greater curse to Scotland than the fiercest enemy from outside. How can I ever rule if my subjects will never unite? You could help me if you chose.'

'What do you want me to do?'

'Make peace with Arran – friends with him if you can. You'll find it easier than you think. He is terrified of you, and that is why he surrounds himself with an army, and so you have to do so too. It is absurd. How am I ever to have a civilized capital if all my nobles go about in it with a tail of several hundred men ready to fight each other at a moment's notice?'

She faced him squarely this time and saw she had impressed him; he was looking very thoughtful.

'Aye,' he agreed soberly, 'and the expense is terrible.'

He stared at her astonished as she bit her lip, made a sound like a suppressed sneeze, and then broke into a peal of irrepressible laughter. He had considered her opinion and come to the conclusion there was something in it; what on earth was there to laugh at?

In a flash of temper he said, 'The Borderer's a useful buffer for the nesh inland Scots against England. It's in my mind, Madam, that you find me useful too as a buffer against your other nobles – to take the kicks you daren't give them.'

And he stalked away.

She was furious; all the more so that he left her before she had the chance to show it. She had practically apologized to him for that very thing, and this was how he took it! Well, but she should not have laughed; she had known it, but could not stop herself. It was ridiculous of him to be angry at that, when he had not been at her public reproof.

But then it struck her – did she know how angry he had been – and was now? It was an uncomfortable thought; she turned sharply from it, turned from one to another in the crowd, joking and laughing with them so that they felt no strangeness with this elegant and lovely creature.

She won the heart of Black Ormiston of the Moss Tower, Bothwell's bailiff, a swarthy stalwart ruffian who stared like an indignant bull, by praising his care of his lord's estate; and learned from him the surprising fact that the reivers, both Scots and English, were apt to levy protection money or 'blackmail' from those on the Border who were willing to pay a yearly subsidy, so that they should be left in peace in the raids.

She heard a great deal from a stocky bow-legged fellow about horses, and the 'gay geldings the English gave the lords at Berwick, that they cracked up as better than any we'd brought out of Scotland —!' the man jerked up his short red beard and shut his mouth.

'What was the matter with them?' she asked.

'Ah, nothing at all, Madam. They'd do fine – as meat for the hounds.'

A grizzled led-captain told her that the Lord's favourite black horse, Corbie, and the Lord himself too (it took Mary an instant to discover that this reverent title referred to Bothwell), were like a pair of mountain cats the way they could see in the blackest night. In fact, his horse seemed to matter rather more to the Borderer than his life; as well it might, seeing that his life so often depended on his being well-mounted. All Eskdale was once lost and won for the sake of a bonny white horse, she was told; and pleased them by remarking that it was no wonder the Hepburn crest was a horse's head: 'And is the Hepburn motto "Horse-sense"?' But there she went too far in jesting on a sacred subject: she was reminded gravely, with a knitting of shaggy brows, that it was 'Keep trust' – 'and well the Lord has proved it to you and yours – Madam.'

That rebuke and belated 'Madam' brought home to her the family likeness between 'the Lord' and his men.

She talked with greybeards who told her escapades of her father when in disguise as the Goodman of Ballengeich; and from a minstrel with a white beard more prophetic than that of Knox, but a merry and irreverent blue eye, she heard how Harry VIII of England had tried to make her father suppress all of their calling, since they were always making comic ballads about him and his unlucky wives.

'But your royal Da, a minstrel himself, knew better than to forbid the heather from growing or the birds from singing. Forbye he had no wish to, for I've seen him hold his sides with laughing at what the songs said of that wicked old sack of rotten guts down in London town.'

'I wish I had known my father.'

'You would have agreed well. Many's the laugh you'd have had together.'

'But all I did was to break his heart. The news that I was a girl, that killed him.'

'Ah well,' said the old man, 'he has more sense now.'

She thought how good it was to be in a land that had never known serfdom like France, so that everyone she spoke to seemed as free and proud as a king.

It was growing late; even Johnnie admitted he 'could not let one more leap or yap out of him'. But all called for one more song before they went to bed, and the minstrels gave them 'Johnnie Armstrong's Goodnight'. Bothwell would have stopped it because of its references to James V as a stern and cruel tyrant, but Mary would not let him.

'You have just told me,' she said haughtily, 'that it's Borderers like Armstrong who protect me from England, for all their unjust reward, so why should I not hear others sing it? Is no one to have the privilege of abusing me but yourself?'

'No,' he admitted, smiling at her.

She could not keep it up, especially when, as they reached the last verse, he said low to her, 'I was a fool to speak so,' and joined in the lines:

> *'What I ha'e done through lack of wit*
> *I never, never can recall.'*

To which she sang with the rest, in answer:

> *'I hope you're all my friends as yet,*
> *And so goodnight unto you all,'*

and for an instant she laid her hand on his.

Yes, she was very forgiving; too much so, that was the trouble, for what was the use of her forgiving him, if she forgave his enemies too, and hers?

He saw her go up the great staircase to undress the bride, followed by her ladies, their shadows rising taller and taller against the wall as they left the light below. Their silk skirts rustled and swept behind them. In front of them went the Queen, her soft velvet dress like a wisp of smoke and as noiseless; her hair bright against the grim stone. She too held up her skirts with one hand while the other rested on that majestic balustrade. She looked down and saw Bothwell watching her, and her hand left the stairway and touched her lips. He saw this without seeing that she did it till afterwards, and at the time he never moved.

Then he went to Johnnie's room to join with d'Elbœuf in undressing the bridegroom.

Johnnie was not drunk, but he was very gay and affectionate, also inclined to reminiscence. He kept reminding them of their raid on Ramsay's house, an unsuitable bachelor recollection, as they pointed out.

'Well, we *were* bachelors then, though we'll never be again.' He put a hand on each of their shoulders and chanted:

> *'For gear will come and gear will gang,*
> *But three brothers again we'll never be.*

'But we will. We've sworn to hold our next New Year Revels at Coldinghame all of us – yes, you too, d'Elbœuf, for you've vowed never to refuse a drink – and I'll get Mary to promise to be with us again, and what's the betting but there'll be a fine young newcomer as well, a lad bred of Stewart and Hepburn stock? Which reminds me —'

And he started for the door.

'He is charming, your Johnnie,' said d'Elbœuf after they had left him in Jan's room, 'a child, but of the most delightful.'

He took his host's arm as they walked down the passage. '*What* a wedding!' he breathed, 'I have never seen anything like it in France.'

And the Prince of the house of Guise who had seen his eldest brother's wedding to Anne d'Este, daughter of the Duke of Ferrara and granddaughter of Louis XII, a wedding more royal than that of many kings, who had seen the wedding of his niece Mary to the Dauphin, 'to describe which was to describe all the glories of the Renaissance', spoke as sincerely as he spoke truly; for certainly he had never enjoyed any wedding in France half as much.

Yes, it had gone off well, Bothwell agreed, and told himself that it had been worth the outlay, though he would have to sell yet more land to meet his debts.

He went to his room, well pleased. The Queen was sleeping under his roof; they had quarrelled but they had made it up; there was no doubt but that she was friendly to him. And she had been quite sound about Arran; he could not afford, from any angle, to keep up that feud.

Yes, in spite of his enemies he had done pretty well for himself. Here he was, still three years under thirty, and already looked like becoming one of the most trusted friends and councillors of the Queen. It was a great thing that she liked Jan and that she was so fond of Johnnie; it all ought to help. Tomorrow morning she would ride away over the haugh to Borthwick Castle; would she ever sleep under his roof again? She might.

It was strange to think that she was there now, in the great room in the south wing, in the beautiful bed from Dunbar Castle in which, according to a family legend, Patrick Hepburn, Lord of Hailes, had slept a century ago with Queen Joan, widow of James I, when they defended Dunbar together against her subjects. He didn't know if there were any truth in that tale of an amour during the siege; his father had liked to think there was – but then he would. He rather wished he had told the Queen of it and seen how she'd take it; he could still do so tomorrow, but breakfast was not so good a time.

He stretched his arms above his head in a cracking yawn. 'Ah-a-ah well,' he gaped, 'that's over. It *was* a wedding!'

WITHIN A MONTH there was another wedding in the family, that of the Lord James to Agnes Keith, daughter of the Earl Marischal – 'And here comes James' "long love",' whispered Johnnie wickedly as tall Lady Agnes, with long thin neck and nose rather blue on that raw day, came stepping high and mincingly like a crane in her gorgeous robes beside the husband whose tenacious affections were now at last rewarded 'after long love'.

There was far more state at their wedding than at the other; many said low and significantly that it could scarcely have been more royal if he had been King. But the most outspokenly unfriendly criticism of it came from James' chief friend. His pomp 'caused great offence to the godly', declared Mr Knox, meaning himself. He accused James of 'growing cold' and 'seeking too much his own advancement'; he was busier over ratifying his new honours and lands than the new Church of Scotland, which had not yet been ratified by the Crown. He showed less penetration in his complaint that James 'yielded to Mary's appetite'; for he himself, far more direct and honest than James, was incapable of the deep subtlety of the Bastard's game.

The wedding sermon gave Knox his best opportunity to hector his friend and patron. In his self-appointed task of 'keeping all men right' he had taken matrimony as his special prerogative; there was nothing he liked better than to hear complaints and settle differences between man and wife. In this instance he laid some fairly fruitful seeds for such differences, for he threatened the bride from the pulpit by telling the bridegroom that if he were 'found fainter' in his zeal for the Church after this, then 'it will be said that your wife has changed your nature'.

The guests glanced sideways at each other with pursed lips; the wife looked down her nose as determinedly as the husband.

The Earl of Arran remained sunk in profound gloom all through the wedding feast, and said he wanted to go back to France. Instead of which he went to bed, though there did not seem to be anything the matter with him. The report went round that the real reason for his going to bed, as for his wish to go to France, was his fear of meeting Bothwell. Mary peremptorily summoned him to Court, disregarding his sick-bed, and ordered him to sign a formal bond of peace between himself and

Bothwell then and there before the Privy Council, overcoming all his protests with a sharp command.

Bothwell had little faith in this, and told her so that evening when the Court were listening to some Italian songs. Four men were singing glees, and the bass had a particularly good voice; he was a very ugly little man, black-dark and misshapen, but with a face so vividly intelligent that Bothwell found himself watching it with interest even while he was telling his doubts to the Queen.

'But what can be done?' she asked.

'I'll see.'

A bold plan had occurred to him, but he would not tell her what it was.

'Who is the bass?' he asked. 'I haven't seen him before.'

'No. My trio wanted a fourth to sing bass and told me of this man in Signor Moretta's train, so I have engaged him. David Rizzio is his name, it's quite well known in his country, for he's a poet.'

'He looks like a monkey.'

'That is what you Scots nobles always think of poets and musicians. When will you tell me your peace plan?'

'When it has succeeded.'

She was gaily confident that whatever it was it would succeed 'if one really wants it to', so certain was she that people preferred friendship to enmity.

'I have just had good proof of it, as even you, my lord Timon of Athens, must agree when I tell you. You won't believe that Queen Elizabeth wants to make friends with me, but what do you think! She has told Lethington in London that if there were no other way to meet me she would come back with him, disguised as his page!'

'Charming! You must have felt yourself in the woods of Amboise again, acting romances with your sister-in-law.'

She took his sneer very well. 'Yes, it was absurd, but she really is determined we shall meet this next summer. It is all being formally arranged, and I am to visit her at York. Don't you think it a good plan?'

'Admirable, Madam. You've everything to gain by showing yourself to the English, and giving them the chance to compare you with Elizabeth.'

'Then it is all the more generous of her.'

'If it happens. But it won't.'

'But I tell you it's settled. How maddeningly provoking you

are! She has sent me this token of it' – she fingered a diamond locket in the shape of a heart that she wore round her neck; 'she writes that it would be easier for her to forget her own heart than mine, "*ce cœur que je garde*".'

His contemptuous laugh astonished her. James and Lethington and Randolph the English Ambassador had been deeply impressed by this gesture from Elizabeth – perhaps, it now struck her, because they knew how she hated to part with her jewels. She herself had returned the compliment by drinking Elizabeth's health in an exquisite gold goblet fashioned by Benvenuto Cellini and had sent it to her as a present. But no, she would not tell Bothwell that.

'And that awkward little affair of Your Grace's ships detained by the English fleet on your voyage here has all been satisfactorily explained, I suppose?' pursued the relentless ironic voice.

'Yes, it has. It was all a complete misunderstanding. They were released as soon as it was cleared up.'

He was silent. She swung round on him so sharply that he thought she would have hit him.

'Think – think – if you can!' she exclaimed. 'We are the smaller, weaker half of an island, split into two warring halves. That can't go on. You've shown it me yourself. Scotland has had to fight to preserve her independence ever since she won it at Bannockburn. The war's gone on ever since then – for two and a half centuries – growing more deadly as chivalry dies and hideous new weapons are created. War now means organized destruction – and we are the poorer country, the smaller population. How can we then, in the long run, survive?'

He was struck by her sense. 'It's true. The growing use of gunpowder is lengthening England's odds against us, and they were already about five to one.'

'So our only hope is friendship with her, and, ultimately, union. We must – we *are* having it. Look!'

She took from her dangling waist-bag an unfinished letter to her uncle the Cardinal, telling him of Elizabeth's assurances of service to the Guises; and pointed proudly to her triumphant sentence describing the feelings of their enemies 'now that they see us, the Queen of England and myself, getting on so well that she orders her Ambassador to do as you direct him.'

He was baffled by the odd ignorance of human nature which he had always noticed in her, in spite of her grasp of affairs that so impressed the politicians, and, just now, himself. Did she

156

really believe that Elizabeth would do what she wanted, just to please her? She was so used to being loved and adored that she simply could not understand the contrary. She would always trust – even Elizabeth.

*   *   *

Bothwell's plan was this. To make a real peace with Arran he must approach him personally, and to arrange this he must have a mediator, one of Arran's friends. But all Arran's friends were Bothwell's enemies, since, though he was of the same religion as they, he had fought for the Queen Regent two years ago and they had fought against her. Nevertheless he decided to go direct to the man who had been the prime mover in that rebellion. It was his way to attack the chief. Besides, John Knox had been a Haddington lad.

So it was to John Knox that he went that wintry night in March, with his hat pulled well down and his cloak pulled well up over his face against the stinging slap of the raw sleet that came whistling and hissing round the corners; also against recognition, since he had no mind that this interview should be known until he knew the result.

John Knox has left a full account of that interview. If Bothwell had also done so, it would probably have been very different. But one thing shows plainly through Knox's account, and that is his pride that James Hepburn should have sought him out. It was no new thing to Knox to be sought out. Everybody came to ask his advice or influence – magistrates how to settle their differences with the craftsmen; burghers how to reclaim their runaway wives; while only last Sunday the Duke of Châtelherault himself had come to supper to meet the English Ambassador and discuss affairs of state.

But for the Hepburn to do so who for generations had been Lord of Hailes and Haddington was quite another matter. It is remarkable that this is the only time in all his numerous writings about himself that Knox has ever mentioned his forebears, and that he did so only to acknowledge Bothwell's overlordship.

He had had warning of this visit, and also its motive, from his friend Mr Barron, a rich merchant to whom Bothwell was deep in debt, and he greeted him with a certain frank sympathy for his difficulties.

'I have borne a good mind to your house, my lord,' he said, 'for my father and grandfathers have served Your Lordship's

157

predecessors. Some have died under their standards. This is a part of the obligation of our Scots kindness.' And he removed Bothwell's wet cloak and offered him a seat by the fire with a gesture more nearly respectful than any that had welcomed the Duke whose daughter he was proposing to marry.

Bothwell had never expected such homely recognition from the rebel who openly aimed at a world revolution of ideas, discarding all ancient loyalties that might interfere with those ideas. He was beginning to acknowledge the kindness when Knox, feeling that enough had been said of such earthly obligations, hastened to speak of God, whose messenger he was and whose majesty Bothwell had offended.

'Therefore my counsel is that you begin at God.'

But if Bothwell had come here to be preached at, he might as well have gone to hear Mr Knox in St Giles' on Sunday. He stretched out a hissing boot against the burning logs (very snug this little study was, with its new light deal panelling to keep out the draughts – the Town Councillors made their minister remarkably comfortable, he noticed) and spoke as man to man.

'Barron told you how matters stand; poor Barron, it's his best hope of seeing any of his money from me, for all I can tell him is, like Willie Dunbar,

> *I cannot tell how it is spended,*
> *But well I wot that is is ended.'*

'Aye, he told me Your Lordship was his chief creditor.'

'And am likely to remain it, as long as I have to keep a following of several hundred rascals in the city, to no profit to themselves or others, poor devils. If Arran and I made up our quarrel, I could live at Court with only a page and a few servants and so save expenses.'

His guest's extremely practical estimate of his difficulties gave Knox no chance for the moment to resume the preacher, except to promise to serve His Lordship if His Lordship would promise to 'continue in godliness'. Since godliness in this case appeared synonymous with economy, His Lordship was very ready to do so.

Unless he could begin to repair his estate it would soon be utterly destroyed, 'and you'll see me sitting in the pillory at the Market Cross wearing a bankrupt's yellow hat!' he chuckled.

Mrs Bowes hurried in with 'a comfortable hot whisky posset to clear the cold night air from His Lordship's stomach' – and, incidentally, from his host's, for she kept reminding him of 'a salty rheum' that had settled on it last week. A thin nervous female, there was still a sort of agitated good looks in her soft tremulous red mouth and eager eyes that opened wide and awed on the Wicked Earl, who ran the critical eye over her that he always accorded to any horse or woman.

Her former son-in-law cut short her chat about the posset and shooed her out of the room as though she were a hen; but not before she had scuttled aimlessly round the table, darted at the candles, and in her efforts to trim them put out one of them, then exclaimed that it would never do to have three candles on the table 'as for a corpse', blamed herself almost tearfully for her heathenish superstition while relighting it, then made a side-pass at the hearth and picked up the poker, but as the blazing fire could require no ministrations she dropped it again with a clatter, then apologized, fluttered, curtsied, departed.

A deep masculine repose settled on the little room, which now seemed much larger and less crowded. The hot whisky posset went down in silence to its appointed place.

'And now,' said Knox ungratefully, 'will anyone deny my words that "it is more than a monster in nature that a woman should reign over men"?'

Bothwell didn't deny it. He had too much on his hands at the moment to take on the relation of the sexes. His host got back to the business of the interview.

Bothwell had in no way acknowledged his fault. Arran's enmity against him had been first aroused by the deadly blows Bothwell had struck at his party, and at Knox himself.

'All I have suffered in the service of Christ Jesus, even those hideous months in the galleys' (the encouraging effect of the posset almost tempted Bothwell to ask if complicity in the murder of his countryman was the service of Christ), 'were as nothing compared to the hurt you did me when you robbed John Cockburn of the bag of gold he was bringing us for the pay of our soldiers. Mutiny followed straight upon it, defeat, flight. That night was the worst of all my memories, when the sword of dolour passed through our hearts.'

'You mean the night of your retreat from Edinburgh?' inquired the soldier, not unsympathetically, but a little puzzled by this description of a military manoeuvre.

But to Knox it was the night 'when the wicked began to spew forth the venom that had lurked before in their cankered hearts. The rabble flung filth and stones at us, their spiteful tongues crying "Traitors!" "Heretics!" and even "Cut their throats!" I would never have believed that our own countrymen could have wished our destruction so unmercifully, and so rejoiced in our adversity.'

'It was the fortune of war,' said Bothwell.

'Aye, you had it then. The Lord Arran gave chase to Crichton within a few hours of the robbery – but the bird had flown.'

'To Big Bess's kitchen, bless her,' Bothwell chuckled, but to himself, for these happy reminiscences would not further the cause in hand. To Knox he said earnestly, 'The hurt I did you was not personal to you – nor Arran – least of all to John Cockburn, a far kinsman, so that I gave orders he should not be killed. A man can as soon make friends with his enemy as with his neighbour – sooner more often. You, who are from the Border, like myself, must know that.'

He had leaned forward as he was speaking, his eyes fixed hard and hot upon the other. Old loyalties, old traditions stirred uneasily in the depths of the preacher who thought he had broken clean away from all such childish ties, into a realm where men held together only by what they thought.

But he could not always be sure of their thoughts, however much he strove to make them the same as his own. Of late he had felt much doubt and discontent with his allies. He had never liked 'Michael Wily' Lethington, a worldly mocking man who had been heard to say that the God of his fathers was nothing but a bogy of the nursery. As for those 'young plants', as he had called Lord James and Arran so tenderly two years ago, they were growing with a twist; James inclining more and more to Lethington's worldly policy, while Arran's zeal was becoming so lopsided that it threatened to uproot his reason.

'My lord,' he said, 'you are a frankly confessed opponent. To talk with such, openly, face to face, as I am used to do, is even something of a relief to me, for I have had to fight with shadows and owlets in the dark.'

'Who hasn't?' said Bothwell, with a touch of exasperation at the self-pity he had already noticed when Knox spoke of the worst of his memories (God's blood, did the man keep a diary only to put 'bad', 'worse' or 'worst' against his days?).

Knox wished to show that his 'shadows and owlets' were more sinister than any that this bold Borderer could have had to face, but it was unwise to complain of his allies, so he spoke instead of the monstrous scandals against him, all without any basis.

'Then we're in the same boat,' said his guest cheerfully, 'since my enemies not only accuse me of seducing more women than I could ever have had time for, but of sodomy as well – even as some of his enemies have accused Calvin.'

Knox's eyes flashed; the approaching entente might have been in grave danger of dissolution, had not Mrs Bowes popped her head in at the door to ask if they were indeed certain, but indeed truly certain, they would not have another hot whisky posset ('*No*,' said Knox), it would not take her a moment to prepare, it was all there ready, and — 'Go *away*, woman!' he exploded, and away she went, bearing with her so much of his wrath that he forgot to attack Bothwell at once. That acute fencer seized the opportunity to leave the subject of the scandalously misunderstood trio of himself, Knox and Calvin for the safer one of reconciliation. The country looked more like settling down into reasonable peace and prosperity than it had done for years; it was incumbent on all parties and their leaders to help that settlement.

'Settlement? The only true settlement of the country, my lord, was last year, when Christ's true Church was established under the rule of the Book of Discipline.'

'Aye, you had your run of rule last year before the Queen returned, but was it so settled? There was open insurrection all the spring and summer, the prisons were chock-full of the common people, for rebelling against your Book of Discipline.'

'The rascal multitude!' exclaimed the democrat from the back street in Haddington.

The nobleman fired back: 'Because they wear hodden grey, do you think their whole lives are to be made drab? They insisted on their old mumming plays and amusements —'

'Abominations!'

'It was Robin Hood against —'

'Christ Jesus!' proclaimed Knox.

' "John Knox" was what I was going to say, but no doubt it's the same thing. In any case, you've proved for yourself that the rule of this country is no easy matter. Think then how hard it is for the Queen, a girl, foreign-bred, and a Catholic ruling Protestants.'

'It is not hard,' said Knox, now quietly and finally, 'it is impossible.'

'You mean that you have decided to make it so?'

'I? I have done nothing. I have let an idolatrous priest say Mass in the Chapel Royal and I have not raised my hand.'

'You raised your voice, though, and pretty loud, the next Sunday.'

'Nothing shall stop my preaching Christ Jesus to be the only Saviour.'

'That was no news before you were born. What has it to do with preaching insurrection?'

'If I had chosen insurrection I should have done more than preach. I have the power. I could have plunged this country into civil war.'

'Another! It's only two years since the last. And to what end? To put the Hamiltons in power?'

'*No*, my lord. I am the servant of God, not the leader of a faction.'

'Well, a faction is all you'd lead in a civil war today, for Arran may be discontented enough to follow you, but you'd not have the Bastard and Lethington as you had last time. *They* hope to find some way of compromise, as England is finding, with the bulk of the people Protestant, though their Queen has crucifixes in her chapel and some sort of modified Mass – and hates the clergy to marry,' he added slyly.

'The false whore!' burst out Knox, touched evidently on a tender spot. 'As I wrote to her, she is an infirm vessel.'

'Maybe, but her seat on the throne is getting firmer. When she came to it, England was weak and divided at home, and all her foreign possessions lost. Yet each year it's stronger, and Elizabeth's position with it. With luck — ' he hastily changed it to 'With God's help – and above all with toleration – the same might be done with Scotland and the Queen here.'

But toleration was not only impossible, but loathsome to Knox. The preacher was at his worst in argument, as Mary had proved, though more painfully, for he was also at his worst with women.

He had now been goaded into a state of excitement wherein nothing but uninterrupted eloquence could appease him, for eloquence, especially in anger, was to him what violent action or drink was to other men. He replied, 'I utterly abhor the blasphemy that men who live according to equity and justice shall be saved, whatever religion they profess.'

Righteousness, then, could not help the Queen, yet he was determined to prove her unrighteous.

'I do not call her a whore, but she was brought up in the most arrant company of whoremongers.' To prove this he repeated incredible stories of former festivities at Queen Catherine's

Court, where at an appropriate moment the lights were put out in order that her husband, King Henri, and the Cardinal de Lorraine and the rest of the company might amuse themselves with the ladies. 'Sire,' the Cardinal had said with a very proper respect, 'the first choice is yours, and I must have the second.' And Knox drew so vivid a picture of the orgy that Bothwell asked him with due innocence if he had been there, and what luck he had had.

The eyes opposite burned in their sockets.

'Do you dare mock this horrible villainy, the direct fruit of the Cardinal's religion?'

'No, for I can't believe it, and if I could, what has it to do with the Queen?'

'*This!*' said Knox loudly. 'That it was in such pastimes that our Queen was brought up.'

'And you are telling all Edinburgh that?'

'That – and more. That this will now be the upbringing of the sons and daughters of the Scots nobles, with fiddlers and dancers at the Queen's Court. They might as well be exercised with flinging upon the floor – and all *the rest that thereby follows*!' – a heated interpretation of the stately Court dances that the reprobate opposite, now cocking a delighted eyebrow, had never imagined.

Knox made it even hotter; 'the reward of dancers,' he said, 'was drink in hell.' The Queen's ladies wore long trains to their skirts that picked up all the dirt on the floor, and what's more, they stuck targets or tassels on them. 'The stinking pride of their targeted tails,' he spat out, 'will provoke God's vengeance not only against these foolish women, but against the whole realm.'

This threat of God's vengeance on the whole nation, for the crime of tolerating their Queen, struck Bothwell as the most dangerous weapon in Knox's armoury. His reputation as a prophet would be used to the utmost among that 'rascal multitude' that he despised, yet knew so well how to inflame.

And what weapon could Mary ever find to withstand it?

The problem made him so thoughtful that he scarcely heard Knox's thunder on yet another matter of national importance.

A chambermaid was with child by a married man, and this was in the Palace, 'almost in the Queen's lap'. Yet Mary would not have her executed as ordered by the Book of Discipline. He quoted a vulgar street song about it, to prove the disastrous effect of the Queen's morals. Mary Livingstone was to marry the Master of Sempill, 'and not before it's necessary, for shame' – though Bothwell, considerably more in the circle of Court gossips than Knox, had never heard any breath of scandal against the pair. Was Knox making a side-blow at another couple?

'You are harsh on weddings,' he remarked, 'even on Lord James'. What had you to say to my sister's?'

'A sufficient woman for such a man,' was the answer.

'Aye, they suffice each other very well, thank you'; but there was a stony glint in his eye that was sufficient to silence Knox for the moment. That eye had seen something feminine and thwarted in the terrible prophet; he was more like a meddling auld wife of Haddington who should be put in the stocks to wear the scold's bridle for his shrill slanders. Here he was complaining of scandals against himself when he was the worst scandalmonger of the lot! The streak of vulgarity, of cruel lack of chivalry, that he had shown in his exultation over the suffering of a dying woman, was now intensifying in his jealous rivalry with her daughter – the rivalry of an old man with a young girl, surely a 'monster in nature'.

Yet, even as he saw this, Bothwell saw the face opposite change; the indignant eyes grew grave and ardent as they removed their gaze to a wider scene.

'You blame my rule that it did not succeed,' Knox said. 'How can the rule of Christ succeed if men will not follow it in their hearts? Earth might be fair as Paradise; no man need starve, whether of bread or learning; if only all men would wish it. But no rule on earth can make them wish it. We took the wealth of the old Church lands to better the lot of the poor, and set up schools with learned masters and ministers in the farthest and wildest places. Yet now the peasants all over the country are complaining that they were better off under their old masters; they are so ground down by their new landowners that many of the labourers are compelled by poverty to leave their land in the hands of their lords. And so the Reformed Church is deformed by the avarice of those very lords that helped to set it up.'

'As always happens. How could you hope to avoid it?'

With a tremendous gesture the preacher swept aside such worldly sophistries – and with them his empty posset cup from the table, but never heard the crash.

'I see no reason why men should not begin to express in their lives that which they have professed in words. If they plead, like dishonest merchants, "The world is evil, how can we live if we don't do as others do?", then it is they who make the world evil. It is the sin that has provoked God again and again to destroy strong realms and flourishing commonwealths. It is the rule of Satan, and as long as men follow it, this world will be hell.'

The cynical guest was uncomfortably impressed both by his passion and his honesty. The man was disappointed in his colleagues, but he would never be disillusioned of his ideals.

'But what remedy can be found?' Bothwell asked.

'Let every man speak the truth with his brother. Let none oppress or defraud another in any business. Let the bowels of mercy appear, for the hatred of the heart is murder before God, and whoso loveth not his brother is a murderer.'

The weak husky voice now speaking was the voice of genius – a genius that brooded like a thunderstorm over the whole country, and could reveal in a lightning flash to every man the conviction that his soul was stronger than fate.

That voice was still echoing in his ears when Bothwell went out of the warm house into a changed world. The wind had dropped while he was inside, the sleet had turned to a brief but heavy fall of snow, and the moon had risen. The dark gusty street on the hillside was quiet now and white, the jagged outline of the tall houses white against the black sky. Snow had covered the mud and smells of the middens, the air was as pure as on the moor; nature seemed to have a sign to show that 'earth might be fair as Paradise'.

'But what odds?' said the young man in the street. 'It will all be trampled black again tomorrow.'

Paris came up to him, his nose peaking up against the moon as he flung back his head in a half-suppressed yawn.

'Are you asleep already, you lazy dog?'

'Yes, my lord. The entertainment in the kitchen was very poor.'

'Well, I'd not say that of the study.'

He had heard the call of a trumpet which, if he followed, and others, would awaken the world from its haunted sleep. For an instant he saw the nightmare wherein men struggle blindly; clutch at an insensate metal and call it riches, at uneasy domination and call it power, and die even while they wrangle in the dark.

Then he gave a harsh laugh and swung his cloak round him. Earth might be fair, might it, if men only practised what they preached? A fine one Knox was to preach that, to plead on behalf of mercy, and against the hatred of the heart, when he himself never ceased to preach that 'the idolater shall die the death'! He hated Mary, and would hate her to the death if he could compass it.

Bothwell turned sharply to Paris behind him.

'Where's that new brothel you'd heard of? I need a rest from family prayers and blood-feuds.'

CHAPTER EIGHT

THAT ODD, not unfriendly interview bore its fruit, though its ripening was delayed a little by a brush between Bothwell and a son of Arran's protégé, John Cockburn, who, said the Hepburns, fired his pistol unprovoked in the face of his father's enemy, missed, and galloped off hell for leather, 'but the Lord's was the better horse'. The Cockburn version was that the young man was out hunting when Bothwell gave chase to him shouting, 'If he's out for a hunt, let him have it!'

In either case, young Cockburn suffered no worse by his adventure than being taken to Berwick and back and then released; but he was a pupil of Knox, so in some sort sacred, and the preacher was gravely displeased. In a short time, however, he, like his forebears, did the service Lord Bothwell had asked of him.

So the enemy Earls met in his presence and that of their friends, who looked forbidding. The truculent Gavin Hamilton whispered scowling instructions to Arran as Bothwell and his company entered. But Arran paid no heed to him, nor to Knox's introductory speech; he was staring at Bothwell and came up to meet him, holding out his hand.

'Words do little,' he said in a low voice. 'If the hearts are upright, no ceremony is needed.'

His sudden gentleness was like that of an animal anxious to make friends; as those startled hare's eyes looked into the other's face, he seemed to be asking reassurance, not merely of Bothwell's enmity but of his own secret fears. Bothwell's astonishment was shot through with both pity and triumph. He had had to set his teeth to come to this meeting, but how easy it was all being made for him! Now that he was face to face with this erratic trembling creature, he knew that he could get him to feed out of his hand. Arran's own hand was clammy and cold, poor wretch – he'd soon show him he had no need to worry. He said:

'Will you dine with me tomorrow, my lord? We might hunt together first.'

All the set speeches prepared by either side for the other to say were stricken dumb. The seconds continued to glare at each other for a bit, but it was of no use, for the principals had retired to a window to discuss the form of sport next morning. But one speech was not to be silenced, John Knox was determined not to leave them until his part in this happy event had been recognized.

'Now, my lords,' he admonished them, 'God has brought you together by the labour of a simple man.' No doubt that labour would be misconstrued by misreport, but he could patiently bear the wrongful judgements of men.

Sure enough, a flood of gossip poured through the town at the sudden amazing spectacle of the enemy Earls, whose rioting over a loose woman had lately been the scandal of Edinburgh, now reconciled by the Prophet, and hunting, dining, going to church together, and paying a friendly call together on Arran's father. What the Duke of Châtelherault thought of it no one could say, but probably he was, as usual, not thinking. What McCrechane, a cook in the High Street, thought and said, was that now the two chief roysterers were allied, Knox would find himself in the cart, and his reputation 'scourged through the town'. But it was the cook who was scourged and made to wear the scold's bridle in the pillory for his blasphemy in speaking against Knox – a punishment that did not show the minister's promised patience under misreport.

Arran clung to his new friend with the desperation of a drowning man, and so voluble and so plausible were the reasons that he gave for this that Bothwell did not guess that the true one was Arran's fear of his own clouding mind.

He talked as they walked up the High Street, occasionally tripping over his own feet in his shambling fashion as he peered round into the other's face, and passers-by stared and shop-keepers peeped from their doors. He talked as they rode back from the hunt, his voice coming in spasmodic gusts, high and shrill, blown away on the wind like the cawing of the nesting rooks over the late March fields. He talked as they sat over dinner, and sobbed as he told Bothwell of 'the beastliness of my father, who's got more money than either faith or God', and yet kept his son so short that he could make no proper show at Court before the Queen. And at mention of the Queen the tears ran down his sallow cheeks. He was betrayed, he said; his party

167

had promised to support his pretensions to her, but they were secretly thwarting them. Baffled desire, and the sudden drop in his political importance, made him furious with his allies, frantic to assert himself.

He had had a royal marriage dangled before his nose ever since his childhood, when Henry VIII had offered his daughter Elizabeth to him. Had his father accepted, Arran would now be Queen Elizabeth's husband.

'And had mine been accepted, I'd now be her stepson,' Bothwell retorted. 'My father proposed for her when she was the Lady Elizabeth – her or her bloody sister Mary, it was all one to my dad as long as it was a princess, he having had a shot at the Queen Regent and missed.'

He flung back his head in a roar of laughter, glad of the chance to turn his companion from his lachrymose mood. 'How many Queens do you want?' he demanded. 'You can't have 'em both, you know.'

Arran took his chaff seriously. He was determined Bothwell should know what value had been set on him by the English Queen.

Elizabeth had sworn openly to 'take a husband that would give the King of France a headache', and everyone knew that she intended Arran, and a joint attempt with him on the Scots Crown. He had been induced to slip away from the French Court and smuggle himself into England; hide in a wood for a fortnight, living only on fruit; hide in Cecil's own house in Westminster while Elizabeth brightly denied that he was in her kingdom; travel north with a false passport from Cecil, and hide with the English Ambassador in Scotland, until he could openly join the rebel lords to fight against the Queen Regent, and send for subsidies from England through their secret agent, John Cockburn.

But then, as a sympathizer sang in Aberdeen,

> 'Curtfoot Bothwell like a limmer lay
> (And traitor tried, yea, and a tyrant too),
> And unawares did wound thee on the way.'

From that moment of the Portmanteau Raid, Arran had dated his decline in importance, and hated and feared James Hepburn more than any other man; but now, in his disgust with his allies, he told him that he was the only man in Scotland he could trust.

Of which Bothwell took instant advantage. He meant to find

out what lay behind that scare last autumn of Arran's supposed intention to kidnap the Queen; by 'gentling' him as he would a nervous horse, he led him on to speak of his fantastic dreams of Mary. Arran got more and more excited; it was his 'right' to have her; he had given up Elizabeth and the hope of two kingdoms for her ('Oho, so it's that way round now, is it?' thought Bothwell with sardonic amusement); he had been in love with her ever since he had seen her, he would go mad if he did not have her.

'And how do you propose to get her?' asked the practical voice on the other side of the little table. They were dining in comfortable privacy in a small room in Bothwell's house, with only Paris to wait on them, and now that dinner was finished he noiselessly left the room. Arran's eyes followed the thin form as it slipped like a shadow through the door, then shot back to the dark face opposite and opened wildly, staring not at Bothwell but at something just behind him, as though he saw a ghost.

The moment hung between them in the flickering candle-light, with the red wine glowing on the table, and Bothwell's hard muscular hand raising his glass, but pausing as he caught that strange look on Arran's face.

'We can speak freely now, there's not even my French page here – not that he'd matter. What is in your mind?'

'The same as that which lurks behind your dark mind,' was the unexpected answer.

Bothwell brought his hand down so sharply on the table that it cracked the stem of his wine-glass.

'What the devil do you mean by that?' he exclaimed in amazement. 'Did *I* ever plan to kidnap the Queen? *Answer* me,' he thundered, as the other cowered at his question.

'No, but you will, you will,' wailed Arran.

'You have gone clean daft with fright.' Then he forced himself to speak more kindly. 'You've nothing to fear from me. Why did you say that the same thing was in both our minds?'

Arran had plainly no idea by now why he had said it. But he made a violent effort to pull himself together and justify it.

'Why should we not be of one mind? Hamiltons and Hepburns filled the town at Christmas when they were ready to fly at each other's throats. If, instead, they had joined forces, the Queen's men from Holyrood would have had no chance against us. You too hate that backslider James, traitor both to his religion and the Queen; you too hate her priests, servants of Satan, who are dragging her soul down into hell.'

'Is it only her soul you're concerned with?' asked Bothwell dryly. 'What of her body?'

'In my arms, safe in Dumbarton Castle,' cried Arran, beside himself now with excitement. Bothwell too seemed to have caught it, for he half rose from his chair with his hands clenched. But Arran never noticed the movement, he was rushing on: 'With Gavin Hamilton and all our clan at my back I'd have power to do it – kill the Bastard, kill Lethington, hack them to pieces, and all else who oppose us — But *you'd* not oppose us?' he demanded suddenly – 'you'd help me? You'll plan it out and put all things in execution?'

'While you stand by and watch, hey? Until I hand the Queen over to you in Dumbarton Castle?'

Bothwell's laugh was harshly disagreeable. Loathing had rushed over him when he had half risen from his chair, but he had sat down again in time before he smashed his fist into that sickly white face before him. His horror had taken him by surprise, and that angry bark of laughter scared Arran off.

He began to disclaim all he had just said, and Bothwell had again to do the human equivalent to 'Woa there, my beauty. Steady now, steady', until he had reassured him, and then he added quite casually, 'You've said how easy it would be to capture the Queen out hunting. Is that what you mean to do?'

'If you would help me.'

'And what do I get out of it?'

'You and I together will rule all,' Arran said impressively.

'Very pretty, but I haven't said yet what I'll do.'

Then, as the poor wretch flinched at his grim tone, he said, 'Put it from you now. Do not speak, no, nor think of it again – do you hear? – until you speak again with me.'

He took him by the hand and looked into his eyes, compelling him to follow his will. Arran stared back, seeing him as the strong man that deep within himself he had despaired of ever being. But it would not be necessary if Bothwell would be it for him. He would only have to stand by while Bothwell put all things in execution.

*   *   *

Next day Mr Knox had another visitor. He had just preached his mid-week sermon, and was walking up and down his study, pulling at his beard while he dictated letters to his secretary, when Lord Arran rushed in, unannounced, having charged up the stairs ahead of the servant.

'I am betrayed,' he gasped out, 'treasonably betrayed! My life is in danger.'

His eyes were full of tears, his twitching hands plucked at his dagger, he glared at the secretary as though he were accusing him of the betrayal, so that the youth, though goggling with curiosity, was thankful that his master curtly signalled to him to leave the room. Arran was incoherently accusing 'one Judas or another' of seeking his life by involving him in a plot against the Queen. Knox insisted on his giving Judas' surname.

'The Lord Bothwell,' whispered Arran fearfully – 'but if he knows I have told you, he will challenge me to combat. That wouldn't be allowed in France,' and he bewailed that he had not gone there as he had first intended.

Bothwell in a plot against the Queen! It sounded the most unlikely thing for that determined royalist. Knox demanded details, heard that the Hepburns were to join with the Hamiltons to murder Lord James and Lethington (that sounded more probable), seize the Queen and hand her over to Arran – 'and so he and I together shall rule all,' declared Arran on a wild note of triumph, then instantly cried that the whole thing had been planned only to ruin him, so that Bothwell could accuse him of treason.

'If you refused, you cannot be held guilty.'

'Yes, yes, yes, I shall be! You don't understand. It is treason if I conceal it. I must tell it – no, I had best write it to the Lord James.'

'You had best do no such thing,' said his mentor in deep disgust. Here was a pretty coil! It would utterly discredit his efforts in bringing the two enemies together if this treason turned out to be the real motive of their friendship. It looked as though the impertinent cook McCrechane would be justified in his malicious opinion, and that Knox's reputation for wisdom and judgement might get a nasty blow.

But he could not believe in it; even discounting all Bothwell's previous record of loyalty, he would never be such a fool as to confide so dangerous a design to his former enemy, within only a few days of their making up their quarrel. It seemed clear that Arran had really gone off his head. He tried to soothe him, but the wretched creature only grew the more frantic and rushed out of the room before Knox could stop him.

All the minister could now do was to write to Lord James and warn him of Arran's condition. He called back his secretary; the Earl had met him as he rushed downstairs and had promptly knocked him down; he was therefore not surprised when his master dictated the words that the Earl of Arran was plainly stricken with a frenzy, and that it would be a grievous mistake if over great credit were given to his inventions.

But James' notion of a grievous mistake did not agree with Knox's. He proposed to take Arran's accusations seriously. Bothwell and Gavin Hamilton were both arrested.

Arran had added a third traitor to his list, and was now accusing his father. The Duke wrote declaring his innocence, both of treason and his son's madness – 'he takes it off his mother'.

The accusations went further and embarrassed even James; for at a public examination Arran declared that he had been deluded by devils and witches, and when asked by what witches, replied,

'Lord James' mother.'

Sometimes he utterly denied all that he had said against Bothwell or Gavin or his father. But when confronted with Bothwell before the Council he again charged him with treason, imputing to him words he had himself used. Bothwell had offered to 'put all things in execution', to capture the Queen, 'hack to pieces' all who opposed him, and take her to Dumbarton for Arran 'to keep her surely or otherwise demean her person'.

At that there was an uproar, for Bothwell was halfway across the Council-room before the other lords could fling themselves on him and hold him back.

'Let me go,' he roared. 'I'll squeeze the lying breath out of your throat, you rat!'

'One of the liveliest Council scenes I ever remember,' purred Lethington, who had not stirred from his comfortable seat.

Bothwell's fury was choking his wits; nothing else mattered beside his longing to wipe out in blood that foul charge against him of offering to procure the Queen for Arran. He challenged him to a fight to the death, and Arran shrieked and claimed the protection of the Council.

Bothwell's blind rage was put down as a mark against him; he could give no answer but threats of violence against his accuser – showing plainly that he had been touched on a sore spot; there was no smoke without a fire, etc.

There had been no witness to that fateful interview between

him and Arran, and each accused the other of the very same words of treasonable intent. The previous rumours of Arran's intention to kidnap the Queen went against him; on the other hand, Lord James was reminding everyone that Bothwell was known to be a desperate fellow – one who would stick at nothing, and ready to fling himself into any bold adventure for the sheer love of the game. His fortunes were in a bad way; he had had to sell much of his lands and was still heavily in debt; he had little to lose. All Edinburgh had been amazed by his sudden reconciliation with Arran; the gossips had always known it must have been for some nefarious purpose.

Knox stood up for him, but then Knox's credit was involved; everyone was laughing at the result of his meddling; for once he had been proved wrong – it was a delectable change. Lethington was never tired of asking the preacher whom he proposed to reconcile next. No, in this case for once, Knox had little power to act.

Bothwell's other partisan was infinitely more helpless, for it was the Queen. Mary refused to believe that Bothwell had meant to hand her over to Arran; the latter was insane, she declared, and his word should not be taken. Bothwell demanded his trial, but Lord James produced most admirable and public-spirited reasons against it. For once he could not get the Queen to listen to them; her growing irritation with him exploded in a violent burst of temper, and he left it to Lethington to manage the explanation.

His dry humour had made him increasingly a favourite of hers; moreover, he was all but betrothed to her dear Mary Fleming who thought him the wisest and gentlest as well as the most charming of men; he was in an excellent position to drop his quiet advice as to the best course to follow. It was perfectly true that a public trial and acquittal would be a disaster to the State, for if Arran were proved guilty of false accusation he must die on the scaffold, even if he were proved also to be now insane. The execution of the next heir to the throne would so rend the country that it would almost certainly lead to another civil war.

And was she so sure that the trial would prove Bothwell altogether innocent? He gave satirical yet half-admiring hints about Bothwell's character: 'A mild fellow like myself is naturally envious of the dashing way he and his house have always been able to use women – Queens, I should have said – as their stock in trade.'

He placed the tips of his long waxen fingers together in five slender arches ('as though he were saying his prayers, the old humbug, when all he's doing it for is to show off his beautiful hands!' Mary observed in amused exasperation) and enumerated the royal scandals in the Hepburn family: James I's widow and the Hepburn of the day; his son, Adam Bothwell and James II's Queen, Mary of Guelders. To bring the story more up to date, there had been that vain, facile, fickle fellow, the Fair Earl, and his advances to her own mother, as well as to Elizabeth of England or alternatively her sister Mary of bloody memory. He made this ancestral gossip so entertaining that Mary could not help laughing, but she pulled him up.

'A man's forebears are not himself – you might as well call me a saint because my great-grandmother was one. Wherein has the present Earl of Bothwell used women (I won't limit it to Queens) to advance his fortunes?'

'There is a Norwegian lady living on his mother's estate at Morham who might tell you more about that,' the quiet voice answered her. 'She is the daughter of an Admiral of high position in his own country. Her name is Anna Throndsen, and she had good reason to think it would be changed to the Countess of Bothwell when she left her home and country for him. The reason is now being dandled on his mother's knee, a fine brat just over a year old.'

'You should sing all that – it sounds exactly like a ballad.' She always found herself speaking more abruptly than usual in contrast with Lethington's smooth periods. She added, 'But I can't see wherein she advanced him.'

'In Flanders eighteen months ago she helped pay his servants, so that he was enabled to come on to Your Grace's Court in France – leaving her behind, of course.'

A hunt in the golden autumn forest of Fontainebleau and a bold stranger who rode up to her and her uncle the Cardinal, and turned out to be her mother's most trusted servant; a talk in which he had brought the keen wind and fierce joy of a night-raid in midwinter on the Border into her warm room with painted walls; a State ball at Orléans when she had listened enthralled to him and her uncle de Guise talking as professional soldiers; – these things, then, had been paid for by that unknown woman in Flanders, to whom he had returned without a word of explanation at the very moment when she herself had had most need of him!

She resolutely shook off the remembrance; she must be fair.

'Well, at least those old ruffians you spoke of wooed for themselves; but you accuse him of wishing to act pandar to my Lord of Arran, whom he has always loathed as I would a spider.'

'M-mm,' purred Master Michael Wily with a soft sidelong look at her; 'if it's a case of pandar, the boot may well have been on the other leg.'

He would not say more, nor did Mary dare probe too deeply, for she felt her face flaming; it was safer to take a leaf out of his own book, and remark sarcastically that he was the prince of romancers. But he only gave her his delightful smile, and contrived a few further hints that too close an inquiry might prove very inconvenient to the man she wished to benefit. It was a great mistake to make such an ugly business too public; 'the more you stir a dung-heap, the worse it stinks. Leave it to settle down. Arran is a deal safer without his wits than when he had the half of them. He is comfortably shut up — '

'And so is his victim,' she broke out indignantly.

Again he gave her that quizzical eye. 'I doubt the Earl of Bothwell would thank you for that description. The poor injured innocent won't suffer too badly from a brief imprisonment. I should think he'd be glad of the rest. However young and bold and active he is, it must be a fatiguing life, baiting all the lords of Scotland. Let him cool his heels for a bit and slide out when the affair has blown over. If it's justice you're concerned with, Arran's punishment is incomparably the heavier, since his will probably be a life-sentence.'

That was no consolation to Mary, who was already so sorry for the poor distraught creature that she had sent him her own carriage that he might take the air, now that it was no longer considered safe that he should ride. Nor could she bear to see the distress of old Châtelherault; it gave her no satisfaction that all his stupid insolence to her had flown; he cried like a child as he knelt before her and protested his innocence. Her belief in it made small odds to James, though he let the old man off with the loss of Dumbarton Castle, a forfeiture that greatly lessened his power. When Bothwell heard of it, he observed: 'That carrion crow has got some fine pickings out of Arran's daft fits!'

Or, as James himself put it, he had great reason to thank heaven for this singular opportunity. It had enabled him to strike a double blow, and ruin the strongest and most ambitious family in Scotland by the same means that he disgraced their former enemy and his own chief stumbling block – an example, as Lethington said on a note of praise that made James slightly restive, 'of exquisite economy'.

I T W A S the beginning of May when Bothwell was imprisoned in Edinburgh Castle, and he remained there for the rest of that wet summer. There was something to be said for Lethington's view of a term in prison as the best chance of rest and peace that a Scots noble was likely to get. Bothwell made good use of it as such; he slept about four times as much as he usually did, and composed verses about his chief adventures, accompanying them on his lute, though it never occurred to him to write down such trivial stuff. Nor was he always solitary; the Captain of the Castle was friendly and often played with him at draughts or dice; and he saw something of the other prisoners, among them some humble fellow-Borderers from Liddesdale whom he himself had sentenced for cattle-thieving to this very prison. They grinned at their former judge with no malice, only a pleased recognition of the equality of fate; they met on friendly terms and discussed the news from the Border. It was bad; Lord James had no one now to hold him in check, and moreover was determined to destroy all those 'thieves and rovers from Teviotdale and Liddesdale' who might prove useful to Bothwell if he got out of prison.

'Hadn't halters enough for 'em all,' said Sym Scott of the Kirkhill, 'but that didn't stop him. Drowned 'em he did, two and twenty of 'em, kicked into the river with their hands bound.'

A deep snarl went up from his listeners; no words could speak their hate of the Bastard. The Queen had been furious, but what use was that? Lord James had made himself twice as powerful as when she had come to Scotland; his policy in asking her to come and 'rule' it was now fully explained; it was the best blind to cloak his own rule.

After four months Bothwell realized how little hope there was of his getting an official release. He was not one to worry about formalities, and had begun to make plans for his escape when he received a surprising sanction of them in a message from the Queen, smuggled in by the Captain's servant; it told him what

176

he knew already, that she had found herself powerless to help him at present, but also that she hoped earnestly he would be able to help himself.

As he read it the bars rattled derisively in his window to the mad tune of the wind that hurled itself round the Castle rock. The rain sloshed down. He took hold of the lower bar and shook it; it was no wonder it rattled, for he had been loosening it gradually.

That night he got it out, squeezed himself through the gap, and in the thick dark of the rain climbed down the wet and slippery face of the Castle rock. It was well it was so dark; not only was he hidden, but the appalling steepness of the climb was hidden from himself. When at last he reached the foot of the cliff he drew himself up, flinging back his head to get the wind and rain full on his face, his bleeding hands outstretched to them; the enormous darkness of the rock towered above him, its summit lost in the rain. He was free, and he began to run, madly, downhill.

*   *   *

Exactly a year before, at the end of August, he had brought the Queen safely to Scotland. Now he was a fugitive, though not, he thought, in any immediate danger of re-arrest. That would be awkward for his captors, when the reason for his first arrest had never been proved. But he felt it as well to retreat to the Castle of Hermitage, now under his command, that hugely massive and ancient stronghold that could hold fifteen hundred men and horse at need. If that need were now at hand he must strengthen its fortifications and lay in provisions, and little enough money he had left for either. Help came unexpectedly.

He heard voices groaning louder and louder through his dreams early one morning. 'No, no, no-o-o-o!' they finally bellowed in his ear as he sprang up awake, to find that a herd of cows, lowing plaintive protest, was being driven up just underneath his window. He threw on his clothes and ran down into the courtyard, which was full of cattle pushing against each other and every object they encountered, with the blind bewildered obstinacy of their kind. A drover and his dog were marshalling them; a woman on horseback rode up with the rosy light of dawn glowing on her worn face and her shrewd, merry, experienced eyes. 'She looks old,' he thought, and 'She'll never look old,' at the same instant.

It was Janet Scott of Buccleuch, who had once been Janet

177

Beton, his former mistress and now very present friend in time of trouble, for she had brought him the cows to stock his larder. Here was a woman worth a dozen buxom young wenches such as the flaxen-haired Fleming or the exotic Anna! He laughed thankfully with her over her 'love-token' as they breakfasted together and sketched plans for his line of conduct, and gossiped over the news from the North.

The Gordons were up. Lord James had taken the Queen for a survey of her Northern counties, in which he had reported signs of trouble. What was more to the point, the Lord James had set his heart on the title and lands of the Earldom of Moray, which the Earl of Huntly held in irregular possession – 'as if he had any chance to keep it, the poor old fat fool, with that one after it!' Janet exclaimed.

There was also a respectable motive for James' hostility ('There always is,' they agreed). A younger son of Huntly's, Sir John, was a wild young man who seemed bent on proving the tag of the Gay Gordons:

> *Ken ye the Gordons' Gramacie?*
> *To curse and swear and damn and lee!*
> *And that's the Gordons' Gramacie.*

He had been imprisoned for the commonplace crime of stabbing an enemy in the street, had broken his ward and fled to the family stronghold at Strathbogie, where Huntly had the insolence to uphold his action and refuse to give him up. No doubt the old Cock o' the North relied on the Queen's favour to the only strong Catholic family in the kingdom.

'He'll soon learn what her favour's worth,' jeered Bothwell.

His companion looked at him with quizzical tenderness. 'You've not had much luck yet with women, have you?'

It was so different from the usual opinion of him that the young man stared in astonishment.

'If you mean by that that the Fleming girl is going to marry old Mother Tabbyskin instead of me, that's not my ill-luck for I never asked her – and when I saw you riding up just now I knew what luck it was that I hadn't.'

'No, it wasn't that. You once made me think of an Eastern fable of a young man who was granted a wish, and chose the gift of pleasing women. But as he stepped out full of pride and plans of the beautiful Queens whose love he'd win, an old witch caught sight of him from the dungeon cell where she lived, and dragged him down to live there for the rest of his days. And so that's all that came of his power to please women.'

'That's a fine tale, my Lady Aesop! And who's the old witch?'

'I can't tell you – maybe it's fate.' She spoke carelessly, then wished she hadn't, for both remembered her reputation for the second sight. She went on quickly, 'I used to think it was myself, as I was twice your age – but then I'd the sense to let you go in time.'

He leaned across the corner of the table to kiss her, and she, pretending to misunderstand him, passed him the ale-jug. They were laughing and pledging each other when the sudden ring and clatter of harness and armed men filled the courtyard with uproar for the second time that morning, but with noise far less leisurely than that of the indignant cows.

Lord George Gordon had come to ask Hepburn aid in men and horses for the Gordon cause. Tall, superb, with that look about him of a lonely eagle, but no trace of his father's pompous arrogance, he came clanking in his armour through the mighty archway into the hall. There he told Bothwell his errand, in front of the strange lady with the notorious reputation, to whom he showed his usual aloof courtesy, but no reserve about his plans.

The Bastard was pushing matters into open warfare, and Huntly and his sons determined in that event to defend Strathbogie against the forces of the Crown. Bothwell told Gordon to go back and tell his father not to be so mad, but the young man himself was plainly touched with a more dangerous madness. Huntly had bragged from the beginning of his intention to marry the Queen to his eldest son; it might be the Gordon hoped to win by force of arms what his father's diplomacy, or lack of it, had failed to achieve.

'Am I to help every man in Scotland who is fool enough to fall in love with the Queen?' Bothwell broke out to him. 'And isn't Arran's fate sufficient warning to you?'

It was no use. Gordon had in his eyes the look which his own men would have called fey. He did not care what his fate might be, and only knew that he must follow it. He rode away, bearing his friend no ill-will for his refusal to join him, and left Bothwell ill at ease.

Had Gordon been at the head of this affair instead of his father it might have been another matter. But he had no confidence in Huntly – the Weathercock o' the North, he called him, for Huntly had once turned against the Queen Regent. Besides, he had made up his mind; he would not be pushed either by his friends or his enemies into open rebellion against the Queen. He wrote to her to assure her of his loyalty, despite the fact that he, like the rebellious Sir John Gordon, had broken his ward; and he urged his friends and neighbours to keep the peace.

In the midst of such virtuous activities, it was a little irritating to get a message from John Knox urging him to the very course he was following, 'so that his crime of prison-breaking might be the more easily pardoned'. But he was grateful for the prophet's continued goodwill – 'there's some decency in the old ruffian after all', was his irreverent comment.

By late autumn the news from the North was dark indeed. Mary had hoped to make peace with Huntly and proposed to stay at Strathbogie, but she was warned of treachery there, and Huntly's own behaviour gave colour to it, for his castle at Inverness closed its gates on her in open revolt.

That stung her to fury, and it was easy for James to rub salt into the wound by pointing out that it was the men of her own faith who were encouraging her troublesome subjects to rebellion against her. She would show her country that if Catholics disobeyed her, they should be punished equally with Protestant rebels.

In high excitement she took the field in person, sleeping and eating out on the open moors as if she were any old campaigner, and with a good deal more enjoyment.

'I have always wished to be a man,' she said, 'to know what pleasure it is to lie all night in the fields and walk the causeway with a Glasgow buckler and broadsword by my side.'

Her words ran like a heath-fire through the ranks; the men were wild with enthusiasm for the lovely girl they had seen riding at their head, sharing the wind and the wet with them. Even Randolph, her quietly hostile English Envoy, was carried away by his admiration; he had 'never seen her merrier, she was never dismayed'. The clans flocked to her aid; the castle at Inverness surrendered; and that, she hoped, was the end of the business.

But Huntly was driven into marching against Lord James' forces and was defeated at Corrichie. The whole clan was crushed, the family ruined, Lord George Gordon imprisoned, and Huntly died of a fall from his horse in an apoplexy. Rumours were flying round the country. One of them, vouched for both by Knox and Buchanan, was that the Queen 'glowmed' when news was brought to her of her victory. Sir John Gordon, the chief occasion of the rebellion, was beheaded at Aberdeen, and the Queen fainted when forced by her brother to witness the execution from a window. It looked as though James' sense of power were getting a little exuberant. But no doubt he felt he could afford it. He had already taken the coveted title of Earl of Moray with its revenues worth £26,000 a year, and laid hands on the splendid furnishings of Strathbogie, now forfeit to the Crown, which he was carrying south for his own apartments in Holyrood.

'He's climbing like a mule,' was Bothwell's comment.

A triumph over James' enemy was sung in St Giles' pulpit next Sunday, when Knox demanded of his congregation, 'Have you not seen one who was greater than any of you, sitting where you now sit, pick his nails and pull down his bonnet over his eyes when idolatry and such vices were rebuked? Did he not say, "When will these knaves finish railing, when will they hold their peace?" Have you not heard me tell him to his face that God would avenge that blasphemy? Now God has punished the Earl of Huntly even as he and you heard me foretell.'

James had more solid reasons for triumph than the divine punishment for picking nails in sermon time. In the last few months he had crushed the heir to the throne, all the Haughty Hamiltons, together with the Queen's boldest and most loyal supporter, the Earl of Bothwell; and now he had destroyed the only strong Catholic power that she could count on in her kingdom – 'And all in the Queen's name, that's the beauty of it!' Bothwell exclaimed to Janet Scott on her next visit, as they walked by the rocky burn that tossed and foamed in spate through the heather just beyond the huge ramparts of Hermitage Castle. 'He has no need to attack his enemies to destroy them – he gets them to destroy themselves.'

'He is eating the artichoke leaf by leaf,' said Janet thoughtfully, 'as Caesar Borgia did with the states of Italy – destroyed them one by one. Go quick to the Queen before that happens to you – as soon as ever she is back in Holyrood.'

And to her he went with a strong force at his back, at the end of November when it had turned bitter cold. A mysterious new disease was striking down one after another in Edinburgh, running through the town as fast as the plague, and yet there were no such definite symptoms as in the plague, only aching limbs and a rheumy nose and a great cough and a sore stomach and above all a high fever. People were calling it the New Acquaintance, and the doctors the Influence. It influenced Bothwell's fortunes, for the Queen was seriously ill in bed for some weeks and could see no one. Lord James, though reported to be sneezing his head off, was, however, more active; he sent out an order to the Earl of Bothwell to return to prison in the Castle of Edinburgh on pain of treason.

All his good behaviour had been for nothing; if he didn't go back to prison he must flee the country. He chose flight, borrowed two thousand crowns from his sister and went to say goodbye to his mother at Morham.

That dark, uncompromising Highland woman stood very stiff and straight as she gave him her blessing and bade him beware of a knife in his shoulder-blades, poison in a friend's cup and the kiss of a woman, 'for there is nothing else you need fear'.

Just like her, he thought, admiring, amused, but slightly subdued, as he left her house for that of his mistress Anna Throndsen. He found her with their son Willie, a sturdy champion not yet two, engaged in playing 'Willie Wastle in his castle', that is to say, in shoving his playfellow, the son of his nurse, down the steps of the house. Willie was already so unruly that Anna despaired of managing him. In fact, she had given up any project of it for the time, for since the decline in her lover's fortunes she was planning to pay a long visit to Scandinavia as soon as the winter was over, and the weather safer for sea-travel.

'I want to go home,' she drawled plaintively in her deep seductive voice. 'You will be leaving me all alone in this strange country. My sister, who is married to a Scot in Shetland, will be home next year to see all the family, so why not I – who am not even married, *hélas*?'

Why not indeed? Since she was *ennuyée* here, '*Hélas!*' repeated Bothwell fiendishly.

She intended to take her furniture with her, even a fine carved bedstead. It seemed a lot of truck to take on a visit. She had already made inquiries about her passport and had learned that she would have liberty to return to Scotland whenever she wished – 'but that will depend on if you still wish it,' she said yearningly.

'More likely on what you can make some other man wish,' he growled.

At that she flew into a rage; did he dare suggest she was going husband-hunting?

182

'Looks like it, when you take your furniture and leave your son behind.'

He found to his annoyance that he was furiously jealous. She was a damned fine woman and his property; how dared she take it for granted that she was free to transfer herself to anyone else? But he choked back his unreasonable emotion; he knew he would be thankful to be rid of her so easily at this awkward time in his affairs, and forced himself to say:

'Why not? I'm no use to you now I'm making tracks for France.'

She answered indignantly that she had always been faithful to him, though he had not been true to his promise. He laughed, she boxed his ears, and he flung her on the bed. They both enjoyed a quarrel, and she looked her handsomest when angry.

Afterwards, when she was twisting up those magnificent great coils of black hair, she showed some sympathy for his misfortunes, but this he did not enjoy; there was something strained about it, and she got a few scratches into her stroking. 'I may be able to raise money for you abroad,' she said. 'It will not be the first time I have helped you with a loan.'

Which he had not repaid, though he had had the value of it several times over in this comfortable house at Morham and its furniture, of which she was taking the best part away with her. But he did not choose to point that out, though his careless glance did fall on the things that she had collected together, and he began to whistle a tune. She flung herself on her knees before him, swore she cared nothing for the 'dirty money', all she wanted was himself. She would leave everything again, her baby son here, as she had left her home and parents in Denmark, if only he would marry her and take her with him on his wanderings, through the whole wide world if need be.

She looked beautiful with her hair tumbling again all over her splendid white shoulders; but her appeal made him shudder. What a clutch this woman would get on him if she could! He suddenly discovered that he was immensely relieved at what had at first piqued him – that she had of her own accord decided to put the North Sea between them.

'You'll be much better off at home,' he said.

She did not cry, as he had feared. There was an expression in those lustrous dark eyes that he had not noticed before. Perhaps he had not noticed her much all along. He had taken her for granted, as he had taken her body; and how much did he really know of her? At this moment he felt he was looking down, not at the Scandinavian Admiral's daughter that he had met among a crowd of jolly sisters, not at the voluptuous Spanish lady that she loved to be told she was like, but at the black elflocks and white strange face of a Lapland witch.

CHAPTER TEN

IN THE last days of the year there was that unusual thing, an ice-storm: the rain as it fell 'froze so vehemently', complained Knox, 'that the earth was but a sheet of ice'. He blamed it, as he had blamed all the bad weather since her arrival in that dark haar, on the Queen; she, the daughter of 'mischievous Mary', was proving to the full as mischievous, especially in the matter of bad harvests, floods and frosts and all occasions when 'neither sun nor moon have performed their appropriate offices'.

After her long illness and convalescence, and a Christmas which she was too sad and listless to enjoy, Mary went at the end of December, informally with very few attendants, to 'make merry' at the New Year with her brother Johnnie at his house at Coldinghame, as she had promised a year ago. She was the only one to keep that promise, for d'Elbœuf had long since gone back to France, and nobody, not even Jan, knew where Bothwell was.

There was one other that Johnnie had vowed should be there – a fine boy a few weeks old, whose arrival had transformed Jan into a preternaturally wise and mature person. She smiled indulgently on the pranks of her husband and his royal guest as though they were a couple of children. All her awe of Mary had gone; how could she feel awe of this girl who went tearing along the frozen shore with Johnnie, dressed in an old suit of his and a pair of long riding-boots to keep out the sea-water – which they didn't? Jan even found herself scolding the Queen.

'Your hands are freezing even in those gloves. Your feet will be wet through again, and you *must* remember you've been ill.'

'Why should I remember? I'm not ill now. I shall remember nothing here that I don't want to remember, nothing, nothing!' she cried in such passionate answer that Jan flung her arms round her and exclaimed, 'Nor you shall, my bairn.'

'Bairn! How many months older are you than me?'

'Years and years,' replied Jan profoundly, 'but I beg Your Grace's pardon.'

'Ah, leave "Your Grace" – I'm sure I've none in these breeks!'

'The sea-water's freezing on them too – come, off with them and into your furred gown; it's spread in front of the fire in your room, and your bath is there – we'll have up a cauldron of boiling water.'

'Jan, Jan, we saw a gull walking on an ice-floe as big as this hall and half a mile or so out to sea – and all along the top of the tide-line there are thousands of poor frozen crabs no bigger than prawns, lying thick as pebbles, all stiff and stark – should I have brought them in for you like a clever housekeeper? How you'd have thanked me, wouldn't you!'

She was chattering all the way upstairs and while Jan took off her ice-wet things and bathed and dressed her: 'Oh I've been dead, dead,' she said, 'but now I'm alive again.'

Jan knew she was not thinking only of her illness, but had the sense to ask no questions. Mary was too much alive, her eyes and cheeks aflame, her whole slender body taut as a bowstring; what would happen to her if she did not soon get a good steady sensible husband to look after her? Johnnie, of whom Jan demanded this, replied airily, 'Oh she'll find one, you'll see. She's a likely lass. I'd ha' married her myself if I hadn't been her brother.'

The north wind howled and rumbled in the chimney, and the huge fire on the hearth went roaring up to meet it; outside, the sea crashed and thundered on the shore. 'God help the sailors!' they prayed. But each was thinking, not of the sailors, but of Bothwell, who most probably was even now on the North Sea, since the last news of him was that he had been seen some days ago making inquiries among the ships in Leith Harbour. But they did not speak of him lest they should increase each other's anxiety; they told stories of ghosts and bogles as they sat as close as they could to the fire, and roasted nuts and watched the ice-blue flames leap up among the red, for the logs were driftwood washed up from some wrecked ship, encrusted with salt and sputtering sea-spray, though blazing all the more fiercely for that. 'New Year's Eve and what will the New Year bring, and I was twenty last month,' thought the Queen, watching for pictures in the fire that should tell her her fate.

She heard a door bang, a quick step outside. Jan sprang up with a joyous shout and with her the dogs, barking madly. A voice rang out, 'Hey there, you rascals! I've kept my vow – now for yours!'

Bothwell swung in through the doorway, the dogs leaping round him, Jan flinging herself on him, the quiet scene flaring up into life and movement, a hundred questions and exclamations – and then he saw the Queen. There was an instant's pause, he gave a quick glance at her face, then swaggered up and dropped on his knees before her in an exaggeratedly penitential attitude.

'This is a bad shock for you, my lord of Bothwell,' she said severely.

'On the contrary, Madam, I am here only to give myself up into your ward again!'

Jan cried impetuously, 'Oh, but Your Grace will never keep him prisoner!'

Mary said sternly, 'I condemn him to imprisonment here in my loyal brother's house, for as long as it is safe for him to stay.'

He kissed both her hands, and sprang up with a shout of laughter. He was half frozen, ravenous, and in tearing spirits. He ate and drank enough for ten men as he told his adventures with as much gusto as if they had been a triumphal progress, instead of his attempt to fly the country in disgrace. He had played stowaway on a boat leaving Leith Harbour, but it had been driven back by storms on to Holy Island, which was garrisoned most inconveniently with English soldiers, so he had made his way across the sands at low tide – 'they were safe enough', he answered their alarmed exclamations, 'frozen hard for the most part' – and walked the twenty miles or so across the Border to Coldinghame.

'Had you not even money to buy a horse?' wailed his sister. 'What's become of the two thousand crowns I lent you?'

'Here, in bills of payment.' He thrust a bundle of papers into Johnnie's hand. 'Keep 'em safe for her. I know what Jan's like with papers – she can't believe they mean money. I mortgaged more land through Barron before I left Edinburgh. Poor old Barron, his wife's left too; run away across the Border, and the ministers in hue and cry after her, Knox writing to all the English bishops to send her back again. Nothing to do with me, I tell you, Johnnie, so it's no use your eyeing me. I'll take Barron's money, but not his wife.'

'Then why no horse?'

'I'd no mind anyone should see me who needn't.'

'Had you no servant?'

'Only my French lad, now hogging it in the kitchens as I'm

doing here. So here I am at your New Year revels, uninvited as I promised – and where's the new guest? Are you calling him James after me?'

'Not I! I'll not be reminded of my precious elder brother every time I call my son. We're giving him your father's name, Francis.'

And Johnnie insisted on showing Bothwell his sleeping nephew – a queer dark elf with pointed ears.

'Has it got its eyes open yet?' the uncle solemnly inquired, to the indignation of the proud father.

'Do you take it for a pup, my lord?' he demanded furiously, then joined in the roar of laughter against himself.

Mary said very little, but laughed as much as any, and watched and listened with shining eyes as if she were drinking in new life with all that careless merriment. As the bells rang out at midnight they all drank to 1563, clinking their cups together, 'and may the luck turn for you', said Johnnie to his brother-in-law, 'as the tide's now turned on the shore outside – listen to it coming roaring in!'

'As *you* will, when your luck's in!' said Jan.

Mary cried, 'Let's go and greet the rising tide and pray that your luck rises with it, my lord!'

She seized the painted fool's bauble that they had been tossing in the hall earlier that evening, and declared they should launch it in honour of his coming voyage. In breeks and boots and the thick woollen scarves of Border warfare muffled round their heads and necks, the four of them ran out from the hot fireside and warm smells of meat and wine, into the breathless glittering night. The wind had gone down, the moon was up, the frosty stars were crackling like white fireworks overhead and —

'The night's enchanted,' cried Mary. 'Look! There are spirits of fire joining battle in the sky!'

Far in the north, spears of fiery and bluish light shot upwards through the dark.

'The Merry Dancers are out,' said Bothwell; and Jan, 'The spirits are riding the Northern Lights.' Mary, who had never seen the Aurora Borealis before, still believed that it was a portent of victorious war.

She had been hushed and silent in the house, a smiling shadow in the background; she was another creature out of doors, a wild young Maenad, drunk on the iced wine of that stinging air, now rushing along the shore away from them, her head back to see the stars and those strange lights in the north, her hair flying out from under her scarf; now leading them headlong over the frozen shore and the pools of ice that glinted between the rocks, down to the very edge of the huge silver-hollowed waves that came rolling and roaring up under the moon. Her bauble went bobbing darkly over them, the wind caught it and drove it this way and that, while they cheered it on, laughing at its vagaries. The tide came up, rushing round the great banks of crusted wavy ice that had frozen in its pattern; it broke over them and broke them up, washing them off the shore so that the sea was dark with floating ice for a long way out.

Mary led her company to help launch the floating islands and push them into the swirling silver-dappled water; they scrunched and splashed through ice and wet, played ducks and drakes with flat pieces of ice, and Mary tore bunches of frozen seaweed off the rocks, so encrusted with ice that each brown globe was only a seed in the heart of an enormous crystal grape. She danced madly with them, tossing and clattering them together like castanets, holding them up for the moon to shine through, calling to the others, 'Come and suck my crystal fruits! or will you only tell me that the grapes are salt?'

This mad laughing creature was something that Bothwell had never seen in her before; it was a shame, he thought, even to coop up such a wild thing in woman's dress, let alone a Queen's stiff robes of state. Well, she had flung all that now to the cold winds!

Next day he was up before the late winter sunrise, and out on the shore to see what promise the sea gave for his further voyaging; and there she was by herself, standing looking out to where the dawn light was gleaming on the nearer water, while the distant sea was still iron-dark.

'Have you been out all night?' he asked. 'I can almost believe it, for I hear Your Grace is an old campaigner now, and asks nothing better than to make the heather your bed and ride all day on the march. It is your turn to tell your adventures.'

But the face she turned on him was no longer that of the spirit of freedom he had seen last night. 'The adventure of hounding a fat old man to his death,' she said. 'It was a brave one, wasn't it!'

He said, 'Well, Huntly fought against your mother for his own ends. You'd already a score to pay.'

But she never heard him. 'I saw him lying there on the cold

stones,' she said, 'with only a cloth of rough Irish frieze flung over him, and stockings of coarse hodden grey. They had taken all the finery he loved so. Do you know that he would have avoided that battle at Corrichie – he had meant to retreat that morning – but they could not wake him before it was ten o'clock? They say his spirits were weighed down with his corpulence; it made him clumsy, helpless – and nervous, since he knew he could not move fast. It's hard to understand that, isn't it, when one's body is light and free to move quickly, and so one's mind too.'

Her passion of pity took him by surprise; he had expected it for Sir John Gordon, a young man accounted the handsomest in Scotland, who was reported to have said on the scaffold that 'he died for love of his Queen', though it was difficult to see how he had expressed it by stabbing a private enemy, breaking prison and raising rebellion.

But her restless sadness was not for him, nor, Bothwell suspected, only for Huntly. She told him her pride in setting out on that campaign, thinking that now at last she had a chance to prove herself the true leader of her people, putting down rebellion with equal justice and no favouritism to those of her own faith – 'A Scot first and a Catholic second,' she said, 'as I had determined to be all along, but no one here will recognize it – though I have been blamed for it by my own Church again and again. The Pope keeps asking me what I have done here for the Faith, and I have to fob him off with excuses. But here, that horrible old man, Knox, tells all my people that I am only waiting my chance to put the Catholics in power and persecute all the rest. So when James told me all that Huntly was working against me, I was glad, glad – fool that I was! – that now they would see the truth. But do people ever see the truth?'

'They see what they want to see. It's not often it happens to be true.'

The white dawn now had spread into the upper sky. The long curved white-crested waves were rolling in at as regular a succession as the march of troops, their foam blown forward like white hair. The curve of a gull's wings flashed against the dark headland towards which they were walking briskly to keep warm.

Mary laughed sadly at his answer. 'That is true of me too,' she said. 'I saw the tall pines standing like black sentinels against the stars when I slept out, wrapped in a great plaid, and smelt the sharp spiced smell of the pine needles and the heather

189

and the bracken, and I thought how the night brought out the star of the Guise, and how you had always fought best in the bright dark – and that now I too was a soldier. I proved it too when the clans came flocking to me at Inverness and stormed the rebel castle; Mackintosh and Fraser and the Graham of Montrose – it was for *me* they fought, and not the Bastard.'

Bothwell drew in his breath sharply. It was the first time she had ever given the Lord James, now Earl of Moray, the title he had borne from birth. But she did not notice; she was busy telling him of the assault at Inverness, so swift and resolute that the castle yielded almost at once and not a man in the attack was killed, 'and their pipes playing them into action as though it were a dance, and those mad kilted Highlanders singing, yelling – do you remember showing me them singing in the court-yard of your castle a year ago, and that wild chant —

> *Little wot ye wha's coming!*
> *Colin's coming, Donald's coming',* —

'Mony a buttock bare's coming!' he joined in.

'Yes, they came to me then! They charged the castle high above the town, and I marched in to the music of the pipes, with the river glittering below and the distant mountains all purple in their pride. I dined in the great hall that night, and they told me stories of the chief, Macbeth, who slew his King there. You are too fond of killing your King's in Scotland.'

'Well, we've not killed a Queen yet. And won't get the chance if you're so stout a warrior. You weren't at Corrichie when Huntly was killed?' he asked, with a sharp return to serious-ness.

'No, thank God!' She hit her thickly gloved hands together and broke into a run, then turned and walked soberly back to him. 'It need not have happened,' she said, 'I'll swear it. He only fought at Corrichie because he believed that half James' army was on his side, and would desert to him as soon as the battle was joined. What had led him to believe that?'

'The Lord James' agents,' said Bothwell boldly.

'Do you know that?'

'No, but I can guess. His spy work is excellent, and the chief work of a spy is to give wrong information to the enemy.'

'Oh God, is war as foul as that?'

'It gets fouler every year, I fancy. But I'm only a rough Borderer. I'm not civilized enough to appreciate the modern methods.'

190

'Need *none* of it have happened? Was James all along engineering trouble for his own ends? – Sir John's private brawl, old Huntly's wish to put the Catholics in power, with himself at the head? *That* was true, but I don't believe he meant to go to war for it. Though James has found papers of Sir John Gordon's proving all sorts of plots against the Government.'

'James is gey good at finding papers to justify what he's already done. I wonder he troubles, seeing that he's now destroyed the only family left in Scotland who might dispute his power.'

She cried in anguish, 'And it is I who have done it! *I* have put him in power. I have set him up to destroy my friends – and if he ever wishes to take the chance, to destroy myself.'

Her cry, in echo to his suspicions, moved him unbearably. He flung his arm round her shoulders, hurrying her forward in a yet faster stride. At that moment she was to him only what she appeared in her man's clothes, a very young, sexless, friendless creature, cruelly perplexed, and his only thought to give her heart – as he would if she were indeed a lad who had been worsted by his enemies.

'You will win through,' he said. 'It's true Scotland's not kind to her Kings, but by God what a race of 'em she's bred! Think of your own father when he was younger than you by four or five years; what chance did *he* have, would you say? A Flodden orphan, seized in his boyhood by the Douglases. Yet he broke away from them, and when he was still only a lad, stole out of Falkland Castle when they thought him in bed, rode all night to Stirling, fell asleep there, and woke to find himself King. What a Stewart King has done, he can do again – a Stewart Queen I mean, and I beg Your Grace's pardon for gripping you! You're shivering under all that wool and leather – let's run to our porridge before they cool.'

As they ran back, the deep red sun came up over the rim of the North Sea, balanced itself on it, flattened at its base like a bubble, and the whole vast sea burst into flame.

*   *   *

They had no more serious talk after that; all that day and the next were spent in what Mary called the chief business of Scotland, the effort to keep warm. The frost was of course too hard for hunting, but they skated and played at curling on a pond near by, and when the short winter daylight died they danced flings and played ball and battledore and shuttlecock and blindman's-buff and hunt-the-slipper and a dozen other noisy romping games.

Mary was in mad spirits, refused to be treated as Queen or called Your Grace, put on a short blue kirtle and a scarlet apron, and showed Jan how to cook French dishes in the kitchen. Some Spanish oranges had been stored there, and she made a new sort of preserve – called after herself, as she told them proudly, for the cook at her grandmother's château of Joinville had made it to tempt her appetite when she was ill; 'Marie est malade', he had muttered again and again as he racked his brains to invent something new for her, and 'Marie-malade' they had called it ever since. They ate the bitter orange jam in her honour, but preferred honey.

She sang them the latest songs from Paris, all new and piping hot, brought by young Châtelard, who had left Scotland with her uncles a year ago, but had just returned, since he could not endure life away from her. Mary had been enchanted to see him again; he could bring her all the latest gossip of Catherine and her Court that he knew how to make so vivid and impudent. And in the delicious pantomime of the elaborate Court dances, half mime, half ballet, there was no one whose steps and gestures so perfectly matched her own. So they danced and chattered, sang his own poems, dressed up and acted impromptu charades in which she played the husband and he the wife and both the fool, so extravagantly that she did not dream his devotion was serious and might be dangerous. Yet even the insouciant Johnnie had seen it, and warned her against flirting with him so openly, to which her indignant reply had been that it was safe just because it was so open — 'Besides, even James has said nothing. What a staid old married man you're growing, to outvie James in prudery!'

She spoke of the young Frenchman now with friendly easy freedom to Bothwell, as she told him the news Châtelard had brought of her uncles. It was disturbing, for there had been a Huguenot attempt to murder the Duc de Guise. The man had been caught and brought before him, and when asked why he had done it, replied, 'for his religion'.

'Well,' said the Guise, 'if your religion teaches you to murder one who has never injured you, mine teaches me to forgive you'; and he let him go free, to the fury of his followers.

'If the Guise is killed,' they threatened, 'then all France will flow with blood.'

Mary begged Bothwell to make her uncle understand the

danger his death would bring to France, since he could never make him regard it for himself. And to her uncle she wrote a long letter on behalf of Bothwell, that he should give him the Captaincy of the Scottish Archers. The Guise had a great liking for what he had both seen and heard of Bothwell and would be only too glad to make use of him, as he had told his niece more than once. 'So at least my mother's country will repay you a little for the service you gave her, though my father's has shown you such ingratitude,' she said as she gave him the letter.

*   *   *

The next day after that sunrise walk along the shore, there came another unexpected visitor. Lethington, returning from a diplomatic visit to London, and hearing that the Queen was at Coldinghame, broke his freezing journey there, and sufficiently late in the day to ensure his lying there the night. He rode into the courtyard in the frosty blue twilight when all the company were snowballing each other, so it was too late to hide the fact that Bothwell was present. But Lethington was very friendly to him, and as long as he remained at Coldinghame there was no way in which he could work against him. So his hosts and the Queen were most pressing in their invitations, and he was well content to stay, settled comfortably before the fire in a big arm-chair, with cushions at his back and a rug to keep off the draughts from his feet, and allowed to wear his cap before his Queen to keep off the draughts from his head, 'which is none so thickly thatched as I could wish', and a cup of warm mulled wine in his hand, his furred cloak drawn close about him. He gave himself these elderly invalid airs quite shamelessly, not only for the sake of his comfort, but for his enjoyment of the exasperation they caused in the younger men. Moreover, they enhanced his privileges; he spoke indulgently to his Queen and his hostess as if they were a pair of pretty children, while with leisurely enjoyment he told them all the gossip from England.

Elizabeth was still insisting that her dearest wish was that she and Mary should meet, though she had put off the proposed meeting at York last summer.

Mary declared, 'I don't believe she intends to meet me, or ever did intend it.'

'Console yourself, Madam; if she does not meet you she will scarcely sleep for curiosity. I had to answer a thousand questions concerning your height, complexion, the colour of your hair, your accomplishments, and all in comparison with her own. Judge how precarious was my balance between truth and courtesy. But I compromised. You dance more gracefully than she; this, translated into the language of the English Court, means that she dances 'more high and disposedly' than you. Your Grace is taller than her Grace, and therefore too tall for a woman, I am sorry to inform you, since her Grace is exactly the right height – I have it from her own lips.'

He had had to notice each different dress she wore; it entailed a fresh start of rapture three or four times each day – and more rapture, punctuated by her coy scoldings, when allowed by a courtier to surprise her playing the virginals.

'But she is close on thirty!' exclaimed Mary incredulously.

'Ah, but a Virgin, you must always remember. Her ways in fact were more virginal than her instrument; they left me well satisfied to serve so staid a dowager as Your Grace.'

'Did she ask if I too played the virgin – and the virginals?'

'The latter instrument – yes; and how well? I told her, "Reasonably well – for a Queen!"'

'Monster! I'll have you hanged for that!'

'She'd have me hanged if I'd made it warmer.'

His mission to London had been on the question of Mary's marriage. If she did not marry according to Elizabeth's wishes, Elizabeth would refuse to admit her as her successor. But it looked as though no one that Mary could choose would be according to Elizabeth's wishes.

Obviously the English Queen would not encourage a match for her with any great Continental power that would make Scotland a dangerous neighbour. Lethington had held only secret interviews with the Spanish Ambassador in London to discuss the proposals for Mary's marriage to Don Carlos. But Knox's spies had discovered the matter and he had preached openly against the marriage with 'an infidel: for all Papists are infidels'. So the secret was out, and Mary had only shown how helpless she was when she summoned Knox to the Palace for an angry scene; she had cried so with rage that she had to send her page for more handkerchiefs; and he had summed up their respective positions by assuring her that her tears gave him no more pleasure than those of his little boys when he whipped them.

'What have you to do with my marriage?' she had stormed, 'and what are you in this realm?'

'A subject born within the same,' was his superb answer.

The word 'subject' seemed to have a different meaning in Scotland from in England, where a Puritan writer had had his right hand cut off for expressing his opinion against Elizabeth making any foreign marriage. It was the opinion of Elizabeth herself; but that did not lessen her punishment of his impertinence in daring to discuss her marriage at all. Nor did his punishment lessen his loyalty: the instant his hand was cut off he waved the bleeding stump round his head and shouted, 'God bless the Queen!'

'It seems,' Lethington now said slyly as he told this tale, 'that one Queen may steal a horse, where another may not look over the hedge.'

Mary had had to climb down, and profess entire obedience to Elizabeth over her marriage: she had declared she would only take a suitor of Elizabeth's own choice; and Lethington could now tell her what that choice had been.

He amused himself by tantalizing the company with their questions and guesses and his own ambiguous replies, finished his mulled wine, put down his cup on a stool near by with his usual precise care, placed the tips of his beautiful manicured fingers together, glanced at the eager faces of the two girls, whose combined ages did not quite equal his own, and said, 'The Queen of England has paid Your Grace the tenderest compliment in her power by proposing to give you the man that she loves best herself – though "as a brother", she was careful to assure me. That is, Robert Dudley.'

There was an instant's speechless astonishment. Bothwell's hand flew instinctively to his sword. 'Christ's blood!' he burst out; 'is this a joke of yours to insult the Queen? Robert Dudley – that kept stallion of Elizabeth's!'

'Your Lordship's known eye for horseflesh,' drawled Lethington, 'should judge whether the stallion or the grey mare be the better horse.'

'Is this true?'

'My profession, my lord, obliges me to lie abroad for the good of my country. But not at home.'

'Why, he's not even one of her nobles,' exclaimed Johnnie Stewart.

'Her Majesty noticed that omission,' observed Lethington, 'and has supplied the remedy. She has created him Earl of Leicester, and signified her pleasure in honouring him by tickling his neck during the ceremony.'

There was a crude hoot of mirth from Jan. Mary clenched

her hands till the knuckles showed white. At last she said very low:

'He was believed to have caused the murder of his first wife, Amy Robsart. Is that the reason for the choice of his second?'

Jan gave her a startled glance and flung her arm round her.

'It's monstrous,' she cried. 'Everybody says the English Queen was enceinte by him this last summer and that was why the skirts at her Court have suddenly grown so wide.'

'An admirable instance of petticoat government,' murmured Lethington.

'And you, I suppose,' sneered Bothwell, 'told your good friend of England that it was an admirable notion to pass on her lover as a husband for our Queen?'

'I did indeed,' was the smooth answer, 'and with such grateful consideration for the value she set on him, that I suggested she should first marry him herself, so as to have the enjoyment of him during her lifetime, and then leave the reversion of him in her will, along with her kingdom, to our Queen.'

There was a roar of delight from Johnnie. 'You said that to her face, and left England alive!'

Mary clapped her hands. 'No wonder she calls you the flower of the wits in Scotland! She's proved your thorns sharper than any on her Tudor rose. Oh how I love you for that, dear Michael Wily!'

For the rest of the evening she gave all her attentions to him and none to Bothwell, in rebuke for his rough attack on her most able servant. And Bothwell only made matters worse for himself by returning to the attack once or twice in vain attempt to prick his precious complacency – by which he only called down on himself the light but deadly shafts of his opponent's sarcasm. They pricked him, probed him, made rings round him in which he felt like an enraged bull, longing to charge but bewildered as to his direction. And all the time he had to conform to the polite fiction that this was only a friendly piece of back-chat, when he was itching to get his hands round the scraggy neck of that elderly pussy-cat, with his tabby hair growing grey and his thin ironic lips and his cunning half-sarcastic sympathy that now began to show itself to his Queen, stroking her like a soft paw while underneath one could feel the claws.

Bothwell's chief memory afterwards was that soft casual voice saying things that are never said to a Queen.

'You, Madam, represent the Inquisition, and Knox the Reformation; that is the whole crux of the matter. That is why whatever you say or do will be wrong; and whatever he says or does will be right. It makes no odds at all that you have no intention of bringing in the Inquisition, or of persecuting Protestants, should you ever have the power to do so. I have argued that point with him for hours on end; I have told him that your only wish is to keep your own faith and let your people keep theirs. His unfailing answer is, "We ought to do God's express commandment. Not only ought idolatry to be suppressed, but the idolater ought to die the death." So what chance have you, Madam, since everyone of importance now in Scotland, and in England, knows that the Reformation is right, and the Inquisition wrong?'

'I see. And am I to stand by and listen while he incites my subjects to rebel against me, and ultimately put me to death?'

'It is much the safest thing to do. A martyr is far more dangerous than a bore. Those trumpet notes of his are getting a bit too long drawn out. Edinburgh is complaining that all his preaching is turned to railing. What's more, her pawky sense has guessed the reason: that your growing popularity, and his lack of any definite handle, or even scandal, against you, are gall and wormwood to him.'

'And so it is to be a race between us to prove which is right?'

'No, Madam, I made that clear. He will always be right, whatever he says; just as your brother will always be the "Good Lord James", whatever he does. For they are the Reformation, and you the Inquisition.'

'I am *not*! I am myself, myself, myself!'

'Just so. And so, though you will always be wrong, they will always love you.'

A tapering ice-blue flame had leaped up like a wave of the sea from the heart of the fire as Mary uttered her cry of passionate self-assertion; long afterwards Bothwell saw it as the flame that burned at the heart of her – her fiery integrity as a living soul refusing to be identified with religious or political movements; refusing to be judged by any other standards than the simple human value of her actions, right or wrong.

He too had determined not to be bound by the formulas of other men – not to be disloyal because he was Protestant, nor to be Catholic because he was for the Queen.

But look at the result! Because he belonged to no party, his just treatment was nobody's business. He had stood by the Queen, but the Queen was not strong enough to stand by him. Would she ever be strong enough to stand alone? Lethington was hinting it when he gave her these soothing pats about her growing popularity; he himself had urged it yesterday when he had told her of her father's escape from bondage. But he knew, and had not said, for fear of discouraging her, that the cases were clean different. Her father had had to fight his nobles, as she was doing. He had not had to fight the ministers as well. He had been King of the Commons. But his daughter was a girl alone against the world.

Then, in bald selfish reasoning, what good had he done here, or could ever do, either for the Queen or himself? In spite of all Elizabeth's determination to prevent it, she was pretty certain to marry some foreign prince, especially after this amazing insult of the offer of Dudley; and after a year or so would leave the country. He would then have lost his only well-wisher – he could hardly call her ally; and his worst enemy, the 'Good Lord James', would be still more firmly in power, as Regent in her place.

He would get out of it all long before that – out of it in the next week, with any luck. It was Saturday night now; even Lethington would not flout public opinion by travelling on the Sabbath. He'd not give that tame cat any time to inform against him when he'd finished being stroked by the ladies and gone back to Edinburgh. 'Wait till he has purred his way up to his snug bed with his feet against a wrapped hot brick; wait till I can get Johnnie aside and ask him for a couple of his best horses with their shoes well cocked for the ice – he owes me that, now I've just paid off Jan's loan – and then off tonight "by the ae light o' the moon", off alone with Paris, back along the coast to Berrington, and a boat for France and the Guise; he is the greatest man in Europe, and France is sick of the Medici and her brood, maybe he'll be her King!'

And in any case there were chances in the foreign wars: foreign estates and titles, castles in Spain!

CHAPTER ELEVEN

I T W A S Sunday afternoon, and the little Northumbrian village of Berrington near the coast was sound asleep. John Rively, farmer, slept sounder than any after his dinner of stuffed goose and salted mutton, hot dough cakes and home-brewed ale, the best in the country, he'd say that for it, and had said it at dinner so often that he could scarcely say anything else. But now he was snoring instead, spread out at length in his chair, with his head fallen back and his feet on the hearthstone and his belt unbuckled and his hands clasping the two ends of it as if in unavailing attempt to make them meet across his now unfettered belly, that swelled up in the highest curve of that hill chain of his contours, bulging forehead and podgy nose and chin upon chin. To wake him now was an imprudence that neither his wife nor his nephew John would commit; it was reserved for a stranger.

Someone knocked on the door of the house, and a stertorous awakening snort shook the mountain chain into volcanic upheaval. Silence fell again, and the volcano subsided. But the knock came again, louder and repeated; John Rively opened round glaring eyes, shouted 'Who's that?' in a vain attempt to stave off the evil moment, finally jerked all his curves forward, pulled himself out of his chair and went to the door.

A little man stood there, wrapped in a plaid, a ragged peak of red beard sharpening the point of his narrow face. His eyes were screwed up against the wind and now twinkled up at John Rively's massive face with a sharp shrewish questing look, like that of a small lean terrier investigating an over-fed mastiff.

'Know me?' he repeated Rively's question. 'If you don't know Willie Tatt of Coldinghame, it's likely you'll know of Black Ormiston of the Moss Tower. You're a friend, I think, of the Forster family, and they've had friendly dealings with him in the past bad times, sending him the kindly word when it would be well to thresh his corn and secure his cattle when Sir John Forster was going to march North.'

Rively knew well enough of these unprofessional relations between the English Warden and his Scots neighbours, or enemies, and cultivated them himself whenever possible. With a heavy wink he replied, 'Aye, it's better to have a friend on the wrong side of the fence than two on the right side, I say.'

He had heard of Willie Tatt as a warm man with a snug farm across the Border, and it encouraged him to prove his maxim; whatever he could do for Tatt he'd do – 'and mind you make it tit for Tatt, ha ha, when we meet in the next Border fighting!' ('Though I could eat you then at one mouthful, you starveling red-feathered cock-sparrow!' he added contemptuously to himself.)

Willie Tatt's demands were modest enough at the outset. He had come in a trodd of sheep; some had strayed and he wanted help to collect them. John Rively promised him his nephew as soon as he should return to the house; in the meantime, Tatt must come in and taste his ale. Over the ale, and after Tatt had taken some further soundings as to John Rively's policy and verified that it was based on a sound sense of commercial values, he confided to him that there was more in the matter than a trodd of sheep, and that Rively might get the chance to make a more important ally 'on the wrong side of the fence' than Willie Tatt, one too who would pay more for his benefits.

'My master,' said Tatt, 'has had the bad luck to offend the Queen of Scotland, and has had to leave the country on the quiet. Now, if you could house him and his servant with their horses in those caves you use as cellars behind the house — '

'And how do you know about my cellars?' asked Rively.

It was Willie Tatt's turn to wink. Black Ormiston had informed him that the cellars could be – and had been – used for other purposes than storing kegs of ale.

John Rively was not altogether pleased by this, but he was busy pursuing a subtle piece of statecraft that all but eluded him in the soporific haze of the Sabbath. At last, however, he ran it to earth. Laying a finger like a sausage to the side of his bulbous nose, he said profoundly, 'If your master is upsides with your Queen, it's likely he'll be on the right side of mine?'

'Nothing likelier,' agreed Tatt.

'Who is your master?'

'The Earl of Bothwell.'

Rively's supposition did not look so likely now to him. He had a pretty fair idea of which names among the Scots figured on the pension list from England, in return for their 'goodwill and private information', a list headed by Lord James and including Mr George Buchanan, who was not too learned to be canny, and many more of the Protestant nobles and gentry, also their womenfolk.

But no doubt Bothwell would now be induced to join it, and anyway what odds, so long as Rively got paid? So he agreed to hide the Earl and his servant until they had done their business in Berrington; he could make a shrewd guess at its nature when Willie Tatt said he would want a guide across the sands at low tide next day to the harbour of Holy Island. As soon as they could get a ship his visitors would be off, that was plain. It was money for nothing, and all his curves expanded with geniality.

They were blown to their fullest extent when he greeted the noble Earl himself and his French servant, showed them the cellars and the beds put up in them, and the stout door that could be locked 'as safe and snug as that dungeon in your Lordship's castle of Hermitage where the Dark Knight of Liddesdale threw his friend and horse to starve together.'

And he roared delightedly at the happy reminiscence as he ushered them back to the house to dine, with profuse apologies for 'my meagre and humble fare' in the same breath that he pointed out its excellencies, lamented that he had no wine, 'but this young rascal my nephew knows where to get as good a bottle as any in England when he takes Your Lordship's servant to the harbour tomorrow – it's not for nothing that the French ships call there with the best from Bordeaux – we'll make merry on it tomorrow to make up for this plebeian stuff tonight. Not but what it's the best brew —' and again he told why it was the best, while the 'young rascal' his nephew looked sourly on with a pale contemptuous face, picking up the jug to refill it as soon as it was empty, with an air of weary indifference.

Next day he set off with Tatt for the harbour and the wine in the fishing village, and grumbled about his uncle all through the expedition. He was mean as hell, he said, for all his jovial airs, he made his nephew work for nothing, he would get blood out of a stone, there was nothing he wouldn't do for money. This account of their genial host bore out Bothwell's impression of Rively as a *faux bonhomme* and untrustworthy. Luckily Tatt had found there was a ship that would sail next day, so they would only have to rely on this bag of bombast for one night. They endured his boasting over the wine and young John's sullen silence, and went early to their vault. Bothwell ordered the horses to be ready saddled and his two followers to keep on their clothes, and their weapons by them, and locked the door himself before he went to bed.

The precaution was useless; there were two keys to that door, and it was opened from outside at about four in the morning. The light of torches guttering in the night wind showed four of the Berwick officers at the head of a party from their garrison. Behind the door cowered Rively in his night-shirt, unavailingly trying to keep a blanket wrapped about him, hiding his face in it while the wind revealed his unmistakably bandy legs. Bothwell leaped out of bed at Rively's throat, but he was seized before he could reach him.

'He sent us no information,' said the Under Marshal; 'we're taking him along too for harbouring suspects.'

'But Your Honours,' gasped Rively, seeing the Earl now

securely held by the soldiers, 'I led you straight to this vault, I intended all along to give them up.'

'Much use that was!' exclaimed the Master of Ordnance, in charge of the expedition. 'If Captain Carew here hadn't had word from Edinburgh to search the ship at Holy Island, they'd have sailed in her tomorrow.'

'And they'd have done that,' broke in Captain Carew, conceitedly twirling his moustache, 'if I hadn't searched the village too, and seen your lad buying wine there, so that I guessed you had company.' He looked challengingly at the Master of Ordnance as though he expected to receive promotion for his cleverness on the spot; but the Master only nodded impatiently, grunted, 'Very fine, very fine,' and asked Bothwell if he would dress and go with them quietly to Berwick, or be carried in his shirt.

'I'll dress,' said the prisoner, 'and before I leave this place you'll give me pen and ink and I'll write to my friends in England to demand for what reason, and by what authority, I have been taken prisoner in my bed in time of peace, with no charge preferred against me.'

At this Captain Carew looked somewhat anxiously at his commanding officer, but the Master of Ordnance with a smile granted the prisoner's request, if he would state the names of his English friends. Bothwell unhesitatingly replied with the names of the two antagonists whom he had twice worsted in battle in the Border wars, the Earl of Northumberland and his brother, Sir Henry Percy.

ABROAD

'There is no one in England,' said Bothwell, 'whom I'd sooner kill than Cecil and John Rively.'

'Why John Rively?' asked Sir Henry Percy.

'Because he was the reason I was here last March, am here this March, and if things go no better with me on this journey to London now than they did a year ago, am like to be here next March as well, listening to the spring gales break themselves on these damned grey rocks and the seagulls scream —'

'And your host play the clarinet,' finished Sir Henry, picking up that instrument.

He was a small man, considerably older than Bothwell, very fair, with a tiny pointed chin-tuft of beard already growing white. He spoke seldom and incisively, and never made an unnecessary movement. The effect of his silence, his stillness, the neatly chiselled stony-white of his features, and his hard light unswerving eyes, made one think of a marble knight on a tombstone. All his life he had been compared unfavourably with his elder brother Thomas, the Earl of Northumberland, who was so much taller, handsomer, jollier and more popular, but he knew himself the wiser man and the better soldier, and was content whether other men knew it or not.

His previous encounters with Bothwell in the fighting between Scots and English at the end of the Queen Regent's reign had given him a great respect for his enemy. He had twice nearly fallen into the strong hands of this tall quick dark young man who now lounged opposite him, kicking the table in his impatience, the next instant leaping from his chair to stride up and down and rub his clenched hand against his head, as fiercely restless as some lithe black panther prowling up and down in his cage.

To cage such a creature seemed to the Percy, a usually unemotional observer, an act against nature. He lowered his clarinet from his lips to say, 'They'll not put you in the Tower again, or my own liberty shall go bail for yours!'

But it was an unnecessary remark, so he continued to play instead. His companion whistled the tune in accompaniment, then sang in a deep rollicking voice:

> *'Oh there was horsing, horsing in haste,*
> *And cracking o' whips out o'er the lea,*
> *Until we came to the Till water,*
> *And it was running like the sea.'*

And Bothwell swung round from the window where he had
been staring out at the North Sea that surged up against the
headland of Tynemouth. 'What's put you on to the ballad of
our raid at Haltwellsweir? Our second merry-meeting, wasn't
it? Merrier if I'd caught you! Odd how nearly you were my
prisoner then, and now I'm yours.'

'You were my prisoner a year ago, now you're my guest.' Sir
Henry's voice rebuked not his tactlessness but his inaccuracy, a
thing he disliked far more. These Scots were always too fond of
the dramatic, the coloured antithesis, particularly when they
were half Highland, like this young fellow; his Sinclair mother
had left the mark of her clan on his black hair and high cheek-
bones, as well as on some mental characteristics deprecated by
the Percy. Throckmorton's opinion of Bothwell as 'glorious rash
and hazardous young man' on whom it was well to keep a close
watch, would have been endorsed by Sir Henry from the
moment when he had met his formidable opponent at the signing of the peace treaty between England and Scotland. He had
had to swallow his objections to 'the insolent levity of this
young galliard', and finally to admit that this laughing swaggering young man took his business seriously enough.

There was one clause, the last in the treaty, that Bothwell had
urged: that in neither realm should men be 'put in irons and
fetters or cast into horrible pits', but that 'all prisoners shall be
honestly treated in time coming', a piece of youthful optimism
that had touched the older man.

He had not seen or heard from him again until a year ago last
January, when a letter had reached him from Berwick signed
'your loving friend lawfully, Bothwell'. It claimed 'some little
acquaintance' with him (and Percy readily acknowledged the
force with which he had introduced himself on his raids), told
him that 'being deliberate to go into France to the Queen's
uncles', he had been captured and detained by the English
officers at Berwick, without reason.

He asked Percy to use his influence to get his release, and
offered no compliments nor explanations as to why Percy
should do this for an enemy who had twice worsted him in war
and plagued him while negotiating peace. This omission pleased

Sir Henry as much as the last sentence in the letter annoyed him. 'Excuse my homely writing' wrote Bothwell in a fluent Italian hand, clearly and even beautifully formed, remarkable in a country where his fellow-nobles were apt to write vilely, if at all, yet he must needs point it out by this flamboyant piece of mock modesty.

Percy at once had Bothwell transferred to his charge at Tynemouth, and there he stayed till past the middle of March. Mary asked that he should be returned to Scotland for her 'to deal with him as she thought fit'. That, however, was just what his enemies feared she might be able to do, so they urged Cecil to keep him prisoner in England. Rively was given bail and went to London to help Cecil concoct some charge against the Earl. The English Minister of State was only too willing; he had never forgiven 'that unhonourable and thievish act' of Bothwell's in snatching his secret subsidy to the Scots rebels from John Cockburn.

'I think all the hobgoblins of All Hallows' E'en were out that night!' Bothwell had burst out to Percy, 'for I've been haunted by 'em ever since. Every enemy I've ever made goes back to that night. It wasn't just John Cockburn I knocked on the head – it was John Knox and the Bastard and Arran and Michael Wily and Randolph and Cecil and Queen Elizabeth. They've been out for my blood ever since, every man-jack of them, and won't rest till they get it.'

'You have certainly chosen the most powerful persons in both countries for your foes.' Sir Henry could no more flatter a man's hopes than his person – to his face.

To a man's enemies he took another tone, and wrote to Cecil in high praise of Bothwell's sense and ability. Straight on top of reports from Edinburgh that described their fellow-countryman as 'despiteful out of measure, false and untrue as the devil', Cecil had to consider this letter from his English jailer which plainly told him that 'the Earl is not the man he is reported to be'.

Percy did things thoroughly; he told his brother the Earl of Northumberland, then at Court, to insist that Elizabeth should see his letter to Cecil. The immediate result was that Percy was allowed to give his prisoner the greater freedom he had asked for him; his friends in Scotland were allowed to come and visit him, and Johnnie Stewart told him that Lethington, again riding south to London, had been given special written instructions from Mary to arrange his freedom – news, however, that only encouraged Bothwell to express his fears of the tabby's claws.

He and Percy were summoned to London; they set off towards the end of March and had a delightful leisurely journey riding down through the Midlands, Bothwell exclaiming half in envy, half disgust at 'all these fat meadows; you English are too rich in dirt, it may make for a heavy purse, but it would choke me to ride all day without seeing a hill or hearing the sound of the sea.' Even the towns were flat: his eye pined for the jagged outrageous outline of Edinburgh and Stirling.

Percy was amused. Not all the anxiety of this doubtful mission in an enemy country, on top of a year of hostile plotting and imprisonment in his own, could dash James Hepburn's spirits or subdue the vigour of his interest in everything he saw. He refused to be downed even when, at the end of the journey, they received orders that his destination was the Tower of London.

'Hell and the Tower for good company!' he said with a wry grin. 'Your Queen pays me the compliment of sending me to her former lodging and her mother's. Pray heaven I don't come out of it by the same way as pretty Boleyn!'

The Earl of Northumberland was disgusted with the failure of his efforts on his former enemy's behalf.

'But we'll get you out in no time, trust the Percies for that!' he exclaimed in the exuberant fashion which made him seem so much younger than the still, short figure of his younger brother. 'These new gentry at Court, these sons of the butchers and cheesemongers that King Harry delighted to honour, haven't got it entirely their own way yet. I'm to be made Knight of the Garter – think of that for a man who's had never a draper in the family! And France is working for you too; Philibert Du Croc has orders from the Guises to see to your just treatment – pity the Guise himself is dead. What, did you hear nothing of it on the way here? Shot by a Huguenot lad – one Poltrot, Poltroon I call him – at a range of nine or ten yards – three bullets notched with brimstone and spittle; they say he suffered tortures before the surgeons let him die.'

The Guise murdered! Bothwell was staggered by this piece of news; Sir Henry too, though he had never known him personally, was horrified: 'the best general in all Christendom, and of the greatest courage, courtesy, liberality —'

'Aye, it's the lion that's slaughtered; the wolves howl on,' said his brother. 'Assassination is a dirty way of running politics. It'll lead to no good.'

His rosy eupeptic face, blue-eyed and fair-haired like a child's, shook itself solemnly over the excellent dinner he had provided for his guest in Northumberland House, overlooking the Thames.

'And war too is changing,' he said. 'Your Queen's grandfather lost more than his army when he fell at Flodden. It wasn't just the defeat of his country, it was the defeat of chivalry. Bungled, that battle was. Sheer lunacy, not to understand that the one thing in war is to defeat the enemy!'

'If so,' said Bothwell, 'then treachery and savagery of every kind is to be excused – and is coming to be so excused. James IV was no fool, though he carried the logic of chivalry to its furthest extent. But your logic, carried to its full extent, would mean the end of mankind.'

'What's to be done? You're a modern soldier like myself. In these days of guns we can't still play the knight errant.'

'What have guns to do with it?' interpolated Sir Henry, as quietly as if he did not intend to be heard.

But Bothwell heard and said, 'They have this to do with it – that war is getting more destructive, at the same time as men have lost all restraint of the rule of chivalry, all the old standards of keeping faith to each other, friend and foe. All that our precious new discoveries have brought us is the power to be devils rather than savages!'

Northumberland brought his fist down on the table with a thump that made the glasses ring. 'God's blood, young fellow, must you cut the throat of the whole world? If what you prophesy is true, I'd rather drink myself to death than live to see it.'

But it was Henry Percy, speaking at last, who gave the final word that evening.

'Chivalry was thought of, and made a part of man's nature, centuries before guns were invented. They are an accident of his brain, but chivalry is a part of his soul. He cannot lose that. So chivalry will win in the end, even over guns.'

*　　　*　　　*

The Percies kept faith. In two months Bothwell was released from the Tower, though on parole not to leave the country, and Randolph merrily warned Cecil to 'take heed how you lodge such a guest', begging him not to send the Earl to Dover Castle lest he should seduce Randolph's mother and sister there, not to mention several nieces.

It was high summer. London was appallingly hot and stuffy; plague was rife and people were dying so fast in the poorer parts that they could scarcely get buried before they rotted. The city stank of corruption – and in every sense, for men were saying that bread made of bad corn was spreading the disease; threats of revolution were muttered in the stifling and sulphurous air that hung like a pall over what seemed a doomed city.

Now again Bothwell owed his release to the Percy. Sir Henry offered the hospitality of his huge and ancient Castle of Norham on the Border, which Bothwell had blamed d'Oysel for neglecting to burn on the occasion of the Haltwellsweir raid. He was not so sorry now for that omission, as he breathed the fresh northern air again, and hawked and hunted with jolly Jack Musgrave, Sir Henry's deputy at Norham while he was down south.

The two young men became fast friends as they dined together on the salted eels and salmon, and pipes of malvoisie from the huge vats in the cellars. They found still better sport than hunting, for Musgrave had a quarrel with the Berwick officers; they marched to confiscate his goods, and found the Castle held against them, not only by their compatriot, but by the Scots Earl that they had seized in his bed in Rively's vault last January, and now spoiling for a fight with them. Their assault failed; it was answered by a mysterious party of armed men who made a sudden flying attack on the city one night with squibs and fireballs, and the fiery influence of Musgrave's guest was suspected. An order was sent for Bothwell to be transferred to Alnwick and the more sober charge of Sir John Forster.

Jack Musgrave was furious at losing his comrade. In his gratitude for the good times they had had together, he suggested that his men should ride with slack rein when they escorted Bothwell to Alnwick. With a wink and a tug at his scrubby straw-coloured moustache that gave a frost-bitten look to his red weather-beaten face, he said, 'Then a quick glance over your left shoulder as you near the ford, and away with you across Tweed into the Cheviots. You've friends enough in Scotland to shelter you till you get a boat for France.'

'And break the faith of a Borderer?' demanded Bothwell furiously. 'You can tempt your own men to march-treason if you will, but I'll thank you not to think a Scot is likely to break parole.'

It was their only quarrel, and they made it up in a rollicking debauch of malvoisie the night before Bothwell left his charge for that of Sir John Forster, English Warden of the Middle Marches and Deputy Governor of Berwick, a splendid square rock of a man – and rocklike he stood, for he held the latter post for thirty-seven years.

Here too Bothwell made a real friend in his custodian. His horse-sense came in handy, and he amused himself choosing English geldings for sale in Scotland. They spent Christmas and New Year together with a fair amount of festivity, but it was saddened for Bothwell by news of the sudden death of his young brother-in-law, Johnnie Stewart.

Memories of Johnnie laughing, dancing, singing, on New Year's Eve a year ago at Coldinghame, and two years ago at Crichton at his wedding, crowded in unbearably on his mind. Jan wrote a pathetic bewildered little letter, and Mary, she said, seemed almost as unhappy as herself. She had cried so bitterly; more even than for the Duc de Guise, whose murder had cast her down so terribly; she had sobbed out that God always took from her the people she loved best. She had given Jan a black knitted dress and a cape of squirrel fur. The baby Francis was well, but not in the least like Johnnie; he grew darker and more like a goblin every day.

'Aye, she's crying her heart out now but she'll forget him and marry someone else in a year or two,' so Bothwell told himself rather grimly. Woman's love was of small account; he had had very literal token of that this last summer in his extreme poverty in London, when no Scots merchant there considered his securities sufficient to lend him any money, since all his lands were mortgaged, the command of Hermitage had been given to the head of the Elliots, and Haddington Abbey to Lethington. And at that moment, in his wretched lodging, arrived 'a Portugal piece for a token' from Anna Throndsen in her home in the far North, as if to mock his miserable fortunes.

He had less reason to complain of his Queen than of his mistress, for she now wrote personally yet again to her 'Dearest sister and cousin,' and urged her to grant the Scots Earl liberty to leave England for anywhere abroad where he might wish to go. And she contrived that Lethington and Randolph should write as well, their pens, under her control, being surer weapons than their spoken words. Her determined influence on Bothwell's behalf, and the letters that passed between her and Alnwick, gave rise to wild reports of secret rendezvous between them, and plots for her to recall him to Scotland for a Catholic revival.

He was now said to be 'a great Papist', and 'the Queen thinks to have Bothwell ready to shake out of her pocket against us Protestants. The Mass shall up. Bothwell shall follow with power to put all into execution, and then shall Knox and his preaching be pulled by the ears.' Bothwell would have been astonished to hear it; all his hopes were now fastened on becoming Captain of the Scottish Archers in France, or, to give it its alternative title, of the Bodyguard of the Virgin Mary.

'And they're doing what they can to make it live up to its name,' he chuckled to Henry Percy when at last he rode to Tynemouth again, this time as his guest, early in the March of 1564, on his way south once more to try his luck with Elizabeth. 'They've brought in new regulations that no Archer is to lie on the floor beside the French maids of honour – only sit – and then only if he is married! As I've been twice married by report, with both wives living, I should have special privileges.'

It was good to be again with Percy, telling him all that had happened to him since the Tower gates had swung on him a year ago; of the plague in London and the fireballs at Berwick and the horse-dealing at Alnwick, of the fun he had had with 'that mad demi-lance Cumberland Borderer', Jack Musgrave, and how Sir John Forster had the great town bell of Carlisle ringing within half an hour of getting word that the rude Johnstones were riding into Cumberland.

For the past two years he had been a prisoner or fugitive or exile; they had not betrayed him into the final corruption of self-pity; his vitality was still taut and ringing; but they had made him harder and more cynical, and this Sir Henry noticed particularly when he spoke of his young Queen. He did not blame her that the reward of a loyalty unusual among his fellows had been ruin and exile, but he resented it, and it showed subtly in his tone about her.

He could not see what it was that drove men mad about her. That young fool Châtelard had lost his head over her all too literally; he had been caught hiding in her bedroom and dismissed with a severe warning, 'but like all these French fops he thought himself irresistible, and a few nights later there he was again, and nearer the mark! I've asked when she'd ever have a

210

man in her bed to teach her what the strange beast is like, but under the bed is the nearest she's got to it, and a royal rage is all it taught her. She called to James to come and kill him, and snatched at his sword to do it herself, since he would not – wish I'd seen her!' And his laugh, though admiring, was not pleasant.

'Her brother was probably right,' said Percy; 'it would have caused great scandal for him to kill a man in her bedroom.'

'It caused every bit as much to have him prancing on the scaffold sighing "Oh cruel fair!" and reminding the populace that he was a nephew of the Chevalier Bayard and like him *"sans peur"* though not *"sans reproche"*. I'll swear he enjoyed that last hour as much as any in his life. Knox made good profit from it, of course; said his head was cut off so that it shouldn't tell the secrets of his Queen. What do you think of it all?' he asked, suddenly swinging round in the midst of his restless prowl up and down the room, and confronting the steadfast gaze of his host.

'I think,' said Sir Henry gravely, 'that for a girl just twenty-one and of a rare charm, your Queen is very unhappy in having neither parents nor any disinterested friends and advisers. It will be a miracle if she escapes disaster.'

Bothwell somehow felt rather ashamed of himself, and anxious to show that he agreed. He said, 'Maybe that's the reason she's made this extraordinary appointment lately – taken that Italian fellow, a musician and a poet, not a gentleman, for her private secretary. Her last showed himself too familiar they say, and was discharged – the same old story, she smiled and so he pranced – and so now she feels it safer to take a low-born fellow like David Rizzio.'

'Safer in one respect certainly,' said Percy, 'since he is a foreigner with no particular axe to grind in her country. But from what I have seen of your nobles, I should say that that appointment was full of danger.'

He picked up his clarinet and began to play again, the notes falling clear and round and perfect as drops of water, and with them fell a strange quiet on the whirlpool of hopes and fears, angers and jealousies and suspicions in the young man's restless mind. Could there ever be any harmony in the jangled confusion of his or anyone else's affairs? Percy seemed to find it; was it in his music, his liking for old-fashioned poets, such as Chaucer, his refusal to be discouraged by the contorted actions

211

of others? Most men wanted it; even Knox sought it, furiously, desperately, never seeing how one half of him destroyed what the other half intended.

And suddenly, as so often in these last three months, he was stabbed with a vision of Johnnie's brief glancing happiness, leaping across the crowded scene of his life in one gay shout of song, and now of Jan left crying over the cradle of her 'goblin baby', in a black knitted frock and squirrel cape, when only a day or two ago it seemed she had come riding towards him in his old clothes, the autumn sunlight on her face, a creature so wild and childishly ignorant that she did not even know she was in love with her young lover.

*   *   *

Next day he rode south once more on his quest for an interview with Queen Elizabeth, his cause fortified not only by the letters of his Queen and her Ministers, but by those of his recent hosts. Sir John Forster, though proudly stating that 'we that inhabit Northumberland are not acquainted with any learned or rare phrases', had added his praise of his guest to Percy's assurance that Bothwell's behaviour 'has been both courteous and honourable', and, he emphasized, *'keeping his promise'*. He had heard from Jack Musgrave, not Bothwell, how that young man had 'Kept trust'.

His journey south a year ago had ended in the Tower. This journey ended in nothing. For six months he kicked his heels in or near London, getting tantalizing glimpses of Elizabeth hunting, riding through the city, dancing, flirting, a stiff figure blazing with jewels, set about with wired ruffs and stuffed out skirts like the spread tail of a peacock. Sometimes he was near enough to catch the high vibrant tones of her voice, but he never got the interview he asked for until nearly the middle of September.

Then, at a little place some miles north of London called Harrow-on-the-Hill, he waited to see her, in company with a farmer who wished to obtain the royal leave to build a school on his land there. He had been applying for this leave for years, but the Queen had a passion for keeping people in suspense – and well Bothwell knew it too after these eighteen months!

At last he knelt before her and kissed her hand, a hand as beautiful as that of his own Queen, but older, thinner, harder, longer, so long that it looked dangerous; those white fingers flashing with rings in the sunlight would be claw-like in age, nor would they ever let go of anything or anyone that had fallen into their power. The sinister impression left him at the sound of her hearty voice, one that would carry across the hunting-field as well as any man's, and now ringing with amusement.

'Is this the naughty fellow that my sister of Scotland was so anxious to have returned to her for punishment? He doesn't look as though he would be much afraid. Yet she has shown how severe she can be to a rash young man.'

Châtelard's unlucky attempt on Mary's virtue was plainly of great interest to her, for she referred to it again while com-missioning Bothwell to take letters to her Ambassador in France. But he did not by any means get the popular impression of a frivolous young woman 'entirely given over to love, hunt-ing, hawking and dancing, consuming day and night with trifles'.

The tiny Tudor mouth had tightened. Those quick bright eyes were as wary as when he had had his first glimpse of her years ago as a powerless girl beset with enemies and dangers; they were also of a remarkable steadiness. For all their alert apprehension it would be very difficult to frighten her or to put her off her course; it would be still more difficult to discover what that course really was. He thought that the astute Leth-ington had for once shown a rather foolish optimism when he had laughed at her timid and vacillating nature, and declared that he would soon 'make her sit upon her tail and whine like a whipped hound'.

For once he found himself considering these points before those of her person, which he then admitted, but dispassion-ately, to be handsome.

*　　*　　*

So now he was free, and not as a fugitive, for the first time for two and a half years. He went to France; was made Captain of the Scottish Archers; six months later, in the March of 1565, he suddenly appeared in Scotland, to the astonished consterna-tion of his friends and foes alike. What could have possessed him to throw away his hard-won security and his new honours to make this reckless dash home into the midst of a host of enemies agog to clap him into prison?

The Cardinal de Lorraine had summoned him in February to ask his opinion on some disturbing rumours he had had con-cerning his niece. Young Lord Henry Darnley, of Catholic up-bringing, had just been permitted by Elizabeth to cross the Border into Scotland. His busily intriguing mother, Countess

Meg, was the daughter of Henry VIII's sister, Margaret Tudor, by her second marriage with Lord Angus, and was therefore Elizabeth's first cousin. She had been imprisoned in the Tower of London, but a year ago Elizabeth had released her, summoned the whole family to the English Court and made a great deal of them, especially the boy Darnley, who was officially recognized everywhere as first Prince of the blood. It was said that she had secretly acknowledged him as her heir. His father, the Earl of Lennox, had been exiled from his Scottish estates for his treachery to Mary's mother, and was now restored to them by Elizabeth's special request to Mary, which she had immediately after revoked in her usual way; but Mary had coolly obeyed the first request and not the second or third.

'And now here's that great chick been sent crowing cock-a-hoop after the old rooster!' The Cardinal had no opinion of young Darnley, a spoilt mother's darling, reared on an exaggerated sense of his importance as heir, though remotely, to the English and Scots Crowns. He was tall, fair and good-looking in 'a vacant English way', the Cardinal said unkindly, a jolly youth, mad on pleasure, good at games, a keen horseman and the women all liked him. Elizabeth had done so, or had seemed to, though that might be part of her game – 'and God knows what that really is'. What disturbed him was that Mary had seemed to take to him when she welcomed him at Wemyss Castle on the Firth of Forth.

The Cardinal was furious with his niece. Was the loveliest Princess of her day, and not merely Princess, for 'I have never seen her equal, either among high or low,' declared the connoisseur, to throw herself away on this insignificant lad? She had won the admiration, no, the adoration of her subjects; her beauty, birth and position had led the greatest Princes in Europe to woo her. 'Spain, France, Sweden, they are all on the cards. She might marry anyone.'

'But she hasn't – that's the trouble,' Bothwell answered bluntly. 'For four years she's had unseen lovers dangled before her, while all she's had to content her eyes have been dour Protestants, or ruffians like Ruthven – or myself! She's sick for someone of her own kind and upbringing – the Châtelard business showed that. There's no such easy prey as a virgin.'

The Cardinal could hardly boggle at such plain speaking, having invited it. He was beside himself with personal anxiety, for Mary's marriageable asset was the trump card in his suit; he was also fearful that she was in a mood to be rash enough to

214

marry Darnley, which would provoke Elizabeth. However much the two Queens might play at friendship, it was bound to come to a life-and-death struggle between them.

To Bothwell there came a sudden painful vision of Mary speaking to him with triumphant pleasure in that friendship; behind the memory of her eager face there now hovered the image of the thin hand that he had kissed at Harrow-on-the-Hill.

He sprang to his feet. 'I'll go back now, Your Highness, and find out what's afoot.'

The Cardinal was foolish enough for one moment to show his amazement, although this was exactly what he had been hoping to contrive. 'Is it safe enough?' he asked.

'I'll soon see!'

And he left Paris next day.

No sooner was the news out of his landing in Scotland than the Lord James ran to the Queen in a rage that showed his terror.

'Is it by your will or your advice that my enemy's back? He has sworn to be the death of me and of Lethington on his return. Scotland will not hold us both. Either he or I must leave it.'

Those delicate arched brows of his half-sister, so maddeningly like their father's, nearly reached her ash-gold hair. 'In that case, dear James,' – but no, she must not say it, whatever happened she must not drive him into open enmity just now. Tonight there was to be a banquet and ball in honour of their distinguished guest, Lord Darnley; things must go on smoothly for a few days, a few weeks – was it so much to ask, even in Scotland?

'Lord Bothwell has always done me good service. I cannot hate him as you do.'

'He has never answered for his crimes.'

'How could he, since he was never given the trial he demanded?'

'Give it him now, then, and put him to the horn.'

Mary took up the plan of the tables at the banquet that evening, and asked his advice on a question of precedence.

He stormed at her; his bullying had of late grown much more open. 'You do not mind threats against my life, that's plain enough. But you shall hear what else he's said in France, against yourself. There is solid proof of it from Dandie Pringle.'

To his disgusted bewilderment she began to giggle. 'Oh your

Scottish names!' she gasped through her irrepressible laughter. 'Are they always those of little dogs?'

She scored as usual, but as usual James won.

A few weeks later Bothwell suddenly arrived at his mother's house at Morham.

'The hunt is up,' he told that impassive lady. 'I'll be put to the horn in a few days now.'

Along with 'thieves, foreigners and wolves' he was to be, with three blasts of the horn, proclaimed outlaw and at the mercy of any citizen who could kill or capture him, if he did not give himself up on the 2nd of May to justice in the Edinburgh Tolbooth, from whichever of his houses he was now occupying – Crichton, Hailes, Morham, Haddington, Duns, Lauder, Selkirk, Hawick, Hermitage or Jedburgh.

He had answered the summons submissively, promising to appear, but in the meantime he had taken the precaution of turning out the Elliot who had supplanted him at Hermitage, had barricaded its gates and gathered round him in that fortress a stout company of dalesmen and moss-troopers. But a siege would land him nowhere, and he believed in the Bruce's maxim for warfare, that the strongest walls were the woods and caves in the hillside.

One of his men, Gabriel Sempill, came galloping back from Edinburgh late one night at a panic-stricken pace and staggered exhausted into the great hall, where Bothwell was eating supper, to warn him that the Lord James with a great company of horsemen and all the clans of Scott and Kerr, the Hepburns' hereditary foes on the Border, were marching upon Hermitage. Bothwell gave the order to horse, and his men took to the hill for that night.

The march on Hermitage proved a false alarm, but it had been prompted by facts. The Lord James was collecting a mighty force of six thousand armed men to support his charges against Bothwell at the trial; and his brother-in-law the Earl of Argyll was Lord Justice. Against such strong advocates for the prosecution Bothwell felt absence his best argument.

'Let them convict me of treason! I'll set my sail by the dog-star and be off again before they catch me.'

'What are the charges?' asked his mother coolly.

'The old one, of "treasonable attempt against the Queen's noble person", revealed by Lord Arran. And some brand-new ones piping hot from Dandie Pringle of *lèse-majesté*. No, Willie, you young rascal, I'll not ride you on my boot again. Off

216

with you and play with the other puppies!' He rolled the child over with his foot, and Willie shouted in delight and gnawed his boot in imitation of the hound puppies sprawling with him on the hearth.

'Lèse-majesté?' demanded his mother. 'How did Dandie Pringle get that? I thought he had left your service.'

'And is now servant to James Murray of Purdovis – though I never knew that, and thought Purdovis my friend, had him to dinner at my lodging in Paris, filled him up with plenty of good wine – filled myself too, I suppose, if I ever said the half of what he is now reporting, backed up by Pringle, who must have been couched at the keyhole.'

'What did you, or they, say?'

'That the two Queens of Scotland and England rolled together would not make one honest woman. That's true enough, I remember saying it, and God's blood! haven't I had reason! Kicked out like a dog from Scotland, twice over, after all I've done — '

'Your last words are more dangerous to you than any of lèse-majesté,' said his mother quietly. 'Once a man – or woman – begins to count up "all I've done", they might as well hang themselves.'

He looked at her dark still face, and remembered he had once seen her crying when his father had divorced her so that he might be free to marry the Regent. That must have been the only time she had counted up all she had done for her husband and two young children.

He said hurriedly, 'You're right. I was a fool. But I can't believe I was such a fool as to call the Queen the Cardinal's whore, however drunk I was.'

'Did you ever think it?'

'Lord no, not really. They were together when I saw her first, walking down a street in Paris, and a very pretty pair they made, and he knew it.'

'You were jealous.'

He stared at her astonished, it sounded so ridiculous. Could she be right? She generally was.

'As a matter of fact, she's had too little experience, not too much. She's proving that fast enough now, running mad after her spring fancy, a conceited lad with not a hair on his baby face.'

For it was common property that Mary was head over heels in love with Darnley and did not care who knew it. She was dancing or hunting with him all the time, or singing or playing the lute, for he was an accomplished lad, and Meg Lennox, his mother, had brought him up with an eye to this very business. Mary was throwing her bonnet over the windmill with a vengeance, playing outrageous pranks too, dressing up with her Maries as burghers' wives, and teasing and coaxing the passers-by for contributions to a banquet; this she did in the streets of Edinburgh in broad daylight, not heeding who recognized her.

And now that Darnley had fallen sick of the measles, as if to show what a child he was, Mary was nursing him so devotedly that she sat up with him all night when his fever was high, to the great scandal of Queen Elizabeth, who hoped that the report would be contradicted 'for her dear sister's own sake'.

Bothwell, who had seen her tenderness with the sick boy, King François, guessed that her nursing of Darnley, even through that unprepossessing illness, was probably the very thing to convince Mary of her love for him.

Elizabeth had taken alarm; she was performing one of her famous right-about turns and demanding his return to England. But opposition only inflamed Mary's high spirits into angry resolve to take her own way. James had already opposed the match, and she had had her first open quarrel with him, in a blaze of white-hot rage on her part which ended in her sending dispatches to Lethington at the English Court, telling him to inform the Queen openly that she would follow her own choice in her marriage, and nobody else's. To tell Elizabeth to mind her own business must have given her as much satisfaction as to lose her temper with James after keeping it for nearly four years, Bothwell remarked with a chuckle to his mother.

Her gossip was not all of royalty; some was from their own town. Haddington folk were annoyed that their 'great little man', John Knox, having failed to bring off his marriage to the Duke of Châtelherault's eldest daughter, had fallen back on a fifteen-year-old girl, Margaret Stewart, daughter of Lord Ochiltree, and a distant cousin to the Queen. Here was a wedding of January and May with a vengeance; it had done him great discredit, and Bothwell asked sardonically if the Prophet's powers had so failed him that he could not foretell his own horns. Haddington was supplying news all round. The new schoolmaster evidently thought Knox had not gone far enough in his contempt of the sacraments; he had just baptized a cat in the name of the Father, Son and Holy Ghost.

His time at Morham was necessarily short; it was the end of April and he must be well out of the country before the 2nd of May. He had achieved nothing by his dash to Scotland; he could not go near Edinburgh, so he had not even seen the Queen, and this preposterous report of his accusing her of incest had put her into a royal rage. She had sworn he 'should never again receive favours at her hands' — 'And much odds *that's* likely to make to me!' he snorted. 'All I've got by this jaunt is the loss of my Captaincy of the Archers.'

'You seem to have lost some of your shirts too,' remarked his mother. 'Where are those two I wove for you on my hand-loom?'

She was annoyed, for they had taken her longer than any; the linen thread was so fine it was all but impossible to keep it from breaking, and moreover she had embroidered the front of them with gold thread to match the small gold buttons, an heirloom from the Sinclair family.

'They were stolen, I suppose?'

'Aye, by Wat Murray, my head groom. I found it out just after – and a parcel of dirty work with it that I can't make head or tail of, except that there was a plot to murder me while I was in France, brewed by Lethington, they said, though I suspect the Bastard rather – not that Mother Tabbyskin would make any unnecessary effort to keep me alive. A compliment they should still so fear me, even in exile!'

'They will fear you as long as you are alive. You are the only man strong enough to serve the Queen against them, if she is ever strong enough to call on your service. What was the plot?'

She sat on the edge of the bed where she had been laying out his linen in neat piles, while he lounged against the window. He looked at the fields outside under a late light fall of snow which sparkled almost pink in the sun between the brilliant blue shadows. Crows swooped down on it and strutted here and there, pecking for food; the small scarlet figure of Willie came hopping and hallooing in among them, waving his arms round his head and shooing away the big black birds that rose flapping and cawing round him.

He said, 'It was when I took the hill with the Liddesdale men from Hermitage near a month ago that Wat seized the chance to steal the shirts and sell 'em to a travelling packman. I threw him into prison and swore to hang him. I was angry,' he added apologetically, fancying some disapproval in his mother's silence. 'He said he could tell of a plot against me if I'd promise

219

to let him off – so I did, and out came this tale of our Michael Wily commissioning the Laird of Pittencrieff, then in France, to bribe my servants to poison me. My barber had the stuff all ready mixed to give me, but at the last moment his heart failed him – so Wat said. Then later they had another shot and tiptoed upstairs one night to stab me, the six of them, while I was sitting reading in my room. But there again they stuck, on the third stair up, shivering and whispering, the dirty cowards, until at last they slunk away – and I of course never knew a thing about it. For they didn't try again.'

She looked at the alert forcible face, dark against the cold spring sunshine. She had told him to beware of the poison in a friendly cup, of the knife between his shoulder-blades, and it seemed he didn't even have to fear these, so powerful was the effect of this man on those weak criminals as he sat in his room alone and unaware, his back to the door, leaning forward over his book by the light of the lamp. So she saw him, very clearly, for an instant, and said, 'Was it your book of "One Hundred and Twenty Stories of Battle" that you were reading?'

He nodded, smiling. It was odd how she guessed things.

'And they all stayed with you after that?'

'All but Dandie Pringle, as you know, who left me and got this chance to poison the Queen's ears against me, as he hadn't the nerve to pour it into my mouth. The rest were there at Hermitage, and told a mass of contradictions when I questioned them on Wat's story. I threatened torture, had it applied, to begin with, but what truth can one get from a coward when he's shrieking from pain or fear? He's only wondering which answer will save him a turn of the rack. I got sick of the whole thing and let 'em all off. I've kept Paris in my service, since whatever part he played in it was from fear of the others – Wat admitted to threatening to cut his throat if he didn't join them. There's no doubt Wat was the ruling spirit.'

'Yet you let him off too?'

'Yes. Well, I'd promised to before he disclosed it. I've told you, I was sick of their whining lies, and I'd more important things to see to. And they of all men are the least likely to try that game on me again.'

The Highland woman looked rather strangely at the Hasty Hepburn who in a temper would hang his groom for stealing a couple of shirts, but whose rage cooled so quickly after discovering a plot of such concerted treachery.

She did not take after her son, as Bothwell noted four months later when he heard that Wat had been killed by one of his Sinclair cousins.

But by then he had still more important things to see to.

*   *   *

He sailed for France just before his trial at Edinburgh, where a Hepburn cousin, the Laird of Riccarton, pleaded that his personal absence should not be prejudicial to the Earl, 'since he has so potent an enemy as the Lord James, Earl of Moray'. But in spite of the legal arguments supplied by Lord James' six thousand armed supporters, the Earl of Argyll did not condemn Bothwell in his absence to be put to the horn. People said that this was due to the Queen, as hasty as any Hepburn in forgiveness as in anger; she still, they complained, wished well to that 'blasphemous and irreverent speaker'.

His speech grew a deal more blasphemous and irreverent as he kicked his heels in Paris, waiting for the Queen's summons that he was certain now would come, for the split between her and Lord James grew more and more open. A letter from her was actually sent at the beginning of July, but it never reached Bothwell, as the Laird of Riccarton, who bore it, was captured and detained by the English at Berwick. James was now in secret league with Elizabeth against the royal lovers, and sealed orders were out in both countries to detain the Earl, 'enemy to all honest men', should he make a second venture home.

Mary's second summons, by a more wary messenger, reached him at the end of August, and with it the news of all Scotland in arms. At last James was in open conflict against his half-sister and had raised an armed force, with the help of money and musketry from Elizabeth.

It was James, not Bothwell, whom Mary had 'put to the horn' – a piece of news that made Bothwell give such a yell of joy that Paris, now suffering a nervous and almost agonized devotion to his master, fled from the room in terror lest he had suddenly gone mad. But a following shout quickly recalled him.

'Pack my things, you rabbit! Summon the rest of my scoundrels. I leave Paris today.'

And he left – 'no man knows whither', reported the English spies in Paris. He moved so fast as to outwit as well as outride them: to Brussels, then to Antwerp, then Flushing; bought guns and powder in the Netherlands, and laid a red-herring trail that hoodwinked them into thinking he intended a landing in Ireland to help O'Neill's rebellion.

221

The English fleet were deployed to catch him as he sailed for Scotland with his munitions in two small pinnaces. Seven ships were not thought too many for the job. To make sure of the man so feared by the English Ministers, who a year ago had written him down as 'of no force now', four warships were sent to watch for him between Ireland and the west coast of Scotland, while two more waited for him off the east coast, and yet another pursued him under command of the great explorer, Anthony Jenkinson.

But the seamanship of the Lord High Admiral of Scotland proved a match for Elizabeth's famous sailor, and his couple of little boats sped too fast for the warship to catch up with them. They reached the mouth of Tweed, where, however, two other ships were waiting to blockade him. As Bothwell's pinnaces sailed up to Eyemouth, the wind fell dead just when they lay within range of the enemy guns, which started firing salvo after salvo, all wide of the mark; but the men began to panic, caught in that sudden awful calm on the hot blue sea, with the cannon-balls hissing and spluttering in the placid water all round them, and they helpless with their sails fallen limp and idle. Bothwell coolly ordered them to man the oars, and soon their light boats had run the blockade and were unloading in double-quick time at the harbour. In less than an hour he had got all his arms ashore, ordered horses, and was riding at the gallop towards Holyrood.

The tourelles of the long grey palace, and behind them the glowing curves of the hills sweeping up to Arthur's Seat, rose again before him, after nearly three years. Hot, tired, excited, his clothes dusty, sweating with the speed at which he had ridden in the baking mid-September sunshine, he came into the long gallery, heard the tinkling of music, and saw two figures. One of them, a tall fair young man, stood leaning over the back of the chair in which the other was sitting; but as Bothwell tramped towards them in his riding-boots she uprose in a sudden rush of silken skirts like the uprising of a fountain; she ran towards him with both hands outstretched.

He knelt to kiss them, looked up, and fell in love.

Part III

LOVERS' MEETING

CHAPTER ONE

HE HAD not seen her for over two and a half years, and by
now they had both changed.

As he stood there looking down on her so strangely and in-
tently, she felt an odd tremor, a new fear of this man who
seemed so much older and more powerful than she remembered
him, perhaps more sinister. She had counted so certainly on his
'ruffianly fidelity' (Who had said that of him?), but those who
invoked the devil to their aid had to pay a price – and there was
devil as well as Galliard now in this man; that earlier gaiety was
still fiercer, more savage and cynical, and deeper – was it deeper
in sin as well as in his dearly bought knowledge of the world, so
much of it bought from her?

All this she saw in that first instant, and never knew it till
long after.

And he, looking down on her, saw that gone was the douce
young girl who bent over her embroidery in the Council
chamber and was so gentle and obedient to her bastard brother.
Now, when still three months short of twenty-three, she was a
woman whose senses as well as affections had at last been
roused, and stimulated by rage with her enemies. 'The foundation of this marriage was despite and anger,' said the English
statesmen, but bodily passion had been added to her rapturous
defiance of the distant Queen and the ever-present brother who
had hemmed her in and hectored her ever since she had come to
her kingdom.

She was now free, a glorious creature, all fire and fierce spirit,
fit to mate even with a Borderer, in the opinion of one of them.

She had acted as boldly and promptly in the face of rebellion
as he could wish, and was as eager to tell him of it as he to
assure her that he had safely brought her all the munitions 'that
credit could buy', and an offer from his old friend d'Oysel of
two thousand men if needed.

'But they won't be needed,' she cried. 'I've my own men here,
my own countrymen; even this wicked old town of Edinburgh
with all its tottering houses leering down on me have sided with

223

me against James. And that all happened only a fortnight ago – oh, there is so much to tell you.'

She could hardly bear to let him go to wash and change his dusty clothes before supping with them, so she insisted; and the youth beside her looked rather sulky about it, but was very gracious and jolly later as he welcomed him at the little table ('Had a drink or two in the meantime,' Bothwell decided, noting his heightened colour and greater flow of speech).

They sat in a small room where the life-size figures of huntsmen and stags on the tapestries wavered and shook with an odd appearance of coming to life every time the pages brushed against them with their heavy gold dishes, coming from the darkness of the narrow spiral stone stairway into the dazzle of reflected light from the sunset. It made that tiny room glow as though it were inside a hollow jewel; it struck red sparks on the dish of plain beaten silver that held dark grapes and polished red apples and green figs in the middle of the oval French table; it threw red shadows from the wine-glasses like long pools of blood on the white cloth; it winked and glittered on the emeralds and diamonds that studded the agate hilt of the dagger in Darnley's belt. Bothwell had seen that dagger before, in Mary's hand when she had dubbed him Lord of Misrule at Jan's wedding; it was a present to her father from François I, 'but nothing's too fine for her to hand over to him', he thought.

Never had he seen her eyes so wide-open or so brilliant; gone was all their veiled, subdued look, the lazy eyes of a girl who loved to lie in bed all day. She was awake now and sparkling with an energy that was no mere girlish excitement, but concentrated on her purpose with a force and intensity unusual he thought in a woman.

She had defied everyone, from Mr Knox to the Pope himself, for she had not waited to get his Dispensation for marriage between cousins before she married Darnley. On the other hand, she had dared to celebrate Easter quite openly this year, and to object when the priest was tied to the market cross and, as Knox jocosely proclaimed, 'the boys served him with his Easter eggs', pelting him for hours until he was insensible.

She had outwitted James, who had opposed the marriage because he feared that Darnley 'would do little to forward the cause of Christ'. In these pious interests he had planned to kidnap both the lovers at Loch Leven and hand them over to England. Mary heard of it, coolly made no change of plan, but got up extra early that morning and galloped with her company past Loch Leven while James was still in bed.

'I must have had more kidnapping attempts against me than any woman in Europe, but you Scots are such bunglers, you never succeed.'

'Perhaps we've not yet had the right incentive,' remarked her guest, but refused to explain himself.

That attempt, known as the Raid of Beith, had forced James' hand into open rebellion. He calculated, with some reason on the face of it, that he had as good a chance to raise the country now in the name of religion against the Queen as he had had when he raised it against her mother the Regent. So he marched into Edinburgh with an armed force at the end of August, when the young couple had had just a month's peaceful honeymoon; preached the glory of God and offered the people good pay to defend it. But to throw rotten eggs at a tied-up priest was one thing; it was another to take up arms against the young Queen whom they had enjoyed having in their midst for four years. They heard his exhortations in icy silence, and then frankly begged him and his men to leave the city. The Castle guns, opening fire on him, gave point to the appeal; also the news that Mary with her hastily improvised army was advancing on the town. James fled from Edinburgh in the middle of the night, as once before he had been forced to do. 'This is the day of my cross and persecution,' he announced.

Knox also made himself scarce, with his accustomed dignity. 'Although I have appeared to play the faint-hearted and feeble soldier,' he wrote from Kyle, where he had established himself and family, 'the cause I remit to God.' This was perhaps a fair way of shelving his responsibility, since he had been charged with praying publicly for the rebels (and given the excellent answer that it was lawful to pray for all men); also for the most remarkable addition to his wedding sermons.

The new young King, though a Catholic, had thought it well to try and propitiate Knox by attending his sermon at St Giles' in a throne specially built for the purpose, and the preacher, by his own account, 'took occasion to speak of the government of wicked Princes, who for the sins of the people were sent as tyrants and scourges to plague them', the wicked Princes being specified as 'boys and women'. Other words which, he complained, appeared bitter in the King's ears, were that 'God justly punished Ahab because he would not take order with that harlot Jezebel'.

The sermon had lasted an hour and a half longer than the time appointed, and the young King was so late for dinner that he refused angrily to eat it at all, but went straight to his hawking. The Council punished Knox for his attack on the Royal Family by desiring him to abstain from preaching for a fortnight, and the preacher was publishing his sermon to show 'upon how small occasions great offence is now conceived'. But on hearing that Darnley was advancing with the Queen's army, absence struck him as the better defence.

Yet he could admire the spirit of his enemy, 'Mischievous Mary'. She rode at the head of her troops in more danger from storm and flood than from her foes, head-on against the raging wind and rain; she braved a torrent that had turned suddenly from a brook into a roaring river; several of her horsemen were drowned and many utterly exhausted, 'Yet,' declared Knox, 'the Queen's courage increased man-like so much that she was ever with the foremost.'

She told Bothwell now of that adventure with pride and laughter – if he'd been there he'd have called her a good moss-trooper – 'and better than some, who were shouting "The water winna ride, we'll all be drowned." But we swam it, horse and man, and Queen too!' Drenched to the skin all over they were when they arrived at Callendar that night, and her hair such a tangled dripping coil she thought it would have to be cut.

'Has that wicked old magician the power to raise tempests against me, and turn little streams into murderous torrents? – and what do I care if he has? He's not been able to turn the hearts of my people. We rode into Edinburgh to be greeted rapturously as King and Queen – that was worth a wetting. And for the first time since I came home, I *was* Queen! Oh, I must show you! Wait! Look!'

She sprang from the table and ran into the next room, returning with two scrolls – she could not wait for a servant to find them, she said in answer to Darnley's annoyed question. They were copies of her Proclamations to her people – one at her wedding, the other at her triumphant entry into her capital. She spread them on the table, pointing out to him the sentences of which she was most proud.

'Neither my conscience nor yours ought to be forced. You have entire freedom of religion – pray allow me the same privilege.'

They had been signed by her the week before, 'in the *first* and twenty-third year of our reign', to mark that for the first time she would indeed rule, instead of allowing even her former privileges to be taken away from her. Bothwell could not help smiling as he read her indignant statement that 'when We ourselves were of less age, and at our first returning into this our Realm, We had free choice of our Council, and now when We are at our full maturity, shall We be brought back to the state of pupils and be put under tutory?'

James' true intention in his rebellion was nothing but his own rule; *this* is the "quarrel of Religion" they made you believe they had in hand; for which they would have you hazard your lands, lives and goods as rebels against your natural Prince. To speak plainly, they would be kings themselves.'

'Plain as a pikestaff,' was Bothwell's comment, 'though I never knew before that the "s" at the end of the name showed James to be a plural noun.'

'Oh, that was Davie's doing. He wouldn't let me mention him by name, so he had to be "They" throughout. Don't you like my last sentence?'

This was a reminder to her people that 'under our wings you have enjoyed the possession of your goods and lived at liberty of your conscience', and should continue to do so. So she saw herself in her full maturity of twenty-two and three-quarter years as a mother-bird to the dour Edinburgh citizens! Well, she would certainly have to play that role with that great cock-chick beside her for some time yet, if she were ever to train him to anything more useful than crowing and flapping his wings. Harry, she called him, and when he got rumbustious, 'Bluff King Hal', but there was an implied compliment in her teasing, since it was a reminder not only of his new royal title but of his mother's Tudor blood that made him an heir to the English Crown.

He too was eager to show off about their adventures, though Bothwell could not see that he had done anything very much in them beyond annoying an unnecessary number of people. Of this he boasted with a boyish glee that was rather engaging – 'I stirred 'em up a bit, there's no doubt of that. *I* showed I wasn't going to stand any nonsense – told the Great Bastard to his face that he owned too much land; that was before all the trouble began.'

'It began soon after, I should imagine,' remarked Bothwell. Mary was quick to put out a sheltering wing.

'It was Rob's fault. He showed the King a map of Scotland

with all James' possessions coloured red, so that it was startled out of him.'

It sounded as though something of Johnnie Stewart's impish spirit had descended on his brother Robert.

Darnley had helped drive old Châtelherault into the opposite camp by threatening to get up from his bed to break his bald pate for him. Once again Mary contrived to let drop that this was when Darnley was feverish with measles. She would have a busy time of it covering up his tracks. Bothwell meanly wanted to see how she would explain Darnley's behaviour in drawing his dagger on the Justice-Clerk, his own adherent, who had brought him disappointing news. Probably the real excuse would have been drink, for he was drinking fairly heavily now and as a matter of course. He tried to make Bothwell match him glass for glass, but though he had a head far stronger than the boy's he refused to follow his lead.

'I have had occasion to doubt what I have said in drink.' He looked at the Queen as he spoke; it was an odd apology for *lèse-majesté*, but he thought that she accepted it.

He listened to the eager boasting of these two children; they had done their job remarkably well so far, or rather she had. The vigour and promptness of her actions, the clear sense and sincerity of her proclamations, had at the very outset utterly disconcerted her powerful opponents. It was plain that James, for all that he was the leader of the popular – and profitable – Protestant party, did not hold the affections of the people as she had come to do.

That hold would strengthen – 'if only young Master Cock-a-hoop doesn't spoil it all'. But he was not quite twenty, and his head turned by his good fortune and adoring mother, and now it seemed an adoring wife. He might learn sense in time, and even without much of that quality he was a good showpiece, with his head carried high and his bold, boyishly insolent stare and his knowing talk of sports and horses and wines and the haughty shyness collapsing suddenly into a loud jolly laugh. Vain as a peacock, of course, but people were often taken at their own valuation, as he had been taken by Mary. Only why in God's name had she again got to take a boy younger than herself? There was plenty of time for him to grow up, but —

She of course was laying all her triumph as a tribute at his feet. That was just what she would do in her generosity. 'After four years he's opened my cage and set me free at last,' she said, and flapped her arms like wings 'to see if it's really true.' It was her marriage had done this, since it had driven James into open revolt. It should also assure her of the English succession, and of the support of the Catholic powers. The Pope had quite overlooked her hasty dispensing with his Dispensation and had written his warm approval and congratulations; so had Philip of Spain: they had even sent some money to help her in the face of her subjects' rebellion, and promises of more. It was little Davie who had worked all that.

Who was Davie? Why, David Rizzio, of course. Davie should have been there at supper with them, but he was working so hard that he would not join them till later. 'We owe everything to Davie,' she said; her hand rested a moment on the young man's beside her, and he caught at it.

'I had wit enough to woo the prettiest girl in Europe without Master Davie to show me how,' he cried.

Bothwell had heard that her secretary Rizzio had helped to work the affair more than anyone: but his look showed his surprise that the Queen should have asked him to supper – a singer. She answered it indignantly. Davie was their friend, and the best they had in Scotland. She had found she could trust him as she could not trust her Secretary of State, Lethington ('And that's no news to me,' muttered Bothwell), and then when Darnley came they had made instant friends, Darnley staying at his lodgings, sleeping in his bed and playing tennis with him, and Davie had promised him to help him and had kept his word.

Bothwell was amused to see that Darnley did not like these reminders; 'they don't fit in with his picture of himself as a haughty young English nobleman – he doesn't like to be beholden to an Italian singer for his lady's favour'.

He expected to dislike Rizzio himself; it was intolerable that this beggar on horseback, possibly a Popish spy, should rise to such power.

But when the little man appeared in the dark doorway of their glowing room with the suddenness of a brightly painted jack-in-the-box in his over-gorgeous clothes sparkling with too many jewels, and his broad ugly face, all smiles, and brilliant black eyes beaming up at them, an enormous bouquet of deep red roses in his hand 'for the Rose of all roses', chattering in bad English and good French indiscriminately and equally fluently, joking, grinning, greeting the strange Scots lord with instant trustful friendliness as a friend of the young couple to whom he was obviously devoted – then Bothwell found to his great surprise that he did not dislike him at all.

He was so short as to be almost a dwarf, his shoulders were hunched, his head was big and his face pitted from the small-pox; but his misshapen ugliness had no effect on his spirit, he was a really merry fellow and his eyes sparkled with intelligence. He was delighted with himself, the position he had won, the rich clothes he wore, the services he had done his adored mistress and the splendid young Prince he had befriended and helped to marry to her, and now with this new arrival of the Queen's strongest man of action, a fine soldier and man of the frontiers, who would set her safely and surely on the throne that she had only occupied till now as a stalking-horse for her half-brother.

'There is only one thing to be done with that one,' he said of James, and drew his hand across his throat with a sharp click, then laughed up into Mary's face with the daring impudence of a child who has said something that the grown-ups may scold but will secretly like. The astonishing mixture of simplicity and subtlety was one that Bothwell had met before in those of his nation, but he saw that it baffled the English youth completely.

Darnley had seen Rizzio managing Mary's foreign diplomacy, conducting her correspondence with the Pope and Philip of Spain, wary, cunning, sharp as a needle, and quite unscrupulous in his determination to get his dear mistress what she wanted by any means, boasting of them to Darnley to show how clever were his hints and lies and promises. He was greedy too of jewels and gifts and the fine clothes that only emphasized how unaccustomed he was to wear them; he took all he could get, chuckling with unabashed pleasure and calling it his booty. 'I am as gay with trinkets as one of your Border wives after a raid!'

So that the English lad could not believe in the other side of the picture; the upstart, greedy, cunning adventurer, of the race that had become a byword for guile and treachery, could not be genuinely this merry little fellow who frisked and yapped round him and his lovely Mary; he must be playing a part – and what insolence to bring her roses! And then he played and sang so much too well; of course Darnley played and sang well too, but like a gentleman, whereas Rizzio was a professional who had wormed his way up from the gutter by his gifts.

Mary had demanded music, and Rizzio was tinkling a very pretty and expensive guitar made of ebony and ivory inlaid with

230

tortoise-shell and mother-of-pearl. With his broad face beaming blandly as the sun over his instrument, he told them that he had sung in the streets of Genoa as a ragged little boy and sold lucky charms to keep off the Evil Eye – 'and a grand trade I did with them, for my back was more crooked then than now, and it's lucky to deal with a hunchback – look at the luck I've brought these two young Princes – and myself too. I have had the best of luck ever since I was born.'

The disgusted pity that Bothwell was accustomed to feel for any weakness or deformity was impossible in this case; and he could have cheered the little man for making it so. Pity in a woman is of a different stuff; it was that quality, mixed with admiration of his gay courage, and her gratitude, that made Mary coax and pet him and chaff him tenderly; Darnley would be an ass if he didn't see that.

The glow was fading from the little room, but Mary would not have candles put on the table; it was so pleasant to sit there in the half-dusk, talking desultorily and listening to Davie's music that began as a wittily tripping accompaniment to his and their talk, an illustration of it, such as a solemn thrumming of the strings during any discussion of the Lords of the Congregation: *pom pom prrrom te pom*, here comes the Great Bastard and his 'long love' – *te wee tiddledly we wee* went the thin notes, somehow irresistibly like Lady Agnes – into whose rapacious hands Queen Elizabeth had actually disgorged £3,000 to help the rebellion, 'and what's the betting that Agnes helps herself to a good helping of it?' *Te wee*. Would Elizabeth (the guitar suddenly gave an extraordinarily clever imitation of a schoolgirl playing the virginals, the notes prancing up and down very 'high and disposedly' like the strutting of a peacock) really give the rebels more help and money? Lord James had her written promise, of which Davie's spy work had obtained a copy; but all four were agreed that as the rebellion had failed so far – *prrimp presto prrimp* – the peacock stepped discreetly away.

Bothwell gave his advice that they should release Lord George Gordon and restore him to his father's titles and lands as Earl of Huntly.

'I did that more than a month ago,' cried Mary proudly, 'the first moment that I broke with James.'

· The guitar miraculously became the pipes, playing the Gay Gordons into the presence, exalted, hare-brained, magnificent. It changed to a sinister note; the hoot of owls, the mew of cats were heard in the wild witches' dance that whirled through the room as they discussed Darnley's kinsman, that grey elderly savagely bad-tempered invalid, Lord Ruthven, who had shown his hand on their side. He was an adept in black magic; Mary had once complained that it was unsuitable that a sorcerer who practised the Black Mass should be a member of her Privy Council.

The talk died. The four of them sat in this dim tiny scented room with the clear green light of the September evening outside the little window, the shadowy figures on the tapestry behind them, and the music deepening, glowing, binding them now to silence.

After all his adventures, imprisonment, escapes and the attempts of murderers against him, James Hepburn was sitting here with the Queen, whose tip-tilted face beside him now shone grave and lovely like the young moon in the dusk. His body told him he was in love; he had been that many times, but never before had his mind and fancy flamed with it, telling him that life was a thing of greater beauty and danger than he had dreamed of.

It was the first time, too, that he had ever sat beside a woman with whom he had fallen in love, and felt her unconscious of him.

For Mary's spirit had raced out of the room on the deep notes of Rizzio's exultant song; the thrumming of his guitar was an echo to her of galloping horses and the blood tingling in her veins; she felt the furious wet wind again in her face as she braved the roaring torrent of the Carron, there where King Arthur had fought his last battle, and where she rode at the head of her troops to defend her right to reign, her right to love, to defend the man by her side that she had chosen herself in the teeth of her enemies.

He had faults as she had seen already, he was proud, violent-tempered – well but she had liked that, she was so herself though she had learned to school her temper. Anyway, he had not had one single quarrel with herself; they had laughed about it, saying it was the right thing to have a quarrel. And he would not go on drinking now his life had suddenly become so full of new excitement and importance. She had insisted on his being given the title of King, on his being treated with all royal honours equally with herself.

She thought of all she would give and do for him, of all he would become as he grew to full manhood with power and responsibility in his hands. 'My life, my lovely life,' she murmured to herself in ecstasy as the music flowed over her, lifted her on a wave of glorious sound, and she saw her life unrolling before her like a bright tapestry away into a sunlit distance, and herself riding down it with the tall youth glittering in blue and gold beside her; then turned her head, saw the eyes of the man on her other side, saw them deep on her as he had never looked at her before, saw, stopped, caught her breath and wondered – what lies ahead?

CHAPTER TWO

BOTHWELL'S LIFE was moving at its old headlong speed. He at once sent his lawyer, Mr David Chalmers, to London with dispatches to the French Ambassador, and though Chalmers had just ridden to Eyemouth to meet him, and back to Edinburgh at his master's own furious pace, he was now bidden to make the ride of four hundred miles in four days – 'and I may allow you an extra half day for accidents, but no more,' said his lord – and was obeyed.

In that time Bothwell was reinstated on the Council, and as Lieutenant of the Border; rallied the Border clans to his command; drew up plans for the coming campaign, in which he counted on collecting fifteen thousand men at Stirling to round up the rebels at Dumfries; and, also within those four days, followed up his commands to the clans in person, riding all through Teviotdale and Liddesdale, Nithsdale and Annandale, to assure himself of the exact strength of those 'barons and gentlemen of the dales' who had by now already sworn to him 'truly to serve the King and Queen – and in especial James Hepburn, Earl of Bothwell'.

The Johnstones and the Jardines, the Crabbed Kerrs, the Turnbulls and the Bold Rutherfords, names that have rung through a hundred ballads, flocked to follow him.

> But the Elliots wouldn' wi' him ride,
> And they rue it to this day.

For Rob Elliot of Redheugh had been turned out of his command of Hermitage Castle by Bothwell on his brief and breathless visit to Scotland this last spring; and in his rage he had transferred his clan's allegiance to the Queen of England, and got fifty pounds from Sir John Forster, the English Warden, for

233

doing so. Bothwell threatened, but Sir John had bribed, and Bothwell won over only part of the clan to his Queen's service. That put him in a furious temper as he rode back to Holyrood at the end of the four days, swearing that as soon as he could spare the time he would burn the Elliot's peel towers and get Rob of Redheugh's head.

His return did nothing to sweeten his mood, for he found that his Lieutenancy had been supplemented by the appointment of Darnley's father, the Earl of Lennox, as Lieutenant of the Western Border, so as to cope with the special emergencies of these troubled times. That was the official explanation: the true one was that Darnley had been hotly indignant at Bothwell's appointment; the Lieutenancy was the highest and most important office in the kingdom, it should therefore be held by the King's father. Mary had flatly refused, and they had their first quarrel; and it was not the right thing! She could not bear it, to see him go red and angry and hear him shout at her, and such silly things; there was a dreadful moment when she wondered if she were really beginning to dislike her young 'bluff King Hal'. If she saw her gay lad turn into a sulky lout, what would she do?

Her terror was lest she should lose her love for him; not lest he should lose his for her. To make herself see him again as she wished, she gave Lennox the supplementary appointment of the Western Marches; she told herself that it could not matter much, since Bothwell held the chief command.

But Darnley would not step back on the pedestal where she had placed him; he took her concession as a tribute to his firmness, and traded on it unexpectedly when Mary wanted to put Bothwell at the head of her army. She sat stunned while Darnley explained to the Council in a casual offhand manner that it was also his father's right to lead an action against the rebels near Dumfries.

'He may have the right to – he hasn't the chance,' exclaimed Bothwell. 'He's away keeping the Campbells off his lands.'

'He's preventing the Campbells from joining forces with the rebels' cavalry,' corrected Darnley with a haughty glance at the Borderer under half-shut eyes. Bothwell was imperturbable.

'Whichever it is, he's away, and can't march on Dumfries.'

'He can when he returns.'

'And give the rebels time to escape?'

Mary reminded Darnley that she had recalled Bothwell expressly to put him at the head of their army; that he had already collected that army from his Borderers, as large as all the rebel forces at Dumfries.

'He hasn't got the Elliots, though,' said Darnley.

Mary looked at him in a dull wonder: he seemed really pleased with his score.

So he was. There they all were yammering away at this deadly Council table on this glorious September morning when they might be out hawking; if he couldn't get any other fun he'd put a spoke in their wheels, he'd show them that he could make a decision and stick to it as well as they. He had liked Bothwell, a bold adventurer, with a good pair of hands for a horse; useful at need, no doubt. But it would never do to let him get the upper hand; Mary couldn't see that, of course, a girl wouldn't, and all these men round her only said, 'Yes, yes' to whatever she suggested.

All this he told himself, but rather uneasily, while deep down beneath his manly firmness a small child lay on the floor and kicked and screamed to be noticed. Certainly everybody had to notice Darnley; their plans held up while they argued, tried to persuade him, and finally had to leave the Council in despair.

They collected together in little groups after it, grumbling in low tones, and the older men said that the young ass was the spit and image of his grandfather the Earl of Angus, whom Margaret Tudor had married after the death of her first husband, James IV. For Angus also had been a handsome haughty fool, who also, oddly enough, had married a Queen of Scotland when he was only nineteen, and had had his head badly turned by it.

'Aye,' they chuckled, 'and she spelt his name Anguish to the end of her life – and good reason he gave her for it, and Scotland too.'

'Well, she got rid of him at last, and so may this Queen.'

Mary was hoping only to win Darnley over. Would she succeed with him? Bothwell doubted it. She was not the type of *maîtresse femme*, for all that she had twice over proved herself an inspiring leader in a campaign. But that was as a warrior, not a woman. Those very qualities of courage and generosity, that had served her so well with men in action, went against her in the feminine battle she now had to wage, of getting what she wanted out of a man in love with her. There was little of the coquette in her and much of the Queen; her desire was not to conquer, but the deeper and more passionate one, to be conquered; hers was the love royal, the wish not to take but to give.

235

And to Darnley, as many of her followers had already for some time complained, she had given 'all honour that can be given to a man by a wife, all praises, all dignities as to her husband and King', and what was more, 'given over to him her whole will to be ruled and guided as he likes'.

'Yet one thing she has not given him, I'll swear,' said Bothwell, as his friend Gordon told him of these earlier reports; he would not say what that was. There kept echoing in his head the line that Harry Percy used to quote from Chaucer where the humane old poet says:

Men say, I not, that she gave him her heart.

He did not believe in Mary's love for that pink and white jackanapes; she was trying too hard to love him: she was too eager to overload him with honours and gifts (the tailor's bill she was running up for him must be pretty heavy, with all those curled feathers and silver lace). In all this he guessed that she was trying to persuade herself, rather than Darnley, of her love for him. Passion there had been, that was certain, but he doubted that it had survived in her after the first night; that selfish cub was sure to have disappointed her, though she was too proud and probably too ignorant to admit it even to herself. It was her imagination that had fallen in love with this tall young Prince of her dreams, mad on horses as she was – 'He should never have dismounted,' said Bothwell to Gordon.

The two were greater friends than ever. Gordon's three years' imprisonment had been as lenient as Mary could contrive, but it was a crippling experience for a young man in the height of his vigour. But neither time nor circumstance seemed to have the power to affect that grave yet reckless young Highlander. His first act on his release was to bring his mother, Lady Huntly, to Court, with a bodyguard of four younger brothers and his sister Jean. Neither mother nor brothers laid the blame on the Queen for the way their house had been crushed and the old lord done to death – 'The poor lassie was helpless,' said Lady Huntly. No one knew what Jean thought, but she was only a girl, and the youngest, just twenty, and did not count.

Gordon was as much in love with the Queen as before, and in the same aloof way. He had the air of a spectator at a play, waiting to see what would happen, and knowing that he could not influence it. Neither he nor Bothwell spoke of their love for Mary.

In spite of all Mary's vehement support of Bothwell as the

better man, Darnley won the contest, and the army had to wait for Lennox as its Commander-in-Chief. He was to command the vanguard, Bothwell the main body, together with the young King; and George Gordon, Earl of Huntly, the rear.

'So we get our sops thrown to us to soothe our tender feelings, and the line of march was drawn up in order of rank as if it were a State banquet! God's blood! We've lost a week by this fooling, and the rebels are withdrawing to Carlisle without a scratch. I'd have wiped them out by now if she'd stuck to my having the command.'

'It's not her doing that you haven't,' said Gordon.

'Don't I know it! It's never her doing. It used to be the Bastard's doing, and now it's this spoilt mother's darling – wife's darling. We're ruled by whatever man rules her, and she's made a rotten choice.'

'There was no other.'

That was true, as he grudgingly admitted. Darnley was no fit match in rank to the Queen, but Arran had been the only other diplomatic possibility for her in two kingdoms. Darnley's claim as heir to them was thinner than Arran's, yet a child born of him and Mary would certainly be in the direct succession to them both. Mary's headlong fancy for the only young man who had any right to make open love to her had been prompted in the first place by her policy of union with England.

The campaign was very pretty, in Bothwell's sardonic comment, a sartorial success. Darnley was undoubtedly the chief triumph for the tailors, in a gilded corselet over his chamois-leather riding-suit, and overcoat of buffalo hide to keep out the chill of an early October cold spell. He was already wearing his new winter gloves, another present from Mary, perfumed and velvet-lined. She herself was not so elaborate, though she had been advised to wear a light breastplate under the plaid she loved as a riding-cloak, and was very proud of the brace of pistols at her holster. She wore a steel cap and let her hair fly free from under it, for it was impossible to keep it pinned up.

They rode over Crawford Moor, where her father had hoped to find gold – 'but all the gold here is growing on the whin,' she laughed as she gazed out over the bright hillside. They held a Council of War at Castlehill, a rude old fortress of Robert the Bruce, whose daughter had married a Stewart and so brought that family to the throne of Scotland. 'It came with a lass, it will go with a lass,' James V had murmured on his death-bed

237

when he heard that his child was a girl. But it should not go; she was riding at the head of her armies to see to that.

Her enemies were already on the road to Carlisle, and Bothwell pleaded vehemently at the Council of War that he should go after them with a couple of thousand men, cut off their line of retreat and exterminate their whole army. It was not allowed; but all the same, his speed and the size of the army he had so instantly collected caused the utter collapse of the rebels. Their followers deserted and scattered; their ringleaders fled ignominiously out of the country to the protection of the Queen of England. And all with practically no bloodshed; that was what delighted Mary!

'I think it's been a glorious campaign,' she said haughtily, in answer to Bothwell's disparaging remarks.

'Do you so, Madam? I think it's been no campaign at all. It was just a chase-about raid.'

And the Chase-about Raid it was called ever after.

Cecil and Elizabeth cursed the day when James Hepburn had so coolly run the gauntlet of their ships and out-sailed one of their greatest captains. For eighteen months they had had him in their hands, and let him go as 'of no force now' – and here he was back in Scotland, thwarting all their plans. There was nothing to be done but one of Elizabeth's complete right-about turns. Those £3,000 that she had smuggled to James' wife had apparently been nothing but a premature christening gift for Lady Agnes' expected baby (a safe assumption, as she was generally expecting one). As to it being sent for the rebel troops, Elizabeth 'never meant any such thing in that way'. James had to retract his angry reminders of her Ambassador's 'faithful promises' and *your own handwriting, confirming the same*, and play a carefully rehearsed comedy with her for the benefit of the French Ambassador, who was concealed behind a curtain while James solemnly told Elizabeth that she had never given him either money or promises, and Elizabeth told James to 'get you out of my presence for an unworthy traitor'. She was then immensely surprised to see the French Ambassador step forward and coyly admit that he had heard every word. She knew that he knew that she knew he had been there all the time; but that did not matter, appearances were preserved; and some money was sent in secret after the 'unworthy traitor' to make the curtain lecture worth his while.

'Note diligently,' wrote Knox in the margin of his page describing James' strange reception by his ally; and three times over: the second time, 'Note diligently Queen Elizabeth,' and the third, 'Here mark either deep dissimulation or a great inconstancy.'

Mary could scarcely believe her triumph. After four years of servitude in her own kingdom she now reigned supreme. Scotland was hers at last, and England must become hers in time. She had kept her word to Elizabeth, married an English subject, and by choosing the one nearest the throne had assured the English succession for their heir.

By honourable dealing, she had actually outmanoeuvred the tricky English Queen; she had the best proof of this in its recognition all through England itself. Important members of Elizabeth's own Court, more, of her own Council, were already trying to come to terms with Mary, assuring her of their loyal service when she should be their royal mistress.

There was even an overture from Cecil.

Elizabeth had made a surprising success of her eight years' reign, but she was nearing her middle thirties and still a childless spinster and reputed sickly: it was rumoured that she was incapable of child-bearing. Her star had now begun to set, while Mary's, so long kept in such dark eclipse, was suddenly shooting up the sky. The mightiest powers in Europe, the Papacy and Spain, were delighted with her, and almost embarrassing in their offers of support. And all the Catholics in England, some said the greater part of the population, were of course in wild jubilation, many of them beseeching Mary not to wait for the death of her cousin, 'Boleyn's bastard', but march south now to 'her rightful inheritance'; the great Catholic lords of the North offered full help of arms and men and money. But this would mean a civil war, the very thing that Mary dreaded with more than her adult reason, for her loathing of it was a legacy from the horrors of her childhood in France. All she wanted of her enemies was their absence.

Her 'desire to have all men live as they wish, which so offends the conscience of the godly', appeared to them after all to have its points.

The rebels began to make peace overtures. They recognized that their best mediator would be Rizzio; James climbed down so far as to write him a very humble letter from England, with the present of a fine diamond; the little Italian promptly stuck it in his cap and capered about, with some outrageously merry remarks about James' advances to him. Lethington too was making a careful cat-like approach to him; and it

239

was Rizzio who got a pardon for Châtelherault, to Darnley's disgust.

The young man began to complain that this precious Master Davie had finer horses than himself. The nobles scowled at the little upstart and shouldered him out of their way, but all the notice Davie took of that was to mimic their lordly bad manners to Mary so comically that she sobbed with laughter.

Neither guessed that he was being used as a weapon against her. Her enemies could still work her harm from a distance. In England, James began to spread the report that 'his sister hated him because he knew that concerning her which respect would not suffer him to reveal.' Elizabeth repeated these dark hints to the French Ambassador. They spread slowly nearer and nearer home, in reversal to the usual process of scandal.

But the seed had been sown there too. At the very beginning of their acquaintance, James had contrived to suggest suspicions of Rizzio to Darnley. The youth ignored them while he was certain of Mary's obvious passion for himself. When he was not so certain, he would begin to remember them again.

Bothwell did not hear the faint breath of scandal that was creeping up against the Queen like a wreath of fog from outside her kingdom. He was far too busy to be much at Court. He had first remained at Dumfries in command of his Borderers, to keep watch all along the Border against the rebels; he had all the fords across the rivers guarded, and the hill passes, so that there should be no communication between them and Scotland.

When it was clear that 'the rats have not a tooth left to gnaw with', he turned his vigorous attention to working up the Queen's artillery. Now at last he was able to carry out his plan of putting all artillery into double equipage to serve both as siege guns and field batteries; he appointed a Controller of Artillery, with authority to place wrights and gunners near all the fortresses, to cut timber for the wheels and platforms, supply iron for the mountings, and lead and stone for the ammunition. Timber was felled all that winter on the Tay and sent down by sea to Leith Harbour. He arranged for continuous labour and regular wages, and ensured the exact number of draught oxen to be sent by each stock-owner to Leith for drawing the timber.

There was some pleasure among all this business: a brush or two with the English at Berwick who had objected to his guard on the Border passes; more than a brush with the Elliots, whose peel towers he now burned as he had threatened, in accordance with his powers as Lieutenant of the Border 'to ride with fire and sword' upon those houses that had disobeyed his call to arms. Rob Elliot of Redheugh sought safety with Sir John Forster, but Forster had to go cannily, for the English Queen was anxious to appoint a peace conference, with Forster and the Earl of Berwick as the English Commissioners.

Once again Bothwell stood in her way. He was chosen by Mary as the chief Scottish delegate instead of the easy 'tractable' nominees that Elizabeth had wanted. In vain did her Envoy, Randolph, protest and even storm at the Scottish Queen, declaring that she had chosen the very man most hated by the Queen of England.

The delicate girl lying back on her pillows only laughed at the indignant little man's attempts to bully her out of her right to choose her own representative. She apologized charmingly for receiving him in bed, but she had not slept well. Randolph's gallantry was more disconcerting than his anger.

'I expect,' he said archly, 'Your Grace has something in your belly to keep you awake.'

'Do you really like that man?' she asked later of Beton, who had held a long flirtation with Randolph.

Beton tossed her impudent curls; the corners of her mouth went up in a hard little shut smile.

'He thinks so. You may find it useful that he does, Madam.'

'He's a spy, of course. Have you been spying on the spy? Is it something about Elizabeth? Will it affect me?'

'It is something about Elizabeth. It has affected you. I don't know how much it will.' Beton spoke more slowly than usual. Mary threw a pillow at her.

'Beton, you teasing monkey, tell me quick!'

'No, Madam, give me time. I like to make sure of my facts.'

Mary gave in good-humouredly. 'And so you let Randolph make love to you, merely to make use of him for me?'

Beton was instantly again the casual cynical young woman of the world. 'He is well enough to flirt with – and to work up others. I like handsome Sandy Ogilvie better.'

'So does Lady Jean Gordon, I fancy.'

'She may, but she's a dull creature.'

'All the same, I have a notion that she will always get what she wants in the end.'

'The end of my life then!' and Beton laughed at so incredible a thought. She was already secretly engaged to the fickle swain, she admitted.

Kisses and congratulations, laughing promises of secrecy and a wedding dress, they could not keep off the chill dismay that struck at Mary's heart before she recognized its cause. Was it that Sandy was not good enough for the most brilliant of her Maries? No, it struck nearer home – the knowledge that Jean would now be thankful to save herself from the ignominious position of the jilted, by encouraging a lover of far greater power and importance than young Alexander Ogilvie of Boyne.

He was not the only man who had noticed the Lady Jean Gordon. She was too pale and her nose rather too long, but her figure was beautiful, full-formed, and carried with the conscious voluptuous grace of a much older woman. Her whole air and manner were of a remarkable composure for her age: whatever the cause of her silence, it was certainly not from any shyness or diffidence.

Bothwell had noticed her deliberately on his rare appearances at Court, for he was glad of the chance given him by a fine young woman to distract his attention from the Queen. Mary's presence was now an acute discomfort to him; it was bad enough in absence to hear in his mind some sudden echo of that magic voice, the tingling vibrant excitement of it, ringing across the serious business that he had in hand, sometimes even waking him just as he was falling asleep, so that he started up imagining for one wild instant that he had heard her speak. While away from her he could tire his body and drug his mind with the furious speed of all his activities; when with her, the only relief for his tormented senses, as he watched her with that pampered boy, was to behave with rather more than his accustomed ungraciousness to her.

It was becoming the fashion for the young Protestant nobles to attend Mass in the Queen's chapel occasionally as a courtesy, and also as a relief from the long sermons of their own ministers. But Bothwell still refused to do so, flatly and bluntly; he would not give any handle to the notion that because he supported the Queen he must therefore be 'a great Papist'. The world had gone mad over tying labels, generally the wrong ones, on to everybody.

'You are the Inquisition' – that still expressed the common opinion of Mary.

He did not explain this, but laughed when she thought he would come, 'if only for the music, as many do. We're having the new Palestrina Mass. Davie got a copy of it from Rome. He still sings the bass.'

'Aye, they call him a base fellow.'

'What a stupid joke! I thought you liked him.'

'I do. My only objection to him is that he's served you too well.'

Again he would not say why, and when she cited the Protestants at Court who attended Mass, he jeered at them. 'They're used to changing their coat – more often than their linen, some of them. Even that may follow, now you're civilizing us all so fast.'

How rude and sneering he'd grown in his long absence! He would probably never quite forgive her for it. So she still spoke gently, though urgently, as she explained that this particular Mass was a State occasion of international importance. Monsieur Rambouillet, a nobleman from the French Court, was being sent to confer on Darnley a high honour of ecclesiastical origin, the Knighthood of the Cockle, of the Order of St Michael. This decoration had not been given to a Scot since half a century ago when François I had bestowed it on his friend the Franco-bred Duke of Albany, 'Magnificent Uncle' of James V, who had left his fair wide lands in France to come and be Governor of Scotland during his nephew's minority. Tremendous preparations had then been made for the Collar of the Cockle; the Palace of Holyrood had been repaired (even the drainage sewers, which were never its strong point) and partly rebuilt; all the lords and barons throughout the kingdom were summoned to attend the ceremony in St Giles' Cathedral in new robes of cloth-of-gold, crimson satin, purple velvet and black taffetas. Albany ever after bore the Cockle shells round the border of his coat of arms.

She told all this to Bothwell, almost begging him to understand her eagerness that the occasion should not fall too far short of that earlier splendour. St Giles' was now Protestant, and closed to her; the ceremony could only be held in her private chapel, but at least let her and Darnley have the support of her greatest nobles!

Even this failed to move him. He said that he would meet the Frenchman at the banquet that his old friend, the merchant, Barron, was giving in honour of the occasion, and that would certainly impress Rambouillet if Barron told the full list of Bothwell's debts to him as an after-dinner story.

She shrugged her shoulders; she might have known it, he would do nothing to please her. Serve her, yes, he had proved that again and again, but that was his loyalty, the one tribute he paid to morality. But he cared nothing for her happiness or unhappiness—and nothing for what she thought of him, any more than he cared what the world thought. She felt as much envy as irritation. If only she could be like that, carefree, insolently regardless of others' opinion!

For she was indeed desperately anxious about the effect Darnley would make on Rambouillet, and through him on all her family and friends in France; all the more so since Beton had at last told her her discovery from Randolph. But that she would not, dared not think of now, for she must seem confident and secure – more, a radiantly happy bride; and the best way to seem that was to feel it.

Her Maries helped her into a new dress for the banquet that glimmered with gold tissue, and twisted the pearls in her shining hair and dabbed a touch of rouge on her cheeks, the first time she had ever used it, for she had always been proud of the peculiarly transparent whiteness of her skin, but today it made her cheeks look thin and her eyes hollow, and that would never do. She picked up her little silver-backed looking-glass she had brought from France, the first ever seen in Scotland, where mirrors were made of polished metal.

Gazing into it this dull wintry afternoon when the candles had been lit since morning against the grey light, she saw that white face like a ghost looking back at her – 'and so I shall be one day', she thought, 'and other faces then will look back from this glass, the faces of my children and grandchildren and great-grandchildren, and something of me will look out from their eyes'.

That gave her confidence again in the future. After all, if anyone had told her a year ago what her position would be today, she would have run mad with joy. For she would walk to Mr Barron's house (they were going, as they often did, on foot) and pass under that overhanging house at the foot of the Netherbow, knowing that that old man Knox was no longer peering down from his study window at her like a crow from its nest, most literally 'overlooking' her with the evil eye, since all that he could see would be stored up to use against her. Now she had got rid of Knox, as she had got rid of James and all her enemies; there would soon not be a single pensioner of England here to work against her.

Only French opinion remained to be convinced; and that she knew to be largely personal – her uncles were so fond of her, they were unlikely to think any match good enough for her. Rambouillet must tell them – oh, but how she wished Rambouillet could see him now!

For at that moment Darnley had come swinging in on her from his ride, with the great buffalo-hide coat making him look so much a man and every inch a king – and what a lot of inches there were as he leaned over her shoulder to peer into her glass and laugh at all the pretty little objects on her dressing-table!

'Rouge? So you've come to it at last. I like your pink cheeks. There wasn't much game to be had. The birds are too cold to fly. There'll be snow before night, I swear. How much longer will you sit and fiddle with these pots and pans before you're ready?'

'I'm ready now. Oh, Harry, I wish you could come like that! I love you in those great boots.'

'Only in them?'

'And in that great coat.'

'Only in that?'

'Off with you, silly, and make yourself gorgeous. What will you wear?'

'Oh, I don't know. Anthony will see to it.' He swaggered off with an air of manly indifference, manifestly feigned, for he delighted in all the fine clothes Mary had ordered for his trousseau and the proud evidence of the hundreds of pounds she had spent on him. She wandered into the little anteroom and sat waiting for him, smiling, assured, all that former vague uneasiness dispelled by the sight of his jolly boyish face fresh from the keen air.

He was a long time dressing. He always was a dawdler. Royalty oughtn't to be late. Time took twice as long when one was waiting. She picked up a book – Ronsard's new poems that he had sent her with a charming flattering inscription; she dipped into it, noted a prettily pedantic phrase, a diminutive or two, musical as the tinkle of little bells – *'ondelette'*, *'doucelette'* – saw something about eating strawberries in a wood by a fountain, looked up at the lowering sky outside and remarked, 'How very improbable!' and saw her jewelled watch on the table.

There was no doubt now they would be late. She sent a message to Darnley to urge haste; walked round the room, took up another book in a white vellum cover with gold tooling, more poems and a treatise on poetry by Ronsard's gentle young friend, du Bellay, who had died on his return to the Loire country for which he had always been so homesick. As she read of the winnowing flail in the summer heat and the dust dancing in the barn door, she saw the silvery light breaking through low clouds over that wide soft-flowing river, the flat fields of waving corn and little homely blue-grey roofs pointing upwards at absurd angles; and majestic châteaux rising by that river, rich with carving and the new painted glass, more delicate than the old stained glass, the châteaux of Chambord and Amboise, Chenonceaux and Blois, where she and François had loved to stay, the little town of Orléans on the river's edge, where François had died.

These elegant arabesques of words, interweaving like the sinuous lines of that architecture, where stone had been made supple and slender as the reeds by the Loire, wove their spell round her and lulled her back into their world of refined and learned dreamers, a world so civilized that the style in verse mattered more than its content, and the introduction of a Greek word into the French language more than the civil wars of religion that raged while they were being written. The strongest passions in this intimate and delicate poetry were ennui at the world's affairs, or the sense of loss that steals on one with the slow passing of the days; the controversy in this prose treatise was on no more dangerous a theme than the defence of the French language against the Latin. But now she had ceased to notice what she read, for 'we shall be late', she kept saying to herself, 'we shall be late, late, so late'.

CHAPTER THREE

DARNLEY CAME into the room. As she laid down her book and sprang to meet him, she saw that he had come back quite different.

'Harry, you're not well. Don't worry – I can easily explain. You know you said what a tedious business it would be – long speeches – all so polite! I envy you, not coming.'

'Not coming – what do you mean? Want to keep me out of it, do you? We'll see about that.'

He stood there magnificent in white and gold, 'but he is quite different', she said to herself, and 'I knew it. I knew this would happen.' His eyes were staring over her head, vacant and blue as glass; his face sagged, his full mouth drooping open, his restless hands plucking nervously at his sleeves, his dagger, the tight buttons at his throat, unable to finish anything they began to do. Only his hair remained unchanged, that curling chicken-yellow hair that looked almost ridiculously young when he was fresh with riding, but now sat on that red heavy face as grotesquely as a wig.

It was impossible to dissuade him from coming. She could only hope the cold air would sting him fairly sober as they walked up the hill. But she would not be able to prevent him drinking at the banquet – it was bound to happen. And now it was happening and she watching it, talking to Rambouillet very fast so as to keep his attention, talking, talking – what about? Ronsard and du Bellay, of course: how lucky that she had just been looking at them!

J'offre ces violettes
Ces lis et ces fleurettes.

'Daring innovators,' Rambouillet called them; they had made a revolution in French poetry, the Sorbonne was fighting it desperately. Wars, wars everywhere and revolutions, even in verse and language! She nodded with grave concern; she agreed it was all part of the revolutionary spirit of the age; she thought, a great many young men drank, especially in this country, Rambouillet would know that. If only Harry would not talk so much and so loudly, and insist on Rambouillet's two pages drinking with him glass for glass; he roared with laughter when one of them tripped forward and fell. It must be something very strong – 'aqua composita', Harry was calling it in a loud pompous voice, a mixture of whisky and brandy and other stuffs which he had insisted on his servant Anthony mixing for him. He had refused Barron's wines, to the dour disgust of their sturdily respectable host, who had been prepared to be so genial. Neither he nor Rambouillet would touch the stuff, and Rambouillet looked down his pointed beard every time Harry tried to catch his eye, though he addressed him with icy deference as the King.

'The King!' He ought to be drinking with the scullions in the pantry; it was grotesque that he should be here beside her, with his new decoration of the Order of the Cockle round his neck and his hands groping up over it while he interrupted her talk with Rambouillet to make some foul joke about the Order of the Cuckold. He went on interrupting them; he was determined to show that he was as important as his wife, even though he hadn't yet got the Crown Matrimonial – and why *hadn't* he got it, he'd like to know?

'The Crown Matrimonial?' Rambouillet inquired with polite interest. 'That, I take it, confers equal powers on the consort, and in the event of the Sovereign's death leaves him the throne?'

Darnley, only hazily distinguishing the cool crisp French words from among the loud blurr in his ears, was somehow disconcerted by the dispassionate inquiry: it made him want to assert himself on his own merits.

He began to brag of the support and encouragement given them by the Pope and Spain: 'They want us to lead an army into England, of course. We could do it, too, like a shot – look how we chased those rascals over the Border. But Mary's so weak – she hates war and yet she loves fighting – just like a woman, ha ha ha! We Catholics ought to conquer England and convert her over again – she's used to it, isn't she? Been converted three times already – Protestant under King Hal, Catholic under Bloody Mary, Protestant under his bastard Elizabeth – and now Catholic again under the next King Hal. That makes it all fair and square, doesn't it? But Mary doesn't care a rap for the Church – gets their backing and does nothing for it, and doesn't mean to. Says people ought to worship as they wish – can you imagine such stuff? And yet there she sits up night after night with little Davie, writing letters to the Pope and King Philip to make 'em think her a good Catholic – or says she does – and if she doesn't, what *are* they doing, I should like to know? Have you any more of that aqua composita, Anthony? – if not, just mix it again.'

Mary had stopped thinking. Rambouillet, the representative of French Catholicism, had heard that she meant to do nothing active for their religion; their rigidly Protestant host, Mr Barron, a friend of Knox, had heard she sat up night after night writing letters to the Pope and Spain through Rizzio; and everyone present had seen and heard that her husband, who demanded full rights as King of Scotland, was a babbling sot who could be trusted rather less than a mischievous child.

She made a sign to Anthony, but her husband saw it and turned round on her in a sudden rush of fury. 'Not the first servant you've tampered with behind my back, I'll be sworn. Like servants, don't you – like to do them honour and tell them to go against me – *I* know – you think I don't, but *I* know.'

She rose, trembling all over, stunned and shaken as if he had crashed his fist into her face, as indeed for an instant she had thought he was going to do. They had all got up, they were saying things, Harry was shouting. She began to cry, wildly, helplessly. Someone threw a cloak round her, took her arm, was

248

leading her away so fast that her steps tottered, but the hand on her arm held her up; and now there was cold air on her face and darkness round her, no more faces round her, staring shocked faces, contemptuous pitying faces, no more of that heated face that had slipped into so dire a change from everything she knew in it, shifting and twisting itself as it blared out worse and still worse things.

There was only the cold air and the black jagged roofs against the stars.

'Steady now, steady,' said a voice close beside her; 'there's no need to force the pace.'

She went on through the darkness, held up by Bothwell's arm.

CHAPTER FOUR

H E T O O K her up the narrow spiral stairway into the tiny room where they had supped that first evening of his homecoming. A fire of pine-logs and fir-cones burned in the corner. A small lamp of perfumed oil hanging by a gold chain swung gently in the draught as they came in, and filled the room with moving shadows. He set her in a chair and poured out wine from a flagon on the little oval table that had been pushed to one side. She asked for water to mix with it, as was her custom, and she added it from a tall silver jug. It was the first time she had spoken at all; and now she said dully, 'My feet are cold.'

He flung himself down on his knees before her, dragged off her shoes without waiting to unfasten them, and began to rub her feet with such exasperated violence that she pulled them away, thinking that he was angry with her. But at that he caught them again in his hands and began to kiss them, and then sprang up and snatched her to him, kissing her face, her hair, her throat and shoulders, blindly, furiously, and the next moment his hands tore at her dress. She gave a cry so full of anguish that it reached him even through his deaf passion.

'I am with child by him. If you hurt that, all is gone.'

He let go of her as violently as he had gripped her; he thrust her from him and stood there with his hands clenched. He forgot everything but the sight of her face before him, white and still among the warm swinging lights and shadows, and the knowledge that they were alone together in this small bright scented room, and that he must not touch her.

'Say that again,' he said at last in a low voice that seemed to come from a long way off; and then, 'What was it you were telling me?'

She began to cry again, not wildly this time, but like an unhappy child.

'Why are you crying?'

Again it was that strange voice. He might have been speaking in his sleep. She shivered as she said, 'Have you gone mad?'

'Is it mad to love you?'

'Now you must be mad. All these years you've never been in love with me.'

'Never till now, when you're with child by another man.' His own words woke him from that trance. He turned to the table and poured himself out some wine. 'Drink yours,' he said, without turning his head. It reassured her immeasurably to hear that curt command in his own voice again. It was as practical as a doctor's as he asked her if she were certain about the child, and when it should be born.

'In May or June,' she answered, and began to laugh hysterically as she sipped her watered wine. 'That horrible nightmare, Harry's face, all their faces, everything crashing round me – what a time to tell me you love me! Why, you were never even polite to me. We've always quarrelled. You've only paid me two compliments in all these years, and they were more on behalf of Scotland than yourself.'

He could look at her now, and even feel grim amusement in her unconscious admission. So she, who had been paid such thousands of compliments, could remember his two – which he could not!

'Did I ever pay you compliments?'

'Why yes, at your sister's wedding – something about my making Scotland a fief of Elfland. And long ago, in France, you told me to come back here and be such a Queen as they would make songs and stories of until the end of time. Do you still think that?'

'God knows what Scotland will do with you! We've got to think what you can do with her. This child, that will be your highest card against your enemies. It secures the succession, it will be Sovereign of Scotland and England both. You must guard yourself in these next months as if you were made of glass. You were ill lately. You must not be.'

'I was only tired out, I think. That mad campaign last summer, and then this autumn.'

'A bad start for breeding. No matter. You'll rest now.'

'Yes, if only —'

'There's no "if only". Keep friends with the King till the child's born. Does he take other women?'

'Yes. It must have been my fault. He said I was cold.'

So he was right. Darnley had disappointed, probably repelled her physically as soon as they were married. The thought gave him a fierce stab of exultation. But he repeated, 'All the same, keep friends with him. You don't want him shouting about the place that your child is none of his. What did he mean about Rizzio?'

'I sit up late with him, of course. He's my private secretary. Even Harry could think nothing of that except when he's mad drunk. I love Davie, he is adorable, utterly faithful, but, but – well, you have seen him.'

'You mean he's deformed?'

'Yes, and of low birth.'

Once again he was astonished by her ignorance of the world. 'You'll find neither a protection against scandal – and your husband seems anxious to make one.' His taut dry-voiced control suddenly snapped. He broke out, 'Didn't I say you'd always trust the wrong man! Elizabeth at least has an eye for one.'

'She's shown that, I suppose, with Leicester.' Mary's voice went cool and ironic as his flamed.

'True, I'll give you her Dudley for your Darnley. But at least she didn't marry him.'

'Because Cecil would not allow it.'

'Nor would I have allowed it. Christ's blood, why wasn't I here! Only the little Italian, and he must needs spoil you, must put whatever sugar-plum into your mouth you cried for, however bad for you.'

'I *didn't* cry for Darnley. It's true I wanted to marry. For me not to do so, that would be impossible, you know – and I had just begun to know it. But I had given up all my hopes of a great Continental alliance – no, not because Elizabeth was determined to thwart them, but because I'd learned – by now – that union with England matters so desperately.'

'And the man, as usual, didn't matter!'

She stamped with rage. 'I told Randolph in joke that I'd have no husband but Elizabeth! *Now* do you understand? I'd even have taken Leicester if there'd been no other way. Then Darnley came North, and I thought there was. My eye for a man may not be as true as Elizabeth's, but then I didn't have him by my side a whole year as she had, studying him with a view to this very purpose.'

'*What* purpose?'

'Her purpose in marrying him to me, of course.'

He thought her light-headed. Elizabeth, he said, might have wanted to side-track her from the Spanish marriage, but she could not have actually wanted a marriage which should combine all the Catholics in England under Darnley with those in Scotland under Mary, and ensure their Catholic heir for the English throne.

'It was *not* ensured – that was one of the chief points of her game. She meant me to marry without any promise from her of the succession. And so I did.'

'Then why did she try to stop the marriage? Recall his father and himself to England, send Throckmorton – you like him – up here to dissuade you? Throw his mother into prison to punish her for managing it?'

'That's just the way she works – gets people to do what she wants, and then punishes them so as to hide that it's her doing. Yes, and all that she did to stop the marriage she did just too late, havered and hesitated to make people think she didn't know her own mind, to make them think as I thought – fool that I was – that I had outmanoeuvred her. When all along I was being tricked and betrayed into marrying the very man she had intended for me from the beginning.'

He still looked incredulous.

'Won't you see it even now?' she cried. 'That was why she paid me the insult of offering Leicester as a husband. She even suggested that she and her Sweet Robin and I should form one household 'at her charge'! And to make it clear, she went on flirting with him more openly and intimately than ever – all to show the world I could not win him from her. It was to goad me into marrying someone else in haste – into marrying the very man she knew would be my ruin.'

He was now utterly disgusted. Even her condition, with child by a mate whom she had suddenly discovered to be despicable, did not excuse such hysteria. 'It's all the most damnable feminine stuff – it's too far-fetched. Machiavelli himself could never think of anything so subtle.'

'Machiavelli wasn't a woman.'

'Even a woman couldn't be such a devil.'

'I have proof of it – her own Ambassador's letter to Cecil.

One of my servants saw it in Randolph's rooms – never mind how – but here are the very words.'

She unlocked a minute cabinet and gave him a paper with a woman's handwriting on it – Beton's, as he guessed. 'And as to Machiavelli,' she added, 'that is her chief boast – that they call her "the Florentine".'

He sat on a chair near the lamp and read the copy of Randolph's letter, the original of which was now in Cecil's files in London. Of Mary's marriage to Darnley the Envoy had written: 'a greater plague to her there cannot be, nor a greater benefit to our Queen's Majesty. My whole care is how to avoid suspicion that our Queen's Majesty was the whole means and worker of it.'

Mary watched him read it; a small vein on his forehead stood out like a knot of whipcord; he scrunched the letter in his hand and burst out into a string of appalling oaths. When at last he could speak coherently he said, 'Yes, this is woman's work. Not even the Borgia could have laid a snare so devilish.'

'She means to destroy me utterly, both body and soul – to corrupt my soul with hatred.'

'You shall not be destroyed. You are warned.'

He straightened out the crumpled letter and handed it back to her. 'This fellow Randolph, can you get rid of him?'

'I've done so,' she answered proudly; 'at least, I should have, but he just won't go! Davie's collected evidence that he handed over the English money to finance the rebellion last summer. He's had to admit it and has been dismissed. But, in spite of that, he's shut himself up in his quarters and refused to budge.'

'I'll ferret him out,' said Bothwell with satisfaction. 'I'll send Black Ormiston to him tomorrow morning with half a dozen of our fellows.'

'You won't hurt him?'

'Lord, no. We must keep as fair a show as we can, both with him and his Queen.'

Then he asked about Darnley. Had he shown jealousy of other men as well as Rizzio – 'of me, for example?'

'No, how should he? I have seen so little of you. There was the matter of your command of the army, and your Lieutenancy of the Border, he was jealous of them, but that was for his father.'

'Hum,' said Bothwell, and was silent so long that she asked of what he was thinking.

'Of getting married,' was the unexpected reply.

The blood rushed burning up into her face; she cried out as sharply as if he had struck her. 'Married! *You* – now!'

'"Now" seems the right time. There's not been time before. Here I am, close on thirty-one, settling down in my own country after my – unavoidable absence, shall we call it? And having at last won the favour of my Sovereign – at least, I hope I have. All I need now is a wife to make me respectable.'

'I'd rather she made you happy.'

'Would you so?' he asked. 'Are you sure?'

He looked at her and she looked back. They did not move, but their faces seemed to swim nearer and nearer to each other. The silence grew loud and breathless.

He swung up from his chair. 'Don't drive me too far, or I shall forget.'

'I think I want you to forget,' came in a whisper.

'Do you?' He was across the room to her, and his hands hovered for an instant over her shoulders, but he flung away again. 'If I touch you, it's all over. I'll not do it. Your child is the one thing that matters now. I'm going.'

Going, and she would be left alone to bear Darnley's child; all these weeks and months ahead of her till then must be lived through alone. 'How *can* I do it?' she cried. 'What if it has a big chicken-tufted head and red face like his tonight? And a chicken heart and loose slobbering mouth? Let it go, it will never be a child of mine. If it were born now I'd kill it with my own hands.'

He turned back to her, came slowly across the room and deliberately laid his hand on her shoulder, which before he had not dared trust himself to touch. Now, though his hand lay so heavy on her, there was no passion in it; her cry had driven it from him, and he was forcing it from her too.

'Listen,' he said, 'the child in your womb is not a person yet. Do not think of it as that until there is need. All that matters now is that it shall be born, whole and sane, to protect your throne for the time being. It is your army, which you must muster together before you can fight. What's the sense of trying to foretell the quality of that army years hence? You are not living then, but *now*.'

The dry rattling sobbing in her throat relaxed under that hard pressure; it held her so firm that she ceased to shake. Her eyes grew less wild as she looked up at him, and presently her trembling lips forced themselves into a smile and she said, almost in her natural voice, 'Whom are you thinking of marrying?'

'I don't know. Whom would you suggest?'

Again it seemed that a knife was going through her.

'I think you like Jean Gordon,' she said. 'I've seen you look at her, and no wonder, for she is beautiful – and only twenty' (This came with a gulp, for she had just had her twenty-third birthday.); 'her breeding, her manners and behaviour are perfect And she is the sister of your greatest friend.'

'She might do. I should like to marry Gordon's sister, and it would combine the Highlands with the Border. That would strengthen us.'

'And you think her beautiful too, don't you?' she insisted.

'Yes,' he said smiling, 'she's my type.'

'And I'm not?'

'Not a bit.' He took away his hand from her shoulder. 'That is why you are so dangerous.'

And now she had got to let him go, there was no help for it, though she weakly said she did not know what she should do – if she went to bed she would never sleep, and there was no Davie here tonight to play at cards with her.

He swore at that 'as roughly as a husband,' she thought, and made her promise that she would never sit up alone with Davie again, but always have someone at hand 'to prove your innocence to any who may seek the contrary. And now don't think, especially of what may happen. Whatever it may be, it hasn't happened yet.'

She promised to read and not go on thinking. She watched him go down the dark narrow stairway; and then turned back into the flickering lights and shadows. This small room, so bright within its shadowy tapestries, always seemed to be waiting for something to happen; she had thought this evening as they entered its warm intimacy that it was for her and Bothwell – but nothing had happened; she wished it had, and whatever it was waiting for, 'it hasn't happened yet', she repeated to herself.

She must obey him, pull herself together before she fell to dreaming, dawdling, sitting before the fire and thinking over all he had said and she had said, and all she might have said, and wished she had not said and wished she had made him say, until half the night had slipped past outside the Palace, and the moon slid down the sky.

'Is it mad to love you?'

'Never till now, when you're with child by another man.'

255

'Did I ever pay you compliments?'

'Christ's blood, why wasn't I here!'

But *that* she must not remember, must not think of. She sprang up from the stool where she had sunk down by the fire, and moved round the room, quick and glancing in her golden dress like some swift bright bird, touched the chair where he had sat, perched on the edge of the table and turned her head this way and that, seeking some object to distract her thoughts.

There were her shoes, fallen on their side where he had pulled them off, the diamond buckles still fastened; she must not look at them.

There was du Bellay's book beside her, open where she had left it; she had promised Bothwell she would read. She picked it up and held it where she sat, and stared at the page, on and on, and never saw the words.

CHAPTER FIVE

JAMES HEPBURN, as usual, wasted no time. At ten o'clock next morning Black Ormiston of the Moss Tower paid his call on Mr Randolph of London, with the half-dozen of 'our fellows', no more and no less, that Bothwell had specified as exactly sufficient for the purpose the night before. After a brief talk with the Black Laird, a man of few words, Mr Randolph, 'perceiving himself narrowly encompassed', finished his packing in less than an hour, and was escorted out of Edinburgh to Berwick.

Bothwell joined the little cavalcade once they were clear of the town, and asked Randolph point-blank why his Queen had objected to him as the Scots delegate for the Peace Commission. The little Envoy, accustomed to the circumambient language of diplomacy, blinked at this like an owl in daylight. He could not tell Bothwell the true objection: that it had proved impossible to get him on the pension list from England, to ensure his working against his own Queen. He therefore referred darkly to 'things' spoken by the Earl injurious to the English Queen.

'That old scandal!' said Bothwell impatiently. It seemed little enough for her to complain of – that she and Mary rolled together were not enough to make one honest woman! She ought to be flattered by her company! He made his usual amends, a challenge to any man who dared say he had ever spoken dishonourably of the English Queen. Randolph promised politely to report the challenge; he then made his own complaint, of his removal from the Scots Court, saying venomously that he knew well enough who was the chief cause and adviser of his dismissal. He was accusing Mary's secretary – naturally enough, since Rizzio had collected the proof of his treacherous conduct. What Bothwell did not like was the gleam of mysterious satisfaction that had shot across his face in that unguarded spasm of anger. What scheme did he know to be hatching against his enemies at Court? And whom would it attack? Rizzio alone? Others with him? The Queen herself?

Further questions only shut up that prim pursed button of the Envoy's mouth. Anyway, he would be safe out of the country in a few hours, and under Ormiston's guard till then. Bothwell parted company with him and watched that narrow bent back ambling away towards Berwick among the broad alert upright backs of his rank-riders.

He would have been less satisfied could he have had a glimpse of Randolph's next post-bag to London, sent from the security of Berwick Castle. In it he told Robert Dudley, Earl of Leicester, that 'there is a bait laid for Signor David.' Of Mary herself, and her husband and his father Lennox, he wrote that 'there are practices in hand contrived between the father and the son to come by the Crown against her will,' and hinted darkly of 'many things grievouser and worse than these – yes, of things against her own person.'

To Elizabeth he wrote more discreetly that it was scarcely worth while for her to work further for the return of Lord James, or even for himself to forward her latest letters on his behalf; since that return should soon be effected by means of a 'matter of no small consequence, which is intended in Scotland.'

All of which was evidently more intelligible to Elizabeth and her Ministers than it would have been to Bothwell.

That indefatigable fellow was acting yet again with his accustomed speed in yet another business; he was getting married, and within the month. Gordon was delighted to have this close tie with his friend. He came down very handsomely over the dowry, as Bothwell told him, while mentioning that his own finances, in spite of recent honours, were still somewhat shaky.

'Jean will help you in that better than most men could do,' the Gordon solemnly assured him. 'Yes, you may laugh, but she has the best business head in the family. She's done more than anyone to pull the estates together after my father's death; got a coal-mine started on them, and salt-pans. Not a farthing wasted in all her transactions. I tell you, you couldn't do better than put your affairs in her hands.'

This unusual praise of a young and lovely bride did not seem to inspire the bridegroom to any degree of passion. He looked rather blankly at Gordon and said he was afraid he hadn't got a coal-mine for his wife to play with – perhaps a few loads of peat off the bog might amuse her. And his humour grew more sardonic when he asked if it were Jean's head for business that had prompted her conversion and her brother's to the Reformed Religion. Fortunately Gordon, so quick and fiery to take offence with others, never seemed to mind what the Hepburn said to him; the grave and haughty Highlander and the cynical Borderer understood each other far too well.

Where Gordon was generous, Mary was lavish. She gave the bride the materials for her wedding dress from the stores of gorgeous Eastern silks and woven treasure she had brought from France – a dozen yards of the finest cloth of silver and half a dozen yards of white taffeta to line the sleeves and train, boxes of pearls to sew all over it.

'Aren't you rather overdoing it, your contrast with the Virgin?' Bothwell demanded in his mocking fashion of his Queen. '*She'd* have had me to the Tower for marrying – and on top of saying I loved her – but you give us a wedding like an Emperor's.'

Her soft under-lip trembled; she bit it and said with valiant lightness, 'But I like gorgeous weddings. I got the taste at fifteen. And just think of all the gay weddings we've had at Court since I came home.'

'It's what I am thinking. And in double the time at the English Court, none.'

And he went off to commission a French artist at Court to paint his and his bride's miniatures in an oval case side by side, and had his first sitting straightaway. It was a tedious business, and his impatience communicated itself to the portrait, the eyes alert and fierce, a permanent frown carving a rut between his brows and running sharp lines from nose to mouth. There were iron-grey threads in the rough dark hair. He wore the doublet of ribbed gold silk he had ordered for his wedding, with gold buttons and a very narrow pleated white ruff. Jean was painted in a tiny blue and gold cap far back on her fine forehead, and her narrow ruff pinned close up to her long shapely chin. She would not wear her wedding dress for the portrait, to her mother's deep disappointment. She, as well as all her nine sons, had always been a little afraid of Jean, the youngest girl, who had from babyhood managed to establish that as a unique and privileged position. Her father had worshipped her, and the fat foolish loquacious old fellow was the only member of her family for whom the silent scornful girl had ever felt real affection.

Lady Huntly frankly adored the Queen and wished Jean did too, but girls were so hard nowadays. Was she pleased with this fine match to the rising power in the kingdom? She had accepted the offer in her calm way, as her indisputable right; but Lady Huntly knew that she had been piqued by Sandy Ogilvie's defection to Mary Beton, though in any case Jean would have been far too ambitious to let young Sandy stand in the way of a more important marriage. She certainly signified her desire to make the offer a firm one; for she pointed out that as there had been a marriage between the families four generations back, it would be advisable to get the Papal Dispensation for marriage between cousins; Protestant as they were, the Pope was still useful legally. Her eldest brother, with unusual gaiety in his pleasure over the match, chaffed her on her cautious foresight: 'You don't mean to give him any loophole for escape later!'

'He has shown he knows how to use it, by the reports of his former marriages,' she replied, with no hint even of irony in her grave young voice.

Gordon felt a twinge of anxiety for his friend. But Bothwell of all men would know how to ride a grey mare.

Lady Huntly showed no such coolness for her future son-in-law. She told him all about the Queen's magnificent presents, and Bothwell had the sense to keep it dark that he had happened to come in on her just when she was looking them out with her own hands. The stout old lady would purr like a stroked cat over it, but the girl standing so still by her side – well, there was another sort of cat there! He enjoyed the challenge implied in Jean's manner to him; to conquer her would give him something to do and think about; of all things, he could never have stood a gentle and loving bride at this moment. It intrigued him that she showed no eagerness to obey her mother, who insisted, in transparent excuse to give the young people a moment together alone, that she should take her lover to the sewing-room to see her maid sewing on all those lovely pearls – 'such a clever girl, Bessie Crawford, though only a blacksmith's daughter.'

Jean led him up the stairs without a word, and he followed her into a long low room where the February sunshine slanted in through little crooked panes of greenish glass. Again he saw those moonlight-coloured waves of silver stuff billowing and flowing away, this time round a seated figure, dark against the window, with black head bent low over her work. Bessie Crawford raised her head to show eyes black as sloes and a white skin; she began to rise to make a curtsy, but Jean motioned her to stay where she was. 'You'll drop the pearls,' she said.

It gave him an odd sensation to see in those busy hands the globed translucent drops that he had last seen trickling through the Queen's long fingers. Pearls and waves of silver, of their very essence they belonged to her, 'the Mermaid'. This dress should be for her, this wedding — It was the first time the thought had occurred to him, and it went through him with a cold thrust like steel.

Jean had left the room, so quietly that he only now heard her going downstairs. Had his thoughts been louder than her footsteps? She was credited with witchcraft, the usual tribute to any woman with some learning. He turned to follow her, nodding goodbye to the sewing-maid and hoping she would like it when she came to Crichton.

'If I stay so long in my young lady's service,' said the girl smoothly.

'Why, it's not till the end of the month!'

'She doesn't keep her servants so long as a rule,' was the demure answer.

He chuckled at her impudence.

*   *   *

Of all the grand weddings Mary had so proudly counted at her Court, this was the most superb. She herself had two new dresses made for it, one all white and the other crimson, braided with black and gold.

Bothwell insisted on the Protestant Church for the ceremony, though Mary artfully pleaded the feelings of the bride's mother.

'If I won't do it for you, d'you think I would for my mother-in-law?' he demanded.

It was the only satisfaction she got. 'And I shall wear the white at the banquet instead, as I like it better,' she said to Beton. 'The Kirk of the Canongate shan't have the honour of my prettiest dress!'

The Kirk was so crowded that many people could not see the handsome couple at all, though they stood on stools brought for the purpose.

The Queen signed the marriage contract together with Bothwell's friend, Long Geordie Seton, the Hepburn lawyer Mr David Chalmers, all the Gordon brothers, and their mother the Dowager Countess, who, dimpling coyly all over her wise old face, admitted she could not write, and had to have her hand guided by the Bishop of Galloway.

A tremendous banquet followed at Kinloch House, and everyone said what a regal and sumptuous figure the bride made. The Queen, in her white dress, though many knew her now to be with child, looked far slighter, younger, more like her bridesmaid than her wedded Sovereign.

Darnley said so, rather too loudly, though he actually refrained from getting drunk, for he was determined to make it up with Mary at this wedding. They danced together, except for the opening Dance Royal of the Galliard, when etiquette demanded that he should lead out the bride, and the bridegroom the Queen.

'I have danced this before with him,' thought Mary, 'and I shall do it again. Why does it seem as though it were the only time we have ever danced together?'

There were five more nights of dancing and banqueting in Edinburgh, and five days of tournaments in the tiltyard of the Castle, and all the citizens attending them congratulated Mary on having brought back the old glory when Edinburgh had been the scene of chivalry as courtly as any in Italy or France.

'Ah, those were the days!' sighed old Lady Huntly as she sat beside Mary at the jousts in the cold spring sunshine, and told her that this tiltyard used to be known as the Field of Remembrance, between the Castle of the Maidens and the Secret Pavilion. That great oak at the end was where the knights hung their shields in challenge; 'and for five *weeks* on end, not days; it was called the Tree of Hope which grows in the Garden of Patience, bearing the Leaves of Pleasure, the Flower of Nobility, and the Fruit of Honour.'

For the first time since she had met her, Mary saw Jean smile. Her mother said rather sadly that for all Jeannie was so clever, she never looked at a book of romance.

'But I do, Lady Huntly,' said Mary. 'I was reading Tristram and Iseult all through again the other day. And I love Sir Launcelot.'

'I think all girls do, even nowadays,' said the old lady, patting her knee – 'Jeannie, too, don't you?'

'I know nothing about him, Madam, except that he was the Queen's lover.'

Jean was born old, thought her mother with a sigh.

But Mary loved to hear all she could tell of those gayer and gentler days. 'Oh, if I had seen Edinburgh then! And my grandfather – the most splendid young King in Europe – did you ever see him, Madam?'

'I did indeed, in this very Field of Remembrance. Five years old I was, and proud to be taken to my first tournament – and in whose honour do you think it was held? Not for the Tudor rose, Queen Margaret, but for a Black Lady – a negress that had been captured in a Portuguese ship, and the wild young King must needs make her Queen of the Tournament, and himself her Savage Knight, to joust for his lady against all comers. And at the banquet a magic cloud came down from the ceiling, a most ingenious invention of Bishop Forman's – there are no bishops like him now, all this theology has spoiled the clergy. The cloud bore her up over our heads in all her spangles like a glittering black angel – or ape! Willie Dunbar wrote an absurd poem to her, saying how

> *In her rich apparel,*
> *She blazed as bright as a tar barrel.'*

And she laughed so much that her light tawny wig had to be set straight by Jean, who blushed very red for her mother; it was bad enough that she could never remember to have her grey eyebrows made up to match the wig. But Lady Huntly, no whit disturbed, only said, 'Thank you, my bairn.'

Bothwell won joust after joust, and laid his prize before his bride, whose scarf he wore bound round his arm. Mary thought of Queen Guinevere watching Sir Launcelot at the jousts when he wore Elaine's sleeve. Her old French romances and Bothwell's ballads and legends of the Border, though so much rougher, met in the same great-hearted world of chivalry; the chivalry of friendship, whether between man and man or man and woman. 'Well is he that hath a trusty friend,' Guinevere said when Launcelot rode to her rescue – as Bothwell had done to her own. She suddenly found herself looking at the Field of Remembrance through a mist of tears.

*   *   *

262

The Queen had proved her desire to have all men live as they wish by allowing Knox to return this winter to preach in St Giles'. Bothwell carried off his brother-in-law to hear him the Sunday after the wedding. The Queen had thought he could not refuse her the return compliment of hearing Mass with her 'this once', as she had attended his Protestant wedding; in her eagerness she took him by the hand and said, 'Won't you come with me?'

'Where, Madam?' he asked, with his hard hot eyes upon her. 'I'll leave you to go to God alone.'

And to Knox he went with Gordon.

In the fading daylight of that wintry day in early spring the little figure of the preacher hunched over his pulpit looked older and feebler than when Bothwell had last seen it more than three years ago. His voice too was hoarser even than usual, with the croak of a sore throat that sometimes took away his voice altogether. But his fierce whisper, determined to make itself heard, hissed through the darkening church. That intent crouched form, the sweep of his black winged arm in the gloom, seemed charged with some dreadful purpose; the sibilant voice urged its meaning forward like a serpent hissing as it struck.

And what was its meaning? Why was he telling the story of Queen Esther and the faithful Mordecai whose services had been forgotten? Why did he rail again and again on that lying, spying knave, the villain Haman? The whole sermon was an incitement to hate, rising higher and shriller, until that weak bodiless voice seemed to whisper a prophecy: 'So they hanged Haman high upon the gallows he had prepared for Mordecai.'

'Well,' said Bothwell as they came out of the church, 'for the faithful Mordecai read the Bastard, I suppose, and for Haman, David Rizzio. How long has he been preaching holy murder?'

Gordon could not believe the preacher to be so bold. 'He has only just crept back out of his hiding-hole.'

'Aye, he moves fast enough at a gun or the clash of a sword. But put that one into a pulpit and he'd preach death and damnation to God Himself.'

And he thought it worth while to speak a word of warning to Rizzio. But the little man showed flamboyant confidence. 'Those great Scots lords, they brag, they talk very big – pouf!' and he blew himself out – 'but they will not act. They are like geese strutting one after the other.'

'Are they so? You'll find they can fly all together like geese and strike at the same mark. Be careful not to give them that mark, that's all I say.'

'My lord, do not be angry with me. I speak to you as my friend, who have nothing to do with these geese – all birds of a feather. But you are the lone eagle, and I' – he struck himself absurdly on his squat black and white velvet doublet – 'am the lone magpie. Now I will tell you why I am safe. A fortune-teller has told me to beware of a bastard. But as long as I am here,' and he laid his finger vulgarly to his nose, 'the Bastard stays at a safe distance in England.'

Bothwell was astonished at his simplicity.

'God knows what distance is safe for that one. Nor is he, by a long shot, the only bastard in Scotland.'

But he could not stay to argue. He had his honeymoon to see to; he could spare a week at Seton House before returning in time for the opening of Parliament. He told Gordon to keep what watch he could at Court, and rode off to Seton with Jean.

The honeymoon might have been more of a success if she had not worn black the first day, in mourning for her lost love, having just had the news of Sandy Ogilvie's open engagement to Mary Beton. Her husband roared with laughter at the insult, tore the dress off her back, and threatened to dress it with his whip if she ever wore widow's weeds at him again. If she had laughed back it would have won him to her faster than anything, for her childish gesture of defiance had amused and excited him. But he had frightened her more than he intended, or realized, and fear always made Jean sullen. Nor had anyone ever heard her laugh since her father died.

So she sulked, and he cursed and yawned, and meeting a girl in the passage whose black eyes glanced merrily at him, he remembered it was Bessie Crawford and said, 'What, the faithful retainer! Are you still in Her Ladyship's service?'

'And in His Lordship's, sir,' she said, curtsying.

He tweaked the saucy coloured handkerchief she wore on her black head, and laughed as he passed on.

CHAPTER SIX

THE WEEK'S honeymoon was over, Bothwell back in Edinburgh, and the next day, Thursday, he rode in the procession to open Parliament, bearing the sceptre, while his brother-in-law, George Gordon, Earl of Huntly, bore the crown. Mary wore her new crimson dress with the flowing sleeves lined with glistening white, and all her company were particularly magnificent, for this was the first Parliament since her marriage and the over-throwal of the Bastard, who was to be tried, in his absence, for his rebellion last summer.

But there was one notable exception, the King himself, who had preferred to go hawking on the sands of Leith. It was his way of showing that he ought to be given the Crown Matri-monial.

'He blames Davie that he has not got it,' Mary contrived to tell Bothwell, 'but it is impossible.'

He thought her face looked thin and strained under the rouge, which did not suit her in the daylight and at close vision. She was nearing the seventh month of her pregnancy, a ticklish time, and she did not look fit for it, and one never knew what next that young idiot might do to upset her. Bothwell, who had never before considered the bearing of children as much differ-ent from the production of a litter of puppies, now found himself hideously anxious. He suggested a hunt next day to distract her mind, was abashed that she had to remind him that it would not be safe for her to ride hard.

Two months more and she would be free, and this precious burden within her, safe.

All she wanted now was to be as quiet as possible; on Satur-day she got up late and watched her husband playing tennis with Davie all the afternoon. Davie, though so short and squat, was an uncannily quick and forcible player and held his own untiringly against the tall graceful golden-haired youth. It de-lighted her to see them playing together, it showed that Harry had already forgotten his sulks and sense of grievance against Davie.

They came up to her now, laughing and mopping their fore-heads; it had been a grand game, a close game, but Davie had won at the end, and Harry rather surprisingly took it quite good-humouredly. 'I'll get the better of you next time,' he said, draw-ing his fine linen shirt-sleeve across his hot face with a jolly boyish gesture and then flinging his coat over his shoulders for he was still too hot to get into it.

He was going to dine in the town tonight with some friends – 'You don't mind, do you, *chérie*?' he asked Mary, who won-dered if she were looking very ill. Nothing else could explain such consideration from him after his months of neglect. But of course Harry hadn't found it amusing to dance attendance on an ailing wife; now her time was getting near, he had at last begun to realize the importance of her health. She was so happy at that that she squeezed his hand, but he pulled it away and muttered something apologetic about it being too hot and sticky. She laughed and told him to enjoy himself tonight and she would too, for she was having a little informal supper-party for her half-brother Lord Robert and her half-sister the Countess of Argyll (really her father had been very thoughtful in providing her with so many half-relations) and Davie here, who would give them some music first – they would all make music; with the four of them they should have some charming madrigals.

He smiled at her in a gentle absent-minded fashion and said, 'Well, don't tire yourself. You've got to be careful now, you know.'

He was strangely unlike himself. But it was a very pleasant way of being unlike himself. Certainly nothing to worry about. She went to lie down for an hour, then put on a loose filmy grey dress with hanging sleeves to hide her figure, and joined her guests in the little anteroom. She could never come into that room without looking to see if Bothwell were still there, standing, watching her as he had stood and watched her that night after the banquet.

Others were there instead: dear Davie, still smiling all over his face at his victory at tennis, for he had the vanity of the small and misshapen, prouder of his athletic prowess than of all his wits or his musical and poetic genius. Rob was there, so merry and affectionate, so like but never really like his brother Johnnie. Alison was there, the fat jolly Countess of Argyll, in high spirits at getting away from her dour husband, whom she could never abide. It was a gay little company.

The cold pale green light of the March evening made the small room seem like a cave under water; their voices trilled out into it as they sang their madrigals, and mingled with the long fluting notes of a nesting blackbird in a pear tree near by. Then a man's deep voice rang out alone into the still air, the magnificent voice of David Rizzio.

Soon the pale gloaming and its one star were shut out with silk curtains; candles were lit, supper was served, with Arthur Erskine, the Captain of the Guard, in attendance. It was Lent, but Mary had been ordered meat by her doctor and they laughed over her special privileges, Lady Argyll advising her always to be with child each spring. They had just finished

266

supper, and were sipping their wine and eating sweets out of a carved silver dish, when Darnley suddenly appeared in the doorway at the top of the little spiral stairway that led straight up into this room.

Mary looked up startled. Whatever could have brought him away from his merry-making in the town? He was drunk, of course, she knew him well enough to see that at the first glance, but it was in a quiet dazed way, thank heaven.

She at once asked if he would not join them, and tried to make room for him between herself and Lord Robert, though it was difficult to get even four round that oval French table. He grinned at her in a vacant silly way, lurched over to her and put an arm round her shoulders, too drunk, it seemed, even to speak.

She could not bear that foolish grinning face hanging over her. She looked down instead at his hand; it was twitching and plucking at the agate-hilted dagger that she had given him. The emeralds and diamonds winked back at her between his fumbling fingers; he was always restless, always fidgeting with something or other, but tonight his hand seemed almost convulsive. What could be the matter with him?

There was a gasp from the table, a sudden stir; she saw the gaunt form and livid face of Lord Ruthven coming in at the door where just now Darnley had entered. She saw murder in that dreadful yellow face, in the staring eyes, before she saw his drawn sword and steel cap and the breastplate over his loose bedgown. She knew what he had come for before he spoke in the ghastly wheezing voice of a very sick man.

'Let that man David come out of Your Majesty's chamber, where he has been too long.' And he rapped out at Darnley as to a dog, 'Sir, take the Queen!'

For she had already sprung up and in front of Rizzio, who cowered down behind her, clutching at her dress, while Darnley stood and gaped like a man in a dream.

'Is this your work?' she demanded, with sudden horrible conviction.

'I know nothing about it,' he stammered thickly. His red face was turning grey.

She turned on Ruthven. 'On pain of treason, I command you to go,' she cried; and to Arthur Erskine, 'Take him away!'

Erskine drew his sword. Ruthven shouted, 'Lay a hand on me at your peril!'

His shout was a signal. Men came crowding in now at both

doors, men with drawn swords or daggers, their faces agape like hounds for blood. Rizzio yelled, 'Justice! Justice!' Mary cried to him frantically, 'The King will prevent it – he has not forgotten all you have done for him.'

Did Darnley even hear her? He stood there shaking, gibbering, while the armed men surged past him, knocking over the table. There was a crash of glass and silver, the candles fell and went out, Lady Argyll had the presence of mind to snatch one and hold it up high or the room would have been in total darkness. Lord Robert and Arthur Erskine were at once overpowered, pinioned, and dragged off down the stairway.

A man thrust at Rizzio across Mary so that his blood spurted out over her dress. He still clung to it, but Kerr of Fawdonside bent back his middle finger till in agony he had to let go, and then Ruthven seized her and thrust her into Darnley's hands, telling her as she fought and struggled that no harm was intended to her person. She laughed, dreadfully, for while Darnley held her down by force in a chair, Kerr pushed a pistol against her side. She tried to hold it off. 'You are hurting the child!' she cried; then as they pushed and thrust against her she saw that that was indeed part of their intention. But what she was seeing and hearing in front of her should surely be enough for their purpose.

Davie was being stabbed again and again, and screaming in a horrible thin whine unlike any human voice, and Darnley never spoke to save him, but pressed her down, down into the chair as if he were falling on her. Blood was on her dress, blood was spurting everywhere; that huddled, writhing, whining thing on the floor was being dragged into the bed-chamber and finished off there, all the men thrusting after it, panting and grunting in their blood-lust. Darnley went too. There came a moment's silence, and then the sound of something soft and heavy rattling and bumping down the bedroom stairs.

Ruthven came back, fell into a chair, with a refinement of courtesy asked her pardon for sitting in her presence, and called for a drink, 'for God's sake.' He was moribund; it seemed for a moment that there would be another death before her eyes.

As he sat there gasping and holding his side, there came an uproar from the end of the gallery. Men came in and told him that the Lords Bothwell and Huntly were trying to force an entry with a few scullions. Ruthven laughed in answer, with a dry rattling hollow sound in his throat.

'Much good they'll do against five hundred men!' he wheezed. 'I'll soon settle the scullions.'

She fainted at that. He finished his drink, dragged himself together, and with two of his servants holding him up by the arms, limped down the stairs.

CHAPTER SEVEN

THE HEPBURN was supping with the Gordon that evening in his quarters at Holyrood. They had walked first in the gardens, where a blackbird was singing like mad on a branch of budding pear blossom. The huge shape of Arthur's Seat rose dark against the pale evening sky, and the tourelles of the Palace pierced it with tapering points graceful as those of a château in Touraine. From one of them came the sound of music and a man's deep voice singing a triumphant song. They stood for a moment to listen, then saw lights warm and golden in the window; the curtains were drawn across it and there was silence.

They went indoors, and Lord Atholl joined them at supper. They talked of the impending trial of Lord James and his colleagues. Atholl was of opinion that it would come to nothing. 'The Bastard has too strong a party, and none knows where it spreads. It works underground.'

Bothwell gave a cracking yawn of disgust. 'I hate politics,' he said in explanation. 'I think I hate all mankind and all their filthy little businesses.'

These Timonesque reflections were interrupted by a shout:

'A Douglas! A Douglas!' The war-cry was ringing through the Palace, and the hurried tramp of armed men, hundreds of them.

Bothwell sprang to his feet with an oath, pushed back his plate and gave a shout to his servants. 'Call your men too,' he told the others. 'What the devil is this? Are the Douglases out?' And then as he realized the smallness of their numbers he called to the cooks and scullions to follow too, and to bring their spits for weapons.

They ran in the direction of the shouting, and Bothwell turned cold with fear as he realized it was coming from the Queen's apartments.

They flung themselves against the door of the gallery that led to them, and found it barred and held fast. They sent back some of the servants for crowbars. Bothwell shouted to the men on the other side to let him and the Earls of Huntly and Atholl pass. They called back that they were holding the doors for the Earl of Morton, the head of the Douglas clan, and had orders to let none pass.

More men came running past; Bothwell seized one of them and spun him round.

'What's the business? Is it an attempt on the Queen?'

'No, no, only that Popish rascal Rizzio.' He grinned as the servants came running back with the crowbars. 'You'll find that no good, my lord. There are five hundred men in all about the Palace, the gates are closed and the porter's keys taken.'

Bothwell let him go and turned to the others. 'We may as well go back and finish our supper, Gordon.' He winked as he spoke; they must go cannily for the moment. Atholl left them for his own quarters, Gordon and Bothwell sat down to plates of congealed gravy.

They had not long to wait before Lord Ruthven came limping in, held up by two servants. He fell panting into a chair, and they gave him drink with expressions of respectful sympathy. Bothwell insisted on making it whisky instead of wine. 'You need it, my lord.' He further said it was a good thing the Italian was dead – 'we want no foreigners here.'

The invalid, gulping down raw whisky as if it were water, gasped out, 'We should have hanged him; we brought the rope for it, but there wasn't time.'

Bothwell filled his glass again. The blue lips writhed in a grin and repeated. 'No time. We made short work of him. Come and see.' He poured the second glassful down his throat, then dragged himself up and led them down the passage to the porter's lodge. There on a wooden chest lay a lumpish blood-boultered body, the gashed and twisted face scarcely recognizable as that of David Rizzio.

The porter was leaning over it, fingering the jewelled hilt of a dagger stuck deep in the ribs; he sprang back and began talking very fast, to distract their attention from what he had been doing.

'Aye, there he lies,' he said, 'and right it is he should. It's his due. That chest was all he had to lie on when he first came to this place, and for all he jumped so high in the world it's all he's got to lie on now, the niggardly knave.'

'Wasn't free enough with drink-money for you, hey?' said Bothwell. 'Well, you'll get enough out of him dead.'

'My lord, I've not touched the body except to count the

thrusts in it – fifty-six in all. Hardly room for 'em all on a little fellow like him. And this whinger here, it's the King's, and should go back to him, but it's a tough job to pull out.'

He gave another tug, and out came the dagger, which Bothwell had also recognized. Ruthven held out his hand for it, and turned with a grin to Bothwell.

'Here you see the outward sign and proof that we acted in the King's business, led and instigated by the King. This rascal David stood between him and the Crown Matrimonial, lay between him and his wife.'

Gordon's hand flew to his sword, but Bothwell moved in front of him so quickly as to hide the gesture.

'And the Douglases?' he said. 'Why are they in it?'

'As we're all in it, all good Protestants who'll never stand by and see a base-born Popish intriguer rule this kingdom and the Queen. They're Darnley's kinsmen too, aren't they?'

They were, but a stronger and more likely motive was Morton's personal grievance (he had been afraid that Rizzio's influence would deprive him of the Chancellorship), combined with the hereditary policy of his Douglas clan in its venomous rivalry with the royal Stewarts.

'All sound men are with us,' said Ruthven. 'Lethington said a month ago we must chop at the root of the evil.'

'Lethington? And is James Stewart with you too?'

'That he is – and in the flesh before many hours are out. He's left Newcastle and should be here in Edinburgh by dawn, and the rest of the exiles with him. That slave there thought to pull him down in the coming trial, but the noose has been fitted round his own neck instead.'

'So they hanged Haman high upon the gallows he had prepared for Mordecai.' The weak bodiless voice of the preacher seemed to be whispering in exultation over the mutilated corpse.

'What of the Queen?' cried Gordon hoarsely. 'Was this done in her presence?'

'We dragged him away from her, into the next room, and killed him there. She's safe with her husband – if she doesn't like that, let her learn to, as an honest woman should.' Again there came that ghastly writhing of the lips, grinning back from the pallid gums. Ruthven had been in bed for over three months with inflammation of the liver and kidney disease. It gave Bothwell his opportunity at last for revenge.

'I hope indeed, my lord,' he said, with a grave sympathy that

271

showed he had no hope at all, 'that this death here tonight will not cause your own.'

The yellow eyeballs swivelled round on him like those of a startled horse. 'You'd best stay close in your quarters,' was the frightened man's retort. 'The whole place is under guard. There are eighty armed men about the Queen's room alone. None will pass in or out of the Palace except by our command. I will go and tell Atholl of the matter, and trust he'll show as much care for his skin as you have done.'

And the terrible old man hobbled off between his supporters. The Earls of Huntly and Bothwell went back obediently to Bothwell's rooms and there discussed their plans. Inside the Palace they were prisoners, for even if Atholl gave active help, which they doubted, they would be a mere handful against five hundred men, who had already taken up all the strategic points.

They must escape from Holyrood in order to rescue the Queen and raise an armed force on her behalf. So much Bothwell said, and briskly, for Gordon was overcome with rage and loathing. 'If she should have a miscarriage — '

'That's what they're working for, of course, and her death with it. But with luck it's their plot we'll make abortive.'

'My mother would help,' said Gordon. 'If we could only get into the town and up to Huntly House — '

'We must get there. There's a window along here that looks on the lion-pit. That won't be guarded.'

'Except by the lions,' observed Gordon.

'It's a cold night – they'll be inside. Anyway, we'll take the chance.'

And the two Earls jumped out of a first-floor window into the lion-pit.

CHAPTER EIGHT

IN ONE way the conspirators succeeded in their purpose. There *was* a forced birth that night: the birth of a new creature in Mary, one 'hard as steel when offended, cold as ice in danger', the heart of a man of war in the body of a young woman three months past her twenty-third birthday and nearing her first childbed. With her unusual power of concentration she now shut her mind to everything but that moment ahead of her. Nothing else mattered. She had just seen her trusted friend and servant hacked to death, but that was not the only, nor the

272

chief aim of her enemies. They could have chosen any other moment to dispatch him, and far more easily. It was done in her presence in order to produce her miscarriage, and in all probability her death. They had succeeded in the first part of their attack; they should not succeed in the second.

She had fainted, but no one helped her to come to herself; her half-sister had been dragged away from her, as well as Lord Robert and Arthur Erskine; she struggled back to consciousness slowly, unwillingly, to the dreadful awakening that was no continuation of a nightmare, as she at first thought, but the unbelievable truth.

Under her nearly closed eyelids she saw the familiar scene of her bedroom round her, but horribly distorted, as in delirium. There was blood spattered over the chimney-piece where they had struck the final blows. Her hand touched thick drying blood on her dress. She was lying, not on her bed, but hunched in a chair; she felt so ill she thought she must be dying. None of her women were here to look after her. Instead, there was the tramp and clank of armed men marching round about her room.

She was a prisoner here, and these were her jailers. The ghoulish Ruthven limped in and out with the help of his servants, as though he were not free to die until he had done all the evil required of him by his master, Satan; he croaked and gasped out his commands to the youth he sneeringly addressed as his King.

She shut her eyes fast, thinking that when she opened them again he would be gone, and when she opened them he was – but she now saw in front of her the bestial pudgy face of the Earl of Morton with his little pig's eyes winking out above his ragged red whiskers. Morton – head of the Douglases – yes, this was the man who had had a minister tortured and hanged for rebuking his adultery with the widow of a man that he had murdered.

And then she heard the thick fury of Lord Lindsay's flurrying voice, blaring and roaring out orders, threats and oaths indiscriminately. He was excited to frenzy, as always by bloodshed. In the first weeks of her arrival in Scotland he had led the riot against the priest in her chapel with Arran, and yelled with blood-lust as madly as that poor lunatic. She had seen as little as she could of him since then; but now he was here, in her bedchamber, together with Morton and Ruthven.

She was in hell and in the power of the devils, and all the

time there was one slender young shape, like an angel with fair hair, moving restlessly about, hovering over her when her eyes were closed, sliding away from her when they were open. That fair form in blue and gold was a worse devil than these savage old men, for he had played tennis and joked with his victim all this afternoon, so as to lull any suspicions he might have; he had been sweetly attentive and considerate to herself.

'You don't mind, do you, *chérie*?' – and then that gentle, absent-minded, foolishly loving smile. Did Judas smile so when he kissed Jesus the same night that he betrayed Him?

'You've got to be careful now, you know.' He had said that when plotting this thrust at their child's life and her own. To get a woman with child and use that child as a weapon against her, a knife in her womb to be turned on herself – such treachery was past all human thought. 'But then he doesn't think, he drinks,' she told herself, and all his brains were rotted at the roots. She watched him under those half-shut lids as he drifted about her room, uneasy, unhappy, almost as much a prisoner of these brutal murderers as she was herself. He didn't realize it, of course – he realized nothing. But he could be made to do so. And a plan began to form itself behind the white ravaged mask of her face.

She had heard the uproar at the end of the gallery die down; but now that she could think again she did not believe Ruthven would dare have the Earls Bothwell and Huntly murdered at this juncture. They were more likely to have been taken prisoner. But to what end?

Now there came another uproar, from outside the Palace this time. She heard the clanging of the Common Bell away in the town; the hurried, uneven hammer-strokes upon it came hurtling down the hillside on the night wind. Someone must have got out of the Palace and given the alarm to the citizens; they were arming, they were calling to each other, hurrying down the long steep street to her defence. She heard the running tread of hundreds of feet, and the clamour as they beat upon the locked gates. Now they were shouting from the outer courtyard, and the light of their torches flared across the ceiling. There was a hush while someone parleyed with them, but a murmur grew, a muttering growl of dissatisfaction, then shouts louder than before. She could hear now that they were calling, 'The Queen! Let us see the Queen!'

She had lain cramped and huddled in her chair for about two hours, apparently lifeless; now she sprang in one movement to the window and got her hands on the latch. But before she could open it Lord Lindsay seized her arms and wrenched her back.

'Show yourself at that window,' he shouted, 'say one word to them, and I'll cut you in collops and throw you down the wall!'

His mouth seemed to slip over his face, his eyes glared; she was staring into the face of a wild beast. The next moment he threw her with all his force back into the chair; she gave a low moan and lay limp, her eyes shut, her mouth half open and saliva running from it. That brought Darnley to her side, fumbling, inarticulate. He rubbed his hand over her head in some vague attempt at reassurance. Deliberately she laid her cheek against it; it was cold and blue, she felt as though she were caressing a snake. This hand, too, had struck down Davie; under her eyelids she saw his belt, and that his dagger was missing from it. Her father's dagger, her wedding present to Darnley, that dagger had been used by her young husband to kill her friend, perhaps her child, perhaps herself. Its steel had entered her own heart; she felt nothing now, not even horror, as she laid her lips against that hand and whispered, 'Speak to the people, Harry. Tell them I am in danger.'

'Yes, yes, I'll do it,' he stammered.

The noise outside was growing; there was the clash of weapons, and the shouting came louder and angrier for the Queen. Darnley had left her side and was hurriedly conferring in low tones with Lindsay and Morton. Then he went to the window and opened it, and her hopes rose fast.

'My Lord Provost and loyal citizens of Edinburgh!' she heard him cry, and then, 'Justice has been done on a criminal within the Palace, a spy and infidel, the foreigner David Rizzio. But the Queen and I are safe. All is well. Return quietly to your homes. The Queen is quite safe, she is with me, and surrounded by her loyal servants.'

A shriek, piercing and agonized, from behind him was strangled as Lord Lindsay thrust his hand over the Queen's mouth. Then Darnley closed the window. This time she fainted again in good earnest.

When she came to at last she was quite alone. The guards marched up and down outside, but there was no one with her in the room where that night David had been murdered. She was light-headed for a time, for she had found herself whispering to him, telling him she would avenge him. Then she grew afraid that she heard him answer her. How foolish to be afraid of

Davie's ghost, who would never harm her, as would all these living men about her door. She crawled to the bed and lay there, hour after hour. At first she shrieked wildly, but nobody came. Then she lay silent.

Some time next morning Lord Lindsay brought her food, but she would not touch it. She gasped out that she was very ill and must have her women.

'Aye, and pass out from here in their clothes!' he snorted. 'Do you think I don't know your tricks?'

Her answer was a cry with her hands at her side, and he flung away from her.

Again there was silence, on and on, it seemed for ever. Was she to be left here alone to miscarry and die? She began to scream with a sound that frightened even herself.

And again Lindsay came back, but this time there was someone with him.

'Now mind,' he was saying, 'no woman is going to come out of here muffled up to the eyes; whoever comes out shall show her face, and if it's the Queen's, so much the worse for her. No, there's a better way than that!'

And closing the door, he stood there in the room, leaning against it, while Lady Huntly ran over to the bed and took that crouched figure in her arms, soothing her with her plump hands.

'My bairn, my bairn,' she murmured.

Mary clung to her but could not speak.

Lady Huntly bathed her face, asked if she had had food. It was now four o'clock on Sunday afternoon, and Mary had had none since supper the evening before. Rounding on Lord Lindsay, Lady Huntly demanded to know if he meant to starve the Queen to death.

'I brought her food,' he said sullenly, 'and she'd have none of it.'

'Very likely, from such hands as yours.'

She bustled out, and presently came back with a servant bearing a tray. Lord Lindsay, still on guard, insisted on examining all the dishes. Then Lady Huntly, paying no more attention to him than if he had been a doorpost, coaxed the Queen to eat and drink, chatting away as if there were nothing abnormal in the situation.

'And now we must get you to bed,' she said cheerfully.

Mary shuddered. 'Not here – in this room —' but Lady Huntly pressed her arm and she was silent.

Even now it was difficult to get rid of Lord Lindsay, but the old lady told him roundly that if he insisted on staying to watch the Queen undress, she would bring a charge of attempted rape against him. At that he hurriedly departed, telling them he would give them five minutes and no more.

As soon as the door shut on him, Lady Huntly whispered very fast as she undressed the Queen, 'I've been trying to get in here ever since last night. My son and Lord Bothwell escaped from the Palace and came and told me. Now they're planning to rescue you. Lord Bothwell gave me a long rope to smuggle in to you on a covered dish, but you saw how it was, they are examining everything that comes in. Luckily I waited to see if that would be so.'

Mary's heart had given a great leap. So Bothwell was not a prisoner. Hope, life, anything now was possible. She asked what the rope would be for, and was told that Bothwell planned to lower her in a chair from the clock tower. So different was the change in her mood since she had heard of his safety that she began to laugh unsteadily.

'How like him! *He* climbed down the Castle rock in the dark, so he thinks a woman seven months gone with child can swing down from a clock tower!'

'Yes, I told him it was impossible. But he has so great an opinion of you he swore you'd manage anything.'

'So I will, I will!' Her heart was soaring now. She would prove herself to him. 'That's impossible, the guard anyway would make it so. But I've another plan. I'll tell him. Give me a scrap of paper from that writing-desk – there's the ink – quick!'

Lady Huntly brought them to her just as Lord Lindsay began to thump on the door.

The Dowager gave the usual formula. 'Wait one moment,' she called impressively: then, as he presently banged again, she went to the door and said in a lower voice through the keyhole that the Queen was on the *chaise percée*. Mary took the hint and seated herself on that article of domestic furniture while she scribbled her note. She was in her bed-gown by now. Lady Huntly hurried back to her, put away the pen and ink, and just had time to shove the note inside the neck of her dress before Lord Lindsay, disregarding their exclamations, pushed into the room.

'How dare you enter at this moment?' exclaimed the Dowager.

He was somewhat disconcerted to find that the Queen

actually was on the *chaise percée*, and roared back, 'How dare you stay here muttering and whispering long past the time I gave you? You'll go now, whatever excuse you trump up, and you'll not come back.'

She helped the Queen into bed, speaking the while as though she were continuing a conversation – 'and as I was telling Your Majesty, the King has dissolved your new Parliament, at midday today. There was a proclamation read at the Market Cross telling all the members of Parliament, only just assembled, to leave Edinburgh within three hours, on pain of death.'

She plumped up the pillows and coolly confronted Lindsay. 'Yes, my lord, and it's no treason to tell your Queen what everyone in Edinburgh has been told by order of you and your fellows. Nor is it treason to tell her that Lord James is back in Edinburgh, with the rest of the exiles. Oh, and yes, Madam – did I mention that the proclamation has declared that there will now be no trial of your half-brother and his fellow-rebels, and no danger either to them or their property? So now you see why they have returned.'

And she marched out past Lord Lindsay and went back to Huntly House, where she found her son and Bothwell secreted in a back room, having disregarded the decree of banishment 'within three hours on pain of death'. The Earl of Atholl had taken the hint and made for the safety of the hills with his followers.

They sprang up demanding news of her before Lady Huntly was inside the room. She began to unbutton the neck of her dress as she replied that the Queen was a deal better than she'd any reason to hope, 'but for all that, my lord, your plan will never do, as indeed I told you. But she has another, which she tells you of in this note. Read it quick and tell me what it is.'

He snatched it; it looked absurdly short, too short to tell any plan. 'What in hell does she mean?' he exclaimed as he scanned it, frowning. 'She says nothing here of how she means to do it. Has she gone mad?'

'Small wonder if she had!' exclaimed the old lady. 'But for pity's sake, what is in the note?'

'There's nothing in it, nothing! She tells me to wait for her at the village just before Seton, tomorrow night, from midnight on.'

*   *   *

That evening Mary obtained leave from her jailers to send for her half-brother. Waiting for him, she grew so restless that she rose and dressed herself again. At last, after some hours, the door opened and she saw the familiar impressive figure, the long grave face in its fringe of sparse beard.

The faithful Mordecai had returned.

CHAPTER NINE

IN THAT moment a strange thing happened.

James' hour of triumph had come at last, after all his waiting and plotting; his open rebellion; defeat and humiliation. But he had worked against his half-sister while away from her, used others to do his dirty work while he himself abstained from personal violence, which he disliked. He had only to make a dignified appearance when everything had been carried out according to plan.

This time there had been no hitch anywhere. For weeks past, messengers had carried constant secret communications between him at Newcastle and the conspirators round Ruthven's sick-bed in Edinburgh; as also between Randolph, still lurking on the English side of the frontier at Berwick, and the English Queen and her Ministers in London. Cecil had already in-formed 'Countess Meg' Lennox of the plot of her son's approaching triumph.

For this was an arrangement between the two gangs of plotters, formerly enemies, now allies. At the head of the old gang was the Protestant James, who had opposed Darnley be-cause he feared 'he would do little to forward the cause of Christ,' but who now swore to procure him the Crown Matri-monial, and 'to spare neither life nor death in supporting his quarrel against all his enemies without exception'. At the head of the new gang was the Catholic Darnley, the hope of his religion throughout England and Scotland, who now swore to establish the Protestant religion and restore James and the other rebel Protestant lords to their full powers and estates.

There was also, in case of accidents, which seemed only too likely to those who knew him, a Proclamation all ready to hand, signed by Darnley, in which he took all the responsibility for the murder of Rizzio 'though it were in the very presence of the Queen'. That presence was insisted on as the main objective, since her probable miscarriage and death would leave the ground clear of all obstacles to all the parties concerned.

And this elaborate conspiracy, whispered of in London,

Berwick, Newcastle and Edinburgh, had been kept secret and proved successful. The Queen was still alive, but Rizzio was as dead as fifty-six stabs could make him. Her Dominican friar, Father Black, had also been murdered in the Palace that same night. The Parliament had been dissolved, its members banished, and Mary was a helpless prisoner.

It only remained for James, who had arrived, as planned, several hours after the actual killing, to tidy up things and give them an air of respectability. And then he would be – as he had seen himself in his dreams ever since he could remember – the Regent of Scotland, all-powerful, with no one, certainly not a drunken young fool calling himself King, in his way.

But it is not quite true that nothing succeeds like success. There is a core of weakness in it. James in exile, disappointed, afraid, could scheme against and slander the half-sister who had loaded him with honours and riches, and feel no more remorse for it than if he were a devil.

But James in his complete triumph, with nothing to fear from her, seeing before him this white piteous wraith who looked as though she might indeed die before his eyes, was taken unawares. For perhaps the only time in his life he was conquered, for a moment, by that insidious power, pity. His eyes filled with tears.

Mary saw it and flung herself into his arms. 'Oh,' she cried, 'if only you had been here, you would never have let them treat me like this!'

And she too was sincere, although she knew that he must be in the plot.

But for a moment their minds had ceased to work; their arms were round each other; he was stroking her hair, calling her 'little sister'; she was clinging to him, sobbing; the same blood was in them both; he, who could remember their father so well, had seen it again and again in her likeness to that strange, fair, laughing King, and though it had never moved him before, it did now. And that same blood was pregnant in her now, to produce another Stewart King – if this last night's work did not prevent it. For the first time he felt some horror at that thought; it was true, he told himself, if he had been here he would not have let them treat her like this – not quite like this.

And he told her he was gravely displeased with Lindsay, he would speak to him very strongly, and that she should have her women with her.

The strange moment was past. He was pretending he had had nothing to do with the plot that he had instigated; she must pretend to believe in his pretence. There was more that she must do.

'And Harry,' she said tearfully; 'he has not been near me all day. Perhaps they would not let him come to me. Please tell him, dear James, that I should feel easier if I might see him for a little – but not with those others!' she added with a violent shudder.

So by James' consent, indeed order, Darnley came, very sheepish and unwilling, to see his wife, and at last she could speak with him alone.

*　　*　　*

'I'll tell you what it really is,' said Darnley, 'you never thought my rank good enough for you. I know the scorn you have for the base-born. Queen Catherine, the daughter of Lorenzo the Magnificent, is only the banker's daughter to you!'

'Oh God,' sighed Mary, 'that silly thing said by a pert child in a temper over her Latin lesson – is it always to be remembered against me?'

'And you've called Elizabeth the alderman's granddaughter.'

'But, Harry, you've said things like that about her too. Anne Boleyn, the alderman's daughter, was no relation of yours.'

'Oh, it's not just the Boleyn blood you sneer at. You Stewarts look on us Tudors as a pack of greedy Welsh upstarts, *I* know.'

Bewildered, she wondered where all this family pride was leading. 'It's only your grandmother, and mine, who was a Tudor.'

'There you go again, rubbing in now that even my Tudor claim to the English throne doesn't amount to much. I dare say it doesn't. I dare say I'm a nobody and that you're the daughter of a hundred kings on the one side and go back to Charlemagne on the other. I dare say you only took me because you couldn't get anyone better – your two merchants' daughters saw to that! But suppose I am of mean degree – all the same, I *am* your husband, and you promised that I should be your equal in all things. And look how you kept your promise! You gave me a lot of honours, it's true, revived the royal title of Duke of Albany for me, made people call me King, and so forth. But what's the use of giving me the name of King if you don't give me the power of one? I've said it all along, I ought to have the Crown Matrimonial, with full powers as King, and to continue as King if you —'

'If I die as a result of this last night's work?' she finished quietly.

He went crimson. 'It wasn't *my* work,' he mumbled; 'at least, it wasn't I who thought of it.'

'I can well believe that,' she said in the same soft tone.

He was deceived by her apparent gentleness and dropped down on his knee beside her chair. 'Oh, Mary, why has it all gone wrong? It was all Davie's doing. You – so proud and superior to all the Medicis and Tudors – no one good enough to be your husband – and then you could take up with that little rat from the Genoese gutters!'

'A servant is not a husband, Harry.'

'Damned near it at times, I'll be bound,' he muttered.

'I cannot believe that you mean it when you talk like that,' she said wearily.

'No, but, Mary – Mary, listen! It was Davie this, Davie that, from the very beginning. Davie got us married. Davie worked up the Pope and Spain on our side, Davie got in touch with the English Catholics, discovered James' plot to kidnap us —'

'But, Harry, he *did*. You're not denying it, are you?'

'No, but I was sick to death of hearing it.'

She looked at him with a slow, new amazement. She had thought there was nothing left for her to learn about Darnley, but only now did she begin to realize where the ingratitude of a mean nature could sink. The haughty youth of whom the nobles complained that he 'seemed a monarch of the world' had not been too proud to toady the Italian gutter-rat, play tennis with him, share his bed, and use his help to win his Queen, even sing the love-songs Davie wrote for his purpose – as Harry had let out with his usual naïvety.

But he was too proud to remember all this afterwards, except as an excuse to murder him.

He looked up at her and saw her face like stone. Was she still thinking of that wretched little fellow? Why must she go on thinking about him now he was dead? That white mask-like face began to worry him. He had made himself master now; it was absurd that he should feel nervous with her. Yet his hands would keep twitching; he twisted them together, he felt for the dagger that he always liked to fidget with, and found it gone – and then saw her eyes following his hands.

'What if it *was* a murder?' he broke out. 'Not that I had anything to do with it, I'll swear that to you, on the Cross if you like. But suppose it *was* – well, it's not the first murder in

Scotland, and it won't be the last – not by a long shot! It saved the trouble and uncertainty of a trial. It's a sort of justice. Davie was getting too much power. It was best to get rid of him. It's a sharp form of politics, that's all. Assassination has always been a weapon in politics – not pretty, but then politics aren't.'

She wondered who had taught him all this. She thought she could detect a rather cracked echo from that mellifluous-sounding politician, James.

'And to commit the murder in front of a pregnant woman,' she said, 'handling her roughly the while, so that with luck it may be not one murder but two, or rather three – does it make it right to call that, too, a sharp form of politics?'

She was too clever for him. He should never have let her argue. He had a better way in the old days of their courting – take her in his arms and kiss her. But somehow that had not outlasted their marriage. He got up and began to wander about the room, baffled and unhappy.

She saw that it had been no good talking to him. How silly to waste time! Involuntarily she looked at her watch. It was close on midnight. Tomorrow at midnight, or soon after, was the time she had appointed to keep tryst with Bothwell. And how much time, if any, would she be able to get tomorrow with Darnley? She had encouraged him to talk because she had got to find out what was in his mind before she could put what she wanted into it.

He saw her look at her watch. 'You'd best go to bed,' he said, glad of the excuse to go. 'So had I. There's a Council Meeting tomorrow morning, and I promised the old Bastard I'd be there.' (A glance at her to see how she took this news, but she showed nothing.) 'And today was pretty full, I can tell you – arranging the Proclamation at the Market Cross, and then the public meeting with James and the rest of the exiles to show we were all friends together.' (That would rub in how he was being recognized as King, and carrying out all his kingly duties.) 'And we all went to one of old Knox's endless sermons – and Lord! if you think murder wrong, just you go and listen to the Man of God! *He* called it a "most godly deed" and "worthy of all praise", and he ought to know what's godly, oughtn't he?'

'Are you going to be a Protestant now, Harry?'

'No, of course not. But it's good sense to keep in with them.'

'And the Pope, and Spain, and all the English Catholics who were so eager for your succession? Have you stopped keeping in with them? How are *they* going to take it, your joining up with their worst enemies and swearing to uphold Protestantism as the only religion?'

'Who told you that?'

So it *was* true. It was bound to be, of course.

She ignored his question. 'Do you think I've no friends outside Scotland?' she demanded. 'There are my uncles in France, they will avenge me, and all good Catholics will join them. You've turned against those of your own faith; they will turn on you.'

He gaped at her. It seemed it was the first time that had struck him. 'Anyway,' he said thoughtfully, 'the Catholics haven't any position here.'

'Nor have you, a Catholic. Why do you imagine James and Morton and Lindsay and Ruthven, all rabid Protestants, should want to put you in power? You are as much a foreigner here as I, English-bred, as I am French, and Catholic-bred, which they hate worse than either. You were friends with none of them here before this plot began; they hated you, and you rather gloried in it. Why should they suddenly change round and love you so much that they should consent to make you an absolute monarch over them? Of course they haven't changed. They don't ever mean you to be King. They are using you simply to get rid of me. As soon as that is done, they'll get rid of you.'

At last that had got him. His mouth fell open. He gasped out, 'They couldn't be such traitors!'

She could hardly restrain herself from breaking into cruel laughter.

'Oh yes, they are traitors,' she said lightly, 'and they will betray you – just as they (she had nearly said "you") have betrayed me.'

'But – but what can I do then? What *shall* I do?'

'You can't do anything, Harry. You've joined with them against me. So now you'll just have to wait till they join against you.'

This new, cool little voice, so quietly and dispassionately saying these deadly things, did it really belong to herself?

'But, Mary – Mary, I'm not against you. I'm not really. I thought you were against me. You were so cold.'

She began to cry in a soft weak feminine way. He had seen her cry with rage, but never like this. He did not notice that, though she was sobbing, she shed no tears.

'Oh, Harry, I wasn't, but I thought you didn't love me any more. You took other women.'

'I'd never have looked at another woman if you'd really cared about me.'

'I did care, but I was ill after that campaign, and then I was pregnant and the doctor said — '

'Damn the meddling old fool! You ought to have listened to me.'

'Yes,' she said meekly. 'And I will now, always. Oh, what a fool I am! There will be no "always" now; we are both their prisoners, and God knows what they'll do with us.'

'They shan't touch us, I'll swear it. Oh, Mary, don't cry so. I'll get us out of it somehow. I'll manage it all.'

He tried to put a brave face on it, but he was shaking as though he had the ague. Suddenly he flung himself down beside her and put his head in her lap.

'Oh, my God!' he wailed. 'What have I done? Is it all a trap? Will they shut us both up and kill us secretly? Mary, is there no way out? You're so clever and strong, don't give way now, don't cry. For God's sake, do be some help.'

She looked down with dry eyes on that ruffled chicken-yellow head. She raised her hand, then deliberately laid it on his hair, then forced herself to stroke it again and again. After all, it was no more than to stroke a wig. She had once thought, when he was drunk, that it was like a wig. She swallowed, moistened her lips, practised silently inside her head the tone that she must use.

'I'll try, Harry. But it's not easy. We'd best leave it now and get some sleep.'

'I'll not sleep a wink all night.'

'You must. You've got to go to the Council tomorrow morning. Come and see me after it, will you, and I'll see if I can think of anything by then.'

'Can't I stay here tonight?'

'*No!*' It was surprised out of her, but she hastened to cover it. 'Of course not – it would be madness. They think they've got you away from me to act against me. Whatever happens, you mustn't let them guess you've made it up with me – if you have,' she added wistfully.

'I have, indeed I have, Mary. Oh, Mary, you will think of something, won't you?'

'And you'll notice all they say at the Council tomorrow so as to tell me afterwards, won't you?' She was speaking more cheerfully, she seemed to be forcing herself to take courage. 'We mustn't lose heart. I shan't if I know you are with me again, as we were last summer. Oh, Harry, wasn't it grand – the forced marches, that ride past Loch Leven under James' very nose when the water was still all grey in the dawn – and then the Carron in spate, having to swim it on our horses. What a fine honeymoon we've had! And we'll have it again.'

Well, he wasn't sure about that. There was no fun in getting up early – still less in getting wet through and all but drowned.

There was always something going wrong in Scotland, floods, sermons, murders. Why had he ever left home? He wished he was dead, he wished he was at home with a cold, and his mother putting him to bed. Mary had nursed him well through the measles, but she wasn't the same. Old Countess Meg, even when she scolded, she made one feel so safe. He began to cry.

She put her arms round his head and hoped he would not raise his face. But at last he did, and it was all red and blubbered with tears. She bent her head quickly and kissed his hair.

CHAPTER TEN

ALL THAT night she wondered if she had not said enough to bind him to her – or alternatively had said too much, and that he would betray it to her enemies. He seemed incapable of keeping a secret, even when it was against himself to betray it. The astonishing thing was that he had kept this one so long beforehand. She must have been very blind. True, he had been avoiding her lately, and she had been too glad to wonder why.

Whenever she began to doze she dreamed that he had run straight to James and told him all she had said. In terror she woke herself up again and again. She had not dared confide her plan to him, but she would have to do so some time – as late as possible, so as to give him the less time to betray it. Even the fear of his colleagues that she had planted in him might give him away; they would notice a difference in him, they would get everything out of him, they would not let him come back to her after the Council; she was doomed, and there was no escape.

Her waiting-maid, Margaret Carwood, was with her, but Mary let her sleep; it was consoling that anyone could sleep there in that room. At last, when it was daylight, she herself slept for a little, and woke to hear the blackbird singing in the pear tree as she had heard him sing, with them, an hour before Davie was killed. That somehow gave her courage. These murderers could not kill everything that sang, not the birds, nor the returning spring.

She was astonished to find how hungry she was at breakfast, till she remembered that that hurried, agitated meal Lady Huntly had brought her, taken in front of Lord Lindsay, had been all that she had eaten yesterday. She made Carwood dress her very carefully. Then there was nothing for it but to wait till Darnley came to her after the Council – if he came. But she had some inquiries to make, some messages to send by Carwood, who was allowed to pass in and out through the guards on the pretext of getting medicines for her.

The mid-day bell sounded up in the town for 'noon-shanks', the pause in the morning's work when all workmen had their noonday draught of ale. The Council must be over. Had Darnley given away everything at it? Would they not let him come back to her? Would he never come? But he came.

He had got over his fright. He was a little subdued, but no longer cowed or lachrymose. He frowned and winked at Margaret Carwood when Mary asked him what had been said at the Council. Mary told Carwood to go into the anteroom.

'But she is part of our plan,' she said, 'she will have to help us.'

'What, you *have* a plan, then? You told me you'd none.'

'I told you I'd think of one. But it may depend on what happened at the Council. What did they say?'

'Oh, the usual things, upholding the Protestant religion and so forth.' He was sheepish again, and she had some little difficulty in getting out of him that it had been agreed to remove her to Stirling Castle 'for greater safety'.

'Yes, the safety of a prison cell where I shall conveniently die.'

'Mary!' His pained voice carried no conviction.

She saw that he had slipped right back from the position where she had got him last night, and the reason for this was soon forthcoming; the Council had summoned their fresh Parliament to bestow on Darnley the Crown Matrimonial and the government of the country. This had so flattering a sound that he could not believe they didn't really mean it. She had to begin all over again.

He was soon telling her that he had only swung back again because she could offer no alternative. 'Now tell your plan and I'll see if it's feasible.'

He was becoming quite lordly again. After all, the Council

287

had formally offered him the Crown Matrimonial that morning!

It was a desperate matter to tell her plan to anyone so slippery. 'How *can* I trust you? You do not care what happens to me as long as you think there is a chance of getting what you want out of them. You will leave me to be starved to death most likely in a cell in Stirling far away from all help.'

That shocked him. He had not thought, nor wished to think, what was likely to happen to her at Stirling.

She had soon worked it all over again.

And then she had to let him know her plan.

If he could get the jailers to remove the guards round her room, then he and she and Margaret Carwood would steal tonight down a back stair into the pantries and butler's offices and squeeze out through a broken gap in the wall that Margaret had discovered near the door, which would of course be locked. That would get them into the Abbey graveyard, and there Arthur Erskine would be waiting with horses. They would ride clear of Edinburgh, meet Gordon and Bothwell, who alone had remained loyal, and make for the safety of one of Bothwell's Border fortresses, where he would raise an army for them in a few days most probably, as he had done before.

'And then,' she cried, 'we shall be able to do what we like instead of always being bullied by these foul old men.'

The scheme certainly had its points. He'd always wanted to pull James' long nose. And now Davie was out of the way he would be able to get all he wanted out of Mary.

'But how can I get them to shift the guards? They'll never do it.'

'Tell them how ill I am. It's true enough. Tell them if only they will stop pestering me I'll forgive them everything. Bring them here to be pardoned, formally. James likes things to look well.'

Darnley promised to manage everything. He was full of confidence now. When she asked for a list of the conspirators in the murder plot, he gave it instantly, never realizing that he could not have done this if he had not been one of them. Nor did it seem to embarrass him that the name of his father was on the list.

She asked who had struck the first blow, and was told one of Morton's men, George Douglas the bastard.

So the prophetic warning had been right after all, and about as much use as prophetic warnings ever were.

Darnley briskly hurried off to give her offer to the ringleaders.

They were naturally suspicious and told him her fair speaking was nothing but policy. Ruthven said bluntly that they had no need of pardon from a prisoner. But James reproved him for that. She had been exact in her gauging of him. He would greatly prefer some sort of legal covering for his actions. A signed pardon for the acts of violence committed in her presence might prove useful; anyway, it was respectable. He would be very glad, too, of her free consent to being removed to Stirling. So he and Lord Ruthven and the Earl of Morton went with Darnley later on in the afternoon to the little anteroom leading into the Queen's chamber.

It was about halfpast four. The cloud of budding white pearblossom, a little whiter than two days ago, was blowing outside the window in the March wind and sunshine. There was a dark stain on the floor of the bright tiny room. The three lords waited while the boy fetched his wife.

After a little time he brought her in. She was deadly white and there were deep shadows under her eyes. Her hair had been brushed very smooth and shining, straight down on either side of her face. She was wearing a simple gown of deep blue; its close-fitting bodice, in contrast with the full skirt hanging in heavy folds, emphasized her pregnancy. She looked like a very young Madonna in an early Italian picture, her shoulders touchingly slight, her bosom small, her slender neck rising from it like the white stalk of a bluebell.

She stood looking at them, at the gross Morton, the ghastly Ruthven, the grave, dignified James. They knelt, and her eyes followed the course of Morton's massive knee, which came down full on the bloodstain. James asked for the royal pardon and restoration of estates; he added pointedly that mercy was 'advantageous and necessary to Kings, for their own safety.'

Morton, edging his knee away from the bloodstain, said that the loss of one meanly born man did not matter much, at any rate not as much as the ruin of many lords.

Ruthven said nothing.

Mary said she was not bloodthirsty nor greedy for their lands and goods. She would be only too glad to forget the past – and here she gave a little gasp and choked with tears.

They discussed the terms of their safeguard, but she got weary and told them to draw up what document they wished, and she would sign it. She went back into the bedchamber with Darnley and James, while through the open door came the sound of Morton's and Ruthven's voices arguing the terms. She began to laugh rather strangely.

'It is so funny,' she said, 'to hear that old yellow fellow haggling away for his future when you can see he has only a few weeks to live!'

Her brother and husband were shocked.

She was very restless. She could not sit still, though she was too weak to walk by herself. She walked up and down the room between them, leaning on both their arms, up and down, up and down, for a whole hour, talking, all three, of such silly things, none of them meaning anything, but they must go on talking, she must anyway, to show she trusted them, to make them trust her.

Yes, she would willingly go to Stirling; she would much rather her baby were born there in the high clean air of that huge castle rock – much rather than at Holyrood, so damp, and with all the smells of Edinburgh wafting down to it; it was good of dear James to think of it for her. (She was pleased to see that caused him some discomfort.) She would do anything they wanted, sign anything, if only they would not go on treating her like a criminal. It would be dreadful if her baby were born a prisoner, with the sound of armed men clanking about her door. James said he would see, he would do what he could.

She said pettishly, 'If that's all you will promise, I'll say the same to your pardon.' She stood still, withdrawing her arm, and looked straight at him. 'I'll have nothing to do with it, unless you get the guard removed this very evening.'

He promised.

It was after six o'clock when Morton and Ruthven presented their document, and James scanned it, touched it up and showed it to her. But she could not take it in, the writing shook so, she said. Would James read it to her? He did, and she had to ask him to repeat several sentences. She was obviously distracted and in great pain. Ruthven thought it well to hurry things up. He dipped the pen in the ink and presented it to her.

'Will Your Majesty be pleased to sign?'

She stared up at him with wild uncomprehending eyes. He thrust the pen into her hand, but she dropped it and clasped her hands to her side with a scream so full of animal anguish that even Ruthven fell back abashed. Margaret Carwood came rushing to her, and others of her women. Her screams went on, hideous, unabated.

'The doctor!' cried Carwood, 'and the midwife, on the

instant!' She flapped a cloth in Ruthven's face. 'Out of the room, all you men!'

'She can sign first, she's not unconscious,' he said. 'I'll guide her hand.'

'Get away!' yelled Darnley, beside himself.

And James, so frequently a father these last few years, led Ruthven away. 'We must wait till this is over,' he said low to him. 'After all, it may not be necessary.'

Ruthven gave a grin of understanding.

Darnley was rushing about, quite distracted. He had sent his own man, Anthony Standen, for the doctor. Now he hovered in the anteroom, when Carwood came and plucked his arm and whispered to him, 'The Queen wishes to speak to you.'

Was it her last message to him? Those frightful screams! He wished he had never heard them. He wished he had been a better husband. He was surprised at the brisk note in Carwood's whisper. Women had no heart really. He trembled as she led him up to that contorted blue figure on the bed. He bent his head to it; Mary raised hers and said very low, 'Remind them, they've promised to withdraw the guards tonight.'

What did it mean? How could she ride tonight, straight after a miscarriage, after that agony? Those eyes that he had just seen all clouded and screwed up with pain, they were looking up at him, now quite clear and calm. One of them slowly shut in a wink.

*　　　*　　　*

Would they dismiss the guard? Hours seemed to go by, and still they were outside. But now the beleaguered party were re-inforced by the doctor and midwife. They complained that their patient was in a very grave condition, that she was semi-delirious, and kept screaming that there were armed men in the Palace only waiting to burst in and hack her to pieces. It certainly didn't seem necessary to keep guard on anyone as ill as that, but Ruthven and Morton were still reluctant to give way. Darnley had the bright notion of saying he would keep guard over her himself, he and his men who were in the Palace. That seemed safe enough, since he was more deeply committed against her than any of them. So they left him in charge, with-drew their men, and went off to hold a convivial supper-party at Morton's house to celebrate the occasion.

Mary at once dispatched Margaret Carwood with a message to Arthur Erskine. She kept Darnley by her side, for after play-ing up so well to the lords he was suffering a collapse of nerves.

'Nothing's safe yet,' he kept saying. 'Any of the household may notice something is in the wind and carry the word to Morton's house.'

That was true, of course. They would have to wait till everyone was asleep in bed. Never did the household seem to go to bed so late as on that night.

'There are too many in this,' he repeated again and again, 'it's bound to leak out. That old doctor and the midwife, you ought to have kept them here – I told you you ought to. It's bound to get out now. And so many of us escaping, someone's sure to notice when we go. Erskine and Traquair and me and you and Anthony and Carwood. Why should Carwood come?'

'I *must* have one woman with me, Harry, in case — '

'Oh yes, that everlasting child. But why Traquair?'

'Margaret must ride pillion behind him, as I'm doing with Erskine.'

'You could ride with me.'

And he ruled out one after the other of their party till it seemed that they themselves had better stay behind.

She had to buoy up his spirits by treating the whole thing as a joke. She mimicked James walking up and down the room with his solemn voice, his portentous clearing of the throat, his gentlemanly decorum – Davie himself couldn't have done it better, he declared in spontaneous admiration. He cursed himself the next moment for his thoughtlessness, but she paid no heed to it, only gave him a narrow glance. She was wrought up to a pitch very near hysteria, and just prevented it by making herself 'hard as steel, cold as ice in danger'.

It was close on midnight before it was judged safe enough to make the attempt. She was very quiet now, but her eyes were blazing with excitement like a cat's in the dark. He thought she looked like a lovely young witch muffled in her dark cloak. Had she laid a spell on him that he was doing this mad thing? He would give anything now to get out of it. And if only he could get a drink! 'Mary, don't let's do it. It's such a frightful risk.'

'Erskine will be very careful, Harry. He's bringing a safe horse, it shan't jolt the child.'

'Damn the child!' His hoarse whisper was nearly a scream. 'Think of *me*! I've sworn to guard you!'

'Too late now to think of that. Think of them instead tomorrow morning, all their long faces, coming here and finding we have given them the slip.'

But her laughter could not cheer him now. He could have

killed her in his rage of fear as he and she and Margaret and Anthony went creaking and cracking down the wooden back stair into the butler's quarters. Did ever boards and doors make such a noise? Someone was sure to hear them, someone was sure to be about. Mary had said if they were it wouldn't matter, for they were her own French servants and would never betray her. But how did she know? Anyone would betray anyone if it were made worth their while. He stopped dead for a moment, thinking he heard a heavy tread. It was only the thumping of his heart.

Now they were in the sculleries. 'Pouf, what a smell!' whispered Mary.

'It's the washing up,' Margaret whispered back.

How could they add to the danger by whispering such stuff?

Then he whispered himself, for he saw a keg of whisky. It was just what he needed. 'I must have a drink,' he told Mary. They tried to prevent him, but it was impossible. He snatched a cup and helped himself. He tried to take another, but Anthony seized his arm and made him put it down.

'Oh, very well,' he said aloud in an off-hand way. 'Anyway, I feel better for that.'

It was striking midnight when they reached the ruinous gap in the outer wall and squeezed through into the keen night air, the frosty stars overhead, the dark shape of the hills rising sharp against them. They were in the burial-ground of the old Abbey and had to pick their way through the mounds. A new one had just been dug. Mary stood still, looking down on it.

'Come on,' muttered Darnley, then suddenly realized for whom that grave had been dug. 'Poor Davie,' he whimpered. 'I wish it hadn't happened.'

A strange new fear came to him by the grave of that mangled body; and beside him, dreadfully still, that cloaked figure with the hidden face. It was as though someone quite unknown were standing there. He put out a hand and touched her timidly.

'*Mary!*' he whispered.

She turned and walked swiftly away.

There was nothing for him now but to follow her.

They were outside the walls, and there were the horses, and Erskine, the Captain of the Guard, and Traquair, the Master of Horse. The two women rode pillion behind them. As they mounted, Erskine told them he had got into touch with the Earl of Bothwell, who had decided that his fortress of Dunbar would be their safest refuge. It meant a ride of thirty miles in the dark

– 'No matter, we'll manage it,' said Darnley, his teeth chattering.

He rode off ahead with his servant Anthony. As soon as they were out of the town he set his horse at a brisk canter, and the two men behind, with the double burden on their horses, had great difficulty in keeping up with him. Mary was intensely anxious to go gently; she found it a great strain holding on to Erskine; with her arms thus occupied, she could not keep her cloak wrapped round her, and grew so cold that she was afraid her numbed grip would not keep hold.

They had ridden for about an hour and a half when Darnley came thudding back to them. 'There are soldiers about here,' he gasped out. 'We'd best stick all together and go slap through them hell for leather. Quick, or we'll all be murdered.'

And he lashed out with his whip on the hindquarters of Mary's horse so that it plunged sideways.

'You'll kill the child!' she cried.

'What of it? We can make another. Come *on*!'

'Ride on yourself,' she answered.

Without a word, he spurred his horse to the gallop and disappeared into the darkness.

The soldiers he had observed were now coming up to them, dark shapes of horsemen, several of them.

'Is that Erskine?' said Bothwell's voice.

CHAPTER ELEVEN

H E H A D lifted her on to his own horse and was carrying her in the crook of his left arm on his saddle-bow, with his great cloak wrapped right round her, binding her securely to him. The release of that strain on her waist muscles, when she had been sitting sideways on the pillion and twisting round to clasp Erskine's broad waist, gave her intense relief; and now the warmth of his body was coming through to her so that her blood, which had seemed quite congealed, began to thaw and creep back through her veins. He slipped his reins for a moment into the hand that was holding her, and put his right hand inside the cloak to feel her hands; they were still like bits of ice.

'Put your little frog's paws in mine for a moment,' he said, enclosing them both in his grasp, and then begged Her Majesty's pardon, with a smile that she could hear in his voice.

'It's too dark for majesty,' she said drowsily.

'Too cold, you mean.'

'All cats are grey – I mean all queens are cold in the dark.'

She was surprised to hear his chuckle, for she hardly knew what she was murmuring; ease, warmth, the sudden, even violent cessation of fear and struggle, and above all of the strain of trying to get and then keep a hold on Darnley, were plunging her into a deep wave of peacefulness that engulfed her like sleep – and for three nights and days now she had had practically no sleep. She was riding for her life, with only this small company of men to protect her from the hosts of her enemies who might even now be in pursuit, yet she had never in her life felt as safe as now, in these fierce arms.

She fell asleep, though not too deeply to lose consciousness of those arms round her, and the gentle jogging of his horse, which seemed to know by instinct what was required of it and picked its way along that rough track over the moors in the dark without any jolt or jar. For a little time she lost the memory of what lay behind this moment, or expectation of what lay ahead. All her life lay here in this movement together through the bright dark.

It might have been years later that she heard the clip-clopping of a loose shoe on the horse's hoof. Bothwell would not exchange horses with any other of the men. The Night Hawk, he said, was the best horse he'd ever had, barring old Corbie, for night work; they were close by Broomhousebanks and nearing their journey's end at Dunbar, and had well lessened the danger of pursuit in this direction; they could afford to lose ten minutes or so at a little forge he knew close by. It showed a cool nerve but sound reasoning, for he had all along refused to hurry, because of the Queen's condition, and this shoe was necessary.

A cluster of little houses showed their shapes solidly before them; the night was fading, the stars paler, the rough ground glimmering with frost. She saw this, and the high chimney of a smithy just before her; she smelt cow-byres, heard the horses' hoofs clattering on cobbles instead of thudding and squelching on the moor. The Night Hawk stood still beneath her, champed his bit and shook his jingling harness; a man dismounted beside them and hammered loudly on the door, but no one came. Bothwell snatched the lance from him and thrust it through the casement window; that brought a scurry of footsteps and frightened voices within the house, the scraping of bolts drawn back, then a dim gaping face, anxious questions and peremptory answers. She was lifted down and carried into the blacksmith's forge, for it was warmer there than in his cottage. Bothwell left her while he went to set out a picket. She sat on the shaft of a barrow and watched the blacksmith blow up the fire. The darkness leaped away from the place; some of it ran in long shadows up the walls and ceiling and lurked there till chased away altogether by the flames. The smith was a young man in a leather apron and a shirt that left his arms and neck bare. He had the face of a Roman emperor on a coin she had seen in France. An old man, his father as she saw, came up to her with a horn mug of ale in his hand. His benignant bearded face was that of an apostle, not an emperor.

'The lord told me to bring ye a hot drink,' he said. 'This is the best I can do, but wait now till I stir it for ye.' He thrust an iron bar into the furnace to get red-hot, and stood looking down at her with interest, but it was plain he had no idea who she was. 'That's a braw horse of the lord's,' he said, 'but his foot is going a bit tender from carrying the both of ye, and with a loose shoe at this latter end.'

'He's not hurt it, has he?'

'Ah no, a good night's rest and feed is all he'll be needing. There was a French knight in these parts when I was a laddie, used to bathe his horse's hoofs in wine when they went foot-weary.'

'A French knight! Who was he?'

'We called him Beauty round here. He'd some such sounding name and he was a beauty to look at too, always wore white armour and a white scarf round his sleeve in honour of his leddy the Queen of France.'

'Was this in my – my lord the late King's time?' She had nearly said 'my father's'!

'Aye, but the King was a wee bairn then and the great Duke Albany was Governor, and he left his friend Beauty or Bawty here in charge as Warden of the Marches while he was away a while in France. A sair while it was for Beauty, and well that your horse should be shod before going by the Stony Moor – Battie's Bog they call it now after him, ever since his day.'

'Did his horse sink in it?'

'It did, for it had too many heavy French trappings on it and a new French curb it didn't well like. Forbye, he was riding for his life towards Dunbar with all Hume's men after him in their coats of Kendal-green, and had little heed to spare to his going.'

He pulled the bar out of the furnace. It was red-hot and he

leaned over her, stirring her ale, which hissed furiously and rose higher and higher in a smooth creamy froth. His shadow soared behind him, it blackened all the ceiling. Tink tonk, tink tonk went his son's hammer on the red-hot shoe he was reshaping to fit the Night Hawk's hoof. Shadows were stealing out again, sharp and pointed from behind the spears stacked in a corner. She sipped the warm ale, it was very soothing. The rising shadows as the fire died down again, and the swinging of the hammer, were becoming part of a dream spun by the old man's gruff, gentle, monotonous voice. Was she really here or only dreaming of something she had heard long ago? Was it she herself, or the French knight, who was fleeing towards Dunbar?

> *'Thou'rt safe if thou canst reach Dunbar*
> *Afore the gloaming's grey.'*

Who was singing that? The old man, as he stirred her ale and told her to wake up now and drink it before she dropped the mug out of her hand.

'Tell me the rest,' she said.

Well, he had been out looking the hill, a wee lad minding his father's herd, and himself saw that furious pursuit of the Warden and his handful of Frenchmen, and the running fight down in the dale along the banks of the Bluidy Burn, as the stream was now known; 'from Langton Tower they'd come across the Corney Ford, by Pouterlaney and down eastward towards Duns' Grueldykes, and it was in the bog near old Cramecrook's house that he was laired, and I saw it all with these two eyes; I heard the shouting and the yelling and the clash of their arms down in the dale, and I ran along the hill just in time to see his horse flounder in the quivering marsh among the white bog-reeds. Eh, but I stood there aghast to see that slaughter down below, and the men of the Merse all riding up round him and his handful of men, and their long spears glinting in the sunlight. It was Tom Trotter cut off his head and held it up by its long long hair, and Sir David Hume of Wedderburn tied it to his saddle-bow and rode off light and gay. They stripped him of his white armour and his braw duds, and the song they sing now tells you he was buried where he fell,

> *On Broomhousebanks without a Mass*
> *Or prayer his soul to save,*

but that last's not true, for I and my father and brothers buried the puir French bodies that very night as they lay gaping at the moon, buried them there in the bog and said a prayer for them. It was a sair pity for him that he came to this land, for he was a great knight in his own country.

> *The leddies of France may wail and mourn,*
> *May wail and mourn full sair,*
> *For the bonny Bawty's long brown locks*
> *They'll ne'er see waving mair.'*

Now indeed she was dreaming, for she had heard this story before, but in another language, another voice, old too, but a woman's, talking French; and suddenly she remembered the anxious tone of her grandmother de Guise, as she warned her that when she left France she would be going to a country far rougher and more savage; and told her of the dreadful fate in some obscure skirmish on the Scottish Border that befell the famous Chevalier Blanc, Seigneur de la Bastie of Dauphiné.

The crisp delicate old voice echoed strangely here in the blacksmith's forge where her granddaughter sat on the shaft of a barrow and stared at a stack of spears, perhaps the very same spears that had done de la Bastie to his death.

> *'I'll never get hame to my ain dear land*
> *That lies sweet o'er the sea.'*

It was the old man singing that as he took her mug from her; was it of de la Bastie, or of her own despairing homesickness for France?

Bothwell saw that the tears were running down her face when he came back into the forge.

'You'll be safe now,' he told her as they lifted her into his arms again on his horse's back; 'once over Batty's Bog and it's not far on to Dunbar, and look, the dawn's coming up.'

But would they reach Dunbar 'afore the gloaming's grey'? And would the Night Hawk with its double burden not flounder in the quivering marsh, where now she could see the glimmer of the white bog-reeds?

She did not speak her fears, but she could not stop the tears from running down.

'Seven centuries lie buried there,' she said.

He thought she was light-headed and tried to give her some vague comfort, but she said again, 'It lies there in the bog, the grave of the Auld Alliance that Charlemagne made with Scotland. Friendship between Crown and Crown, king and king, people and people, he set that down in his charter, the Golden

298

Bull, seven hundred and seventy-seven years ago – and its climax came with my marriage – the Queen of Scotland to the King of France. But it came too late: the Scots had killed de la Bastie; they hounded my mother to the death, as you said yourself; and now are hounding me.'

'Let them! They'll not get you.' His arms tightened round her.

But still she cried, 'Is it all over? Will England have her way in the long run and take this country to her own?'

'Only when the child that is in your womb is born to wear both Crowns, and then, and then only, the countries will be one. England will never conquer us; it is we, in your little body here, who will give her a King.'

*   *   *

They reached Dunbar when it was fully light, but the sun had not shown itself and a thin rain was falling. The North Sea rolled up in grey tossing waves to the little harbour and the blood-red fortress of the castle on its edge. The huge bulk of the Bass Rock out to sea was blurred with rain, its white cliffs faintly shining like a ghost-ship in the mist.

When they lifted Mary from off the horse, she stood dazed and rubbed her eyes. 'But it's all quite different,' she said. 'Just now I saw that rock clear, like pearl, and birds flying up round it with wings of fire.'

Joy and awe had swept her up, exalting her, dizzying her; but now that wave had flowed past and she did not know why she had felt it; it did not belong to this drear moment at all as she stood before the empty castle and the rain-drummed sea, and the rain fell on her.

A closely serried line of redshanks stood at the edge of the surf below, fishing for bits of flotsam with their black bills; they had nothing to do with those birds of fire that she had seen proudly soaring and floating round the Bass Rock, now grown invisible in the advancing rain. She felt very near tears.

They went into the hall, which was quite bare and very cold.

Anthony Standen came slowly down the stairs towards them, looking sheepish and indignant. The King, he said, had never drawn rein till he got here, drank a half-pint of whisky, and was now dead asleep, rolled in his cloak on a bare bedstead upstairs.

'Good,' said Bothwell with satisfaction.

They gathered round her, he and the other leaders who had

ridden with him and whom she now saw clearly for the first time: Gordon, and the fathers of three of her Maries, the grave kindly Lord Fleming, jolly Lord Livingstone with his red face and bushy grey beard, and Bothwell's old friend, lean and lantern-jawed, the chief of the Long Setons.

'And now there's but one Mary to do duty to three fathers!' she said, smiling up at them as they hovered, anxious and rather helpless, not knowing what could be done for her beyond lighting fires everywhere, as the soldiers were already doing. The place was almost entirely unfurnished, and Margaret Carwood, exhausted by her constant anxiety of the last three days and nights, was distracted to find herself the only woman in this grim fortress, and no doctor, 'and anything may happen any minute,' she muttered, wringing her hands. Her mistress ought to be got straight to bed, but where were the blankets? They would all be damp and must be aired.

'So they will be very soon,' said Mary, who was sitting on a bench by the now crackling fire in the hall, 'and I can tell you I am not going to bed till I have had some breakfast. I am ravenous, as you all must be. What can we eat?'

Some dry oatcake was discovered and kegs of ale, and a grinning soldier brought in his helmet full of eggs that he had found in the hen-roosts, and thought would be more to the fancy of a breeding woman than the salt beef which was all there was in the larders.

But who was to cook them? for Carwood was upstairs routing out the bedding. Mary cried that she would make omelettes for them all. There was a procession of the lords and the Queen into the kitchen; frying-pan and bowl and wooden spoon were found and wiped, and she set to work as chief cook with a zest that amazed them when they thought of it afterwards. At the moment they were so thankful to have reached the fortress safely and to find her not desperately ill as they had feared, that they were all in the highest spirits and it seemed quite natural that she should be too. She chaffed her three fathers and set them, most undutifully they declared, to beat the eggs and chop some herbs that yet another enterprising soldier had found at her command in the herb plot. The omelettes were delicious, and she heated the oatcake and stirred the ale with a red-hot poker – it wasn't in the Court of France she had learned that trick, so where was it? they demanded, laughing.

'This very night in the blacksmith's forge, so you see how good it is for queens to go among their people.'

She was not her father's daughter for nothing, they told her.

'No, and in more ways than one, for with your help I have escaped from my captors as he did, and shall wake up to find I am indeed Sovereign of Scotland.'

She looked at Bothwell, who three years ago in the winter sunrise at Coldinghame had given her courage by telling her of that. He was astounded by the happiness in her face.

She was using herself to the uttermost, and glorying in it. This was to be alive: to find what she could do, and do it – and to do it beside the man who had done more than any other to show her how. The comforts and refinements that she had been taught to look on as necessities mattered no more than a straw blown away in the wind; her hair was a tangled mass of elf-locks and her face unwashed and unpowdered, but that did not matter, as it would have done with Darnley. But not with him.

As he took the frying-pan from her hands, the man who loved courage more than anything looked at her with worship in his eyes. She would always rise to the occasion in danger, he knew. But to be able to joke and cook and cheer her waiting-maid after these three days and nights, and with such simple, carefree gaiety, was even better.

The roughest of his men would not have treated a foaling mare or cow as her enemies had treated this delicate pampered girl from the Court of France – shut her up alone to die of a miscarriage, untended. But she had survived their brutality, outwitted and escaped them, travelled thirty miles on horseback at night, and was now cooking their breakfast.

CHAPTER TWELVE

BOTHWELL ALSO rose to the occasion. This time it was in just three days that he mustered four thousand fully armed men round them. On Tuesday morning they arrived at Dunbar; by Thursday night there was their army complete, drawn from the dalesmen and rank-riders, besides four companies of trained infantry and a substantial backing of artillery. Cattle too had been driven in, the larders stocked, and it would be as hard to assail their position with their backs to the North Sea as to 'ding down Tantallon or build a brig to the Bass'.

The effect of his army was as quick as its muster. It encouraged all the nobles who were hesitatingly watching the course of events to come riding up to Dunbar at the head of their retainers; Atholl descended from the hasty retreat he beat into the mountains over the weekend; Hume, who at that same moment had been escorting the Lord James back to Edinburgh, now rode up to serve the Queen; the Earl Marischal, though father-in-law to the Bastard, the Earls of Caithness, Cassillis, Crawford and Sutherland, all followed suit; and the Hamiltons sent word from Edinburgh that they and all the town were only waiting to give the Queen a right royal welcome on her return to her capital.

And that was by no means its chief effect. The band of conspirators in Edinburgh saw at once that the game was up. They saw it really from that first moment on Tuesday morning when they returned to Holyrood with their Act of Pardon all ready but for her signature, to find that the Queen had neither died nor miscarried but had escaped from their power, *with* her husband – that took some time to swallow, even by those who knew their Darnley – and had fled, no one knew where.

Very soon they heard that she was at Dunbar with Bothwell in command of an army whose force increased hourly with every fresh report. That settled it. The most conspicuous of the murderers, Morton, Ruthven and Lindsay at the head of them, fled precipitately over the Border to the safety of England and the very same quarters at Newcastle that James and his fellows had left for Scotland in such high hopes a few days before.

'So they'll find their nests kept warm for them,' chuckled Bothwell.

He roared with laughter when those lords that were less conspicuously incriminated came riding up to Dunbar to crave their pardon from their 'justly incensed Queen'.

'Here comes the first flock of turtle doves,' he said; 'all the carrion crows will now be of the same feather.'

Sure enough, the Lord James, while keeping a safe distance, sent assurances that he had broken off all connection with those who 'had committed the vile act.' Darnley was hurt that James had sent no message to him.

And Knox, once again finding that absence makes the heart grow stronger, hastily disappeared until people should have forgotten his last Sunday's sermon in praise of those who had executed 'just punishment on that knave David.'

Mary's spirit and Bothwell's strength had saved her throne and given her complete victory. She rode back in triumph into the city from which she had fled so desperately just one week before. Beside her and her husband rode Bothwell at the head of his Borderers and professional infantry; behind them, all the lords who had flocked to her at Dunbar, with their troops; the Hamiltons, with the warlike Abbot, Gavin, at their head, rode out from Edinburgh to meet her and joined their forces to her army; all the townspeople poured out into the street, and roared themselves hoarse in her welcome. They were all her loyal and devoted servants, and once again an upward glance at that over-hanging upper window in the house at the foot of Netherbow showed her that she was no longer 'overlooked'.

The cavalcade stopped in the High Street in front of the house of the Bishop of Dunkeld which had been prepared for her, for she could not face those haunted rooms in Holyrood. She would move up to the Castle as soon as it was got ready for her, and await her baby's birth in the security of that mighty stronghold; in the meantime, Bothwell did his best to turn the episcopal mansion into a fortress by placing his field-guns before its doors and billeting his soldiers in all the nearest houses.

Mary was now living in the very heart of her capital, and made to feel every moment how her people adored her for her courage and resourcefulness, and with that mixture of amuse-ment in their admiration that is more endearing than any holy awe. There was a lass for you, who could stand up to a murder when seven months gone and not miscarry, outwit even the Great Bastard, steal away under his very nose, long as it was (and not for the first time either!), and come riding back before a week was out at the head of an army! Her bairn should have the spirit of Wallace.

Sympathy also came from England. Elizabeth wrote at once to express it, and her admiration for her cousin's magnificent spirit. That was sincere; a wistful envy peeped out between the lines from the older woman, whose lifelong struggle to fortify her position and her kingdom held no such spectacular ad-venture. Her indignation with Darnley was sincere enough too; she flatly refused to believe the protestations he wrote to her of his own innocence of the murder plot. 'Damnable liar!' she roared. 'If I'd been in my cousin's place I'd have snatched his dagger and stabbed him with it myself.'

Cecil, more consistently, still tried to wring some advantage by spreading the scandal that 'a deformed and base menial' had been killed 'in her arms'.

Elizabeth's practical sympathy showed itself in fact far more on behalf of the chief murderers who had taken refuge in her country; she refused to send them back for their trial, as requested. One never knew when Scottish rebels might come in handy – a consideration that weighed more than the Bastard's secret intercessions. For James, while declaring in Scotland his complete dissociation from them, wrote to England begging protection for his 'dear friends' who 'for my sake have given this adventure'. So Morton and Lindsay stayed on safely in England; but Ruthven's liver and kidneys quickly paid the price of his over-exertions; he died convinced that he was one of the Saved, by a vision of angels descending from heaven to bear his soul thither. His death-bed greatly encouraged his friend Morton in Calvin's doctrine that by no sin of his could the sinner lose his place among the elect.

The charges against the criminals were read in court: of gathering five hundred men 'armed with secret armour in the silence of night' within the Palace, who 'reft the keys of the porter, closed the gates, and slew the late Secretary David Rizzio in the presence of our Sovereign Lady; and put violent hands on her most noble person, held, detained and pressed the same most awfully and treasonably – giving to Her Majesty occasion by the sight of the said cruel slaughter and by the thrusting of her person in violent manner, to part with her birth.'

Only two of the most active ringleaders were executed. Darnley, zealously blackening others in order to whitewash himself, thought this insufficient, and succeeded in bringing two more prisoners, both safely obscure, a saddler and a merchant, to the foot of the gallows. But Bothwell called the Queen's attention to the matter with his usual vigour.

'Is it your wish, Madam, that the small fry should be sacrificed while all the big fish escape? It is not? Then give me your ring, quick.'

And he rode up with it himself in token of their pardon, just in time to save their lives.

He also saved from outlawry three fellow-lairds from Lothian; true, one of them, though a neighbour, was an old enemy, no less than that John Cockburn whose clinking money-bags from England had echoed so strangely in the crises of Bothwell's life these last seven years – 'But he gave me the best raid of my life, for all it's given me the most trouble ever after.'

And so, not very logically, Cockburn also escaped the net. But when it came to the big fish, Bothwell's intentions were ruthless enough, though his opportunities were slight. The exiles in England were outlawed in their absence, that was all that could be done about them. And Darnley was an impossible case. Mary had used him to effect her escape; without him she could not have contrived it, and she insisted that he should not therefore be made to suffer by it. This was also politic, since to accuse him of the murder was to strengthen the scandal that he had killed Rizzio out of jealousy of his wife's lover, a scandal that aimed, of course, at throwing a doubt on the legitimacy of her child and its right to the succession. It was for this reason as much as for the hope of a miscarriage that the murder was planned for when Rizzio was with her – if possible alone, but Bothwell's stern warning to her earlier had prevented that.

Darnley co-operated heartily by declaring before the Council that he had known nothing about the conspiracy and 'never counselled, commanded, consented, assisted or approved the same'. He thought it would be a good idea to have that down in writing, and posted his signed declaration of innocence at the Market Cross. It was very annoying that just after he had done this his former confederates placed in Mary's hand a copy of their bond to secure her Crown for himself, at the price of her dishonour and possible death. And there was his name topping the list. Luckily she didn't seem to take much notice of it.

He was quite unprepared for this spitefulness on the part of his former friends. Even his father, now in exile on his Lennox estates for his share in the plot, was furious that Darnley had left him behind in Holyrood on the night of his flight – he might at least have warned him, he said. He swore a solemn oath that he would never look upon his son's face again.

'Lepers don't care to look in the glass,' was Bothwell's comment.

Darnley's high hopes of getting all he wanted out of Mary now Davie was out of the way were badly disappointed. He found himself farther off from the Crown Matrimonial than ever; he did not even have the authority he had had before all this fuss : she allowed him no share now in the practical administration; he was being pushed further and further into the background.

'John Thompson's man' who has to do as his wife bids, that was the servants' name for him, as Anthony insolently let him know. Even Anthony had turned against him; he kept on making sneering reminders of Darnley's 'superb horsemanship' on that cursed night when he made such remarkably good going.

The nobles at Court showed even more openly their contempt for his cowardice and treachery, and Mary did not seem able to bear him to come near her – it was monstrously unfair, when after all it was he who had helped her to escape.

Since everybody avoided him he tried to avoid them, pretended to be ill and went to bed so as not to have to greet the new French Ambassador, Philibert Du Croc; but even that would not do, for Du Croc came to him instead, reproached him for his behaviour, and then wrote home: 'There is not one person in the kingdom, from the highest to the lowest, that regards him.' He added, on the other hand, that everywhere 'the Queen is beloved, esteemed, and honoured.'

It was the secret fountainhead of the conspiracy that Bothwell longed to quench. The Bastard's head was already forfeit two or three times over, he told the Queen, and begged her to remove it. She had a horror of condemning her half-brother to death in cold blood, he knew that, but she owed it to herself, her throne, and her unborn child. James was skulking in the Highlands, along with Lethington and Argyll, powerless and discredited, but that would not last long.

'This is his second open attempt to dethrone you,' he warned her, 'and within the past year. He's failed this time, as he failed last summer. The third time he may be lucky.'

James had kept most discreetly in the background of the plot; his name did not appear in the list of conspirators, but Bothwell could procure definite proofs of his guilt from George Douglas, the other bastard, now in exile in England, who proposed to buy his pardon by the evidence he could furnish that James and Lethington too, together with 'others that the Queen knew not of, were the designers and purpose-makers of the slaughter of David.' It would not be easy to get George Douglas back into Scotland, as Elizabeth, terrified of a full exposure of the plot, had ordered her Warden of the Marches to prevent it by putting him under a strong guard.

'And do you hope to bring Elizabeth to book too?' asked Mary, with that ironic flicker of her eyelids.

'No, but I can bring her servant James,' he answered doggedly. 'That mad fellow Jack Musgrave would help me, I know. He'd have smuggled me across the Border if I'd agreed to break parole; well, he can smuggle George Douglas instead. We'll manage it.'

But she still showed indifference, and he lost his temper. 'I wish to save your throne, perhaps your life. Are you unwilling to attend to so slight a matter?'

'Very,' she replied with a strange smile.

He found her face inscrutable, especially now she looked so tired. Her eyes were veiled; she seemed to be brooding over some secret.

They were walking on the battlements of Edinburgh Castle, where she was now lodged. High up on that towering crag she could see the smoke of Auld Reekie rising far below in blue wreaths in the windy sunshine of early May. The blossoming fruit trees in the orchards were no bigger than dandelion clocks. Away in the distance, with the white foam flecking its blue, and here and there the flash of a white sail, the wide Firth of Forth broadened out towards the open sea.

'Do you see that sail?' she said. 'A fishing-boat going straight out to sea on this stormy day, to catch mackerel and herring for the fishwives to sell and bawl out their wares down in that little ant-heap far below. Those tall spying houses used to hang over and oppress me when I lay below them in Holyrood – and now they're nothing but an ant-heap beneath my feet. Wasn't I right to prepare so high a nest for my eaglet's eyrie?'

'You were right to take the strongest fortress in Scotland for it. God's blood, Madam, do you realize that that hour of your helplessness is just the one that James may seize to bring back Morton and his crew, perhaps even to invite an invasion from England? What steps are you taking to guard against it?'

'I am inviting James and Argyll to come and attend me here in the Castle with their wives.'

He was speechless.

'No,' she said, 'it is not as mad as it sounds. It will be more difficult for them to plot against me under the same roof, even though I am occupied with an *accouchement*.'

'With your midwife as your guard?'

'Lord Erskine will command the guns here. They can do nothing while under his eye. And it will keep them clear of the Border, which you will guard.'

'You are going to pardon James!'

'It is what I promised him.'

'You never signed the promise.'

'No, for heaven knows what they put in that paper for me to sign – a deal more than I ever said. But I did most solemnly promise James to forgive him and restore him to his estates.'

'A promise wrung from you in such conditions – you were

307

alone, with your back to the wall, fighting your battle single-handed against the most desperate odds. You had to snatch what weapons you could.'

'That is an excuse that can always be given. If we use it for the spoken word we shall come to do so for the written one also. It will be the end of all faith and honour between men and men, nation and nation.'

'It's ended *now*! When has James ever kept faith with you? He's been working against you from the beginning, long before you ever came back to the country. If you fight fair while he fights foul, he's bound to get the better of you.'

'Will you come indoors?' she said. 'I would like to show you something.'

They went into the Castle. One of the soldiers on guard peered at them round the buttress. Bothwell, who remembered faces, even when seen once in a troop, placed him as one of Lennox's men, and therefore probably a spy of Darnley's. He would speak to Erskine and have him hanged if anything could be proved against him; if not, removed.

She led him into a little room, where an attempt had been made to disguise the fortress by hanging bright tapestries over the massive stone walls. The window was a small square of glass in a five-foot-deep embrasure; silken cushions had been spread over this stone window-seat; she sat down there, and picking up a book that lay open beside her, read out the following passage:

' "Our experience has been that those princes who have done great things have held good faith of little account. They have known how to circumvent the intellect of men by craft, and in the end have overcome those who had relied upon their word." '
She looked up and said:

'I have just been wondering if Machiavelli were indeed right, and now you tell me that he is. If so, there is no hope for the world – not for a long long time, when men may begin at last to learn that such wisdom is the worst folly. And by that time the world may lie in ruins.'

Surely he had heard this before – not in her words, nor her voice, now low and clear beside him, but in a harsh yet weak and husky voice that breathed, 'Let every man speak the truth with his brother. Let none oppress or defraud another in any business.'

He shook the memory from him. What had that old fraud to do with it? Let men practise what they preached, then indeed earth might be fair as Paradise!

'But this,' he said, 'is all havers, it is part of your condition.'

'It is what you yourself have taught me – the faith of a Borderer.'

'I've never spoken of any such thing to you.' His voice sounded almost disgusted.

She laughed. 'You had no need to. You've shown it. It's there in the Hepburn motto, "Keep Trust". You've just told me you refused Jack Musgrave when he wanted you to break your parole – and to your captors who held you in ward unjustly.'

He flushed a deep red. 'That was different. On the marches if a man breaks his word to his enemy his own clan will put him to death to wipe out the disgrace of march-treason. That is held by both sides.'

'And are you telling me that no one else can hold it?'

'I doubt if a Sovereign can. It's not statecraft.'

'The State is only the sum total of human lives within it. You cannot have one law for men and another for nations.'

He looked down on her sitting there with her hands lying so white and still in her lap. 'Christ's heart!' he cried suddenly. 'What do I care for all this? It's your life or death that matters. You've got to destroy James before he strikes at you for the third time.'

'He may not have the time.'

It came to him then, cold and deep within him, the reason for her resignation. She did not believe she would survive the birth of her child. It was small wonder. But worst danger of all was the wish to die that now was evident in her.

He flung himself down on his knees before her and caught at those limp hands, crushing them in his grasp without knowing what he was doing or what he could say to give her heart, and hope. When his words did come, it was in a torrent of rage that startled himself.

'So that's the outgate you're hoping for! You think to die and escape your trials. You *shall not* have such easy victory! You – who have been braver than any woman, or man either, that I've ever known – are you to turn coward now, and leave the kingdom to be torn yet again, as it was at your own birth when your father died for lack of courage to go on?'

'It's true,' she whispered. 'I am afraid to live.'

'Better to accept defeat – is that it? Better to sit than to walk, better to lie than to sit, better to sleep than to lie, better to die than to sleep! Look at me. Open your eyes. Swear to me that you won't give in.'

She looked, and her eyes were not veiled now; they were like bright swords.

'I'll swear it.'

'You *want* to live, remember.'

'If I do, it's because you've made me.'

He bent his head on her hands but did not kiss them. She felt his tears on them. Then he got to his feet, clumsily, blunderingly, and moved towards the door without looking back at her.

'Where are you going?' she cried.

'Back to the work you've set me. There's nothing I can do here.'

CHAPTER THIRTEEN

I T   I S not surprising that immediately after such unwonted exaltation of the spirit Bothwell took a mistress, the first time he 'had ado with any woman since he was married,' as his servants observed with some apparent surprise. As he had been married a bare three months, this was not a strong tribute. The Rizzio murder had early interrupted the course of his matrimony, and it did not run any the more smoothly for it now that they were together at Haddington Abbey, which he had reclaimed from Lethington. Jean did not show any obvious feminine jealousy over the amount of time that her husband had had perforce to spend away from her and with the Queen. But when her brother Gordon repeated to her the Queen's public praise of Bothwell's 'force and dexterity', and 'how suddenly by his providence not only were We delivered out of prison, but also the whole company of conspirators dissolved and We recovered our former obedience', then Jean's silence was positively deafening.

Gordon's own aloofness was stirred to a brotherly blundering; he had been badly disappointed at the way this marriage was going, and now indignantly rubbed in that all men – 'I say all *men*,' he repeated, glowering down at that impassive female figure, 'recognize that nothing of importance is now done without Bothwell; he stands higher than any man in the country, and damnably lucky you are to have married him instead of that nincompoop Ogilvie who left you for the Beton girl – and for very shame you might have had the decency to send them a wedding present!' he delivered as a final shot.

Jean went on sewing.

Gordon was not the only man to reflect how insidious a weapon was the needle.

Mary's exquisite embroidering of her designs through all the wrangling of politics had sometimes reminded her Council that the beauty she was making would last long after their discords had ceased to have a meaning; that there was a heart of peace and harmony in the world, however troubled its state, to those who cared to create instead of destroy.

> *'Queen Mary sat in her bower*
> *Sewing a silver seam.'*

That was the picture of her that her subjects sang as they went about their work in the steep crowded noisy streets of the hill-town, and looked up at the towering crag of Edinburgh Castle where their Prince would be born.

A refuge to Mary, a weapon to Jean, the needle provided another and piquant instrument to her sewing-maid Bessie Crawford. Her sleek dark head in its bright cap bent over her sewing, her quick hand darted backwards and forwards, the tip of her tongue peeped out between her white teeth and passed slowly from side to side as she sewed, while a very low humming sound came from her red lips; intent, industrious, demure, she looked as happy as a little cat lapping cream; then she saw that the Earl was watching her; the humming stopped, the tip of the tongue went in, but her eyelids never fluttered, and her fingers flew faster than ever, drawing the needle and its scarlet thread backwards and forwards in its endless rhythm.

'Stop pretending you haven't seen me,' he said, 'and come here.'

Down went her hand as fast as a shot bird, and the needle and its scarlet thread, and all the coloured silk in her lap into a pool at her feet. She dropped a curtsy and came over to him; she did not know how much depended on her walk. If she had minced up to him, as he half expected, he would have thrust her out of his sight. But she was neither timid nor too bold, she came directly up to him and looked him in the face. He took her round chin between his finger and thumb, pinching the soft firm flesh, turned it this way and that, scanning her face. Her eyes fell before his look, her lips parted in a quick intake of breath, and then were crushed by his mouth. She met his kiss eagerly, springing forward into his arms.

'So you'll enter His Lordship's service,' he said. 'Go up into the little room in the steeple and wait for me there.'

But they were observed as they came down.

Bessie had not libelled her mistress when she said she did not keep her servants long; Jean's own letters have left it on record that the difficulty of finding honest and faithful servants was one of her chief domestic troubles; her most poignant complaint was that she 'had no peace because of the oft-changing of her servants'.

She certainly had good reason to get rid of Bessie, and did, within only a few days of that excursion up the steeple. Bessie went back to her father the blacksmith, but as his smithy was in Haddington town, and as Willy Crawford had a very proper sense that 'the nobility and gentry should have every justice', this only made Bothwell's brief visits to her rather more convenient.

He had been acerbated to fury by his unsatisfied love and anxiety for Mary, and the irritation of his wife's passive hostility; added to this, Anna Throndsen had started again on long reproachful letters from Scandinavia since she had heard of his marriage. His nerves and senses found something of the relief they craved in the moments of entirely animal union with the rapturously acceptant Bessie. Gossips were on the look-out for the Earl's tall figure in the dark cloak that concealed his white doublet as he passed down the back streets of Haddington, where once he had fled on a very different errand, with a bag of gold under his arm, to the kitchen of a bigger and a better Bess.

The gossip at once reached Jean. It was only three weeks since they had come to Haddington, and already Bessie had been seduced, dismissed, and re-established in her connection with her lord and master. With his accustomed speed in love as in war, Bothwell now quenched the ensuing storm with his wife. Their quarrel was quite like the old days with Anna, he reflected, with amused contempt of himself as well as of both women; his passion had flamed as suddenly as her wounded pride, and conquered her utterly for the moment; in recognition of which he wrote out in suitably loving terms a deed of gift of his lands, houses and castle of Nether Hailes for the period of her life. For a woman of Jean's sense of property and administrative powers this was an excellent equivalent of the necklace usually given in such cases; it was of greater value, and provided her with an estate and occupation apart from his side.

His own occupations gave him little enough time either for

wife or mistress. Just over the Border on the English side, Morton and his fellows were prowling up and down, only waiting their opportunity to break through. Nor could he himself keep watch there all the time, for he was continually riding to and from Edinburgh to attend the Privy Council, which meekly passed all the Acts proposed by him. In these few weeks he brought forward two to promote order on land and sea: Courts of Justice to be held on every royal progress, and piracy checked by cancelling letters of search, even those that had been issued to his own sea-captains; two preventive game laws, one against the shooting of deer, which were growing scarce, and the other against foreigners fishing in the Highland lochs; a Currency Act to stop false money being imported from Flanders; and two Acts directly aimed against Mary's own indiscriminate charity, forbidding further shameless and indiscreet begging of benefits from her private purse (which left her barely enough for her own living): and limiting the number of pardons issued in the future by the Queen, who had 'oft times shown mercy without occasion.'

His lawyer, Mr Chalmers, told him the Queen had made her will, remembering everybody, and showing particular generosity to Darnley. Bothwell could see from that how she had welcomed death; she was free to forgive when she had no more to fear. There were magnificent bequests of jewels to his wife, rivalling those to the Crown of Scotland; to himself, a ring with a great diamond, and a jewelled plaque of her own symbol, a mermaid on a dolphin's back, an enchanting thing made by an Italian artist for the Mermaid, bride of the 'Dolphin of France'.

One fine early-summer morning as he rode towards the capital he heard the crash and roar of the guns thundering out from the Castle, set spurs to his horse and galloped the rest of the way until he came clattering up the High Street, and had to slacken his speed among the hosts of people who were flocking out into it. Every door stood open, every window was alive with faces, the city hummed like a hive with anxious eager questioning voices. 'A boy,' he was told in answer to his demand. 'She's the lighter of a son, God bless her bonny face! A braw big laddie, they're saying.'

'Big' – and some other fool came running downhill saying she'd just heard from one of the kitchen-maids herself that she'd been told that the bairn had a bonny big head!

Big – and a big head – after all she'd gone through, and her hips as slight as those of a lass of fifteen! He had always thought the stock too fine to breed from.

He pushed his horse through the crowd and reached the Grassmarket at the foot of the Castle Rock, and looked up that sheer height to the window that he knew to be that of her bedroom. Others were hanging about there too, staring up, waiting for any more shreds of news. Sir James Melville had been waiting here on horseback ever since dawn, they told him, and the instant the baby was safely born, Mary Beton, now Ogilvie, had leaned out of that window over the sheer drop of the cliff and let down a ring and a letter on a cord. Melville had caught them and galloped off to take the news to Queen Elizabeth in London, as fast as fresh horses posted all the way could carry him.

Inside the Castle he could get no news that reassured him. The Queen had had a long and terrible labour; the doctors, and what was even more important, the midwife, Margaret Houston, had not believed it possible that she could live. But she had made such a fight for her life that by her will alone she had won through.

('You *want* to live, remember.'

'If I do, it's because you've made me.')

But it was too early yet to know if he had succeeded; she was lying up there, limp and exhausted and grey with her agony, and who could tell yet if she would recover from it?

Round him the busy, complacent voices buzzed against his ears, talking again and again of this brat that might even now cost her her life, a 'fat bouncing boy' – Du Croc had said his godfathers would feel the weight of him when it came to the christening.

He was the living spit of the King, they said, with sly triumph in their tones, for that would dispose of any lying rumours that suggested Signor Davie as the father. And they went on repeating descriptions of the big sloping head and blue eyes set very wide apart, until Bothwell went out on the battlements to cool his head of the raging desire that filled him to kill both Darnley and his son together.

*   *   *

Up in the small stone room with the one little window looking down over the Grassmarket, the figure in the bed at last moved its head on the pillow. It was night by now and the candles were shaded from the patient's eyes, but the curtains

314

had been drawn back from the window to give her air, and showed a square of sky that was one red glow. Bonfires were blazing on the heights all through Scotland; five hundred were afire in Edinburgh alone, and with that smoky glow there came the surging roar of voices, cheering, singing, shouting with joy in the town below.

She heard them and opened her eyes and saw the sky all red for joy of her son who would be King of Scotland, and of England. They brought him for her to look at.

Presently, when she was stronger, they brought Darnley in to see her and the baby. The room was full of people. He stood awkwardly, looking down on her face that seemed to have been spun all over with a cobweb of tiny fine lines of pain. Margaret Houston drew back a shawl, and there, tucked into Mary's arm, lay a crumpled red scrap that opened its mouth and yawned in a terrifying manner. Mary spoke in a voice only just above a whisper: 'My lord, God has given me a son begotten by none but you.'

He blushed crimson, and not knowing what to say, stooped and kissed the infant. But still that relentless whisper went on, as if it were stealing into the room from the other side of the world. 'Here I protest to God, this is your son and no other man's son. I desire that all here bear witness. For he is so much your own son that I fear it will be the worse for him hereafter.'

*   *   *

Sir James Melville came back loaded with congratulations and gossip. All the Catholics in England were of course overjoyed; the Moderates too were well pleased, and far more eager now to give Mary their support than before. But there was tough opposition from the new gentry created by Henry VIII's Reformation, whose power and property might be jeopardized by a Catholic succession – although even Bloody Mary, with all her Parliament re-converting themselves Catholic on their knees, had never been able to get back from them a single foot of Church lands.

Queen Elizabeth herself, at Melville's interview, had declared the news gave her such happiness that it had instantly cured her of a dangerous sickness. This was rather odd, as when Melville arrived the night before at Greenwich Palace on the river Thames, he had found Elizabeth in the midst of her Court, dancing in her usual indefatigable fashion. Melville, still in his riding-boots and dusty travelling-dress, had not dared enter the ballroom, but sought out Cecil, who was working in an ante-chamber ('I believe the little man never stops writing even in his sleep – if he ever sleeps!'), and told him to give Her Majesty the news.

With small precise steps the Minister threaded his way through the dancers and whispered in the Queen's ear, while Melville watched from the doorway.

She tottered to a seat and turned her face away from the room, leaning it against her hand. The music fell silent, the dancers still. Her ladies gathered anxiously round her. In that fateful, questioning pause, a harsh high voice was heard sobbing out, 'The Queen of Scots is mother of a fair son, while I am but a barren stock.'

It was, as Bothwell remarked, a strange assumption for a virgin.

And the more militant of her subjects were determined she should not assume it. She was at once besieged with demands, indeed commands, to marry and produce an heir, or else to nominate her successor. The first, she said, was her own business and nobody else's; the second, was to ask her to dig her grave before she was dead. She told the House of Lords that they were a knot of hare-brains: the House of Commons, that they were a lot of inexperienced schoolboys; and a deputation of bishops, that they were merely 'her creatures – doctors, not bishops, avaricious and immoral, who had once dared call her a bastard'.

And while she roared at them, her Parliament roared back that papers were being printed calling the Scottish Queen's son ' "Prince of Scotland and England" – and *Scotland* before *England*! Whoever heard or read *that* before this time?'

CHAPTER FOURTEEN

THE BRUTAL occupation of pain was over; all emotion and excitement were over. Here she lay, and the faces moved round her and went away, swam over her and went away, the voices hummed far, far away. One face stayed, thoughtful, mocking, of rare but irregular beauty. Something of herself looked down at her through those questing eyes, something of herself was always just about to speak with those mobile, delicate lips. It was an oval face, framed in bright hair under a velvet cap; against the dark robe a fine hand was raised, holding a small white carnation; he was a little amused at having to do this, he told her – for he was speaking with her all the time, though no sound came from those secret smiling lips.

The portrait was by Holbein, of her grandfather James IV, the king who had been denied the grave of a beggar, the scientist who believed the fairy-tale that men could learn to fly, the heretic who wished to lead a Crusade to the Holy Land, the philosopher who found no answer to his questions, the man whose passionate curiosity of mind and body bridged the gulf between two ages.

She had been only semi-conscious for a long time after the effort of her speech to Darnley; and when she revived again, that first shock of his son's close likeness to himself passed into anxiety for the odd little creature. Born whole and sane almost by a miracle, it was too much of a miracle that he should be strong. His legs were particularly weak; his sloping bulbous head had the look of an infant prematurely born – odd, as his birth was not premature, as had been expected. His tongue was too large for his mouth, which slobbered in consequence even more than most babies. He showed great intelligence, but more timidity, and cried with terror when Mary dangled a bright jewel before his eyes to make him 'take notice'.

' "Illegitimate!" ' his wet-nurse exclaimed to her friends. 'It's my belief he *is*. That one is no son of the Queen – the King must have given birth to him when we weren't looking!'

She was Margaret, Lady Reres, younger sister of Bothwell's early love, Janet Scott of Buccleuch, a plump jolly coarse woman, an excellent nurse to both mother and baby; she understood Mary's utter physical weakness well enough to keep her attention on the next short stage only, on the coming Christening. It would be an affair of the highest international importance. Elizabeth, as godmother, had promised a gold font in which to baptize the heir to both Crowns, and it was passionately hoped through the kingdoms that she would then make a public statement recognizing him as this. The silken banners with the Leopards of England, taken from Edward II at Bannockburn, would decorate the chapel at Stirling; to Mary this was a symbol that the wars that had been waged almost continuously since then between the two countries would be exorcized by the holy water that baptized the future King of them both.

This was no fancy: it had grown to be the backbone of her policy, as it had been of that young man with the carnation in

317

his hand. She must carry on his work. He had made Scotland a European Power, as she had been told she was doing in her marriage as a child with France. But now the Auld Alliance was dead, and she had known it, finally, when she had drunk warmed ale in a blacksmith's forge. Alliance with England was what Scotland *must* have now.

If only she and Elizabeth could meet! She had acted as Mary's most insidious enemy, 'but that is because we don't know each other', said Mary. If only they could sit together at a table and talk things over perfectly frankly, saying what they wanted of each other, they would surely do more for their countries than by scratching at each other in the dark.

Strength lay in agreement; division was death. 'She is a cleverer woman than I, she must know that too. We could work together then for a real victory, this whole island to be one country, just as my grandfather united the Isles and Western Highlands to Scotland, and got all the nobles together to join with him, and sought friendship with Henry VIII by marriage with his sister.'

'And was refused Christian burial by his brother-in-law, after dying in battle against him,' finished old Sir Richard Maitland in his silvery voice.

This delightful octogenarian was the father of 'Michael Wily' Maitland of Lethington and resembled him in his refinement of looks and intellect, the gentle suavity of his manner and the deadly cynicism of his remarks. Sir Richard, like his son, had for convenience adopted the new formula of the Protestants, but detested them for having burnt the libraries and charter-chests in the monasteries. Lethington had carried his father's disillusionment a stage further, in his contempt for old-fashioned notions of honour as well as of religion. Both father and son were agnostic and unmoral, but Sir Richard still held that there were certain things a man could not do and consider himself a gentleman; he regretted that his cleverest son had a crude strain of folly in him somewhere that made him ambitious.

Sir Richard was himself entirely devoid of that quality. He could not see why a Maitland should ever wish to add anything to his name. To want power was merely to add to your labours and decrease your pleasures. And what more money could one want than would pay for dainty cooking, good wine, a sheltered garden, and the leisure to collect and copy old manuscripts? This last almost amounted to a passion with him; not quite, for he had never been so unbalanced as to endure any discomfort for his pursuit. That he left to his daughter, a thin austere devoted woman who would ride all day in the rain for the chance of finding some hitherto unknown poem in a neighbour's muniment-chest.

Sir Richard told Mary there was only one invention in this past century that really mattered. 'What does it matter *how* men kill each other? They will always do it. Your grandfather tried to band all the countries of Europe together in a league of Christendom – but why? To defend it against the advances of the Turks. Nations will only make peace with each other in order to make war on someone else. When I was a boy I watched the building of his fleet down here below in Leith Harbour, the ships coming in with logs for it from Norway, and all the trees in Fife cut down for the *Great Michael* alone, the largest ship in the world. He made Scotland a sea-power – but he lost it all. The *Great Michael* was sold after Flodden, and his greatest Captain, Sir Andrew Barton, was killed by King Henry's sailors; his name is now nothing but an old song. *That* has lasted, though his ships haven't. None of these things last. But your grandfather did something really useful when he got Walter Chepman to set up a printing press here in the High Street, and he knew it. More than once I've seen him there, for I was always in the place myself when I came home as a young man of twenty; and the King would stroll in to see what was being printed, and even help set up the type with his own fingers, just as in the dockyard he helped build his ships himself, and practised surgery as well as he played the lute.'

With those long fingers that rather disdainfully held up a white carnation – yes, she could see the young man in the portrait doing all that.

She lay back on her cushions on the battlements where she had been carried that she might feel the sea-wind from the Firth of Forth, and heard the precise amused old voice telling her of the plays and poems of that time; but most had already disappeared, because no copy had been made of them. 'And so it comes that out of all his earlier fellows that Willie Dunbar mentions in his lament for dead poets, almost a dozen have vanished clean out of present memory.

Timor mortis conturbat me,

so he sang, for the fear of death troubled him. It troubles me worse for the death of their poems.'

'A poem can't die,' she answered.

'Is this a new creed of immortality? Please convert me, Madam.'

She smiled, but could not say it. She had watched that big white cloud sail past in the high summer sky, gracious and proud as a tall ship at sea, and believed that nothing that had happened after to the *Great Michael* could matter as much as the fact that it had been built. Ships, poems, the League of Christendom itself, the minds of men that wished and planned these things would not die. That was why for many years in Scotland people had refused to believe that James IV had fallen in battle: he had been spirited away, they said, and would return to bring the Golden Age again.

They were right, she thought. He had not died.

* * *

Sir Richard Maitland did not show any sentimental yearning to see his son again before his own presumably near demise ('At eighty, one does not take long views'), though he admitted that the young rogue's conversation amused him more than most. But he suggested that Mary would show sense in getting his wits to work for her instead of against her. She admitted frankly that she desperately needed Michael Wily's brains to straighten out the tangle of the kingdom's finances. But could she trust him not to work against her whenever it was to his own advantage?

'No, you could not,' was the reply in that sweet, faint old voice, 'nor any other of those clever brains you have about you. Only for his own advantage. The boy would not work against you for the sheer pleasure of destroying a lovely thing.'

'But who would, and why?'

'Your tutor, Mr George Buchanan, for one, now busily writing praises of your chaste motherhood to the hope of two great nations. His Latin is the only part of it that comes easily to him. He would much rather write some of those virulent satires of his, wherein he gambols as playfully as an elephant, and against you. So he will, the moment you are down, and so will hundreds of other clever men of the same calibre, who may never have seen you, may live long after you are dead, but will hate you nevertheless. It is your own fault, Madam, in being charming. That is a crime such men can never forgive.'

She thought the old gentleman must be senile after all. She had never really liked Mr George Buchanan; he had always been fulsome to her, and his fat red cheeks wobbled with joy whenever he could tell or hint at some dirty piece of scandal. He had been a small farmer's son and a pauper scholar; nevertheless she had given him the Abbey of Crossraguel with its temporalities worth £500 a year, and only a month ago created him the Principal of St Leonard's. How could he hate her?

'Feminine charm such as Your Grace's,' those silvery tones answered her, 'is a challenge that his perverse instincts are unable to accept, and therefore resent. He, and his kind, wish to avenge their own thwarted natures by revenging themselves on you.'

'Oh,' said Mary as a light dawned, 'I remember now what my lord of Bothwell once called him.' And she gleefully repeated his pothouse phrase.

'My lord of Bothwell has his own way of putting things,' said Sir Richard, 'one that is scarcely compatible with feminine charm.'

She was quite pleased to find that she could shock him.

*   *   *

So Michael Wily, like a faithful Mordecai, returned, and there was to be a banquet to help on a reconciliation between them and Bothwell. She explained to him how she needed Lethington for her diplomacy and finance, as she needed Bothwell's strong arm in war to protect herself and the baby Prince.

'Very pretty,' he growled, 'and you think we can all make friends by dining together!'

He saw the difficulty, all but impossibility, of Mary's doing without them – unless, as he wished, she would put them to death. Deeply as he hated James, he was even more consumed with jealousy of Lethington. It had extended to his father, 'since you no longer wish to speak with anyone under eighty!'

He naturally could not understand that in her physical and emotional exhaustion she found his enormous vigour overpowering, and shrank from it as she would at this moment from a nor'-east gale.

'Have you never been ill or tired yourself?' she asked. 'If you were, I suppose you'd feel as weak as a horse!'

What was she driving at? He was not asking her to do anything. No, the thing was plain enough; she'd fallen in love with him and now fallen out again.

He did not see that she had fallen out of love with love itself;

321

that any sexual emotion was abhorrent to her for the time being, after all she had suffered from it in body and mind. He told himself that he had served her turn, and now that he was no longer immediately necessary he was being pushed again into the background. He was damned if he'd stand that.

It was very hot; Erskine of Mar offered the Queen the hospitality of his castle of Alloa; she longed to be on the moors again and by the sea, but dreaded the effort of the journey. Bothwell suggested that one of his sea-captains, William Blackadder, and his crew should take her by boat up the Firth of Forth, and she would then have nothing to do but lie on deck, he added crossly, for he was disgusted at her not making a quicker recovery. Anger, pity, and fear for her, he could never look at her now without a mixture of those uncomfortable emotions, and the last two were painfully unaccustomed. But for a moment he was won to something tenderer by the delight and gratitude in her face.

'To sail up the coast in one of your ships! It's what I've always longed for. And you will be in charge, my Lord High Admiral, as you were when you stole me away from France!'

But he would not come. Her 'watchdog James' would be with her as well as Mar – he'd not spoil so harmonious a company. The next instant he regretted his sneer and said Blackadder would manage the voyage perfectly, he was a useful fellow ('and would have been more so if I'd got the chance to use him!' he added to himself). For Lethington, before his pardon, had planned to go to France, and Bothwell had blithely detailed Blackadder to pursue him at sea, capture his ship, and drop him overboard. George Buchanan was not entirely libellous for once when he described Bothwell's sea-captains as 'famous pirates'.

But that happy opportunity had been missed, the wind taken out of Bothwell's piratical sails, and Blackadder left with the gentle task of transporting a sick girl and her baby to 'the sweet seat of Alloa.'

By mid-August she was strong enough to ride again, and Bothwell saw her at a grand royal hunting-party, which James and Darnley also attended, on the high downs of Ettrick Forest. The sight of her once again on horseback, with the quick colour in her cheeks and the light in her eyes as of old, brought back his unbearable longing for her. He had thought her cold, ungrateful, uncertain, weak, preferring a lot of tame treacherous cats to himself, but when he saw her in front of him he could not go on hating her; they rode together for a time over the waving bent, now in pearly flower, and there they were talking as though they had never parted and he had never been angry with her.

As they sat their horses waiting for the others to come up, watching the silver lights and shadows chasing each other over the rolling hills, she told him that Darnley was giving trouble. While in Edinburgh he had 'vagabondized every night', and she had scarcely seen him, but when she was at Alloa he had suddenly turned up and made a scene, demanding 'bed and board' with his wife, 'just as though I were a lodging-house keeper!' she said with a desperate little laugh. The doctor had told him it was impossible, and he had flung away in a temper within a couple of hours of his arrival. He simply could not understand why everything should not be just the same between them as before Rizzio's murder; and now that he found her so unforgiving, he was writing abroad to the Catholic Princes complaining of her lack of zeal for the faith; that she was getting their sympathy and protective interest on false pretences.

'He can't really think that would endear him to me, but he doesn't seem to mind *what* I feel for him as long as it is something – if it can't be the old fondness, then let it be fear, or just irritation!'

'And when you are stronger,' he burst out, 'will you then give him his demands?'

She met his eyes fairly. Her own were clear, with the silver-golden lights of the day reflected in them, and her hair blowing round her face as soft as thistledown.

'No,' she said in a voice so low he scarcely heard it. She had whispered a pledge to him.

*   *   *

She gave Darnley more presents and induced him to make official appearances with her. They rode together to Stirling to place the Prince under the charge of Lord and Lady Mar, with Bothwell in command of his bodyguard. There the young couple stayed for a little with their baby, and Mary carried him up and down the prim paths of the formal garden that James IV had made, and watched the white peacock, of the same breed that he had installed, spread its tail like a great mother-of-pearl fan in the sun, and tried to think her child was growing less like his father every day.

But his father grew more and more like himself, and by September she fled back alone to Edinburgh.

Work, that was the only thing for her now. Even then she could not really take in the problem of modern finance. She sat day after day in Exchequer House with Lethington, and heard how prices were rising and money falling with the influx of new gold through Spain from the Indies; how this vast increase of yellow metal, for which men went and killed each other, would in the long run ruin Europe. Why then had men made gold their master?

Lethington shrugged and advised her to ask his father.

But he was, as always, sympathetic over her own immediate problems; he had often complained at the Council that it was most unfair the Queen should have to pay the Protestant ministers' stipend out of her own privy purse – if she were to meet all their demands, he told them, 'she will not have enough at the end of the year to buy herself a pair of shoes.'

But what else could she do? The enormous wealth taken from the old Church, which was to have endowed the new, had found its way into the lay pockets of the Lords of the Congregation, and she could not let the poor ministers starve.

'And has Your Grace understood so ungraceful a subject as your revenues?' asked Mr George Buchanan with what he intended as a courtly smile.

'I have understood the Council will vote twelve thousand for the Christening,' she replied crisply; 'with that, and Masques written by the finest Latin scholar in Europe, we should impress the foreign Ambassadors.'

The finest Latin scholar contorted both person and speech as he bowed over a return compliment so elaborate that he had difficulty in unwinding himself from its coils.

She came to his rescue with inquiries after the famous French pupils he had taught while holding the chair of Latin at the new College of Guienne at Bordeaux. For France had sheltered Mr Buchanan when both Scotland and England had turned him out, and he seldom missed a chance of telling Mary that her mother country was *summa humanitas*. Young Michel de Montaigne and Monsieur Scaliger owed their early eminence entirely to the fact that he had given them their first floggings, so he chuckled with reminiscent pleasure. Montaigne had been a pampered brat whose father had given orders he was to be awakened always by music, lest the tender brain of childhood should be injured by a more sudden process; but George Buchanan had soon put a stop to such nonsense. The ill effects of that early spoiling persisted, however; he was already, though a young man, wishing to retire to a life of 'quiet and in-difference to all things.' To his former tutor, a shrewd and inde-fatigable man of business, passionately ambitious, this was the worst sign he had yet seen of the decadence of modern youth.

Montaigne had been made Gentleman of the Bedchamber at the French Court at a very early age, and King Henri II had delighted in his conversation; Mary herself, the thoughtful child King Henri had loved to have near him, had often leaned against her father-in-law's chair and watched that strange young man with the melancholy smile looking at her under the heavy lids of his dreaming eyes, while he made little restless movements, kicking his feet together in a most unconventional manner for a royal audience, and talked and talked, and decided nothing.

But once he had left his 'perhaps' and 'I think' and 'it is possible' and all his gentle qualifications, and burst out in his rather loud voice at the news of fresh Spanish victories in Mexico. Politics! The greatness of Empire! The moral duty to civilize the savage and teach him true religion! What did it all amount to but that great cities were levelled to the ground, nations exterminated, the richest and most beautiful countries wrecked – to provide Europe with pearl and pepper! 'Mechanic victories!' shouted that odd young man.

'King Henri thought him remarkable,' she said.

'Yes, yes.' The stout black indignant form heaved himself up and down the room in agitation that was somehow pathetic, so helpless was all the talent and energy of the careerist in conflict with the man of genius. 'I've told him again and again, he might get anywhere. And yet look at him! He wishes only to read old books, to talk with gardeners and carpenters, he who has entertained kings! That is the result of having "a well-born soul" as he calls it! A well-born purse, rather. All young men should be born poor, as I was. Vanity and egoism, they will ruin the most promising career ever launched. Scaliger, too, says Montaigne's interest in everything that concerns himself will swamp all his energies. What will it matter to the rest of the world whether he likes radishes, must drink his wine from a glass, wears silk stockings winter and summer? Yet that is all he wishes to do, draw himself with a pen in his essays as painters draw their own portraits with a crayon. He cares nothing for worldly prospects nor fame, does not want to be read or quoted after he is dead, thinks learning nothing to be proud of, and the cleverest men apt to be foolish, the laws mere conventions, and habits and customs a timid convenience. He wishes only, he says, to be "a master of the art of life".'

And he mopped his brow, which was damp with rage and a real concern for the pupil who might have done even better than himself.

Mary had never liked him so well as now, for he had forgotten he was speaking to a woman, that strange faintly unpleasant species that had to be approached in a particular manner with placatory smirks and compliments; for once he was speaking sincerely, and, though with disapproval, of one of the men who made France '*summa humanitas*'.

'But,' said he, 'let us turn to more important matters,' and he produced his Latin Masque. She looked at it as they walked in the garden at the back of Exchequer House that still, golden September day. Some very tall sunflowers had raised their heads over the wall from the next garden; Mary looked up and laughed to see their black faces framed in glistening gold peering down at her. 'A whole row of Black Ladies for a Savage Knight to tilt for!' she exclaimed. 'Whose garden is that?'

Mr Buchanan, disgusted that her attention should be diverted from his Muse, replied with a touch of acid, 'Is it possible Your Grace does not know? That is the garden of Mr David Chalmers, one of my Lord Bothwell's creatures.'

'His lawyer, you mean,' she answered, and thought yes, it was true, he really was leering. It was strange that so much learning could not create the '*âme bien née*'.

CHAPTER FIFTEEN

MONSIEUR D'OYSEL, over on a diplomatic visit to the French Ambassador, Philibert Du Croc, simply could not understand it. His fat pink hands flapped in the face of his old comrade in arms, the Earl of Bothwell, as he wheezed and panted his astonishment. He had left Scotland six years ago, and now he found it a different country. Then all had been darkness – war with England, civil war, and worse than all, war with those one believed friendly: 'Never could one tell here the friend from the enemy, for he who was with us in the morning might go over to the other side before dinner. No wonder that poor gallant lady died of it. Yet her daughter, a young girl, comes, and pouf! in five years she makes daylight. There has been no war with England. She has put down two civil wars against her as soon as they began. She escapes alone, enceinte, from five hundred armed guards. She crushes all her enemies within a week, then gives a natural birth to her infant and does not die. I tell you it is incredible, impossible!'

Bothwell quickly informed him that he had something to do with the crushing of her enemies and the squashing of the civil wars.

D'Oysel flapped away this information. 'My friend, you are a fine soldier and you lead men *gaillardement*. It is known. Also you are seven years older than when you raided the English trenches and then lamented your Hobs and your Willies – it is possible you have learned some sense.' (There was very nearly an explosion at this, but d'Oysel with a glance at his companion's face did not wait for it.) 'But that does not detract from the miracle of this young thing, with but one of her nobles both strong and loyal to her, making such headway in a country all but foreign to her, and the most part hostile. Who has she had to advise her? No one but her bastard brother and your Scots Machiavelli, who, it is now plain, have worked only for their own ends from the beginning. But she has refused to serve their ends – or that of others. She has refused to obey the Pope and put down Protestantism, refused even to give his Legate an official audience. On the other hand, she has refused to obey John Knox and turn Protestant, although she has been threatened with murder again and again in his sermons if she does not do so – and those threats of Knox, they arrive, it is known. Yet she holds her way between the two faiths, and will have tolerance for both, and, in spite of the ministers, she has succeeded. The country has answered for her and not for the Bastard. All Europe is impressed, the English Queen envious and afraid, her enemies cowed.' He drew breath, then demanded,

'How is it then, this miracle? She has no troops of her own, no great allies, since she will not join the Catholic League – no, it is her own, the miracle – her generosity, her wish for peace, her trust in her people; rather than her charm and beauty.'

He undid another button of his doublet and leaned back, contemplating his wisdom and Bothwell's wine together with placid satisfaction. His face had grown more completely spherical in the six years since Bothwell had last seen it in the inn-garden at Paris: it was now a perfect harvest-moon with its attendant satellites of chins.

But suddenly its celestial calm was shattered by a convulsion from within; the blue eyes blazed, the fluffy tufts of eyebrows

327

shot up into the pink forehead, the mouth opened in a round indignant O; he was confounded, he was outraged, he demanded of what were the men made in Scotland, and was their Queen indeed a woman and not a mermaid? How was it that even now she was nearly twenty-four there had been no real scandals about her in spite of all the attempts of the ministers, civil and religious, to work them up? Rizzio? Pouf! Cecil's efforts to blacken her over that had made him a laughing-stock in France. Châtelard? Pah! She was not of the type to kill her lovers. It was seen.

No, she was cold; and he gave a furnace sigh at the reproach; compliments on her beauty, however subtle, did not amuse her (obviously his own vanity had been piqued); it delighted her far more 'to hear of hardihood and valiancy'. She never heeded Ronsard's warning to make the most of her young beauty before it faded like the rose. And in a rich surprising tenor, his hand to his heart, leaning amorously towards his companion, he chanted,

> 'Cueillez, cueillez votre jeunesse:
> Comme à cette fleur, la vieillesse
> Fera tenir votre beauté.'

'No need to goggle at me. I've always made the most of my beauty.'

D'Oysel ignored such triviality on a subject as serious as that of food. He wagged his fat finger and said reproachfully that the act of sex could give the Queen no pleasure, only disgust; it was evident in the repulsion she felt for Darnley. She could no more bear him even to lay a hand on her sleeve than if he were a gross spider.

'Christ's heart, and do you blame her?' Bothwell broke out at last, suddenly moved from his silent amusement in those crisp, final, infinitely certain tones that put everything so neatly into categories for the sheer pleasure of arrangement.

'Blame? How you confuse things, my friend. I say that one has never – but *never* – pleased her. It is seen. She could not hold him faithful to her for even a few weeks after their marriage, and why? Because she did not wish to. Nor does she wish to console herself. Again why? Because he has rendered her a great service: he has disgusted her with men. That is an advantage certainly, to a Queen. To a woman, no!'

'Because a sickly cub has disappointed her, you think —' but he could not go on.

'Aha, you are *touché*! You are not then all stone.'

'It's the first I've heard of it.'

'Oh, you have your blacksmith's and foreign admiral's daughters, it is known. How goes it with your Norwegian lady? Is she the reason you have been too preoccupied this past year to make love to your beautiful young Queen?'

'More likely that my Queen has been too preoccupied with a dangerous childbirth to allow me,' said Bothwell, hoping his explanation was the true one.

D'Oysel was not to be steered off Anna. His infallible nose for gossip had already discovered that that importunate lady had made use of her passport to pay a second visit to Scotland this summer, encouraged thereto by the news she had obtained that Bothwell's marriage was not a success. But neither was her attempt to revive the past. Bothwell was none too pleased at her return. To lodge her again on his mother's estate would have made her far too conspicuous; he gave her one of his peel towers and visited her occasionally and in secret. Poor Anna, lonely, bored and disappointed, poured out her feelings in her sonnets, complaining of the pale tearful wife, in love with another, who had won from her 'her true husband in the sight of God'. Had she not left her friends and country twice over for him, placed her son, her goods and her own subject heart in his absolute power? These complaints were easier to endure than her expressions of abject humility, when she 'kissed his hands' and told him she was trying to make herself worthy of his love.

But even if Bothwell shared her opinion of his wife's 'feigned tears' and 'writings rouged with learning' (Lady Jean had recently been both plaintive and pedantic, in a belated attempt to win her husband's affections), he had no intention of deserting her for Anna. So the Norwegian had now gone home again, and continued to write letters, mostly in verse. He did not answer them – but he kept them.

'You are too fortunate, my friend, that is your trouble,' the bland voice of his companion rounded off the troublesome episode. 'You have a fair lady come sighing for you out of the far North and you are ungrateful. You have a beautiful young wife who now regrets her childish folly and wishes you to love her, it is seen; but you shrug, you say it is too late. My young friend, beware of women. They are more dangerous than serpents when they are scorned.'

'Oh, God damn you for an old wiseacre!' Bothwell answered.

And d'Oysel with mountainous tact spoke instead of Darnley's odd behaviour politically.

'He would cut off his nose to spite his face, that one, but that is dangerous, for with it would go some other noses too.' He pressed a finger on the pudgy button in the middle of his own face, squashing it flat into his cheeks while his little eyes glared out on either side of it with an expression of appalling cunning.

'Playing with a pup will end in a howl,' observed Bothwell, 'and there's not a Scot now who doesn't know it and fight shy of him.'

Darnley had indeed set to work to find fresh allies. In May, before his son was born, he had already tried to get away to Flanders, and the two comrades now debated this obscure move. Could it be that he had hoped to meet King Philip of Spain, who had been expected to arrive in Flanders in May with an army to crush the Netherland Protestants and their English backers? Bothwell had some evidence to support this notion.

'The pup's got into touch with some English spies, that I know. One of them was in the Tower with me and released later, a fellow called Arthur Pole, who talked big of being able to raise the Catholics for King Philip if he should invade England. He tried to get me into it, and couldn't understand that though I was an enemy of Elizabeth I was no friend of Philip's. He'll find his mistake with the English Catholics too, I'm thinking – they'll not fight for Philip, however much Elizabeth stamps on 'em; but these fish, who think wars are made only for words, forget there's such a thing as flesh and blood. Pole's furnished Darnley with a chart of the Scilly Isles and plans of Scarborough Castle which the young ass left lying about in his usual artless fashion. What's the betting he means to join King Philip in a descent on the English Coast?'

'Scarborough – Scilly – Flanders! Your pup roams wide.'

'Maybe he's heard that "a ganging fit will aye get something, if it's only a thorn or a broken toe",' Bothwell remarked dryly.

There was no doubt about the 'ganging fit'. Darnley had a ship ready manned in the Clyde to take him abroad. On Michaelmas night about ten o'clock he had ridden to Edinburgh, but hearing that the Queen was sitting with some of her great lords, refused to enter. She had run out herself into the raw foggy night air of the courtyard, taken him by the hand and let him in. That evening, alone with him, she had tried to discover what he intended to do on this mysterious voyage, but failed.

For so fair a creature, d'Oysel complained, she was singularly deficient as a Delilah.

She had next day to admit to her Council that she had been able to get nothing from her husband about his plans: it was agreed that he should be questioned publicly. The Frenchman Du Croc and d'Oysel were there; Du Croc asked in flowery terms how he could wish 'to relinquish so beautiful a Queen and so royal a realm'; Mary took his hand before them all and asked him to say outright what grievance he had that made him act against her, seek to blacken her name with the Catholic Powers, and now secretly to leave the kingdom.

It was the moment he had rehearsed inside his head for weeks; he would tell her in front of everybody how shamefully she had treated him, ignored him, got all she wanted from him, even a son and heir, and then denied him any real power, turned everybody against him. And here was the moment, and Mary standing before him, grave, beautiful, her cold fingers just touching his, her eyes meeting his so cool and calm – for the first time he thought what strange eyes they were, always changing colour, but now they seemed to have no colour, they were the eyes of a mermaid.

And as he turned his head he saw James' long contemptuous nose, Bothwell's fiery glance of disgust, and Lethington's fingertips gently tapping each other.

His courage ebbed out of him; if he began to speak of his injuries he would burst into tears and they would all laugh at him. He mumbled that he 'never intended any voyage or had any discontent'. He thought he saw a smile pass round. He *must* show that he was to be reckoned with, yes and feared.

He took away his hand with a gesture of tremendous dignity, and in a tone of sinister importance he said, 'Adieu, Madam, you shall not see my face for a long time.' Then he rammed his hat over his eyes and strode out of the room.

From Corstorphine that very same day he wrote to her complaining of the scornful looks and treatment given him by her 'great lords'.

But he had at last succeeded in one of his aims, for the 'great lords' decided they could no longer ignore him. No sooner had he ridden off than a conference was held by the Lord James, Lethington and Argyll, with the Earls of Bothwell and Huntly, pledging to support each other in disobeying the King when his orders conflicted with the Queen's. This curious combination of old enemies showed their sense of the urgent need for unity against a common danger.

*　　*　　*

Bothwell's uneasiness was not merely because of Darnley. It was in Mary's very success that the danger lay. Her toleration was winning more and more of the milder Protestants to her side, and even to her religion; as the ministers were still very much a minority (there were not nearly enough of them for all the parishes), this was driving them to desperation. And a Scotland strengthened by unity, as she was strengthening it, was the last thing England wanted. There were English attempts to stir up trouble, Morton and Lindsay being very helpful as agents. Was the Lord James engineering the trouble for his own purpose? The old Abbot of Kelso, William Kerr, was murdered by two of his own relatives, who struck off his head 'because', it was rumoured, 'the Lord Bastard wanted to shut his mouth'. The Abbot had known too much about the Rizzio murder plot and who was in it. Bothwell's office as Lieutenant made it his duty to ride against the Kerrs and punish their murder of their kinsman, but his scouts warned him of opposition being organized against him all along the Border; also, on the English side, of a widespread plot working against him personally, either to kill or capture him for England.

To counter this he called a Royal Progress with a Court of Justice at Jedburgh, which, of course, James would also attend. 'Set a thief to catch a thief'; he grinned as he thought of James sitting in judgement on the very crimes he had instigated.

He did not explain his motives to Mary, but she gladly agreed to this; her Progresses had always had effect, she told her Lieutenant.

'On the partridges anyway,' he answered her. 'I hear their price goes up to half a crown apiece as soon as you appear.'

'It's the purveyors' fault. They take all the profit and poke their noses into everything, and those are so long they stretch from here to France over even a bottle of Bordeaux.'

So she appointed a tariff to 'put the purveyors' noses out of joint' and keep down the prices of board and lodging at Jedburgh during her visit: bed and bedding at a shilling a night; a man's 'ordinary', with braised beef, mutton and roast, at one and four; good ale at fivepence a pint; finest bread at fourpence the pound; and stabling for a horse at twopence the twenty-four hours.

Old Sir Richard Maitland quoted to her from his own verses how

> *Of Liddesdale the common thieves*
> *None dare sleep for their mischieves.*

He warned her in especial to beware of the three Jocks – the Laird's Jock ('Takes hen and cock'), Jock o' the Side ('A greater thief ne'er did ride') and the famous or infamous Little Jock o' the Park ('rips chest and ark'), for

> *They leave not spindle, spoon nor spit,*
> *Bed, bolster, blanket, shirt nor sheet.*

He watched her ride off in her spirits, the hoofs of her mare Black Agnes clattering merrily on the cobblestones of Edinburgh High Street, and all her Court in attendance. She turned to wave her quirt at the old man with a flourish: she never looked so well as on horseback: it was a graceful fashion, this new-fangled side-saddle that she had introduced into Scotland.

CHAPTER SIXTEEN

MARY HAD put off the Assizes till October so as to give time for the harvest to be gathered in first. Bothwell had ridden ahead two days before with three hundred horse to round up 'the common thieves'. Hermitage Castle was his headquarters, and on the first day he filled it with prisoners from the Armstrong clan who were conducting a happy little war on the Johnstones of Nithsdale. These he would take on with him to be tried at Jedburgh when he had added to the bag. Next day it was the turn of the Elliots, now his determined enemies.

One got up early to catch an Elliot; as the Night Hawk clattered across the drawbridge over the moat the ground was still dark, and a white cow moved through the dim shapes of some fruit trees as slowly as the moon through clouds. A brown owl rose heavy and blundering from almost under his horse's hoofs and flapped away into the shadow of the Castle. His 'lambs' came jingling after him, the hoofs of their mounts beating a merry rattle like that of kettle-drums on the hollow planks of the bridge.

They rode over the open moor, the dawn breaking in streaks

of pale light behind the hills that lay like sleeping giants all round them. The wind was from the west, driving and tossing the clouds before it in dark flying banners now flushed with red. The sun climbed over the edge of the still dark hills, and the foam of Witterhope Burn was turned to blood – then silver. Water ran everywhere, brawling in the burn, whispering hidden in the squelching bogs where the treacherous moss gleamed brilliant as emerald; the sun struck the autumn bracken and turned it to a flare of gold on the hillside, and the heather a fiery purple; the wind rippled and tore the bent like a running sea.

For all the brightness of the morning there was the smell of rain on the wind together with the sharp earthy freshness of wet moss and bog water and the brave smell of horses and leather. By the faith of his body, but it was good to be on this work again, with the wind in his face as he rode west, and the creak of the saddle beneath him, and the Night Hawk's throbbing muscles springing forward under the press of his knees! Round him rode his lambs as on their old forays together: Wee Willie Wallocky now grown to a stalwart stocky young man, who'd been in at many a death since he'd squeaked with excitement to see John Cockburn drop from his saddle that All Hallows' dawn seven years ago; Long Fargy longer than ever, but filled out from the lean lanky youth he was then to a fine broad-shouldered fellow; older men who'd ridden in many a Martinmas raid of a less legal nature than this, and new lads eager to try their spurs for the first time.

They rode up to Gibby Elliot of the Shaws, whose peel stood on the banks of the Witterhope Burn, and would have ridden past, for old Gibby never rode a raid, which gave him small credit with these ministers of the law! There was no 'riding' at the Shaws, they jeered; old Gibby had lain in so long at peace with his neighbours that his horses had grown too fat to stir out of their stall.

But Gibby was out at his gates waiting for them with a big jug of ale and two or three horn mugs to offer stirrup-cups to the leaders.

'This is paying blackmail to the Lord Lieutenant,' he said with a wink as he handed them up, 'so mind you never take the fray to me.'

'Not I!' laughed his overlord; 'it's ill work taking the breeks off a Highlander. I know peace is your over-word, my douce quiet man. But there are others a wee thought of your own kin

334

who sing a different tune; with them it's aye, "Who brings the fray to me?"'

'Maybe. I'll not answer for 'em. I'd rather pay blackmail to be left unraided than rescue-money for my neighbours' succour when raided. But it's a lie to say I ever *took* blackmail from any man and then refused him succour. No, my lord, I can say to all, as I said to Jamie Telfer of the Fair Dodhead,

> Go seek your succour where ye paid blackmail,
> For, man, ye ne'er paid money to me.'

He tipped up the jug and filled the mugs again with gnarled old hands knotted with rheumatism, a complaint he had suffered from early youth, which may have accounted for his strangely peaceable behaviour. His small screwed-up eyes twinkled wisely under his grizzled brows.

'I hear you took a big haul of Armstrongs from the Tarras Moss yesterday. You'll need stout locks for Jock o' the Side. It's no' so long since Mangerton's lads carried him away from an English prison, fetters and all. And now he'll rue the day that made the Galliard Lord Lieutenant.'

'Reivers shouldn't be ruers. He's never lacked good beef nor ale as long as his neighbours' lasted. He'll still feed free of expense in prison!'

'Have you warned the water, my lord?'

'Everywhere south of Lousy Lauder – from Borthwick Water to Priesthaughswire and the Currors o' the Lee, and as we came down the Hermitage Slack two days syne I left word on Willie of Gorrinberry. He'll obey a royal summons, so will the Coultart Cleugh and Gaudilands and Commonside and Allanhaugh. But what of your own kin, Gibby? Will they ride with me to Jedburgh, or must I take them in shackles?'

'Well now, I doubt Little Jock Elliot o' the Park will come whinnying up to eat out of your hand.' He rested a confidential hand on the Night Hawk's bridle. 'All the years I've lived I've never known a worse summer for trouble, except in the invasions – and there's been more than one sign that those might start again at any moment. You've got all the fords of Liddel set?'

'Not a salmon leaps in the moonlight but it's known and named and a message sent to its mother. Every ford is watched, the Dunkin and Door-Loup, the Willie-ford, Water-slack and Black-rock and Muckle Trout-tub o' Liddel.'

He said the names for the sheer pleasure of hearing them ring out again like the clang of bells. Three years he'd missed out of his life on these moors – he was making up for them now!

Old Elliot of the Shaws looked up into those hot reddish-brown eyes, of the very colour of the trout waters he'd been naming, and saw the blazing gaiety that was racing through his veins, making him more alive than any mere mortal had the right to be.

Was it true, then, that he was the Devil's man? True or no, to one creaking old man it gave new life to see the reckless arrogance of that head and hear that dangerous laughter.

Gibby's stiff-jointed fingers stroked the Night Hawk's neck while, forgetful of the New Religion's ban on saints and charms, he murmured the invocation to safety for those who would ride the autumn bogs:

> '*Matthew, Mark, Luke and John,*
> *Hold the horse that you ride on,*
> *Hold him fast and hold him sure*
> *Till you win o'er the misty moor.*'

He dipped a mug into the ale-jug for himself and held it up, pledging his visitor. 'Here's to more friends like yourself, and less need of 'em!'

'And may the mouse never leave your meal-poke with the tear in its eye!' responded the Lord Lieutenant, clinking his mug against his host's and tossing it off.

He wheeled the Night Hawk round, waved his thanks for Gibby's hospitality and hallooed his men on to the hunt. They answered him with a shout and cantered after him, following the Witterhope Burn to where it joined the Liddel Water, with the Tower of Redheugh across the burn to their right. The land here between the two streams was known as the Park, the terrain of the redoubtable Little Jock Elliot.

But when they came to his peel tower 'away was himself'. The doors were locked, and they smashed them in with a hewn tree that was lying handy, but 'not a thing about the place but an old rusty sword without a sheath that wouldn't fell a mouse,' Willie Wallocky reported as he came out, a grin splitting his freckled face from ear to ear.

'Better an empty house than an ill tenant,' muttered Soft Wat, who'd no wish to meet Jock o' the Park face to face. But he'd no luck, for the Lord's voice was ringing out, 'So he's taken the hill – and the better hunting for us! After him, lads, and hell for leather!'

They galloped on down Liddel Water. The towers of Mangerton and Whithaugh rose stark and grey on the hillside against a torn strip of blue among the racing clouds. Those towers too were empty, for their Armstrong owners had been taken yesterday to the Hermitage prisons, and Little Jock Elliot should join them 'afore the gloaming's grey'. So the hunters swore, and suddenly their leader turned in his saddle and shouted a view-halloo.

Bothwell had sighted their quarry among the heather. Now, clamped on his saddle, with the Night Hawk stretching out at a hand-gallop under him, and the Elliots flying before him and his men sweeping up behind him and the ground thudding like thunder under their horses' hoofs, and the dark moor and the wind and the wide sky all round him, there was nothing in the world he could not do!

But the Elliots had had a good start and their horses were fresh: they scattered, and some were soon clean lost to view. One short stocky figure on a dappled gelding was galloping hard towards the Kershope Burn.

'After him, Hawk!' He dug his spurs into the Night Hawk's flanks and the horse's quivering muscles responded nobly, sharing his joy in the pursuit, plunging forward over the wet heavy ground, forgetful of the travelling he had already made that day, straining every nerve and sinew in answer to the grip of his master's knees, the caress of his hand.

Jock o' the Park looked back and saw one horseman close on his heels. Only one. The rest were now outdistanced. But that was the Lord Lieutenant himself, whom Jock feared as he would the devil. He flogged on his mount, but his pursuer came thundering down the slope, gaining ground steadily, and they were neck to neck as they came down to Kershope o' the Lily Lea.

Here the ground was a shaking morass and both riders had to check their pace.

'Yield to the Queen's justice!' shouted Bothwell.

'If I do, will you give me my life?' came Little Jock's shout in answer.

'*I'd* be content. But you'll have to abide by the law.'

That last word was too much for Jock. He sprang from his gelding, which was already floundering among the livid green and burnt-red mosses. On foot there was still a chance he might escape the Lord Lieutenant on this marshy ground. Bothwell brought up his pistol and fired, and Jock stumbled as a bullet hit his thigh. The Night Hawk plunged after him, squelching fountains of water up from the drenched ground. In another minute the horse's weight would bog both himself and rider.

Bothwell dropped his smoking pistol and leaped from the saddle – on to a loose log hidden in the marsh, which turned under his foot and brought him down headlong. As he scrambled for a footing, Little Jock sprang back on to a firm tussock of bent, swung his two-handed sword back over his shoulder and hacked at the man below him. Three blows he struck, wounding him in the head, in the body, in the left hand as it shot up to defend the right, that was dragging out his whinger from his belt. But Bothwell struck upwards twice, at Elliot's chest. Two wounds he gave him; at the first, Jock dropped his sword; but as he dealt the second, Bothwell fell forward on his face and lay still, the blood pouring from his three wounds. Jock dragged himself through the reeds and long grasses some little distance before he fainted dead away.

*   *   *

Gibby Elliot of the Shaws stood at his gate yet again that day, when the clouds had covered the evening sky, and rain and battering hail swept past on the wind, striking down in long silver spears. But Gibby stood there at his gates and paid no heed to his bare head nor his aching bones, and saw a company of men coming riding very slowly up the Witterhope Burn, and among them some on foot, carrying a hurdle between them, and on it the body of the Lord Lieutenant.

CHAPTER SEVENTEEN

WORD TRAVELS fast in wild country. 'The Queen has lost a man she could trust, of whom she has but few,' so the report was written; and by word of mouth went faster: 'Lord Bothwell lies dead in Liddesdale.' Queen Mary heard it low down by Borthwick Water as she travelled by way of Melrose to Jedburgh:

> *My lord lies dead in Liddesdale,*
> *And his hunting it is done.*

His horse had bogged in his headlong pursuit, and Jock o' the Park had killed him and left him lying in his blood upon the moor and moss.

There was nothing she could do. She could not speak. She rode on towards Melrose.

The triple head of the Eildon Hill rose in sudden purple from the green plain, and the sky was blue as midsummer. Once he had told her she would make all Scotland a fief of Elfland, like the Eildon Hill where True Thomas had followed the Queen of Faery.

The grey ruins of Melrose Abbey towered above her. Once he had stood with legs apart and hands on his belt, laughing down at her with hot bright eyes, when she had accused him of threatening the monks of Melrose for neglecting to pay their fees – 'Do you know a better way to get money out of monks – Madam?'

She rode between Lord James and Lethington (Darnley had refused to come), and everywhere people ran out to cheer and wave to her and throw gay autumn flowers, marigolds and big yellow daisies and late roses, and she smiled and bowed and spoke her pleasure, and smiled, and smiled.

And then she came to Jedburgh, where she was to have held her Court of Justice with him. She came to a stone house with a corner tower, set in an orchard where the trees were heavy with fruit, the yellow and polished green of the apples in the evening sun glistening like lamps hung among the dark leaves. She heard the splashing ripple of the river Jed flowing under its old hump-backed bridge down below the orchard. She went up the winding stone stair with its rail on the left side – for the house had been built for the Kerrs, who were all left-handed. She went into a small room with a wide window looking out towards the blue hills. There were tapestries on the walls showing Jacob coming to claim his reward of Laban's daughter after his seven years' service for her.

Seven years he had served her mother and herself since he had snatched the bag of gold from the English agents that October night, and now here was his reward this bright October day – that he lay dead in Liddesdale, and his hunting it was done.

She sat in a chair by the window, it may have been only for five minutes but it seemed as many hours, before Mary Fleming, now just married to Maitland of Lethington, burst into the quiet room and filled it with a whirlwind of rushing silks, flushed cheeks, and warm plump arms flung comfortingly round her.

'*Madame ma mie*, my little darling, it is all a tangle, I cannot find out yet for certain, but I believe there is hope – anyway he is not yet dead. Oh, Madam, I know you will be glad as I am, for whoever else we may marry, we'll never get a man like that!'

And the happily devoted bride of the most brilliant intellectual in Scotland had tears of joy running down her face. The two friends clung together, laughing, kissing, crying, that numbed passivity of Mary's all broken up by dear Fleming's golden warmth of hope.

It was an odd twist of news she had heard. The report of Bothwell's death had sped like the wind across the moor and reached Hermitage long before his men's slow return on foot with the hurdle bearing his unconscious body. The Armstrong prisoners, taken a day before, had snatched their chance of the general consternation to attack their warders, seize the keys of the fortress and make themselves masters of their jailers. So that when Bothwell's men came back, it was to find that redoubtable Armstrong, Jock o' the Side, in command, and refusing them admittance to their own castle. At any moment the Elliots might take advantage of the situation to make a counter-attack. And all this time the blood was soaking through the roughly improvised bandages of their all but lifeless leader on the hurdle.

It was Gibby Elliot of the Shaws who saved the situation and, for the time anyway, the life of his neighbour: he had accompanied that sad returning party and so was able to make the very practical suggestion that the Armstrongs should be given their liberty and safe departure to their homes if they consented to give up the keys of the fortress. This they did, and Bothwell was at last carried into the Castle and put to bed to be nursed of his wounds, which were said to be mortal.

'But would he go through all that to die after all?' exclaimed Fleming. 'No, he'll live, if only to catch Jock o' the Side all over again – yes, and Little Jock o' the Park too, for though they all said at first that *he* was dead of Bothwell's dying stroke, yet now there's a rumour that the Elliots carried him off the moor alive and with a good chance to be hanged for sheep-stealing next year instead of this. You see how it is – rumours always put the worst first. My lord is dead; then, my lord's wounds are fatal; then we'll hear there's a chance of recovery after all!'

There would be, if only she could go and nurse him! She had nursed François, she had nursed Darnley, but now she could not go to Bothwell to nurse him. She could only wait and wonder who was by his bedside to give him life and hope and determination to live, as once he had given her. Would Jean do that? She could not believe it. But perhaps he would do it himself; he would surely fight for his life on a sick-bed as on the moor.

And now they heard that he was hanging between life and death – that he was in grave danger from his wounds, but not, it seemed, that he was dying.

His condition had prevented the wide attendance at the Assizes that had been hoped for. As before, the thieves of Liddesdale felt they could ride safe now Bothwell was not there to deal with them. And a mass of business was silting up that could not be done without him. The Court had been at Jedburgh a week when a message came from Hermitage that Bothwell insisted he was now well enough to see visitors and discuss business. A visit of the Queen, George Gordon Earl of Huntly, and the two chief officers of the Assizes, Lord James and Mr Secretary Lethington, was instantly proposed for the very next day if the weather held tolerably fine, for weather made a deal of difference in travelling across country at this time of the year. They must start at daybreak in order to return by the same evening, for there was no accommodation for women in that massive fortress.

Was the Queen in a fit condition for riding sixty miles in all, across trackless moors and swamps, with the chance of getting wet to the skin, when she was by no means fully recovered from her agonizing labour of four months ago and had been often ill since then with that mysterious sharp pain in her side? Mary Fleming was very doubtful of her taking the risk of so much exertion 'for what will after all only be an official visit of a couple of hours at most, and then talking business all the time with your officers of justice.'

'And are *they* to pay my official visit for me? Is my brother the Lord James and your husband, Mr Secretary Lethington, both of them, as you well know, his unfriends, to convey a patronizing royal message of thanks for his service and condolence for what it cost him?'

'No, Madam, I will,' was the answer with a roguish glance.

'Devil doubt you! Here I am beginning to talk like my lord of Bothwell already, so potent in his influence even at this distance! No, Fleming, you shan't steal a march on me. We'll ride together, and thank God for one whole day on the hill and the heather after holding justice in a stuffy court day after day.'

So they rode together, across Swinnie Moor down into the dale of Rule Water towards Windburgh Hill where the fairies

341

were often heard piping and holding their revels at night. From a small pit-murk loch high up on the hill, haunted by a water-kelpie, rose the stream of the Slitrig which they now rode through at the shallows after crossing Earlside Moor, and then up, up the broad hillsides, with Black Agnes' hoofs squelching into the soaking mosses, and the heather swept back by the wind, its shining grey stems writhing and twisting like wreaths of smoke in the sunlight; up over the crest till they saw the Allan Water run like a sparkling ribbon on the other side; then up the Priesthaugh Burn until the mighty heads of Cauldcleuch and Greatmoor Hill reared themselves up like thunder against the white towering clouds.

'This is the country I am Queen of!' thought Mary with a rush of such pride and joy in her land as she had never known till then – perhaps because of her chief servant in that land, who more than any other had shown her what it was; and to whom she was riding.

They crossed the dyke of the Catrail high up on the hills, that Border more ancient than any between Scotland and England, made by the Picts centuries before the Romans came, to mark off the boundary between kingdoms whose very names were long forgotten. Now, as they neared Hermitage, they peered down into more than one deep and sudden hollow, gashed into the hills by narrow streams that ran almost hidden by the steepness of the slopes that they had carved. 'Beef-tubs' these were called, very handy for hiding cattle.

They were coming down on to Hermitage Water, when suddenly before them in that wide and lonely place there stood a circle of hoary stones, their shadows attendant on the bright grass; so still, so silent and aware, they seemed to have been waiting there from before the beginning of time for the Queen of Scots to come riding down over the moor towards them. Involuntarily she drew rein and sat looking at that Druid circle that had once peopled this solitude with its strange company of worshippers. Human sacrifices had been made on these stones: 'They look as though they remember,' she said low to Gordon as they rode on.

And then they came in view of the Castle, a huge old granite block on the banks of the stream that brawled and tossed over its rocky bed just below those mighty walls. She drew a deep breath as she rode in under that towering grey arch. So this was Bothwell's chief fortress: she would have known it.

*   *   *

'So you came by the Nine Stone Rig – didn't you count them? Yes, there are nine. Human sacrifice? – I don't know about that, but they boiled Lord Soulis in a cauldron slung between them, so it's said – it was he who built most of this castle, years before the Bruce, so that's long enough ago for you. Why boil him? Why not? He deserved it, no doubt. The holders of Hermitage have been great rascals most of 'em. And it's a queer thing, but no spreat nor bent has ever grown within the Nine Stone Rig since then until this day. I've noticed it myself – Madam.'

'Spreat and bent – that's hair-grass, isn't it? – I remember you and your sister telling me – but how are you, my lord? You've never answered.'

'I'm as weak as a horse,' he said, grinning, and she laughed with such sheer happiness in her voice as he had not heard since she had cooked eggs for them at Dunbar.

They must talk sense, they must talk business, but it did not matter; whatever they said, or was said by the sage faces round them, seemed said in joke to amuse only them.

'So it's been a douce quiet Assizes without me – not a hanging among the lot, only fines!'

'Well —'

'Well indeed for them when the Queen holds justice! But you've had a poor show of prisoners, I'll say that, and that's my fault, laid low here like a forfoughten hound and letting Little Jock o' the Park and Jock o' the Side and every man Jock of them all slip through my fingers. My wounds? They're nothing, they're healing fast now and I'll be in Jedburgh within the week. It was the thought of my folly in letting the Night Hawk bog that kept bursting them open – that I should give him Tam o' the Linn's stabling! – what, don't you know how

> Tam o' the Linn gaed over the moss
> To seek a stable till his horse,
> The moss was open and Tam fell in,
> "Dod! I've stabled myself!" quo' Tam o' the Linn.'

A gaunt dark woman, whom Mary remembered to have seen at his sister Jan's wedding, leaned over him and laid a hand on his arm and told her son he'd talk himself into a fever again at this rate; and certainly the one unbandaged eye was very bright as it fastened on the slight figure sitting beside him in the amber velvet riding-dress.

Very French she looked and fashionable, and like a dashing

343

page, the padded shoulder-puffs of her dress sprouting upwards, as cock-a-hoop as a pair of budding wings, and so he all but told her in front of them all! She looked like a golden pheasant with that amber light in her hair and eyes as well as on her dress, and the curls clustering so neat and close and tight to her gallant little head – the head of a boy, he'd always seen that, and like a boy's her stiff collar went high up to her ears. The ruby buttons were unfastened at the neck, where the narrow ruff of creamy linen inside the collar rose up on either side of that small firmly rounded chin, and the tender line of the throat showed just as far as the absurdly childish hollows of the 'salt-cellars' at its base.

His eyes devoured every detail of her sitting there dandling her silly little golden-feathered cap on her knee, a cap just big enough to cover the tip of her ear, and how much good would it be to her if she ran into a storm of rain on the way back? So she had put on her prettiest Paris gauds to come riding over the moor to him in his grim fortress in Liddesdale. He lay here on a rough bed strewn with deer-skins, and these stark old walls towered behind her, and that slit of a window let in a slanting beam of light on her velvet sleeve, and her eyes laughed at him and the corners of her closed mouth curled up as though every moment it would break open in laughter. 'Why do you laugh, Madam?'

'I am glad to see you better, my lord.'

No, it did not matter what they said or didn't say nor who heard them; they were speaking together without that.

He heard himself arranging for a Court of Oyer and Terminer to be held here by him, authorized by the Queen, and settling what papers must be brought over for it by messenger from Jedburgh tomorrow; he heard Mary conferring the post of Keeper of the Seals on his mother's brother, George Sinclair, with pretty graciousness.

And then his mother turned them all out in her uncompromising fashion, just as she had turned out the Lady Jean when she bore down upon them a few days ago and disapproved of the way in which her son's wife was nursing her son. Hermitage could hold fifteen hundred men at a pinch, but there was not room enough in it for two women when they were Jean and the Lady of Morham! He chuckled over this as he watched his mother move about his bed, bringing him a cooling drink, seeing to fresh bandages for his wounds, and all the time he still saw beside him that gallant figure with the boyish head, and now

344

muttered to himself as he had done to her when she leaned over him to say goodbye, 'we shall ride together again.'

*   *   *

The weather changed soon after they had started back on the return journey: the rain-clouds marched up terrible as an army with banners, ragged black banners that overwhelmed all the sky; the rain charged down in hosts of ice-cold arrows; the streams shouted and tossed their white manes under it; the ground swelled with it, the glittering mosses bubbled as though the whole round crust of the earth were breaking, and the water below pushing through again to flood the world.

And below the towering bulk of Cauldcleugh Head that stood black behind the driving rain, between Liddesdale and Teviot-dale, Black Agnes bogged. They dragged Mary from the saddle, her golden dress smeared thick all over with black peat mud, and herself drenched to the skin with the icy bog water. She called to them to save Black Agnes, and would not leave till they had succeeded in hauling out the plunging terrified mare.

As she rode on again, drenched and frozen, a shuddering began to run through her veins and left her now hot, now cold, and the pain in her side stabbed like the thrust of a knife, yet her wild gaiety cheered on the whole miserable soaked party, even poor Lethington, who shivered like a wet cat. His nose was blue, and James' red and raw, and Fleming's hair all out of curl. Only the Gordon enjoyed the ride as Mary did, holding his proud head aloft like a wet eagle, though even he could not touch her strange exultation. She was being christened anew to her country, she told him, laughing as the rain ran down her face.

She was riding in spirit with the man she had left lying wounded on his bed, riding through the land he watched and guarded for her, that sweeping waste of moorland, now silent of all but the rush of rain and river and the long cry of the curlews tossed in the storm-wind, but ready always to leap into furious life, into fiery cressets on the peel towers blazing their warning from hill to hill, into the thunder of galloping horses, the war-shouts of their riders, the clash of arms.

The sky did not clear again till the first star peeped out and the young moon swung between the flying clouds and they saw the ruined arches of Jedburgh Abbey like lacework against the pale evening. They had reached the end of the ride. But she was deadly cold and they had to lift her down from the saddle.

345

Next day she lay in the tapestried room upstairs, so ill that already the doctors were despairing of her life. Violent sickness and vomiting of blood and a raging fever continued for some days; she could not live, they said, and when on the seventh day, after long delirium, she became conscious for a time, she knew it from their eyes and her own heart.

The little room was filled with the golden quiet of the late October evening. Cows lowed, going by below to be milked; birds twittered, flitting among the fruitful apple boughs; the river rippled and murmured under the old stone bridge; like the echo of the sea in a shell, the room took the echo of these sounds into the heart of its stillness. Behind the silent, frightened faces round the bed hung the figure of Jacob, come to claim his reward after seven years' service.

She lay there, waiting to speak for the last time. When she had made her confession and received unction, she felt strength ebbing from her as the warm light ebbed from the room. She whispered that her nobles should come to her bedside; they gathered round her, James nearest to her, his long yellow face hovering over her; now close above her, now so far away she could scarcely distinguish it among the clouds that drifted before her eyes.

What could she say to that face so distant from her all her life, now soon to be divided for ever by death? But perhaps death was not the great division; life was that.

When James lay dying as she now lay, would he not know what she now knew – would not any man or woman, even Elizabeth, know this in death: that to triumph by stirring up hate and discord *must* fail in the end? In death, as with God, only love counted: and hate and fear drifted away impalpable as clouds. What did it matter now to her that her husband had tried to kill their child, that her brother had worked with her enemies to bring about her ruin? She was free of them now, and nothing they had done now mattered to her – only what she had done.

'If you knew, if you only knew —' she began to say, and then her voice failed, the darkness swept over her again, but presently she heard herself speaking through it, speaking of 'love, unity and charity. All goodness comes of unity and concord, and from discord all desolations.'

She placed her son in their care, begging them to see that he did not take any harm 'through either his father or his mother': strange words, but how else could she warn them of his father?

346

or ask that they should not punish her son for his mother's religion?

'I have never tried to press your conscience,' she whispered, 'nor troubled you to worship any other way than you thought right. I beg you will do the same with those of the Old Faith.'

It was what they had never done; why should they then when she lay dead? But they would do it if they only knew —

'If you knew what it is to be in extremity, as I am – and have to render count of your faults, as I do, then you would never press them.'

The faint words fell in the stillness, hardly to be heard even in that dim shell of quiet. It was growing very dark; she could see no face near her now. Her hand groped out and touched a long cold hand, heavily ringed; she clutched it desperately before she should sink for ever into that dark. Her voice came again, clearer now, calling him: 'I pray you, brother, Earl of Moray, that – you – trouble – *none.*'

Then her hand died in his; her eyes were closed. They laid a feather to her lips but it did not stir. Her limbs grew cold and stiff, all the beauty of her face was carved in marble.

'She is dead,' they said, and the word ran through the house and the little town, out into the countryside. Candles were lit in the small still room, and her maids filled it with weeping. They opened the window wide to let her spirit go free out over the moonlit hills.

CHAPTER EIGHTEEN

ONCE AGAIN she was not to have 'such easy victory'.

She passed through the gates of death – and came back.

She was dead, and for several hours; all the doctors said it, for the heart had ceased to beat, there was no breath, no pulse of life in any vein, and it was recorded that 'Her Majesty became dead', but that her surgeon, Nau, 'a perfect man of his craft, would not give the matter over'. For more than four hours he worked to restore the circulation to that cold and rigid body, by continuous rubbing, drawing of her limbs and tight bandaging, until at last the blood rushed back in a sudden great sweat, and he knew that she lived.

When she recovered consciousness she found that James had already collected her jewels. He returned them in hasty confusion, giving several disinterested reasons for his action.

347

Some days later she was out of danger, and then at last Darnley was induced by his companions to leave his hunting to pay a visit of kind inquiries to his wife. He remarked that she was always ill – first there had been that baby, and now this. If she were really getting better, when was he going to bed and board with her again? She had better make up her mind to it or she might be sorry. So there was no room for him and his retinue in this poky little house? That was why she had chosen it, he supposed, even though it had let her in for being ill in a room the size of a cupboard! Very royal!

He stayed in an old house in the town, royally large and spacious, and departed next morning, leaving her considerably the worse for his visit. His swaggering air of mysterious confidence had worried her far more than his heartlessness.

Within a couple of days she learned the reason for it.

For months past Darnley had been busy, as even Knox knew and noted down, 'complaining of the state of the country that it was out of order, and giving the whole blame to the Queen for not managing the Catholic cause aright'. He had now informed Spain, France and Pope Pius V that it was no use to attempt their Counter-Reformation in Scotland as long as Mary was on the throne.

She had, while ill at Jedburgh, to make a formal protest to the Spanish Embassy in London to try and clear herself of the charge that 'she was dubious in the Faith'. The Pope had been gravely disappointed that she had not shown more 'good and holy resolution' by executing her half-brother, and the other Protestant rebels, even when warned that His Holiness would withdraw his subsidies if no better use were made of them 'for the service of God in Scotland'. It was just what the Papal Nuncio, Vincenzo Laureo, had already feared; 'the danger', he had written, 'is that the Queen in her excessive kindness would not consent to such an act'. He made a stronger attempt at blackmail. If Mary would not work more actively for the destruction of heretics in her country, she was told, then 'the King himself could execute it'.

So Darnley had offered to take her place on the throne as the necessary figurehead for the Catholic Powers in Scotland! This was the reason of his defiant swagger and threat that she 'might be sorry'; the reason too of his attempts to get abroad and into personal touch with King Philip.

She was left defenceless; those great distant figures in the background of her life, the Pope and Philip of Spain, whom she had never seen but always counted on as her friends, had now grown strange and sinister. They even had a disquieting resemblance to John Knox.

All these months Darnley had been setting spies on her and her correspondence; she knew that now, and could see the meaning for a hundred little unexplained happenings. Fear fell on her of these new unseen enemies, and loathing of her husband. She lay back on her pillows and heard the autumnal evening song of the birds and envied them, wishing that God had never given man a soul to be so abused against Him.

Then there came another visitor, and with him the wind outside, keen and rough from the hills, blowing away those darkening shadows. This was the Earl of Bothwell, who had got himself carried to Jedburgh in a horse-litter across the pathless moors rather sooner than his wounds were fit for such painfully rough going. His left arm was in a sling and his body wound still troubled him a good deal, especially after this reckless journey; the bandages still covered the scar on his forehead near the left eye; that would stay for life: 'Luckily my eye isn't hurt, so it's only yours, Madam, that will be offended by it.'

'Oh, you are monstrous!'

'So my mirror told me – but d'Oysel assures me that I need not lose all hope of favour from women. An honourable scar — '

'You deserve another for talking so. Fair rewards Your Lordship has got in my service!'

'I'll get others,' he said low, and that forbidding eye under the bandage looked rather strangely at her.

She told him how she'd followed his example and 'stabled herself' in the moss like Tam o' the Linn – 'a fine pair of moss-troopers we've made!'

'Well, you've made the bog famous already. I hear they're calling it Queen's Mire now.'

'That's a muddy compliment! And I lost my prettiest spur there, chased silver it was. Is there any chance it will ever be found?'

'Maybe – this year, next year, a hundred years hence. You'll win more spurs than you lose. And we'll not let this couple of silly accidents spoil our plans either; we'll carry out that Royal Progress through the Border towns as soon as you're well enough. Have you got the gauds you promised yourself for it? You must make old Forster open his eyes when you get to Berwick and swear there's a fairer Queen on this side of the Border than on his own.'

Was it still possible? Yes, of course it was, he told her.

He got her to walk with him, at first just in the orchard, and then down on to that humped bridge, where they leaned over and counted the rippling circles of the rising trout, and he told her how the barricades at both ends of the bridge had been put up to defend the town from the English in the last invasion, and showed her the deep tree-shaded pool where witches were tested to see if they sank innocently or floated unholily – that was Jedburgh Justice for witches!

By the second week in November she was well enough to ride out in royal state from Jedburgh, with Bothwell and Gordon, James and Lethington close behind her, a glittering train of white and scarlet and black velvet. To Kelso and Home Castle, Langton and Wedderburn they went, and up on Halidon Hill above Berwick, where the English guns thundered out the royal salute from the frontier town, and that sturdy old bulldog, Sir John Forster, now in command there, rode out to meet her at the head of sixty captains and chief citizens, and fell so deep in love in five minutes that he rode all the way to Eyemouth beside her, to the great amusement of his former guest, Lord Bothwell.

In spite of their illnesses and the escapes of the Armstrongs and Elliots, 'in spite even of Your Grace's incurable clemency', Bothwell told her, the main object of the Assizes had been achieved – to squash the plot to bring the Earl of Morton back to power on a *coup d'état*.

But there were other plots. No one could make out what Darnley and his old fox of a father were now brewing between them (for Lennox had long ago swallowed his paternal indignation). As before, those farthest away seemed to know most about it. D'Oysel got word from home of a rumour that was flying round Paris of a design of theirs to seize the baby Prince, imprison Mary and set up a Regency. Any such attempt would certainly be seized on by Morton's crew as the chance to attack from over the Border, probably with an English army. It would be safer to have them back in the country, as even Bothwell now agreed.

She had her best chance yet to unite all her nobles together at the Christening. The day was getting very near, December 17th. She would hardly dare breathe till it was over, so important was it that it should be a success, so dangerous the many forces working against it.

Darnley wrote and told her flatly that he was not going to attend it. This would amount to a public declaration of the child's bastardy by his father. He had conceived a dislike of his son, due indeed to jealousy, but not of Rizzio. This goggling slavering brat, that in some revolting way did remind him of his own image in the glass, had cut him for once and all out of the direct line of the succession. He had lost his chance of the Crown Matrimonial, and now, even if Mary died, it was his son and not himself who would be heir.

His letter threw Mary into a paroxysm of despair; she cried out that she was chained to this hateful boy, and that if she could not escape she must kill herself. 'There will be little need for her to lay hands on herself,' declared her doctor, Nau; 'her husband is doing all that is necessary.'

Others were getting desperate about Darnley. At the pleasant Castle of Craigmillar, two miles from Edinburgh, where Mary, again avoiding Holyrood, went for a fortnight's convalescence at the end of November, there were continual conferences for 'the putting forth by one way or other of the young fool and proud tyrant'. A King who denied his heir's legitimacy and intrigued with foreign Powers against his wife, Sovereign and country, was an impossibility for all concerned. But Lord James, at the head of the proceedings, was determined that they should go cannily. It was not safe to kill a King. Once divorced, he would no longer be King; it would then be constitutional to arrest him on some very obvious charges of high treason; and if he should happen to resist arrest (or even if he didn't), then nobody could be blamed if he unfortunately got killed in the tussle.

This happy *dénouement* was discussed privately; the divorce openly in Council with the Queen. The Protestant Church had made adultery a ground for divorce (it had also made it a capital crime, to be punished by hanging, but nobody paid much attention to that). Darnley had obligingly furnished innumerable grounds, but Mary doubted lest her Catholic Church would, against its usual custom, recognize them. An annulment was then suggested, since the Pope's Dispensation for the Queen's marriage to her cousin had not arrived in time for their wedding. But again Mary saw the flaw; to declare her marriage illegal would logically declare her child illegitimate.

'Not a bit of it,' said Bothwell; 'my parents' marriage was annulled on grounds of consanguinity, but no man shall call me a bastard.'

She was too shaken to be encouraged. Darnley divorced, at liberty to wander about Europe blackening her name and their son's birthright to the two kingdoms, would be as sinister a danger as his presence in the country. She could see no way out anywhere, and felt too ill and nervous to try. She had better give it all up to retire to France. She began to speak of this, but encountered a furious look from the Earl of Bothwell.

Lethington's smooth voice poured oil on the troubled waters. If the Catholic Archbishop's judicial Court were re-established, it could arrange a divorce that would satisfy both religions. There would be violent protests from the Kirk at legalizing a Catholic body, but James Earl of Moray could be trusted to bribe them with his usual discretion. He told the Queen to rest assured that 'we shall find the means that Your Grace shall be quit of him without prejudice to your son.' He smiled sidelong at James, unable to resist a scratch at that determinedly stainless character. 'Although my Lord of Moray, here present, be little less scrupulous for a Protestant than Your Grace is for a Papist, I am assured he will *look through his fingers* at it.'

James stiffened. Mary, sensitive to his air of disapproval and Lethington's jibe, was uncertain what they meant, and insisted that they should arrange nothing contrary to her honour.

Lethington soothed her. 'Madam, let us guide the matter. Your Grace shall see nothing but what is good and approved by Parliament.'

She was beyond coping with the matter any further. She must give all her strength and mind to the Christening. Some responsible person had to be at Stirling to attend the enormous preparations, since Darnley would not. Some of the Ambassadors were already arriving and had to be received. So Bothwell set off there immediately after the Council, and she told him to write her full particulars of all the business.

Then, as decided, she had to set to work to meet Darnley and get him to join her at Craigmillar, overcome his threats and get him after all to accompany her to Stirling for the ceremony. So they had meals together as before, though she kept her bedroom barred.

She had some success, with the result that Darnley became very jaunty and jolly at her 'making up to him' again. He was jocose about Bothwell's face wound and its probable effect on his *bonnes fortunes*, at which Mary fired up; looking at his flushed overfed face, she remarked that it wouldn't do *him* any harm to be 'daggered a little like my Lord Bothwell', and was startled, not for the first time, by her fierce longing to snatch his knife from him and do it herself.

She had still to arrange her State entry into Stirling. She wrote to Bothwell rather peremptorily that he had promised to send her news, but 'I can learn none. As for me, if I hear no other matter from you, according to my commission I bring the man Monday to Craigmillar. He is the merriest that ever you saw and does all he can to make me believe he loves me – wherein I take so much pleasure that I never come near him but the pain in my side takes me.' She wanted Bothwell to know how Darnley sickened her. Then she prayed him to send her word from Stirling.

It was a rather curt letter, and it could no more strike her that it could ever be used against her than it could have occurred to Lethington that his jeer at the virtuous James, conveniently 'looking through his fingers' at the slight to his Protestant scruples, would be used as evidence that a murder had been openly discussed at the Queen's Council table.

Only in one thing was the Queen's letter unbusinesslike. It had no address, and was dated only 'this Saturday'.

CHAPTER NINETEEN

FOR THE first time for two generations Stirling was cosmopolitan once again. French, Spanish, Italian, the accents of Savoy and Piedmont, the narrowed vowels of cultured English voices, the soft sound of Gaelic, were heard everywhere in the little streets. The great Castle on that mighty rock upspringing from the plain was ablaze with light in every window, and its ramparts carved up the sky against the December moon. From those starry windows in the enormous darkness there came the sound of Italian songs, the thin tingling music of foreign fiddles, the high sweet call of flutes, the beat and rhythm of dancing feet. The little town was packed; it was hard to find stabling for all the horses of the foreign retinues in the barns, for they were full of visitors from all over Scotland, even shaggy bare-legged Highlanders from the farthest mountains of the North-West, who had tramped all this way through the midwinter snows to see the one great royal spectacle of their lives, and catch their only glimpse of the young lovely Queen.

They saw her riding full tilt down the steep path from the Castle, a gay, wild creature, her horse's cloth-of-gold caparison streeling out in the wind of her speed like the sun itself flying through the wintry scene, her Court scattered far behind her like a hunting-field. Fresh air always went to Mary's head; but inside the Castle the impression was the same, though quieter: the Ambassadors saw a young mother shining with serene happiness as she showed them the solemn slobbering baby, six months old. Here was the Mary of Delight who for years had been a legend in Europe; her subtle eyes, her swift glancing smile that made all on whom it lighted feel they were her intimate friends, her free natural speech that held the dignity of a Queen because she never had to think of it. She wore the chain of diamonds and pendant from her baby's godfather, Charles IX of France, that sad-eyed, excitable youth whose message after six and a half years was that he still envied his brother François, who 'died young but lived happy since he was married to her'.

She had been Queen Consort of France, all her power and splendour dependent on François; here she was sole Sovereign in her own right, as was Elizabeth in England. But Mary held the future of both kingdoms in her arms.

It was the hour of her supreme triumph and she exulted in it, looking round her on the representatives of all the countries come to this cold Northern land so far away to do her honour. And with her own people she was triumphant; she had so won her way in the hearts of this fiercely Protestant country that no protest had been made against the Catholic Archbishop baptizing their Prince with the full ceremony of the Catholic Church.

Not quite the full ceremony, for she refused to allow the use of the spittle by the Archbishop, showing a sense of the superior importance of hygiene to that of the religious service. 'I'll not have a pocky priest spit in my child's mouth!'

'That's a sound estimate of His Grace, seeing the Italian doctor got 1800 gold crowns off him for curing him of it.'

'I didn't know that. Anyway, it's a filthy apish trick, rather in scorn than in imitation of Christ.'

'Your Grace is no bigot, I'll say that.'

'My lord of Bothwell should know, since he's still bigot enough to refuse to attend the Prince's baptism.'

'Bigot! I! Do you think I'm acting for my religion?'

'What is your religion?'

'To hell with the Pope!' he grinned. 'And with all foreign interference.'

He took her hand and swept her forward into the stately movement of the dance. Three steps to the right, three to the left, and he went on speaking: 'Didn't Your Grace yourself have the Papal Legate intercepted in Paris so that he shouldn't come on here to give you his master's commands?'

She tapped out some little intricate steps in mocking answer.

'And apart from foreign policy?' she asked.

'Why, I never fancied our home-grown monks in their long black petticoats, like a lot of old women lording it over the land. No man should play the master without a sword to make his title good.'

She floated round him as he spoke, a cloud of silver gossamer, their hands still touching, and as he swung her back to him, laughed up into his face.

'Here's flat treason, to decry petticoat government to me!'

'That's another matter. I've seen you wear the breeches better than most.'

His glance swept her, stripped her too, she felt; she blushed, and a new strange fear followed her unwonted shyness. She held up the great peacock fan from the Duke of Savoy, its colours painted in sapphires and emeralds, before a face grown very thoughtful for that bright occasion. Scandal said that the Lord Bothwell feared to encounter a crucifix or the Sign of the Cross because he had sold his soul to the devil.

The music drew to a close. On its last long-drawn notes he led her back to the side of the hall, and she said low, 'When you lay at Hermitage, so ill you were thought to be dying, was your religion then still only protest?'

His eyes softened at the anxious note in her voice, but he would not ease it.

'My gramercy was that of old Kennedy's fifty years ago, before Protestantism was thought of —

> *I will no priests for me to sing,*
> *Nor yet no bells for me to ring,*
> *But ae bagpipe to play a spring.'*

In the face of that pagan arrogance she shivered; was his pride so fierce that he scorned the need of even God's help? She seemed to be standing beside him, not in that hot crowded enclosed place, but alone with him on the wide moor under the windy sky – alone in all the world, with not a single ally, human or divine.

The vision passed swifter than the flash of a bird's wing; the music died, the dancers bowed, the buzz of talk rose shrill and clattering against the storm-swept night outside, where the wind and hail drummed against the Castle rock.

She had to dance next with Sir Christopher Hatton, a favourite of Queen Elizabeth's, and considered the best dancer in England; she had to meet Mr Carey, who was a great-nephew of Anne Boleyn's, and so vain of the connection that he would scarcely admit any English family to be noble that had not contributed a member of it to the block; she had to look pleased with the Earl of Bedford's 'merry message' from his Queen, who had sent a gold font studded with jewels as Christening present to her godson. It had been big enough when ordered at the baby's birth, Elizabeth had said, but if he had outgrown it by now, well then it would do for the next! Bedford, an extraordinary little man, very short but immensely consequential, beamed with pride in Elizabeth's genial wit, though he must have recognized the sting in it since she had also given him instructions to ignore Darnley completely and never address him as King.

It was easy to obey, since Darnley was nowhere to be seen. He was in Stirling Castle, that was all that was known; some said he was sulking, some that he was ill, some that the tailor hadn't finished his coat of cloth of gold in time for the baptism – but as the King had expressly stated that he would not go to the baptism at all, why, asked the indignant tailor, should he fash himself to finish a coat that would not be needed, when all the new coats of the great lords were crying out to be finished in time?

It had been a pretty notion of the young Queen to have each noble and his retinue in a different colour: James in green with linings of red and gold, Argyll in red, and Bothwell in blue, the colour that in blazonry represents loyalty, as she reminded him; she did not add that the linings she had chosen for it, white and silver, were her own special colours.

All the barons of Scotland stood in two files from the door of the royal nursery to the door of the Chapel Royal, each holding an immense lighted candle of pure wax – no guttering stinking tallow to light the Prince! From under his bedspread of ten yards of patterned cloth of silver the Countess of Argyll lifted him up, placed him in a shallow basket like a broad-brimmed hat, and put this in the arms of His Excellency the French Ambassador. Monsieur Du Croc had now good occasion to feel his weight as he had prophesied, and the dapper little man wore an expression of portentous anxiety as the baby dribbled, rolled

356

his large eyes, and made a sudden grab at the ambassadorial beard.

'Goo?' inquired the Prince, and with growing persistence, looking from left to right as they proceeded down the lane of baronial candle-bearers, 'Goo goo guggug *goo*?' Everyone agreed that he showed remarkable intelligence. The Catholic nobles followed, the Earl of Atholl and the Lords of Dunkeld and Dunblane bearing the great serge and cude-cloth, the Earl of Eglinton the salt-vat, Lord Ross the basin and ewer. In the chapel doorway stood the Archbishop in his mitre, with the great gold crozier in his hand; behind him candles glimmered on the rich vestments of the priests and an armoury of pastoral staves and gold crucifixes; incense swung to and fro, the chanting of Latin rose and fell; three bishops, the Prior of Whithorn, deans and archdeacons, stood in attendance to baptize in the Catholic faith, and in a Protestant font, this heir to two Protestant kingdoms.

The Countess of Argyll, acting as Queen Elizabeth's proxy, received him from Du Croc's arms (she had been warned by the Kirk she would have to do penance for this, but it was worth it): the Primate gave him the names of James and Charles, sponsored by the Sovereigns of England and France; the heralds proclaimed them three times and all his titles with a mighty blast of trumpets. The Protestant nobles, among them James Earl of Moray, George Gordon Earl of Huntly, Bothwell and the English Earl of Bedford, watched from the door. The music soared; the future King James VI of Scotland and James I of England was carried back to his crib. His father was nowhere to be seen.

'The Queen's brought her donkey to the water,' said Bothwell, 'but she can't make him drink.'

He was not at the hawking nor any of the hunts, not even the hunting of the wild bull in the great park. He was not at the dancing, nor at the vast banquets (most of the tables in the great hall seated sixty apiece): he missed all the Latin Masques by George Buchanan, the French ones by Sebastian (Bastien) Pagez, Mary's highly cultivated pastry-cook; and with them he missed a surprising impromptu effect which occurred in a woodland scene of singing naiads dragged in on a platform by satyrs up to the dining-tables. There the satyrs handed dishes of figs from Malaga and sugared fruits from Venice and Cyprus to the Queen and all her noble and ambassadorial guests. But when these furred and painted waiters, with cloven feet and shaggy tails, served the Earl of Bedford and his escort of eighty English gentlemen, they so far forgot their manners that they put their hands behind them and wagged their tails at the Englishmen.

There was nearly an international incident. It was well known by all the French and Scots there present that Englishmen had tails; had not '*tailard*' always been the name for an Englishman all over Europe? And the knowledge was deeply resented by the English. Anne Boleyn's haughty great-nephew had to be restrained from thrashing the nearest satyr with his own tail. Sir Christopher Hatton blamed the stage manager and told Sir James Melville that if the Queen were not present he would stick a dagger into the heart of that French knave Bastien. Melville made him drink more wine instead, and the stately Sir Christopher then decided that the most dignified protest he could make would be to sit on the floor behind the table where he should not see the rest of this shocking spectacle. He insisted on a Mr Linguish accompanying him in this aloof position; it took the combined efforts of the Queen and the Earl of Bedford to induce them to abandon it.

The festivities had their effect even on the Good Lord James' austere wife, Lady Agnes, who kissed the Earl of Bedford, as the pompous little Englishman himself indignantly stated, 'without his leave'.

The official climax to the jollities was a sham fight out in the churchyard under the glittering December stars; the whole company trooped out to see a fortress attacked by centaurs, demons and Highlanders, lanzknechts and Moors. Fire-balls and fire-spears were the weapons, shooting in flame against the night; finally, in a furious explosion, amid a roar of cheers and laughter, the fort was blown up by gunpowder. At the end of this gorgeous firework display, which had taken six weeks to prepare at a cost of £190 17s. 5d., the laughing, chattering, shivering party returned indoors, to be met by scared servants important with news.

Darnley had received a message from his father and within the last few minutes had fled from Stirling.

CHAPTER TWENTY

STIRLING CASTLE was an island cliff looking down on an eddying sea of blown mist; when the wind tore it apart for an instant, a strip of brown woods or gleaming water showed small and clear, framed in cloud. 'This is my life,' thought Mary. 'I can see only glimpses here and there of what is going on in it, knowing nothing of what is round me.'

News and rumours came flying every hour, giving a sudden brief picture of little groups of men going about their business, some of it straightforward, some mysterious, some sinister, all of it affecting herself, though she did not know how.

One was of the Catholic Consistory Court, restored the day before Darnley fled from Stirling, that it might find a convenient formula for the Queen's divorce.

Another was of a company of men riding over the snow-scarred hills of the Border, at their head a stout man whose small pig's eyes flickered out with a look of gross cunning above his bushy red whiskers. This was the Earl of Morton and his Douglas kinsmen returning from exile after the pardon that the Queen had given them, as was agreed, immediately after the baptism. The Douglases, Darnley's kinsmen, were now his deadly enemies, and had sworn to avenge his betrayal of them after Rizzio's murder.

There was that rumour that the Council were planning to arrest him and kill him if he resisted. So one of Lord Eglinton's servants told the Town Clerk of Glasgow, and the Town Clerk told the Provost, and the Provost told Lennox, and Lennox sent a messenger to tell Darnley, and that, on top of Morton's approach, and the re-establishment of the Archbishop's Court, was enough to send him flying from Stirling, and behind him the hosts of men with which Lennox had filled the little city.

That scene of urgent flight quickly melted into one more passive: of Darnley lying mysteriously ill in his father's house at Glasgow. There were whispers of poison; the doctors said small-pox, but the symptoms seemed to be the same as he had shown when ill some months before. At that time the report had reached England that Darnley had the pox, and this recurrence of the disease seemed to confirm it. The wretched youth who had been so proud of his looks lay in bed in a darkened room and wore a silk mask to hide the spots on his face; this picture was unbearably painful, and Mary turned away from it to send her own doctor to him and order fine linen to be made up into night-shirts for him and a blue satin coat to wear in bed.

But another scene near by that darkened sickroom impinged upon it, the grey outline of a tall English ship riding at anchor in the wintry fogs of the Clyde. What was that ghost-ship still waiting for, what orders from Darnley, even now that he lay so desperately ill? Helpless as he might be, the plans that he had helped contrive were going forward; here and there in other countries, the mist that surrounded her lifted a corner of its thick curtain to show a distant warning.

The Duchess of Palma in the Netherlands, the Spanish Ambassador in London, had heard from Paris of a plot forming in Scotland against the Queen; the Archbishop of Glasgow, now in Paris, sought an interview with Catherine de Medici to discover what she knew of it. It would take a very wily man to discover what Catherine chose to conceal. But her ironic praise of Mary's mercifulness to her enemies suggested that she might find good reason to regret it. The Archbishop paid attention to that hint, vague as it was, and dispatched one of the Scottish archers to urge Mary 'to take heed to yourself' and see that her guards were 'diligent in their office', as he feared 'some surprise to be trafficked to your contrary'.

Ambassadors and Archbishops sitting at their inlaid escritoires in foreign capitals, their ringed hands in their furred sleeves, their big quill pens and the serpentine trail of pointed Italian handwriting staining the white paper for centuries to come with dark warnings of what might happen within the next few weeks, or even days – these minute vignettes could be discerned for an instant, but threw no light on the hidden scheme.

That she must discover herself; no other could do it. They all told her so, even Bothwell, though he plainly loathed the thought of her going near Darnley; but the danger was too great to think of that. At any moment he might die, and the plot in which he was involved march on without him, and their one possible source of information on it would die with him.

Mary must go to Glasgow, and under strong guard, for it was a stronghold of the Lennoxes, and get Darnley away from it as soon as he was well enough to be moved. Together with Gordon, towards the end of January he escorted her part of the way there, but not all, for Darnley was more nervous and jealous of Bothwell than of all the other lords, and she must allay his fears. Besides, the Elliots were giving serious trouble again in Liddesdale. So, halfway on their ride west between

Edinburgh and Glasgow, he swung off towards Hermitage. He had but just come from Whittinghame, the house of one William Douglas, where he had met Morton and Lethington, and all he would say to Mary about that oddly mixed company for him was that they had had a pleasant walk in the garden – a strange pleasure for this icy foggy January!

At Lord Livingstone's house he took his farewell.

'Write to me,' he said.

'And if I discover nothing?'

'Then write that. But you must discover what he is up to. You must get him away from Glasgow and under our watch till your divorce rids you of him.'

'*Must – must!*' – it had a strange echo from a subject.

She did not see that his very hatred of the work he was forcing on her made him so harsh and peremptory. Fear too, for could he trust her to carry out this business? She was pitiful, tender; she must not be so now or she would mar everything. Nursing him through measles without any thought to her own danger had first won her to this rotten-hearted boy. Would the pox have the same effect? he asked himself savagely. It was not thought to be infectious, that was one consolation; all the same – 'Take care,' he urged her, 'don't kiss him, however much he begs you,' and the scar above his eye seemed to turn livid as he said it. 'Short of that, use all means. Promise him anything – everything.'

'Even myself?' she asked very low.

'Even that. You shall never keep the promise. I swear it.'

She shuddered, sick at the hateful task before her. At that moment she hated the man that now knelt to her, kissed her hand in farewell, outwardly courteous and subservient, yet mastering her with his insistent command that she should do this thing against her nature. Was it indeed the Gay Galliard that they had danced together? They seemed now to be dancing between swords.

She watched him ride off to the clean air of the hills, to the Border fighting that he loved, to open enemies, and danger only to the body.

Then she rode on, it seemed quite alone, in the midst of her guards through the dense grey air.

Just outside Glasgow she was met by Thomas Crawford, a servant of Darnley's. He had a message from Lennox, apologizing for his failure to escort her himself into the city; he was afraid to do so, Crawford said, because of her displeasure at the extraordinary number of his men he had installed in Stirling at the time of the Christening. She sat silent; erect and still on her horse, while under her cold level eyes the glib fluency of the messenger broke up into nervous stammering.

At last she said, 'There is no recipe against fear.'

Lennox's fear, said the messenger, was only because she had shown anger.

'He would not be afraid if he were guiltless,' she replied.

'The Earl of Lennox wishes nothing better than that the secrets of every man's heart were written on his face.'

The eyes of the Queen glittered like ice; sitting there before him so straight and alert she had the look of an unsheathed blade.

'Have you any further commission?' she demanded.

'No, Madam.'

'Then hold your peace'; and she rode on through the frosty mist.

In some ways she found her task all too easy. That was the most horrible thing to her about this creature of wax that seemed to have no centre, no soul of its own at all, but lay ready to be moulded by whatever hands touched it. Darnley might be plotting her downfall, even her death, but now that he was ill and miserable he was as genuinely thankful to see her as a sick child that has been naughty, but knows his mother will now forgive him everything. All his excuses and pleas were on that ground.

'I am young,' he told her again and again. He had made mistakes, he had been led astray, but it was by people older than himself, and she had forgiven them, so why could she not forgive him?

All she had to do was to say she did forgive him, to promise him that all should be between them as before. It was the hardest thing she had ever done in her life.

The sickroom was unbearably stuffy, for the doctors would allow no window open to the wintry air, and the patient's breath was poisonous. She felt herself infected by his close presence, yet sat on through the night, all her nerves taut as a bowstring. When he slept, she had no desire to do so, nor even to lie down and rest. She walked up and down restlessly, softly, in heelless slippers; to the fire where the clean flames roared and sparkled up the chimney, back to the bed and stood looking down on that uneasy feverish sleep that still made demands on her, muttering her name, moaning in agonized self-pity; then remembered her promise to write a full account to Bothwell, and turned to the little writing-table behind the bed curtains and sat there, at first staring at nothing, tapping the quill pen against her teeth, unable to think of a word, then pulling a paper towards her and jotting down items here and there as a sort of rough memorandum, and then at last finding the words flow so fast that her pen had hard work to keep up with them.

She had never written like this before, to him or to anyone. She was not indeed writing to anyone but herself. Her heart was pent up with perilous matter; she must release it or she would scream aloud, run clean mad and stab the sleeping form in the bed and then herself. She must write it all down, somehow, anyhow, though she would probably destroy it by the morning. That did not matter; she must write now.

The flaming logs died down to a steady glow, all their sputtering silent, only now and then a faint crackling whisper; the candles burned down deep into their sockets, their pointed flames descending lower, lower before her eyes. The room grew cold round her. The city lay outside asleep in the darkness, much of it hostile to her; Lennox, it's overlord, had worked that. Men slept, but their ill intentions were awake, they went on continuously. Through this sleeping house a relentless current of life was flowing, bearing her away on its stream, she did not know where. Her round jewelled watch with the gold stars lay on the table, ticking in the silence. The tiny feet of time marched inexorably on and away; she saw them marching past against the descending candle-flames; each minute had a face drawn by a child, two dots and a dash and a spiked hand. Not one looked back. Each carried a load so small she could not distinguish it; yet this army of ants was carrying away the world piecemeal.

She wrote: 'I am weary and am asleep and yet I cannot forbear writing as long as there is any paper.'

She wrote: 'He prayed me to come again, which I did. He told me his grief – that I was the cause of his sickness, because of the sorrow he had, that I was so strange to him. And (said he) "I admit that I have done amiss, but so have many other of your subjects and you have well pardoned them.

' "I am young.

' "If I may obtain this pardon I protest I will not make fault again. And I ask nothing but that we may be at bed and table together as husband and wife; and if you will not, I will never rise from this bed. God knows I am punished to have made my

God of you and had no other mind but of you. If I thought, when anybody does any wrong to me, that I might make my moan of it to you, I would open it to no other." I made as though I thought all to be true and that I would think upon it.'

She wrote: 'He then used so many kinds of flatteries so coolly and so wisely as you would marvel at. He would not let me go but would have me to watch with him. He had always tears in his eyes. He salutes every man, even the meanest, and makes much of them that they may take pity of him. You never heard one speak better nor more humbly; and if I had not proof of his heart to be as wax, and that mine were not diamond, no one but you could prevent my having pity on him.'

That looked as though she did think all – or some – to be true that Darnley had said. True, it was his instinct to confide in her. Yet in these five days and nights of watching by him, feeding him and talking with so much apparent frankness, he had made his moan to her certainly, expressed his abject submission, but not told her what she had hoped to discover. He had denied any plots against her, any intention to go in the English ship; she had drawn a blank there. Her deceitful kindness had won this, however – his promise to go with her wherever she wished as soon as he was well enough.

'But to make him trust me I had to feign to him; and therefore when he desired me to promise that when he should be well we should make but one bed, I told him, feigning to believe his fair promises, that if he did not change his mind by then, I was contented. I do here a work that I hate. You would laugh to see me so trimly make a lie, or at least dissemble and mingle truth with it. You make me dissemble so much that I am afraid thereof with horror, and you make me almost play the part of a traitor —

'Alas, and I never deceived anybody.'

And she wrote: 'Burn this letter, for it is too dangerous.'

CHAPTER TWENTY-ONE

THREE EARLS sat at the dice on red velvet cushions fringed with gold. They were in carnival dress: the Earl of Argyll in purple with a turquoise satin lining to his cloak; Gordon, Earl of Huntly, in crimson with primrose-coloured taffeta; the Earl of Bothwell in black velvet passemented with silver. They rattled the dice on to a low stool-table covered with a green velvet cloth, and called the numbers from time to time. They were sitting just within the King's bedroom. He lay in his blue satin coat and black mask in the great bed with hangings and palliasse of violet velvet and silk, edged with gold and silver. Beside him sat the Queen in a high chair, her feet resting on the little Turkey carpet beside the bed; she wore a gala dress of white and gold; her furred mantle had slipped to the floor and lay there like a couched beast.

A small antechamber opened beyond the bed, furnished only with hangings of the Coney-Catcher tapestry and, enthroned in royal state, formerly consecrated to the use of a Cardinal, the King's majestic commode, upholstered in velvet, under a tas-selled canopy of red and yellow shot taffeta, and fitted with twin pans.

The same famous tapestry hung in the reception-room be-yond the bedroom; through the open doors the long narrow room could be seen, full of moving colours as the ladies and gentlemen in attendance on the Queen and on the great nobles in the bedchamber walked to and fro under the flickering torches. Behind them rose the royal dais and canopy and double Chair of State of black velvet fringed with Venice gold. The hum of voices rose and fell, the crackles of laughter. It was Carnival Sunday, the 9th of February, and a gala day for other reasons; there had been the farewell banquet to Signor di Moretta, the Envoy from Savoy, and the double wedding of French 'Bastien', a great favourite with Mary for all his ill tail-wagging fame, to one of her women, Christine Hogg, also of her faithful maid-in-waiting, Margaret Carwood, to John Stewart of Tullymet.

'So I said to her when I kissed her in the church, "You are my Cousin Meg now," and she curtsied and said, "All Stewarts arena' sib to the King" – it seems it's a proverb.'

'And a very sound one,' Darnley growled from the bed. He never could get over Mary's familiarity with her lesser servants. He did not want to hear about the weddings, nor the banquet to the Savoyard, since Mary had prevented his seeing him as he had wished, although he had a perfectly good reason for it. 'Can't a fellow see a man about a horse?' he muttered.

Mary had not believed that the reason for Darnley's eagerness for the interview. Signor di Moretta was in close touch with the Papal Nuncio and might well be a secret emissary of Spain, a near ally of Savoy. But she too could not give her true reasons, so she said, 'Rizzio was Moretta's servant before he was ours, and Moretta thought the world of him. It wouldn't have been very comfortable for him to meet you.'

'Why bring that up? After all this time!'

'It's not yet a year since his death. Eleven months to the very day.'

So she still remembered even the exact date! 'I thought you'd promised to forgive and forget.'

She was silent, and he pushed his comfit box towards her, saying coaxingly, 'A sweet to my sweeting.'

'He's sweating to be sweet!' murmured Bothwell as he rattled the dice. The more prudent Gordon hastily inquired about the raid Bothwell had led a couple of weeks ago. He had taken a dozen prisoners, among them 'an Elliot of the best', but as he was bringing them home, Martin Elliot of Braidley counter-attacked in great force. Bothwell had routed him, but at the cost of several of his men's lives, among them a brother of Black Ormiston, and Bothwell in attempting to save him had only by a chance escaped death himself.

'You'll never be content till you're brought home feet fore-most,' grunted Gordon.

'I've done that this autumn and none the worse for it,' said his brother-in-law indifferently, and discussed Martin Elliot's surprise tactics with the admiration he was apt to give to an enemy.

The air of the moors was blowing into that corner of the stifling room, so it seemed to Mary, catching fragments of their talk while Darnley continued to make tentative overtures of affection. He seemed extraordinarily nervous tonight; she could not think what was the matter with him. He showed her a letter he had just written to his father in which he told him of his 'good health which is the sooner come through the good treatment of such as have this good while concealed their good will; I mean of my love the Queen which I assure you has all this while and still does use herself like a natural and loving wife'.

It gave her a pang to see the trusting, boyishly punning words. He could not help it that he was so shallow, and she hated herself for being so deep.

'Oh Harry!' she sighed, 'that is kind of you,' but rather oddly he too seemed embarrassed. She could not see his expression under the black taffeta mask, and he went on speaking hur-riedly, telling her that Crawford was taking the letter within the hour, starting this very night for Glasgow.

At mention of Crawford her friendly impulse chilled. Crawford had made difficulties when she had brought Darnley away from Glasgow as soon as he was well enough to be moved; he had objected to Craigmillar, which Mary had chosen for the rest of his quarantine because of its good air, and Darnley had followed instead Sir James Balfour's suggestion that they should take an empty house purchased only lately by Balfour's brother, a Canon of Holyrood.

This was the old Provost's house at Kirk o' Field, about half a mile from Holyrood. The church of St Mary in the Fields had fallen into ruin, but the houses round were stately. Hamilton House, belonging to the Duke of Châtelherault, stood within a stone's throw of the Provost's house, and Douglas House on the other side; the nearest was the new Provost's house, also owned by the convenient Canon, and joined by a gallery and cellars to the old Provost's house. The air was high and out of range of the noise and smells of the city; behind the house were gardens and an orchard, just within the city wall that had been built after Flodden to defend the capital; in this wall was a postern gate through which one could pass direct into the open country.

Mary had furnished the house sumptuously from the Holyrood plenishings, and had a small bed in green and gold put up for her own use in the little room below Darnley's bedroom, where she had slept most of this last week because Darnley had been so absurdly eager that they should be under one roof again. The house was very suitable for the period of quarantine, and her only objection to it was its owner, for Sir James Balfour enjoyed the reputation of the worst man in Scotland. Years ago he had been implicated in the murder of Cardinal Beton, and rowed in the same galley with John Knox on that account, but in spite of this recommendation the preacher had no good to say of him. He had become a Catholic when Darnley's brief ascendancy looked like putting the Catholics in power, and Mary could only wonder uneasily as to how far he was in Darnley's counsels and in touch with the secret agents of the Catholic League.

But the house was convenient; so near Holyrood that she and her Court could ride down in gala dress after the banquet given to Moretta for a couple of hours' visit to Darnley, and now back again to the Palace at eleven o'clock for the wedding dance she was giving for the two newly married couples.

Bothwell's page, Paris, was now in her service, for it amused her to hear him talk in French of Paris and his experiences as a gutter-student at the Sorbonne. He brought her a message at this moment from Lethington to say that the ball was ready to start. She sprang up gladly and bade Darnley goodnight, but to her astonishment he was utterly disconcerted at her leaving him. Why should she go out in the middle of a bitter February night just to please the servants? She flashed out that Carwood had been a deal more than that when she had helped them escape from Holyrood.

There again! She didn't seem able to get away from the thought of Rizzio's murder. And she had promised to spend the night here, his last night of quarantine: James and Lethington and Bothwell had all been going to stay and escort them back to Holyrood in state early tomorrow morning, and now it had all fallen through, so he cried in angry complaint. Lethington had found that he had to stay in Edinburgh, for no very clear reason; and James had hurried out of the city that morning, not even waiting to attend Moretta's farewell banquet, to the Envoy's great offence. And now Mary would not stay either; she would go to the ball with Bothwell and the other lords in attendance on her, she would dance with them and never think of him lying here sick, all alone except for a few servants.

What was all the fuss about? They would all be back here early tomorrow morning, she reminded him, and take him back to Holyrood with them.

He caught at her hand and she tried to take it away. Bothwell had risen from the dicing-table and was coming towards them; she felt the blood rushing to her face in furious disgust that he should see Darnley holding her hand. 'Let go,' she commanded, and pulled, but he held her so fast that he tugged off one of her rings.

'There,' she said, trying to laugh off her anger and his absurd importunity, 'I'll leave it with you as a pledge that we'll be back here at dawn tomorrow, and then we'll all ride back to Holyrood on those new great horses you've been longing to try.'

But the mention of the horses seemed to agitate him worse than ever. 'I dare say I shan't be well enough to ride after all,' he said. 'I know I shan't be if you fret me like this.'

She gave a despairing sigh. What should she do? Had she better stay after all? But Bothwell picked up her cloak and put it round her shoulders. 'They are all waiting,' he said.

'Yes, you'll heed him!' – Darnley's voice was strident – 'you never heed me.'

She could stand no more. Followed by Bothwell and the

other two lords, she passed into the reception-room and all the bright company streamed out after her down the spiral staircase. They went out into the cold dark where the waiting servants had been standing by the burning braziers to keep warm, stamping their feet on the freezing slush, and now ran here and there to fetch the horses for their lords and ladies. Voices called and answered, the horses neighed and tramped, clanking their harness. The Queen stood just within the doorway, lifting her face to the wind after that breathless crowded air, watching the torches throw their tossing yellow glare on the black-shadowed confusion. Paris brought up Black Agnes to the door. Bothwell lifted Mary up into the saddle before she could move forward into the muddy snow.

He rode beside her slowly on into the dark. She looked back at the old Provost's house; there were lines of light at the edges of the curtains in Darnley's room and in the gallery where some of his servants slept. The new Provost's house, connected with the old by this gallery, was all dark, as were the other houses near. Only one light showed in a window at a little distance; she asked which it was, and was told Hamilton House.

They came out of the darkness and the trodden snow into the wedding ball at Holyrood, some of the company in fancy dress and most of them in masks. The two brides, Christine and Margaret, ran forward to greet their mistress; curtsying to her in the bridal dresses that she had given them, they exclaimed how happy they were that she had come.

'And I too,' she cried, catching a hand of each. Her furred cloak fell from her shoulders and all the brightness of her white and gold shone out: her eyes were lit with relief and happiness, she looked like the flare of some unearthly candle. 'I must dance for joy,' she laughed, and a tall masked figure in black velvet and silver led her out to the Dance Royal of the Galliard. Bold reddish-brown eyes looked down at her through the slits in the black silk. What was in the heart of this man beside her, with whom she could speak – and write – yes, and think – as she had never done with any other human being, yet who had never made love to her since that night just over a year ago, when she had stopped him with the despairing cry that she was with child by Darnley?

She danced with the two bridegrooms, she danced with the chief guests, she lost herself in this world of music and flowing movement and shifting lights and colours. 'I wish I were a burn on the hillside,' she said, 'to dance for ever.'

'For ever' lasted an hour. A little after midnight Paris came and whispered to her that the lords Bothwell and Traquair desired a private word with her. She said goodnight and kissed the brides, and left for her own apartments.

There awaiting her were the two lords in charge of her bodyguard, for Bothwell commanded the horse and Traquair the foot. They were still in their gala dress and carried their masks. Their news was rather absurdly vague; a servant of Darnley's called Sandy Durham had just lately been discharged from his service (because, it was said, he had set his own bed on fire!), and it was now known that he had had a long talk with the Lord James very early that morning. Bothwell believed that this gave the clue to James' sudden departure from Edinburgh just after that interview, rather than its ostensible reason, his wife's pregnancy.

'James' absences are apt to be pregnant,' he remarked.

There were other danger signs. Lennox had moved from Glasgow to Linlithgow, less than twenty miles away; Kerr of Fawdonside, who had threatened and nearly injured the Queen with his pistol, and whom she refused to pardon with the rest of Rizzio's murderers, was lurking in the countryside and had boasted that there would soon be a change at Court and himself back in favour. And Bothwell did not like the extraordinary insistence of Darnley's on the Queen staying that night at Kirk o' Field. He urged her not to go back there early tomorrow morning to escort him here to Holyrood. Traquair added his entreaties. They were appointing extra guards round Holyrood; let her stay here under their eye for the present till they could discover if indeed anything definite threatened her. He went off to see to the guards, leaving Bothwell still arguing with her, or rather commanding.

'You are not to go back to that house,' he said, 'I'll not have it, till I've found out more.'

She was sick of plots and mysteries, and said, life was not worth living if one had always to be warding off shadows.

'Shadows don't move of themselves. If they are there, it's because there's something behind them.'

'When I sat up nearly all night at Glasgow, I wrote to you all the time of that pocky fellow, curse him, and there were so many pleasant things I could have written instead. What a waste it is – and whatever happens to us after death, we only live here once!'

She laughed up at him as she spoke, and found herself desperately wanting him to take her in his arms and kiss her, madly, devouringly, as he had done that time a year ago. Ever since then she had been ill or terribly harassed or both; only now in this last hour, while dancing, had she suddenly begun to feel free of the painful effects of her baby's birth, free to live and love like other women.

But Bothwell's face was shut; only the scar over the eye showed bluish-red, as it did when he was stirred; but she felt it was not she who stirred him but that sixth sense that he possessed in action.

'I smell danger,' he said, and that excited him more than the perfume of her hair. Had he fallen clean out of love with her? Was it Darnley or Darnley's child had done that, or was it herself, unable all these past months to feel bodily passion?

Before she knew what she was doing, she held out her hands to him. 'I love you,' she said, 'and that I think we have both known for a long time past. But now I love you as once you told me you loved me. Is that gone from you, and has mine come too late?'

For an instant he stared, and still his face did not change; he did not move, nor take her outstretched hands; she wondered if he had heard her. Then he turned and left her.

CHAPTER TWENTY-TWO

CENTAURS AND demons were dancing round her, and satyrs who took their tails in their hands and wagged them; and Queen Elizabeth, who sat hidden somewhere in the darkness, cried in the huge Tudor voice of her father and her sister Mary of Bloody memory, 'They have insulted my Englishmen. The war with Scotland has only lasted two hundred and fifty years. It must go on for three hundred.' So the demons and centaurs danced out from behind the gravestones and stormed the fortress, and against the darkness there shot up spears and balls of fire and 'all other things pleasant for the sight of man', so then she knew it was only the fireworks display in Stirling churchyard after the Christening, for those words were from the order in the account book. It was a great relief to know that, for now she knew there was nobody in the fortress, which they were blowing up with gunpowder, but what a roar it made, what a heavy rumbling and crash after crash – *was* there no one in the fortress? Surely Darnley was in it, lying there in his black mask, clutching her ring – or was he galloping away? – thud, thud went his horse's hoofs, but the roar of the explosion swallowed them, it swallowed everything, the whole world was tumbling about her, and she woke with a cry.

The roar was still going on. It sounded as though a whole house were being blown up into the air and was now crashing in ruins.

*   *   *

The old Provost's house at Kirk o' Field was blown up by gunpowder at two o'clock on Monday morning and totally destroyed. Not one stone was left standing upon another; even the arched vaults below the building were 'dung in dross to the very groundstone'. Only the gallery which rested on the Flodden Wall was preserved sufficiently to save the lives of the servants who slept in it. There were but few of them, for most had been given leave to attend the wedding ball. Among the rubbish-heap of stones and debris only one broken body had been found – and it was not Darnley's.

His was discovered later in the garden, at some little distance from the house, and with it the body of his valet, William Taylor, who slept in his room. Both were clad only in their linen night-shirts, which were drawn up, exposing their naked bodies nearly to their necks. Taylor also wore a cap and one slipper. It was thought at first that they had been blown out of bed to this distance, but that was soon proved impossible. There was not a mark on either of their bodies, not a hair singed, nor any sprinkling of dust or powder. Still stranger, Darnley's sable-furred dressing-gown of purple velvet lay close by, carefully folded, with belt and dagger, also a pair of his slippers, a quilt, and, oddest of all, a chair from the bedroom stood upright on the snowy ground beside them under the bare trees.

Bothwell gave this report to the Queen early that same morning while she was still in bed. He had just returned from leading a party of soldiers to Kirk o' Field to examine the scene of the crime, and had had the King's body carried to the new Provost's house. She listened stupefied, asking him again and again what could have happened.

He shrugged: 'The strangest accident! A thunderbolt came out of the sky, I suppose, and burnt up the King's house!'

His sardonic flippancy appalled her. She pulled herself together enough to tell him coldly that that was not very likely.

'Nor is it likely that an explosion that wrecked such a house to its foundations (some of the walls are thirteen feet thick) could blow two men out of an upper room, clean through the falling roof and walls, and with them a chair, quilt, slippers, and neatly folded dressing-gown, and deposit them all perfectly intact on the ground some sixty to eighty paces away! I tell you there's no bruise or fracture anywhere on him. He's dead, and that's all you can say. Better bring it in as "Act of God or the King's Enemy!" In this case the two should be synonymous.'

She was stunned by his brutality. When she had heard the first bare report, 'The King is dead,' her heart had given a great leap, telling her she was free; but the mystery and horror of it all had quickly overwhelmed her, and so now did this rough, casual, almost joking air of Bothwell's. She tried to think it the result of strain and bewilderment; he certainly looked tired and harassed, he had been up all night, a thing he had done often enough on a raid, but detective work such as this was another matter.

'After I left you last night,' he went on, and her face flamed at the recollection of that leave-taking, but he was evidently not thinking of it, nor noticed that she was. How could she have held out her hands to him those few hours ago and asked his love? She could not believe it as she looked at his jaw thrust out like a clenched fist, at his fierce eyes, and heard his caustic remarks go straight to the subject and blast it. It was hard sense, no doubt, uncompromisingly practical, to realize Darnley was better out of the way – but not like this! If he could see nothing of the pity and terror of it, even to her, then he must be cruel as the sea, relentless as the grave.

But he saw nothing of her thoughts. He was busy telling her how he had gone carefully round all the guards newly appointed by Traquair and then began to go to bed, when Paris burst in on him with a piece of news that aroused his suspicions afresh.

Archie Douglas had during that day moved down to Douglas House at Kirk o' Field with some of his servants – by order, it was believed, of the Lord James, just before the latter's hurried departure from Edinburgh early that morning. Archie Douglas was apt to play the part of hired bravo to his clan; if there were dirty work to do at Kirk o' Field, he would prove a handy weapon for it. 'So,' Bothwell told the Queen, 'I flung on some clothes and went and knocked up Black Ormiston at his lodging in the Canongate. He was in bed, of course, but belted his gown and came straight on with me to knock up Jock Hepburn and young Hay of Talla who was sleeping at Jock's house, sturdy rascals both of them, and it looked as though we might have need of several. We collected Wilson and Powrie too and went down to Kirk o' Field, giving our names openly to the watchmen at the gates.'

The note of rough defiance was again in his voice, and she wondered at it, for of course he would give his name openly while going on his errand of investigation. And why did he not continue?

'Do speak!' she cried. 'What did you see at Kirk o' Field?'

'What everyone in Edinburgh heard. We were close to the house when suddenly there was a flash as though lightning had risen from the ground. It gave a roar and blew up into the air. Jock Hepburn ran me back just in time to prevent some of it falling on us. When it was all over we picked ourselves up and counted each other to make sure we were all there. The building was nothing but a rubbish-heap, even the great arches of the vaults beneath were lying in pieces. The house must have been completely undermined, or else a huge store of gunpowder placed in those vaults.'

So Darnley had been murdered within three hours of his having implored her to stay with him that night. It was as though he had begged her protection – in vain.

'But what protection could I have been?' she said, pursuing her thoughts aloud. 'I should only have been blown up too. That must indeed have been the intention.'

'Of course it was the intention!' Bothwell burst out vehemently, 'you, and all the leaders of the Government – it was the merest chance that you weren't there last night or early this morning, and James and Lethington – not so much chance where they were concerned, I fancy.'

And he fell silent, remembering the message that had come from Lethington reminding her to return in haste to Holyrood.

'James – Lethington – are you suggesting that *they* could have known anything of this? And the Douglases gathering at Douglas House – and the light in Hamilton House, are the Hamiltons in it too?'

'God knows who *isn't* in it – half Scotland it seems, one way or t'other.'

She stared at him wildly. The whole thing was like an evil dream, inconsequent and horrible.

'He felt he was in danger,' she cried, appealing for some sign of pity from him, however faint. 'You remember how nervous he was last night, he was almost frantic that I should stay with him.'

'I do remember,' said Bothwell grimly.

Margaret Carwood, now Stewart, came into the room carrying a tray, put it down by the Queen's bed, and began to draw the curtains against the dark February morning and light the candles. She told Mary in firm answer to her expostulations that no matter if she were a bride last night, she'd have no one else looking after her mistress this morning, so let her eat her nice fresh egg and drink her milk before they cooled while she hung the black velvet on the walls in accordance with the rules of royal widowhood.

'You'll not play that hideous foolery *now*!' exclaimed Bothwell.

'Indeed, I think we're all too much in the dark already,' said Mary, and then wished she had not fallen in with him so meekly. How dared he tell her what or what not to do about her mourning?

Meg did not even hear such havers. A queen was a queen, and a widow was a widow, however she had come by such widowhood, and she proceeded to hang up the black velvet draped over her arm.

There was a timid knock, and Paris slipped into the room with a message for his former master. Bothwell took his leave of the Queen and followed him out of the room.

'They have arrested Will Blackadder,' said Paris.

Bothwell swore. What could they have against the sea-captain?

Nothing, it appeared, but that he was drinking late last night with Willie Henderson, 'Bloody Wits' to his friends, and ran out into the streets at the noise of the explosion to see what it was. So, as the magistrates had found no one else to arrest, they arrested him.

'And who – who may they not arrest next?' stammered Paris, who was shaking from head to foot.

'Anyone they fancy, I should think,' said Bothwell surlily. 'Why should you look so white in the gills when half the nobles and gentry of Scotland stand a good chance to lose lands and life over this?'

*   *   *

'I have talked with Du Croc,' said d'Oysel; 'I will tell you to whom he points as *le vrai traître*. Who owns the two Provost's houses at Kirk o' Field? Who suggested that the King should

375

stay there when he refused to go to Criagmillar? Who alone
would know that the houses, the old and the new, were connected not only by the gallery on the wall, but by doors between
the cellars of both, underground? It is important, those cellars.
For there are fools who say that the gunpowder was carried into
the old Provost's house in a portmanteau and barrel on the back
of a grey nag on the Sunday, and placed in the Queen's bedroom below the King's, by those who knew that she would stay
at Holyrood that night. Now you and I, my friend, who know
gunpowder, know that even several barrelsful would not blow
up any house to its foundations, certainly not its cellars, unless
it were placed in them. An explosion does not go down, but up.
Therefore that gunpowder must have been conveyed into the
cellars from those of the adjoining house by someone who had
the keys of both. And who could that be but its owner, and, as I
tell you, the true traitor, Sir James Balfour.'

'By whose orders?' asked Bothwell. 'And were the King and
his valet first strangled in their sleep, and then carried outside?
Or did they go for a nice brisk walk in their shifts in the snow
at two o'clock in the morning, in order to be strangled outside
by the tails of their shirts? And in either case, did the murderers, having then finished their job, blow up the practically
empty house, just in order to tell everybody all about it?'

'True. One does not burn a house to roast a goose, particularly when the goose is out of it. Nor does one use gunpowder to
kill a man when poison or a knife or even the tail of a shirt, as
was probably used in this case, could do it quicker, more
secretly and more surely. One can never be certain of gunpowder – even in this case one of the servants escaped alive from
beneath the ruins. There could only be one reason – no, two –
for employing gunpowder; the first, that it should kill a large
number of people; the second, that it should spread panic and
so help to manoeuvre a revolution.'

'We know all that,' said Bothwell irritably; 'it was in the
account issued by the Council the same morning.'

That first straightforward official account had stated that 'the
authors of this wickedness failed but by a very little in destroying the Queen with the great part of the nobility and gentry in
her suite who were with the King in his chamber until almost
midnight. And by chance only Her Majesty did not remain
there the whole night.'

'But they did not think of mentioning the chair,' Bothwell
broke out.

'What chair?'

'The chair in the garden beside the two nearly naked bodies, and with it the quilt, the slippers, the furred velvet gown with belt and dagger, all neatly placed there in the snow. Nobody says anything about them, they are too trifling to be considered. But a sketch was made of the scene on the morning of the crime, before anything was touched. An artist does not muddle the evidence by thinking whether it's important or not – he puts down what he sees. And he saw Darnley's clothes ready to put on – and an oak chair, presumably to sit on while he puts them on. Careful fellow, Taylor, very useful valet – always takes a chair out into the snow at two in the morning when his master has a whim to dress there instead of in his room after a two months' illness!'

'You joke, always you joke, till you make the whole world seem mad.'

'Seem? – it *is* mad! Or else – something frightened the King so badly in the middle of the night that he ran out of the house without even waiting for his gown and slippers. It frightened Taylor too, but not as urgently, since he stayed to collect all those things. He'd put on a cap and one of his shoes before his master must have yelled to him to come on at all costs.'

D'Oysel leaped from his chair with the effect almost of another explosion.

'Listen, my friend! Either the King knew there was gunpowder in the house, or he did not. It is agreed, yes? no? Very well, then, if he knew of it, and the two of them smelt smoke, the King would know that the danger was more immediate than that of fire; he would run out barefoot, all but naked. His servant, no! *He* thinks there is fire, but he does not think an explosion, so he waits to collect these things for his master and follows him more slowly. It is seen.' His finger shot out:

'But how does the King know of gunpowder in the house? In two ways only is it possible. First, does somebody warn him? No – for in that case he would have made it public, or at the least he would have moved at once and not stayed to be blown up. There remains only the second way. The King knew there was gunpowder in the house because *he himself had ordered – or allowed – it to be put there.*'

And having flung round eyes, tufted eyebrows and plump pink hands upwards, he collapsed into his chair again so violently that he bounced. He then observed Bothwell's face, grinning, not in startled amazement at his friend's brilliant piece of detective work, but in amused appreciation.

'Do not tell me you thought of all this before!' the Frenchman exclaimed in fury.

'Certainly I thought of it. Remember I *saw* that chair before you only heard of it. Besides, I have now had some confirmation. All but two of the King's servants survived, as you know. I wouldn't have them examined by torture – you can get no truth from a man by that – he says only what he thinks you wish him to say. But they've talked. One of them did more than talk. Sandy Durham, you remember, was dismissed for setting fire to his bedding, certainly the quickest way to get his discharge from a house full of gunpowder! The others, who were there that night, tell you the usual things – the pious state of mind of the two victims just before their death; how Taylor sang psalms which proved singularly appropriate. Psalms always are, have you noticed? Then Darnley talked of Rizzio's murder. It worried him badly that the Queen had mentioned it that evening. Then at last he drank goodnight to them and reminded them that his new horses were to be saddled early the next morning for him to ride to Holyrood. But at what hour and in what place do you think he ordered them to stand ready for him? At five o'clock in the morning – and in the south garden, under the Flodden Wall, where there is the postern gate through which one can ride direct into the open country – without having to pass any of the city guards. That certainly strikes one as the more likely direction for his ride than Holyrood, in the pitch dark of a February morning at five o'clock after a severe illness.'

'The horses are ordered for five o'clock,' repeated d'Oysel. 'The house blows up at two – three hours at least, then, before it was intended – by whom?'

'Presumably by the man who also intended to ride away in time from it,' said Bothwell.

*   *   *

Lord James, an astute psychologist, once observed that rumour was more powerful than fact. It was to prove so now.

The King had sung psalms just before his death (or his servant did; it made no odds); the King had been disturbed because the Queen had talked of Rizzio's murder – and why had she done so on the very night when his slayer was to meet his death?

It was said that the Italian's ghost no longer haunted the anteroom at Holyrood.

'The spirit of a King has been sent to appease the ghost of a fiddler,' said George Buchanan, low, glancing out of the corners of his little eyes.

But how long a train of ghosts would be sent trooping after him to appease the spirit of the royal victim? Bothwell had not spoken in joke when he said that half Scotland seemed to be implicated in this affair one way or another. Certainly there had been more than one plot afoot that dark February night, though in the public mind they were all confused together as one.

The first was the Gunpowder Plot to blow up the Queen and leaders of her Government and so clear the way for a *coup d'état*. This was the 'surprise' of which the Archbishop of Glasgow had already received some vague warning in Paris, and had written to her to beware of it. The second was the plot to kill the King. It could have no connection with the Gunpowder Plot, except in as far as it was probably precipitated by some discovery of it.

For evidence of the Gunpowder Plot one would need to question the Spanish Ambassador in Paris; Pope Pius V; King Philip II, who was known to be awaiting a convenient moment to invade England, and would certainly find it in the overthrow of the Protestant Government in Scotland and consequent confusion; also the Ambassador of his ally, Savoy, Signor di Moretta, who left Edinburgh for London the day after the crime.

Not only was it impossible to make inquiry of such persons; it would ruin Mary's chances of any future help or alliance with the European Powers of her own faith. There was, as always, little hope of arriving at the truth of a piece of international villainy, conceived by foreign rulers.

But the secondary plot, to kill the King, involved so many to whose obvious advantage it was to kill him, that for many years to come there was a steady procession of victims to appease that hungry ghost of the lad who was to succeed, when dead, in killing far more people even than he had tried to kill when alive.

Bothwell saw clearly that it would now be a *sauve qui peut* among all those connected with the King's death, to see how each could fasten the suspicion on someone else.

On the day following the crime the Queen wrote to Lennox,

promised justice for his murdered son and invited him to Edinburgh to take part in the investigation. A whole week passed before he answered, with a request for a Parliamentary inquiry. Mary answered that she had already summoned Parliament 'and would leave undone nothing which may further a clear trial'. But she had done far more than that, and immediately, having at once offered a reward of £2,000, a yearly rent, and free pardon to anyone who could give any information concerning the crime.

Balfours, Douglases, Hepburns, Hamiltons, all had been on or near the scene of the crime at the moment that it happened. A velvet slipper of Archibald Douglas was found in the garden and considered clear proof of guilt, though, as he was reported to have worn armour all that night, it was scarcely likely that he should have kept on his dressing-slippers to walk all that distance from Douglas House in the snow. Slightly stronger evidence against the Douglases was provided by some humble neighbours who ran to their doors 'when the crack raised' and swore they heard Darnley pleading for his life in the garden, crying, 'Pity me, *kinsmen!*' – a term that could only have applied to that clan.

On the other hand, the sudden and convenient absence of the Lord James and Lethington was almost equally incriminating to such experts in 'throwing the stone without seeming to move the hand'. James, however, as if to show that for once in his life even he could be incautious in this singularly blundering affair, was reported to have said on Sunday evening, 'This night the King will be free of all his troubles.'

Such reports could lead nowhere; nor did the evidence.

The public, baulked of fresh sensations in the way of arrests, had to feed instead on rumours. High feeding they proved, for by now they were being artificially induced by hidden masters of propaganda, and engineered towards a given direction. There were no more whispers of James' prophetic utterance, or his private interviews at St Andrews with Morton, the head of the Douglas clan.

Instead, people were saying how Bothwell had given Hay a brown horse and Jock Hepburn a white, and told his servants they 'should never want so long as he had.'

They were saying that when the Queen rode down in brilliant torchlit procession to Kirk o' Field that fatal night, if any of her Court had cared to look behind, they might have seen two packhorses laden with bags of gunpowder led by two of Bothwell's serving-men and, as if this were not a sufficiently open manner of advertising the crime, Bothwell himself helped to carry in the powder and lay it in the Queen's bedroom underneath the King's, before joining the gay party upstairs, his gala dress in no way deranged by so grubby a job.

The same did not apply to his page, who appeared before the company all covered with gunpowder, so that the Queen cried out, 'Jesu, Paris, how begrimed you are!' At which his master showed distinct annoyance that Paris should not have taken the simple precaution of washing his face and hands.

At this point the story showed signs of breaking down, and it was easier to fall back on the pathos of Darnley's fate when not yet twenty-one. People remembered instances of that 'fair, jolly young man', riding at full gallop, shouting to his huntsmen, drinking and dicing in the most friendly fashion at low taverns, paying royally (with his wife's money) for the women he procured there. No doubt his wife had borne him a grudge for it; that was the worst of women, they were jealous, even when they themselves gave cause of jealousy. She had never forgiven Rizzio's murder.

That illness of the King, there had been something mysterious about it; many said it was not really small-pox. John Knox said and wrote outright (being still at a safe distance) that it was poison. He even proceeded to extol the dead youth whom, when alive, he had to his face compared with Ahab. He admitted that Darnley had been 'from his youth mis-led up in Popery'; but laid great stress on that youth, his 'tragical end', and his 'comely stature – none was like unto him within this island'; most admirable of all, he was 'prompt and ready for all games and sports'. Yet no one had seen the Queen weep as a widow should. After four days' darkness it was noted with horror that she had opened her windows for a time to let in light and air. The doctors had in fact ordered it, and declared that she was in danger of utter collapse. Exhausted, stunned, she gazed on the embalmed body of her husband as it lay in state, and gave 'no outward sign of joy or sorrow'.

Knox's literary rival, Buchanan, could do better than that, and declared that the Queen 'greedily beheld the dead body'. It was buried by torchlight in the vault at Holyrood five days after the murder.

The next night an anonymous placard was pinned to the door of the Tolbooth, accusing as the King's murderers 'the Earl of Bothwell, Sir James Balfour, Mr David Chalmers, black Mr

John Spens, who was the principal deviser of the murder, and the Queen assenting thereto, through the persuasion of the Earl of Bothwell and the witchcraft of the Lady Buccleuch'.

The Lady Buccleuch was Bothwell's former love, Janet Scott, whose charms, in whatever sense, seemed as remote from this noisy deed of violence as John Spens, whom Knox admired for his piety and 'gentle nature'. The anonymous accuser seemed indeed conscious that he might be shooting rather too much at random, for he ended with the qualification, 'And if this be not true, ask Gilbert Balfour.'

Bothwell rode past the Tolbooth next morning, leaned from his saddle and tore the poster from the wall with his whinger. He went on to the Palace, demanded to see the Queen, and found her in her rooms that were again conventionally darkened, looking by candlelight at a copy of the same placard. She raised a white face to him, her eyes staring aghast from deep pits of shadow. He was across the room in one stride, snatched the paper out of her hand and threw it in the fire.

'What shall I do?' she said in a whisper.

'Get out of this black hole and down to Geordie Seton's place – with a strong bodyguard. I'll appoint two hundred soldiers to attend you. I'll meet you there this afternoon, on the links. What you need is a good game of golf.'

CHAPTER TWENTY-THREE

SETON HOUSE, on the shore of the Firth of Forth, some miles from Edinburgh, lay in pleasant open pasture-land where the wind tasted salt from the sea. Mary Seton, the gentlest and most devoted of her four Maries, was the only one still unmarried; she had, in fact, determined that she would be a nun 'when you no longer need me', so she told her mistress, though every day that day seemed farther off, to them both. She was as proud as her long lean father to welcome the Queen yet again to their home.

The Protestant reporters noted with shocked glee how she 'exercized right openly in the fields with goif' in company with her hosts and Bothwell and Gordon. Golf had been put down by law, as it kept the players from practice at the long-bow and made the Scots inferior shots to the English; but as the gun was now gradually ousting the bow, golf would certainly come more and more into fashion – and one of the best things to be said for gunpowder, Bothwell declared. But just to show what law-abiding citizens they were, they gave archery its due too, and he and Mary won a contest with Gordon and Seton at the shooting-butts, of which the prize was a dinner given by the losing side. It was a merry dinner, and the pipers with more appropriateness than tact played a tune called 'Well is me since I am free'.

Among her friends, in the clean sea-winds and frosty sunshine, she could almost believe it as she swung her golf club and sent the ball flying over the green sheep-nibbled turf. Her eyes began to lose their haunted look: there were even moments when she was wildly gay and quite forgot the world outside all round her, the forces that were making history, indifferent to her fate.

She was soon reminded. She had to go back at times to Edinburgh to receive the envoys from other countries, to listen to their shocked condolences and know that they were watching avidly for any signs of guilty conscience. For Catherine de Medici had at once expressed her conviction that her former daughter-in-law had been at the bottom of the crime, and would have dissolved the Scottish Guard in France in token of her virtuous indignation, had her son Charles allowed it. Du Croc, now in Paris, wrote to warn Mary that she was being 'wrongously calumniated', and to beg her to take speedy and furious vengeance in proof of her innocence.

Elizabeth wrote letters that seemed full of generous frankness, perhaps were really so, despite the scratch in begging her to take 'revenge on those who have done you *tel plaisir*, as most people say. Show the world what a noble princess and loyal woman you are.'

But her ignoble and disloyal cousin refused to avert suspicion by having even a few helpless commoners tortured, hanged and quartered. 'Damned careless of you,' was Bothwell's comment, but his grin was admiring.

She broke out in sudden passion, 'The whole world is ruled by hate. I'll never submit to it. Do what they will, I will go my own way.'

'One's own way is the only way,' he said.

Each had drawn a sword in challenge to the world, and knew they stood together against it.

That world was closing in on her, nearer and nearer. Once she had feared one old man spying down on her from his eyrie in Edinburgh. Now all those tall crooked houses were conspiring against her; there were faces peeping from behind the window-shutters instead of leaning out to gaze frankly on her, figures in doorways muttering suspicion. The very wind whispered and shrieked against her, scurrying round corners with its foul breath of middens and stale fish and blown onion skins and sour rags and old men's envious rage, screaming and hissing against what they might not enjoy.

No light had been thrown on the murder by the Board of Inquiry. Darkness took up the theme. A voice was heard in the streets at midnight, calling down vengeance on the murderer of the King; anonymous posters were pinned night after night on the Market Cross, on church doors, on the city gates, then even on the gates of Holyrood Palace.

They offered to disclose all, even the name of the writer, if the reward of £2,000 were immediately placed in the hands of an intermediary. They blackened more and more names; there were rough drawings of a man with a scar on his forehead, and beneath them the words, 'Here is the murderer.' Then came a drawing of an arm brandishing a sword, and above it the letters, very large, M. R.; a mermaid was shown luring her lovers down beneath the sea: Bothwell succeeded in tracing it to the hand of James Murray of Purdovis, the professional libeller who had spread slanders against him when he was exiled in France. But he had already made his escape, leaving behind him the most outspoken of all the libels: 'Farewell, gentle Henry, but a vengeance on Mary.'

Lennox took up the publicity campaign and had a broadsheet circulated which pointed the undeniable truth:

> *The farther in filth ye stamp, no doubt*
> *The fouler shall your shoes come out.*

It also promised God's vengeance for

> *The slaughter of that innocent lamb:*

to which someone unkindly added a verse about the lamb's father,

> *That bleating old bell-wether ram.*

A Tragical Ballad of Earl Bothwell that found its way up by word of mouth from England told how

> *Lord Bothwell kept a privy watch*
> *Underneath his castle wall,*

and in reply to the young King's cry for pity,

> *'I'll pity thee as much,' he said,*
> *'And as much favour I'll show to thee*
> *As thou had on the Queen's chamberlain*
> *That day that thou doomed him to die.'*

That Darnley's murder had been in revenge for Rizzio's, appealed strongly to the public's sense of drama; it made tragedy simple and coherent, an artistic whole, and something they could all understand.

'What the devil is this, my lord?' asked one of his Hepburn kinsmen, 'that everyone suspects you and cries a vengeance?'

They did not like the look of things. Was their lord, the strongest man now in Scotland, to be hounded to death by a pack of invisible foes? These voices at midnight, these verses, these painted papers found in the morning no one knew where next, it was not canny. And they were having effect on their master; he swore he would wash his hands in the blood of these poison-pen men, but he could not catch them any more than the birds that drop filth on one's head.

His hand went too easily to his dagger these days. He kept a bodyguard of fifty round him – extravagant, so it seemed to his clansmen, who did not know all his reasons for it.

For the Lord James had got in touch with Lennox, and the Protestant leaders were holding secret conclaves with the Catholics; it looked as if the heads of both the murder plots would now combine to use Darnley's death as a means to ruin both Bothwell and the Queen. And from the Border he got word that Cecil's spies were at work again, rounding up all those 'who seem to mislike Bothwell's greatness'. Worse, his enemies showed a dangerous amity. He was invited by Lord James to the dinner he gave to the English Envoy, and never had the Bastard shown himself so genial to him. After that, it was no surprise to his guest to hear that assurances had been sent to England that 'Bothwell and his accomplices should lose their lives ere midsummer'.

Lennox was demanding the trial of those mentioned in the anonymous placards. Mary asked which, since there were so many inconsistent names, all 'so different and contrarious'. Lennox chose out eight, with Bothwell at the head.

She showed his letter to Bothwell, who barely glanced at it, flung it on the table and said, 'Tell him to come to the Tolbooth and prosecute me, and I'll stand my trial as he asks. I'll broach it to the Council tomorrow. Fifteen days' notice have to be given' (he was counting on his fingers, drumming them on the table). 'What's today? March 27th. That brings it to Saturday the 12th of April for the hearing.'

He drew himself up, squaring his shoulders with a sigh of relief. 'By the faith of my body, it will be good to get down to it in the open, and get it over!'

'But it will give all your enemies their opportunity,' she cried. 'They are certain to find their way into the jury, among the judges.'

'Let 'em! I've got a fortnight to prepare my case.'

'Who will help you? What legal advisers?'

'I can't tell you their names, for they'll be a fair number. The Good Lord James showed the way last time he called me to trial two years ago, and packed the town with six thousand of his armed troops to support the verdict. This time it's my turn. I can count on four thousand.'

*   *   *

Lennox had urged the utmost speed in justice, but now, on receiving notice of the Act of Council appointing Bothwell's trial, signed, rather oddly among the other names, by Bothwell himself, he pleaded that he had not had sufficient time to prepare his charges. Two months since the murder seemed a fair time, but perhaps 'charges' signified supporters for he had only mustered three thousand as against Bothwell's four.

More ominous still, his new ally Lord James suddenly found that he wished to go abroad. He made his will, with surprising friendliness appointing Bothwell as secondary executor to Mary, and left Scotland for France via London, just three days before the date of the trial. Another 'pregnant absence'? Lennox had some reason to fear it. He wrote to Queen Elizabeth to beg her to intercede for a postponement, and did not attend the trial himself.

Very early on the morning of April 12th a messenger from England, John Selby, arrived at Holyrood, sweating from the haste with which he had galloped with his guide since before dawn from Berwick. He bore a letter from his Queen which must be delivered at once to the Queen of Scots. The servants laughed at him; it was only six o'clock and the Queen still fast asleep. John Selby went to cool his heels in the Edinburgh streets and found them bristling with Hepburn pikes. The town was so full it was all but impossible to get breakfast at any tavern: there was no meat to be had, the Hepburns had snaffled the lot, and he had to make do with burnt porridge and coarse fish served half-cold.

Back he went to the Palace in a very bad temper about nine o'clock, and found the courtyard also full of Hepburns, men and horses, so full that he literally could not push his way through them, nor find anyone to take his letter into the Palace. They had guessed that his message was to postpone their master's trial, and were not going to let him through if they could help it. Selby was furious, Selby was pompous (was he not Provost Marshal of Berwick?), but it was no use.

Then two men appeared in the doorway, the one tall and dark with a scar on his forehead, moving quick and impatient as he flung his cloak round him, the other slight, stooping, already huddled in his cloak; and at once all the lairds and gentry standing beside their horses sprang into the saddle. The guide told Selby that these two were Bothwell and Lethington; and the Provost Marshal, with a Herculean push, succeeded in getting through to them and once again explained his errand in a flood of outraged indignation.

'Best wait until after the trial,' was the brief comment of the taller man; 'the Queen won't be able to attend to any business till then.'

'But, my lord — !' Selby checked. He couldn't very well explain to the Earl of Bothwell that his errand was precisely to get that trial postponed so as to collect more evidence against him.

But that the Earl knew it was shown by his genial aside, not very low, to the guide: 'So it's you, Rushety you rascal – you ought to be hanged for bringing him here at an awkward moment like this.'

'Your Honour knows well I had no choice but to guide him,' Rushety pleaded without any great sign of alarm.

'Guide him – why not? Guide him into a peat-hag if you'd any sense.'

Lethington laid a hand on Bothwell's arm to stop these scarcely diplomatic passages. 'Is your letter,' he asked suavely of John Selby, 'from the Council, or from the Queen of England herself?'

'From the Queen's own august hand.'

'In that case, I will deliver it with my own obsequious hand,' and Lethington took it into the Palace.

All the men waited in the saddle, their horses champed and

fidgeted, eager to be off. Half an hour passed like an eternity to Bothwell.

Then Lethington reappeared, gracefully apologetic. The Queen had been, and still was, very ill; she was in a deep sleep and the doctor said she must not be disturbed; he feared it was unlikely that Selby would get any answer now before the trial, especially as this delay had already made the accused half an hour late for it. He mounted, turned his horse's head, and looked up at the Palace with a smile as he took off his hat and bowed. There at an upper window was his wife, formerly Mary Fleming.

Bothwell followed his example, and at that moment the Queen appeared beside Fleming, and both the women smiled and nodded to him.

'The Queen must have woken up,' was Lethington's blandly superfluous comment to the scandalized Mr Selby.

It was just like her not to care who saw her nor what was thought, Bothwell reflected, and with gratitude, for that sign of goodwill heartened him greatly as he rode up towards the Tolbooth through the crowded streets.

. A great noble going to his trial for the King's murder was not a thing that happened every day. All the shops had stopped work, all the doors and windows were thronged with gaping faces, people were packed like herrings all the way up the outside staircases and on the roofs. They ought to cheer him for providing them with such entertainment. Once again the Gay Galliard, he turned in his saddle to see the pikes of his followers glittering in the April sunshine, rose in his stirrups and gave them a lusty cheer, which they answered in a roar like a breaking wave of the sea.

Then he asked Lethington, did the Queen know anything as yet of that business of the letter?

'No,' was the Secretary's gentle answer. 'It would only make for trouble to refuse the English Queen's request to put off the trial. Elizabeth herself could hardly expect it when delivered, as is her wont, at the eleventh hour and fifty-ninth moment. She has given her threat, or shall we call it "cousinly warning", just too late, which was doubtless just what she'd intended.'

Bothwell gave a short but picturesque description of Elizabeth's interference, but it did not relieve his feelings. Once again he was seeing the hand that he had kissed at Harrow-on-the-Hill, the hand that had written this letter. Behind all the foes surrounding him and his Queen was this woman whom he knew

388

to be more dangerous than all; and with her at this very moment was James, giving his account of Kirk o' Field, of Mary and of Bothwell himself.

Lethington was being positively genial in his sly mocking way as he ambled along beside him on his palfrey ('like a smug prelate', in Bothwell's irritable opinion) and assured him of the success of his trial. Success, that was the one hold he could have over such men. Let go of that and they would turn and rend him.

Inside the Tolbooth, stone-chill and dark, he looked on the faces of many such men. He knew Morton and Lindsay, whom he had outwitted after Rizzio's murder, to be as really hostile to him as Lethington: the Lord Justice Argyll was no friend to him; John Hamilton was Arran's brother and bore him a life-long feud; Sandy Ogilvie, a grudge for marrying his sweetheart Jean; Caithness was James' new ally; he had quarrelled with Herries; Pitcairn, MacGill, Balnaves, Rothes and Boyle, Sempill and Forbes had all come up against him in the old troubles when they had worked for England and he for the Queen Regent. Not more than a third of those present were friendly or even neutral, and yet people were repeating Buchanan's saying that the judges were 'not chosen to judge but to acquit', a lie flatly disproved by the list of their names.

Well, what of it? The true judges were the pikemen outside! Would it come to open violence? Bothwell rather wished it would; he was on surer ground there. But no, he knew that whatever happened this verdict must not go against him.

As he heard his indictment for 'the treasonable and abominable slaughter' of the King 'under silence of night in his own lodging beside the Kirk o' Field', his face went dark.

Black Ormiston plucked at his cloak. 'What the devil is this, my lord?' he whispered. 'You might look so if you were going to the deed!'

'Hold your tongue,' muttered his master.

Lennox's servant, Cunningham, answered to his master's name, and pleaded for a postponement of forty days to collect evidence, the accused to stay in prison meantime; although Lennox's own letters to the Queen, now read in court, demanded 'immediate justice'. So the trial went on – not very long, for no evidence whatever was produced. The jury withdrew, and by seven o'clock that evening 'acquitted the said Earl Bothwell of art and part of the said slaughter of the King'.

*　　*　　*

At that same hour Elizabeth's letter was handed to Mary. Whatever her intention in sending it too late to serve any possible purpose, there was a strange note of truth in the urgency of its warning: 'For the love of God, Madam, use such sincerity and prudence in this matter, which touches you so nearly, that all the world may believe you innocent of so enormous a crime.'

That was not mere spite. It had come straight from the he rt, as though, for once, the English Queen were trying to use her own sorely won experience of life, not to damage but to help her much younger rival. Elizabeth had lost her reputation as the alleged mistress of Robert Dudley; had very nearly lost her throne by the report that she meant to marry him a.ter his wife's mysterious death.

But there could be no such report concerning herself and Bothwell. In any case, the letter could make no odds.

*   *   *

James Hepburn was out in the air again, and free, with 'this jolly acquittal'; Lennox had hastily set sail in a ship down the west coast; and *now* he could whistle, 'Wha dare meddle wi' me?'

He felt he could defy the world, and did, by bills stuck up on the Tolbooth door, offering to 'oppose his body to any gentleman born' who dared now to charge him with the murder. To round it off, he also challenged Sir William Drury, the English Marshal at Berwick, for repeating the slanders made against him two years ago.

It stirred up a fresh crop of placards, offering to prove by force of arms that Bothwell was 'chief and author of the foul and horrible murder', helped by accomplices – and here followed a completely new list of fourteen names not mentioned before, including this time Captain Blackadder, young Hay of Talla, Sandy Durham, Black Ormiston and Harry Lauder. And still the doughty champion refused to disclose his identity.

Times were changing. Challenges weren't what they had been. The whole thing had been made ridiculous, a thing more trying than any danger to the Galliard's temper. He lost it, furiously, shockingly – with the Queen of all people!

Just at this moment of his relief and triumph, on the Sunday the very day after his trial, she must needs go and have a full blast of her infernal religious mummery, a special solemn Mass with dirges sung for the King's soul in the Chapel Royal before a memorial bed of cloth of silver and crimson velvet, and a canopy of ancient cloth of gold cut from the pavilions of Edward II, captured by the Scots at Bannockburn. Very fitting that young Darnley should wear the gauds of that degenerate Southron King, but was he any the warmer for them? A pity then he didn't have 'em the night he lay naked in the snow at Kirk o' Field!

But the climax of his disgust and wrath came when he found that Mary had sat up nearly all that night in the chapel, on her knees beside that painted gallimaufry – to pray for the soul of Henry Darnley.

'As if all your prayers could pluck that trash out of hell!'

She turned on him in a white rage. 'You have never known what pity is. At least show decency.'

So he'd knocked *that* spark out of her, for all she'd looked so listless and hollow-eyed! How dared she mourn him? He'd no pity for her making herself ill with such foolery – and for Darnley, '*Pity*, for the man who planned to blow you to pieces!'

'I'll not believe it. There's no clear proof.'

'There's no clear proof of anything in this coil. It's clear, though, that he knew of the gunpowder. And the horses —'

'Yes, I know. All ready to take him away. But might he not have meant to take me away too in the confusion, to escape together as we did before? He was vicious, weak, helpless somehow – it's not fair to judge him like other men. There was something in him would always have prevented him from growing up. But he was *not* a monster. He *couldn't* have begged me to stay that night, intending me to die that horrible death. He did love me in a way.'

'So they've made even you believe in their "gentle Henry", "that innocent lamb!" You refuse then to be free – you'll tie yourself even to his corpse!'

He was too angry to see that she was pleading so passionately, not to him but to herself. Those hours of kneeling in the chapel last night had come after weeks of nervous collapse. She could not write any letters, not even in answer to her uncle the Cardinal nor her grandmother. A strange apathy had overwhelmed her, a dull disbelief in all the world. She had hated Darnley so that her whole spirit seemed shrunk and withered by it. All last night she had prayed to be delivered from that hate. So she had tried to believe that her young husband was not wholly vile; but here was Bothwell dragging his soul down again into hell – and with it, hers.

Ruthlessly he stripped her of her illusions, reminded her that Darnley had planned her destruction as horribly, as treacherously, a year ago, and only helped to save her from it in order to save himself.

'Did he not kiss you then, and beg you to take care of yourself the same night that he betrayed you? Did he not play tennis and joke with Davie just before he and his fellows worried him to death like a pack of hounds? Yet you still believe in his love for you. You pray for him, try to see good in him, cock him up and heap finery on him in death as in life, hang the Bruce's battle spoils upon his tomb, bury him beside your own father among the Kings of Scotland! Nothing's too good for this rat that should be left to rot in a sewer.'

She gave a cry of sheer physical anguish, her hands to her side. 'Oh, you too! – you are hateful. It is true, you hurt both body and soul.'

Her cry went through him. He flung himself on his knees before her, and his arms round her body, locking her in his grasp. She could not see his face, for his head was pressed against her, that rough, leonine head; his great shoulders were shaking, some extraordinary emotion seemed to be convulsing him.

'Yes, it is true,' he was saying. 'I am hateful. But don't let us hate, or it will be the end of us both.'

Trembling, she said, 'No, no, don't let us hate. Hate is killing me. Remember he was the father of my son.'

He sprang up from her as violently as he had flung himself down, his face was terrible.

'By the blood of Christ, I will remember it always!'

He went from her too quickly to see that she had fainted.

CHAPTER TWENTY-FOUR

AFTER THAT she could never see him again – never, never, never, she kept moaning low to herself, to the terror of Mary Seton's tender heart, who did not know what had happened to throw her mistress back into this piteous state.

But she had to see him again, and at once. On Wednesday she had to attend Parliament, with Bothwell again bearing the sceptre before her. She noticed that the usual escort of Edinburgh bailies had been exchanged for solid ranks of hagbutters, doubtless by Bothwell's command. So he still felt her to be in grave danger; but small odds would the soldiers make to her who had once found her safety in the hearts of her people. 'God bless that sweet face!' they had called when she rode to her first Parliament; but now it was 'God save Your Grace – if you are innocent of the King's death!'

So now they had said it – in the street in the open daylight, before the Lords of her Parliament, surrounded as she was by the muskets of her soldiers; they had cried out to her face what they had whispered behind their window-shutters, muttered in the dark of their doorways; this was the voice of her people, that Greek chorus in the drama of her life that had praised and blessed her, and now shouted aloud its hideous suspicion.

Bothwell had rapped out an order to the captain of the musketeers to arrest those who had shouted, but her temper, stung by the insult, flared up at him for giving the order without her leave, and her voice rang out forbidding it; he expostulated, and she said in a voice of ice, 'Do you indeed wield the sceptre, my lord?'

She saw the anger in his face, knew herself a fool for all reasons to have said it, for indeed he was all-powerful now and knew it, and so did all else. Everything in that week's Parliament was ordered by him, and no one opposed a syllable. The Assembly issued a proclamation that on pain of death no one should further calumniate him or his. An Act was passed against anonymous placards and the 'liberty to back-bite', which aimed at causing disturbance among the people.

But the only material advantage Bothwell reaped from this Parliament, that was utterly subservient to him, was that the lands of the old Church, already appointed to him and other Protestant lords, were confirmed in their possession. Mary let the measure pass with a small wry smile, and asked herself, did *she* indeed wield the sceptre?

But one Act came entirely from her, though it bore the stamp of his hearty approval. It removed any traces of the old Catholic laws that penalized the Reformed religion, it gave the Protestants 'full surety' in that religion, and promised that 'no foreign person or other pretending jurisdiction may interfere with it'. She had snapped her fingers in the face of the Pope and Philip of Spain and their pious requests for the blood of her subjects! Nor was the Act merely negative; it commanded all her subjects to 'live in perfect amity', whatever might be their religious differences.

This was a law of universal toleration such as no other

country in Europe had as yet even dreamed of passing; it expressed an ideal of freedom and of friendship as the only true bond of society. As she heard it read, she thought, 'I have done one thing for my country, perhaps mankind.' The warm pride that filled her veins went glowing up into her thin white cheeks; the men round her who had seen before them only a desperately tired girl, hardly conscious of what they were saying, now stared anew, amazed at this bright spirit. Touched to momentary recognition of the greatness of her hopes, the Parliament expressed their gratitude in a vote of thanks that 'Her Highness ever since her arrival has attempted no thing contrary to the estate of religion which Her Majesty found here standing.' Then on their knees they prayed for her 'long life and good and happy government'.

She rode back to the Palace of Holyrood in an exquisite late April evening of bird-song and budding daffodils in the gardens of the Canongate, a sky washed clear by showers, and wet roofs gleaming in the last rays of the sun. A child flung a bunch of primroses to her, she caught and kissed them and waved them, laughing as she rode on. A stump of rainbow made a splash of iridescent light low over Arthur's Seat as she turned her horse into the gates of Holyrood, and the pear tree outside her turret was in blossom as on that evening a year ago when Davie had sung for the last time. Yet even that did not sadden her now. Whatever had happened, or might happen, even to the law she had just appointed, nothing could alter the fact that the desire for goodwill among all men had been expressed in the law of her land.

'Madam!' cried Seton in awestruck tones when she saw her, and burst into tears. 'You look so – so happy!'

'And is that a reason for crying?' Mary kissed her, laughing, and added, 'Yes, I am happy, and I am going straight to bed, and tomorrow down with you again to dear Seton.'

The Queen had looked so radiant, Seton told Fleming later that evening, 'it was as though a star had passed. I fear she's not long for this world.'

Fleming scoffed; happiness never killed anybody; the Queen had taken one of her sudden turns for the better, that was all. 'You know how it is with her, she changes in a flash, one moment in the depths, and the next like all the birds in the air. I wish she could know some real happiness, God knows! There's one bold fellow who I swear is longing to give it her.'

'The Lord Bothwell?' murmured Seton, shocked – 'but you know they say – and indeed it looks very like —'

'Indeed and it does – and so it does for at least a score of others. It's my belief there's not a man among our nobles who *didn't* plan to kill the King, and that's why they made such a mess of it, all jostling up against each other. So unless the Queen takes a foreigner, she'll have to stay a chaste widow for ever.'

Poor Seton, shuddering, hid her face in her hands. These ghastly weeks were proving too much for her, to the more robust Fleming's annoyance, for what possible help could it be to their darling to creep about like a frightened mouse instead of heartening her by a pretence that everything was normal?

So she spoke more flippantly than she felt when Seton asked, 'How *can* you joke about such a thing?' and replied, 'I dare say the men who did it can. Listen!'

She opened the shutter and leaned from the window-seat where they were talking. The night was mild. A soft rain fell pattering in the garden. In the wall of the opposite tower a window blazed with yellow light, open to the warm night, and from it came the sound of men's voices, many of them, loud and jovial, with every now and then a great burst of laughter.

'What a noise!' said Seton, leaning out beside her. 'I hope the Queen can't hear them from the other side. She wanted to sleep early. She's not slept properly for so many nights. Someone must be giving a great dinner-party, but I'd heard nothing of it, had you?'

'It's a man's dinner only. Lord Bothwell is feasting his friends to celebrate his "jolly acquittal" – twenty-eight of them, Morton and Argyll among them, and a large sprinkling of bishops to give a smack of religion to nine earls and seven barons.'

'Argyll – Morton – bishops – those aren't his friends!'

'Friends or foes, he's keeping them all in hand. Give them pause to think how jealous they are of him, and they'd all be at his throat. But he strikes too quick for them. The Galliard does things in grand style!'

'How do you know all these things?' Seton was admiring but a little uneasy, for Fleming had grown very worldly-wise since she had married Lethington. Of course that was why she knew so much; she seemed indeed to know rather more than she told.

The party grew noisier; snatches of song came rolling out

into the night, and long shadows of moving figures passed across the shining spears of rain illuminated by the window. They could distinguish Bothwell's deep voice singing a verse from the song of the Outlaw Murray,

'I'll own no king in Christendie,'

and it was followed by a roar of laughter from them all, so huge and inconsequent that it frightened Seton.

'They sound very drunk,' she said disapprovingly.

'But on the best French wines, trust the Galliard for that!' murmured Fleming on a pensive note.

'I cannot bear your Galliard,' her gentle companion broke out with sudden passion. 'And I thank Heaven the Queen comes down to Seton tomorrow I know she hates him too.'

'Do you really, my little nun?' Fleming's tone was maddeningly amused.

'You don't know her as I do. They are always quarrelling, they have done so from the very beginning, and sometimes he is so brutal he makes her ill. I found her in a dead faint after he had been with her on Monday.'

'Oh, but she has always been subject to fainting. Remember how frightened the doctors in France were about her.'

'This was different. She could do nothing but weep after it.'

'Ah, but you don't know her as I do,' said Fleming.

In that proud and fond belief each had put her finger on the secret of Mary's charm, both to her friends and enemies. Just as no painter could ever produce a portrait of her that was in the least like any other portrait of her, so no one who ever thought of her, either with love or hate, either in her lifetime or long years after she was dead, could ever believe that anyone else knew Mary Stewart.

CHAPTER TWENTY-FIVE

MARY SETON'S thankfulness was short-lived. The dinner-party followed the closing of Parliament on Saturday. The Queen went down to Seton with her bodyguard of hagbutters on the Sunday morning; Bothwell followed that evening. They had just finished supper in the great hall when he arrived and said at once he wished to speak to her alone. His friend Geordie Seton unfolded his long limbs from his chair like some angular mathematical instrument and cocked a grizzled eyebrow at him as he led off his silently indignant little daughter.

Mary went over to the fireplace and sat warming her hands, though the evening was very mild. She had not spoken with him, except formally in public, since their quarrel six days ago, and wondered if he had come to apologize – 'for the first time in his life, I should think!' He seemed ill at ease, but she would not make it easy for him. He followed her and stood leaning his arm against the chimney-piece, looking down at the fire.

At last he said in a harse, constrained voice, 'This can't go on. I'd have given you more time if I could, for the look of things, but it's too dangerous. Separate, we're vulnerable. To-gether, we'd be twice as strong. If you would consent to marry me now —'

'If I would *what*?'

She could not believe she had heard him correctly. For so practised a lover, James Hepburn was showing himself singu-larly maladroit. He squared his shoulders and repeated, 'I said, marry. Has it so strange a sound? I've served you well enough, haven't I? All this last year I've established order and peace for you in Scotland.'

That indeed was true. 'One man worthy of the name has worked this miracle!'; she had glowed with pride in that opinion from France. He was still speaking.

'Who else has stood by you? Fleming and Geordie Seton here whom you're so fond of, and Livingstone jollying you as if you were a kitten, all damned fatherly' – he savaged the words, but clipped them off and added dryly, 'but they've not a tenth part of my power, nor has the Gordon, for all he holds the key to the Highlands and worships the ground you walk on.'

Again there was that contained rage in his voice. How dared he think he had the right to show jealousy? Yet before she realized she was doing so, she sought to appease it.

'I? But it's you he worships – his mother and everyone says he's "at your entire devotion".'

He muttered, 'Aye, devotion this and that! There's been enough of it by all accounts. I've been at yours and your mother's devotion since I first drew sword, playing the faithful watchdog, as you once were pleased to fancy your precious brother in the role. Has it never struck you I might ask my reward?'

'What then do you want?' There was a cruel scorn in her voice. Nor did it spare herself. 'There was a night not long ago when I would have given myself gladly to you, but you paid no heed – you walked away and left me without a word.' He made a quick turn towards her, but she put up her hand with a forbidding gesture, as royal as it was unconscious. 'That's all past. I'm now an eternity more old. And I cannot make merchandise of myself. You could have taken me then of my free giving, but you cannot claim me as a reward.'

'What – *that* night? There was no time.'

She gave a laugh that stung with contempt, and he swore. 'Madam, are we to talk of philandering *now*? The case is too desperate – as it was then. Was I to be made blind and deaf by your love that night when danger lurked all round you? – as it does now. To make common headway against it we must marry.'

'*Must? Marry?* I think you have gone mad.'

The Queen who had had the greatest Princes in Europe suing for her hand was speaking now; her candid amazement, more potent even than her scorn, reminded him of it; but to no good purpose.

'It would not be the first time you married beneath you. What if Darnley had a Tudor grandmother – are the Hepburns to count themselves lower than those tainted Welsh upstarts? Or Robert Dudley, brand-new Earl of Leicester? At least I know myself the better man.'

She had fallen silent. What the devil was she thinking?

At last she raised those strange level eyes and looked at him, and her voice came very low. 'Did you kill the King?'

It was the last thing he had expected. But he answered quick and loud, '*No*. By the faith of a Borderer, I can swear to that.'

'You've no need to. I know you would not lie to me.'

He turned and kicked at a log. 'I'm not lying,' he said sullenly.

Yet there was something she was unsure of; was he keeping something back from her? He had spoken to her with such brutal frankness the morning after the crime – but his very brutality made her doubtful; he could never mention Darnley except as a snake that any man had a right to trample.

He turned on her again and said angrily, 'You ask that only to put me off.'

'No,' she said gravely. 'Only to show you how impossible it is, what you suggest. For if even I can ask that question, how many others through all the world are asking it?'.

'God's blood, I've stood my trial, haven't I? and been

398

acquitted, and got an Act of Parliament to forbid anyone to charge me with it again on pain of death!'

'So did Robert Dudley, Earl of Leicester, but Elizabeth did not marry him.'

'No, she's kept him instead all these years as her tame stallion to give her such pleasure as she's capable of. But I'm no woman's game, nor Queen's either, for that hole-and-corner business. What I take, I take in the open, nor do I think would you yourself do otherwise. Well then, will you not marry me – Madam?'

The familiar belated 'Madam', the very poor attempt to make it sound humble, was no longer amusing; it was insufferable. 'You seem to have forgotten one objection – your wife.'

'Oh, *that*!' He sounded relieved. 'She has consented to divorce me.'

'On what grounds?'

'Adultery last summer – with Bessie Crawford, the black-smith's daughter,' he said with a grin. To her it was de-liberate effrontery.

The whole thing was ridiculous. He could not be even in-tending her to take it seriously. She said so, dismissing the sub-ject without giving as much as a glance at him. It was as well she did not, or she would have seen his clenched fist. He could not trust himself to speak. He put his hand in his doublet and pulled out a folded paper and handed it to her. There was a great deal of writing on it, and a very long list of signatures.

'What in the world is all this?' she asked wearily.

He did not answer. She gave him a startled look, but his face was now black against the firelight and candles behind him. She read on. Earls, barons, bishops, a great many of them, had signed some document declaring themselves ready to uphold James Hepburn, Earl of Bothwell, 'and maintain his innocence by the law of arms, remembering the antiquity of his house and the honourable service of himself and his forebears'.

So Bothwell, the lone wolf, had entered into one of the 'bonds' he so despised; what desperate impulse had driven him to it? She read on; that the Queen was now 'destitute of a hus-band, in which solitary state the common weal may not permit her to remain. In case the affectionate and hearty service of the Earl of Bothwell may move Her Majesty so far to humble her-self as (preferring one of her native-born subjects unto all foreign Princes) to take to husband the said Earl,' then the undersigned would swear to 'further the marriage, hold its adversaries as their own enemies, spend life and goods in its defence, or else be accounted in all time hereafter as unworthy and faithless traitors'.

'When did you get this done?' she asked with dangerous quiet.

'Last night at Holyrood.'

'At the dinner you gave to your friends – I heard some echoes of your revelry. It must have been indeed a merry one to induce them to sign – this!' and she crumpled the bond in her hand and stood up, her face flaming. 'So you discussed this marriage over your wine with all these men! The compliment is too vinous for my taste – or for your security. Do you really think the half of them will stand by you when sober? Your enemies would never allow this match. Nor would my friends.'

'*Who* are your friends?'

'The Cardinal of Lorraine would scarcely welcome you as his nephew; nor the King of France call you brother.'

'Much help have they been to you ever since you came here!'

'I have borne your insults too long, my lord. Go, and never speak of this again.'

As always, she looked glorious in a rage, taut and vibrant with life, her eyes as bright as swords. He suddenly remembered that there was only one way to convince a woman. He swooped on her and caught her up in his arms, his kisses striking against her, stifling her as she tried to cry out, his arms crushing her furious struggles.

But in that same instant there came a growing uproar outside, the clank of armed men hurrying nearer. He thrust her back into her chair, and turned to face a body of the hagbutter guards who were noisily pushing one of their number before them into the hall, encouraging him with cries of 'There he is' – 'Say it now' – 'Say it!'

The ringleader, a big fellow, red in the face, with the hot indignant eye of a hen, shouted very fast, 'Give us our wages! Not a penny's pay have we seen for eight weeks! Give us our rights or — '

He got no further, for Bothwell had leaped across the hall and taken him by the throat, shaking the burly soldier as though he were a rat and forcing him down on to his knees. The men thronged round, afraid to interfere but crying mercy for their comrade, who seemed on the point of being choked to death; but Bothwell neither saw nor heard them. The Queen sprang up and cried out to him to let go. He heard that. He had lowered himself to attack one of her soldiers in her presence with his naked hands – out of anger at the interruption. Only as he loosened his hands did he recognize the hint of mutiny.

'Let that teach you to thrust into the Queen's presence to demand your wages,' he said, trying to give the proper judicial touch to his insensate fury.

The man was tenderly feeling his throat and in no eagerness to resume the theme. His fellows took it up in muttered growls of indignation; they were only demanding their rights, their pay had been in arrears for two months.

Traquair was in command of the foot soldiers, so that it was no affair of Bothwell's, who commanded the horse. The Queen, however, was in no mood for such masculine subtleties. She asked how much was owing to them, and when she heard, said sharply, 'Then give them two crowns apiece from my purse and let them go.'

She stood by the window as they shuffled out, mumbling their shame-faced thanks; she saw them pass below in the late April dusk, shadowy figures talking low among themselves and chuckling, and heard one say, 'Small wonder the Earl was black angered that we spoiled his sport.'

She was trembling with rage, but saw to it that her hands were still before she turned and looked him in the face and said, 'I shall do my best to forget this insult. At least I can thank you for making it clear that I could never love you.'

'You lie, and you know it. You loved me that night you asked my love.'

'With your experience, my lord, you should know even better than I what such love is worth. And such as it was, it is over – for ever. Now go.'

She turned again to the window. The room was very silent. When she looked round again she found that he had gone.

Little Mary Seton came running into the hall. 'Oh, Madam, he has gone already! I am so glad! Madam, there is the first cuckoo we've heard, on the other side of the Castle. Do come and hear him before it gets quite dark.'

CHAPTER TWENTY-SIX

SHE COULD not stay at Seton. She left the next morning to pay a private visit to her baby son at Stirling, and would only take a small escort of about thirty horsemen, with Gordon and Lethington in charge. No, she would not take Mary Seton as she begged. 'What odds?' she said. 'I shall be back in Edinburgh on Wednesday.' She wanted to escape from everybody, even her best friend. Thank heaven there was still her baby, who could not talk and turn her affection to irritation, as did Seton's anxious solicitude; or to hatred, as did Bothwell's abominable behaviour.

But she hated herself worse. It was her doing that he had changed so to her. She had cheapened herself to him that night when she had asked his love and he had left her without even troubling to reply; she saw now how he must have despised her for it, he who was accustomed to women making fools of themselves for him. The proof of it had been in the contemptuous insolence of that proposal; he had actually got the consent of her lords before asking hers – because he could take that for granted! And so much for granted that he had not troubled to woo her, had made not even any pretence at love, or wish for her love; no doubt he felt he had no need to, since she had held out her hands and offered herself, 'just like any courtesan of the Paris streets!' she told herself miserably.

She would never love any man again; she would devote herself from now on only to her kingdom and her son, and she heaved a deep sigh of relief at the contemplation of those respectable emotions, patriotism and maternity.

But the visit to Jamie was not an immediate success. It was some time since he had seen his mother, he did not like her black clothes, worst of all, she gave him a diamond safety-pin to fasten his bib which made him howl with terror. Lady Mar told Mary that he could not bear the flash of jewels or steel and they had to be careful how they used knives before him. It was unthinkable that any Stewart should be a coward. Did little Jamie unconsciously remember the daggers that had flashed before his mother's eyes in the anteroom at Holyrood so soon before he himself was born? But theories of pre-natal influence had not yet been exalted into a religion, one that in any case bore no consolation. Her solitaire proved more successful than the safety-pin; Jamie gurgled with delight over the little figure of a Cupid as a Court Fool, and the great pendant pearls which he tried to tug off. Mary left it in his fat hands.

On the Wednesday she set off back again, but Edinburgh suddenly seemed unbearable; she must have one more day's respite from those prying houses. She had failed to find much comfort in her baby; now she sought it in the memory of her mother, and on a sudden whim decided to spend the night at

Linlithgow, her mother's favourite palace, where she herself had been born.

Linlithgow's foundations were so old that none knew what race of giants had first built it; her father had added to it and adorned it with stained glass and carving by French artists in honour of his bride from France. It seemed still to linger under the influence of that tall gracious lady with the calm eyes and wise smile. Mary had trotted along with her hand in that rather large, firm, capable hand when they went to throw bread to the swans who came sweeping up over the loch towards them, their great wings upreared, superb as avenging angels; but she was never afraid of them when with her mother.

She went straight to the loch below the Castle walls as soon as she arrived this fine spring evening, and once again the swans came sweeping up to be fed. 'How much smaller they seem now!' she thought, and yet she herself was just the same as that little girl in a rose-coloured snood listening to her mother's soft French voice telling her that her kind grandmother de Guise had just sent her a thousand pins for her birthday and this pretty little watch with the gold stars. The watch had ticked on ever since, minutes, hours, days, years it had ticked out, and yet it was just the same, 'and I too, for here I am the same as ever inside'.

The evening was full of light, the loch water gleamed, the wild daffodils and primroses on its shore shone out like faint lamps. Little wooded islets touched with pale green lay dreaming in that wan water; long ago a fairy hound had been found on one of them chained to a tree, so her mother had told her, but could not tell her what happened after that.

A missel-thrush sang quick and bold on a willow tree; the boughs, though still bare, were outlined in dark gold, and fell like a fountain against the dimly rosy sky. They called that bird the storm-cock up here because it sings in all weathers. 'Yes, he's no fair-weather friend, he's proved that,' she told herself involuntarily – and then remembered she had driven him away.

Would he perhaps never come back?

It was unthinkable that James Hepburn should leave her service – and if he did, what should she do?

But what else could she have done? Surely her mother would have approved. *She* had sent his father packing when he had dared propose marriage, but far more decorously. She had encouraged him first, though, when it had suited her to win the

403

Fair Earl's service with hopes of her favour. Was it possible that the house of Hepburn had some reason to feel aggrieved at its treatment by widowed Queens?

The moon, nearly half full, was growing clearer in the pale sky; it would be a lovely night. She sighed for no reason that she knew of, and wondered how long she must wear this hideous black; no wonder Jamie cried at sight of it. 'This is the Palace of Widowed Queens,' she thought, looking up at the turret window of Queen Margaret's Bower where her Tudor grandmother had watched to see King James IV come riding back from Flodden – but he never came back.

In this haunted twilight she herself seemed only a ghost – and of one who had never lived. She was twice a widow, who had never really known what it was to be a wife. Tomorrow would be St Mark's Eve, the anniversary of her wedding nine years ago to the Dauphin of France, and she the loveliest bride that age had seen, so the poets had told her and the courtiers and Ambassadors and her admiring uncles and father-in-law, all adoring her; but the poor sickly child, her bridegroom, two years younger than herself, had clung to her crying after all the fatigue and nervous excitement of the day. The wedding had never been consummated.

'For me not to marry, you know it is impossible'; but she developed too late to know it for a very long time. And then all her curiosity and awakening desire had been disillusioned by Darnley from the first night of their marriage.

It was love itself she was wanting, and so had been fool enough to think she could have it from Bothwell, who took women as casually as he took wine, and despised them for being so taken. 'Oh!' she cried aloud in pain so sharp that she could not bear it in silence, and pressed to her burning face the hands that she had held out to him, asking for him.

She could stay here no longer. She went back to the Palace through the central courtyard, under the superb carved gateway built by her father, where his cockle-shell of St Michael and motto, 'tremor immensi oceani', spoke of the troubling of the great sea. Lighted windows were making bright orange-coloured squares all round the great quadrangle. Yet there was still light enough from the sunset to see the figures on the eastern wall of the Three Estates of the Commonwealth, a priest for the Church, a knight for the Nobles, a labourer for the Commons, all equally important to that 'King of the Commons'.

Yes, she and her father would have agreed well.

> *So we'll go no more a-roving*
> *So late into the night.*

But why had *he* sung that, the unquenchable rover?

She went in and to bed in the room where the carved stag stood under the tree and the words ran in stone, *'Belle à vous seule.'*

She read in bed, on and on, for she knew she would not sleep. Old Sir Richard Maitland had sent her a book of English verses, Tottel's Miscellany, printed ten years ago. He had told her that she would be interested in tracing the influence of the Italian poets on the verses of Sir Thomas Wyatt. She did not notice that. She heard Bothwell's deep voice in all his words.

> *Forget not yet the tried intent*
> *Of such a truth as I have meant;*
> *My great travail so gladly spent,*
> *Forget not yet!*

This was himself, speaking of his 'steadfast faith yet never moved', of his 'service such as none could tell', his 'great assays' – and – oh God! had he too not some reason to speak of her own 'scornful ways' and his 'painful patience in delays'?

She turned the page, and found no escape from his reproach.

> *And wilt thou leave me thus,*
> *That hath loved thee so long*
> *In weal and woe among?*
> *And is thy heart so strong*
> *As for to leave me thus?*
> *Say nay! Say nay!*

No, her heart was not so strong, she felt that it was breaking. She sprang out of bed and flung her furred cloak round her; she could lie still no longer here in the great chamber where she had been born just after Sir Thomas Wyatt had died. He had loved King Harry's Queen, the fair frail Anne Boleyn, who had given birth to Elizabeth ten years before Mary herself lay in that beautifully carved cradle that still stood in the corner of the room.

She was walking up and down in her white feathered slippers on the coloured French tiles, trying to distract her thoughts with the strange tangle of human lives. Here was this English politician, dead before she was born, speaking for Bothwell and herself alone. 'Farewell, unjust!' He might well call her that. 'Farewell, unkissed!' Yes, he had gone, and not even kissed her hand.

She went to the window and looked out on a ghost-white world; the jagged shadow of the Castle lay black upon the moonlit loch where the mist rose in thin wraith-like forms. Two dim figures on the shore were just passing into that shadow, and her heart gave a leap, for she thought in that instant that one of them walked like Bothwell, but in the next she knew that it was only because his image was so clear in her mind, for she could not have recognized him in this light and at that distance. And he of all men would never come back, at midnight, to gaze up at her window like the pathetic scorned lover of romance. He would shrug and go his way – Sir Thomas Wyatt had just told her so.

> *May chance thee lie withered and old,*
> *The winter nights that are so cold,*
> *Plaining in vain unto the moon:*
> *Thy wishes then dare not be told:*
> *Care then who list! for I have done.*

And suddenly, with a shuddering inarticulate cry, she clutched at the window-sill, for she felt as though a new self were being born within her, here in this room where her body had been born twenty-four years ago, and never come alive till now – now, when every nerve of her was tingling in an agony of regret and longing.

Those two shadows by the loch might have been their two selves walking together in the enchanted night. 'We shall have moonlight again,' he had said that reivers' over-word years ago to her in France, and it had echoed ever since; but she had sent him away, she would never feel those fierce arms round her again, nor those kisses that had struck like blows, giving her no chance at the time to know how she desired them. Now, too late, she knew.

She slid to the floor, her head against the window-sill and whispered brokenly,

> *'We'll go no more a-roving*
> *Let the moon shine ne'er so bright.'*

*   *   *

Mary's first fancy had been right. It was Bothwell she had seen on the shore of the loch, but he had not come to gaze at her window. He had paid a secret visit at midnight in order to talk with George Gordon, Earl of Huntly, to Gordon's surprise, for his brother-in-law had just set about collecting a large force of men for a raid into Liddesdale, so what was he doing up here? Bothwell had got him out of the Castle, away from any possible eavesdropper, and was now walking with him up and down, talking in low, urgent, imperative tones while the Gordon stalked beside him in silence.

Bothwell had already discussed with him his project of marrying the Queen, and Gordon had given his consent to the divorce as gladly as he had given it to the marriage. A year and two months had been more than long enough to prove it a failure, nor was it Bothwell whom Gordon blamed for this. The admiration that his unpractical nature had felt for his sister's businesslike qualities had turned to dislike; he was harsher than Bothwell when Jean flatly refused to give up the lands she had acquired as Countess of Bothwell. Her husband excused her, 'it's little else she's had from me, after all', and promptly bought her off with the promise of the fairest of his castles, Crichton, and all its goods. Everything should have gone as merrily as a wedding bell, or a collusive divorce court decree. Only the Queen's consent was needed, and he had now to admit to Gordon that he had failed to win it.

'Then,' said Gordon, 'there is no more to do.'

Bothwell swore. 'You think that, do you; that I am to take my dismissal like a whipped hound, after all I've done for her!'

An echo of his mother's quiet voice struck on his unwilling mind: 'once a man begins to count up "all I've done" he might as well hang himself'. He hastily expanded it to – 'and after all I've put up with from her! Are you, too, going to prove yourself my unfriend? I had thought you'd stand by me if all else turned against me.'

'And why will they?'

'Because, I tell you, I will marry her, whoever will or will not – yes, whether she herself will or will not.'

Gordon stood still and faced his friend. 'What devilry is this?' he asked.

'It's no devilry to carry off the woman I love, and who loves me – I know she does. I was a clumsy fool with her. I'd never have bungled so with any other woman. But needs must when the devil drives. I've sworn to have her, and there's an end. Either I'll lose all in an hour or I'll bring it to pass.'

They made a strange contrast even in that wan and misty

light, the dark scarred face confronting with furious defiance the other's stern calm. Gordon said no more than, 'You cannot do this thing.'

'Christ's blood, man, but I love her. I've waited for her.'

Even then Gordon did not speak of his own love for her. He said, 'She is a great Queen, and are you to use her as if she were the spoil of a Border foray?'

Bothwell drew in his breath sharply, it sounded like exultation. Gordon's hand flew to his sword, but in the same instant he dropped it, turned and walked away. Bothwell stared after that lonely figure; for the first time in his life he knew what it was to feel dismay. It could not be that Gordon had turned against him.

He saw him walk through the huge gateway, and then followed him, into the central courtyard of the Castle. A cold fear had fallen on him that Gordon had already gone inside the Castle, but no, he was standing by the fountain, where the figure of the mermaid threw a fantastic shadow on the glimmering dew.

He went up to him and said, 'What will you do? Will you now warn her against me? It will make no odds, I tell you – except to you and me. Are you going to be my enemy?'

Gordon was so still that he seemed not to have heard. His pale forehead stood up like a rock in the light of the moon; in the hollows carved beneath it his strange light eyes looked through the other, out beyond him at something he had seen long before, when he had watched Bothwell in the Dance Royal of the Galliard with Mary in the torch-lit hall of Crichton – and had turned his head away.

At last he said, 'No, I'll not meddle with that which I have seen. You must dree your own weird, and I wish it may come to good. But that cannot be.'

'Good or ill, I must do it. I've waited long enough. I can wait no longer.'

'Then go your way and I'll not help you or gainsay you. But this I tell you, that if you take her and do not win her to you, then I will not rest till I have your life.'

He went into the Castle. Bothwell rode away. The courtyard was left empty in the moonlight except for the stone mermaid that would stay there for centuries after the two friends were dead, and the woman they both loved.

CHAPTER TWENTY-SEVEN

NEXT DAY she started late in the afternoon with her cortège of thirty men. One had to be a hard rider to keep up with the Queen. She drew in her horse and waited for the breathless Lethington. Edinburgh was only a few miles off among the hills that lay chequered with flying shadows in the stormy evening sunshine. They were now looking down on the river Almond, which they would have to cross either by the ferry or bridge – 'but I beg Your Grace's filial piety won't go so far downstream as the Auld Brig of Cramond, for then we'll all have to wait while Jock Howison's Jock's Jock fetches a jug and basin and towel for you to wash your hands'.

'Will he see they're as dirty as that? And what have they to do with my filial piety?'

'Only that your royal father was once set on by six ruffians at that bridge when he was riding alone in rough clothes. And the old Jock Howison of that day, who was cutting his oats near by, came to the unknown traveller's aid with his sickle, and so won a fair estate – and with it the privilege for him and his heirs of bringing wherewithal to wash the hands of every Sovereign of Scotland who crossed the Brig of Cramond ever after, in memory of your father who washed his bloody hands there after the fight.'

'And did old Jock Howison really not know he was the King?'

'Not till he came to the Palace next day as summoned, and seeing his Master Redhead of the fight there, said, "Why, the King must be either you or I, since we're the only two with our hats on." '

Mary laughed with pleasure. 'And that only in my father's time! It sounds like the days of romance. What a pity they're at an end!'

'One can never be sure of that,' said Lethington.

They moved forward towards the new bridge, and as they crossed it they saw the low ground below the hills dark with horsemen. Before she had time even to look back to where Gordon rode with young James Borthwick, some of them had already ridden up to her. At the head of them was Bothwell, who took her bridle and turned her horse's head.

'I've been watching the water for you since morning,' he said. 'You cannot go on to Edinburgh with your handful of men.

The Lennox men are out. I have over eight hundred here who'll bring you safe to Dunbar.'

So he had come back, and once again to the rescue. Relief and gratitude filled her eyes with tears; was there any man in the world so magnanimous? She tried to stammer out her thanks, but never had it been so hard to speak them. He did not want to listen to her; his face was like a mask. He made his men fall in behind her and ordered them forward; her little band, now closely surrounded by his men, were fiercely arguing and disputing. James Borthwick succeeded in thrusting his horse forward and calling to the Queen to know if it were her pleasure that they should all ride to Dunbar.

'Indeed yes, since it's my Lord Bothwell's advice,' she called back, but then turned to Bothwell and suggested that young Borthwick should, instead of accompanying them, ride straight to Edinburgh to warn the authorities of the rising, and call the citizens to arms. He did not seem to welcome the suggestion, though it was the obvious thing to do, but he did not gainsay it, and Borthwick started off. Captain Blackadder spoke a few words to him, low, before he rode away, and then the whole little army swung into the route for Dunbar, with Mary, Bothwell and Blackadder at the head of it, and far away, near the end of the long line of eight hundred horsemen, Lethington and Gordon and her thirty soldiers, with Bothwell's men guarding the rear.

She was full of eager questions, to which Bothwell replied somewhat surlily; but that naturally did not surprise her after her dismissal of him at their last meeting. When had he heard of the rising? How was it he had been able to come so quickly to her aid? Where had he and his men been last night? He told her, at his house of Calder close by here.

'But why Calder? That was no use for a raid into Liddesdale.'

'You're in the right of it, Madam. But it turned out very handy for watching your route from Linlithgow!' He had some right to that sardonic tone, she thought, in echo from her last night's repentance. She was in danger, so he came and rescued her, as he had done again and again. She began again tentatively to speak her thanks, but he cut her short with amazing rudeness, saying that her thanks were the last thing he wanted of her. She had thought she hated him; now she wondered if she had made him hate her.

But for all his scowling face beside her, she could not quite

410

believe it; he *must* feel, as she did, how natural it was for them to be riding off together on another adventure. And the evening was so lovely; as they passed Edinburgh Castle, perched up on its rock, now just within a mile of them, it looked like a fairy city that had floated down from the flaming sunset clouds. The Common Bell clanging within the city, summoning her loyal citizens to arms in her defence, chimed absurdly with the cuckoos shouting near her. The very birds of spring had joined in this adventure and were singing in concert with her heart.

A roar, a puff of smoke, another and then another came from that fairy city on the great rock. The guns of Edinburgh Castle had opened fire on them.

They hit no one; it would be luck if cannon nearly a mile off managed to hit a moving target. And the target was quickly moving out of range. As they galloped past the city they looked back and saw the Town Bands hurrying out through the city gates after them, but as these were on foot they would have no chance to catch up with the horsemen.

Bothwell rode apart a little way with Captain Blackadder.

'What the devil did you say to young Borthwick?'

'Why, that all was being done with the Queen's consent – but it's plain he doesn't believe it, since he's got them to attack us.'

'Who gave you leave to speak that lie of the Queen's consent?'

The muttered tone was so enraged that Blackadder edged his horse away. He had only thought to ease matters, 'and anyway,' he argued, 'if she's not yet given her consent, she'll soon have to.'

The two men rode on together, still talking in low voices. Mary had nothing but the moss-troopers now close round her, and no chance to ask any explanation of the extraordinary conduct of her loyal citizens of Edinburgh. The sky darkened as the clouds marched across it, trailing their long grey skirts over the hills, and now a spurt of rain fell, stinging her face. The wind had turned colder; it would be a long ride to Dunbar. Why did Bothwell not come back to her? Why did he leave her so long alone, and why had he separated her by the whole length of his column from Gordon and Lethington? Was he deliberately preventing them from coming up to her?

Fear grew – but not of the citizens of Edinburgh. They had been warned of a rising; but it was on Bothwell and his troops that they had fired. What reason had they to take him for the rebel? Was he – could he – after all his loyal service – become a rebel? It was not possible. But she had thought so many and such violently contradictory things of him in the last three days that now almost anything seemed possible. Were his enemies right about him after all, and Sir Thomas Wyatt all wrong?

Night came down on her, but not at the exquisite lingering pace of yesterday, the sun setting, the moon rising as if to slow music in the formal measure of some gracious pavan of the skies. Now it was driven in scurrying gusts of wind and rain, and the moon went in and out among the clouds like a hunted thing. 'Thou'rt safe if thou canst reach Dunbar.' *Would* she be safe at Dunbar?

At last, far off, she heard the roaring of the sea.

It was midnight when they reached Dunbar. The soldiers held up torches on either side of the drawbridge, her horse's hoofs clattered hollowly over it, and those roaring waves, now very near, came thundering and crashing on the rocks below the Castle. She had none of her women with her, but one of the garrison's wives took her upstairs to a room that had been hastily furnished as a bedroom for her, put out her things and helped her out of her wet riding-dress into a loose gown. Some hot broth and cold chicken, bread and wine, were laid out on a little table.

She was very tired, but could not go to bed until Bothwell, and Gordon and Lethington too, came and told her what was happening. She told the woman to let them know she was expecting them; to which however she only shook her head, and said she could not say what was the Lord's will.

It was an uncomfortable reminder that Bothwell's power was absolute in his own fortresses, where the Sovereign herself was regarded only as the Queen of Fife and Lothian. Dunbar was Hepburn to the very bone of its blood-red rock; it was known as Lord Patrick's Stronghold ever since Bothwell's great-great-great-grandfather had defended it with the widowed Queen of James I against his subjects. She had died here after a few weeks, the chronicle did not say how or why – nor if Lord Patrick had been her lover, though she remembered Bothwell telling her something of the sort years ago – yes, at breakfast at Crichton, the morning after his sister's wedding – and asking her with an impudent cock of his eyebrow how had she slept in Queen Joan's and Lord Patrick's bed!

How young they had all been then! He had been so found of Johnnie, and surely of herself too in his odd mocking way. He could not turn against her now. But why did he not come?

Why did none of them come? She looked round her at the massive stone walls; the terrifying question flashed into her mind: Did Gordon and Lethington not come because they were his prisoners? Was she herself his prisoner? Suddenly she remembered his coming towards her down the long gallery at Holyrood, coming in answer to her call for aid. She had seen then that he had changed; thought something that she had not thought of since – that those who called the devil to their aid had sooner or later to pay a price.

She shook herself: she would not get worked up by these foolish fancies; this was a dismal flight compared with her last to this place, but that was all. She drank her broth, warming her feet by the fire.

She heard a man's tread on the stone stair; there came a knock on the door, and Bothwell stood inside the room, stood still by the door, not advancing to her, but staring, almost as if he had not expected to see her there. A stranger had entered the room.

She tried to shut out her fear; she exclaimed, 'What does it all mean? Have you had fresh news? But this is the strongest of your fortresses.'

'Yes,' he said, and still stood there by the door: then, slowly, as though talking to himself rather than her, 'I have loved you too long, I think, and now I've nothing left to say of it, I've said it so often in my mind. I've been dazed with love of you and could not think clearly. You've stood between me and sleep – the only woman who ever did that – when absent.'

She scarcely heard his words, only that twisted laugh at the end of them. Her voice came sharp and angry with the fear she tried to control. 'Why aren't Gordon and Lethington with you? Why have you brought me here? You said an enemy, but there's been no sign of one – unless it's yourself!'

'I've never been your enemy. Don't make me so now. You know I love you.'

'What use to talk of love —'

'None! You don't even listen.'

'Not to a rebel – if you are that.'

Their voices clashed like swords. His eyes were narrowed to slits of angry light. He brushed his hand across them and still did not move from the door; he said, 'I've been blind mad for you. I don't want to be now. I blundered at Seton and spoilt it all. Now I've had to do this.'

She gave a gasping cry, 'Then this is all a trick! You

413

pretended a rising in order to carry me off yourself – *you* – whom I thought my most loyal servant!'

· 'Is it disloyal to love you – crave you – as you've shown you do me, for all you've gone back on it! There's been too much of this havering.'

And suddenly he was across the room and had caught her up, kissing her, not roughly as at Seton, but with a bewildering intensity that made her forget everything but that she was in his arms, as she had longed to be last night. But tonight she was his prisoner. That came back into her drowning consciousness, and with it a furious and desperate pride. She would never be a willing captive. She struck out at his face and tore herself away and shrieked for help. He let her go, and waited that she might hear the echo of her voice die away and none answer.

'Who's to come to your help in "the strongest of my fortresses"?'

She saw how she had maddened him, and now made a wild attempt to plead.

'There is yourself – my faithful friend.'

'Am I to come to your rescue again, even against myself?'

He was laughing, with the laughter that his men knew well, for they had heard it often enough in battle; she knew only that it was the laugh of a stranger, and a devil. It roused her own fighting spirit again. Even now her astonished pride could not believe that her subject would actually dare to force her body. Not even her husband and royal cousin Darnley, when sick and craving for her, had dared attempt it.

His hands came down on her, and she stood quite still under them, so certain was she of the mastery.

'You will get nothing of me but of my own will,' she said, her voice small and cold as a stiletto.

His answer was to seize her. In the shock of his attack all her newly reawakened love of him now turned again to hatred, and she fought with frenzy to defend herself, tearing his hard hands with her teeth, trying to tear his lips too as they crushed down on hers, not to kiss but to batter resistance out of her. She roused all his brutality, his determination to conquer. At last he conquered.

He looked at her lying only half-conscious, at the bruises on her delicate throat and breasts that were still round and small, her body still immature in spite of childbirth. He forced some wine between her lips; it revived her, but was strong and made her choke, and she asked for water to mix with it.

'No, drink it as it is, you need it – and will again,' he told her grimly. She flung up her arm in a wild weak gesture and sent the cup full in his face. He laughed with delight that her spirit was still unbroken, even while he forced more wine down her throat.

Spluttering, she told him, 'I will have your head for this. I will send for the Provost of Dunbar tomorrow and tell him of your treason.'

'Send for him, then, and your tame cat Lethington, and see what succour they can give you!' And he poured out wine for himself in the same cup, singing,

> 'Go seek your succour where ye paid blackmail,
> For, Ma'am, ye ne'er paid money to me!'

Her head fell back on the pillow. 'And I doubted less of you than any subject that I have!' she said in a low voice.

That did not move him, except to some amusement. 'What reason had you to doubt any man, who know nothing of them?'

But there he stretched his mockery too far, and a sudden pity caught him unawares. He knew that he loved her helplessness even while he abused it, that her frankness and trustfulness had worked against her and always would, with others as well as himself; and that he would not have it otherwise. He walked away from her to the window and stood staring, seeing nothing; thinking how he had first seen her in Paris, and said that night at dinner that she was too young for him – and so she was still.

He did not want to think of that now when at last after all these years he had her at his mercy; it was better to be angry with her, fighting her. She had had good use of him; it was her turn to pay.

'I paid high enough for intent to ravish you when I had none,' he said, 'a sort of Jedburgh Justice that I should now enjoy the crime for which I went into prison and exile!'

And he turned back again to remind himself and her of his new mastery. But when he reached the bed and lifted back the tumbled hair that had fallen over her face, he saw that she had fainted outright. He was not much surprised, for she had fought so furiously and he must have hurt her badly; he made sure that he had not actually harmed her, then set to work to bring her round, first to consciousness, then to ease and quiet and to acceptance of him. He did not speak nor let her do so, but used all his practised cunning as a lover that had made women follow him blindly; used it cynically, almost mechanically, knowing that he could make her 'like her pleasure as well as another'.

But this magic gentleness after cruelty, so new to her after Darnley's boyishly clumsy and selfish notion of love-making, aroused something new in her – and in him. His deliberate intention to win her over was forgotten in a strange new pleasure, that of watching her bewildered delight in his caresses. She turned to him with the wonder of a child and the rapture of a woman, giving him all the ecstasy of her body in undemanding, unquestioning gratitude, giving as utterly, as royally, as she had just now withstood him, her greatness of spirit as clear in surrender as in conflict. He was abashed and conquered by it. All his artifice, his clever tricks learned from a score of women, seemed cheap to him, a base coinage which this royal creature accepted in her ignorance, but still more in her generosity, as pure gold.

So it was that now, when he had made her his prisoner, his victim, literally since he had conquered her – at the very moment when with others he would have shrugged, amused, 'She is like all the rest,' he was instead brought for the first time in his life to real humility and tenderness, and wished he had coin to give her that had not been debased ever since his dissolute boyhood. His peacock father, his sensual old uncle at Spynie had made his upbringing; and all his life, though he despised them, he had followed the lines they had laid down.

He knew that he would be proud of having subdued her so easily and so soon after her furious repudiation of him, that he would even tease her with it, gently; yet it was not till now when he had utterly subjugated her that he himself knelt to her in spirit. So he did now in act. 'My Queen,' he said, and kissed her hand.

It was the first time he had ever truly done her homage.

CHAPTER TWENTY-EIGHT

BUT HE found next day that she would not consent to marry him. Her denial was no reaction from the violence of passion the night before; it was clear and considered. He was astonished at the coolness with which she kept her head when physically and emotionally she had been swept off her feet; her lifelong political training in France had taught her to keep her thoughts free from her passions, years before those passions could be roused.

He admired it even while it infuriated him. All through that day he coaxed, pleaded, finally bullied, and still she said it was impossible. His fellow-nobles had been blackly jealous of his power before this; there was not one of them who would stand him on the throne; they would at once combine together to pull him down. Even the men of the Border, who had followed him so devotedly as their own overlord and lieutenant, would bitterly resent him in the position of that age-old bogy, their hereditary foe and tyrant, the King of Fife and Lothian. He had given her many instances in the past of this jealous instinct against the authority of even their legitimate monarch; she used them against him now with damnable logic. How coolly she faced him, telling him that! He knew it better than she, and for that very reason wanted to shake the breath out of her body before she should finish saying it.

But he was certain he could override all such jealousies and enmities; he had got his lambs feeding out of his hand, they'd never turn against him. As for the nobles, they'd bite if they got the chance, of course, but he'd not give them that chance. He knew that France and the Catholic Powers would never support the match, that England would seize the chance to stir up all the trouble that she could against them – were they to be downed by that?

She took fire from his defiance; yet still that cool brain of hers went on reasoning; she saw, what his furious impulse had ignored, that dangerous as it was in any case for them to marry, it was madness to do so after he had kidnapped and carried her off. Either he would be regarded as a criminal ravisher (for which the punishment by law was death) who had coerced her by brute force into consent to the marriage; or she would be suspected of having connived at the whole scheme, perhaps instigated it, in order to save her face in marrying so soon after her husband's death.

'They will say you were my lover all along. Already they say you murdered him; now they will say you did it in order to marry me, and that I approved.'

' "They say – what say they? Let them say!" Do you care what the rabble shouts?'

His towering arrogance could not believe that he alone was not a match for the whole pack of them. It made him say the worst thing he could have said to her: 'There's no need for all this talk. You're my prisoner. I've sworn to marry you, whoever will or will not – yes, whether you yourself will or will not.'

'Then indeed there's no need for more talk,' she said in that low, ice-cold voice that she could use like a whip.

He felt his anger rising, his hands went out – to do what? He had ravished her; he might kill her; he could never force her to submit. He went quickly out of the room, out of the Castle, knowing only that for the moment he must leave her.

Left alone, Mary's high courage collapsed into frightened sobbing. His look had terrified her, and his silent going from her.

If only she had stayed safely in France! She even found herself longing for James' unalterable respectability, for Lethington's suave manners. And it was just then that Lethington with precise delicate steps came into the room. There was no time to be lost, and he had left the door open for a speedy retreat. Quickly yet unhurryingly, with a quiet matter-of-factness that sounded unbelievably reassuring, he told her that he had contrived to get a message sent secretly to the Provost of Dunbar to arrange for her rescue – if she indeed desired her freedom. The implied doubt stung her; it was just what she had pointed out to Bothwell, that her consent to him now would look like her connivance beforehand.

'Indeed I desire it,' she cried indignantly. But what could be done? Dunbar was impregnable, the key of the East Coast from Leith Harbour to Berwick-on-Tweed, defended by the sea on three sides of it, and now by close on a thousand men as well as some cannon. It was impossible for the Provost to raise men to attack it, nor would she have a civil war. 'A boat under the Castle walls — ' she said it at the same moment that Lethington was making the same suggestion, and he smiled with gentle humour.

'It is no wonder that we think alike, since the poets seem to be the authority for our plans. Many Queens have made history, it is left for you, Madam, to make romance.'

Here was the modern gentleman, to whom it was as unthinkable to ravish a Queen as to get a divorce for her through the medium of a blacksmith's daughter. The reminder he gave her of the civilized world that she seemed to have lost for ever was too much for her; she laughed and began to cry again at the same moment. She looked so pretty in spite of her tears that he felt really sorry for her and patted her shoulder, then stroked that shining head bowed over the arm of her chair. He had always wondered if her hair felt as soft as it looked; it did.

'There, there,' he murmured somewhat fatuously, 'it will be all the same in a hundred years' time.'

It struck his speculative mind that Elizabeth's smirched, shrewd childhood had learned more of men at thirteen than Darnley's widow knew even now; the English Queen could exploit her love-affairs to her advantage, where the Scots Queen was taken by surprise, perhaps to her own ruin, as well as to that of the men who loved her. So headlong a career as Bothwell's must shortly crash in disaster; the sooner he helped to dissociate her from it, the better for himself.

Suddenly the Queen leaped from her chair and thrust him away so violently that only the wall prevented him from falling. Before he had recovered his balance she dashed in front of him, and he saw Bothwell's murderous eyes above her head, and his hand raised to strike with his whinger.

With his other hand Bothwell seized her to drag her away from Lethington, but she screamed and flung herself on the arm that held the knife, crying, 'I have seen a man murdered – don't, don't let me see it again!'

He dropped his arm; through the choking red mist before his eyes some sense came to him that he must not do her more hurt.

'I'll not kill him in front of you,' he said.

'You *shall not* kill him, or your life will pay the forfeit, I swear it, as soon as I am free.'

'Aye, he was plotting your escape, I know that. And you'd trust yourself to that double-dyed traitor rather than to me! You'll get no more chance of that.'

He went to the door, called to the guards, and told them to take Lethington away and keep him in his rooms under lock and key. Lethington wiped his forehead with his fine silk handkerchief as he was led away.

Bothwell turned to Mary. She had fallen back into her chair and was trembling violently from head to foot. He could not speak to her, and his eyes were clouded as though he saw her not as herself but as part of his rage and hatred. His hand was still gripping his whinger, the knuckles white, and she gave a little moan of fear – 'Your hands – they are murderers!'

He rammed the knife back into its sheath, and walked away from her and then back, up and down, restlessly, ceaselessly; would he never stop prowling up and down, never speak, never turn and look at her? She had given herself body and soul in the night to this man, and now awaked to find him 'the two-footed beast' that his enemies called him.

419

At last she had to ask it. 'You will not kill him?'

'No, I will not.'

He came back and stood before her, with desperation in his eyes, and yet there was also a proud humility.

'I have made you hate me. I would give the world to undo it, but what's the use of that? I go mad with rage, it comes up hot in my throat, choking me, and hot like fire in my eyes, and hot, hot in my hands with the longing to stab and smash and kill, and then I know and care for nothing but that. It's made me blunder and do things to my own hurt, and that just lately. Now I *must* win you. I'd fight the whole world to do it – but what's the good of that if I make you hate me?'

It was the appeal that he had flung at her only ten days ago, after the night she had sat up praying in the chapel, and it had haunted her ever since; now it rose to her own lips – 'Oh don't let us hate, or it will be the end of us both.'

He was on his knees before her, his arms round her. 'Hate or love, or both, as I think it is, you cannot, you *shall* not escape me now. Swear to me you will never try to again. Don't you know you cannot? You are mine. You know it.'

Her voice came small and frightened. 'I think you would kill me to possess me. Did your ancestor kill Queen Joan – here in his stronghold?'

He sprang up with an oath, 'Who told you that fable?'

'No one. I never knew there was a fable, only that she died here —'

'A hundred years ago! What have their old ghosts to do with us?'

The stories, based only on conjecture, of Lord Patrick's Stronghold, had never troubled him before, but now he could not bear to think there was any possibility of their truth. He wished he had brought her anywhere but to this grim fortress. He would get her out of it. He did not, even now, trust himself to stay here with her after that access of unsatisfied rage. Nor did he want to win her by drugging her senses with pleasure as he had done last night.

A new pride had come to him and a new honesty, though he did not recognize it as that; he thought it was only what he now said: 'For God's sake, let us get our heads clear on the hill!' And he caught her hands and swung her to her feet. 'You'll not stay mewed up in these old stones, my falcon gentle. Will you come out with me?'

'Chained to your wrist?' she asked, with a little desperate gasp of laughter in her relief at his change of mood.

'Aye, as a falcon gentle should be. Do you think I'd dare let you out of my grasp now? I'll carry you on the Night Hawk, as I did when I brought you here before – if you will come,' he added humbly, for she was hesitating, and he saw her exhaustion and her fear. 'You can trust yourself to me on my horse better than in this room.'

She felt that he too was helpless. What could they ever do to escape each other?

'We may ride to the ends of the world, we'll find no outgate from ourselves.'

'No, but we'll find fresh air and a cool forehead,' he said with a sudden return of his practical common sense.

So she rode again in his arms through the long twilight of the Northern spring, with the North Sea glimmering before them. The sight and sound of that grey stormy ocean was art and part of all his homes, as was the bare hillside on which they rode, the wind whistling in their faces, the thud of his horse's hoofs beneath them, throbbing through her body and his, the very pulse of his life and hers. For more than an hour they did not talk at all, but heard only the long rippling cry of the curlews and scream of the gulls, then, as they neared the cliffs, the shouting and the shattering of the waves below. The sky faded but did not thicken; the huge rocks of the Bass and Tantallon stood up like storm-clouds in that strange dark light, pure and cold, that seemed of the distilled essence of sky and water.

When at last he spoke he told her of his forebears, the Vikings who had come to Scotland in ships painted like dragons from over the North Sea, pirates who had discovered the Americas long centuries before Columbus, and had voyaged in their frail galleys among the outland terrors of the Curdled Ocean.

'You speak as if you had been of them.'

'Well, I expect a man is what is in his blood.'

She too could remember the immense open solitude of those Northern seas where the islands lay very near the edge of the world. Some kind rough sailor voice had told her that, when she had sailed to France at five years old on the Northern route, all round the coast of Scotland, the Orkneys and Hebrides.

'Do you remember how I wanted to travel back that way from France and you would not let me? It was almost our first real quarrel!'

He drew in his breath sharply at her return to the old

intimacy. She never noticed it out here on the hillside where it was so natural for them to be together.

'What is it?' she asked.

'I thought I had driven you away for ever, but I don't think now that that can be. You are myself, and I am you. It's true there's no outgate, for I cannot escape myself, nor can you. Do you still wish it?'

'I wish only that we were on a boat together alone, to sail out over the sea at the wind's will.'

*　　*　　*

The next day, which was Saturday, the doors of Gordon's rooms were unlocked. Bothwell came in. His friend stood up and faced him. They both looked older.

'I have won her consent,' said Bothwell. 'Your guards are dismissed. You are free. Will you go, or stay with me?'

'I will go,' said Gordon, for once the more practical of the two, 'and get Jean to hurry on the divorce.'

CHAPTER TWENTY-NINE

THEY HAD ten days in peace at Dunbar; that was the length of time that it was reckoned afterwards, and they shortened even that, saying 'it passed in a moment'. But a moment, or a thousand years, both were true, and they knew it.

The little gold-starred watch, that Etienne Hubert had made years ago for her in Rouen, lay on her table now at Dunbar; so it had lain at Holyrood, ticking out the agonizing moments till Darnley should come in, late and drunk, for the dinner in his honour; so it had lain at Glasgow when she had sat writing through the night in his sickroom, hearing that procession of minutes trip by her in the silence, seeing their faces all turned towards her, and not one look back. That army of ants was carrying away the world piecemeal; Darnley was dead, their enemies were gathering together against them at Stirling; soon they would have to go to Edinburgh and face the outside world.

But it could not carry away the life that was now, had been, and would always be their life together. That lay behind time, beyond the world, outside their bodies; never to be invaded by chance or enmity; no more to be measured by her watch than happiness by the false measure of possession, whether of wealth, of power, or even of the loved person.

All their earlier friendship, growing into love, was with them now, and made part of this rapture of sheer living that swept both spirit and body into a white-hot flame of ecstasy. In that flame there shone out precious things that had lain hidden in the secret unconscious life that they had shared. 'You are myself,' he had said, and she had known it long before, when she rode to him at Hermitage and spoke to him with a dozen others standing by, and rode back to Jedburgh to pass through the gates of death, and they opened the window to let her spirit go free out over the moonlit hills. She had passed then beyond the agony of dying, into the bliss of death, deeper than sleep, making her one with all that she loved in him. And he, so nearly dead of his wounds, had then found that same release of spirit, clouded since in his furious passions of baffled desire and fear lest he should never get her; but now, in this sudden breathless calm, remembered.

He saw with new eyes the miracle of her body and of his, and of the happiness he gave her. With new eyes he saw the spring, as she wandered to and fro discovering fresh buds in this wind-blown garden above the yellow seaweed and wet rocks; and the wind tossed her song towards him:

'Thank love, that list ye to his mercies call!'

Her hands were full of early forget-me-not found in a sheltered corner below the red sandstone wall; she came running to him, and in both their minds there rose the vision of a garden in France six years ago when all the ground before them had shimmered with those pale blue flowers. There too they had had 'almost their first quarrel' (they could never decide which was really the first) there in the Jardin de l'Amour Repenti.

He took her hands with the flowers in them between his own, and said, 'I swear you shall never repent my love.'

That trust was kept, for she never did repent it.

CHAPTER THIRTY

H E   L E D her horse into Edinburgh himself, on foot and bareheaded, and all his men had laid aside their pikes to show she was not now a prisoner. That was on the 6th of May, and the date of their wedding was fixed for the 15th, the Thursday of the following week. The banns were to be called on Sunday at St Giles'. But Mr Craig, the minister there during Mr John

Knox's continued absence during these dangerous times, refused to read them. Instead, he publicly charged Bothwell from the pulpit with ravishing the Queen and keeping her in captivity; with adultery; arranging a collusive divorce with his wife; and finally with the murder of the King, 'which this marriage will confirm'. He was sent for to the Castle, and repeated his charge to Bothwell's face for as long as he was allowed to speak; at last the Earl cut him short and sent him away, but in full liberty. Craig's courage was great, but it was obvious that he had no need to fear tyranny.

After that it was plain that the position must be cleared, and Mary made a public statement that though Bothwell had abducted her against her will, yet she had now come to give her free consent to the marriage. Bothwell advised her to write this too to her friend the Bishop of Dunblane, who was about to go to France.

'Clear the decks. I'll not have it said there was any collusion on your part over the abduction, as in Jean's over the divorce. Tell him the truth and lay the blame where it is due, on me. It's true it was a rape – admit it. Tell him too, if you will, I'd do it again!'

She did not quite say that, but tried to make it as respectable as she could for the old Bishop's eyes, and Bothwell laughed at what she wrote, but let it go.

He would have none of the titles or appanages of a king such as she had showered on Darnley.

'Give me only what was mine for centuries, which your father, that "Good Poor Man's King and murderer of the nobles", took away. My blood was Prince of Orkney when Malcolm Canmore reigned in Scotland and the Stewarts hadn't yet left Brittany.'

That last laughing flare-up of his old grudge against her family was appeased when she sat on her throne under the Canopy of State in the Abbey of Holyrood. The Gordon bore the crown before her, the heralds in coat armour passed in procession, and a blue banner showed Bothwell's arms with the addition of a golden ship with silver sails on an azure sea for Orkney; Bothwell himself in a furred red robe was led in between two earls and knelt before her: she placed the coronet for Duke of Orkney and Lord of Shetland on his head with her own hands, as once she had placed a crown of silver paper and named him Lord of Misrule. *Absit omen!* Would his present followers turn and rend him?

There was little time or money for pageantry, or wedding presents either. Instead, Mary gladly suggested melting down the gold font sent by Queen Elizabeth at the Christening, for pay for the beginning of a small regular army that Bothwell was anxious to form – 'a better trinket than any other I could give you!'

And in sharp contrast to all the sumptuous clothes and jewels she had lavished on Darnley at their wedding, he would accept from her nothing but some fur off an old cloak of her mother's to put on his dressing-gown; and one superb enamelled and pearl chain – not for himself, but to send as the accustomed gift to his stepson, Prince James.

To his sister Jan, who had just been remarried to the Earl of Caithness' eldest son, she gave a crimson satin and sequinned petticoat and a dashing coat of black taffeta and silver, at the same time recommending her nephew and godson, Jan's fatherless little boy, Francis, to the Abbey of Kelso.

But for her own trousseau, and then not till the last minute, she had some new linings put on an old gown and petticoat, and an old black velvet done up with some gold braid. 'Do you mind?' she asked, thinking of her first wedding, when she had worn a silver train twelve yards long, and a single jewel in her tiara was worth £500,000.

'What do I care for your clothes, now I can see you lovelier than I ever have, in none!' But he had heard the wistful note in her voice, and added, kissing her, 'It's you, my dearling, who must miss your gauds – you who once set the fashion for them through France and Europe.'

She looked up into his face and laughed. 'What do I care? I'd follow you to the end of the world in a white petticoat!'

It was not always so happy between them. He was madly jealous, 'the most jealous man alive', complained the many men whom she had treated in delightful casual fashion as her intimate friends; 'so beastly and suspicious that he would not let her look at anybody, or anybody look at her, though he knew that she liked her pleasure as well as anybody'.

The high-spirited, pleasure-loving girl who had no check on her personal conduct ever since she was eighteen years old, naturally took this very badly; there were some violent scenes in which they stormed at each other like thunder and lightning. Often he made her cry, hated himself for it, swore that he knew her to be true to him, and then found that hot flare of rage take him in the throat again, longing to kill Lethington for laughing

425

with her, Melville for gossiping with her, Gordon for walking in silence with her, John Hamilton because she gave him a horse, and all of them for looking at her, 'as though they'd eat you – yes, even old Mother Tabbyskin thirsty to be lapping cream'.

She saw nothing in such looks; she had had them from childhood, and would have thought something had gone wrong if any man did not look at her in a kind of eager or pensive dream.

'It is nothing to the way they paid court to me in France,' and *that* made it no better; he was as jealous as he was proud that her young charm had dazzled the most brilliantly civilized Court in Europe.

'And I am not civilized, I suppose. I can read Latin and talk French and Danish and write a better hand than most, but I can never give you what your fine French scholars and poets did – I who would give you the whole world if I could.'

'And then lock me up so that no man should ever see me!'

It was true – but so was the other.

'There is a torment in love, I think,' he said, with a puzzled humility strange in him. 'I have waited too long for you, and now I can never have enough. Sometimes I fear we'll not have the time.'

'We have all time. Nothing can part us now.'

'A pretty fancy!' he said bitterly, then caught her to him and swore that it was true – not fate itself could part them now.

Fear for her heightened the tension. He insisted on armed guards before her chamber door, and was watchful of whomsoever approached her. He felt he scarcely dared breathe until the marriage contract was signed the day before the wedding. It mentioned the nomination by 'the most part of the nobility' of 'the noble prince, now Duke of Orkney' as bridegroom to the Queen, in view of his 'magnanimity, courage and constant truth which has preserved Her Majesty's person from great dangers'. A clause was inserted by his orders that all documents should be signed by both Queen and Duke, and none by the Duke alone.

So there it was, signed now, and for a moment he could relax at ease as he sat drinking with Gordon after supper on the eve of the wedding. The Envoy, Sir James Melville, whose bright little eyes a year ago had spied out Elizabeth's discomfort at the birth of Mary's son, interrupted them with a congratulatory visit, but the Duke, with dangerous urbanity, had quickly got rid of him by progressively bawdy talk until the correct Melville went off to lodge his protest – in his diary.

'So much for our squeamish busybody!' Bothwell remarked

with satisfaction as he leaned back in his chair. 'His brother has just gone to England, and I'm pretty certain it's to ask English aid against us. Melville himself has been tampering with Balfour and advising him not to give up his temporary command of Edinburgh Castle. I don't trust Balfour – a bludgeon-faced lawyer.'

'Why then,' asked the Gordon in his deliberate way, 'did you take the command from Sir James Cockburn? Was it because he fired the guns on you when you galloped the Queen past the Castle rock?'

'God no! He'd heard she'd been captured and carried off, he was quite right to fire on me. He's getting his reward, for I'm appointing him Controller of the Customs, a job he's long been asking for.'

'Still, what need was there to give the Castle to Balfour?'

'The worst need in the world – blackmail. He asked for the temporary command and I had to shut his mouth till the wedding was over. I know enough to swing him ten times over, but he's been clever enough to leave no proofs, trust the lawyer for that! But *he* knew — ' He put back his head and poured what was left in his glass down his throat, then rapped the glass back on the table and added quickly. 'Well, it wouldn't do if he chose the wedding eve, this very evening, to tell the Queen who lit the fuse of the gunpowder that blew up the Old Provost's House at Kirk o' Field!'

'Who did?'

'Myself, of course,' said Bothwell.

There was silence for a minute. He poured out more wine for them both with a steady hand, but Gordon's shook a little as he raised his glass to his lips. Then he said, 'But you did not put the powder there?'

The Hepburn was hurt. '*Would* I lay down a cellarful of gunpowder to blow up a man – which didn't, as it happened, kill him after all? I'd have done the job with a knife, and far better. No, you know what we all agreed upon, that as soon as he was divorced he should be arrested for treason and conveniently killed in the scuffle. All very neat and respectable. But I must needs go and spoil it by losing my temper!'

It was a blessed relief to be telling this to Gordon at last. He did not like his reason for keeping it from him before, but he told that too. 'I was afraid you wouldn't back this marriage if you knew.'

And then he told what he had done on that February night of

427

Carnival Sunday, when he, with a few of his followers, had gone down to investigate at Kirk o' Field. He had found Sir James Balfour near the outside door into the cells, and questioned him searchingly. Balfour, seeing the game was up, had ratted and admitted there was a plot to blow up the Queen and leaders of her Government and set Darnley on the throne. Bothwell had insisted on seeing the cellars himself. There lay the proof of the story in the barrels of gunpowder that had been dragged during the day from the vaults of the adjoining empty house, through the connecting cellar doors. And upstairs lay Darnley, who was to escape in time on his famous 'great horses' through the postern gate and get off scot-free from the effects of his treachery.

Not if Bothwell knew it! He'd pay Darnley in his own coin and hoist him with his own powder! He lit the fuse himself. It took some time to burn. Impatient, he returned to the house to hurry it up, and at that moment the train took fire, and Jock Hepburn threw him back just in time to prevent the house falling on him. That pause had given Darnley time to smell the burning fuse and dash out of the house into the South garden – only to be met there by his Douglas kinsmen. They had come on a separate murder plot against him. It was certain now that they had done the actual killing; but it was Bothwell's firing of the gunpowder that sent him into their hands.

Ever since that night he had cursed himself, not for his crime, but his superfluous folly.

'I'd meant to kill him, God knows, unless someone else did the job for me. That I knew to be best, because of the Queen. There were so many others determined to have his life. I had only to sit still and wait!'

'The one thing you could not do – not when you saw red. No,' Gordon repeated slowly. 'God set you the one thing you could not do.'

'I'd have excused Him for that if He hadn't set me a nest of rats to deal with. They turn so fast to attack their allies, it's a marvel they don't bite off their own tails.'

The coalition forming against him at Stirling included practically all those lords who had recently signed his bond to support him in his marriage. But now they had just signed another, 'by the faith and truth in their bodies, to put the Queen at liberty and punish the murderer of the King'.

'A lot of good wine was wasted in getting them to sign mine first! And now they say it wasn't even the wine, but that I had two hundred hagbutters outside the doors of Ainslie's tavern to put the fear of God into them, and so they signed "for peril of their lives"!'

'At Ainslie's? But they dined here at Holyrood, not at Ainslie's. All the Palace saw and heard it, and that there were no guards.'

'What does that matter to them? Twenty-eight lies make a truth. Their sole idea of society is to sign a bond together to kill someone, and then another to kill the man who did it.'

The Stirling coalition had arranged a novel form of propaganda, a play showing the 'Murder of Darnley and the Fate of Bothwell' – which fate was hanging, so vividly performed that the actor who represented Bothwell was all but strangled in good earnest.

Bothwell told this with savage amusement, but Gordon took it strangely. 'A play to catch the conscience,' he said slowly, 'a play within the play of our tangled lives. What if those lives themselves should be nothing but a play, acted to give sport to God?'

This blasphemy was too much for his 'blasphemous and irreverent' friend.

'If I thought that, I'd worship the Devil outright, as fools say I do.'

Gordon was pursuing his own thought.

'You are both the hero and the villain of it. The Queen is your victim, but you too are one – love's victims both of you, and a terrible beauty is born of this union, though few will have eyes to see it.'

Bothwell's joke on this description of his possible progeny faded in uneasiness on Gordon's account. He had noticed the strained look in his eyes as he signed the marriage contract with the other lords this morning; it had struck him then that he had been growing even more remote from his fellow-men these last days. Was Gordon to lose his wits for love of the Queen, as Arran had done? A stab of dismay shot through him at the notion, but he thrust it quickly from him. The cases were clean different; Arran would have gone mad anyway, but Gordon had a sound brain, afflicted only with too much imagination. He loved the Queen; this was a bad time for him.

He got up and laid a hand on his shoulder and said, 'We're all three of us love's victims, I think, one way or t'other, but none of us would have it otherwise.'

*   *   *

They were married now; however morally irregular the proceedings, she was legally his: nothing could alter that. In spite of drinking late with Gordon the night before, he had been up before dawn on the day, so anxious was he to be on guard against anything that might even now prevent the ceremony. All that he found was one more placard on the gates of the Palace, a scholar's this time, for it was a line from Ovid that he recognized from his schooldays: *'Mense malas maio nubere vulgus ait.'*

> *They say*
> *That wantons marry*
> *In the month of May.*

He tore it down, and went to meet the Queen, who was ready for him by four o'clock. The wedding took place in the Great Hall at Holyrood, performed by the Protestant Bishop of Orkney and attended by a large number of nobles, both Protestant and Catholic; the Primate of Scotland and the Bishops of Ross and Dunblane representing the Catholic clergy, although Bothwell had insisted on the Protestant ceremony. It had cost him a half-day's quarrel with the Queen; she had had to salve both conscience and pride by showing him her assurance to France that though she had had to give in to her husband in this, 'she would never leave her Church for any man on earth'.

She must have seen or been told of that last detestable placard, for that evening after the public banquet he found her reading Malory's 'Morte d'Arthur', and as he leaned over her shoulder to look at it, she took his hand and pointed his finger to the words: 'It giveth unto all lovers courage, that lusty month of May – and lovers then call again to their mind old gentleness and old service. Therefore all ye that be lovers call unto your remembrance the month of May like as did Queen Guinevere, for while she lived she was a true lover and therefore she had a good end.'

'And yet,' said she, 'men called Queen Guinevere a wanton too, and would have burned her for her love.'

For answer he in turn took her hand and led it farther down the page to the words: 'anon we shall deface and lay apart true love for little or nought, that cost much thing; this is no wisdom nor stability, but it is feebleness of nature and great disworship'.

'Let those bawdy tom-cats scatter their filth on the walls! The great gentleman who wrote this book long ago knew more about you than they do. And people will know it again, for time is the mother of truth.'

She laid her cheek down upon his hand. 'You have come to my help always when I had need of you, as Launcelot did to Guinevere – I want all to know the truth about you.'

She felt that hard lean hand go rigid under her cheek. 'Leave me out of it,' he said gruffly.

*　　　*　　　*

They were 'quiet and merry together', so people observed when they went out; the gossips noticed an absurd little scene when he walked beside her, bare-headed in respect, and she snatched the cap from his hand, laughing, and clapped it on his head.

There was a water pageant at Leith, and she watched him ride at the ring in a tourney, and conduct a sham fight with those precious new troops, the five hundred horse and two hundred foot he had added to her guard of two hundred hagbutters, which were costing them more than their few simple shows.

As the month came to an end, and June danced in on them in showers of blown fruit blossom and gusts of flying rain and sudden sunshine, they seemed to have been married for years, so natural and inevitable was it that they should now be riding out together every day, sleeping in each other's arms at night, dining informally with the citizens, who were increasingly friendly, planning and working together at the business of the State. For the sheer luxury of the contrast she would remember how difficult it was to get Darnley to give the smallest show of interest in such business, though demanding absolute power in it.

James Hepburn attended all five Council meetings in the week following the wedding. He at once overhauled the arrangements for the Council sessions, tightening up the number of attendances necessary, and hurried through a fresh Act against the false coinage from abroad that was being imported to 'the great scathe and detriment of the commonweal'. 'I mayn't understand the Exchequer like your Michael Wily,' he told Mary, 'but this I do know, that the falsifying of money will lead to the ruin of the State. That red-haired vixen on the English throne is blamed for parsimony, but with money going rotten everywhere there will come a time when she, or her successors, can no longer keep the country going on it – and that she knows, even better than her Ministers.'

He had great plans too for the navy. The world was opening so wide and fast, a whole new continent piecing itself together, bit by bit, and were the Scots to be left mewed up in their half of this old island while the English made fresh hunting-grounds in the mighty river of Plate, and ranged along the coasts of Chili and Peru and all the backside of Nova Hispania?

Would they ever have time enough to carry out all they hoped? No matter; their hope was the greatest part of it. So Mary believed. That was why some years ago she had had those strange words embroidered on her Canopy of State: 'In my End is my Beginning'.

His most difficult and delicate job was to announce the marriage to the Courts of France and England. Mr Secretary Lethington, anxiously conciliatory, offered his subtle pen for the purpose, but James Hepburn preferred to write unaided to his brother monarchs. 'Now for ourselves,' he wrote to France, 'somewhat we speak though briefly. We cannot marvel indeed that this marriage, and the rumour that preceded it, appear right strange to you. The blame indeed we must confess and underlie, in so far as some things may appear omitted in cere- monies and counsel-taking as otherwise ought to have been done.'

This under-statement he read out with a quick glance at Mary, and was glad to see her smile. She laid her hand on his at the next sentence. 'Her Majesty might well have married with men of greater birth and estimation, but never with one more affectionately inclined to do her honour and service.'

Was this so unsuitable a 'kinsman' for Charles IX of France and the Cardinal of Lorraine? The bold candour of his words, their simple and unconscious dignity, struck her as so manly as to be indeed kingly.

To the English Queen he admitted that he knew her to have been offended with him, yet allowed no trace in his letter of the servility that was almost a formula in such cases; neither was there any hint of arrogance; he merely mentioned 'the mis- reports of my unfriends', and declared himself 'careful to see your two Majesties' amity and intelligence continued by all good offices'.

'But it will never make amends to her, or to you either, for that unlucky remark that you two Queens wouldn't make one honest woman!'

'I think now,' she said, 'that one honest woman is worth more than two Queens. You say the false currency of money will bring ruin to the State. I say that false political ideas will bring even worse. I believe Machiavelli to have been not only a villain

432

but a fool, though it may take hundreds of years to prove him so. To make friends, that is the only sane policy.'

'Aye – with a standing army to back it!'

* * *

Gordon's doubt had been justified. Balfour had politely refused the diplomatic overtures to make him give up his command of the Castle of Edinburgh. He still had the power to turn informer against him to the Queen, and Bothwell dared not take the risk of her learning from anyone else what he would give the world to hide from her for ever. So he himself now told her, as he had told Gordon, the whole truth of himself and Darnley's death.

She sat very still. Only her fingers moved a little, pulling at a ring. At last she said in a dazed voice, 'I think I've known it all along. Ever since that morning you told me so roughly of his death. But I *would* not know.' And then presently, 'You said at Seton you did not kill him — ' she raised her eyes as she spoke, and then again fell silent, looking at that lean rugged face. She saw how the hair had thinned and turned grey on the temples, the eyes sunk deep in their sockets, yet their fiery glance always on the alert. She had known how the tension of the last few months had told on him; now for the first time she knew how great that tension had been, and sought desperately to lighten it. 'It was true,' she said, 'you did not. It was not the explosion that killed him.'

Bothwell gave a somewhat dubious grunt. 'That's what I said to myself, of course. But the main thing was that I couldn't tell you that I was his murderer when I was asking you to marry me.'

At one stroke his innate, almost brutal honesty had stripped her of all the pitiful defences she was trying to build up round them. Once before, while dancing with him in a crowded ballroom, she had felt she was alone with him in all the world, with not a single ally, human or divine.

And now that fleeting vision had come true.

She gave a terrible cry. 'I am married to my husband's murderer – nothing can alter that, not all the reasons for it. You killed him, and within three months you married me. All the world will think you did it for that.'

'So I would have, and for that alone, if there'd been no other way to get you. You cannot look on him as your husband – he'd twice plotted your destruction.'

'The world doesn't know that. He was allowed to clear himself of the Rizzio murder. No evidence can be brought of the international plot. All Europe will condemn me.'

'Let them, as long as you hold Scotland, and we *will* hold it.'

His bravado could give her no comfort. The weakness of despair had fallen on her. She knew now how desperate her cause must look to all men. But to God, who had seen into their hearts from the beginning, seen what she half saw and shut her eyes to – to God her cause must have been abandoned long ago. The maimed rites of their marriage, as they seemed to her, held not even in a church but the Great Hall, like any other secular business of the State, were justified; for how could she ever have looked for God's blessing on their union?

'We are lost – lost,' she cried, and her head fell on the table, on her clenched frantic hands. He bent over her and tried to raise her, but she would not look at him. To his horror, he found her clutching at his dagger to turn it on herself. He wrenched it from her and flung it away.

Even in her frenzy she was generous, for she cried that she was as guilty as he; 'I hated him – I longed for his death. I had murder in my heart.'

He could do nothing with her, for she could not bear him near her, and cried that Darnley's strangled body would now always lie between them. At that, despair seized him too, but in fury; he cursed Darnley, and himself.

What he could not do to quiet her was done at last by her lifelong training in good manners. There were visitors at Holyrood; she had to go and welcome them; he saw her pull herself together, compose her face into a mask of courtesy and go downstairs, a changed woman; yet able to smile and speak the right compliments, ask the right questions, and above all show that warm friendliness, that natural intimacy, that made every man think he alone was the one whom the Queen really wished to see. Often that gift had made him storm at her for a born wanton; now that even her coquetry expressed her courage, he could have worshipped her for it.

They got through that evening somehow, though it lasted a lifetime.

That night when he came to her, he stood with his back against the door, not daring to advance, and said, 'That I did it, I cannot care for that – I am glad that I did my own work instead of leaving it to others. But I cheated you. I ought to have told you before our marriage. I knew that, and I wouldn't do it, for if I had, you would never have married me.'

He saw the slight figure in her white draperies sitting on the bed, her face turned towards him, but her eyes strange and blank as they had been all the evening.

He said, 'I cheated you into this. If you cannot bear it, I must and will free you. It will be easy, for many people believe that you are still my prisoner and that that is why I keep guards about you. I have only to confess that I got your consent by force.'

He turned to go, his hands blundering with the latch, thick and blind, but as he did so, there came a rushing movement behind him, her hands were on his arm, her eyes were looking at him, seeing him, they were alive, aflame.

'I thank God you did not tell me!' she said, 'and if God will not hear me, then I thank love. If I suffer for it to the end of my life, I have had more happiness with you than many have ever dreamed of.'

CHAPTER THIRTY-ONE

JAMES, EARL OF MORAY, sat looking down his long nose at the papers that Mr George Buchanan had laid before him. They were not State papers. One batch of them bore the intriguing title 'The Detection of Mary Stewart', and read rather like one of the more lurid modern Italian novels. But James showed no sign of entertainment; his nose seemed to grow longer and longer as he perused it, and at last he laid it down with the remark, 'I could wish, Mr Buchanan, that your logic were equal to your Latin.'

He flicked the pages over with a disdainful finger. 'I asked you to find what matter you could against the Queen, and you have, I grant you, raked up enough mud to blacken a dozen women. But while working on the principle that mud sticks if you throw enough of it, you seem to have overlooked the fact that the one half of this mud obliterates the other half.'

Mr Buchanan's red-rimmed, sensitive little eyes blinked furiously. He felt as raw as if he were again a novice awaiting judgement on his first manuscript. A literary rival had lately described him in the vigorous style of the time as a 'bawdy fellow' and 'dunghill puddle and sink of filth'; he wondered if his pure-minded patron had been influenced by this adverse criticism.

'*Qui tetigerit picem* —' he began.

'I have no concern with your indecency,' was the chill reply, 'but your inconsistency. Your statements contradict each other, sometimes even on the same page. You describe Bothwell as a brutal ravisher who brought the Queen back into Edinburgh "under a vain pretence of liberty". And *yet* you say the Queen begged him to carry her off! Then, too, you quote Lethington, Melville and others who describe his unreasonable jealousy of her. And *yet* you say he is utterly indifferent to her! The two things are incompatible.'

'But he has corresponded with, even visited Lady Jean at Crichton.'

'Naturally, since he bribed her with Crichton and has had to settle up his estate there. Also he must be trying to get hold of that Dispensation for her marriage to him, which could prove the Queen's illegal.'

The inexorable finger flicked on, turning the pages backwards. James noted that Mary had ridden headlong to Bothwell at Hermitage last October in order to indulge her bodily lust (with a desperately wounded man, in the space of two hours, and in the presence of her Secretary of State and other witnesses, including James himself); that her intrigue with him had begun last September (when she was still very ill from childbirth) in Edinburgh at Exchequer House, which Bothwell had visited through the garden door from Mr Chalmers' house, and after an initial rape (though closely surrounded by her attendant ladies, courtiers and guards) so pleased her that she continually sent for him through Lady Reres, a fat aged bawd (Lady Reres being young enough to act as wet-nurse to the baby Prince, whom she was suckling at the time, miles away at Stirling); that last August she had taken a pleasure cruise up the Forth to Alloa with Bothwell and his pirate crew, 'such company as no honest man, let alone woman, would adventure life or honour among' —

'But good God, man!' exclaimed James, startled for once into an oath, 'do you realize what you have written? The Lord Bothwell was never on the boat. And I – I was there!'

It was a most unfortunate slip. Mr Buchanan promised it should be rectified, and mentally resolved that it should not. It was the first time he had tried his hand on a story of this sort, and he had enjoyed it; his subject had run away with him. He was not going to have his fine literary frenzy cramped by these pedantic demands for accuracy.

James threw down the manuscript.

'This scrap-heap of obscene rubbish is worse than useless. It can be disproved by everyone in Scotland.'

'But not abroad,' said Mr Buchanan slyly.

'True.' James pulled his long nose thoughtfully. 'It may have some effect here. The French will listen to a bawdy tale where they will ignore serious argument.'

He looked disapprovingly through the window at the line of coquettish little blue pointed roofs, clear indication of a light-minded race. It would be very good to be back again in Scotland.

But he would not venture it yet, not while Bothwell was still in the saddle. Buchanan had brought a note from Kirkaldy of Grange, the best soldier in the rebel coalition, asking him to come over and head it. But, as he now explained at some length in answer, he did more good in directing the operations from behind the scenes. Propaganda was by far the most important weapon in this affair.

'Aye,' chuckled Mr Buchanan, 'she'd not be the first to die of scandal!'

James said rather hurriedly, 'Those placards are doing good work out here. I have ordered several batches of them to be printed in London and sent to Paris. But it is the campaign at home that matters most.'

Mr Buchanan assured him that that was well in hand. 'Mr Knox, though also at a distance, is directing it. All the ministers are preaching hot cannons. God will avenge Himself on the country if it does not punish the guilty. Already the farmers are saying there is foot-rot among this year's lambs. The women in particular are being worked up into a frenzy; they are told that the Queen "has no more liberty, nor privilege, to commit murder and adultery than any other private person". That is excellent, it touches their rights.' He gave a hearty laugh. 'Why should they deny themselves the pleasure of adultery and hus-band-murder if the Queen may indulge herself?'

James pondered this outburst of the democratic spirit. He did not want it pushed to extremes. The punishment for husband-murder was for the woman to be burnt alive.

'The ministers are being very austere,' was his comment. Then he roused himself to what was the really important issue. 'Still, they are on the right course. What we must have is a moral Crusade, the country roused to righteous fury, and marching as one man to put down this reign of blood and indecency.'

'But there's been no blood.'

The Lord James regarded him sternly.

'Have you forgotten the murder of the King?' he demanded.

Buchanan's dropped jaw increased his resemblance to an em-purpled codfish. He knew – and James knew that he knew – that the ruling nobles had agreed to murder Darnley; he had a shrewd guess that James himself had ordered Archie Douglas and his band of cut-throats down to Kirk o' Field for that very purpose. But his political training helped him to a quick recovery.

'Then,' he said brightly, 'we must show that the Queen lured the King to Kirk o' Field so that Bothwell should blow up his house with gunpowder.'

'Certainly. The trouble is' – James fingered his thin black beard – 'it is difficult to explain such a violent and self-advertising method of murder, when she could have easily poisoned him without anyone being the wiser. Nor is it conceivable that she should have arranged an abduction which would obviously play into the hands of Bothwell's enemies. There are many who are ready and willing to believe her a criminal. But no one who has spoken with her will believe her a fool.'

'Ah, but the folly of women in love — ' Buchanan began indulgently.

'I did not know, Mr Buchanan, that you had experience of the subject.'

The great Latinist had not just made a very trying Channel crossing in order to be insulted. His heavy black-robed figure surged up out of his chair with a volcanic dignity that swept half his papers on the floor. Fortunately at that moment a French servant entered with a tray of refreshments. James waved a lofty hand towards it.

'Eat, if you are inclined.'

Buchanan ate and drank with uneasy greed under the other's abstemious eye.

Thawed by excellent Bordeaux, he saw the folly of offending his patron, and remembered that he had been promised the office of Moderator of the Kirk (worth £500 a year) if he helped him to power. So he sought how to give better satisfaction than by his severely criticized detective story, and told him that a few papers belonging to Bothwell had just been – well – got hold of, which might come in handy. They had not at first struck him as of importance, being principally love-letters and poems, 'very bad', from one or two women, and a brief note about business

438

from the Queen. But it had since occurred to him that if only they could get hold of more of the Queen's letters, a profitable combination might be made of both sets of correspondence, which could be worked up to prove her guilt. To use passages of her own composition would make them far more convincing; incriminating sentences could be added, and the whole copied out by someone who had long experience of the Queen's easy handwriting.

'I have heard nothing of this matter, nor do I wish to hear,' said James severely.

'But Mr Secretary Lethington may be more interested.'

'Lethington?' exclaimed James. 'But he is now on the side of the Queen.'

'The Chameleon,' replied the scholar, ponderously playful, 'changes colour to suit his surroundings. So does the Secretary bird. The combination that the Lords are forming against Bothwell is now strong enough for Lethington to join it. Just before I sailed he left the Court, and without taking his leave. And,' he continued, warming to his theme as he gulped down another glass of Bordeaux, 'I showed him the note from the Queen among my Lord Bothwell's papers. It is curt and businesslike, but it could be used almost as it stands. It is dated only "this Saturday", and is unaddressed, but was evidently written at Craigmillar shortly before the Christening. Put the word "Glasgow" at the top, and it will suggest that it is written during her visit to the King there, just before he went to Kirk o' Field, and that she was luring him to his doom.'

He balanced a top-heavy lump of butter on his crust of delicious French bread and crammed it into his mouth. James avoided looking at that gobbling turkey-cock and his pleasure in this atrocious suggestion.

His cold and indeterminate mind had long used religion as a tool. Now the weapon turned against him; for an instant he wondered what it should profit him if he gained the whole world and lost his own soul.

But there was no room for the old simple standards of Christianity in modern statecraft. Not for him the luxury of the private virtues, gratitude, pity, personal honour. He must make the great abnegation and devote, not only his life but his virtue to the public good.

In pained resignation to the Divine Will he said, 'My sister was once the creature on earth dearest to me.' (Yes, his eyes had once filled with tears for her. Never had they done that for anyone else.) 'If she would renounce this godless marriage, I would find it in my heart to love her as much as ever I did. But if she do not, she must pay the price of her guilt, for she *must* be guilty. She *is* guilty. Prove it then. I do not wish to know how. But as for this filthy trash, this "Detection of Mary Stewart",' – and he spat out the title like a foul taste, his scorn for his vile tools making some amends to him for his use of them – 'it may pass muster in England or the Continent, but I advise you to suppress it in Scotland, where no one now living can believe a word of it.'

The indignant author flung out a black-sleeved arm in a gesture as portentous as that of Mr Knox. 'I,' he prophesied, 'write for posterity.'

CHAPTER THIRTY-TWO

'THE DANCE has begun!' said Bothwell, and she laughed with him in sheer light-heartedness. This was no dancing floor. They stood on the battlements of Borthwick Castle and saw the dark masses of horsemen on the horizon advancing against them.

'We're in luck,' she cried. 'An hour or two later, the Castle would have been surrounded, and you cut off from me.'

'I'd have got through to you somehow. There must be at least a thousand altogether over there.'

She strained her eyes into the distance, but good as they were they could not equal his hawk gaze, trained from childhood in Border warfare. Like a hawk he looked on this eyrie of Borthwick tower, his head held high, his eyes fierce and cool as they watched the oncoming of his enemies. A sick spasm beset her at the thought of how nearly he might have fallen into their hands, but she quickly fought it down.

He had brought her here after just a month at Edinburgh, on the day that Lethington's desertion had given the first quiet signal that it was no longer safe for the Queen to stay at Holyrood Palace. Bothwell had already summoned all 'lords, landed men and substantial yeomen' to muster at Melrose on the 15th of June with arms and a fortnight's provisions, on the usual pretext of disciplinary measures on the Border. But things were moving too fast to wait for the muster. So he placed the Queen in this massive stronghold, under the guardianship of the loyal Lord Borthwick and his men, and the addition of his own artillery and a hundred and fifty of his two hundred hagbutters.

With the remaining fifty he himself left the Castle quietly at night, the first time that he had left her since he had carried her off to Dunbar, and rode to Melrose to collect any early comers that might have come in, in response to the summons for next week. But no one had yet done so; all he could do in the time was to leave his fifty hagbutters and their Captain there to hurry things up as best they might, and ride back with only one or two men to Borthwick.

No sooner had he sat down to eat and drink and tell Mary his adventures than one of his outposts came galloping up with news of an army of cavalry advancing on them from the north. Down went their knives, and up they sprang from the table to scamper up the stone stairs to the top of the tower. They gazed out over the wide rolling sweep of country, all sparkling and waving with the feathery shoots of the young bracken in the mid-day sunshine, and saw those dark clouds moving over the northern skyline towards them, and laughed, for the dance had begun, and they were in luck, since they were together.

Once before, Bothwell had stood on this tower, and given a roar of laughter to see his house and barns of Crichton go up in smoke; and now he flung his arm round Mary. 'Here's a prettier piece of Venetian glass than any that Arran's troopers smashed!' he cried as he kissed her.

They ran downstairs, clatter clatter as they went round and round, faster and faster, the two of them whirling together down that dark spiral stair. Whisht! Here they were at the bottom, she the Queen again, and he the Commander, calling in a stern purposeful voice for Lord Borthwick, and marching off with him to see to the defences of the Castle.

Within the hour a party of troopers came galloping up hell for leather and battered on the gates, shouting that the rebels were after them.

'We are loyal. Let us in or we are all dead men,' they called, but Bothwell insisted on having a leisurely look at them first.

'Just what I thought – young Kerr of Cessford's among them. That's the gay lad who helped murder his kinsman, the old Abbot of Kelso, for knowing too much about the Bastard. Well, the Hepburns have always known too much about the Crabbed Kerrs!'

Mary thought his suspicions very harsh, but they were soon proved right. As the main body of horsemen came up under the

Earl of Morton, whose huge bulk and orange-coloured whiskers were plainly to be seen in their midst, the Kerrs drew back and joined them, showing that their cry for succour had been nothing but a ruse to enter the Castle.

That having failed, there was nothing for their army to do but fire their muskets in futile attack against those enormous stones; then, coming nearer, they yelled insults at the Duke of Orkney and his Queen. Mary slipped away and appeared on the tower to answer them and appeal to her subjects' loyalty – to Bothwell's fury when he found how she had exposed herself to their fire. He himself was even more reckless, for so enraged was he by their taunts, daring him to come out and support his challenge to single combat, that his men had to hold him back from rushing out to pull Morton's whiskers.

Midsummer madness had fallen on both of them, old Lord Borthwick declared when they at last sat down to eat a ravenous supper after their interrupted dinner. He was a bad-tempered old man, mortally sick of a disreputable disease. Now as he watched these two young things in their hour of danger and desperate venture joking together so light-heartedly, he felt that if his whole life were given to him again, he would gladly throw it all away for one hour of such happiness as now danced like a flame between them.

'Midsummer madness,' he growled with some reason later that night when James Hepburn made one of his lightning decisions. The Castle could stand a siege indefinitely, but what use would that be to the Queen? He must get out to raise an army for her, and lead it in the field.

How the devil did he hope to cut his way out through what had now proved to be over twelve hundred men? And Lord Borthwick started counting up the numbers he could take from the garrison, but Bothwell cut him short.

'One is all I'll take, if that. But who was that great gaunt hag I saw with a bundle in the courtyard?'

'Muckle Meg the laundress!'

'She'll do. I'll go out in her hooded cloak, now while it's raining and pit-murk. I've done it before.'

Yes, he'd done it before in Sandybed's kitchen, turning the spit in Big Bess's clothes; he'd watched from Borthwick tower before; he had lived through all this before and was living it over again now – but now there was Mary beside him, and for the first time he knew what it was to feel another's agony as his own.

It had been bad enough for her to see him leave the shelter of the Castle with only fifty men, but that was safety itself compared with this mad escapade, going blindly out into the night alone among all those wolves who had howled for his blood. She touched his chamois-leather sleeve, it felt like a nice horse, much smoother than his hand, and that she dared not touch, not with this new piercing knowledge that the least joint of his little finger was more precious to her than her whole body.

'Let me be the one you'll take. I can disguise myself too – I've done it.'

He could not let her take so hideous a risk; she must stay in the practically impregnable safety of the Castle till he came with reinforcements to rescue her. She turned away, fighting back the tears and words that might even now bind him here to her: she must again be brave on his account, not only on her own. And she laughed as he swung the old woman's cloak round him, stooped in admirable disguise of his height, and hobbled out into the darkness.

One of his men went too, at a little distance, and was caught. But Bothwell, though within a stone's throw of him, got through safely to Haddington. From their prisoner the besiegers learned that the Duke of Orkney was no longer at Borthwick. His absence put them in an awkward position; if they stayed, they could no longer pretend that they were acting only against him and not against the Queen.

So the next morning those inside the Castle saw their enemies raise the siege and march off. Mary at once sent word to Bothwell that they had gone, and she would join him that very night, at a little distance from the Castle, in case of any spies on the lookout for his return there.

But she reckoned without her host. Lord Borthwick swore explosively that she had been put in his charge and should not leave it on any such prank. His 'duty to his Sovereign'? God's blood, his duty was to his friend, not to a skittering lass who'd got a man to look after her at last, but too late, it seemed, to learn how to obey him. 'A pretty time I'd have of it from that mad young fellow of yours if any harm came to you! You'll stay in your room, Madam, under lock and key if there's another word on the matter!'

And his thunderous roar was followed by a succession of oaths. Mary assured him smilingly of her complete submission, ran upstairs at top speed, shut the door behind her, flung out her arms and cried, 'Quick, my girls! Get a suit of young Willie

Crookston's clothes from him. He's about my size. And tell him not to breathe a word of it.'

That night, when most in the Castle were asleep, there stole out of her room a gallant young page with a big hat jammed down over a face alight with mischief, accompanied by a couple of quaking girls, also in their stockinged feet, and with bundles of sheets in their arms. Noiselessly they felt their way down the turret stair and into the great banqueting hall. This was as far as they could descend without danger of meeting any of the servants or the guards below. The window was twenty-eight feet from the ground, but Mary was not to be daunted by that – Bothwell had jumped out of a first-floor window into a lion-pit for her, and she was quite prepared to do as much by him. They knotted the sheets together and one end of them to an enormous table-leg; then she climbed out of the window down this improvised rope, waved a hand to the two girls above who were drawing up the sheets, slipped through the low postern gate through which Bothwell had escaped, and was soon outside the walls in open country.

Now she had to find the rendezvous she had appointed, the Devil's Pool, farther down Borthwick Water, about a mile from the Castle; she had thought she could not miss it, she had only to follow the water. But to do so at night, through seeping bogs and tangled thickets, stumbling and scrambling and sinking up to her knees, was harder than she had foreseen, though luckily it was a perfect June night, the long-drawn-out Northern twilight never deepening into real darkness. The twisted trees crouched against it like the black forms of waiting foes; at any point they might turn into them, spring out, and capture her.

Yet she scarcely felt fear, so lovely was the night, so certain was she of finding her lover in it, blown towards him on the shifting summer breeze as naturally and inevitably as the pollen dust of trees to find its mate. Only when at last she saw something stir among them, her heart gave a leap of panic terror. What if it should not be himself?

But it was.

He leaped from his saddle, seized her, hugged her, shook her, swore at her. 'How *dared* you do it? I'd have stopped it if there'd been time – there wasn't. Yet I've been waiting here for ever!'

It was the first time she had ever seen him shaken, and she scolded him for it as soon as she could get her breath in his grip – 'an old campaigner like you to lose your nerve with a bit of night-watching, and here am I on my first trial as a moss-trooper! – would I make a good one for your troop?'

'It's what I thought the first moment I clapped eyes on you: you ought to have been a boy.'

'So my father said, and cursed me for not being one: "The Devil take it!" he said. *Has* the Devil taken me?' And she clung to him laughing as he swung her up into his arms, then mounted her in the saddle (a man's) of a close-cropped cob that he had led with him. He himself was on the Night Hawk.

He had sent word to his hagbutters to meet him at Dunbar with all the men they could muster. And now they themselves rode there together yet again, for the third time.

'We shall ride together again,' he had promised her that at Hermitage. And tonight yet again they went a-roving by the light of the moon; they saw it drift in and out of the calm, towering clouds, cast changing shadows down the deep glens, and through its flying formless glimpses moved on together, two passing shadows, conscious that they were one.

The glow-worms were all out over Crichton Moor, innumerable tiny points of greenish light beneath their feet, and the vast spangled sky above their heads. The bright dark was theirs. 'We're riding over the stars,' she said, laughing low in her delight.

They did not speak again till they were clear of this part, where outposts might be lurking. They rode slow and carefully, the creak of their saddles and the thud of their horses' hoofs making a monotonous rhythm among the wandering sounds of the moorland that followed the fitful outbreak of the wind among the hills, sounds that to the shepherds who lived on these haunted moors were the echo of bells and bridle-rings of elfin riders making

> *Merry and merry and twice so merry*
> *By the ae light o' the moon.*

No good thing was it to meet such riders. A cow-herd had been thrown into Borthwick Water in spate by the dwellers on the Fairy Knowe. That great mound now raised its head above them, and then the mighty tumulus of the Mote where the Druids had once assembled; the broad brows of the Lammermuir Hills were like snow mountains when the moon shone on them. They rode over their lower slopes, far away now from the Borthwick country and Crichton, where the Lady Jean slept in her curtained bed ('hugging that Dispensation under her pillow, no doubt', he thought with a snort of mirth – as if any parchment could divide them now!).

She could not believe that this magic night would ever end; she knew that it would not, that they would always ride together over the stars.

The air tasted salt. They had left the hills and reached the low turf-covered slopes that stretched towards the sea, all silvergrey under the spangling of dew; some cattle stirring in the dawn-mist shone faintly luminous like dim planets moving through the gleaming haze. Birds darted silently here and there in dark flashes, intent and secret.

He spoke of his confidence in subduing Scotland for her, of her hopes of England.

She said, 'I would not care if I lost them both, so long as I can follow you.'

She said, 'I'll not have one man killed to keep me Queen. If they don't want me, let them go, and we'll make another kingdom. You have Orkney and Shetland. Let us build our fleet and create an Empire of the Waves – and never see Edinburgh again!'

He scouted the notion; were all the hopes she had had ever since her childhood of three great kingdoms, France or Spain added to Scotland and England, to dwindle now to those wild islands in the far North?

But he shared her pleasure in the thought; as she longed to see his swiftness and desperate will mastering the winds and tempests, so he knew her to be as proper a Queen of the Sea as of the hills. She had a royal quality of freedom. 'You are free as air,' he said.

'And why not King and Queen of that too? My grandfather believed that men could learn to fly, and kept a mechanic to discover how.'

'Aye, and he nearly broke his neck jumping off the rock of Stirling in the attempt!'

'That doesn't show it won't be made again. Whatever man has dreamed, that he will do. And our dreams will live on after us when we are dead.'

He turned his head to look at her delicate face lifted against the unearthly light.

'You should make death proud,' he said. 'I think you look on it as our marriage night.'

When they looked ahead again, they saw the sea. She checked

her cob, rising in her stirrups with a cry. 'Look! It has come true! I saw it like this in your arms when you first brought me to Dunbar.'

Yes, she had seen it then like this; the solan geese rising and swirling in dizzying tangle about the pearl-white rock of the Bass; while still the sea slept dull and pewter-coloured, their wings caught that light that was over the edge of the world; they turned to fire as the first long arm of the sunrise all but touched the last lingering finger of the sunset.

There before them was the meaning of her strange overword: 'In my End is my Beginning.'

CHAPTER THIRTY-THREE

ALL THAT morning he worked, while Mary went to bed in one of his shirts. When she woke, nearly at mid-day, the sun was on her face and he was sitting beside her.

'You have been here all the time, haven't you?'

He hooted with indignant laughter and told her all he had done: sending out her royal summons to all loyal subjects between the ages of sixteen and sixty to arm themselves and come instantly to her support; receiving a deputation of burgesses from Edinburgh 'who hope to keep a foot in both camps till they see which wins'; getting messengers through to Gordon and Balfour in Edinburgh; enlisting the fishermen from Crail farther up the coast to run a service for them in case they were beleaguered here at Dunbar.

She stretched her arms above her ruffled head, the great linen sleeves falling away from their round childish curves, and gave him an odd little important smile and told him that she was certain she was with child.

There was no holding him at this news; he caught her up in that absurd flapping shirt, so much too big for her, and walked about the room with her in his arms, and crowed his triumph as though he were the only man in the world worthy to beget a child on her.

'Aye, there's the blood of the proud Guise and the fine, sad Stewart in you, too much so for strength. But now you'll have Border blood to thicken the brew, and it's many a grand lad I'll sire on you!'

But there were to be no more pranks such as last night's climb from an upper window and roaming the country by herself.

And he cursed the agitation he had given her at Borthwick. From now on she must be calm and placid.

It was a pity that such excellent physician's injunctions had to be accompanied by marching orders. But they could not leave the rebels to make more headway. These had entered Edinburgh under the Earls of Morton, Mar and Atholl, without much difficulty, and at once issued a proclamation, summoning the citizens to arms. But the people did not join as was expected. It looked as though the rebellion might fade away for lack of support.

On top of this good news came better from Balfour. If Bothwell and the Queen would march at once on Edinburgh, he would turn the Castle guns on the rebels as they marched out of the city gates. But he would have to come to terms with them if Bothwell remained inactive at Dunbar. It was the last thing Bothwell had wanted to do; but now that he knew Mary to be with child, he seriously considered their staying in this sea-fortress. They were safe at Dunbar.

She scouted the notion; a pretty pair of Sovereigns they'd be to stay skulking here instead of marching out to claim their kingdom! He had said it would never do to let themselves be bottled up in a castle instead of taking the field.

He nodded, but frowned, biting his knuckle as he always did when doubtful. Balfour was the crux of the matter. He did not trust him an inch. Might his message be a lure to get them out of their stronghold? But then there was a mysterious move of Gordon's; he had joined him in the Castle, and must know of this offer, had probably prompted it. Yes, that must be the real reason of the message, that Gordon had established his power over Balfour and would force him to carry out his promise loyally.

So they rode out of Dunbar with as many moss-troopers as they had collected in under twenty-nine hours, their two hundred hagbutters, sixty cavalry regulars and the three siege guns that Bothwell had installed at Dunbar and made convertible into field batteries. All the way along their line of march, loyalists fell in and swelled their ranks; Border lairds, and Geordie Seton and Yester and old Borthwick, who scolded her ferociously for the trick she'd played on him.

It would not do for her to ride at the head of her troops in boy's dress, so she had borrowed some clothes at Dunbar: a full kilted scarlet skirt which because of her slender height only reached just below her knees, white linen sleeves tied back in points, and a velvet hat that proved too hot to wear, so she carried it in her hand. The simple dress made her look ridiculously young, not at all like the burgher's wife from whom it had been borrowed, but rather his tall young daughter riding to school, so Bothwell told her, and chaffed her outrageously for the loss of her snood, that Scottish symbol of maidenhood. She wished she could have made a more queenly show before her hastily mustered troops; Scotland never gave her a chance to show off, she said, thinking of her first entry on a borrowed nag. But he swore that she looked far lovelier without her gauds: she was never meant to be caged up in stiff State robes; and she remembered the French courtiers had thought her 'barbaric' Highland costume more becoming than her most exquisite dresses.

'So you'll believe me, if a Frenchman said it first!'

That night they halted at Seton House. It was very late and he made her go straight to bed, and there lay with her wrapped in his arms until she fell asleep, her small round head tucked into his breast, the slight body relaxed against his in utter peace, a part of him even more than when awake and fervent with the rapture of his desire. Was it true, then, what she seemed to believe, that in death lay the fullest possession? For the first time he was torn with the poignant mystery of love. He watched the gentle breathing of her parted lips, the dusky gold of her eyelashes lying so still on her pale cheeks. He would not kiss her lest the vehemence of his tenderness should wake her, but stole away from her to rise and dress before dawn.

And he had to get her up again after only a few hours in bed to join him on horseback by five o'clock, for he had had intelligence that the rebels, reinforced with Highland troops, had marched out of Edinburgh at two that morning – with impunity it seemed, for he could not hear that the Castle guns had ever been fired on them. What then was Gordon doing? He sent another messenger to him. Those that they had sent previously might well have fallen into enemy hands; so, almost certainly, had Gordon's to him.

Another baffling factor was that the very important reinforcements of Lord Fleming and Lord John Hamilton had not yet arrived. They had been in touch with each other the previous day and had sent word to Bothwell that they were on their way to him. They would certainly come up some time during the morning, and he sent word back of his line of march to meet the rebels near Musselburgh.

He seemed to be everywhere at once as he rode up and down inspecting his ranks, and Mary noted his look of sardonic vigilance as he came back to her, furious that the most part of them had not brought rations as commanded, not even their waterbottles, a serious matter on a grilling day. It was Sunday the 15th of June, the day he had appointed nearly a fortnight ago for the Border muster at Melrose.

Spring and summer seemed to have stood still this year, for them to pack a lifetime within a few short weeks. But now – 'I am not living just now,' she thought, 'I am only waiting till I live again.'

She sat blinking her hot eyelids to gaze at the hills that were painted flat like pale blue shadows against the noonday heat haze. The hours had droned and dozed on, and still nothing happened; still no sign of Fleming and John Hamilton, still no message from Gordon, still no encounter with the enemy; only a persistent manoeuvring of both armies all the morning for the advantage of the ground.

Bothwell had proved his quality as a general by securing his position on the high ground of Carberry Hill, and placing his field guns so that they commanded the slope up which the enemy would have to advance to the attack, after first crossing the small ravine and burn at the foot of the hill. The position was excellent for defence, and defence only was possible, for the Queen was utterly determined that she should not have the onus of opening battle on her subjects. It was sound politically, he had to admit, though grudgingly, for honourable scruples were of small use with a dishonourable enemy.

'My honour's my own,' she told him, 'I can't change it to suit my enemy.'

The military argument for the defensive, while waiting for his allies, had more force with him, for the confederate lords with all their retainers had the advantage in numbers, and particularly in trained cavalry. He saw too some foreign troops among them, slow solid mercenaries from the Rhine whom he had recognized by their odd custom of keeping 'the better knee' bared for climbing escalades. But despite their strength, their army sat on the hillside opposite about a mile away and seemed in no hurry to attack. As they were on the western hill they were no doubt waiting for the afternoon, so that Bothwell's army should have the disadvantage of the sun in its eyes.

But there might be a thunderstorm – if only there were a

thunderstorm! It was hot enough for one in all conscience; the sun had a brazen glare; a few stiffly carved clouds were moving up against the parching wind; the heat had that foreboding quality that waits for the roll of thunder and the livid flash of lightning. It was part of this strange unnatural day that after half a dozen cold stormy Scottish summers she should sit on a hillside on a rock that was almost too hot to bear, and pray for a tempest!

The water question was serious in other ways, for some of the men had slunk off to drink from the burn upstream, and got captured by the enemy. She was astonished to see how coolly Bothwell could keep his temper over this, since it was done and therefore inevitable. He had brought her water, but she felt that no amount of it would quench her thirst: her lips and throat were dry and sore, and she could eat nothing, though she pretended she had done so; any food brought on a sick and dizzy sensation. Whatever she did, she would *not* faint this day. She was feeling ill from the first effects of pregnancy; but neither that nor her anxiety depressed her; she was strung up to a point where courage comes without effort, and all the men who saw and spoke with her believed her entirely confident.

She sat under the small shade afforded by the great Standard of Scotland, its red lion rampant against a yellow ground. Everything round her was red and yellow – the brass on the guns flashing in front of her, the hillside burning with the gold of whin and broom and buttercups, with scarlet sorrel and bright red bilberry and the young shoots of the bracken stretching out their uncrumpling rusty-coloured fists. At her feet was a jewelled mosaic of minute flowers, as brilliant as any in the Italian paintings at home, and no taller than the short sheep-nibbled turf; flaming pink, blue far brighter than the sky, and the tiny astonished faces of wild pansies; all these glories of the unconsidered grass made her long to enjoy them here alone, instead of staring at them hour after hour, waiting for the enemy to attack, while the sun slipped farther to the west, and still the storm did not break, either in the air or between the hostile armies.

What was happening beneath the bright surface of this summer day? The men were grumbling, doubtful; she saw it in their faces. She believed that many had slipped away as well as that small company at the burn. She was conscious of their uneasy murmurs all round her though she could not hear them, conscious of both heaviness and excitement, a foreboding

451

worse than thunder in the air. Something was going on that she did not know about; she would have to know soon. As she rose and walked a little way to stretch her cramped legs, she knew.

Right in front of the vanguard of their army, the enemy had planted their banner, stretched between two pikes in the full light of the sun. It was a large sheet painted in garish colours with figures more than life-size – the naked corpse of a man lying under a tree, and beside him a crowned infant with the words coming out of his mouth, 'Judge and avenge my cause, O Lord.'

Bothwell jeered at it when next he came up from among his troops.

'No men worth their salt would bother their heads about that. It's their thirst that's worrying them, and the delay; but I can't afford to lose the advantage of this ground by attacking, not until Fleming and John Hamilton come up.'

She was certain at that moment that they would not come, and that he was too. But he seemed entirely calm and cheerful. She somehow forced herself to feel it too, since that was the best way to seem it, but deep down she could not lightly dismiss this new form of propaganda. It was crude but effective, striking at the very roots of an army's belief in victory, the belief that it has a right to victory. Ordeal by combat was still practised as a form of justice on the Border, in the faith that God would give conquest to the innocent.

She suggested riding with him again down the ranks to talk with the men; this had already had great effect, for her air of careless courage had obviously heartened them at the time. He welcomed it gladly if she were not too tired, he asked anxiously, and then broke off with an exclamation of delight – 'By the faith of my body, they're on the move at last!'

A troop of the enemy's horse, about fifty of them, were trotting down the opposite hill, past their outposts, and coming towards them. But no general movement followed, and he saw at once that they were intending a parley.

The French Ambassador, Philibert Du Croc, had come to try and bring about a peaceful settlement, and with him Monsieur d'Oysel, who had lately revisited Scotland with diplomatic messages from Paris for his chief. He had been personally gratified to find that Bothwell had taken to heart his reproaches on being 'all stone', and had refuted them by ravishing the Queen, having ('it is seen') first murdered the King. He thought Mary far more *sympathique* as the probable murderess of an odious husband than as the sexually cold 'mermaid' he had first believed her; and was inclined to congratulate Bothwell on her having paid him the greatest compliment possible in a woman.

Du Croc shared his opinion, though not so affectionately, and more from a natural tendency, cultivated by Catherine de Medici's diplomacy, to believe the worst of everyone.

He was as dry, crisp, small, neat and elegant as his companion was large, loose, unbuttoned and fluid, flapping his handkerchief about his moist face, the steam exuding from his bald head whenever he uncovered it, like the dawn mist rising from a rosy mountain.

The two Frenchmen were brought to the Queen while Bothwell was busy again with his troops, and Du Croc, after kissing her hand with brisk reverence, spoke of the horrors of civil war, how shocking a thing it would be if so good a Princess as herself should wage battle against her devoted subjects.

'They have an odd way of showing their devotion,' she replied coolly, looking with tired eyes at the straight small figure before her, dapper and dark, that cut up the sunlight into a dozen smart points and angles as he waved that sharply peaked hat in his hand. How dared he advise her not to make war on her subjects, when she had twice forgiven them for making war on her?

And this was the third time.

Her nobles, he said, longed to surrender and kneel before her, if she would separate from the Duke of Orkney.

'Monsieur,' said the Queen, 'you must have heard the Proclamation of these lords, publishing their intentions. Three are acknowledged. The first, "to deliver me from the captivity and prison in which I am kept by the Earl of Bothwell"; the second, "to avenge the death of the King"; the third, "to save the Prince".

'It is a strange impudence to pretend to "save the Prince", who is now in their hands alone; stranger, to "avenge the King's death", of which they one and all acquitted the Duke of Orkney; strangest of all, to deliver me, who am no prisoner, and to insist on separating me from the very man whom they vowed, in writing, to support in marrying me. The harangues have one object only, to confuse and disturb the public mind. But I cannot believe they would have effect on the diplomatic.'

And after this severely formal and incisive speech she gave him a sudden smile, so intimate, dazzling and mischievous, that his discomfort was changed in a flash to the discovery that he was the one civilized man to whom she could talk as an equal among a tribe of savages.

He shrugged, but with a world of sympathetic comprehension. 'You know what they are!' he murmured, his eyebrows two acute black angles against the sun.

'I know. Tell them I will overlook everything, on one condition – that they will leave my husband alone.'

'*Their* only condition, Madam, is that you leave him.'

'That,' she said, 'I will never do.'

At that moment Bothwell rode up on his black charger. Du Croc, seeing the look that passed between them, knew that his job was hopeless. They would never give up each other unless – yes, that might possibly work with such types, both passionate and headstrong – they did it for each other's sake.

Bothwell asked straight out, 'What are they at? Am I alone the object of their enmity?'

Du Croc answered, 'The nobles are the Queen's loyal and humble servants, and,' he added in a lower tone that only Bothwell and the Queen could hear, 'your mortal enemies.'

But Bothwell was determined that his men should hear, and his answer rang out through the scorching air:

'Their hatred is from envy of my favour. Fortune is free to any who can win her. There is not a man of them but wishes himself in my place.'

He looked at the girl standing there in the short scarlet skirt, her bright hair waving in the hot breeze, and never had she felt herself so much a Queen. His pride in her brought tears to her eyes; she longed to tell him that they were because she was so happy.

He was not the only one to see them. 'The Queen,' said Du Croc, 'is full of goodness. She cannot bear to shed the blood of her subjects.'

'The best way to prevent it,' said Bothwell, 'is for the subjects to return home. Tell them,' he added, 'that if they prefer it to a battle, I will meet any champion of equal rank that they care to send out against me in a single combat.'

'It is what they themselves proposed,' Du Croc replied, 'to send a round dozen such champions, one after the other, so that if the first fail, the twelfth may succeed! I hardly thought it worth while to repeat so impossible a programme.'

The Queen gave a sharp cry. 'They mean to wear you down by a succession of duels till the last can kill you easily!'

'When the Queen and your army, left leaderless,' finished Du Croc, 'would be at their mercy.'

He assured them that he would do his best to negotiate with the rebels by conveying to them the Queen's promise of a free pardon if they would disband. He rode off, d'Oysel accompanying him only to the bottom of the hill. The Ambassador outlined the dispatches he would send by him the next day to the King of France. Du Croc was taking long views; he thought it likely that Bothwell would have to leave Scotland, and in that case it would be excellent to secure his services for France.

'I shall feel bound to acknowledge to His Majesty that the Duke seems to me a great captain, showing undaunted confidence in the face of appalling difficulties. He is a gay and skilful leader. I have taken real pleasure in watching him and his movements this day, for he sees how determined his enemies are against him, he knows he cannot count on the half of his men, yet he shows not the least sign of weakness or wavering.'

'What has happened to his accursed allies?' d'Oysel let out on a perspiring groan. 'There's not a single lord of note on his side.'

'I'd rate his chances all the higher for that, since it leaves him sole command. But he hasn't the men. And those he has, don't see why they should fight to make him King.'

D'Oysel repeated his words to Bothwell on his return; they aroused an uncomfortable echo of Mary's warnings against the marriage. He had thought that nothing could make his 'lambs' turn against him. Now he was not sure. D'Oysel pressed the advantage home. 'In any case, you'll never get moss-troopers in inferior numbers to cross a ravine and charge uphill against trained professional soldiers, many of them foreign.'

'Yes, I saw their Cologne blades, curse 'em. But my men don't lack courage – you've seen that in the old wars here.'

'A thousand times, my friend. But you have not the half of them here. And this is not a war fought for any issue that's clear or acceptable to them. They are not being invaded; they hear that the Queen is in no danger; the lords declare their devotion to her; their only demand is that she shall separate from you. Well then – separate!'

Bothwell swung round on him, but d'Oysel was waving his fat hands in explanatory gesture. 'It is for the moment only. Give yourself time. Get into touch with Gordon – he holds most of the Highlands – with the Hamiltons and Fleming.'

'I *was* in touch. I sent them my line of march. I've been

expecting them every moment. I know well I've not got the strength to attack until they come up. And Gordon's in Edinburgh Castle – I don't know what it means – only I know Gordon wouldn't have failed me.'

D'Oysel flapped a vast shrug that threatened to heave his melting bulk out of his clothes. He saw now that his friend's cool gay courage, that had so impressed Du Croc, was hiding a desperate perplexity, and he admired it the more for that. The young man was no fool; he could see as plainly as his older and more experienced friend that he was playing a losing game. Far better to leave it, then, till a better moment.

'They have sworn to safeguard the Queen,' he said. 'Let her go with them now. She may be able to secure the Prince, and then they can no longer hold him as a hostage over her. In a week or two you will have assembled your allies and more troops.'

'I'll never trust her to them. Something must be done. I'll pull the men together somehow. They've begun to drift away fast – it's this cursed inaction, it's sapping them.'

D'Oysel saw in his angry eyes a glimpse of the baulked rage that had been steadily eating into his heart during these maddening hours of inaction. But in a flash it disappeared and his voice rang out with the old confidence, now that at last he could make a decisive gesture.

'If I show them a good fight it will put heart into them as nothing else could. Explain that to the Queen. I can't wait.'

Before d'Oysel could expostulate he sprang on to his war-horse, rode to the front of the army, and sent a herald to the enemy's lines with a challenge to single combat.

The other side took a long time finding someone to accept. At last they put forward the professional libeller, James Murray of Purdovis. A bonnet laird (let alone one of his character) was scarcely an equal champion; if Bothwell were to meet his enemies one after the other it was essential to begin with the most important. He named the Earl of Morton for his opponent. Morton accepted, chose the broadsword for his weapon, delayed in coming forward, and finally sent word that he would give up the privilege of the duel to his friend, Lord Lindsay.

As well he as another, said Bothwell, who had not forgotten Lindsay's threat, after Rizzio's murder, to 'cut the Queen in collops'.

She was in sheer panic terror for him; whether he won or

456

lost, it would make no odds, they would all fall on him in a body and hack him to pieces.

Bothwell could believe many things of the confederate lords, but not that they would use the sacred trust of chivalry to cover treachery. Her agony stabbed him but spurred his anger. 'For God's sake, don't try to hold me back from giving battle in the only way that's possible now. I'll not be a coward even for you.'

On that he rode out to the place appointed for the duel, leaving her standing there, dry-eyed and still, all her thoughts trembling into nothing, and the whole hot coloured scene round her a white void.

Would he ever come back? If only he would come back she would do anything, anything, she would leave him for the time, go with the lords as they asked, do anything in the world that would bring this hopeless impasse to an end.

Why were they still waiting? Why did the duel not begin? What in the world was Lindsay doing? She stared across at the opposite hill, at the solid phalanxes of lances glittering like sharp white flames, at the hosts of men dark against the light of the sinking sun. What *was* Lindsay doing? He had taken off his armour – an odd preliminary to a duel! Now he was kneeling down in front of the whole army. He was saying his prayers – shouting them rather. The loud harsh voice came echoing across the little ravine in gusts of angry sound. She could even distinguish some of the words: 'Mercy of God ... vicious murderer —' and then in a long howl, 'innocent blood of the King.' It went on and on. She wondered if prayers had ever before been used to fight a delaying action. At last they were over, and Lindsay began to rearm with leisurely formality, the Earl of Morton coming forward to buckle on his sword. But still he did not move to the appointed place.

Instead, his army began to advance, and at the same time a large body of their horse, about two hundred, under Kirkaldy of Grange, left the main body and proceeded on a flanking movement which would hem in the loyal army between cross-fires in the ravine. At once she sent a messenger to Grange to demand a parley, and he arrived before her just as Bothwell galloped up, in a black fury.

He had been appealing to his men, urging them to fight, and found he could do nothing with them. The preparations for the duel had been nothing but a feint on the enemy's part to make their dispositions of troops under cover of it, and cause further

457

disheartening delay. The rot that had begun earlier in the day had now set in irretrievably. He was as mad with rage as a baited bull, and at sight of Grange, who had treacherously begun this flanking movement during the truce appointed for the duel, was blind with desire for his blood. He went straight for him, drawing his sword. Grange's men quickly intervened, while the Queen flung herself on Bothwell's sword-arm.

'He has come here under safeguard,' she cried.

'Under the safeguard of his own treachery!' and to Grange he shouted, 'Fight the duel your leaders have shirked. It was put up as a blind. You shall have it in earnest.'

Grange flatly refused to fight. He had come under safe-conduct to discuss terms with the Queen. He knelt to her, protested his real loyalty, and that all the nobles on his side would certainly surrender and kneel before her if she would separate from the Duke. He bore their offer to agree that the Duke should ride off the field without pursuit, and his army be allowed to depart unharmed.

He was obviously sincere; in the eyes of this rough grizzled soldier was the look that Mary had seen again and again, of a man surprised and captured by her unawares.

While he spoke with her, d'Oysel pleaded with Bothwell that he should give up this now hopeless contest for her sake – 'the hardest thing to a galliard like yourself, my friend, that you can do. But none who knows you can doubt your courage. And nothing else can now be done to preserve her safety.'

Bothwell stared with bloodshot eyes while the sun beat fiercely off his armour. Sweating, dog-tired, he had reached the end of the meanest battle ever *not* fought in history, and knew that his enemies would accuse him of sheltering behind his wife. 'Let them call me a coward! Those here know the contrary. But it is for her – *her* – to go alone with them! What may they not do to her before I can get hold of her again?'

'We are in a civilized country. She is their Queen. They have sworn to serve and respect her. They have given their oath that their only quarrel is against you.'

The Queen left Grange and joined her entreaties to d'Oysel's arguments. This was the only thing that could be done, and she was glad of it, for she could never bear it if a battle were fought that might have been spared. She would win the rebel lords round to her again as she had twice done before. She said nothing of her chief motive, her terror for himself.

There was a sudden movement near them. A boy had

scrambled up out of some whin bushes, torn and breathless. He told Bothwell that he had run nearly all the way from Edinburgh with a message from the Castle.

'From *whom* in the Castle?' rapped out the eager demand.

'From the Earl of Huntly.'

From Gordon at last!

The message was brief. It said only that Gavin and Archbishop Hamilton (both loyalists) were with Gordon in the Castle, and the three would now have the command of it.

That settled it. Gordon would be able to keep a check on the rebels' action towards the Queen, and he himself would soon be in touch with him. So he agreed at last to the Queen's acceptance of the terms, and insisted that Grange should give her a formal safe-conduct as well as his sworn oath.

Then he took his leave of her in the sight of the two armies, thousands of men, every one of whose lives were spared by this decision, but whose blood would be shed in useless slaughter if the courage of the two lovers failed at the supreme test.

It nearly failed. They clung together with many long kisses and did not know how to part, and wild fancies flashed through both their desperate hearts of hurling themselves on their enemies and cutting a way through, either to life or death, it did not matter which, as long as it was together. But he drove them away, forced both her and himself to be cool and sensible, told her, 'It won't be for long,' and she nodded, unable to speak, but knowing out of an even deeper faith that their parting would not be for long.

The clank of arms and harness all round them, the thousands of staring eyes, the brassy glare of those outrageous guns, invented that men should kill each other the more inhumanly because more blindly and impersonally than any previous weapon – all the heat and noise and aching sunlight of this dreadful day-dream would pass away; and the night come.

'We shall have moonlight again,' she whispered on a little broken smile.

She looked so lovely even now with the tears running down her white drawn face, and in that funny childish, almost peasant dress; there was a kind of fragile splendour about her that filled his heart with anguished dread. How could he hope to keep so exquisite a creature?

'You will be true to me?' he asked. 'Swear that you will be true.'

She put her hands between his. 'I will go with you to the

459

world's end.' Yes, whatever that end might be, together or apart. 'I am with you, I am part of you, always.'

D'Oysel came to tell them that they must not delay. The sun was going down. Grange had warned him that he could not answer for his men if the Duke's army stayed longer. The Frenchman was weeping unashamedly. 'It is true, my friend,' he said to Bothwell. 'All men envy you, and always will.'

He drew back while Bothwell kissed Mary once more. 'It won't be for long,' he said again; then put her resolutely from him and walked slowly towards his charger, not once turning his head.

She stood looking after him as he leaped into the saddle and rode east towards Dunbar, followed by about a dozen friends, their shadows stretching before them on the moor that glowed in the sunset.

They rode up the side of a hill where a single pine stood on the crest, its trunk as red as flame beneath its night-black branches. His shadow touched that flaming tree, his black charger reached the crest, then he drew rein for an instant, turned and looked back; then was gone.

'NO MORE A-ROVING'

HE NEVER saw her again.

That is why this story ends there – where their life together ended.

With a treachery which, at that date, had no parallel in history, the confederate lords broke every one of their terms of safe-conduct to the Queen the instant they had her in their power.

They took her, not to Holyrood as they had sworn, to re-instate her in her palace, but to a very old fortified house in the High Street known as the Black Turnpike. They led her there as a prisoner, the banner of Darnley's murdered body held up before her all the way; the route was lengthened so as to lead her past the ruined house of Kirk o' Field, and the soldiers were encouraged to break their ranks to throng round her horse, shouting 'Burn the whore! Burn her! Burn her!'

Kirkaldy of Grange alone tried to restrain them, and rode among them at the risk of his life, laying about him with his sword; but in vain. They were not to be baulked of their sport; nor was the mob of Edinburgh, whose blood-lust had been worked up all that day by the preachers. Prentices, fishwives, loafers and scourings of every nation from the Leith docks had been waiting till ten o'clock that night to see the beautiful 'adulteress and murderess' publicly abased before them. They thronged so thick round her horse that the soldiers had to ride very slowly and in single file; they danced and yelled with laughter to see the Queen's face 'all disfigured with dust and tears'; it seemed at any minute they would tear her from her horse, and to pieces. When at last she was taken into the house they lit bonfires under her window and shrieked that she should be burnt alive.

Her spirit had been unbroken by the treachery of her captors. She had caught Lord Lindsay's hand and swore by it, 'I will have your head for this!'

But that spirit broke before the hideous madness of the mob. She had been without food or shelter from five in the morning; nor did she get any that night; she was put in a room thirteen feet square, without any water to wash her hands or convenience of any kind; her women were kept from her, and the men-at-arms stayed inside the room all night. All night she saw the light of the flames outside leaping on the walls, and heard those horrible cries demanding that she should be thrown to them. Delirium fell on her, and of a curious kind, for she believed that even those wild beasts outside were more human than her captors; she cried to them from her window, as once she had tried to do in captivity at Holyrood, either to kill her outright or to save her. That instinctive trust of hers in the common people was justified; they turned suddenly to pity and indignation, and forced Lethington to go up and visit her when he was trying to pass by her window unobserved, his hat jammed over his eyes.

The lords, 'fearing the anger of the people', moved her secretly from Edinburgh, in the darkness of the following night, to the island fortress in the middle of Loch Leven under the nominal chaperonage of Lord James' mother, the Lady Douglas. Lord Seton got wind of it, and pursued the troops with a body of cavalry, but could not overtake them. At Loch Leven she fell into a practically unconscious state which lasted a fortnight. When she recovered her senses, though still desperately ill, the lords forced their demands on her, but, so Cecil's agent wrote to him, 'though her body be restrained, yet her heart is not dismayed'. She could not be moved by any threats to be divorced 'from a husband with whom she thought to live and die with all the contentment in the world'. If her enemies would let her, she would 'leave her kingdom and dignity and live as a simple demoiselle with him'. But she would 'never consent that he shall fare worse than herself'. And she wrote him a letter, which they seized, calling him 'her dear heart whom she would never forget, nor abandon for absence'.

'Who are your friends?' Bothwell had once asked insolently. She thought now she knew. The Pope said plainly that he would have nothing to do with one who had worked for religious toleration; in France, the two captains, d'Oysel and his old comrade in arms, the gallant Martigues, appealed for three thousand arquebusiers, with which they were certain they could restore her to freedom and power. Catherine de Medici would not allow her son's consent to the plan.

Only Elizabeth showed herself Mary's friend; she refused publicly to believe in the convenient discovery of the incriminating letters of Mary's, of which there was a great deal of talk, but not even copies could yet be shown – 'Rank as stale fish!' was her comment to the Spanish Ambassador. She sent her Envoy,

Sir Nicholas Throckmorton, to Scotland to tell the nobles that whatever Mary's faults, their behaviour was 'strange, unjust and scandalous'.

He found great difficulty in seeing any of the lords. He was never allowed to see the prisoner. He had even to smuggle a letter to her in the scabbard of his messenger's sword, and urged her in it 'for her own sake' to give up her husband. She sent back word that 'she would rather die'. He believed that his presence in the country did indeed save her from being put to death, though it endangered his own life, since the preachers incited the mob to take their own course against him.

For by now that master-demagogue, John Knox, had felt it safe to return, and was once again firmly in the pulpit. He threatened excommunication to all enemies of the Good Lord James; he preached that death itself, even by fire, was too lenient a punishment for the Queen, 'her iniquity deserves more than ten deaths'; he prophesied 'the Great Plague to this whole nation if she is spared'; he prayed God to 'put it into the hearts of the multitude to take the same vengeance upon her that has been taken of Jezebel'.

The multitude took the hint. The Palace of Holyrood was looted, the chapel defiled; its priceless ancient missals made another bonfire.

Lindsay used physical force to make the Queen sign an abdication of her throne to her infant son, but he could not intimidate her by his threats to throw her to the fishes in the loch; nursing her bruised arm, she told him calmly that she did not regard this forced abdication as valid. So did her Keeper of the Seals (Bothwell's kinsman, Thomas Sinclair), who was held down while Lindsay seized his arm to impress the royal seal on the document.

By the end of June Mr Buchanan was given the highest ecclesiastical office in the Scots Kirk, and was later appointed tutor to the little King so as to instruct him in the depravity of his mother and turn him against her. He succeeded.

Posterity has also proved the success of his boast; his scandals have formed the base of ninety per cent. of English and French opinions of Mary Stewart and of Bothwell.

By early August the Lord James returned to Scotland and told his half-sister (by his own account) that she could 'hope for nothing but God's mercy'. Later he relented so far as to think he might save her life; would try to preserve her honour; but for her freedom, she must not hope for it, 'nor was it good for her to have it'. He assumed the Regency, professing great dislike of the responsibility, took charge of his sister's jewels (of which his wife quickly took a still firmer hold) except her famous pearls, which he sold to Elizabeth at reduced prices.

The 'reign of blood and indecency' was over. Not one man had been killed to maintain it.

The reign of the Good Lord James had begun, in an orgy of long-drawn-out executions of the victims who had been filling the torture-chambers since midsummer. They were mostly bonnet lairds, sailors and poor men, servants, tailors. Their confessions regarding the King's murder were extorted by red-hot pincers and hooks, flaying-knives, the rack and the iron boot that crushed the legs to pulp. Even so, the evidence thus produced often proved inconvenient, sometimes even incriminating Lord James; so that it had to be hastily suppressed and the victims hurried to instant trial, sentence and execution, all in the same day. Their broken limbs were packed into wicker baskets and stuck up on the gates of all the chief towns.

Captain Blackadder had to pay with his life, and his brother's, for leaving his wine to gape at a deserted street. Geordie Dalgliesh, Bothwell's tailor, gave the important information that his master was wearing a workaday coat of 'the new sad colour' so as not to spoil his gala Sunday clothes when he went to murder Darnley; this proving inadequate, he tried to stave off further torture by the opportune discovery of a silver casket that held some of Bothwell's papers. Black Mr John Spens got off with his life because he was able to tell his inquisitors where to get hold of two of Bothwell's coffers which contained 'not the least part of his wealth'. The page Paris was kept for months in a dungeon and then tortured, but could not learn to give all the answers satisfactorily, and was hastily hanged without any trial. The Primate Hamilton was executed solely on the evidence of a lighted window on the night of the murder: Black Ormiston, Hay of Talla, Powrie, Wilson and Captain Cullen went to the scaffold, among sixty-two of Bothwell's followers alone.

But the ghost of the fiddler's murderer was not to be appeased by these blood sacrifices. For years to come, the rulers of Scotland walked in terror, each never knowing when his turn would come to be accused by his colleagues of being 'art and part' of the killing of the King, and hurried to a hideous death. 'From discord comes all desolation,' Mary had said; and now they proved it.

The wolves devoured each other. 'Friend' betrayed 'friend'.

The Lord James denounced Lethington when he had no more use for him, and imprisoned him in the Castle of Edinburgh under charge of Kirkaldy of Grange; but Grange, sickened by then of James' and Morton's rule, turned against them, held the Castle with Lethington for the Queen, and struck the last blow in Scotland for the cause that they had formerly betrayed. They had to surrender when Morton poisoned their wells. Lethington took poison rather than face execution. Morton hanged Grange to 'pacify the clamour of the preachers', chiefly John Knox, who had been Grange's greatest friend, but now, while himself dying from the effects of apoplexy, prophesied that Grange, 'whom I have loved so dearly', should be 'hanged in the face of the sun'.

Years later a brother-in-law of Knox accused Morton of the King's murder. Morton was then Regent, and had long held the supreme power, but he too was executed and his red head stuck up on a spike of the Edinburgh Tolbooth.

Darnley's father, Lennox, had been his predecessor in the Regency and, after a few months, had been stabbed in the back.

The Lord James had met his fate much earlier. His reign had lasted barely two and a half years when he was assassinated by a Scots Borderer 'to avenge the shame he had brought on the country'. The shame was his betrayal of the two English Borderers, Thomas Earl of Northumberland and his brother, Sir Henry Percy, who had risen against their own Queen in order to liberate Mary. They escaped across the Border when the rising was put down by Elizabeth with the slaughter in cold blood of eight hundred peasantry; and found refuge among their hereditary foes of the Scottish Border. James outraged their hospitality by handing the English lords over to Elizabeth for execution, and thus put himself beyond the pale of even the lawless ruffians he was accustomed to hang so plentifully. It almost seemed as though the few relics of chivalry they still preserved were a sounder policy than his expediency, when he himself was shot in the street at Linlithgow – 'And we,' cried Knox, 'are left in extreme misery.'

Knox had helped more than any man to put James' party in power, but was powerless to direct it when there. The ministers were poorer under a Protestant Regent than they had been under a Catholic Queen. The nobles plundered the Church livings and threatened to desert it if they did not get their way. Years of civil war, and its resulting famine and then plague, made a desert for many miles round Edinburgh. The substantial citizens that had formed Knox's congregation had to evacuate the city, their houses were wrecked, their trades ruined. It was, as the English Envoy, Lord Hunsdon, observed, 'a pleasant and profitable time for murderers, thieves, and such as live only by the spoils of true men'.

'Extreme misery' – 'this desolation' – was Knox's description of his victory. The last years of his life were soured not only by the public ruin and attempts on his life (an assassin's bullet was fired through his study window), but by the personal attacks of his former friends; many of them turned against him, accused him of cowardice, threatening him with public ignominy at the Kirk Assembly, 'providing he be not fugitive according to his accustomed manner'; of treachery in calling in the English troops 'against his own native country and the liberty thereof'; of blasphemy in speaking of himself as God, and assuming powers of damnation greater than any claimed by a mediaeval Pope.

His cry of misery was such as all her twenty years of imprisonment, and final condemnation to a horrible death, were never able to wring from his victim, Mary. Indignation at her wrongs she showed, and violently; but she never descended to her victor's level of self-pity.

Both she and Bothwell fought as long as they had life and senses. Years of imprisonment could not tame their spirit. They met death unconquered.

The same fate fell on them both that summer. Freedom ended for them both then, and all that was of their life, living – except the hope of it again.

Each had one more flight into free adventure to make, but apart from each other. Together, each flight might well have won success.

Bothwell's lasted till the end of that summer. During that time he made desperate efforts to rescue the Queen, but he had not calculated for such instant and extreme treachery as the lords showed. By hurrying her the next night to an island fortress in the middle of a lake, they secured her from even his daring ingenuity. The other bad surprise for him was the helplessness of Gordon, who had suffered some sort of cerebral stroke, of the same nature as that which had killed his father. He recovered, but he was never again the same man, though it took his friend long to recognize it.

Bothwell had left Dunbar secretly in a fishing-boat and sailed up the Firth of Forth under cover of darkness; within a week of Carberry he rallied more than fifty names of note with their retainers to his side, for now at last they saw the issue clearly. They were not being asked to fight, as they had thought, 'to make James Hepburn King', but to save the Queen. But what they could have done easily before was now too late to do. Her jailers let them know that if any attempt were made at her rescue, then she would most certainly die. This threat of her assassination in prison tied the hands of Bothwell and the loyalists; his enemies' next moves separated them from him. Alarmed at the success he had already made in his campaign, the revolutionary Government now concentrated the whole force of the law and the Kirk against him.

He was outlawed, along with 'thieves, foreigners and wolves', for the crime of killing the King and 'making the Queen promise to marry him, for fear of her life'. This was a remarkable charge, as it flatly contradicted the evidence of collusive abduction in the Casket Letters, which had been 'discovered' ten days previously by the tortured tailor. They were, however, not yet ready for publication – nor ever were, except in 'translations'.

A reward of a thousand crowns was offered for Bothwell's capture, and penalties of death and torture to all who helped him in any way; the continual spectacle of his followers' mangled limbs issuing in baskets from the Tolbooth pointed the warning example. The Lowland lords, even when they remained loyal to Mary, feared to be associated with a man so interdicted; with their retainers, that fear was now being fanned to superstitious terror by threats of God's judgement on the country hissed out from Knox's pulpit.

Bothwell went north to Gordon and succeeded at first in stirring him to interest in his plan to raise a force of Highlanders to make a secret march to the Queen's rescue. But it was no use; Gordon was too ill a man, and soon sank back into the lethargy of his fatalism.

His sister the Lady Jean was now a bosom friend of Lady Agnes, the Lord James' 'long love'. Their tenacity must have been a link in common; both loved and lived long; Jean secured her first love, Sandy Ogilvie of Boyne, many years later as a third husband, and outlived him as well as everybody else in this story. Even as Agnes refused to part with the Queen's jewels she had embezzled, so Jean contrived to keep the castle and lands of Crichton, and its charter-chest, through two successive marriages; kept also, in secret, the Dispensation that would illegitimatize any child of Mary's by Bothwell, not only for the eighty-four years of her life, but for three centuries after her death. Her care was wasted. There was no child.

At the end of July, Mary's doctor recorded her miscarriage at Loch Leven of twins not quite three months gone. Those children that should have been so magnificent, the result of his vigour and her fineness, were destroyed by her terrible experiences before they came to birth. Her only child was that weak-legged abnormal-looking boy by the degenerate Darnley, a changeling who, by some queer anomaly of fate, lived to inherit not only the Crown of his mother's enemy, Elizabeth, but also far more of her qualities, her caution, patience, and love of the crooked and devious ways of diplomacy, than any of his mother's.

Bothwell still had no doubt that he would win Mary to him again; no doubt but that they would have other children together, would together rule their country – or another.

He now thought seriously of that wild fancy of hers on their last ride to Dunbar, that they should 'make another kingdom', an empire of the waves. If he set out to raise something of a fleet, he could scour the seas and get help for the Queen from Sweden or Denmark, until he was strong enough to come down upon Scotland, effect her rescue, and reconquer the country from the coast inwards, as his Viking ancestors had done centuries ago. His hereditary office of Lord High Admiral of Scotland gave him standing among sailors and even pirates; his new titles, but also hereditary in the past, of Duke of Orkney and the Shetland Isles, would have more weight with those remote islanders than his outlawry by the rebel lords; he should have a good chance to recruit his sailors from among their seafaring folk and make use of their harbours. He was in close touch too with the fishermen along the East Coast and *persona grata* with that queer secret brotherhood of theirs, the Free Fishers, invaluable for taking messages along the seaways of Europe.

He stayed with his great-uncle Patrick, the shocking old Bishop of Spynie, while perfecting these plans. This disgraceful old man was now over eighty and looked like a eupeptic white walrus with his enormous snowy moustache and rosy cheeks; his little blue eyes, though sunk in fat, twinkled with unregenerate vitality. He had always felt a proud affection for his young rascal of a great-nephew, which his latest exploits in royal murder and rape had rather increased; when Bothwell had been ruined and imprisoned five years before, he had done his best to help him, and was eager to do so now, quite undeterred by the Government's command in consequence to his tenants, forbidding them to pay their rents.

But his sins had had awkward consequences for his great-nephew, in the shape of rather more than a dozen bastards, most of them jealous of their encroaching cousin. With surprising lack of invention the Bishop had not found enough names to go round, or else he forgot the ones he had baptized before, and so Bothwell was confronted with three angry Patricks, two brace of Johns and Agneses, three Janets, three Adams, and a George. George and two of the Patricks took active measures and plotted together with the Captain of the garrison and an English spy to murder Bothwell. Lethington gave hearty encouragement to the scheme, and even the correct Sir Nicholas Throckmorton showed a cautious interest in it, but disapproved of the plotters' gratuitous suggestion that while they were about it they might as well murder 'the ould busshope' too. But the only man killed was George, for Bothwell and his followers put up a fierce fight, drove his attackers out of the Castle, and replaced the garrison with his own men. This hurt his great-uncle's feelings, since he did not know of the intention against his own life harboured by his unnatural son.

Bothwell felt that he might have outstayed his welcome. Fortunately he was now ready to leave, having collected five small ships and three hundred men to man them – good enough for a beginning. One of the ships he sent down the coast to collect munitions and stores from Dunbar, and take letters to his friends in the South; but the captain, Jock Hepburn, who had pulled him back from the explosion at Kirk o' Field, was caught and executed. Only one regret could he be made to utter. 'I had ships provided,' he said on the scaffold, where so many fellow-victims had sobbed and moaned their remorse, 'but I could not escape.'

The news gave a savage zest to Bothwell's piracy of a Scots vessel carrying provisions of food for the Lord James; he 'masterfully and violently' seized it and its gear. Two more he chartered in proper legal fashion from their owners, a couple of Hanseatic merchants; one, the *Pelican*, from Bremen, he saw lading fish at Sumburgh Head and liked, a tall two-masted ship, well furnished with anti-pirate guns. He now had seven ships and got them over safely to the Orkneys, though the Government had detailed some of their fleet to intercept him, and tried to forestall him by warning the islanders against him. In spite of that, they gave him a warm welcome, and 'began to lean on him'. His plan, only three weeks old, and interrupted by the domestic troubles at Spynie, was already maturing into a success that was badly alarming his enemies. But they held one trump card; Sir James Balfour's brother, Gilbert, the sinister owner of the two Provosts' houses at Kirk o' Field, was sheriff of the Islands and held Kirkwall Castle. He temporized until he could get into touch with the Government and make his terms with them, then fired the Castle guns on the ships lying in the harbour. It looked as though wherever he went in Scotland, Bothwell would find a Balfour brother in the key position of a castle and guns.

His small ships were not strong enough to attack a fortress; he led them out of range of the guns in Scapa Flow and then to the Shetlands. There, as in the Orkneys, he was greeted as the feudal and hereditary overlord; Oliver Sinclair, the ruler or Foude, his mother's kinsman, was in direct descent, as was Bothwell himself, from the royal house of the St Clairs, Dukes of Normandy, who were independent sovereigns of these islands long before the later Bastard of Normandy conquered England. The princely cousins made friends as they walked along the shore of those far Northern seas and discussed their plans for a maritime hegemony, recruited from adventurers in every ocean. It was by no means impossible at that date.

Pirates would be their enemies' name for them, no doubt, but the dividing line between piracy and respectable naval enterprise was still rather more vague than that between soldiers and sailors; certainly the English captains that had begun to be the terror of the Spanish traders were called pirates in all countries but their own. The ethics of their case did not worry James Hepburn; all his concern was to get bigger and better fighting ships, and shock troops aboard them, since the boats he had already collected were too small and frail, and slow sailers at that, to meet any serious naval engagement. But he had great hopes of getting what he wanted in Denmark and Norway.

A report reached them that the Lord James had returned to Scotland. News travelled slowly to these distant islands; they could not know that James had not only already secured the Regency, but had employed a fleet of the combined naval forces of Leith and Dundee to kill or capture those 'notorious and manifest pirates', Bothwell and his followers, with the emphasis on the killing rather than capturing. Bothwell alive and talking at his trial would be as dangerous as at large.

Kirkaldy of Grange eagerly volunteered to lead the expedition, certain that the notorious pirate 'shall either carry me with him or else I shall bring him dead or quick to Edinburgh'. With him went 'the sorcerer of the Orcades', that same sailor Bishop of Orkney who had married them (and managed to insert references to the 'past evil living' of the bridegroom in his wedding sermon); he now sided openly with his enemies, confident, as were Grange and Lethington and most others, that this was the last of Bothwell. Only James with his usual caution remarked dampingly, 'We cannot bargain for the bear's skin until we catch him.'

The first Bothwell heard of the fleet's setting out was as he sat at mid-day dinner with the Foude, when one of his men dashed in breathless with the news that at least eight great ships, heavily armed, had been sighted closing in on Bressay Sound where four of Bothwell's ships lay at anchor. The sailors had acted instantly, knowing they had no chance against such a war fleet, had cut their cables and run up the channel northwards, that is, three of the ships had done so, but the *Swan* (rechristened the *Lame Duck* by the sailors) had been abandoned, since she was too slow to have any chance of escape.

'I'll not leave one ship behind,' Bothwell roared as he leaped up from the table and dashed down to the harbour, collected the *Swan*'s captain and some of her crew and got them aboard with him on what looked like a suicide cruise. The other three ships were well ahead, but the *Swan* with her delayed start had the pursuers hot on her heels and was losing ground steadily all the way up the Sound. Soon the *Unicorn*, the flagship of the Scottish fleet, was so near that they could see who was on board, and with a yell of joy Bothwell recognized Kirkaldy of Grange and the turncoat Bishop of Orkney. They answered him with triumphant shouts, and certainly there seemed no cause for joy on board the *Lame Duck,* now all but overtaken by her foes. But Bothwell had been with her captain over these waters before and knew what he wanted. He got him to take the ship closer into the rocky shore, where most of the bigger ships dared not venture. Only Grange, no seaman, and hot on the chase, insisted on his flagship following close.

The *Lame Duck* with consummate seamanship ran before the wind through the breaking seas, shipping it green all over the decks, and decoyed the *Unicorn* on to a sunken rock over which she herself was just able to pass. Those on board could hear her keel grating on the rock, and there was a ghastly instant when it seemed as though she would stick there as a stationary mark for the *Unicorn*'s guns. But the captain had gauged the shallowness of her draught correctly and she plunged on to safety, came about to the wind and gained the deeps, the water hissing along the gunwale. But the *Unicorn*, following close, struck dead on the rock. There was a horrible rending sound, the rough water poured in through the hole, the ship lurched, staggered and began to sink fast.

Bothwell roared into the wind to Grange as he leaned over the gunwale, 'Here's your safeguard to the Queen, you perjured swine! Take your pork into the pickle tub!'

Some of the sailors were already struggling in the brine, but others had managed to lower the long-boat and were crowding into it, with Grange among them; they fought each other shamelessly, and the Bishop, crowded out, took a flying leap, robes, breastplate and all, from the sinking ship on to a rock and clung there, shrieking to be picked up. His sailors paid no heed to him and were rowing straight past him, when with another magnificent leap he fell plump into the middle of the crowded boat, on top of all the shouting, cursing men, and very nearly upset it. Bothwell's fugitive crew cheered derisively as they sailed away.

'The sea won't cheat the gallows of you,' they yelled.

Bothwell's manoeuvre had held up the whole pursuit, for Grange's other ships had to stop and pick up the survivors, and Bothwell's all got clear away to Unst, the most northerly of the islands.

But he was certain there would be more fighting, and at once, and sent back one of his ships to Scalloway to fetch a detachment that there had been no time to pick up on his flight. Sure enough, up came Grange's ships again, though without Grange or the Bishop, for their taste of the bear's claws had been too much for them. They preferred to stay on dry land with an armed force and hunt up and take back for lingering execution any fugitives of Bothwell's crews who had not been able to join their ships in time, and were easy prey on an island.

In charge of the pursuit on water was yet another candidate for the unfought duel at Carberry, anxious to make up at sea for what they had failed to do on land, James Murray of Purdovis, now laird of Tullibardine. He attacked Bothwell's ships off Unst, and for three hours the three little ships fought a running fight, working out to sea all the time, and with the *Lame Duck* lagging, lagging, lagging all the way. At last she fell to Tullibardine.

Still the detachment from Scalloway had not come up, and still Bothwell fought on, two small ships against seven far bigger and stronger armed, till the *Pelican*, where he was now aboard, had her mainmast shot right away.

It looked like the end, clean and fairly quick in those long icegreen waves. But just when all seemed over, a south-westerly squall surged up, and Bothwell had one more chance to show his seamanship. He took it superbly, extricated his two battered hulks and ran before the wind, leading Tullibardine for sixty miles on their heels before the laird had to give up the chase to the better sailors.

James Hepburn sailed on through the gale, free of his foes, in an exultation that took no count of the stormy sea, the shattering wounds to his two remaining ships, now barely seaworthy; nor that the ship he had sent to Scalloway contained all his worldly goods, clothes and jewels (he had chosen that one so that it might not fall to his enemies); nor that they were short of all provisions and would need a deal of reconditioning before they could make another voyage, if indeed they could reach the end of this one. But what did any of that matter when, by the luck of the world, they were not at the bottom of the sea, but still roving on?

'A-roving, a-roving, since roving's been my ruin' —

The sailors were singing the version of the song that had reached the English ports.

> *'In Amsterdam there lives a maid*
> *And she is mistress of her trade,*
> *And I'll go no more a-roving*
> *With you, fair maid.'*

He had only one regret, that Mary had not been with him to enjoy that fight, the chase, and best of all that consummate stroke of sea-craft that had sunk Grange's ship. It had been a grand afternoon since he had sprung up from the Foude's dinner-table, years ago it seemed now. Well, they would have others, and together. He was just thirty-two and she twenty-four, they still had a good part of their lives and all the world to go a-roving in.

The pale light of Northern late summer stole over the sea,

and the water gleamed out with that strange added life that comes to it in the dark. With the dawn came the coast of Norway, enormous, remote, unearthly, blue beyond blue, melting into snow-capped heights, like mountains at the edge of the world.

They met a German merchant vessel that piloted them in to that fairy shore. 'A 'manifest pirate' would have seized her to refit and revictual himself. Bothwell, it seemed, was more 'notorious' than 'manifest'. But his appearance was manifestly disreputable in old boatswain's clothes, torn and patched up somehow after his long struggle with the sea. The Norwegians were suspicious, so was the Danish captain Aalborg, who was patrolling these waters in search of pirates, for Norway was then a dependency of Denmark. Bothwell could produce no papers, and had to go to Bergen in Aalborg's custody to answer inquiries.

There, with unruffled confidence, before the governor, Eric Rosencrantz, and a commission of twenty-four burghers and magistrates, the ragged sea-rover announced that he was the husband of the Queen who was known as the loveliest woman in Europe; and the supreme governor of all Scotland. Yet such was 'the serenity of his countenance' that it was not doubted. They only questioned the absence of any passport or ship's papers. To which he made his supreme gesture as the Galliard.

Looking round on these solid respectable burghers in their Sunday black, with a smile of weary condescension the man with the head of a king and the old coat of a boatswain replied, 'Being myself the supreme ruler of the land, of whom can I receive authority?'

That he made his effect was shown by the fact that he was referred to after this as 'the Scottish King', even by the King of Denmark. A more immediate and useful result was that he was at once released from custody and allowed to lodge at an inn pending further inquiries. He had no doubt of their issue. There was some question about the actual ownership of the *Pelican*, but Bothwell had chartered her at fifty crowns a month in fair and open market, and no accusation could be brought against him; it would all be settled in a few days when the court would be held.

He looked forward confidently to meeting Frederick II again, this time on equal terms, and asking him for help for the Queen, as seven years before he had asked and received it for her mother. A single raid carried out with vigour from the coast, a hundred sturdy swimmers to cross the loch at night, and they would carry her off. His plans kept his thoughts happily busy as he walked round the narrow horseshoe harbour where the coloured reflections of the painted houses, pink and blue, white and yellow, danced up and down on the wind-ruffled waters like peasant girls bobbing in a ring.

But he did not get his freedom. He did not see his boon companion, Frederick of Denmark.

> *In Bergen town there lived a maid*
> *And she was mistress of her trade.*

Out of the dead past where she had lain forgotten, into the court of inquiry where Bothwell had expected to hear discussed only some technical point of a vessel's ownership, came the woman with the black elf-locks and white strange face of a Lapland witch. Anna Throndsen, cousin to Rosencrantz, appeared in court to enter a claim for the money she had lent him in Flanders seven years before, so that he might go and tender his services to his young Queen at the Court of France.

The wheel had come full circle; in his end was his beginning.

The money charges could have been easily answered by detailing the goods and valuables with which he had since repaid it over and over. Bothwell preferred to say nothing except offer to pay it again with the smaller of his ships and a yearly rent of one hundred dollars from Scotland. The charge was dropped. Now he would be free. His debt to Anna had only detained him for a moment.

But that moment was decisive. With a strange economy of fate, she proved to be the weapon destined to ruin both her faithless lover and the woman he had afterwards loved and served so faithfully. Her letters and the Queen's, found among Bothwell's papers, were interwoven to form the basis of the Casket Letters that eighteen months later were concocted to prove the Queen guilty of murder; her 'Sonnets', which Ronsard later repudiated as not only too rough in style for the Queen's verses, but in far too indifferent French, were employed for the same purpose. Anna was doubly revenged.

During that delay to Bothwell's freedom caused by her action, Rosencrantz discovered more of the upheaval under which he had left Scotland. The custody of this stormy petrel, with the power to hold him as a threat over both the Scottish and English Governments, who were now both clamouring for his blood, would, as King Frederick, that boon companion, heartily agreed, be extremely useful in the game of European politics. So Bothwell was kept in prison, at first 'honourably' and comfortably, on one pretext after another, always thinking that it would soon be cleared up; writing to Frederick his plan for the 'deliverance of the Queen, my princess,' and offering Orkney and Shetland, those former Scandinavian dependencies, in return for Danish aid and ships (an offer which tempted Frederick considerably for a time).

He wrote a full account of the series of conspiracies against the Queen ever since her landing in Scotland, and showed the assassinations and risings to be no mere isolated and haphazard deeds of violence, but the work of a small secret society of men who had made many hidden, and three open attempts to dethrone the Queen and seize the government; and, the third time, succeeded.

Frederick may have been interested when not too fuddled. He certainly paid less attention to the propaganda of Bothwell's enemies than to the opinion of one who had heard many speak of him from their personal knowledge as 'all his lifetime a faithful servant of the Crown, a man valiant and for magnanimous powers above all others; a man ready to undertake and more ready to put into execution'.

But whether Bothwell were faithful or faithless, or Frederick drunk or sober, the Danish King had a clear head for the one point essential to him in the case. Bothwell was useful as his prisoner.

He never came out.

*   *   *

Mary had her last wild meteoric flight into freedom the following May. She had already made an attempt to escape from Loch Leven disguised as a laundress, but though her face was hidden, the hand that Ronsard had sung, 'longue et gresle et délicate', too fair a hand for any but the Queen, betrayed her. The boatmen took her back to captivity. But her courage and determination were unquenchable, and so was her incalculable magic in winning both men and women to her. Even that grim old lady, Lord James' mother, was not proof against it, for she connived at the next attempt, due to the splendid sense of adventure in a schoolboy of fourteen. Willie Douglas scuttled all the boats of the Castle but one, locked the doors, dropped the keys in the loch, where they were not discovered till two and a half centuries later, and rowed Mary to the farther shore himself. For eleven days her suddenly risen star shot across the sky, then sank into darkness.

Her first move was to send Bothwell word, as she had succeeded in doing even while at Loch Leven through the secret services of the fishermen. No prison, she felt, could be strong enough to hold James Hepburn once he knew that she had broken ward! But he was now in Malmö Castle, two previous prisons having been thought insufficient to hold so fiery a spirit. Even the man who broke the stanchions of his window and scaled the Castle Rock of Edinburgh in the wet dark, could not escape past a sentry, through a guard-room always occupied, and connected with the Governor's quarters, and a courtyard filled with the garrison.

His tragedy was Mary's, for the battle he would certainly have won with her present forces (the people flocked to her this time) was lost for lack of a strong leader. The Hamiltons had always been doubtful as to whether their best policy were to marry or murder her; Geordie Seton was faithful as always, but though a good subordinate soldier he was hopeless in higher command; Argyll, the chief of her leaders, collapsed on the battlefield.

Mary saw her army break and fly. She had 'a man's soul in a woman's body'; but she knew that if she rode into that lost battle she would not be cut down among the hordes of the flying; her enemies would be careful to take her prisoner, and lead her again in triumph into Edinburgh to undergo again that torment she had endured less than a year ago – and this time it would end in being burnt alive. For the first and last time in her life she took panic and fled, with only five persons, and soon even that small company had to divide to elude pursuit – fled 'for ninety-two miles across country without stopping or alighting; then slept upon the ground and ate oatmeal without bread and was three nights like the owls, without a female to aid her'. At the end she crossed the Solway Firth in a fisherman's boat and entered Elizabeth's country.

All this past year Elizabeth had been expressing her indignation with the rebel lords; and, since Mary's escape, an Envoy had been sent to Scotland with congratulations to her and instructions to do his utmost to restore her to her throne. Mary had not fully realized that what had chiefly aroused Elizabeth's indignation was the bad example to her own subjects of a neighbouring Queen deposed and imprisoned by a revolutionary Government.

Mary had been bred up in policy; but her instincts had remained simple. She believed in Elizabeth's protestations of friendship and took her at her word. Elizabeth kept her prisoner for nineteen years and then beheaded her.

She was never allowed to see Elizabeth. All her life she had counted on doing that, with her incurable trust in the essential kindness of the individual. But the individual was not considered of importance in this matter: the State was all.

The hate of one old man had wrought her ruin in Scotland: in England it was not hate, but a thing more false to all human values, called political necessity. This it was that made Cecil seek her death unceasingly.

The Casket Letters were used as the pretext to prevent a personal interview between Mary and Elizabeth: they were produced very briefly at an inquiry held in England seven months after Mary's arrival there. No expert in handwriting was permitted to be present; no witnesses were called; and the accused herself was kept at four days' distance from the trial, and not allowed either to see the evidence against her, or to be heard in her own defence, according to English law. Even so, the verdict was Not Proven – but it was decided that Elizabeth could not meet anyone accused, whether correctly or not, of 'such foul stuff'.

So she served a life-sentence (twenty years in all from her capture at Carberry) on an unproved allegation; and then was sentenced to death on the charge of plotting against the woman who had jailed her, in a trial in which, this time, she could speak in her own defence, but was allowed no advocate, and was permitted neither to hear nor see the evidence against her. It took more than three months after the trial to make Elizabeth give the *coup de grâce* to her victim by signing the death-warrant; but they were months of agony to her rather than to Mary.

Death had given Bothwell his release ten years earlier. His young nephew, who was also Mary's nephew, Francis, the last and Wizard Earl of Bothwell, inherited their fire; he told King James VI to his face that he deserved to be hanged if he did not try to rescue his mother; then buckled on his armour as the only fit mourning, and led a raid into England.

Raids, rescue plots, attempts to escape, all now were only part of that long illusion that was fading fast from her.

The death-knell to her hopes of freedom and of Bothwell's had really sounded sixteen years before, though few realized it,

478

in the tocsin that Catherine de Medici had sounded for the massacre of all the Huguenots in Paris on the Eve of St Bartholomew. Mary had thought she had escaped Catherine for ever when she left France; but neither she nor Bothwell nor myriads of others could escape the effects of that hideous power of insensitiveness to individual life and suffering, the devilish inhumanity of putting policy above all human values. Mary's form of religion linked her to the perpetrators of that massacre, and so cut away the support she had begun to win on all sides. She could have won freedom and power by changing that form, but she still refused to 'make merchandise of her religion'; to her it was always a matter for the individual soul, as she had wished to make it in her country. But to others it was a political creed.

The forces of bigotry and cruelty that destroyed these lovers were the same, whether they masked themselves under the name of Catholicism or Protestantism; as they have masked themselves under other names, religious or political, throughout history; but remain the forces of evil. She and her lover stood for the freedom of the spirit, and were therefore denied all freedom – except that of the spirit, which no one could take from them.

Behind her long captivity blazed the fire of their life at its fullest, in which she had never lost faith, but known always that it was theirs eternally. All the early years of their friendship had prepared the fuel for that fire. Its consuming fierceness was due to the very sense of breathless danger and uncertainty. People say she had little joy of her lover, less peace in which to enjoy it – not seeing that in its very desperation, knowing it might at any moment be snatched from them, lay its terrific power.

Love is not measured by time: nor by safety; nor by comfort. A few months she knew she loved Bothwell: a few weeks she enjoyed that love, though shot through with anguish, terror, anger, heart-break of all kinds. Yet in that love – and not in those few weeks, which it far transcended and overflowed – she knew the height of her life. In proof and reward of this, the twenty years of captivity that followed dwindled in retrospect to an insignificant moment, fugitive as a nightmare, compared with those few weeks.

All that happened in those twenty years, and did not happen; the anguished hopes, the bitterness, the frantic beating of wings against the bars, the devotion of boys and girls who rushed to death to set her free, the plans of marriage to English dukes and foreign princes – even to that magnificent prince of adventure,

Don John of Austria, who rode to war like a clear flame in the midst of hidden treacheries, and died with the vow to rescue her on his lips – all these were but thin wraiths of smoke in the light that still smouldered within her from that early fire. Again and again there were plans to divorce her, and she began to acquiesce in them in the hopes of achieving Bothwell's freedom as well as hers; but she never brought them to fruition. She remained wedded to him till his death divided them, ten years before her own.

Their prisons had not prevented their letters to each other; they came by hidden means, generally through the secret service of the fishermen that travelled along the coasts of England and Denmark as well as Scotland. She had heard of his ghastly imprisonment at the end, chained as a mad beast to the pillar where his steps could make only a half-circle round it. But he had been dead now for ten years, his spirit long since freed from that chained carcass. To her he had been always as she had seen him last, looking proudly at her on Carberry Hill – 'There is no man here that does not wish himself in my place' – and then riding up over the crest of the hill till his long shadow touched the flaming pine. With that parting, their life here together ended, and all that came after did not count. The rest was waiting for their order of release.

It did not matter that the end of a life was wretched any more than its beginning. In eternity is neither end nor beginning: it is there at the highest moment of one's life, rather than the last.

'In my end is my beginning,' ran her motto in its strange hopefulness, for she knew that death was not the end, but the beginning of her real life again. The Latin verses that she wrote in those last weeks are like a carillon of bells, a conquering peal of triumph in her deliverance. As her father had died 'on a little smile of laughter', so her soul went singing to its freedom.